S0-BZV-648

Constance Heaven

★ ★ ★

LARKSGHYLL

HEINEMANN · MANDARIN

A Mandarin Paperback

LARKSGHYLL

First published in Great Britain 1986
by William Heinemann Ltd
This edition published 1989
by Heinemann · Mandarin
81 Fulham Road, London SW3 6RB

Copyright © Constance Heaven 1986

ISBN 0 7493 0009 4

A CIP catalogue record for this book is available
from the British Library.

Printed in Great Britain
by Cox & Wyman Ltd, Reading

*This book is sold subject to the condition
that it shall not, by way of trade or otherwise,
be lent, resold, hired out, or otherwise circulated
without the publisher's prior consent in any form
of binding or cover other than that in which
it is published and without a similar condition
including this condition being imposed
on the subsequent purchaser.*

FOR
CECIL WIDDOWS
and our long years of friendship

Know that love is a careless child
    And forgets promise past,
He is blind, he is deaf when he list
    And in faith never fast.

Walsingham, Sir Walter Ralegh

Part One

1

Delphine came into the sitting room of their London lodgings and crossed to the window, pulling back the heavy plush curtains. It was still bitingly cold. The landlady had not seen fit to light a fire and she shivered, but outside there was an unexpected sparkle of spring in the windblown sky. There were fat brown buds on the plane tree that overshadowed the house and a few green daffodil spikes struggled bravely up through the soot-blackened earth. She turned back into the room and was instantly rebellious. The early sunshine showed up distressingly the stained wallpaper with its bare discoloured patches, the scuffed velvet on the chairs, the sagging horsehair sofa and worn carpet. The winter months had been decidedly one of their 'down' periods, she thought humorously, a vivid contrast to the summer before when they had rented spacious rooms in a fashionable street and enjoyed a nodding acquaintance with the rich and famous. Not the *haut ton* of society, perhaps, but precariously on the fringes of it with a hired carriage when it was needed and horses to ride in Hyde Park, where her father's fine figure and dashing style always drew admiring glances from the female population.

She glanced at the clock. It was half past seven already and she would be late if she didn't hurry. Now she was working regularly for Madame Ginette she was expected to be at the salon at eight o'clock precisely.

She wondered where her father was. He was usually up before she was, drinking his coffee, glancing through *The Times* and filled with exciting plans for the day, no matter how late he had been the night before. He was always so buoyant, so sure of himself at even their worst moments, that she had a sudden sharp spasm of alarm. Could he be sick? He had always had splendid health. A slash from a knife in some midnight scuffle, a bullet wound that she suspected had come from some crazy affair of honour on Hampstead Heath, but these she had dealt with easily. She was just about to knock at his door when the

3

landlady came in with a tray and banged it down on the table noisily.

She was a large woman who always looked as if she were bursting out of her cotton gown. Eyes bright as black boot buttons in a suet pudding of a face never missed a thing. Della had a suspicion that she spied on their every movement.

"You'd best get that tea down you, Miss, you're goin' to need it," she said truculently. "Yer Pa's gorn – hooked it – left me a month's rent and took himself orf. Only just in time if you ask me. I know the signs. I've dealt with fly-by-nights before now."

It was a most unpleasant shock, for she had expected nothing of the kind but she was not going to let any of that show on her face.

"Thank you, Mrs Frant," she said coolly. "I knew already that my father was leaving London today but he must have found it necessary to go earlier than he expected."

"So you knew, did you?" The landlady gave a mighty sniff and the black eyes didn't believe a word of it. "Well, you'd best read that then," and one pudgy finger none too clean nudged a packet on the tray. "Very particular he was that you should get it soon as you was up."

"Very well, thank you," she said, pointedly making no move to pick up the packet until, curiosity unsatisfied, the woman waddled regretfully towards the door.

Della followed after her, saw her disappear down the stairs, shut the door tight and went back to take up the packet with fingers that trembled. It was heavier than she expected and when she broke the seal she saw why. Inside there was the purse she had once netted for him of fine silver beads. It felt heavy in her hand as she let it drop on the table and took the letter to the window.

For a second the bold handwriting with its characteristic flourishes shook before her eyes. Then it steadied and she read the brief message.

"My dearest girl," he had written, "by now you will have realized that I've had to make a bolt for it, temporarily I hope, but who can tell? Don't believe all they will say of me. I swear I've not murdered the innocent or robbed the starving. Please God (or should I say the devil!) we'll be together again some day soon. Write to me if you can c/o François, Rue Donjon in Paris – remember that little café where we once took refuge from the flics? I thank the Lord for Madame Ginette. She's a good soul. At least she will see you come to no harm. Give her my best regards and try to think kindly of your Papa who loves you very dearly and always will."

Did he? She had never doubted it before but now she felt suddenly bereft. It was not easy to accept, but she was not going to weep over it. That was something she had learned at school when she was very young. Tears make you horribly vulnerable. Better to laugh however deep the pain and disillusionment. But the blow had been very severe and for a few moments she did come near to tears that morning. It was the clock that saved her. It boomed eight o'clock from the nearby church steeple and now of all times she could not afford to be late. She left the tea untouched and hurried into the bedroom to take up her thick mantle and tie on her bonnet. She locked the letter and purse in one of the drawers. Mrs Frant called up to her from the basement as she went through the hall but she didn't answer. Time to deal with her later.

The streets were crowded with men and women hurrying to work. Tradesmen's carts and horsedrawn cabs surged by splashing up muddy water from the filthy gutters while screaming children jostled her on their way to school. She battled her way through them until she reached Piccadilly and entered a network of small dirty streets.

Perhaps the change was in her, but the bright promise had gone out of the morning. The wind met her at corners raw and very cold. She ran most of the way, partly because she was already so late and partly because she was afraid to think too much about the reason for her father's sudden departure. There were questions she must ask whatever the answer. They had always moved about too much to make close friends but there were just one or two. She wished passionately that Edmund Dent were not abroad. She had met him just a year ago when he was studying law in chambers at the Temple. He was someone to whom she could have turned for advice.

For some inexplicable reason she knew this was not the usual disappearance of a day or so when her father would turn up again, smiling as he casually jingled the guineas in his pocket and saying, "See what I've brought you, my love," then out would come a new silk shawl, a locket on a gold chain, extravagant silk stockings fine as cobwebs and they would laugh and be very happy together even if there was little food in the cupboard and the rent was still unpaid.

She turned into a narrow black door beside an Italian restaurant. Madame Ginette, born Jeanne Reynard, had a small dressmaking establishment in Soho that could hardly yet be dignified by the name of a salon though she had a small but growing number of discerning clients who were beginning to spread her reputation. It was over a year since a disastrous run of bad luck at the races, which the gaming tables did nothing to relieve, had meant that Della had gone out to find herself a job. She had a streak of common sense and a rooted dislike of debt inherited from some hard-headed Yorkshire ancestor. She had done it once or twice before, much to her father's disgust. Paul Darcy Craven, younger son of Geoffrey Darcy Craven of Larksghyll, with a lineage going back four hundred years and a woeful lack of the ready to support it, had an aristocratic distaste for anything labelled "work". But Della went ahead all the same, more often than not hiding it from him. After all, reading novels to elderly ladies, taking the pug for a walk, teaching French verbs to small girls or acting as temporary nursemaid to a fractious baby were all ladylike occupations. It was the fine needlework drilled into her at her Belgian convent that got her the post with Madame Ginette. Then by a stroke of luck, Kitty, who had a flair for design and the ability to transform it into stylish gowns, fell sick and by the merest chance Della, who was clever with her pencil and enjoyed designing clothes she was never rich enough to have made, temporarily took her place and won the grudging respect of Madame when one of her drawings caught the eye of the wealthiest of her customers.

She arrived that morning out of breath and hurried immediately into the tiny cubicle adjacent to the sewing room where she was sometimes allowed to work on her drawings. A young man was there before her lounging against the table. He looked across at her grinning unpleasantly as she shut the door and leaned back against it panting.

"You're late," he said tauntingly.

"I know. I'm sorry."

"Maman has been asking for you most particularly."

"Why?" she glanced at him in alarm. "Did she tell you?"

He shrugged his shoulders but as she brushed past him to hang up her heavy cloak, he caught at her, slipping his arms around her and drawing her back against him, his hands cupping her breasts. She reacted against him furiously.

6

"Monsieur Reynard, please don't do that."

"Why not? Be nice to me and I'll not say a word."

She pulled herself away. "You need not concern yourself. I shall tell her myself."

"Quite the fine lady, aren't we?" he went on spitefully. "Miss Delphine Craven whose Papa calls himself a gentleman and is no better than a card sharp and racing tout."

"He's nothing of the sort."

"Am I a liar then?"

He moved towards her and, nerves on edge, her quick temper flared and she slapped his cheek hard.

"Keep away from me."

He caught her wrist and pulled her against him.

"I could make you sorry for that, my beauty."

She knew she had been unwise but she detested him, the small dark eyes, the sallow greasy skin, the greedy red mouth and hot groping hands. She might have made a very sharp answer indeed if the cutting voice from the door had not jerked them apart.

"Henri, have you nothing better to do than play games with my assistant? Get back to your desk."

"*Oui, Maman, toute de suite.*"

He had a very healthy respect for his mother's biting tongue and slid past her through the doorway.

"I am sorry but I'm late this morning," began Della tentatively but Madame cut her short.

"Never mind about that now. I wish to speak to you, Delphine. You had better come to my room."

Della followed her apprehensively. She knew only too well that Madame did not approve of her son's philanderings in the workroom. Most of the girls tolerated him and giggled among themselves. It was Della's determined dislike of his fumblings, his attempts to catch her unawares, that had pricked his vanity and aroused him to pursue her with a greater ardour.

For a moment Madame Ginette said nothing. She looked at the girl standing in front of her, at the fine silky black hair that, however hard she tried to keep it within bounds, fell into engaging ringlets around her temples and on the slender neck, at the creamy skin, the dark blue smouldering eyes shaded by thick lashes, the slim figure that contrived to look elegant even in the plain dove-grey dress that she had trimmed with bands of purple velvet. She would be sorry to lose her. The girl had class,

7

combined with style and originality, even though it was coupled with a quick temper and a fiery spirit that might need curbing. But the truth was that her father, gentleman though he might be, was running around with a notoriously shady set. Some extremely unpleasant rumours had reached her and she could not afford to offend the middle-aged wives of the rich bankers and industrialists who, with their marriageable daughters, made such a touchy parade of their virtue. It wasn't the aristocracy. They would laugh and snap their fingers when they brought their mistresses to be dressed by her, but the *parvenus*, the *nouveaux riches*, all vying with each other, were different. Jeanne Reynard's grandparents had fled from the guillotine in revolutionary France and she had grown up in a hard world. She had a disillusioned view of society, its hypocrisies and its harsh judgments. There was Henri too. She knew him through and through. He must not be allowed to entangle himself with some penniless girl. She wanted to see him suitably settled, not like his wastrel father who had walked out when his son was six and left her to fight on alone. She drew herself upright, a small dark Frenchwoman in a neat dress of black silk. She had no wish to be unkind, but in this harsh world one must look out for oneself.

She said, "I am sorry, my dear. I am afraid I have some bad news for you."

This was to be an unlucky day. Della had known it from the moment she had read that fatal letter. For a moment the room seemed to swing around her and she clutched at a chair to steady herself.

"Are you unwell? You look very pale."

She braced herself against it. "I'm all right. It's just that I was late and came out without breakfast."

"I'll send out for some coffee."

"No please. I'd far rather hear what you have to say first."

"Very well. The fact is, Delphine, that Kitty is coming back to me. I always promised that she should if she felt the necessity and now it seems that her husband has lost his job and she must support him as well as her child. She really needs the work."

No more than I need it, thought Della, but she raised her head proudly. "I quite understand."

"I did make it clear from the outset that this work of yours might be only temporary."

"Yes, yes, Madame, you did."

8

"You could if you wish go back to the sewing room for a time . . ."

"No," said Della quickly. It was not the work she minded so much, hard and exacting though it was, it was the girls, their coarse laughter, their resentment at her difference from them, Henri's hateful triumph at seeing her reduced again to their level. "No, Madame, I don't think I could do that."

"As you please. You need not leave at once of course. Finish the work you are engaged on. Shall we say at the end of next week?"

She would have liked to walk out that very day, that very moment, but she dare not and in her way Madame was being generous. She swallowed her pride.

"Thank you. I would like to do that."

"Well, that's settled. You must not feel too upset. I am sure there will be many opportunities opening up for you and I shall be glad to give you any recommendation I can." She smiled suddenly as she got up. "And now I think we could both of us do with a pot of good strong coffee."

The hours crept by with torturing slowness. She tried hard to work on a design for a wedding dress, something new and original. It was to be a grand occasion at St George's, Hanover Square; society would be there in strength and she knew Madame Ginette hoped great things from it, but her mind was devoid of ideas. Every sketch she drew seemed worse than the last and she tore them up angrily. How could she concentrate with anxiety growing and growing inside her? What could have happened? Where had her father gone and why? At last she could stand it no longer. It was unheard of to leave the salon early except in the most exceptional circumstances of illness or sudden death, but what did it matter now? She had been virtually dismissed in any case – and unfairly. She knew in her heart that she was far better than Kitty would ever be but there was Henri and something else, something Madame had sensed and held against her, and it seemed suddenly that her life which had been so straightforward had become darkened with a miasma of doubt and suspicion that she could not understand.

She took her cloak and bonnet walking briskly through the workroom ignoring the staring girls and left quickly before anyone could stop her. Outside she ran down the street and across the square in case someone should call after her and then recklessly took a hackney carriage to their lodging suddenly sure that it was all some stupid mistake and her father would be there before her laughing and teasing her for being such a goose as to doubt him. She knew that hopeful fantasy was a delusion as soon as she stepped inside the door and was met by Mrs Frant, frowning and belligerent.

"I'm not used to it, Miss Craven, and that's a fact. This is a respectable house, this is, and those policemen or whatever they call themselves, those 'peelers' with their truncheons and saucy manners comin' here askin' questions, wantin' to know where you were and when I last saw your Pa, on and on they went. I didn't like it above half, I tell you straight."

"Did you tell them?"

"No, I didn't. Never let on, keep a tight mouth, that's what Frant always used to say before he passed on. I got something better to do than answer impudent jackanapes like that treatin' decent-livin' people as if they were no better than criminals. I gave them a piece of my mind, I can tell you, but all the same you'd best look out for yourself, Miss. They'll be back, you mark my words . . ."

She paused for breath and Della managed to escape up the stairs, the coarse voice still pursuing her from the hall below.

"There's someone waitin' for you, Miss. Calls herself a lady, nice enough spoken, but I must say I had me doubts . . ."

The winter day was already drawing in and the room was full of shadows when Della opened the door. A woman who had been sitting at the table rose to her feet as she came in.

"Miss Craven?" she asked.

"Yes. Should I know you?"

"No, but I have a message for you."

"From my father?"

"Yes."

She was suddenly afraid to ask, afraid to know.

"Wait a moment. I'll make a light."

She lit a taper from the fire and busied herself with the candles. Then she turned to face her visitor. She was a good-looking woman in her early thirties, dressed in a handsome gown and mantle of dark green trimmed with black braid. One of the new fashionable hats with a drooping ostrich feather perched at an angle on lustrous red hair gave her a touch of flamboyance.

"You'll be wondering who I am, Miss Craven," she said

quietly and her voice had a soft rich quality. "My name is Lucinda Shaw," and immediately Della knew why the face had been vaguely familiar. She was an actress playing with Charles Kean's company at the Covent Garden Theatre.

"I know you," she said frowning. "My father took me to see *A Winter's Tale* and you were Paulina. You were very good in it."

"Was I?" she smiled slightly. "It's very kind of you to say so but I did not come here to talk about the theatre."

The anxiety flashed back. Della gripped her hands together tightly. "You were going to tell me something about my father."

"Yes. He came to me last night and he asked me to let you know what he was not able to tell you himself."

"Why should he do that?"

"There were reasons. You must know that Paul Craven and I are . . . old friends."

Friends or lovers? The slight hesitation told its own story. Della was not a fool or a prude. She knew women were fascinated by her father and that sometimes he responded to them but he had never introduced his mistresses to his daughter or brought them to their lodging. Now she was confronted by this extremely attractive woman who must have shared his deepest confidence and enjoyed with him the ultimate intimacies. A painful jealousy shook her and for a moment she could not speak.

"I can see you resent my coming here," said Lucinda quietly. "I will tell you what he told me and then I will go."

Della tried hard to bite back her dislike. "No. Please forgive me if I seem so – so distracted. It has been a terrible day and I have not known what to believe. Won't you sit down and I will ask Mrs Frant to bring us some tea."

"Not for me. In any case I must leave soon for the evening performance."

They stood facing one another and the other woman studied the lovely face with the pure lines of youth, the dark blue eyes, alive with anxiety. Paul had told her once of the Irish girl who had been his wife and the first happy years in Rome before she died of a malarial fever leaving him alone with a five-year-old daughter.

She said gently, "How much did your father tell you?"

"Very little, only that he was obliged to leave England as

11

quickly as possible."

"He didn't tell you why?"

"No."

"He didn't tell you he could be arrested for robbery – and worse – ?"

"Worse?"

"For murder?"

The word fell like a stone and Della shuddered. "Oh my God, it can't be true. My father would never be guilty of such a thing, never, never!"

"Neither is he, but there are those who are and have left him to shoulder the guilt."

"I don't understand. How *can* they do that?"

The actress hesitated. How to explain to this innocent young girl? How much did she understand of the complex man who was her father?

She said gently, "Do I need to tell you about Paul? You must know him better than I. He is a gambler in everything – in life, in love, in danger. He could never resist any kind of challenge and this was how it all began. There are men who meet together and play games of chance for the very highest stakes and take the greatest risks. And sometimes during these sessions it happens that one or other of them will cheat, deliberately or in desperation."

"Not my father!" she said quickly, defensively.

"No, not Paul. He would despise such a thing. He is in any case a player of consummate skill."

She paused and Della drew a quick breath.

"Go on please."

"It seems that a gaming session was set up for four of such gamblers which he believed – rashly perhaps – would restore the money he had recently lost and regretted more for your sake than for his own."

"He did not need to think of me – I have never complained," said Della in a muffled voice.

"It was highly dangerous because he was playing with men whom he did not know well."

"Do you know who they were?"

"No, he would not tell me their names. He thought it better that we should not know but I could tell you of a dozen such. In the theatre one meets many such types, mostly young, vicious, unscrupulous and very rich."

"What happened?"

"At some time during the long night for they played until long past midnight it seems that one of the four had such an unprecedented run of luck that the rest were left utterly destitute. I have seen myself what the gambling fever will do. It drives a man beyond reason, he will pledge his wife's jewels, his house, his lands, everything he possesses, even his daughter's honour in the false hope that he will win it back."

"Is that what happened to my father?" asked Della in a stifled voice.

"Not exactly. He always had his skill to fall back upon. He was not easily shaken but one of those four, stripped to the very bone and grown quite desperate, accused the winner of cheating. They quarrelled violently and driven beyond reason, the young fool whipped out a pistol and shot his tormentor through the heart. There was silence then, a moment of horror. They were all fully aware of the danger they were in. Then your father dropped on his knees to try and help the wounded man and someone in blind panic swept the lamp to the floor, plunging the room into darkness. In the confusion your father was struck a stunning blow on the back of the head and when he came to himself again, he was alone in the room with a dead man, the table overturned, the money gone with the cards and his hands and shirt thick with blood."

Lucinda's low rich voice had filled out the picture so vividly that Della could see it all in her mind's eye. She clasped her hands together.

"Do you mean they deserted him?" she whispered.

"It would seem they thought only of saving themselves. If Paul had called for help, who would believe him innocent? Gaming of this kind is as you know strictly forbidden; even the great houses like Crockfords are raided by the police from time to time. How could he explain? There was nothing he could do for the dead man so he thought the best thing was to leave the country, quietly disappear till it blew over."

"And then he went to you?"

"He could not come here in the state he was in. I live in a quiet mews. There he could change his clothes and write the note he brought to this house for you in the early hours of this morning."

"I wish he had told me," said Della dully.

"My dear, how could he? Time was of the utmost import-

13

ance. He had to get away as quickly as possible."

"He told me to write to him in Paris."

"I think that is where he will be making for."

"Mrs Frant said when I came in that the police have been here making enquiries."

"That is what worries me. Did one of those who were with him in that upstairs room inform the police or did someone see him leave the house and recognize him?"

They stared at one another racked with the same fear for the man they both loved.

"What can we do?" said Della hopelessly.

"Nothing, I'm afraid, nothing but wait until we hear from him." Lucinda paused for a moment. "Is there someone you could go to – some relative or close friend you could stay with until all this blows over?"

"No, there is no one, no one at all."

Her father had told her so little of the house where he had grown up. "Larksghyll is in a Yorkshire dale," he had said dryly, "cold as charity with a wind that can whip the hair off your head." Only once had he spoken of his elder brother. "George is a dull dog. We never hit it off as boys and I see no reason why we should now."

"Is he married?" she had asked curiously.

"He was once and had a son." He had looked away from her. "A loathesome brat if he is anything like his father," he had added lightly.

And that was all she knew. She had sensed his unwillingness to talk about it and somehow it had never seemed to matter. She had no yearning to meet this unknown cousin but now it was different. Now it might have helped to know herself not utterly alone in the world.

She was aware that Lucinda was watching her and roused herself to say, "Thank you for coming. I mustn't keep you from the play."

The older woman stretched out a hand and took hers in a warm clasp. "If I can help at any time you need only send a note to me at the theatre."

"It's kind of you but I shall be all right. I'm used to looking after myself."

"I'm sure you are, but there are still times when one needs a friend."

She turned to go and Della stopped her.

14

"There is just one thing. You must have met some of my father's companions. Have you any idea – any clue at all – as to who this man is who did this terrible thing to him?"

"I have known Paul for some time but I did not accompany him everywhere," was the dry reply. "Mr Kean would not have approved of one of his company being seen in gambling hells."

"No, no, of course not, I didn't mean . . ."

"There *is* just something." Lucinda picked up her reticule from the table and fumbled in it for a moment. "I found it in the pocket of the stained coat your father left behind. Is it his or did he perhaps pick it up during that fatal night?"

She held out her hand. In the palm lay a tiny gold ornament that a man might wear on his watch chain. It was in the shape of a skull with diamonds set in the eyeholes. Della looked at it and shuddered. There was something macabre about it that frightened her.

"I've never seen him wear such a thing," she said slowly.

"Take it. You never know. It might lead you somewhere." Lucinda put it into Della's hand. "And now I really must go. Mr Kean is a martinet where punctuality is concerned. Even if you don't appear till the last act, you must be in the theatre half an hour before curtain up. Goodbye for the present, my dear, and good luck."

She went out closing the door quietly behind her and Della stared down at the golden skull. It was exquisitely fashioned but old, she thought, an heirloom perhaps, not what a young man of fashion would wear in these days. Was it a clue to the wretch who had struck her father down so savagely and left him to face whatever might come out of it? She felt at that moment that she could never rest until she had found him and seen him punished, a fierce resolve that was succeeded by a wave of pure despair. She shivered at the utter impossibility of ever making such a discovery and then put it away, trying to pull herself together.

She had the good sense to realize that part of her weary wretchedness was due to the plain fact that she had eaten nothing that day except the pot of coffee she had shared with Madame Ginette. She called down to Mrs Frant for some tea and bread and butter, then took off her bonnet and mantle and poked the fire into a more cheerful blaze.

The tea was brought by Tilly, a skinny twelve-year-old child from the orphanage who slaved from six in the morning till ten

15

at night and never so far as Della knew had so much as half a day off.

"Dunno what I'd do with it if I did have it, Miss. Got nowhere to go 'cept the orphanage really," she had said wistfully once, "and I had enough of that to last me for ever." She thought Miss Delphine the loveliest creature in the whole of her harsh loveless world.

She put the tea tray down on the table and said shyly, "He's goin' to be orlright, isn't he? Your Pa, I mean. Such a handsome gentleman and so kind."

"I hope so, Tilly."

"He give me half a sovereign one day when I said I didn't have no birthday. 'We'll have to invent one for you, won't we?' he says, 'and here's your very first present.'" She pushed a plate towards Della. "The missus was bakin' cakes so I brought you one."

"That's very kind of you, Tilly," said Della and did not know that the cake had been meant for the girl's own tea, given grudgingly by Mrs Frant.

She ate everything hungrily and felt the better for the food and the hot tea. She had been letting her imagination run away with her. Her father would come back, he always did. She had never known him defeated yet. She went to bed trying to tell herself that the next few days would bring reassuring news. Perhaps he would send for her to join him in Paris or even Italy where they had once spent a happy six months tutoring the backward son of a wealthy nobleman and enjoying the cultured society of Florence. If not, then she would go to Mrs Barnet whose agency had supplied her with part-time work from time to time. She would be sorry to be no longer working for Madame Ginette simply because she had enjoyed using for the first time her own initiative and creative ability, but that could not be helped.

These thoughts sustained her all through the next day. She even produced a sketch for a wedding gown that sent the bride-to-be and her mother into ecstasies: the afternoon was spent in deciding the rival attractions of organza or white lace draped over cream satin and caught up with clusters of tiny pink rosebuds.

It was two days later when she came out of the side door of the salon and walked straight into the arms of Henri coming down the road at a great pace. He pinned her against the wall, his face alive with malice and triumph, only a few inches from her own.

"Have you heard the news?"

"What news?" She tried to push him away from her. "Please Monsieur, you are hurting me."

He pressed closer. She could smell the faint hint of garlic on his breath and turned her head away.

"They caught him just as he was stepping on to the packet at Dover, bold as brass – Mr Paul Craven, thief and murderer."

"It's not true," she breathed.

"Oh yes, it is," he crowed. "I had it from one of those new fellows, Detective Inspector he calls himself, boasting of it he was. They'll have him up for trial in no time. A fine finish to all your airs and graces!"

"I don't believe you."

"You very soon will and don't think you can come back here either. Maman won't want any of your sort in the salon, not if I have any say in the matter."

"Don't worry. I never want to come back."

She thrust him aside and walked away down the narrow street going faster and faster while passers-by stared at the wild-eyed girl who pushed blindly past them.

It couldn't be true, it couldn't! Henri was making it up to taunt her, she told herself frantically. But it *was* true and later that night she was sure of it. Her father, her charming, debonair, handsome father was locked into the horror of Newgate gaol and though she begged and pleaded and offered a bribe of money to the sour-faced turnkey, she was not allowed to speak or communicate with him.

2

The weeks that followed were a nightmare from which Della sometimes felt she would never awaken. The owner of the house, horrified at discovering a dead man, had notified the police in considerable alarm and under pressure confessed to what use the room had been put. There were unfortunately witnesses, a street walker pursuing her trade in the early hours of the morning had seen Paul Craven emerge into the street and accosted him, shrinking back in disgust at sight of the blood; a cab driver up all night with a sick horse had recognized him entering the mews where Lucinda had her lodging and described him in some detail. The dead man himself turned out to be the son of a wealthy banker. Jack Hughes was a young man whose scandalous life had already caused grief to his parents but that did not prevent the outraged father from furiously demanding justice on his killer.

It was only ten years since the newly formed Metropolitan Police Force had been set up by Robert Peel, the Home Secretary, and Mr Richard Mayne, the Chief Commissioner whose responsibility it was to train the new body of men, felt its honour and prestige were at stake. They had had the great good luck to apprehend the murderer before he could flee the country but where was the money concerned? Not a penny of it had been found on him and when closely questioned he had maddeningly shrugged his shoulders.

"Find the fellow responsible and you'll doubtless lay hands on the cash," he said flippantly.

Had he passed it onto his mistress or to his daughter? Lucinda was unmercifully grilled while Della was questioned by the great man himself in the dignified panelled room at No. 2 Whitehall Place soon to be known as Scotland Yard. Baffled, Mr Mayne turned frowning to his fellow commissioner after she had been ushered out.

"That young woman is either innocent or a practised liar and I'm damned if I can make up my mind one way or the other. I

18

have a most confounded itch that somewhere we are barking up the wrong tree."

"You're letting yourself be influenced because the fellow is a gentleman and the girl decently bred – can't get away from that," said Colonel Charles Rowan, flicking the cigar ash from the silver lace of his scarlet uniform jacket. "But I've seen some of these gentleman cracksmen – have had 'em in the regiment before now – devilish attractive chaps for the most part too. He'll put up a good show in the dock and impress the jury but he won't get away with it, not with Judge Willis on the bench. If there is anything that gets up that old devil's puritanical nose it's a rogue with looks, wit and the ability to charm half a dozen birds out of any tree."

And Della sitting in the Old Bailey during those fraught days of the trial saw it only too clearly for herself. Her father stood in the dock, tall, handsome, contriving to look elegant still in the clean linen she had been permitted to send in to him, a faint smile on his lips, glancing around the court with a nonchalant air as if it was they who stood trial for their life and not he. She saw the judge frown and bang the desk angrily as a ripple of laughter ran around the spectators at the prisoner's witty answer to an impertinent question and her heart sank.

She felt in these days as if every eye were upon her. Already an enterprising printer had run up some leaflets, and one of them was thrust into her hand as she entered the court. "The fatal effects of gambling," she read, "as shown in the trial and sentence of Paul Darcy Craven, thief and murderer . . ." She crumpled it up fiercely and tossed it aside.

That was the day she saw Edmund Dent in the body of the court. He had not come to see her, but then perhaps he had only just returned from abroad. There had always been the occasional young man who had pressed his attentions on her – some of them believing her easy prey to their amorous advances until frozen off by her father who if necessary could assume an extraordinarily aristocratic air which brought them up short. She had realized with amusement that Edmund probably thought the same of her at first but afterwards it had been different. She was not in love with him, but they had shared an interest in music. He had accompanied them to the opera and took her to hear Grisi sing and Jenny Lind.

It warmed her to see him there and when the court adjourned she pushed her way down to the corridor where he would come out. She started forward as he came through the door with another young man. He looked her full in the face and walked on as if she did not exist. The shock left her speechless. It couldn't be true. He couldn't be so cruel, but she was rapidly learning in these days who her real friends were and they were painfully few.

The judge's summing up filled her with terror. He dwelt on the iniquity of a man with the prisoner's advantages, ruining his career with idle dissipation, emphasized the value of honest work and condemned the wickedness that had deliberately and with no excuse taken the life of another.

He droned on and on until she felt she could not bear it a moment longer and when the jury withdrew and the court rose, she pushed past the people on the benches and stumbled down the steps into the fresher air, coming face to face with a man she had noticed once or twice simply because he was hardly the type one expected to see on the public benches. Tall and thin, his dark blue frock coat fitted the broad shoulders and slim waist to perfection, narrow plaid trousers were strapped under the handmade boots. Handsome in a queer bony way, there was something disturbing about the eyes in the long pale face which looked at her appraisingly as if he knew very well who she was and judged her as her father was being judged. Then he bowed slightly and drew aside to allow her to pass. She shivered as she brushed against him on the crowded staircase and her disquiet persisted while she took deep breaths of the cold wind outside, but was forgotten when she went slowly back to her place.

The jury was obviously undecided and returned a doubtful verdict, not of murder but death without premeditated intent so that now all depended on the judge. He was keenly disappointed that he could not send his victim to the gallows. He frowned at him and pronounced the sentence with heavy relish.

"Transportation for seven years to the penal colony of New South Wales where it is hoped you will learn by hard work and honest endeavour to lead a useful life instead of wasting the opportunities and privileges that up to now have been yours."

Della sat there stunned. She had alternated between hope and despair and now it was all over. He was not to die but transportation to the horrors of Australia could be worse than death – even if he survived the voyage, how would her father

20

ever endure the brutal life of a convict in that frightening unknown continent from which no man ever returned?

She saw the gloating pleasure on Henri Reynard's face as he turned to glare at her and felt sick. Beyond him the chiselled features of the man she had met on the stairs expressed nothing, neither satisfaction nor pity. She let the men and women push past her in chattering noisy groups before she followed them down the passage and into the street. Now it was all over she felt curiously empty. Now she knew the worst, some kind of a decision would have to be made as to her own future, but she felt too tired, too despondent to think or plan. First she must see her father and speak with him. She had only had one brief unsatisfactory moment with him since his arrest. It had been well nigh impossible to talk intimately through thick iron bars in a long narrow room where other prisoners tried desperately to speak to their loved ones and warders tramped up and down watching closely so that not even fingers could touch through the bars.

"Why, Papa, why?" she had asked helplessly. "Why did you not tell them who was responsible, who was with you on that night?"

But he only shook his head. "I did not kill the wretched man, Della, you know that, don't you? You believe me?"

"Yes, of course I do."

"They have no real proof against me. I shall plead 'not guilty' and if there's any justice in England that should be enough. They can't condemn me on hearsay evidence. It will be all right, my love, you will see."

It had seemed impossible to communicate with each other, to make him realize that even old friends were proving unhelpful and shaking their heads doubtfully and in the end his confidence in British justice had been sadly mistaken. The evidence they had gathered, insufficient though it was, was still enough to condemn him to years of living misery.

He was taken to Newgate prison overnight and the next morning she was permitted to see him. She paused for a moment as she entered the room, the ancient stone walls saturated with human misery, smelling horribly of the thousands who had suffered there mingled with the carbolic with which the floor had been scrubbed. How could her father possibly be one among this row of wretched men, some of them looking anxiously towards the door – how to speak to anyone

21

amongst this babble of voices, of women weeping, children crying and the heavy tread of warders as they paraded up and down?

When she saw him she caught her breath with shock. The thick brown hair had been cropped close to the skull. He had lost weight and the disfiguring prison clothes, coarse and rough, hung loosely on the tall figure. But his smile was the same when she ran towards him and ignoring prison regulations thrust both hands through the iron bars and clasped his.

At first she could not speak but they had very little time and there was much to be said.

"When?" she breathed. "When do you have to leave?"

He shrugged his shoulders. "God knows. They don't tell us much but not yet it seems. I'm to be sent to one of the prison hulks in the Thames until the consignment is big enough to be worth shipping to Botany Bay."

"Oh no!" She could not bear the thought of it. The hulks were old rotting ships used as prisons and conditions on them were degrading and filthy beyond imagination. "They can't do that to you, it's not right, it's not just."

"They can, my love. I'm only a man after all and a convicted criminal like all the rest, no better and no worse."

"Oh how can you say that?" And then with a quick glance around her, she came out with the idea she had been brooding over all the previous night. "Papa, I have been thinking. Could I not take a passage to Australia in one of the ships? Could I not follow you out there so that I could be near you?"

"No, no, no!" His reaction was immediate and vehement. "Not that, Della, never that. God knows I've brought you low enough but not life in a convict settlement. I'm a man, I'll live through it somehow, I'll survive, but I could not do it if I knew I had brought you to such a vile place. In any case we could not be together or even speak with each other for months, even years. Promise you won't think of it ever. I could not endure it."

She tried to argue but he demolished the half-formed notion so strongly that she began to see the impossibility of such a thing and reluctantly abandoned it.

She could not bring herself to tell him of her dismissal from the salon nor that most of their fair-weather friends had already begun to look askance and avoid her lest she should ask something from them that they were not prepared to give. Instead she spoke warmly of Lucinda's kindness and he smiled

22

a little.

"She has been a good friend, Della, and utterly trustworthy. Remember that and don't hold it against her because she works in the theatre and because . . ."

"Because you are fond of her? No, Papa, I would never do that."

Then a bell clanged and the few brief minutes were already over.

He said quietly, "I'm not giving up, Della. I'll come through I swear I will and I'll come back."

"You will write . . ."

"If and when I can."

"And I too," she promised as if those letters could fly back and forth between them instead of taking months and months in passage.

She stretched a hand through the bars to touch his face lovingly and one of the warders stepped up behind her.

"None of that, Miss. You know it is forbidden."

"What harm am I doing?" she flashed at him.

Her father took the hand and kissed the palm closing her fingers over it. "My pledge," he said, "that I will return. It's not the end."

It was not till he moved away that she saw the shackles on his ankles and the heavy chain between them and unexpectedly it was that more than anything that brought the tears to her eyes. They blinded her as she ran from the room so that she did not notice the tall elegant figure that lounged in the doorway and followed with his eyes the long line of shuffling men and in particular the one who still contrived to walk with proud head erect.

The sad fact remains that however unhappy one is, however lonely and wretched, one has still to eat and drink and earn a living. Lucinda was unfailingly kind, though Della suspected she was in her own way as miserable at the parting from her lover as she was herself but at least she had the anodyne of unremitting work. Rehearsals during the day and the play at night left her little time to brood.

"Come and stay with me," she urged Della. "It is better than being alone."

But Della was stubborn. To accept charity from her father's mistress, however well meant, was something she found hard to

23

stomach and in any case now that the trial was done with and sentence passed, she must find some sort of work that would provide a living however modest. The guineas in the silver mesh purse, even if spent sparely, would not last long.

Mrs Barnet was not very hopeful. "Ladies of rank are not going to look kindly on a young woman whose father is a gaolbird," she said bluntly. "The fact that your father has been in some measure one of their own kind and once received in their drawing rooms only makes it worse rather than better. They will feel cheated. Don't tell me it is unjust, I know it, but anyone who expects justice or fair treatment in this world is a fool," she went on acidly when Della protested. "Still something may come up. I'll bear it in mind. Call again in a week or two."

The days went by. It was the middle of April and still there had been nothing. Contrary to all expectation, Mrs Frant showed a grumbling kindness and pushed the money back into Della's hand when she went down to the kitchen to hand it over.

"Give it another week or two. Somethin' will turn up. Them Peelers had to blame somebody and your Pa bein' 'andy so to speak, he was the one they jumped on. He'd never murder no one, not a real gent like 'im and that's what I told 'em right at the start."

It was all part of the rooted distrust felt by the independent Londoners of the new police force, quite unjustified since petty crime especially at night had almost halved in the last few years, but Della was grateful for it as she went off to see Mrs Barnet for the third time in as many weeks.

"There *is* something that came up in this morning's post," she said eyeing Della doubtfully, "and I've no one on the books who would seem to have the qualities required."

"And what are they?" asked Della trying hard to hold down the rising hope and so avoid the inevitable disappointment.

"You've done some teaching, I understand," went on Mrs Barnet turning over the papers on her desk.

"Yes, in my last year at the Convent but they were only little ones. Still I *can* speak French and I did take them for piano and singing."

Mrs Barnet sniffed. "I doubt if those abilities will stand you in much stead in Yorkshire."

"Yorkshire!" repeated Della. It seemed as far away as Africa or the Arctic. "Is it a governess that is required?"

"Not precisely – a teacher in a school if you can call it that."

"A school!" Della's heart sank. Her meagre knowledge of teaching scarcely seemed sufficient to fit her for such a post.

"It seems a certain Mr Thomas Clifford who appears to be in the wool trade requires a teacher for the small school he has set up for the children of his factory hands. His former teacher left to be married and he is anxious to fill the post as soon as possible. How would you feel about that?"

"I don't know," said Della slowly. The prospect sounded daunting and Yorkshire very far away from anything she had ever known.

"Take it or leave it," said Mrs Barnet discouragingly. "There is nothing else and I doubt very much if anything more will be required from you than teaching them to read and write and add two and two. You can do that surely. And it's far enough away. News travels slowly to remote places like Castlebridge some thirty miles north of Bradford."

Escape – somewhere totally different – wasn't that what she wanted more than anything just now? She said on impulse, "If you think I'll suit, I'll take it."

"Very well. There will be three months' probation," said Mrs Barnet, "the terms are generous and include a cottage that adjoins the school. One thing I must say however. For your own sake, my dear, I would advise you to change your name."

"Why? I'm not ashamed of my father," said Della fiercely.

"Maybe not, all the same it would be wise. There could be prejudice. I am afraid you must face that."

Della hesitated, everything in her rebelling against it. She said reluctantly, "If you really think it necessary, I could take my mother's name. She came from Ireland – Olivia O'Dowd Lismore."

"Lismore should be sufficient," said Mrs Barnet dryly. "I will write off to Mr Clifford today and let you know his answer."

Within a fortnight came the reply with a generous allowance of money to cover the expense of the long journey.

Lucinda was doubtful when Della told her about it. They were sitting in her dressing room while she made up for the evening performance. It was strange, but Della found she had received more real kindness from the actors in the theatre than from any of her father's so-called friends.

"It's such a very long way off," said Lucinda leaning forward

25

and darkening her eyebrows carefully in the fly-spotted mirror. "Are you sure you won't be very lonely so far away from everyone?"

"I shall be too busy to feel lonely. There is something else too," she went on thoughtfully, "Papa once told me he was born in Yorkshire – some place called Larksghyll – though I must admit he never really said very much about it. Somewhere or other I may have cousins living up there."

"My dear girl, Yorkshire is a huge area. It covers miles and miles and most of it is moorland and rocks and rushing streams, not a house to be seen, nothing but sheep and cows and goats and sometimes not even those. I know it only too well. I've toured there – York, Harrogate, Richmond, Skipton – I've played them all and it took days and days travelling from one to the other jolting in a coach over the worst roads I've ever encountered. The trouble with me is that I'm a town bird. Give me cities. Great wide open spaces terrify me. I like to see life going on around me – and people."

"Just now I don't think I want to see another human face," said Della with a touch of bitterness. "I think I'd find a sheep or a goat much better company."

"I do know how you feel," said Lucinda sympathetically. She had guessed at the pain caused by Edmund Dent's desertion.

"What do you think he will be like – this Thomas Clifford?" asked Della.

"Well," Lucinda leaned back in her chair, "it is true that I *have* met some of these wealthy millowners – don't expect too much – he certainly won't have any fancy society manners. Most of them have had to fight their way up in a tough world and it shows – and another thing – they won't pay out good 'brass' as they call it without expecting a four-fold return for it. So be warned. He could work you very hard."

Della smiled. "You can't frighten me, Lucinda, and I must do something. I can't just sit back and give way while he . . ." she choked a little as she thought of the hell her father must be going through at that very moment. "It's a challenge and Papa always said never resist a challenge. I will write and tell him all about it."

But that letter, carefully penned to sound as cheerful as possible, never reached him. That very day the prisoners on the *Thetis* were taken off, conveyed down the Thames and packed

26

into the hold of a creaking old vessel which set out with its human cargo on the six months' trip to Australia at almost the same time as Miss Delphine Lismore mounted the Peveril of the Peak, the fastest coach on the northern run, in the yard of the Blossoms Inn in Lawrence Lane off Cheapside at eight o'clock in the evening on the first part of her journey to Castlebridge.

3

Twenty-four hours after the Peveril of the Peak took the Great North Road out of London, they drew up in the yard of the Unicorn Inn in Manchester with a tremendous clatter and the triumphant blowing of the coachman's horn, for they prided themselves on their speed and punctuality. All through the night they had raced north with only five-minute stops to change horses and a brief half-hour for breakfast and dinner at midday. Wedged in beside a stout gentleman who took up more than his share of the seat and snored through most of the night, Della had dozed at intervals, waking up with a start when the horses pulled up and the sharp-cornered box on the lap of the lady opposite shot forward and badly bruised her knees.

At Manchester she was to change and take the coach for Skipton. She climbed wearily out, stiff and aching in every bone. The Unicorn was the meeting place of many coaches going in all directions, Kendal, Edinburgh, Liverpool, Chester. The yard was crammed with a jostling crowd of men, women and fretful children, travellers of all shapes and sizes mixed up with horses and dogs, hunting for mislaid baggage, asking questions and angrily demanding instant attention from inn servants rushed off their feet. One young woman travelling alone without a male protector or even a maid to do her bidding was very much at a disadvantage. She stood bewildered and it took several minutes before she could summon up her courage and pull herself together. This was how it would be from now on, so she had better accustom herself to it. She beckoned one of the ostlers and when he came reluctantly, commanded him to carry her tin trunk into the inn and followed after him. It was a cheerful place filled with bustling life with a rich smell of hot food and mulled wine and a huge log fire blazing in the open hearth. She moved bravely towards it glad of the warmth. Travelling north they seemed to have left spring far behind and despite a thick rug her feet were horribly chilled. A man sitting at the end of the long settle grudgingly moved up a little to make room for her and she thanked him gratefully as she sat down and unhooked the neck of her thick cloak.

All the long hours of the day as they drove past fields and farms, open heathland and woods, stopping in country villages or dirty little towns as they came further north, she had been assailed by frightening doubt. The first flush of independence, of feeling she had done the right thing in cutting herself off from all connection with her old life had faded. Perhaps Lucinda had been right after all and the loneliness, the nostalgia for what had gone, would be too much for her, but nostalgia for what, she asked herself severely. Without her father there *was* no home. They had created it together and without him she was lost. Edmund Dent's desertion had bitten deep. She would never rely on friendship again. She had to make a new life for herself, a new hard-working life in this alien place – she began to nod a little – the heat of the fire after the cold outside was making her drowsy. A sharp voice broke into her dreaming and she sat up with a jerk.

"Can I fetch you something, Miss?"

She looked up to see a decent, middle-aged woman with a clean mob cap and white apron looking down at her and realized that the room had thinned a little. Some of the coaches had left, taking their passengers with them. She was not really hungry. Lucinda, accustomed like all actors to long hours of wearying travel, had insisted on packing a small lunchbasket with bread and cheese, cakes and fruit.

"There's nothing gives you the blue devils quicker than hunger," she had said when Della protested and she had been glad of it during the night and day on the coach.

"Could I have some tea and buttered toast?" she asked tentatively, "and could you tell me at what hour the coach for Skipton leaves?"

"Skipton?" The woman looked at her with added interest. "Would you be that Miss Lismore from London?" she asked.

"Yes, that is my name," said Della surprised.

"Aye, well then, 'tis all booked up for you. Tell you the truth I had begun to wonder when the Peveril came in but the driver was in such a rare taking to get his passengers fed and off again, it went clean out o'my head. Mr Clifford sent word to us through one of his carriers. There's a room booked for you and the coach leaves at seven sharp in the morning." She looked around the inn parlour mostly filled with men drinking and

29

smoking at their ease. "If you would prefer it, Miss, I could bring you the tea and toast to your bedroom. It'll be a deal quieter there, more comfortable like. When the night coaches come in, there's a fair old bustle down here, I can tell you."

"Thank you. I'd like that very much."

The kindness that had taken so much trouble on behalf of an unknown employee was very cheering. Maybe Mr Clifford was not such a hard taskmaster as Lucinda had suggested. She followed the woman up a long flight of wooden stairs and was shown into a little room under the eaves.

" 'Tis not much more than a cupboard," she said apologetically, "but we're over full at this time because of the spring fair but we'd not like to disoblige Mr Clifford so mebbe you can make do. I'll have the girl put a hot brick between the sheets."

"It's splendid," she said warmly. "I'm very grateful to you and to Mr Clifford."

"Aye, well, he's allus been a good customer to us."

She bustled around the room pulling things into shape and turning down the bed covers. The millowner was obviously a man for whom mine host at the inn had a hearty respect, thought Della, and was grateful for it.

Half an hour later, sitting on the bed sipping hot tea and munching lavishly buttered toast, she felt the future might not be quite so bleak as she had feared.

The bed was hard but she was too tired to notice and she seemed scarcely to have shut her eyes when there was a knock on the door and it was time to get up.

It was only just fully light when the coach left for Skipton but soon a fugitive sun broke through and she was looking out eagerly on a bare rolling countryside, all soft greys and browns, with the blue of distant hills that gradually grew more rugged. Here and there gaunt black skeletons rose out of the ground that she knew later were disused lead mines or iron smelting houses seeming strangely incongruous in this wide open country. By early afternoon they were driving along Skipton's narrow high street sloping down from the church and castle perched high on its crag picking their way through carts with shouting men and barking dogs. The air was filled with the bleating of sheep in the huge market pens mingled with the long unintelligible bargaining of the auctioneers as the animals were bought and sold. At last they drew up in the inn yard on the borders of the city where she had been told someone would meet her for the last part of her long journey to Castlebridge.

Whoever it was had not yet arrived so she ordered a pot of coffee and took it to the window so that she could watch who came and went. Despite the fatigues of the last two days she was intensely alive, ready to absorb all she could of her new surroundings, trying hard to understand the unfamiliar broad accents of the men who sat at nearby tables occasionally eyeing her curiously. Farmers, she thought, dalesmen in their frieze coats and cord breeches, not a woman amongst them, only the maid with red cheeks and buxom figure who brought the pots of ale and tossed her head at their laughing sallies of wit. Della had seized the opportunity to freshen her hands and face, recomb and pin up her hair, and straighten the simple grey wool travelling dress. A future teacher, she thought, must look prepared for anything, neat, tidy and unobtrusive, not realizing how very far she was from looking any of these things.

It was while she was sitting there that she saw a young man come striding under the arch and into the yard. He was well dressed in a careless country fashion, riding coat of fine brown broadcloth, pale buff breeches, expensive handsewn riding boots. As he came through the gateway a freak of wind caught his hat. It bowled away merrily and he chased after it, corn-coloured hair blowing wildly in the fresh breeze. He grabbed it just as it skimmed towards a dirty puddle and amused she clapped her hands and laughed. He looked up. She saw him stare and frown, then he smiled back with a slight bow and a wave of his hand.

She drew back a little not wishing to appear bold and heard him shout to the ostler.

The boy came running. "The nag's all ready for you, sir, took him down to the farrier meself an hour gone."

"Good. Bring him will you?"

"Aye, sir, I will that."

The young man whistled as he waited and then when the boy came back leading a sturdy brown horse, she saw him lean forward whispering something and when the boy replied, he looked up again with that odd enquiring stare so that she wondered if he had asked her name.

Then he had taken the bridle, vaulted into the saddle, tossed the ostler a coin and rode away without a backward look. She wondered who he was. There had been recognition in his glance and yet she was sure she had never seen him before in her life. She felt a spasm of anxiety. Had he been at the trial? Could he possibly know who she was? It did not seem probable and yet – she thrust the notion away. No doubt she was only imagining it. All the same there had been a charm about him and she thought lightly she would not mind if she were to meet him again and then told herself how absurd it was to feel any interest in a passing traveller.

It was more than an hour later when a small open dog cart drawn by a stout pony drove into the yard and the driver jumped down and came into the inn. He was small and dark, a typical dalesman if she had but known, in leather gaiters, velveteen breeches, moleskin waistcoat and frieze jacket. His face under the round hat was brown and wrinkled as a sundried walnut. He looked keenly around him and then came across to where she sat by the window.

"Be you the young woman up from Lunnon?"

"Yes. I'm Miss Lismore. Are you from Castlebridge?"

"Aye, I am that. From Rokeby Hall. Where's t' box?"

"Outside."

He strode off without another word and she meekly followed after him. He heaved her trunk into the cart with a strength that belied his small stature and then helped her to climb up into the seat beside him. He looked down at her as she settled her skirts around her, then clicked his tongue, glanced up at the sky and brought a rug from the back of the cart and wrapped it closely around her.

"Might be rain," he said laconically, then took up the reins and they were off.

She had not known what to expect but certainly not that they would be driving some ten miles along a road that was little more than a cattle track and still deeply rutted from the winter storms. As the light carriage jolted from side to side and she clung on to the rail to save herself from being thrown out, she could not help envying the traveller who had preceded them. It would have been a great deal more pleasant on horseback cantering along the green turf each side of the road. Stretches of moorland lay all about them with low clumps of gorse and furze. Then they had entered woodland where she thought she glimpsed primroses hidden in green moss and a shy hint of violets. There was the sound of water babbling over a rocky bed and presently they were splashing through a shallow brook. Her companion was the most taciturn individual she had ever encountered. To all her eager questions he gave only an "Aye" or "Nay" or contented himself with a grunt or a shake of the head so that after a while she remained silent and he began to whistle as he urged the pony forward at a good round pace.

At last they came to the top of a gentle rise, turned a corner and he pointed forward with his whip. To her astonishment she saw what looked like a whole village set down in the middle of this wide open country – rows and rows of small houses, black and ugly, tall buildings that seemed to tower against the pale sky and in another few minutes they were rattling over a cobbled road with children staring and women standing at doorways watching with an avid curiosity as they went by. There was a tremendous noise, a hum and clatter of machines as they passed the giant mill buildings themselves, then they were through and driving on for another mile or so before they turned through tall iron gates and up a long sanded drive.

This must be Rokeby Hall and Della looked eagerly around her. The pony scenting his stable and supper quickened his pace just as a white cat shot across the road in front of them followed by a large dog and a small boy. It happened so quickly that for a few seconds there was pandemonium. She saw the child stumble and fall. The driver shouted as he wrenched the horse aside, then he jumped down followed by Della. Her heart in her mouth she ran with him towards the child who lay spreadeagled on the ground. They arrived together gasping with relief to find him quite unhurt, only winded. By some miracle the wheel of the cart had missed him by inches. He sat up laughing as he tried to brush the dirt and gravel from his blue coat.

"That was a danged fule thing to do, Master Peter," said Della's driver severely. "You could've got yourself killed."

"It was Rusty, Rob. He ran away from me and Mamma doesn't like him to chase the Duchess."

"Mebbe, but her ladyship wouldn't want you to go killin' yourself for the sake of her danged cat," growled Rob.

Then an elderly woman, clearly the boy's nurse, came panting up and began scolding him roundly, the dog trotted back, tail wagging, tongue lolling, and Della saw a white streak slink out of the shrubbery and make a beeline for the house.

The nurse still holding tightly to the child's hand turned to look her up and down.

"You'll be Miss Lismore no doubt. I'm Nanny Roberts. The

Master's been held up at the mill but the mistress will be wanting to see you. Rob, take the young lady up to the house." She shook the little boy with a mixture of playfulness and reproach. "Now come along do, Master Peter, and try to behave yourself for once. Just look at what you've done to your nice new coat. What's her ladyship going to say about it? Blame me for it she will."

She walked on still grumbling and dragging her reluctant charge with her followed by the big dog.

"Little varmint that one," muttered Rob as he helped Della back into the cart. "Eh, but he's a right handful and no mistake."

They proceeded towards the house at a more sedate pace until he pulled up in front of broad steps leading up to a pillared portico. He helped her down, dumped her trunk beside her and drove off presumably to the stables leaving her looking a little forlornly about her. It was a large stately house built perhaps fifty years before in a heavy classical style. It took a moment for her to pluck up her courage, go up the steps and raise the massive brass knocker.

An imposing figure opened the door, scanned her briefly and said, "Miss Lismore, I presume?"

"Yes."

"Come this way, Miss."

She followed after him a little timidly. It was all so different from what she had expected and she wished there had been time to draw back, tidy her windblown hair and prepare to make a good impression. They went up the wide staircase, along a passage, the butler knocked at a door and then opened it.

"The young person, your ladyship," he said and stood aside for her to enter.

The room was so utterly unexpected it took her breath away. White and grey panelled walls picked out in gold, elegant furniture upholstered in rose pink damask, rich velvet curtains in the same shade, a luxurious carpet, silver and crystal everywhere that caught the light from the scintillating chandelier, a fitting setting for the exquisite creature who half sat, half lounged on the sofa wearing some delicate confection of cream silk and organza that Della's experience in the salon told her must have cost a fortune. A deep blue sash circled the slender waist and matched the velvet ribbon that looped up

34

curls of ash blonde hair. A sleek white cat emerged from under the silk skirts and spat at Della, green eyes glinting balefully. She quietened it with a languid hand lifting it to her lap.

"Ssh, Duchess." Her eyes roved over Della with an insolent curiosity. "So you're the new schoolmistress. You're rather young for it, aren't you?"

"I'm twenty-three, nearly twenty-four," said Della defensively.

"Are you? Miss Hutton who has just left us admitted to thirty-five and was forty if she were a day. We thought we'd have her for ever but no – she is actully going to be married – to a clergyman no less. It just goes to show, doesn't it? No one need ever give up hope. How long do *you* intend to stay?"

"A long time, I hope, if Mr Clifford finds me suitable."

"I'm afraid my husband has been detained at the mill. Some stupid creature got her arm caught in a machine, I understand, such a fuss over it. I broke nearly every bone in my body when I used to hunt with Papa, but Tom is so very conscientious. He must see to everything himself. Did you have a good journey?"

"Very good, thank you."

So this was her employer's wife, this lovely insolent young woman, surely an extraordinary choice for a self-made mill-owner. The light voice had a kind of languid condescension combined with a subtle mockery. She might have been interviewing a prospective housemaid, thought Della, and prickled with resentment.

"What made you take up teaching?" she went on with an idle curiosity.

"Necessity, Mrs Clifford."

"Really. I should have thought with those looks of yours you could have found more attractive alternatives."

Della understood the implication and felt the colour rise up in her cheeks. "I'm not sure what you mean."

"I think you do, but never mind." She sighed. "Heigh ho, how delightful it must be to pick and choose as you will. You don't know how fortunate you have been."

How easy to say that when you have lived all your days lapped in luxury! Della said tartly, "It is not always so fortunate, believe me."

"Isn't it?" Violet eyes opened wide. "I'm afraid any other opportunities up here will be very limited. Castlebridge is the most God forsaken place imaginable."

35

"From what I saw of it I thought it rather beautiful and I can assure you, Mrs Clifford, that I am not looking for a husband."

"Not even a lover?" She laughed suddenly. "Oh dear, now I've shocked you. If my husband were here he would scold me for talking nonsense to you."

"I'm not shocked," said Della curtly.

Drooping with fatigue, her feet like lumps of ice and longing for a cup of hot tea, Della was aware that she was being laughed at and was in no mood to go on bandying words for the amusement of this idle young woman. She was just about to ask where she was supposed to go now she *had* arrived when there was a knock at the door and Nanny Roberts came in holding the little boy by the hand.

"Master Peter would like to say goodnight, my lady," she said and stared hard at Della as if daring her to make any mention of that unfortunate accident in the drive.

"Oh, splendid. Nanny dear, this is the young person who will be taking over the school in place of Miss Hutton. Perhaps you will see that she is shown the way to the cottage. You can leave Peter with me."

"Shouldn't I wait to see Mr Clifford?" asked Della.

"Oh no," said his wife carelessly. "Heaven knows when he will come back if he ever does tonight." She stretched out a slim hand. "Come along, darling. Come to Mamma."

The child gave a quick look at his nurse and then raced across to climb up on to the sofa and burrow himself into his mother's lap pushing the white cat out of the way.

"Careful now, Duchess will scratch you and don't tear my dress. Papa won't want to buy me a new one, you know." She dismissed Della with a wave of her hand. "You may leave now, Miss Lismore. Nanny will show you where to go."

They certainly made a wonderful picture, she thought, the beautiful woman and the handsome fair-haired child. There was a furious squawk as the boy pushed the cat to the floor and clambered up to put his arms around his mother's neck. Then Della was following the stout elderly woman out of the room.

"The schoolhouse is between the park gates and the mill," she said as they went down the stairs side by side. "I'll fetch the key and send one of the stable lads across with your trunk."

"I would liked to have seen Mr Clifford first."

"Aye, well, he'll be sending for you soon as he gets back I daresay. The mistress doesn't usually concern herself with anything to do with the mill. You see she was Lady Sylvia Farringford, daughter of the Earl of Sterndale, before she married."

And has definitely come down in the world married to a millowner. Della recognized the implication in the old woman's voice. Was it a love match, she wondered cynically, or a case of marrying an old man for his money?

"Has she any other children?" she asked.

"Oh no, she's delicate, you understand," was the reply as if it was something to be proud of rather than deplored. "I nursed her from a baby, such a pretty thing she was, so I ought to know."

Della had a vivid impression of a rare and fragile flower transplanted against its will into very coarse and ordinary soil. Well, it promised to be interesting at any rate. Then they were in the hall and she was being handed a large key, was told firmly which way to go and set out to walk down the drive in the darkening evening.

She realized suddenly how extremely cold and tired she was and wished that someone had offered to come with her or had even had the thoughtfulness to offer a cup of tea and a friendly word before sending her off to find her own way to what was to be her future home.

It was almost dark when she reached the small ugly building that she realized must be the school and beside it the box-like addition which was as far as anything could be from the romantic cottage she had imagined. A scurry of wind blew dirt and rubbish from the gutter against the gloomy brick walls. She tried to conquer a wave of depression, pushed in the heavy key and turned it with some difficulty.

The door creaked open and ice-cold air flowed out to meet her with the dank smell of any place left uninhabited for longer than a week or two in winter. She walked into what seemed to be a front room though the shuttered windows made it very dark. She bumped into a chair, banged her knee against something sharp, then groped her way to a table where to her relief her outstretched hand felt a candlestick with tinder box lying beside it. With some difficulty she struck a light, lit the candles in the two-pronged iron candlestick and looked around her.

It was a square uninviting room sparsely furnished but clean enough except for a thick layer of dust. Taking up the

37

candlestick she explored further. There was a kitchen at the back with a new style iron range for cooking, plain white china on the dresser, stools at the table, everything clean but completely bare, no food in the larder, nothing in the cupboards, not so much as a biscuit or a bag of flour. She wondered how long it was since the last owner had walked out and locked the door. As she stood there a faint rustle attracted her attention. A little team of cockroaches attracted by the light emerged from under the range and moved slowly across the hearth. It was the last straw. She sank down on one of the stools, shivering with cold and so angry that she had the strongest desire to go straight back to the Hall and tell Thomas Clifford and his sneering aristocratic wife that if that was all the welcome they were prepared to extend to a new employee, tired out after two days and nights of travel, then they could find someone else to fill the post and she would take the first opportunity to go back to London. She sat there broodingly for a minute or two when another slight sound made her look up apprehensively. A mouse was perched at the opposite end of the table, bright beady eyes regarding her hopefully, and for some inexplicable reason the tension broke and she began to laugh.

"I'm sorry, mousie dear, but I'm just as hungry as you are," she said wryly.

The mouse scuttled away and she went back resolutely to the sitting room. The first thing to do was to light a fire. After that, well, she didn't know where she could obtain food at this hour but there was still an apple and some cheese in her lunch basket. That would have to suffice till the morning. If this was to be a test of endurance, then she would rise above it. Never admit defeat. She was her father's daughter after all and she stifled a sharp longing for his resourcefulness and his lively company that could turn the most dismal situation into an adventure. She took off her bonnet and cloak, put them on a chair and set to work.

An hour later she was still struggling to get a fire lit. She had found wood and coal and some rather damp newspaper but obstinately they resisted all attempts to make them burst into flames. The wood either flickered and died immediately or burned for a few minutes, then a shower of soot came down the chimney and the fire slowly smouldered out in a cloud of smoke.

Despairingly she sat back on the rag rug, her hair loosened and falling around her shoulders, her face and hands smudged with smoke and soot, and it was at that disheartening moment that the door flew open with a crash.

A man stood framed in the opening, looming large and rather menacing against the night sky. In all the stress that was to come neither of them was ever to forget that first meeting though at the time she sprang to her feet in consternation as he looked about him, anger in every line of his taut body and blazing in the grey eyes.

"Miss Lismore?" he said and took a step inside the room. "I'm Thomas Clifford. I am sorry I wasn't here when you arrived."

"I understand you were detained at the mill."

She ignored his outstretched hand. He had taken her by surprise and she was very conscious of her dishevelled appearance, her hair in ratstails, soot and coal dust everywhere.

"Yes, I was, an unfortunate accident." He moved towards her frowning. "What the devil are you trying to do?"

"I would have thought that was obvious," she replied tartly. "It's extremely cold and I'm doing my best to light a fire."

"But God damn it – I beg your pardon – I gave orders that this place was to be made ready . . ." his eyes swept around the bare room and came back to her.

"You'd better put those things down and come back to the Hall. You can spend the night with us there."

"No," she said obstinately, "no, Mr Clifford. I would rather not. Since this is where I'm going to live, I would prefer to stay here."

"Don't argue with me please."

"I would prefer not to be indebted to you more than I need."

"This is quite ridiculous. You can't remain here and that is flat."

"I'm sorry but here I am and here I intend to stay."

She faced up to him defiantly even if inwardly she trembled. There was a brief battle of wills, then he made an impatient gesture.

"If that is what you want, you had better let me tackle that fire. I think I might make a better job of it."

"I can do it," she said hastily. "It just needs time."

"Not time, just commonsense," he said abruptly and thrust her aside.

He took off his coat, threw it across a chair and knelt by the hearth. In a remarkably short time and much to her annoyance he had it blazing away cheerfully and began to pile up the coal and wood with a skilful hand while she stood watching him.

He was so very different from the stolid man of business that Lucinda had conjured up. He was far younger for one thing, not much more than thirty, she thought, tall and broad-shouldered giving an impression of great power and physical strength. The flickering firelight played on thick rather untidy brown hair, a craggy face with distinctive features, fine eyes under straight brows, a generous mouth but forceful chin. Not a man to suffer fools gladly, she surmised, nor one to be trifled with.

He rose to his feet, brushed the dirt off his hands not very successfully and turned to her.

"I still think you should return to the Hall with me."

"Thank you for lighting the fire. I shall do very well now."

"What about food? Have you supped?"

Pride forced her to say, "I'm not hungry."

He looked at her keenly, then strode out into the kitchen, flinging open the larder and cupboards before he came back to her, his face stormy. Someone was going to have to suffer for their negligence, she thought.

"If you are determined to remain here, I will send the servants with all you need," he said curtly.

"Please do not trouble."

"There is no question of trouble. I had ordered – well, never mind about that. There is no need for you to make a martyr of yourself, Miss Lismore. People who work for me are not expected to starve. I will see that everything is put in order myself and if you will come to the Hall tomorrow morning, we will discuss what your duties will be." He picked up his coat and shrugged himself into it before he said abruptly, "You are a good deal younger than I had expected."

"That is what your wife said." She was nettled by his tone. "I assure you I have had a good deal of experience with children."

"Have you indeed? Did you say you saw my wife?"

"Yes, when I arrived."

"And she sent you down here?"

"Yes."

"I see." Della had an uncomfortable feeling that Mr Thomas Clifford in a temper might be the very devil to deal with. He paused at the door to look back. "When the servants bring the food, please ask if there is anything further you need."

"Thank you."

"I'll see you in the morning. Goodnight, Miss Lismore."

"Goodnight."

He went out and she followed quickly to see him take the bridle of the horse he had tethered to the ring in the wall, spring lightly into the saddle and go at a brisk pace up the street.

She shut the door thoughtfully and went back to the fire which was already spreading a most welcome warmth through the gloomy room. So that was Thomas Clifford. It had been a surprise and she was not sure whether it was going to prove an entirely pleasant one. He did not strike her as an easy man to deal with and she was only too well aware of her deficiencies as a teacher and of the plain fact that she was masquerading under a false name. Yorkshire that had seemed so far away in London did not appear so remote now that she was here. There had been the young man at the Skipton inn who had eyed her so closely. She had a sudden tremor of anxiety about the wisdom of hiding her true identity. Her brief acquaintance with her employer had given her the impression that he would scorn anyone lacking the courage to face up to the truth. It was a distinctly daunting thought.

Still here she was with no alternative but to go through with it so after a few minutes she went out to the kitchen finding to her relief that water was piped to the stone sink and she did not have to pump it up in the yard as she had begun to fear. She washed off the smudges of soot and coal as well as she could and then took the candle and went up the stairs to the bedroom. It was as cold, clean and uninviting as the rest of the house but there was a chest for clothes, a dressing table with a small mirror and the bed neatly piled with sheets and blankets was hung with faded linen curtains. There was a stale unused smell and she was struggling with the window trying to release the stiff catch when she heard a knock and went downstairs again to open the door.

She very nearly laughed out loud at the small procession standing outside, a middle-aged woman in mantle and bonnet with a boy of sixteen or seventeen both carrying large covered baskets while behind them came Rob, her driver of the afternoon, with her baggage upon a barrow. She stood aside for them to come in and thought all three of them must have borne the brunt of their master's sharp displeasure because the woman whom she took to be the housekeeper at the Hall was profuse with apologies as she unpacked the first basket. She set

41

a number of covered dishes in the hearth to keep warm. In the second basket there were provisions of every conceivable kind, butter, cheese, eggs, bread, tea, with a crock of milk – they piled up on the table and she would have carried them through to the larder if Della had not stopped her.

"Please don't trouble. I can do that."

"No trouble, Miss. Is there anything else you need? You see we didn't expect you for a day or two otherwise all this would have been done long since and so I told Mr Clifford," she went on in an aggrieved tone.

And he didn't believe you and neither do I, thought Della, but she only smiled and thanked her.

"It's very good of you and Mr Clifford to do so much for me. I shall get on famously now."

Rob, with the boy's help, had shouldered her trunk upstairs to the bedroom and came down to stand awkwardly at the door.

"When you're ready, Mrs Fenton."

"I'm coming, Rob. You're sure there's nothing else, Miss Lismore?"

"No, nothing, thank you. Goodnight."

"Goodnight, Miss."

She took up the baskets frowning, her whole manner expressing strong disapproval and pushing the boy irritably in front of her.

Della shut the door on them, bolted it and with a childish curiosity went to peep into the covered dishes on the hearth. There was half a roasted chicken, lying on a thick slice of York ham, huge fluffy potatoes daubed with butter, some kind of a fruit pie and a basin of custard cream pudding. It was only then that she realized how hungry she was. She fetched a plate from the kitchen dresser and on impulse crumbled the last of the cheese from her lunch basket and put it on the floor.

"Your share, mousie," she whispered and giggled.

Then she pulled a chair close to the fire, piled her plate and began to eat with a comfortable feeling that by sticking to her resolution and refusing to yield and return to the Hall with him she had scored a tiny victory. She had made him realize if only in a small degree that she was not just a nobody but a person to be reckoned with or at least she hoped she had.

Della was certainly right in one of her assumptions. Thomas

42

Clifford when aroused to anger could be very formidable indeed. He returned to the Hall feeling considerably put out. He prided himself on the just way he dealt with his employees both at the mill and in private and he had been made to look something of a fool by a chit with a smudged face and coal black hands and did not care for it. A few scorching words to the housekeeper sent the servants scurrying to do his bidding and then still smouldering he went up to speak with his wife.

Sylvia was lying on the day bed reading a novel when the door flew open letting in a blast of cold air and sending the white cat flying off the sofa and under the chair with an angry hiss.

She put down the book and looked across at him. "Really, Tom, do you have to come bursting in like a tornado? You've terrified the Duchess."

"Confound the cat! I was not aware that I was expected to knock at my wife's door."

"Don't be absurd. Oh, for goodness sake, come in and don't stand there glaring at me. And shut the door; there is an abominable draught."

"Sorry, my dear." He closed the door gently and then crossed the room to stand looking down at her.

She glanced up at him under long silky lashes. "Well, what have I done wrong now?"

"Did you do as I asked and order the servants to make the schoolhouse ready for Miss Lismore?"

"Yes, of course I did," she said carelessly.

"Are you sure? Mrs Fenton swears she had no instructions of any kind from you."

"If you believe a servant instead of me." She shrugged her shoulders and put down the book on the side table. "In any case what does it matter? I'm quite sure that class of person is well accustomed to looking after herself."

"That's hardly the point is it? And why send Rob with the dog cart to collect her? She is not a new housemaid."

"I needed the carriage myself this afternoon. Am I expected to walk?"

"Don't be ridiculous."

"It's you who are being ridiculous. Why are you making such a fuss about this young woman?"

"I went down to wish her good evening and welcome her to Castlebridge and found her in an icy cold house, no fire, no food, nothing whatever prepared for her."

"Good heavens, it's not such a tragedy surely. She's got a tongue in her head. She had only to ask. If you felt so upset about it, why didn't you bring her back here?"

"She refused to come."

"Well, that was up to her, wasn't it?"

"No, it wasn't. If I had been her, I would have walked out and gone straight back to London." His calm suddenly broke into anger. "You saw the girl, you spoke with her. How do you think she must have felt? God knows, I don't ask much from you. You could at least do as I ask and run the house properly."

"I do run the house but the school is part of the mill. That's your affair, it has nothing to do with me." She got to her feet and walked across the room, slender, graceful, incredibly beautiful. "That was the bargain when I married you, wasn't it? It's bad enough to have to live here in this house, only a stone's throw from everything I detest."

"Don't exaggerate please. You've always been free to go away whenever you wish."

"Oh yes, a few weeks at Scarborough or Harrogate when you let me off the leash. When did we last go to Paris or London or even as far as York for the races?"

It was an old grievance and he frowned. "I'm sorry but you know as well as I do that it has not been easy for me to get away from here for the last year or two."

"And so I have to suffer for it," she said rounding on him. "Is is my fault that the croppers don't care for your new machines and the combers are striking for more wages or that you're so afraid that these Chartists or whatever the fools call themselves will burn your precious mill down as they've done already at Bradford?"

He made an angry gesture. "Don't talk about what you don't understand."

"Oh I understand only too well and it's all so deadly boring. Now you want to waste good money on a school of all things! I thought when Miss Hutton left that would be the end of it. How many take advantage of it? What is the point of trying to teach anything to children of that class? All it does is to make them dissatisfied with their own lives. Papa always said that education was the curse of the working classes and he was right."

The injustice of her bitter tirade struck at him. He watched her with a mingled impatience and despair, the beautiful fragile butterfly whom he had once loved so desperately nothing would suffice but to capture it and pin it down. When had it all begun to go wrong? For a few brief weeks while his father still lived and he had taken her on a wedding trip to Paris and Italy he had been ecstatically proud and happy, then the assassin's bullet had struck down John Henry Clifford one night as he rode home across the moor and the weight of responsibility had fallen on Tom's shoulders when he was not yet ready for it. For a time he had worked night and day to keep his head above water and supply her with the luxury she expected only to find at the end of it that he had lost his wife if in fact he had ever possessed her even though she had borne him a son.

He came up behind her. "Perhaps Lord Sterndale is right about the school. I am sometimes not sure myself but I have to try. You must understand that." He put an arm around her shoulders. "Come and eat with me. I've had nothing all day."

"I've supped already."

"Then drink a glass of wine with me. Please sweetheart."

He gently lifted the heavy hair and kissed the nape of her neck. Momentarily it stirred her and she almost yielded, then some devil of perversity made her jerk away from him.

"I'm tired. I think I'll go to bed."

Chilled he drew back. "Very well, if you wish. In a day or two I intend asking Miss Lismore to spend an evening with us. She's going to feel lonely up here knowing no one. We'll invite a few friends, the Strattons from Farley Grange, the doctor and so on. Arrange it, will you?"

"If I must."

"I'll look in to say goodnight when I come up."

She watched him go shutting the door carefully behind him and then threw herself onto the sofa in a turmoil of mixed emotions, anger, rebellion, frustration, boiling up inside her with a tormented longing for the one man whom she had wanted and who had been denied to her. Five years had not lessened the resentment at being forced into marriage with a man she did not love. The very fact that in his own way he had tried to please her in any way he could made it worse rather than better, by making her feel guilty. She hugged her grievances to her and would not be reconciled.

Later that evening he came up the stairs and halted outside her bedroom door. For the past year they had slept apart more often than not. It was not that she denied herself to him but a martyred submission to his embraces was not what he had ever wanted. He could buy that kind of satisfaction any time he needed it at Bradford or Leeds.

She heard him come up and then pause. After a moment or two he walked away again and perversely she wished he had come in, taken her by force so that afterwards she could reproach and humiliate him and in the anger would find something to still her restless discontent.

4

Tired out after the days of travelling and the stress of arrival, Della slept later than she had intended. Tom Clifford had not mentioned any specific time for her call at the Hall but she felt uneasily that he was the kind of man to be up and about his business early. She washed in cold water, dressed as quickly as she could and hurried downstairs. The fire which she had inexpertly banked up the night before had burned to grey ash. During the years with her father they had always lived in lodgings. She had never before had to deal with the everyday household necessities and felt her deficiencies keenly. Kettle in hand, she was gazing rather helplessly at the black cooking range in the kitchen with its oven, iron bars and boiling rings when there was a knock at the door. She put the kettle down hastily and ran to open it. A quaint little figure confronted her, brown skimpy hair skewered to a knot on top of her head and an old grey shawl pinned around her shoulders. A brown holland skirt reaching to her ankles revealed small feet in overlarge stout clogs. She looked about eleven and was actually fourteen.

"Master mentioned you might be wantin' for someone to come in and do the rough," said the apparition cheerfully.

It took a few seconds for Della to grasp the broad Yorkshire accent, then she reacted gratefully.

"Oh yes, indeed I do. Would you know how to boil a kettle?"

The girl stared and then grinned. "Aye, I can do that reet well. You'll be wantin' a cup o' tea." She limped in and started to unpin the shawl. "I'll reddy up fire while you fetch t'kettle. We'll have it goin' in two shakes."

She knelt down by the hearth raking it expertly to reveal the still glowing embers hidden in the hearth.

"Did Mr Clifford send you?" asked Della coming back with the kettle.

"Aye, he sent word last night. Me Da's one of his foremen at t'mill." She began to blow on the fire, coaxing a flame and carefully building up wood chips and coal. "Me Ma works

47

there too and so did I till me accident.''

''Accident?''

''Aye, got me foot caught in machine. Doctor couldn't seem to straighten it out nohow so me Ma took me place and I stay at home to look after the young uns.''

She sat back on her heels. The fire had already begun to burn up and she thrust the blackened kettle into the heart of it and got awkwardly to her feet.

''Shall I toast you a nice bit o' bread, Miss?''

''No, thank you, I'll just have tea. How many brothers and sisters have you?''

''Four. And proper old demons they are an' all. Miss Hutton wouldn't have 'em in the school, turned 'em out into the yard with clout on their ears and me Da were right mad about it. Ben, he's the eldest and risin' nine, he wants to go into t'mill but me Ma won't have it. Sez he's got to learn his letters first.''

''Does Mr Clifford employ children as young as nine?''

The girl stared at her with faint scorn. ''O' course he does. Some of t'mills start 'em off at five but the Master don't hold with that.'' She looked round the room critically. ''I weren't ever in here before. Miss Hutton didn't have nowt to do with mill folk like us. Proper dismal, en't it? But don't you worry, Miss, I'll soon have it nice and cosy.''

''I'm very grateful. What do I call you?''

''I were christened Lilian Mary,'' said the girl with a hint of pride, ''after me Granny, but everyone calls me Lil.''

An hour later when Della set out to walk up to the Hall, she thought she might have made a friend in these strange new surroundings and felt considerably cheered. She had insisted on the girl sharing a cup of tea with her.

''Oh no, I couldn't,'' she had said shyly, ''I couldn't sit down wi' you at same table, wouldn't be proper.''

''Nonsense, of course it is if I say so.''

''You en't a bit like that Miss Hutton. Thin as a broom handle, she were, and stuck up with it, right full of herself, but were all put on, see, not real, not like you nor her ladyship neither.''

''Have you ever worked up at the Hall?''

Lil gave a hoot of derision. ''Nay, she wouldn't have the likes of me up there, nor would that Mrs Fenton. Her ladyship brought her and Nanny Roberts with her from the castle when she married Mr Clifford and a right bad day that were for the

48

Master or so me Ma always sez," she added darkly.

"What do you mean by that?"

But the girl only shook her head and set to work lighting up the kitchen stove with a great deal of banging and clatter. Maybe Lady Sylvia Farringford had not endeared herself to the ordinary folk of Castlebridge.

It was a morning filled with the bright promise of spring. The sun was shining, the air smelled fresh and sweet, and Della's spirits rose as she walked briskly up the road and turned into the handsome gates of the park. She was humming to herself when halfway along the drive she rounded the corner and saw the horse coming down upon her at a furious gallop. She fell sideways into the laurel hedge and for one terrifying moment glimpsed the hooves rearing up above her. Then the rider, with superb skill, controlled the frightened mare and brought her to a quivering halt. Della scrambled to her feet to find herself confronting Lady Sylvia herself, no longer the fragile kittenish creature lounging on a daybed but trim and elegant and very sure of herself in her closely fitting riding habit.

"Can't you look where you're going?" she demanded, leaning forward to pat the neck of the restive horse soothingly. "You could have caused an accident and you've terrified poor Sheba."

And very nearly killed me, thought Della, swallowing her indignation with difficulty.

"I'm sorry. I didn't expect anyone to be coming so fast."

"So it's you again, is it? The schoolmistress," said Sylvia infusing a world of contempt into the word. "What did you have to say to my husband last night that sent him home in such ill humour?"

"I said nothing to him. Why should I?"

"Yes, indeed, why should you? If you wish to stay here, you had better know your place and mind your manners, Miss Whatever-your-name-is. And now go on up to the house. He is expecting you and he doesn't care to be kept waiting."

She did not give Della time to reply but was off again like an arrow down the drive. The groom behind her, grinned, touched his hat to Della and galloped after her.

Fuming with resentment she brushed off the dust and dead leaves clinging to her skirt and went on towards the house, convinced that for some reason her employer's wife didn't approve of her appointment though she could not imagine why.

If there *was* to be war between them, then she was prepared to fight back. She marched up the steps and rang the bell determined that no one, no matter who she was, was going to ride roughshod over Paul Craven's daughter.

The butler showed her into a room that by its very plainness formed a vivid contrast to the lavish prettiness of his wife's drawing room. Tom Clifford rose from behind his desk as she came in.

"Good morning, Miss Lismore. You slept well, I hope, and are recovered from the effects of your journey up here."

"Quite recovered, thank you."

She looked very different from the smut-smudged waif of the night before. The grey dress with touches of purple velvet had style combined with a quakerish simplicity which was rather belied by the flash in the dark blue eyes raised to his. Della was still feeling highly indignant at his wife's cavalier treatment.

He pulled a chair forward for her. "Do sit down. There are just one or two matters I felt you ought to know before the school reopens next week." He glanced at the papers on his desk. "Mrs Barnet writes that you have had considerable teaching experience in Brussels."

Oh heaven, thought Della to herself, here it comes. "Yes, I did," she said boldly and failed to add it was only for a few terms in her final year.

"All girls, I presume," he went on. "I'm afraid you will find it very different up here. They are mostly the children of the men who work for me. There are about thirty boys and girls up to the age of twelve. You will have an assistant – Abigail, the daughter of Dr Withers – but she only takes the five-year-olds, I'm afraid."

"I understand perfectly," she said calmly.

But did she? He doubted it. What on earth was that damned woman in London thinking of to send him a girl like this? He should have gone himself and interviewed the applicants personally. He would have known at once that this one was quite unsuitable, far too young, too attractive and too well bred. How would she ever control a bunch of lively youngsters for the most part strongly opposed to having any book learning of even the simplest kind rammed into their thick heads. Most of his fellow millowners whom he met at the Exchange in Bradford thought he was crazy to waste money on any such scheme and had already prophesied disaster. All the same he had set it up two years before and obstinately continued with it in the conviction that eventually it would grow and bear fruit.

Watching him, Della saw him frown and felt her heart sink. She had been foolish ever to have accepted a post for which she was so little qualified. He looked up, met her eyes, thought he read an appeal in them and sighed.

"Have you any family, Miss Lismore?" he asked.

"My mother died when I was very young and my father is . . . he is abroad just now."

"I see. Have you any brothers or sisters?"

"No, no one. It has always been just Papa and myself for as long as I can remember."

The faintly forlorn note in her voice touched him. What kind of a father was it who would send a young woman like this to fend for herself in a world of strangers? He abruptly changed his mind. He had been about to suggest as kindly as he could that a mistake had been made, offer her a couple of weeks salary and pay her expenses back to London but he could not do it. It would have felt like kicking a lost puppy that had followed him home. He could not punish her for not being what he had expected. Let it run on for the three months probation period he had originally suggested.

"I am afraid," he said warningly, "you may find your charges very different from well-behaved Belgian schoolgirls."

"Oh they weren't angels, very far from it," she said stoutly. "I had to learn how to use the cane."

"Did you indeed? You terrify me. Well, we shall have to see how it works out, won't we? I hope you will not find the experience too overwhelming."

"I'm tougher than I look," she assured him.

"I'm glad to hear it." He leaned back in his chair. "My wife will be inviting a few friends to spend an evening with us later in the week. I hope you will join the party. It will give you an opportunity to meet your neighbours. We are rather isolated out here at Castlebridge. Mrs Clifford often complains about it."

"It's very kind of you."

"When you have looked the schoolroom over, you can let me know if there is anything further you will require."

"I will do that at once. Is that all, Mr Clifford?"

"I think so." She got up to go and he stopped her. "By the way did Lil Burns call on you this morning?"

"Yes, she did and I was *most* grateful. I must confess I'm not very good at managing fires and – and things like that."

"So I gathered," he replied dryly.

It brought back vividly their meeting of the night before and he smiled. It struck her suddenly that in his own way he was extremely good looking. The smile irradiated his face and lit up his eyes and she thought that behind the sternness there lurked a warmth and a keen sense of humour.

She said impulsively, "I feel I understand so very little about what goes on up here. The children will know far more than I do. I would like to find out about their lives and the lives of their parents. Could I at some time be shown over the mill or is that asking too much?"

She had taken him completely by surprise. His wife's active dislike, her utter lack of interest in his work, had made him believe that all women would feel like that. Miss Hutton had never made such a request. He stared at Della for a moment.

"Do you mean it? Would you really like to see what we do?"

"Yes, I would very much indeed if it is possible."

"Oh yes, it can be arranged. Leave it to me and I will find a suitable time."

"Thank you. I shall look forward to it."

As she turned towards the door, it burst open and the small boy she had seen the day before stood there, square and sturdy, a tiny replica of his father except for the bright gold of his hair.

He stared belligerently at Della. "I'm Peter," he announced. "Who are you?"

"I'm Delphine."

The peaked eyebrows drew together in a frown and he wrinkled his nose. "That sounds funny."

"Peter, remember your manners," reproved his father. "It's unusual certainly, Miss Lismore. May I ask how you came by it?"

"My mother was Irish and very romantic. She found it in a French love story and liked it so much she gave it to me."

"What have you come here for?" demanded the small boy.

"Miss Lismore is going to teach in our school."

"Can I go to the school too, Papa? Can I?"

"Later on when you are older. What are you doing here anyway? Where is Nanny?"

The boy looked guilty. "I've lost her. I was looking for Rusty."

52

"I see. In that case we had better look for him together." He exchanged a glance with Della. "Good day, Miss Lismore."

"Good day, sir. Goodbye, Peter."

But the child was already rummaging in his father's desk. The last she saw of them was Tom Clifford firmly taking the inkpot out of the small hand. So he had a pleasantly human side to him after all.

She walked back to the schoolhouse with the satisfactory feeling that she had surmounted the first obstacle successfully and perhaps now everything would work out better than she had anticipated.

The first thing she saw when she opened the door was a bunch of primroses that Lil must have picked somewhere, pushed into a cup and put in the middle of the table. The room shone with polish and already had a lived-in look while a delightful smell of baking wafted in from the kitchen. There was a plate of freshly cooked scones and she found that the remainder of the chicken had been chopped up with onion and potato, wrapped in a crust of crisp brown pastry and was keeping warm in the oven. It was her first experience of generous hospitality extended to a stranger and it warmed her through and through.

She ate every crumb with healthy appetite, washed up and went up to the bedroom to finish her unpacking. She put her underclothes away carefully in the chest, shook out her few gowns, assembled her books to take downstairs and came across the tiny golden death's head that Lucinda had put into her hand.

The diamond eyes glinted up at her balefully as she turned it over and over in her fingers. It still affected her painfully – her one doubtful clue to the man who had killed and then in panic and shame allowed her father to suffer the burden of his crime. It brought the wretched business of the trial flooding back into her mind. She sat on the bed feeling the old misery sweep over her again. Where was her father now? Still tossing on the seas between here and Australia suffering the evils of the long voyage with its inevitable sickness, filth and squalor. It would be months and months, a year perhaps, before she could hope to hear from him. With an angry reaction she threw the little golden skull away from her. It was a long time before she could bring herself back to the hopeful mood of the morning but at last her own strong spirit came to her rescue. She recovered the

53

gold ornament from the corner where it had rolled. One day, she told herself, one day she would find the man who owned it and then . . . and then . . . she smiled at her own absurd fantasy. What power did she possess to force him to confess and lift the load from her father's innocent shoulders? She looked at it again for a moment weighing it in her hand and then wrapped it in a piece of tissue paper and dropped it into the box where she kept her few pieces of jewellery. She shut the lid with a snap of finality.

It was a few days later when Della entered the drawing room at Rokeby Hall and was keenly aware that all eyes were turned curiously towards her. She had given serious thought to what she should wear. Not that she possessed all that number of gowns to choose from. Her time with Madame Ginette had developed and refined her taste. She had one dress bought in Paris two years ago in one of their flush periods. A full skirt in deep rose corded silk flowed out from the tiny waist and fine lace edged the square-cut neck and the full elbow-length sleeves. The colour, Papa had said, did wonders for the creamy skin and silky black hair. It had a simplicity that made everyone else appear overdressed and its Parisian elegance was recognized immediately and with mixed feelings by every woman in the room. Surely no mere schoolmistress had any right to look so stylish.

Tom Clifford himself came forward to greet her and introduce her to the other guests. There were perhaps a dozen people present but only a few of them stood out afterwards in her memory.

There was Dr Alec Withers, middle-aged, bald-headed, eyes twinkling kindly behind his spectacles and his daughter Abigail, a gawky eighteen in an unbecoming mustard yellow dress that made her look sallow, but smiling and holding out her hand.

"I'm so glad to meet you and do please call me Abbie. You and I must have a good long talk about everything before school starts. I am sorry my brother is not here. Timothy is a doctor like Papa and he is very interested in what Mr Clifford is doing for the children."

There was Miss Lavinia who was Bret Stratton's great aunt, seventy if she was a day, with iron grey hair piled up under a lace cap, a great deal of heavy old-fashioned jewellery and a forthright manner.

"I don't envy you, m'dear," she said shaking Della's hand vigorously. "I'd start off by boxing their ears all round just for good measure. The fiends stole the old donkey that pulls my garden roller and marched him up and down the moor, taking rides in turn till the poor creature was worn to the bone. Took over a week of my cossetting to bring him round again."

"You should have set the dogs on them, Auntie," said Bret laughing.

"I'd have had Tom after me if I had," said the old lady with a sly look at the millowner. "Everyone knows he has a soft spot for the little ruffians."

Then of course there was Bret Stratton himself and his sister Martha. Della had recognized him instantly as the young man she had seen at the inn. He was even more attractive seen at close quarters and he kissed her hand with an accomplished grace.

"Haven't I seen you before, Miss Lismore?"

"Yes, at Skipton," she admitted frankly, "when you nearly lost your hat."

"Of course, that's it, and I remember wondering what on earth such a charming and fashionable young lady was doing in this part of the world. It quite takes my breath away to find that you're the new schoolmistress and absolutely wasted on thirty little clod-hoppers." He grinned at his host. "I must say Tom knows how to pick 'em."

"Don't be absurd, Bret. You're embarrassing Miss Lismore."

"There you are, you see," he went on ruefully, "Martha always keeps me in order."

His sister was older than he, thirty perhaps, wearing a plaid taffeta gown and with a pleasant no-nonsense manner.

"We live at Farley Grange," she explained, "about five miles further up the valley and we farm or at least Bret likes to pretend he does. You must come and visit us."

Above all there was Sylvia who drifted from one guest to the other, lovely as a dream in a gown of lavender silk with diamonds in her ears and a magnificent bracelet on one slender wrist. Apart from one cool nod of recognition she ignored Della almost completely.

It was a pleasant enough evening with a little music and plenty of conversation. Abigail Withers played the piano,

55

someone else sang rather badly. They were all intimate with one another, talking of people and events about which she knew nothing. She would have felt very much out of it if the doctor and Bret had not made sure that she was drawn into the circle.

At one moment during the evening Tom Clifford, watching how her eyes grew large and bright as if with unshed tears as the music rippled through the room, wondered idly if she missed a lover left behind in London, never dreaming that she was remembering that the last time she had heard that melody had been with her father in Paris when she had been wearing the rose-coloured dress for the first time.

It was Bret who gave her the only heart-stopping moment. The servants had brought in refreshments, tea and coffee with delicious cakes. He came to Della with a cup of tea and a silver basket of confectionery and as she took it from him, he suddenly clapped a hand to his forehead.

"By Jove, I remember where I've seen you before. It's suddenly come back to me. It was about six weeks ago at the Old Bailey during that murder trial."

"You must be mistaken, Bret. Young ladies don't attend murder trials," said the doctor.

"Oh don't they just," he said irrepressibly and turned back to Della. "I beg your pardon, Miss Lismore, but do put me out of my misery – am I right? Did I see you there?"

It had given her time to recover her breath. She had never thought anything like this would arise but to admit it might be dangerous. She had to make up her mind quickly. She had to lie and she hated it.

"Dr Withers is right. Young ladies don't attend murder trials," she said evasively.

"No, of course not, silly of me," but he still looked unconvinced and it worried her. Perhaps one day she could admit who she really was but to do so now could only be deeply prejudicial to the good impression she seemed to have made.

Martha was frowning at her brother. "What murder trial was this? You never told me about it."

"Didn't I? I suppose I didn't think you'd be interested. I only looked in one morning just for a lark."

"I hardly think a murder trial can be called a lark," remarked Miss Lavinia severely.

"I didn't say it was, Auntie. I only went because Oliver was going to be there."

"Oliver Craven? What had it to do with him?"

"The fellow on trial was some kind of distant relative, I believe," said Bret with obvious reluctance. "Look – do we have to go on talking about it?"

"Not if you don't want to," said Tom decisively. "Hardly a subject for the drawing room in any case."

"Oliver has been away from Larksghyll for over two years now," said Sylvia taking an interest for the first time. "What has he been doing with himself all this time? Did he tell you?"

"Gallivanting around Europe apparently, France, Switzerland, Italy," Bret seized upon the change of subject with such relief that Della guessed he regretted bringing up the subject of the trial at all and wondered why.

"Actually we went to Newmarket together," he went on, "and that horse he beggared himself to buy some time ago won an outstanding race and he sold it for more than he paid for it."

"Oliver was always a gamester," said Sylvia.

"Lucky at cards, unlucky in love," remarked Miss Lavinia sententiously. "Has he found himself a bride yet, Bret? It would please his poor father if he did."

"Not as far as I know, though all the Mammas are after him to say nothing of the girls."

"Bret, what a thing to say about him!"

"It's true, Sis. Oliver breaks hearts as often and as easily as our latest treasure smashes the family heirlooms."

Amidst the laughter Della sat silent. Her heart was beating faster than usual. Could this Oliver Craven be the cousin her father had once mentioned? How extraordinary that he should be so well known among this circle and yet she could not say so, could not acknowledge the possible relationship without giving herself away. It seemed that he had been present at the trial too? Would he know her if he saw her?

She said at last as casually as she could, "Where is Larksghyll? Is it far from here?"

"About ten miles away beyond Bolton Abbey, a beautiful spot and a lovely old house crumbling to ruin. Oliver neglects it shamefully," said Tom as if he disapproved. "Did he say anything about coming home, Bret?"

"Not a word. Apparently he is intending to spend the summer in the south of France exploring Roman remains at Nîmes and Avignon."

"Never!" exclaimed Miss Lavinia.

"I can't imagine Oliver interested in digging up the past, he finds the present far too fascinating," remarked Sylvia a little acidly.

"Well, that's what he *said*," went on Bret cheerfully, "though I must confess I did wonder if his 'Roman remains' would prove to be a good deal more lively than a buried classical statue."

"He could be running away from his creditors," said Tom dryly. "It wouldn't be the first time."

Papa's "loathesome brat" began to sound distinctly intriguing and for one rebellious moment Della regretted the necessity to hide her identity and so make it impossible to claim kinship.

Later when the party broke up and she was being helped into her warm cloak in the hall, Tom Clifford came across to her.

"You can't walk home alone. I'll send one of the servants with you."

"No need, my dear fellow," interrupted Bret taking charge. "Miss Lismore can come with us in the carriage. There's plenty of room and it will only take Cox a few minutes longer to make the extra journey."

"Please don't trouble, either of you," said Della firmly. "It's no distance and I'm not in the least tired. I can easily walk."

"I can't allow it," began Tom and was silenced by Martha. "We'll look after her. You come with us, my dear, Auntie won't mind. It's not far."

So she gave in and squeezed into the carriage between Miss Lavinia and Martha and was grateful, for the night had grown cold and damp and her bronze evening slippers were very flimsy.

When they pulled up outside the schoolhouse Bret leaped down to help her out. He took her hand in his and she saw him smile in the light of the carriage lamp.

"We shall meet again very soon, I hope. I knew that day in Skipton that we were destined to see one another again. Did you feel the same?"

"I'm afraid I can't remember."

"You will." He kissed her hand gallantly. "Goodbye for the present."

He waited until she had gone into the house before climbing back into the carriage.

"Lord, I'm tired. I'm getting too old for these junketings,"

Miss Lavinia yawned prodigiously and leaned back closing her eyes. Martha slipped an arm through that of her brother.

"Smitten?" she whispered.

"Oh really, Sis. I'm not a schoolboy."

"Aren't you? I keep forgetting."

"You must admit she is very unusual, isn't she?"

"Good enough to eat," said his sister dryly. "I keep wondering what has brought her here to this place and what on earth made Tom engage her. He could have hardly chosen anyone more unsuitable for that school of his."

"Does it matter?"

"Not really, I suppose, but I think the poor girl may be in for a shock." She glanced at the old lady before she said quietly, "Bret, you haven't told me much about your London trip. You and Oliver haven't been up to anything, have you?"

"What do you mean by that, for heaven's sake? I thought you had a soft spot for Oliver."

"I like him, but that has never made me blind to his faults. Oliver is a 'high flier', not really in your class, little brother."

Bret moved away irritably. "Martha, I do wish you'd stop worrying about me. I'm grown up. I can stand on my own feet now."

"You would tell me if there was anything wrong, wouldn't you?"

"Of course I would, like a shot. And there is nothing, nothing at all."

"That's all right then."

Bret patted Martha's hand and then stared out of the window at the dark starless night. His sister expected too much from him, he thought resentfully. He was no longer the little boy who had run to her with all his childish problems. He was fond of her but he had his own life to live. More and more he sought to escape. He sighed and pushed his gloomy thoughts away from him. There was one thing. It looked as if the summer up here in the dales which he had been secretly dreading might prove a great deal more lively than he had anticipated.

In her bedroom at the Hall Sylvia dismissed her maid and began to examine her face closely in the light of the candles in the silver candelabra each side of her dressing table. Something about the flawless skin, the large eyes with their dark lashes, the delicately pencilled eyebrows, seemed to displease her. After a moment or two she frowned, picked up the silver-backed brush and began to attack her hair with long sweeping strokes.

"Shall I do that for you?" asked her husband coming in from his dressing room.

"No, your hand is too heavy."

"You didn't think so once." He came up behind her, took the brush from her and kissed the top of her head. "Thank you, darling, that was a very successful evening."

"Your Miss Whatever-her-name-is certainly found it so." She began to plait loosely the long silky hair and tie it back with a ribbon.

"What makes you say that and she is not *my* Miss Lismore?"

"Isn't she? You spent a good part of the evening mooning over her."

"Did I?" he said mildly. "I was wondering if those unusual looks of hers – that pale skin, black hair and very blue eyes – came from her Irish mother."

Sylvia frowned. "So you've found out that about her already, have you? What else did she confide in you?"

"Nothing much except that she appears to be very much alone in the world, no family, only a father who would appear to have abandoned her."

"Is that what she told you?"

"No. It's only guesswork on my part."

"She was probably putting on an act to win your sympathy."

"I don't think so. She struck me as honest enough." He looked down at his wife quizzically. "Why so waspish, my dear? Don't you like her? Are you jealous?"

"Jealous of a little dressed-up slut making an exhibition of herself as she did! Did you notice how all the men were hovering around her, even Bret and old Alec Withers?"

Sylvia, who was accustomed to be the eagerly sought after star of any gathering she attended, was distinctly piqued.

Tom smiled. "Oh come, aren't you being a little hard on the poor girl? Bret and the others were only trying to make her feel at home in what is after all rather a closed circle. And she probably only has one or two dresses to choose from, not wardrobes crammed with them like you."

"Do you grudge them to me?"

"You know I don't." He suddenly put his hands on her shoulders and turned her to face him. "You know very well that I would have laid the whole world and its treasures at your feet

60

if I could."

"Oh Tom, don't be a fool." And because she was uncertain and unhappy, she leaned her head against him. "I'm sorry," she whispered, "I'm being a pig, aren't I?"

He put his arms around her and buried his face in her hair. The rare and expensive perfume she used intoxicated him. He raised her up from the dressing stool feeling her body pliant under the thin silk. He kissed her hungrily and she responded as she had not done for a very long time and as had happened many times before he thought this time it will be different, this time we will discover something real, something lasting and valuable between us.

But after he had carried her to the bed, after they had made love, she drew apart from him pushing away the arm that would have held her close to his heart and he knew he was wrong and nothing had changed. Many men would have been satisfied with what he had, but Tom Clifford was more perceptive, more sensitive, asking too much perhaps, but he had once been deep in love and had longed for a companionship of mind and body that had only been achieved very briefly for a few months after their son had been born but never again. He had seen her smile at other men and knew he was envied but up to now he had never doubted her loyalty.

When he was sure she slept, he slid quietly from the bed and went to his own room to lie wakeful and unsatisfied. Some time before the dawn he wondered if in one way his wife had been right and he had unwittingly brought a disrupting element into their life up here with this unknown girl, and then dismissed it as a foolish fantasy born of the doubts and anxieties that always plague the sleepless.

5

During the following few days Della was almost happy. The strain and misery of the trial, the corroding anxiety about her father's fate, retreated a little as it must if one is to live and work. She had never before stayed in a place that was completely her own. Plain and unattractive as the rooms were, it pleased her to add a few transforming touches from what she had brought with her. She walked up on to the moor finding flowers blooming in sheltered places and coming back with a cluster of primroses, violets and wood anemones with tall budding branches which she stood in an old pickle jar. Lil stared at them curiously but she was already developing a devotion to her Miss Della and defended her passionately against the criticism of neighbours.

"What's she want with them old sticks in a pot for?" they said disparagingly. "She'm another of the Master's fancy notions. We don't want no lass from Lunnon up here. The Lord knows what she'll be puttin' into the young uns' heads when they'd do a deal better earnin' a few pence a day at t'mill."

Abigail Withers came to call and over a friendly cup of tea said shyly, "I did so admire the dress you wore at Tom Clifford's party. We never see anything like that up here. I make most of my own but somehow they always turn out frumpish however hard I try."

"I'll help you if you like. I know quite a bit about designing and making clothes."

"Oh would you? You're sure it wouldn't be too much trouble."

"Not at all. I love it really. Wouldn't it be fun to have lots and lots of lovely materials and make them up into fabulous gowns?"

Abigail's eyes widened at such an extravagant notion. This girl was so different from the prim and starched Miss Hutton that it quite took her breath away.

Afterwards they went through the schoolroom together. It

was a large, bare, ugly place with windows along one side set deliberately high so that inquisitive youthful eyes could not be distracted by what went on outside. There was a large blackboard, slates for each child on which they could practise their writing and work out their sums, and a pile of tattered reading primers consisting of short extracts from the Bible, one or two tales of a strictly moral nature and a few verses so stultifyingly dull and colourless she could not imagine how they could possibly capture any child's interest.

"It's mostly learning by heart," explained Abbie cheerfully. "The babies know their ABC already and can even repeat it backwards. Then they start to write on their slates. The older ones have sums and dictation and spelling and Miss Hutton had them standing up and reading every day."

It all sounded alarmingly different from the lessons she had given in Brussels and she waited for the opening day with a great deal of trepidation.

School started at eight and long before that she heard them, a bawling, fighting, rowdy collection of boys and girls who clattered noisily into the playground, the bigger girls tugging their small brothers and sisters behind them. Some of the boys of ten and eleven looked nearly as big as she was in their tattered corduroys and hob-nailed boots.

Abigail rang the school bell and silence fell as Della appeared in the doorway. They jostled and pushed each other into line, the girls bobbing a curtsey and mumbling "Mornin' Miss" as they came past her, the boys pulling off their caps and stuffing them into jacket pockets. The day began with a hymn and she was grateful to Abbie who started it off with her pure young voice.

"Gentle Jesus, meek and mild,
Look upon a little child – "

chanted the children in a tuneless roar.

Della looked them over, boys on one side, girls on the other, the little ones gathered together at the far end of the room. She was not to know that these children represented a tiny minority with parents who, by dint of slaving sixteen hours a day at the mill, could afford to keep their children idle and send them to get some book learning and hopefully better themselves.

She started off by telling them her name and asking for theirs. They stared back at her with wooden faces, the girls with their hair tightly screwed back and tied with a tape or old bootlace, aprons over patched cotton dresses, the boys with scrubbed faces and grubby hands, scuffling among themselves when her eye was off them. Mary Ann, Eliza, Polly and Peggy, Ned, Will, Jim and Joe and Tod – she ticked them off one by one. Would she ever know one from the other, she thought despairingly.

The first day went through well enough with the children mostly subdued and in their own way taking her measure. There was no deceiving them; the London voice, the good looks, the elegant dress that made them think of the ladyship up at the Hall with her proud disdainful glance – all these things were going to be fair game. They bided their time. The persecution started about a week later and began with the snake.

The morning hymn was over. She opened her desk to take out the register and it reared its head and began to uncoil its shining length seeking for escape. She was not country bred. She had never seen one at close quarters before. She jumped back with a scream and the class, most of them privy to the joke, fell about with howls of laughter while the reptile, all five feet of it, slithered slowly over the edge and down the legs of the table.

She could not bring herself to touch it. With an effort she gathered herself together and spoke with as much sternness as she could muster.

"Who does this disgusting creature belong to?"

She was greeted with stony silence. By now the snake had reached the floor and began to flow across it. She was growing desperate when one of the bigger boys gave a smothered snort of laughter. She had singled him out already as a bad influence – cocky but stupid, impudent and when he dared, a bully to the little ones.

"Since you find it so amusing, Jem Carter, you can take this – this reptile outside."

"Sure I will, Miss, if you say so." He swaggered down between the benches, picked up the writhing snake in two hands and held it up high.

" 'Tis only a grass snake, Miss, wouldn't hurt a flea."

"I don't care what it is," she said fiercely, "take it out of here at once."

He walked through the door followed by a chorus of smothered giggles until she swung round to glare at them.

"Now that's gone, we will carry on with our arithmetic

lesson."

They brought out their slates with a clatter, still enjoying the joke while she turned to the blackboard setting out a simple sum with a hand that, try as she would, shook with anger and shock.

But that was only the beginning. Their former teacher had possessed a loud hectoring voice, drilled them mercilessly and walked about the classroom with the cane under her arm ready with a sharp rap on the knuckles at the slightest hint of idleness or defiance. Della's attempts to win attention and interest by gentler methods were regarded as weakness and something to be exploited for the amusement of all.

During the next few weeks she thought despairingly that there seemed no end to their ingenuity. One day it was a frog that leaped out of the desk at her and hopped across the floor to stifled giggles. Another day a baby hedgehog peered up at her myopically. The register mysteriously disappeared and when found was covered with large ink blots so that she was obliged to copy it out again. After a scalding rebuke there was peace for a day or two, then when she dipped a pen in the ink she found that it had been emptied and filled with black stinking mud, while all the reading primers had a habit of vanishing when needed so that hours were wasted hunting for them. Mostly she suspected it was the boys, but even at the sewing class the girls could be exasperating. They lost their needles, mislaid the scissors, tangled the sewing cottons so that they could not be unravelled and made deliberate mistakes in the samplers they were working on so that she was constantly hurrying from one to the other instead of teaching the one or two who genuinely wanted to learn.

Abbie sympathized but could do little to help and she had a frightening feeling it was working up to a crescendo. Then Mr Clifford would hear of it and that would be the end of all her high hopes. It would be back to London and starting all over again.

Bret Stratton had got into the habit of calling on her when he was riding through the village on some errand for his sister of which there seemed to be a great many, and she welcomed his light-hearted company. He never stayed long and was all the time in full view of anyone who happened to be watching, but all the same heads were shaken and tongues began to wag about the newcomer with her foreign fancy ways.

65

She had been far too absorbed in her struggle with the school to realize what had been happening in the rest of industrial Yorkshire but she heard something of it when she was invited to take supper with the doctor and his wife and met Abbie's brother Timothy for the first time. He was older than his sister, had completed his medical studies and was working as an assistant doctor in a large practice in Bradford. He was very thin and dark and looked at Della through thick spectacles. He did not say much while they were eating but afterwards when she was telling them of her experiences with the children and trying to make light of them, he put down the paper he was glancing at and looked across at her frowning.

"That troublesome boy you mentioned, Jem Carter, is he the son of Dan Carter, a stocky red-haired man?"

"That's the fellow," said his father forthrightly, "and an obstinate pig-headed bully he is too. His wife has a serious chest condition and ought not to be working in a mill at all with the atmosphere thick with the dust from the wool but will he listen to me when I tell him she is killing herself? He's one of those who always think they know better," and he snorted disgustedly.

"He's worse than that, he's a troublemaker. I've seen him at some of these Chartist rallies in Bradford. He's a rabble rouser with a gift of the gab. He can kindle a mob into frenzy in a couple of shakes."

"Surely you don't attend meetings of that kind, dear," said his mother a little shocked.

"Yes, I do, Mamma, and in some ways I'm in sympathy with the demands they are making and so would you be if you knew what I see daily. The wool trade has been going down these last few years, men have been turned off and their wages cut to the bone. There are weavers earning less than eight pence a day, which means starvation and sickness for their families."

"Aren't you exaggerating, boy?" put in his father.

"No, I'm not," he went on earnestly. "I've attended patients lying on a heap of filthy sacking with no furniture but old boxes and no food but a handful of oatmeal and skimmed milk if they're lucky. If I was to tell you of some of the things I've seen, it would turn you sick, and it's going to get worse instead of better. It's high time the labouring classes had a say in their conditions of work and a vote to choose their own spokesmen."

"That's dangerous talk, Tim," said the doctor reprovingly,

"and I tell you here and now they will never get what they want by gutting some of the factories and burning down houses of millowners."

"I know that," said the young man impatiently, "and of course I don't go along with violence of that kind, but I'm not ashamed of being a radical and, when soldiers are called in and deal out savage punishment, it drives starving men to desperate measures and they don't always think of the results."

Della looked from one to the other. In London they had sometimes talked of these things. She had heard her father dismiss it airily as a few hotheads rampaging through the industrial towns and very soon put down. It had all seemed very far away almost as if it were happening in another country, now suddenly she felt herself to be in the thick of it, it had assumed reality and in a queer way it was both thrilling and disturbing.

"Mr Clifford hasn't dismissed any of his workpeople or cut down their wages," she ventured uncertainly.

"Not yet, but in the end he may be driven to it and then he could have serious trouble on his own doorstep. Castlebridge has been isolated from the bigger towns but if Dan Carter can spread the infection then he will. The assassin who killed Tom's father was never found, was he? It could happen again."

"Oh no, Tim," exclaimed his sister, "how can you talk so gloomily? You'll terrify Miss Lismore. She will think she has come to live among savages."

"I'm sorry but it's true, every word of it, and I'm not taking any of it back," he said obstinately.

"I don't doubt it's true," Dr Withers' cheerful face was sombre for the moment. "I have sometimes wondered if we were sitting on a keg of dynamite. Let's hope it doesn't explode and carry us all with it."

"Really, dear, what a very unpleasant idea," said his wife with a reassuring smile at Della. "Don't you listen to them, it may never happen."

Then the servant came in with a tray of tea and the talk switched to happier things.

Tim offered to walk the half-mile home with Della and said hesitantly that he hoped he hadn't spoiled her evening.

"Given half a chance I do tend to run on," he apologized.

"I understand," she replied warmly. "It makes one's own little troubles seem such trifles that you feel guilty."

"Exactly. I knew you'd understand. Abbie is a good girl but she doesn't know the half of it living here. I don't come over very often, there are too many calls on my time but I expect we shall meet again. Good luck with the school."

"I expect I shall manage." She held out her hand. "Thank you for coming with me."

"Goodnight and watch out for young Jem Carter. His father is a man who bears grudges."

"I'll remember."

And she did remember for a while. The evening had given her a great deal of food for thought. But then when the crisis came and it seemed that Jem Carter was at the bottom of it, she was so angry that it went clean out of her head.

It began in the dinner hour when the children who had brought food with them ate it in the playground. How the dispute started she never knew but words like "danged ugly tyke" and "dirty scab" were flying about and within five minutes a fierce battle was raging in which every boy joyously took part. Silenced temporarily by the bell calling them back to school, they marched in with blackened eyes, bleeding scratches and ripped clothes and within seconds it had broken out again with redoubled force. In no time the whole room was in an uproar with the girls taking part and the little ones huddling together and beginning to cry. Slates were being smashed and benches overturned. Della's command for silence was completely ignored even if it was heard. At last exasperated beyond endurance she marched through the squabbling mob, forcibly dragged apart the two ringleaders and ordered them to behave or they would be reported to higher authority. She had taken them by surprise and there was a lull while they stared at her.

"And who's that?" sneered Jem Carter at last. "The Master or yer fancy man?"

The school gaped at this outrageous insult and to her fury Della knew she blushed.

"Hold out your hand, Jem Carter. For that you'll get six strokes of the cane."

"You touch me and me Da will show you what a cane can do, Miss High-and-Mighty," and the boy spat contemptuously.

Enraged beyond all good sense she raised the cane and struck him across the cheek. Immediately he snatched it out of her hand. He was as tall as she was and a good deal stronger if it

68

came to a struggle. He took a step towards her but she would not draw back and confronted him boldly.

Eyes glued to this fascinating and unprecedented scene no one noticed that the door had opened and Tom Clifford was standing there until he spoke in a voice of thunder.

"What is the meaning of this disgraceful behaviour?"

There was a sudden and complete silence as every head switched to him. One of the little ones burst into loud sobs and was hurriedly hushed by Abbie.

Tom shut the door and advanced into the room. "Jem Carter, may I trouble you for that cane?" he said levelly.

The boy hesitated for an instant, the red wheal on his cheek standing out clearly, then as slowly as he dared he walked down between the silent rows of children. Tom took the cane from him.

"Hold out your hand," he commanded and brought it down with a dozen stinging strokes that made the boy flinch. "Now apologize to your teacher," he went on.

It seemed for a moment that Jem would defy him, then he mumbled a few words hugging his reddened hand against him.

Tom frowned at the silent class who hardly dared to raise their eyes and then came back to Jem.

"Any more scenes like this and I'll have you whipped and the whole school with you, and now dismiss."

Overawed by the drama of it they clattered out past him with frightened faces as if they expected the heavens to fall at any moment and even the boys were hushed for once. Outside a babble of voices broke out with Jem's jeering words floating back to them.

> "Tom, Tom, the piper's son
> Stole a pig and away he ran . . .

Come on all o' you – has the cat bitten out your tongue!"

But very few joined in. They were well aware that the Master's wrath could fall on their parents' heads and fathers were only too apt to take the side of authority so that there might be the devil to pay. They seized their lunch boxes, grabbed a grizzling brother or sister and scuttled off home.

The taunting words died away and Tom Clifford smiled faintly. "Defiant to the last," he said and turned to Della. "How long has this kind of thing been going on?"

"Oh it happens now and again," she said quickly, "but never

69

as bad as today. You must think me a very poor teacher."

"No, I don't think that, only that perhaps you are struggling with a task that is too hard for you."

"Oh no, no, sometimes it's not like that at all. Sometimes I have felt I was really getting through to them. I should never have hit that boy. I'm ashamed that you should have seen what happened today."

"It was quite by chance. I was riding through and heard the uproar." He paused frowning. "You should have told me about it."

"Run to you for help because I can't control a class of thirty children? That would be very poor spirited. Besides what could you have done?"

"I could have given them a sound beating all round."

"And put them against me for ever. No, I must fight my own battles."

"Win or lose?"

"Win or lose."

"Do you always feel like this about everything you undertake?"

"My father taught me never to refuse a challenge."

"Even if it ends in disaster?"

"Even then," but he saw the shadow cross her face and wondered what kind of father it was who produced a girl like this.

Then Abigail appeared in the doorway. "I've made a pot of tea. I thought we needed it."

"Oh Abbie, what a good idea." Della looked at Tom a little doubtfully. "Will you join us?"

"Why not? I don't usually share my wife's tea table but this is different."

Interested eyes watched him through half-closed doors as he followed the two girls into the house. The Master had never been known to take tea with Miss Hutton.

He not only accepted the cup Della poured for him but bit into one of the sultana scones with obvious relish.

"Haven't had one of these since I was a boy," he said thickly. "I'd forgotten how good they are."

"I don't make them, Lil does."

"I'm glad she is making herself so useful." His eyes roved around the room noting the improvements she had made. "Are you comfortable here?"

70

"Oh yes, very comfortable."

Conversation lapsed after a little. Then Abbie excused herself saying her mother would be waiting for her to return home, but Tom Clifford accepted a second cup of tea and then sat absent-mindedly stirring it. Della thought he looked tired as if this was just one more thing after a troublesome day but did not feel she knew him well enough to make any comment.

After a moment he pushed the cup aside and stood up accidentally knocking a book to the floor. He stooped to pick it up glancing at where it had fallen open.

> "I met a lady in the meads
>   Full beautiful – a fairy's child,
> Her hair was long, her foot was light,
>   And her eyes were wild . . ."

It reminded him painfully of Sylvia when he had first seen her, the enchantment that was turning sour. He shook himself free from it.

"Is this what you read to them?"

"Not yet, but I hope to."

"They will think you're out of your mind."

"Why should you say that? Don't you ever read poetry?" she said nettled by his tone.

"I don't have time. I must go. Thank you for the tea."

"Thank *you* for appearing when you did otherwise I don't know what might have happened. I can be quite ferocious when I really lose my temper."

"Is that so?" He smiled at her. "I'm glad you warned me." Then he was suddenly serious. "All the same I'm a little worried about Jem Carter. I think he may cause you more trouble and try to disrupt the others."

"I'll manage," she said sturdily. "But it's a pity because his sister is very different." She paused and then went on resolutely. "I have been worried sometimes because Mary Ann comes with bruises on her face and once she had a black eye. She says she is clumsy and walks into things but I don't believe that. Is it possible that her father or her brother ill-treat her for some reason?"

"It's possible but don't think you can interfere. Dan Carter is a difficult-tempered man. I wouldn't like him to bear you any grudge."

It was what Tim had said and it made her angry. "I'm not

afraid. Why should a father want to hurt his own child?"

"Who knows? There could be reasons."

"I can't think of any," she said obstinately, with a feeling that he was being deliberately evasive.

"Don't take on other people's troubles," he said warningly. "They won't thank you for it. Yorkshire folk are tough and independent. They don't welcome strangers interfering in their affairs. Do you understand?"

"Yes, Mr Clifford," she replied with suspicious meekness.

He gave her a sharp look. "I mean it, Miss Lismore. I was born and brought up here. I know what I'm talking about."

"I'm sure you do and thank you again for coming to my rescue."

"To tell the truth I rather enjoyed it," he confessed with a boyish grin. "Jem Carter is a young bully and needs taking down a peg or two. And now I must go. We are dining out and I'm late already. Goodbye for the moment, Miss Lismore."

She watched him ride away as she had done once before and was not sure how she felt about him. From the very first moment she had looked up and seen him standing in the doorway with the night sky behind him on the day she had arrived, he had disturbed her. He was so different from the other men she had met, more direct, without airs or graces or pretty deceitful words and yet in his own way undeniably attractive. She wondered if that spoiled beautiful wife of his with her offhand insolent charm appreciated her good fortune. Probably not. Her life had been too safe, too pampered, she had never had to fight for her share in the world's riches.

She sighed and went into the house. It had been an upsetting day and she still felt shaken. It was a relief to find him on her side, but how long would it last if it all happened again, as she knew it might, despite her bold words? She wished again passionately that she had not deceived him about herself. He would despise her if he knew and she was surprised to realize how much she would be hurt by his contempt. She piled the teacups on a tray and carried them through to the kitchen trying to push all such unprofitable thoughts out of her mind.

If truth were known Tom Clifford was similarly puzzled by her. She was so totally unlike Sylvia and yet just as far from the simpering daughters of his fellow millowners whom he was forced to entertain or even the fashionable young ladies in some of the great houses to which his wife had given him entry.

72

He had been a lonely child, growing up without brothers or sisters and losing his mother when he was ten years old in the cholera epidemic that had swept West Yorkshire, a disaster that had taken not only his mother and Bret's parents but a great number of poor folk in the farms and mills. He had battled his way through school at Sedbergh, asserting his pride in his father's achievements and holding his own against the sons of the great landowners very much inclined to look down their noses at anything to do with trade. It was there that he had befriended Bret, five years younger than himself, a pretty delicate child, readymade victim of schoolboy malice and bullying, and it was there they had met Oliver Craven, utterly different from both of them, elegant, clever and devilishly handsome. They had formed a queer threesome, Bret openly dazzled by Oliver, Tom half admiring and half distrustful, and yet in some perverse way they had stuck together, getting into scrapes and loyally lying each other out of them. Living within ten miles they grew up in each other's company, arguing, fighting, hunting, with occasional forays into Bradford or Leeds for more disreputable pleasures until the time came for them to go their separate ways. Tom was forced reluctantly into the mill where his father was determined he should learn every phase of the textile trade and Oliver always in debt, sowing his wild oats far and wide, with Bret tagging behind, neglecting his inheritance and causing his sister endless anxiety.

It was at one of the parties at Farley Grange that Tom met Sylvia for the first time and fell utterly and blindingly in love. The Earl of Sterndale's great house lay in Nidderdale in the North Riding but there was some slight family connection with old Miss Lavinia and occasionally Sylvia came to spend a few days with Bret's sister Martha.

She was seventeen, lovely, high-spirited and utterly un-disciplined, a bargain that her father hoped would one day help to recoup the family fortunes. Some of the great families were feeling the pinch after the long years of the Napoleonic wars and when he was approached by the wealthy John Clifford on behalf of his son he was inclined to lend a favourable ear. Heaven knows the girl had caused him enough trouble already!

She was only sixteen when he had found to his considerable anger that his only daughter was daily riding alone across the moors with a young man of whom he utterly disapproved. Confronted with him she confessed herself defiantly in love.

"The fellow is a bounder," raged the Earl to his daughter in no uncertain terms, "a thoroughgoing unprincipled rake," whom he knew from careful enquiry had wasted his inheritance and was as much in debt as he was himself. She had wept, pleaded, argued and finally in desperation bolted with him only to be brought back ignominiously after a couple of days, very nearly damaged goods. It was hushed up of course, the man's name never mentioned, the whole affair shrouded in mystery. She was sent away for a month or two ostensibly visiting a sick relative and when she came back found herself already promised to the wealthy millowner who was only too ready to buy a titled wife for his only son.

"Don't be a fool, girl," the Earl had said to her when she stood before him, white, tearless, her heart seared with agony that the man she loved so desperately had shrugged his shoulders as he let her go, making no attempt to brave out her defiant wilful gesture.

"I'm not forcing you to marry the old man for God's sake," went on her father reasonably. "After all is said and done he is a Clifford and they were great figures in this neighbourhood at one time."

"Hundreds of years ago," she retorted haughtily. "I'm not marrying ancient history."

"Now you listen to me, my girl," said her exasperated father. "After the way you've been going on, you can thank God for your good fortune. Tom Clifford is a personable enough young man, brought up as a gentleman and if I'm any judge the poor devil is besotted with you. Any young woman worth her salt would have him on his knees to her in no time."

Tom Clifford with whom she had flirted at the Strattons simply to hide the love that was eating at her heart – she had even let him kiss her once, purely to deceive Martha's sharp eyes. She contemplated running away again and knew she had not the courage for so desperate a step.

And so they were married and everyone said what a handsome couple they made and how fortunate she was, but nothing had worked out as either of them had expected. Tom could not be fooled so easily. He surrounded her with luxury, gave her everything she asked for, created rooms especially for her in his father's substantial but plainly furnished house and it was only when the hope he cherished of winning her love had at last flickered out that the angry bitterness had grown slowly between them.

He knew nothing of that early passion that bedevilled her and had dismissed contemptuously the sly hints and innuendoes that occasionally reached his ears, but for this last year he could not but be aware of the canker that ate at the heart of their marriage and slowly destroyed it.

Some of this was passing through his mind as he rode towards the Hall possessed by a restless dissatisfaction. He had never looked at another woman since his marriage. At first because no one else measured up to Sylvia in his eyes, and for the past year or so because it went against his own particular code of conduct. But now more than once he had found his thoughts wandering to Della. There was something about her, something strange and hidden that intrigued him. She was plainly unfit for the task she had taken on and yet he admired the courage and determination with which she was tackling it. Sooner or later he would have to find a substitute and then what? He shied away from making a decision. His hard-headed acquaintances would have thought him out of his mind. They never employed anyone except to their own advantage. Well, to hell with them! What he did was his own affair. Mentally he shrugged his shoulders as he trotted up the drive and saw Peter come tumbling down the steps and race towards him. He pulled up, leaned down and scooped up the boy, setting him in front of him on the horse.

"You're late, Papa," said his son accusingly.

"Am I? Isn't it time for you to be in bed?"

"I wouldn't go. Nanny is cross and so is Mamma. I've been waiting *hours*. Where have you been?"

"Punishing naughty boys at the school."

"Did you beat them?"

"Yes."

"Would you beat me if I were naughty?"

"Certainly."

They grinned at one another in perfect love and trust.

The boy started on a new theme. "Papa, when can I have a pony of my own? Mamma says I am too young."

"She may be right. Your Mamma knows a great deal more about horses than I do. Perhaps when you are five."

"But that's not for *ages*. It will be nearly Christmas."

"All the better. It can be a combined present. You shall come with me to the horse fair in the autumn and we will choose him together."

"Promise?"

He wetted his finger and held it up solemnly. "Promise – wet or dry."

At the house he let the boy slip to the ground and dismounted. One of the stable lads ran to take his horse and father and son went into the house hand in hand. Peter was the one priceless gift Sylvia had given him and for that he would be prepared to forgive her a very great deal.

6

For a few days life went on peacefully. Tom Clifford's dramatic appearance had shocked the children into good behaviour. Della guessed it wouldn't last long but it gave her a welcome breathing space. Jem was absent and when she questioned his sister, the girl shook her head.

"He en't comin' no more, Miss, and neither will I, not after the summer. Me Da says I'm old enough to be earnin'."

"But that's such a pity. You were getting on so well."

Mary Ann looked away. "Aye, but me Da don't care nothin' about me, see. It's only me Ma who wants me to come to the school."

"And what about you? Don't you want to come?"

"I shall miss the readin'. I liked that. 'Twere like lookin' out of a window and seein' a new world outside."

"I'll lend you books, Mary Ann, suitable ones you can read for yourself."

"I don't know," she said doubtfully.

"You must try," she urged. "You've got brains, you could make something of yourself."

The girl had been one of the brightest of her pupils and it made her angry that the tough brutal father should prevent her from improving herself. She looked shyly pleased and frightened at the same time. She was tall for her age with a slim grace about her that made her stand out from the others. With her hair washed and combed, her face unbruised and a clean cotton frock, she could be very pretty.

Della had known it was only a lull and it broke at the end of the following week. She was up early that morning busily putting coal into the stove which she had learned to master and filling the kettle for breakfast when Lil came bursting in, filled a bucket with water, snatched up a scrubbing brush and rushed out again.

"What is it? What has happened?"

Della followed her through the front door and then stopped

horrified. The message was plain, written in foot-high capitals along the school wall.

"Git out, ye dirty whoor, and stay out!"

For a moment she was stunned. The savagery of it struck her like a physical blow. Surely she had not deserved this. For a sickening minute she wondered if they had found out about her father and this was their way of showing it, but somehow she knew that that discovery would have been expressed differently. There was an ugly mean spite about this that was very disturbing.

Lil said furiously, "It's that Jem. Our Benjie heard him boastin' night before last about what he was goin' to do to you, the dirty tyke. I wish I had him here. I'd teach him summat."

She dipped her brush in the bucket and slapped it vigorously against the wall, scrubbing at the letters but they were not that easily washed away. They had only succeeded in getting rid of part of it when a cheerful voice broke in on them.

"What do you two girls think you are doing on this lovely morning?"

"You can see perfectly well what we're doing," said Della acidly.

Bret pulled up his horse to look closer and his voice changed. "My God, who the devil did that?"

"I don't know and I don't care but I'm not having it stared at by everyone who passes by." She scrubbed away harder than ever.

Bret swung himself from his horse. "Lend me a brush and I'll give you a hand."

"Thank you but we're quite capable of dealing with it ourselves," said Della icily.

"As you like." He grinned ruefully. "But don't turn on me. I'm not responsible for this dastardly attack."

Della paused and let fall the brush. "I'm sorry. It's just that it was so – so horrible to come out and see something like this."

"I should say it was. It must be those confounded children. You wait till Tom hears about it. He'll scalp the little demons."

"No," said Della quickly, "no, don't tell him, please don't. When it's all washed out, it will be forgotten and surely that's better. You don't want to worry him with such – such foolery."

"He's bound to hear about it but if that's what you really want . . ."

"It is, it is. I'd rather ignore it than make a big issue out of it." She shivered suddenly as if a bleak wind had blown against her.

"You go in, Miss," said Lil. "I'll finish this. The kettle will be on the boil by now."

"So it will and the children will be coming in to school soon. I'm sorry, Mr Stratton, but I can't stand and chat. I've work to do."

She went back into the house and Bret followed her.

"I won't keep you a minute, I promise, but Martha would like to know if you'd care to spend the day with us on Sunday."

She had gone into the kitchen, had taken down the canister and was measuring tea into the pot.

"Perhaps she'd rather I didn't come when she hears about all this."

"Good Lord, do you think my sister would take any notice of dirty-minded village brats? Do come. I'm afraid it's a five mile walk up the valley but I'll fetch you in the carriage immediately after church."

She still hesitated. "I don't know . . ." and he came closer, taking her hand in his.

"I mean it. I'm not just saying it because of that filthy rubbish on the wall outside."

"If you're sure . . ."

"I'm very sure. Martha has been talking of it ever since that first evening we met."

She gave in. "Very well. I'd love to come."

She raised her eyes to his and he drowned in their blue depths and thought there were very few young women of his acquaintance who could look so devastatingly attractive at seven o'clock in the morning in a water-splashed apron with wisps of dark hair blowing across her forehead and straying on to the white neck.

"Good," he said. "I'll pick you up soon after twelve."

The kettle boiled. She withdrew her hand and filled the teapot.

"Will you take a cup with us?"

"Thank you, no. Martha will be waiting to breakfast with me. Till Sunday then."

"Till Sunday."

She smiled and went with him to the door. His cheerful friendly manner, his ready invitation, had taken some of the sting out of the morning.

Lil stared after him. "He's a real nice gentleman, that Mr Stratton, and he fancies the look of you, Miss Della. Anyone can see that."

"Don't be silly. Is the wall clean?"

Lil dumped the scrubbing brush into her bucket. "Aye, cleaner than it's been for many a long month. Silly danged fool! I don't know what that Jem thinks he's up to, scrawling dirty words on brick walls. I'd like to see our Ben do a thing like that. He'd get such a beating he wouldn't sit down for a week!"

But Della knew very well that it wasn't only Jem. It must be his father behind him who had inspired the insult and maybe there were others in it too. She wondered if in hitting out at her they were also striking at Tom Clifford because he had brought her there. It was an unpleasant thought.

Bret was waiting for her outside the square-towered church which must have belonged to the original village and was now streaked with soot and smoke from the working of the mill. She glimpsed Tom Clifford in the front pew with Sylvia beside him stylishly incongruous among this plainly dressed community in her corded silk gown, the drooping ostrich feathers in her hat mingling with the ash blonde hair.

Heads were turned to stare as Bret handed Della into the dashing two-horse carriage before he took his seat beside her and whipped up the pair to a smart trot. They drove through a rolling open countryside with the blue grey hills beyond them and the meadows alive with grazing sheep and lambs. It became wilder as they climbed, with the occasional ripple of a sparkling stream babbling over grey stones. The May sun had brought out the flowers and here and there patches of bright colour starred the fields and hedgerows.

Farley Grange was an unexpected delight. Screened by trees as they trotted down the winding drive, she caught glimpses of crenellated turrets and walls of silvery stone. Rokeby Hall stood large, square and handsome, its owner asserting proudly, "I made this. This is my work created from nothing," but the Grange had stood for more than two centuries. It was an aristocrat, a little faded perhaps, but still beautiful, still with its own style and grace.

"What a lovely house," she exclaimed when Bret handed her down and she saw the central tower, the long wings with their mullioned windows, the curving graceful steps leading to the pillared portico.

"Do you think so?" Bret carelessly tossed the reins to a boy who had appeared from the stables. "Martha adores it, always has since she was a child. I can never shift her out of it but sometimes I feel it is a prison in which I am trapped."

To Della who had never belonged anywhere, who had not lived long enough in any place to think of it as home, his attitude seemed like sacrilege.

"Oh Bret, how can you say such a thing! You don't know how fortunate you are," she exclaimed without thinking.

"You called me Bret," he said delightedly. "Does that mean I may call you Della?"

"If you wish of course and if we are going to be friends."

"Is that how you think of me? I should like that."

He took her arm and pressed it as they went together up the steps and into a lofty timbered hall which smelled pleasantly of beeswax and the spicy scent of the potpourri of dried flower petals that filled a great porcelain bowl on the oak table. A maid appeared to take her bonnet and shawl and then she was warmly greeted by Martha.

"I'm so glad you got here safely and were not too shaken up. I don't always trust Bret's driving."

"Oh I say," he exclaimed, "that's not fair."

"He forgets he's not driving down to Brighton with some of his rackety London friends," went on his sister and took Della's hand. "Come in to the fire. This sunshine is treacherous. It looks warm but the wind can be bleak up here in the hills."

Huge logs burned on the wide hearth filling the room with the sweet fragrance of applewood and Della crossed to greet Miss Lavinia who was in a stiff old-fashioned Sunday gown of rustling black silk, white lace on the piled grey hair surmounted by a coquettish velvet bow.

"Forgive my not getting up. Rheumatics plague my old bones," she said cheerfully. "Well, young lady, I hear you've already engaged in hostilities with those young rapscallions at Castlebridge. I'm glad to see you're still whole and in one piece."

"I'm not made of porcelain," said Della smiling. "I don't break easily."

"That's more than can be said for some of the young females Bret has brought here," said the old lady tartly.

"At least you will admit they were all beautiful, Auntie."

"Beauty is not everything, not by a long chalk. Come and help me up, boy, and what about luncheon, Martha, I'm feeling peckish?"

Bret hauled his aunt to her feet and they all went into the dining room together.

It was a day Della was to enjoy immensely, partly because Martha's unaffected manner made her feel instantly at home. Until that moment she had not realized how lonely she had been, how tensed up to fight, how nerve-rackingly on the defensive. Now she relaxed and blossomed in the friendliness of her hosts.

She found out very soon that it was Martha who dominated the household. Nominally of course it all belonged to Bret. He was the master of Farley Grange and its long history, of the wide acres, the many farms, the flocks of sheep and herds of cattle, but it was Martha who knew to a nicety the right value to be placed upon ewes and new lambs, who argued over the selling price of fleeces with Tom Clifford, who went to the hiring fairs and stock sales with her estate manager and selected the new rams with skill, who examined the horses for breeding and then left the actual bargaining to him remaining watchful in the background. No self-respecting auctioneer would willingly bargain with a woman and she refused to be cheated simply because of her sex.

After luncheon, with the day still so fine and bright, Bret suggested he might show Della the gardens and frowned when Martha said blandly that she would come with them.

"Aunt Lavvy likes to take a nap in the afternoon," she added lightly, ignoring her brother's obvious annoyance. She glanced at Della's sandals. "But you can't go walking up here in those, my dear. Better borrow a pair of my short boots."

Della laughed and pulled them on before they walked out, all three of them, to admire Martha's rose plot just coming into bloom and the crimson ramblers that climbed up the stone walls. They followed a rustic path through the woodland until they came out to where a small temple had been built on the top of a knoll.

"My great-great-uncle set it up," said Martha. "He liked the view across the valley. You can just see the ruins of Bolton Abbey if there is no mist and beyond is Bardon Lodge where the Cliffords lived in the fourteenth century."

"Is Tom Clifford descended from them?" asked Della

lightly.

"Some people like to say so though there's a bar sinister somewhere," said Bret laughing. "Some unscrupulous Clifford who took a pretty servant girl to his bed. They used to rag him about it at school."

"Oh Bret really! I'm sure Miss Lismore doesn't want to listen to ancient scandals probably untrue. In any case Tom Clifford can stand on his own feet. He doesn't need a long line of ancestors behind him."

"Not like us," murmured Bret mischievously. "Anyway who cares? We are ourselves, aren't we?"

"I like to think so," said Della sturdily and then found herself thinking suddenly of Larksghyll and the family on whom her father had turned his back. Nevertheless it must also be part of her own past and she was aware of an intense curiosity to find out more, to explore into it for herself and perhaps for her father so far away from her now.

"You look very serious. What are you thinking about?" asked Bret quietly.

"Nothing important," she said quickly.

They returned home by the way of the stables and she stopped to admire the huge Cleveland farm horses and the half a dozen others whose heads peered down at her over the half doors.

Martha said, "Do you ride, Miss Lismore?"

"Oh yes, not as much as I would have liked because Father and I were mostly living in cities."

"Borrow one of our nags," said Bret impulsively, "any time you wish. I'd be very happy to show you some of our beauty spots."

"I'd enjoy that above all things, but I have very little spare time."

"Then we must make time. Can't let Tom work you too hard," he went on gaily.

"Bret, you forget," interrupted his sister reprovingly. "Miss Lismore is not here entirely for pleasure. But all the same," she went on, turning to Della, "I'd be very pleased to loan you a horse on a Sunday if you would like to see some of our very splendid country up here."

"Thank you. I will remember that."

They returned to the house for tea with hot pikelets and toasted scones served with cream and strawberry conserve.

Miss Lavinia, wideawake now and wiping her fingers fastidiously on a linen napkin, smiled across at her.

"Come and sit by me, my dear. I love a gossip. Bret and Martha have monopolized your company long enough."

The old lady pushed aside her embroidery frame and patted the sofa. "On this side, my right ear is a little hard of hearing. Now tell me," she went on as Della settled herself, "how are you getting on with Tom Clifford?"

"He has been very kind," said Della cautiously. "I don't see much of him."

"Except when he rescues you from the mob and takes tea with you afterwards, eh?" She smiled at Della's look of surprise. "Oh yes, I know all about that, nothing much escapes my notice, you know. No harm in it of course, none at all, but be careful, my dear. We're a small closed community up here and there are some in Castlebridge who would be glad to find bricks to hurl at him if they could."

"But why? What have I done wrong, apart from not being a very good schoolmistress?"

"Perhaps that is exactly why," she said bluntly. "They ask themselves why a hard-headed business man like Tom Clifford should employ anyone quite as unsuitable and as attractive as you are."

Della felt herself colour. "But that's ridiculous."

"Is it?" said Miss Lavinia dryly. "I knew Tom's father. Now he was quite a different kettle of fish. He built that mill up from nothing and deliberately picked Castlebridge half way between the great woollen merchants in Bradford and the farming communities of the dales who were his first suppliers of fleeces. He told me once that he had seen both his parents die miserably in poverty so that when prosperity came to him he was determined to hold on to it and make sure that his son should never suffer in the same way. He was loyal to those who worked for him wholeheartedly but anyone who rebelled or went on strike or who questioned his authority was out and no pleading would move him to take the rebel back. The worst disservice he ever did his son was to get himself killed too early."

"I heard about that. Did they ever find out who did it?"

"The verdict was robbery with violence by persons unknown, but there had been trouble at the mill shortly before, when he installed some new machines. No use asking me details, my dear, all I know is how to knit a stocking and turn a heel, but it meant cutting down on the number of workers. There were riots, ugly scenes in the streets. For a time he slept at the mill each night with a loaded pistol beside him. It's my belief that one of them knew he would be returning from Bradford that evening and ambushed him on his way home, but they could prove nothing. The money he was carrying was gone and they called it simply robbery and so it was but I'm pretty certain there are men now working the looms who could tell a very different story. Tom was in Paris at the time with his bride and had to return forthwith to pick up the pieces."

"It must have been a terrible shock."

"It was. He was attached to his father but he pulled round, with no help at all from that silly flighty wife of his."

"Lady Sylvia is wonderfully beautiful."

"Beauty!" snorted Miss Lavinia. "What good is that to a man when all's said and done? He needs a wife to be at his back, supporting him, keeping his bed warm and giving him children, not spending his money on fine clothes and expensive jaunts here, there and everywhere. I know all about Sylvia Farringford. Her father, Sterndale, was my mother's cousin. He spoiled her outrageously and then when she became too difficult to control, he married her off with a good profit to himself. One day Tom is going to wake up to his bad bargain if he hasn't done so already," went on Miss Lavinia forthrightly. "I'll tell you something about him, my dear, he is a divided man. One part of him is like his father, hard and tough as oak, but the other part is too compassionate, too inclined to listen to idealistic fools like Timothy Withers."

"But is he such a fool?" argued Della. "What he told me when I was with him and the doctor seemed to make very good sense."

"Anyone who believes he can change the rulers of this country at a drop of a hat *is* a fool. Change has to grow in the public mind and that takes time. Given that, Tom may be able to do it but not if they put him up against a wall and threaten him. He can be persuaded but not broken."

She's a wise old bird in her own way, thought Della, drinking it all in and beginning to understand more about the man who was occupying rather more of her thoughts than he should.

"It's Martha he ought to have married not that self-willed young woman with her fancy ways."

"Was Martha in love with him?" whispered Della intrigued.

"Martha? Oh dear no, when do young women do the sensible thing? She lost her heart to that handsome rogue, Oliver Craven, when she was barely fourteen, not that it ever got her anywhere and she'd die rather than admit it."

That name again. It had a curious way of cropping up.

"Did you ever go to Larksghyll?" she asked.

"Only once. Oliver's father is something of a recluse, has been for years, doesn't entertain at all. There was some mystery, some tragedy connected with his wife. Some say one thing, some another. I never knew the ins and outs of it. I did not come here until after the death of the Strattons in that shocking epidemic when Martha was only twelve. Mary Stratton was my niece. I couldn't leave the child alone with her little brother in this great house so there was nothing else for it but to pack up and come. Someone had to take charge at Farley Grange."

"Did you ever regret it?"

"Sometimes. It was a far cry from my peaceful existence in the Cathedral Close at Chester but at least it was not dull. Youngsters in and out of the house all the time. I saw them growing up together, Tom and Martha and Oliver with their friends, and Bret tagging along after them trying to catch up, poor boy."

She raised her glasses and peered short-sightedly at Della. "It's very odd but when we first met you reminded me of someone and I couldn't place it. Now I've suddenly remembered – that dark hair and very blue eyes – there's a portrait at Larksghyll."

Della was startled. "A portrait? Of whom?"

"I haven't the faintest idea. It was hanging in a room that I blundered into by accident, a kind of lumber room full of discarded furniture and boxes. But it hung under the light and caught my eye, a very handsome young woman whoever she was."

"I've never been to Larksghyll in my life."

"No, why should you? It's just one of those inexplicable coincidences," said Miss Lavinia comfortably. "And now I can see Martha bearing down on me. I'm keeping you too long, my dear, and it's time for you to leave. Come and see me again."

"Of course I will. I would like to very much if Martha will ask me."

"I've no doubt we shall be seeing a great deal of one another during the summer," said Martha warmly, taking her arm. In the hall she kissed her cheek. "Goodbye for the present. Take care of her, Bret. Drive carefully now."

The light was beginning to fade by the time they pulled up outside the schoolhouse and Bret helped her to alight.

She held out her hand impulsively. "Thank you again and your sister for a lovely day. I have enjoyed it so much."

"Let's repeat it often," he said. "Come again soon."

He pressed her hand before raising it to his lips, then climbed back into the driver's seat and whipped up the horses. She watched him go and waved to him when he looked round brandishing his whip.

She had turned back to the house and was taking out her key when the door opened and a man appeared just inside. She stepped back with a stifled cry before she recognized Tom Clifford.

"I'm sorry if I startled you," he said, "I stopped by because I wanted a word with you. When I found you were out, I thought you would probably not be long so I waited for a few minutes."

"I see." She went past him into the house. "How did you get in?"

"Oh we hold keys to all the mill premises. It's necessary in case of any trouble."

She untied the ribbons of her bonnet and put it carefully on the table before turning to face him, strong indignation surging through her at the casual way he spoke of invading her privacy as if he had the right to step in and out of her life as he wished.

"What was it you wanted to speak to me about?" she said coldly.

"I only heard yesterday of what happened here a few mornings ago. Why didn't you tell me?"

"If you mean that stupid writing on the wall, why should I? It was meant for me and I preferred to ignore it. It was not your concern."

"But it was. Any insult directed against someone in my charge *must* be my concern. Do you know who was responsible?"

"No and even if I did, I wouldn't tell you."

He frowned. "Why?"

"Because it seemed to me nothing but silly schoolboy spite and best forgotten."

"And if I choose to think differently?"

"That's your affair, but please don't take up the cudgels on my account."

"And you're not frightened by it?"

"Good heavens, no. I'm not a child to be scared of bogeymen. I have had to cope with far worse things than that."

She thought of tradespeople badgering for unpaid bills when the purse was empty, police harassment in the last few weeks before she had fled from London.

He was looking at her curiously.

"What kind of things?"

"Does it matter?"

"No, I suppose not, but if any more unpleasantness occurs, perhaps you will be good enough to let me know so that I can deal with it."

"Very well – *if* I think it necessary."

He came to the table to pick up his hat. "I saw that Bret was with you. Have you spent the day at Farley Grange?"

"Yes, I have. Anything wrong in that?"

"No, no, of course not," he said hastily. "Martha and her aunt are good friends of ours. Did you have an enjoyable visit?"

"Very enjoyable, thank you. But we did do a great deal of walking during the afternoon and I am rather tired."

"Yes, of course, I'm sorry. I will go at once." He took up his hat and moved towards the door and abruptly her irritation vanished and she took a step after him.

"Thank you for coming. It was kind of you to take the trouble."

"No trouble. I felt I owed you an apology." He paused before turning back to her. "If you would still like to see something of the work we undertake at the mill, would one day next week suit you?"

He had taken her by surprise. "Oh yes, yes, I should like that."

"Shall we say Saturday then, the weekend after next?"

"Yes, and thank you."

"Goodnight, Miss Lismore."

"Goodnight."

He went out closing the door after him. Inside the room it was almost dark by now and she felt the shadows draw closer, shutting her into gloom and loneliness. The quiet pleasures of the day seemed suddenly very far away and she almost called him back with any excuse, just to see him standing there, strong and reassuring. The insult had somehow linked them together. "Whore" they had called her for no reason, simply because she was a stranger and different from them. What would happen when they knew the real truth? Would they be sympathetic or would they drive her out from amongst them? She shivered and then told herself not to be so foolish. She thought of her father enduring so much unjustly and bit back the self-pity. She had chosen to do this and she would carry it through. Resolutely she lit the candles and then saw the open book lying on the table. He must have been looking through it before she came in.

> "There be none of Beauty's daughters
>   With a magic like Thee;
> And like music on the waters
>   Is thy sweet voice to me . . ."

Was it his wife he was thinking of when he read Byron's lines – that lovely dazzling bewitching wife of his that Miss Lavinia condemned so roundly? She suddenly slammed the book shut, aware of danger. She was being tempted to think about Tom Clifford far too much and that could only lead to disaster. Best to turn to practical things. She went out to the kitchen. It was time for supper and bed before the week's work started again.

7

Della had never before been inside any kind of factory and what she saw that morning both enthralled and shocked her. The incessant clatter of the great machines that combed, carded and spun the wool was deafening as she went up the steps of the smoke-grimed building with its tall tower belching out black smoke. All around her was the strong smell of raw wool mingled with oil, a peculiarly sickening odour that near overwhelmed her as she was led down a passage and up a flight of stone stairs to the first floor. The thunder of the machines retreated a little as she was shown into a spacious office but it was still there like a great pulsing dynamo in the background as Tom got up from behind the desk and moved forward to greet her.

"So you did come after all."

"Of course I did. Why shouldn't I?"

"It did occur to me that you might have thought better of it."

"Oh no. I've been looking forward to it all the week."

The room had a kind of ordered chaos. There were cabinets against the walls stuffed with papers, and shelves bulging with gigantic leather-bound ledgers. In one corner stood a tall desk with a high stool behind it on which perched a long thin man, his face and hair as grey as his holland work coat. He stood up at a nod from his employer, looked curiously at Della through thick spectacles, and slid out of the room like a grey shadow.

"Seth Barker, my chief clerk," said Tom, "who knows almost more about my affairs than I do. May I offer you some refreshment? Some coffee or a glass of wine?"

"Nothing, thank you."

"Then where would you like to start?"

She smiled at him. "I'm not sure. From the beginning I think. I am so woefully ignorant. I know absolutely nothing. How does a fleece from the back of one of those sheep I've seen grazing out on the fells become the fine broadcloth of the coat you're wearing at this very minute?"

"That's a tall order," he said, laughing. "But I'll do my best

90

to make it come alive."

They started in the basement where the great piles of fleeces all folded in the same traditional way had been carried in and were being swiftly and expertly sorted and graded.

"How can they possibly tell one from the other?" she asked curiously.

"By feel mostly after years of experience. After they have been sorted the fleeces must be washed and cleaned to get rid of all the grit, dirt and grease. Are you sure you want to go through with this?"

"Yes," she said firmly, "right through to the end."

For over two hours she listened to him as they went from one process to the next, fascinated as much by what he told her as by what he revealed of himself. On his own subject Tom could speak well and eloquently. She saw how the scoured raw wool was first converted into a gossamer-like substance and then became continuous threads. He went on to explain those magic words "tops" and "noils", not that she was very much wiser at the end of it except that she learned that "tops" were long fibres that lay parallel to each other and became worsted, and "noils" were short fibres that lie in different directions and became fine woollen material.

"How can you possibly know so much?" she asked, her head buzzing.

"Am I being unbearably tedious? My father made me go through every process of the trade when I was still a boy and on holiday from school just as he had to do. You see before we had the machines to do this work for us, making cloth was a cottage industry. All these processes you've been watching were done by hand, all the sorting and cleaning, the combing and carding, the weaving on the heavy handlooms, were done in the workers' own houses. As each piece of cloth came off the loom, it was spread on the floor, was soaked and beaten and trampled upon and then hung out on the hooked racks called tenters to dry in the open air. Afterwards there was another washing process, more drying on the tenters and only then was it stamped by an official and sent to market. In the Middle Ages English cloth was sold all over Europe, the finest to be found anywhere in the world."

"It sounds unbelievable."

"Oh it's true enough. That was how my grandfather worked and found himself without a living, his skill no longer needed

91

when the first machines began to be invented. When my father built this mill and the houses for his workers, some of them still had plots of ground where they grew a few vegetables and fattened a pig in the backyard."

"And now?"

"Now it has grown from fifty employees to hundreds, more houses have had to be built, there are not enough home-grown fleeces and we import from Australia and sometimes we still cannot work enough hours to fulfil the orders from all over the world."

"It must make you feel very proud."

"Sometimes. My father always looked forward, every new invention was a challenge to him and he had it installed and it was that which cost him his life. Progress helps some and damns others and they killed him for it." For a moment he looked grim. "It's an inevitable progression but there are times when it worries me."

"I was told that it was robbery that led to your father's death."

"That was the official verdict but there were other factors and only a few months earlier he had installed a new machine that did the work of twenty men. It led to redundancies. He recognized the necessity and regretted it, but he was a hard man and his own father had suffered in the same way."

She sensed it was something he did not want to talk about so she asked no more questions and they went on to watch the great looms at work. The incessant noise made it difficult to make oneself heard and she stared in silence at the long rows of machines shuttling back and forth. Here the workers were mainly women, while children of nine or ten crawled along the floor in between the machines making sure that the cloth did not become entangled. The overseer, a short thickset man with a tough brutal face and a bristle of coarse red hair, strode up and down between the rows keeping a watchful eye to see that no one stopped or even slackened in their work.

"I think you've seen enough of that," shouted Tom above the unceasing clatter and was taking her arm to lead her from the room when it happened. A young girl working almost in front of them suddenly gave a strangled gasp and fell forward over her loom. In an instant the overseer had reached her and struck her across the back.

"Now then, that's the third time, get back to your work or

it'll be the worse for you."

"Let her be," said Tom. "Can't you see the woman is sick?"

"No more sick than I be, Master," growled the man. "She's no more than a lazy slut. I've been watchin' her all t'week."

He would have struck her again if Tom had not caught his wrist.

"I said let her be, Carter."

The girl had dragged herself upright, her face as white as paper, and Della saw that she was heavily pregnant.

"Thank 'ee, sir, thank 'ee," she gasped.

"Better see Dr Withers at his Monday clinic," said Tom gruffly.

"I know her sort, dirty bitch," muttered Carter. "Let one go and you'll have 'em all cryin' off."

"That's my affair," said Tom curtly. "It's near enough closing time. Let the girl go and don't dock her wage."

Carter went on muttering to himself as the girl walked unsteadily down the long room. He shot a glance of such venom at Tom that it startled Della. What possible grudge could he hold against him?

"Is that man Jem's father?" she whispered when they were outside in the passage.

"Yes. He works well enough but sometimes goes too far. It's not easy to steer a line between good business and compassion."

"Should any young woman be working in her condition?"

"I happen to know that Peg is seventeen and has no husband. Who am I to deny her the few pence she earns here to keep her and her child alive?" he said harshly.

The grim reality of it shocked her and yet it was no more than she had seen in London. Even in Madame Ginette's sewing room there had been days when her fingers had been sore to the bone and her eyes felt full of grit from the exacting work and her establishment was a paradise compared with the sweatshops in the slums of Stepney and Hackney which some of the girls had talked about.

She had already learned a great deal that morning and had begun to understand Miss Lavinia's assessment of Tom Clifford as a divided man. She realized too that there were problems on both sides and Tim Withers with his ardent campaign for better conditions was not a ready made solution for workers or employers.

93

Back in his office she sank down into a chair with a little sigh and he looked down at her apologetically.

"I've tired you out and no wonder. I don't often have so interested an audience. Martha Stratton is the only lady of my acquaintance who has listened as faithfully as you have done and that's because she always wanted to know what happened to the fleeces I buy from her."

He fetched a decanter of wine from a cabinet and poured a glass of Madeira for both of them.

"Will you take it with me?"

She sipped the rich dark wine and nibbled the biscuit he offered her thinking how strange it was that she should feel so completely at ease with him.

"Would it be too much if I asked to see some of the finished cloth you sell?"

"No, not at all. When you have drunk your wine, we'll go to the packing room."

"I shall feel quite differently now when I see Martha's sheep grazing on the hills," she went on gaily. "Bret – Mr Stratton I mean – has offered to loan me a horse so that I can explore some of the countryside."

"There was no need for Bret to trouble himself," he said quickly. "You had only to ask. There are a couple of suitable horses in my stables besides my wife's Sheba. You are welcome to borrow either of those any time you wish."

She smiled a little to herself. It was so obvious that he resented anyone he employed being beholden to anyone else.

"That's very kind of you, Mr Clifford. I would be very grateful. Martha was telling me about some of the beauty spots, places like Bolton Abbey and Bardon Tower."

"And Bret told you, I presume, that I have Clifford blood, is that so?"

"It *was* mentioned. Have you?"

He laughed with a touch of exasperation. "God knows but Bret loves to tease me about it and it's anyone's guess. I've no particular thought about it one way or the other. We are all descended from someone and they were a pretty bloodthirsty crew by all accounts. Only one of them has ever intrigued me and that was because the boys used to rib me about it at school. Oliver Craven, devil that he is, started it. I bloodied more than one nose for calling 'Shepherd Lord' after me."

"Was Oliver Craven a particular friend of yours?" she asked, curiosity about this cousin of hers rising up again.

He shrugged his shoulders. "Perhaps. Oliver was everything I was not, handsome, elegant, with a lineage as long as your arm but we did do a lot of wild things together at one time until he went to Oxford and I was pushed into the mill."

"Tell me about the Shepherd Lord?" she asked. "Who was he?"

"Oh it's all ancient local history, years back in the fifteenth century. It seems that in the Wars of the Roses the Cliffords fought for the Red Rose of Lancaster and when the Yorkist Edward became King he pursued them with dire vengeance. The last heir was a boy of seven and he was smuggled out of Skipton Castle by his nurse and hidden amongst the peasants with whom he grew up working in the fields and herding sheep like any other son of the family. Then after the battle of Bosworth and the death of Richard III, the Red Rose triumphed and legend has it that one day up through the feudal majesty of the House of Lords there tramped a ploughman with horny hands and heavy boots, the last of the Cliffords come to claim his inheritance. He rebuilt Bardon Tower as a hunting lodge and he is said to have loved it above all his richer possessions."

"What a lovely romantic story. Can I go there?"

"It's a ruin now but it's in a rarely beautiful valley so you might think it worth a visit." He took the empty glass from her hand. "What power is it you possess?" he said half in jest. "I haven't talked about that for years, not to anyone."

"It's my schoolmistress technique – persuading children to talk."

"Is it? I must be careful and guard my tongue. Shall we go to the packing rooms now?"

It was there that she saw the great rolls of fine woollen cloth, black and grey and rich sombre colours which would be made into frock coats, morning dress and evening wear for wealthy men in England and Europe.

"We have been experimenting this past year," he said, "with a different cloth, one more suitable for ladies." He beckoned one of the men who brought a roll of material in a deep moss green, spreading it a little so that she could let it run through her fingers. It was as fine and supple as silk.

"I could see that being used in all kinds of ways," she said enthusiastically when the man had rolled it up again and taken

95

it away. "Why don't you send out some designs with it to your customers, something like this?"

She looked around her, picked up a black crayon used for marking the bales, drew a sheet of the wrapping paper towards her and began to sketch a jacket falling to the hips with a fashionable flounce and graceful bell-shaped sleeves. "It would be far better made up in your material than in velvet or silk and so much warmer."

"Where did you learn to do this?"

He was standing close behind her, one hand on her shoulder as he leaned over to watch and suddenly she felt breathless.

"Madame Ginette had a dressmaking salon in London. I worked there for a time."

"In between teaching children in Brussels?"

There was a hint of laughter in his voice.

"I did teach, you know," she said quickly twisting round to look up at him. "I was not lying."

"Did I say so?"

For an instant their eyes met. She was very aware of his arm lying across her shoulders, his face only a few inches from her own. There was a stillness between them that seemed extraordinary in this bleak workroom with men working stolidly in the background and the distant incessant hum of the machines. Then he broke it. He picked up the drawing.

"It's a revolutionary idea but interesting. Could you do more of them for me?"

"Yes, if you really want me to."

"I'll think about it. I've never known it done before. Perhaps I'll be able to steal a march on my colleagues in the trade next time I meet them in Bradford."

She was not sure if he really meant it or if he was only teasing her, but it was as if they had suddenly drawn very close together and she was a little frightened of it. Absorbed in each other, neither of them had noticed that Sylvia had come in until she spoke.

"I'm sorry to disturb you, Tom, but had you forgotten that I am leaving today to spend a few days with Father?"

He looked around startled and Della got hurriedly to her feet.

"I must go. I've taken up far too much of your time already."

"Don't let me drive you away, Miss Lismore," said Sylvia sweetly. "Is touring the mill part of the school syllabus?"

"Miss Lismore thought she would like to see for herself

96

where most of the parents of her pupils spend their working hours," said Tom.

"How very conscientious. I don't remember Miss Hutton ever feeling the necessity."

"How did you know where we were?" said her husband.

"Your clerk told me. Did he do wrong?"

"No, of course not."

"I really must go." Della sensing the hostility was only too anxious to escape. "Thank you for showing me around. It has been fascinating. Good day, Mr Clifford – Mrs Clifford," and she almost ran from the room.

The workers were already beginning to stream out of the building. It was the one day when the factory closed at five instead of the usual eight o'clock and as she went quickly down the steps she saw the handsome carriage waiting outside. She wondered how long Sylvia had stood there watching them before she spoke, not that they had done anything wrong. It was her own instinctive response to him that made her feel guilty and the sooner she put it out of her mind the better.

Back in the mill Tom wondered about Sylvia too before he said apologetically, "My dear, I really am very sorry. How could I have been so stupid? I was quite sure it was tomorrow that you were leaving us. Are you taking the boy with you?"

"Father has not been at all well as you know. A noisy child is the last thing he needs."

"I'll take you to the carriage."

"What was that woman doing here?"

"Exactly what I said. Miss Lismore asked me some time ago if she could see something of the mill's working."

"She certainly knows the right way to ingratiate herself with you."

"Oh come, that's being ridiculous."

"Is it? Did you find her so absorbing that you couldn't be bothered to see your wife on her way?"

"You know perfectly well it was nothing of the kind." He had taken her arm as they moved towards the door. "How long will you be away?"

She shrugged her shoulders. "I don't know for certain. I may go on to Harrogate. Father spoke of taking the waters there."

"Bret will never forgive you if you are not back for the fête at Farley Grange, so don't make it too long. In any case I'm going to miss you horribly."

"Are you? Why don't you come with me?"

He spread his hands helplessly. "My dear, how can I at such short notice?"

"You could if you really wished to." She frowned. "The mill has always meant more to you than I do."

"That's nonsense and you know it." He kissed her gently before putting her in the carriage and closing the door.

She leaned from the window. "Don't fall in love with the schoolmistress while I'm gone."

"I'll try not to." He laughed and waved his hand. "Goodbye, my dear, and remember me to Lord Sterndale."

It was a jest of course but there was a warning beneath it that brought him up with a jolt. He watched the carriage bowl away down the street before he went slowly back up the steps. The last of the office staff were coming out and touched their caps to him. He responded automatically. It was all nonsense of course. It was Sylvia whom he loved despite the arguments, the barbed hurting words, the quarrels that had been so frequent of late and over such stupid and unnecessary trifles. Perhaps all marriages were like that and it was only he who had cherished an impossible ideal and yet that day he had gained a sudden glimpse of what might have been, of a warmth of companionship, of two minds that ran together and beneath it that subtle intangible response of the flesh. There was something mysterious about Della, something hidden that he longed to probe and find out for himself. She was too damnably attractive. It might be wise to dismiss her when the three months of probation were up but would that be fair? It was still some weeks away. He need make no decision yet. He picked up the drawing she had sketched and carried it to his office. It was a novel idea, but had an appeal. If she proved to have a talent for it, he could pay her for them. He could discuss them with her. The prospect pleased him and he chose to forget that in even considering such a thing, he was already beginning to forge closer links between them.

It was a few weeks later when Della took advantage of Tom's offer and made up her mind to borrow one of his horses. Summer had come at last to the bleak north, long lovely days when the glimpses she had of the open moors and the hills beyond were an irresistible temptation and she longed to escape from the schoolroom, the smell of chalk, the tremendous effort to force knowledge into closed minds that resisted with every breath, the close, stifling, ever-present reek of unwashed children. She walked up to the Hall one Saturday evening and found Rob in the tackroom surrounded by horse gear which he was working on, while the small son of the house squatted on the floor in front of him, one arm around the big dog lying beside him. He looked up frowning as Della appeared in the doorway.

"You can't come in here," he said imperiously, "this place belongs to me and Rob."

"That's no way to speak to a lady," said the groom reprovingly, "you stand up and say good evening nicely now."

"Must I?"

"Aye, you must and do it now – no argument."

Peter got to his feet, said "Good evening" sulkily and flopped down again. "Go on, Rob, about when you rode Blue Mist in the races," he went on, pointedly turning his back on Della.

"Aye well, that tale will keep till tomorrow. It's about time for your supper and bed so off with you before Nanny catches up with you and gives you a spanking."

"She wouldn't do that, she wouldn't dare!"

"Wouldn't she now? Well maybe one of these days I'll do it for her."

The boy giggled, not believing a word of it, and got up with obvious reluctance taking hold of Rusty's collar and stalking out without another word to either of them.

"He's a rare one. Proper little tartar when he grows up if the Master don't look out."

"I thought Mr Clifford seemed very fond of his son," said Della smiling.

"Ah aye, he is that, too fond, daren't lift a finger to him or her ladyship would raise the devil." He looked at her questioningly. "Would you be wantin' summat, Miss?"

"Yes. Mr Clifford mentioned I could borrow one of his horses."

"Aye, so he told me."

"Would it be all right tomorrow about nine o'clock?"

He looked her up and down consideringly. "Ridin' the dales en't like trottin' in the park," he said, "you'd better take Tansy. She's a nice quiet mare not like her ladyship's Sheba who'd throw you as soon as look at you. And Tansy knows the fells better than most. Do you want one of the lads to go with you?"

"No, I think I'll be quite safe. I have ridden before you know."

"Aye, I guessed as much. She'll be redded up for you, come mornin'."

"Thank you." She turned to go and then came back. "Rob, how far is it to Larksghyll?"

He rubbed harder at the brass in his band. "Not above ten mile. You take road to Bardon Tower, then follow on beside the river." He put the brass aside and glanced up. "What would you be wantin' at Larksghyll, Miss?"

"Nothing in particular. I just thought it seemed rather a pleasant way to ride."

"Aye, it's pretty enough. Weren't thinkin' of callin' on old Mr Craven, were you?"

"No. Why?"

"He don't welcome strangers, not when young Mr Oliver en't there. One of the lads chased a dog into the park and got a shot up the backside for it if you'll pardon my sayin' so, Miss."

"I don't think I will be trespassing, Rob, so it is not likely to happen to me."

"And get ye back before dark. There's a tale or two about that valley. Larksghyll, they call it, but there's some as would rather name it Devilsghyll."

"Rob, you're laughing at me."

"No such thing, Miss, just givin' ye fair warnin'."

"Of what?"

"You can smile, Miss, but I tell you I've seen 'em come in, white as paper and shakin' like a leaf in a gale, talkin' of bein' chased by a danged great black hound out o' hell, and that's the Gospel truth."

There was not a glimmer of a smile on the long melancholy leather-brown face, but she was perfectly certain that the laconic dalesman was taking a rise out of the city miss up from London who thought herself so clever.

"I'll remember," she said demurely.

"You'd better," he went on darkly. "I'll ask Cook to put up somethin' tasty for you in the saddlebag. You'll be havin' a long day of it I shouldn't wonder."

"That's very kind of you to take so much trouble."

"No trouble, Miss. It's what Mr Clifford ordered."

The old Mr Craven Rob referred to must be her uncle, her father's brother, she thought, as she walked back to the schoolhouse, and he could not be as old as all that. Paul Craven had been forty-seven on his last birthday so his elder brother could only be in his early fifties. Perhaps he had earned the title because he lived such a solitary life. She was curious to know why. Her father had spoken so rarely of his old home. Open as the day about everything else in his life, on that subject he had always been a closed book so that she had often wondered if there was some mystery connected with it, some dark secret that had driven him from his home and about which he did not want to be reminded even by her. It had never troubled her before, but now it did, now when Larksghyll was so close and her unknown cousin so intimately linked with Tom and Bret. Sometimes it seemed that a sort of destiny had brought her to this place. What would happen, she thought, if she were to walk into Larksghyll, say "I'm Delphine, Paul's daughter. Didn't you care when he was indicted for a murder he didn't commit? Did you bear him such a bitter hatred that you didn't lift a finger to help him in his desperate need?" Would he turn the gun on her as he did on the boy who had innocently pursued a dog? Not that she was going to do any such thing. She was here under an assumed name and that was how it must remain, though now and then she did wonder what would happen when Oliver Craven came home to Larksghyll. It felt like living on a knifepoint but she was still curious. She wanted to see the house where her father had spent his boyhood, the countryside he must have known so well, the rivers he must have fished, the sweet green valleys where perhaps he had walked with her mother, the Irish girl from the mountains of Tara whom he had loved so well.

Tansy was ready for her when she walked up to the Hall on the following morning. Rob gave her a hand into the saddle and pushed a package into the leather satchel. Sylvia was still away and there was no sign of Tom Clifford or his son as she trotted down the drive. A slight haze lay across the hills promising a fine day and she set out filled with eager anticipation.

Following Rob's directions, she came first to Bolton Abbey. The old grey stone arches and sculptured ruins were splendidly set against the brilliant green turf of the meadows with the blue hills rising majestically behind. Rarely beautiful, Tom had called it, and he was right, she thought, riding Tansy gently along the river bank, pausing to count the thirty-seven stepping stones across the water and then going on to what was called the Strid, a narrow cleft cut in the limestone through which the Wharfe roared to become a furious millstream creaming with foam, fierce and dangerous. She felt the spray ice-cold on her face as she pulled up remembering the legend Martha had told her, the sad tale of Lady Alice Romilly who had built the sanctuary in memory of her son who had once tried to leap the narrow chasm and been dashed to death in the savage torrent.

She followed the path as Rob had instructed her until she reached Bardon Tower. The stone was ancient and crumbling. A board warned of danger but she tethered Tansy securely and climbed up the steps with the strong conviction that whether he believed in the ancient family link or not this was a place Tom had spoken of with love. It commanded a superb view. Leaning on the parapet she could see across a great stretch of the dales in every direction – towards Harrogate and Skipton and the moors of Ilkley. What Tom had told her of the Shepherd Lord had spiked her interest. Somewhere in some far-off history lesson she had heard about him, and it was here, so they said, that he had watched the stars and dabbled in alchemy searching for the philosopher's stone that would transmute base metal into gold, an elusive dream never to be realized.

"Love had he found in huts where poor men lie," the poet had written. Tom liked to think himself the hard-headed business man ambitious for his prosperous mill, satisfying the demands of his wayward extravagant wife and yet there was a lot more to him than that; a divided man but a fascinating one, she was thinking dreamily when the sound of voices brought her back to earth with a start.

Bardon Tower and Bolton Abbey were famous beauty spots and, early though it was, a party of visitors had already arrived, leaving their horses and carriages and coming along the path. She had no wish to meet up with them so she climbed quickly down the steps, scrambled onto Tansy's back and trotted on beside the river.

The sweet freshness of the air, the feeling of freedom under a blue sky with blown fleecy clouds were unusual delights for Della and she savoured them slowly as she rode on, seeing only the sheep scattered across fields hazed with golden flowers and meeting the occasional shepherd or brown-faced countryman trudging along with his dog at his heels. They called a greeting to her and she waved back feeling very content. She had always preferred to be alone rather than be forced into uncongenial company. When she stopped beside a small stream to eat her lunch, she looked up to see half a dozen cows gathered around her watching with mild curiosity as she tucked hungrily into the ham and fresh baked rolls, the creamy Wensleydale cheese and the rosy winter-stored apple that the kitchen at the Hall had packed for her.

It was late afternoon by the time she came to Larksghyll through a small tumbledown village of stone-built cottages that looked as if they were falling into decay. There was a Sunday look about it and as she passed the church she heard the drone of childish voices repeating their hard learned lesson and thanked heaven she had been spared taking a Sunday-school class.

The road divided, one fork going straight on and the other dwindling to a grassy track leading to two massive stone gateposts. This must be Larksghyll. Her heart beating a little faster she ventured down the bridle path. The iron gates stood open, one of them rusted and sunk so deep into the earth, it could not have been closed for many years. An overgrown drive bordered by giant hollies wound away from the gates.

Did she dare risk going any further? For an instant she drew back, then her resolution hardened. She could not come all this way and not see the house itself. That would be cowardice. She slid from the saddle, tethered Tansy to the iron hook in the gatepost and stepped inside. It was very quiet with that afternoon stillness when for a little even the birds are silent and not even a mouse stirs. The moss under her feet made no sound as she moved slowly up the path keeping close against the holly hedge. Then the drive curved and unexpectedly she was looking at the house so very different from what she had expected that it nearly took her breath away.

It was far larger for one thing and badly neglected. At one end there lay what must be the oldest part, a stone tower heavily coated with ivy with an iron-bound door, then the house built on to it, black and white beams, deeply mullioned windows rising to a steeply pointed gabled roof and tall chimneys. No one about, not a sound from anywhere, no barking dogs, no sun-basking cats, it might have been a house in a dream or some ancient fairy tale. She stared at it, longing to peer into the long windows on the ground floor but hesitating to cross the semi-circular stretch of grass with its round weedy pond where a cracked stone statue no longer spouted a fountain of sparkling water and a cluster of reeds swayed in the slight breeze with a faint ghostly rustle.

A curious strangled sound made her spin around. A man who must have emerged from the thicket stood a few paces from her. He was tall and gaunt, leaning on a stick and wearing a snuff-coloured jacket and breeches, a scarf tucked untidily around his scraggy neck, a shock of brown hair liberally sprinkled with grey. All this she took in swiftly but it was his face that held her, a sudden flashing resemblance to her father, not as she had last seen him but as he might be in years to come. It held her spellbound. She saw his eyes widen with a look of joyful recognition. He muttered something and she thought dazedly, he knows me, he knows who I am, in a moment he will say, "You must be Paul's girl!" and she would fling her arms round him and they would laugh together. Then the light faded like a lamp abruptly quenched, his expression darkened and he frowned.

"Who are you? What are you doing here?" he said in a harsh rusty tone.

"I – I was just looking at the house," she stammered.

"Get out, d'you hear? Go away!" He took a step towards her raising the stick in his hand. "Don't you know that this is private?"

"I'm sorry – I didn't mean to intrude . . ."

"Get out!" he snarled and lifted the stick so threateningly that she turned and fled, stumbling in her haste with a feeling that he was coming behind her like the Archangel Michael driving Eve out of Paradise.

She reached the gate before she dared to look back but he had not followed her after all. He was standing just where the drive curved staring at her and then he slowly turned his back and limped towards the house.

The mare thrust a questing nose against her shoulder and still shaken, still out of breath, she leaned against her neck grateful to feel something warm and alive. A little calmer now, she was remembering what he had said at that first startling encounter.

"Olivia! At last!"

Her mother's name – so he had thought she was her mother – but he must know she was dead and if he had seen the likeness, why had he not guessed who she must be? Why the sudden change to anger, to something dark and fearful and bitter? Was he mad or deluded or what? There was no immediate answer.

She rode back slowly, so disturbed by her uncle's strange reaction, her thoughts so busy with searching for an explanation, that she missed her way and suddenly woke up to the realization that she had not the faintest idea where she was. She looked around her. The moors stretched endlessly in every direction, utterly unfamiliar. Somewhere she must have taken the wrong turn. With the coming of evening the mist had come down again and was rolling across the fields in patchy clouds. Should she go on or return and try to find the right road? But that might take even longer. She urged the tired horse forward in the hope of meeting someone or passing a cottage where she could enquire but the road remained empty and she was beginning to despair when she glimpsed a signpost crazily hanging by one nail to a decaying wooden post but pointing hopefully to the right. The letters were half obliterated by time and weather but she thought she could distinguish Castlebridge and gratefully turned down the bridle road.

It led steeply downhill and to her dismay dwindled to a grassy path through a wood of alder and ash. The mist gathered thicker there and the trees arching over her head made it very dark. She was not normally timid but there was something eerie about the lonely track and she began to wish she had retraced her steps and found her original road. Against her will Rob's dire warnings ran through her mind. "It's all rubbish," she told herself stoutly, "there are no such things as devil hounds or ghost dogs," and then nearly jumped out of her skin when there was a curious bleating cry and a heavy body bumped against her. Tansy gave a nervous start and leaped forward. She hung on to the reins, gave a quick look back, saw the dark shape that lumbered after them and panicked. The mare sensed her fear and reacted strongly. Long branches tore her hat from her head and clutched at her hair as they raced on in a crazy gallop emerging out of the trees and flying along the track through the thickening mist until they collided with something. There was an excited barking, the mare whinneyed and reared, she hung on to the saddle for dear life and a voice said loudly: "What the devil is going on?"

She felt rather than saw that another horse had come up beside her, strong hands had come down on her reins and the same voice was saying, "Shut up for God's sake, Rusty. There, there, Tansy old girl, whoa now, whoa my beauty!"

The mist in its unpredictable way rolled away and in the momentary clearing she saw it was Tom Clifford who was beside her, holding the bridle firmly with his own and looking down at her with a frown.

"I've never known Tansy bolt before. What frightened her?"

She was still too shaken to think clearly. "I'm not sure – something bumped into us – I thought it was coming after us."

"Probably a sheep. The silly creatures sometimes stray from the flock and then they panic." She saw him smile in the half light. "Has Rob been filling you up with his tales of ghoulies and ghosties?"

"It seems so silly, doesn't it?" she confessed more than a little ashamed.

"You're not the only one. I've seen grown men who ought to know better arrive home with their hair standing on end and babbling of demon dogs chasing after them."

They were riding back quietly side by side and she glanced up at him shyly.

"Is it so very late?"

"After nine. I came looking for you. Rob told me you'd been gone since early morning and with the darkness and the mist I felt responsible. People do get lost on the moors, you know."

"I'm sorry to have caused so much trouble. I went further than I intended."

"Did you reach Larksghyll?"

"Yes. How did you know?"

"Rob mentioned you were asking about it. Did you have any particular reason for going there?"

"No, not really."

"It's a fine old house, isn't it? When Oliver is at home he sometimes opens up the place and his father shuts himself into the tower. When I visited there as a boy he used to terrify me but now I realize he is just a very lonely and unhappy man."

"And yet he does have a son."

"Yes, he has a son."

She was aware that Tom knew more than he intended to say and had a strong desire to tell him everything about herself, about her father. It would have been such a relief to have someone whom she could confide in, someone to whom she could turn for advice in this awkward situation, but if she did, he would despise her for her deception. She would feel obliged to leave, go back to London and she knew now she wanted to

106

stay. She had a queer certainty that the answer to everything lay here at Larksghyll, that here she would find out who it was who had killed and allowed her father to suffer the penalty, and she wanted to see it through to the end. So she said nothing and they spoke of other trivial things until they reached the stables.

After the chilling meeting with her uncle Tom's lively concern, the trouble he had taken to look for her, warmed her through and through. She thanked him for it but refused to let him accompany her back to the schoolhouse.

"It is only a step," she protested. "I can easily walk."

"You'll do no such thing. It is dark already," he insisted. "I'll come with you and bring Tansy back with me."

So she gave in and though he did not come with her into the house he stood at the door for a moment or two pressing her hand warmly before he rode away and all those prying eyes that watched her coming and going took careful note of it. So that was what the schoolmistress got up to when the Master's wife was away.

Part Two

JUNE TO OCTOBER
1840

8

The coach to Harrogate left Skipton at eleven o'clock and Bret offered to drive Della to the posting inn. When he drew into the yard there was the usual bustle of passengers arguing about luggage and their bookings, or seizing the opportunity of a last cup of ale or nip of brandy before they set off again. Bret helped her down from the carriage, put her small valise into the coach and drew her to one side.

"Wish I was coming with you," he said ruefully, "but Martha keeps my nose to the grindstone these days. She says I ought to buckle down to learning how the estate works instead of running off to London and leaving it all to her."

"And she's quite right."

"No, not you too." Bret wrinkled his nose like a small boy. "She keeps telling me it is high time I found a good wife and settled down, not that she'd really like that one little bit. She's been ruling the roost too long, and anyway who would want to marry me?"

"A very many very nice girls – Abigail Withers for one."

"Abbie! You can't be serious. I've known her since she was a squalling baby. She and Tim make a good pair. They spend so much time doing good and worrying about other people's troubles, they have forgotten how to enjoy themselves." He gave her a quick sidelong look. "Now you are quite different. Would you take me on?"

"Is that a proposal, sir?" and she laughed up at him.

He took hold of her hand. "It could be. Della, do you think. . . ?" He was suddenly serious.

"I'm not thinking about anything except my holiday at Harrogate," she said, quickly withdrawing her hand, "and I don't want to be married to anyone, not for a very long time. And there's our driver. He is mounting the box. It's time I took my place."

"How long will you be away?" he asked handing her into the coach.

111

"A couple of days, no more."

"Is that all the time Tom allows you?"

"I haven't asked him. Goodbye and thank you for bringing me here." She waved to him as the coach jolted forward.

She liked Bret but she certainly didn't want to encourage anything more than simple friendship. Martha wouldn't approve anyway and she wondered if it was his sister's dominant personality that made him so restless and eager to escape. She leaned back against the cushioned seat with a pleasant feeling of freedom from responsibility even if it was only for a brief weekend. The letter from Lucinda had arrived some time after the adventure at Larksghyll. The theatrical company in which she was playing was on its summer tour, she had written, and would be at Harrogate in a few weeks. Was there any chance of Della coming over to meet her there?

"You go," said Abigail when she consulted her. "Leave on Saturday and come back on Monday. I can take charge of the school for one day. Miss Hutton went off more than once."

"Are you sure Mr Clifford won't object?"

"He needn't know a thing about it. You go, Della, and enjoy yourself. I wish I could come with you. I've never met an actress or seen a play – not a real one," she went on enviously.

To Abigail, who had never been to London, Harrogate, where the rich came to take the waters and attend the races, dancing and gambling the night away, represented the height of fashion and luxury to which a hard-working doctor's daughter could hardly hope to aspire.

The day was warm and with the windows tight shut it was stuffy inside the coach and smelled of hay and horse dung and the strong peppermints the gentleman beside her kept popping into his mouth to calm his dyspepsia, but she didn't really care. The journey was not a long one and the road wound through some of the loveliest of the Yorkshire dales. They arrived promptly at Harrogate and Della went straight to the theatre where Lucinda was rehearsing. The smell of paint, size, cheap perfume and human sweat with a faint unmistakable reek of drains hit her as she went down the narrow dark passage, so that she wondered how Lucinda could endure it until she remembered it was part of her life just as the rank smell of sheeps' wool and grease was part of Tom Clifford's working day. She was alarmed to realize how large a part he had begun to play in her thoughts. It must stop here and now, she told

112

herself severely, as she knocked on the dressing room door.

At one time she would never have believed that she would be so glad to see her father's mistress again but circumstances had brought them very close and when Lucinda came to meet her with outstretched hands, they clung together for a few moments, cheek to cheek.

"I'm so very happy to be here," she murmured at last, "and I've so much to tell you."

"You're to stay with me in my lodgings. My landlady is a very decent soul and we can be on our own there, the rest of the company are staying elsewhere. We can talk all night if we wish," which was what they very nearly did, but that was not until much later. First Della had to see the play.

It was a small theatre but charmingly painted in white and gold and packed to the doors on that Saturday evening with an appreciative and highly fashionable audience. Lucinda had booked a seat for her in the second row of the stalls, while the more rowdy playgoers were herded into the back of the pit or the balcony above her head. There was only one box each side of the stage reserved for distinguished company but only one of them was occupied when Della took her seat. The play was *Hamlet* with Mr Macready as guest star in the title part. She had seen the famous tragedian once before as Othello in London, when her father had whispered wickedly, "If his dramatic pauses go on very much longer, I shall be constrained to shout a prompt!" But, with all his eccentricities, the great actor had the power to hold an audience spellbound, while Lucinda, no mean actress, was to play Gertrude, so Della settled down to enjoy herself.

It was not until the intermission that she happened to glance at the empty box. Two people who must have arrived late were now seated on the red velvet chairs. One of them to her surprise was Sylvia Clifford in a gown of palest pink satin with roses at her waist and in her ash blonde hair. The man beside her turned his head slightly and Della drew a quick breath. It was the man she had seen at the trial, the man with the long sardonic features, the high-bridged nose and narrowed eyes who had studied her so closely. He leaned forward to whisper something and Sylvia turned to him. There was intimacy in the smile she gave him and a caress in the way he replaced the silk shawl that had fallen from her slim shoulders. Della quickly looked away, holding up her programme to shield her face, but she need not have worried. The couple appeared far too absorbed in one another to notice anyone else.

All during the second half, while Hamlet knelt at his mother's feet, fought with Laertes in Ophelia's grave and died tragically, she found herself speculating about Sylvia Clifford. What on earth was she doing at the theatre with a man not her husband when Tom believed her to be at Sterndale Castle? It seemed almost unbelievable and yet, to be fair, for all she knew, he could be her brother or her cousin or an old friend of long standing, except that no brother or cousin or friend would surely exchange such looks.

She was still puzzling over it when after the performance she went round to Lucinda's dressing room, but it was the play they discussed while the actress removed her make-up.

"Did you enjoy it?"

"Oh yes, very much indeed. You were wonderful."

"Macready is really something, isn't he?"

"What is he like to act with?"

"My dear, absolutely terrifying. One word missed, one move slightly out of place, and he's down on you like the wrath of God. The queer thing is that he has an absolute contempt for the profession. In his opinion actors are the lowest form of life."

"And yet he is an actor himself. I call that disgusting hypocrisy when he makes his living out of the theatre," said Della indignantly.

"I suppose it is but even though he is such an appalling snob and thinks fate has let him down by not making him a landed gentleman, I have to admire the way he studies his parts. He may drive his company nearly out of their wits at rehearsals but he does not spare himself and just once in a way he'll actually give you a word of praise."

She was soon dressed and they went out of the theatre to be met at the stage door by a little crowd. "Waiting for Macready of course," whispered Lucinda but she smiled graciously as one or two of them pushed forward, holding out programmes to be autographed.

They walked the short distance to her lodgings. She had a little sitting room to herself and while she tackled a hearty supper which, like most actors, she found the best meal of the day, Della talked and talked.

"Well, I must say," she said pouring a last cup of tea and leaning back comfortably, "Thomas Clifford sounds a paragon

114

among millowners. You're not falling in love with him, I hope."

"Of course I'm not. How could I? He's married."

"I've never known that to stop people falling in love," remarked Lucinda dryly.

"Well, it should and anyway I'm not," said Della so emphatically that Lucinda, who had been only half serious, looked at her keenly.

"I must say teaching those appalling children sounds quite dreadful to me. Do you think you will stay up here in Yorkshire?" she asked curiously.

"Oh it has its good moments as well as the awful ones and I'd like to stay for a while at any rate. I hate to admit defeat and there is something else."

"And what's that? Another suitor? Has the young man with a tough sister stolen your heart?"

"No, he has not and stop teasing. It's nothing like that. The fact is I've actually been to Papa's old home and very strange it was," and she began to tell Lucinda about Larksghyll and all that had happened there.

"It sounds exactly like one of the melodramas we used to play all around the provinces when I first started in the business," said Lucinda smiling. "Is this cousin of yours – what's his name? Oliver Craven? Is he married?"

"Apparently not."

"Has it ever struck you that if anything happens to him or his father then you would inherit Larksghyll?"

"Would I?" Della looked startled. "I never thought of that, but I suppose Papa would be next of kin."

"Except that as a convicted felon he could not inherit anything so that only leaves you."

Della stared at her for a moment, then she said abruptly, "My uncle is still alive and so is Oliver, so it doesn't apply, does it?"

"No, but it could."

"I don't remember ever talking about such a thing." Up to then as if by mutual consent they had neither of them spoken of the man they both loved. And it was only now that Della said slowly, "It's nearly five months since the ship sailed. It must be nearing Botany Bay by now. If only we could be told something. I feel sometimes I can't bear not knowing how he is, whether he is sick or well, how he is enduring the horrors or facing up to the future. I still miss him terribly."

Lucinda said quietly, "Believe me, I understand. Night after night I dream of him and he seems so near to me that when I wake and remember what has happened, it is absolute hell. He's out of my reach. I can't get anywhere near him and I feel that if we ever do meet again, I shall not even know him. He will be utterly changed into a stranger."

"You really love him, don't you?" said Della gently. "Forgive me for asking but did he ever ask you to marry him?"

"Yes, once. I told him no. We were from two different worlds."

"Does that matter when two people are in love?"

"It would matter very much if he were the owner of Larksghyll," said Lucinda with a touch of bitterness. "Actors are rogues and vagabonds and actresses for the most part notorious whores."

"That's not true," said Della shocked.

"Oh, yes it is. You'd be surprised how many people still hold that view and yet some of us live far more decent lives than those who condemn us." She smiled wryly. "But that's the way of it, my dear. It used to make me angry but now I simply shrug my shoulders and ignore it."

"How did you and Papa meet? You've never told me."

"In the silliest way possible." Lucinda smiled reminiscently. "It was one night about two years ago after I had given him a black eye."

"You'd given him what?"

"Sounds ridiculous, doesn't it? I was on my way home from the theatre. Rashly I took a short cut through a dark little alley in St Giles and a man sprang at me grabbing at my purse. I was only just working again after a long time of living at starvation level so what money I had was very precious to me. I fought back. Then another man joined in. I thought he was an accomplice and swung my fist at him with all my strength, but it was your father coming to my rescue." Lucinda gave a little gurgle of laughter. "The other man took off and there was I with my saviour who had a very sore eye and a very bloody nose."

"So you took him home with you."

"It was the least I could do. I had no raw steak to put on his eye but I could offer to bathe it and lend him an extra handkerchief. At first he refused and then he came. He didn't share my bed if that's what you are thinking. It was all very

116

commonplace and very proper. We sat and talked and I made tea and had a strong impression that he was lonely."

"Lonely?" repeated Della a shade indignantly.

"Oh I know that he had you but you're his daughter and that's not the same. A man like your father needs a companion as well as a lover. I'd had a hard struggle to get where I was. My parents were strolling players rarely ever achieving anything beyond playing in barns and innyards. I always wanted something better and I had to fight for it."

"I admire you for that," said Della warmly.

"We found we shared a realistic view of life and an ability to laugh when things were tough. It was mutual liking at first, love came afterwards, but there *was* one thing," went on Lucinda thoughtfully," and what you said about Larksghyll reminded me of it. Paul spoke freely about himself, about your mother and about you, but always I was aware that there was something he held back, something which had power to haunt him almost as if he were ashamed of it."

"Ashamed?" Della frowned.

"Perhaps I'm using the wrong word but with all his gaiety, the light-hearted way he took life in his stride, it was there." Then she smiled. "I'm probably talking nonsense."

"No, you're not. Sometimes I felt it too. It's one of the reasons why I must stay up here. I want to find out the truth."

"You may not like it when you do."

"Perhaps not, but I still would rather know the worst than just live in ignorance."

It was not until they were undressing for bed in the room they were to share that Della mentioned the latecomers to the box at the theatre and asked Lucinda if she had noticed them.

"I can't say I did," she replied, pulling her nightgown over her head. "You can see the audience from the stage at times, but I always avoid it if I can. It's horribly disconcerting to be tearing a passion to tatters and suddenly be aware of a face looking at you contemptuously or yawning with boredom or even sound asleep and snoring. I wonder sometimes why I act at all," she went on with a huge yawn, "it must be a kind of masochism – you love your suffering."

It was the next morning when Della saw Sylvia again. She and Lucinda had gone to the Pump Room where the fashionable gathered after church to sip glasses of the disgusting if health-giving water which tasted of bad eggs, drowning the taste afterwards in coffee or chocolate. They were sitting at a table at one side when she saw Sylvia come in, strikingly dressed in green and white striped taffeta. All eyes turned to her as she swept unseeingly past them.

"My stars, but she's a beauty and doesn't she know it? And what a dress! That must have cost her husband a pretty penny. I'd give my eye teeth for one like that," said Lucinda enviously.

A man at the further end of the room rose as she approached, the same man who had accompanied her at the theatre, modishly attired in a pale blue coat and fawn pantaloons.

"Do you know them?" asked Lucinda watching Della's face curiously.

"I know her, but not the man. She is Tom Clifford's wife."

"Is she, by Jove!" Lucinda gave an unladylike whistle of surprise. "Not precisely the wife of a millowner, I should have thought."

"She is the daughter of Lord Sterndale. They were the two whom I saw at the theatre last night. Lucinda, do you know who the man is?"

"Never seen him before in my life but he's handsome, isn't he, in a devilish kind of way? Are they lovers, do you suppose?"

"I hope not."

"I'd be very surprised if they're not. There's something about them, can't you see it? The way they look at each other, a recklessness, a carelessness of danger. The world around them might not exist."

"You're being ridiculous."

"Am I? I don't think so. You forget, my child, I'm more experienced in these matters than you are," she went on half-serious, half-jesting.

They chatted of other things while they drank their chocolate but Della found it difficult to keep her eyes off the handsome couple and presently saw them leave. As the gentleman passed their table he glanced idly in their direction, his eyes fell on Della and the faintest smile curved the thin lips and then vanished.

"I thought you said you didn't know him," whispered Lucinda.

"Neither do I. But I did see him at Papa's trial, only for an instant but it's a face you remember."

"It surely is and so is yours, my dear. He certainly remembered you. Does he know who you are?"

"I've no idea, only that somehow he frightened me. He still does."

"Don't look so scared. After all what can he do to you? Tell Sylvia Clifford who you are perhaps and then she could tell her husband. Well, it's not a crime to be the daughter of a condemned man," said Lucinda sturdily. "The most you're guilty of is hiding it from him and that's surely excusable."

"Yes, I suppose so. It's just a feeling I have."

She still felt uneasy and the knowledge that they might run into him again in the small circle of Harrogate society rather spoiled the rest of her short stay.

Sylvia had come to Harrogate with her father with no knowledge of whom she was going to meet there. They were staying at the Royal Crescent Hotel and Lord Sterndale immediately embarked on a course of medical treatment to counteract the effects of a year's hard drinking and hard living, leaving his daughter to amuse herself as best she could. She had her maid with her and plenty of acquaintances among the visitors who thronged the fashionable little town.

"Enjoy yourself, my dear," he said indulgently, "but discreetly please. I don't want black looks from that priggish, hard-working husband of yours."

"Really, Papa, do you have to say that? I live quiet as a mouse these days."

"Well, if you've not sobered down after five years of marriage, then you never will, I suppose," he said dryly and patted her cheek. "You're in remarkably good looks, puss, is there someone here already who has taken your fancy?"

"No, of course there isn't, how could there be?" she answered rather too quickly and changed the subject. "Isn't it time for your usual draught of spa water?"

"It tastes so foul, it must be good for you," sighed her father. "The only thing is the damned doctor refuses to let me drown it in brandy."

Sylvia went back to her own room, her hands shaking a little as she dressed for the evening. She pressed her hands against her hot cheeks. After the lethargy and boredom of the last few weeks, excitement ran through her like a flame.

She had been out early that morning with a riding party when she had glimpsed the man she liked to think of as her destiny, the man to whom she had given her love, utterly and completely at sixteen, and had never afterwards been able to tear him out of her thoughts and dreams. She had not expected him to be there and in a momentary panic she spurred her horse forward. A few minutes later, cantering across the soft turf, she knew he was riding after her. When he drew alongside he put his hand on her bridle.

"You are not running away from me, are you, Sylvia?" he said silkily.

"Yes, that's exactly what I am doing." She looked down at the slender hand that had such a surprising strength and raised her riding crop.

"They're all watching us. If you strike me, you'll cause a most unpleasant scandal and you wouldn't want that, would you? I don't think Tom would care for it at all."

"Don't speak of Tom please."

"Why not? I was always very fond of Tom Clifford, still am for that matter. Such a worthy character. Far more worthy than I ever was."

"Tom is a good man. Far better than you could ever be."

"Oh I agree absolutely," he paused giving her a swift amused glance, "not so much fun though, I imagine, a trifle stodgy, a little too earnest perhaps. Isn't that so?"

"Please go away and leave me alone," she said violently.

"You know marriage suits you," he went on, looking at her critically through half-closed eyes. "You're far more beautiful than you were when we indulged in that stupid little escapade all those years ago. You were somewhat skinny then, as I remember, all enormous eyes and bird-like bones. Now you are a woman and *tout à fait ravissante*."

She turned on him passionately. "How *can* you say that? I loved you. I would have gone anywhere with you, shared the worst that could happen, starved with you if it were necessary and you didn't care – you've never cared – you handed me back as if – as if – " her voice choked and she turned away her face.

"Oh my dearest, isn't that being a little melodramatic? How could I do such a thing to you? Your father would have cut us off with the proverbial shilling whilst I . . ." he shrugged his shoulders, "I could hardly have kept you in hair ribbons. I gave you up for your own good but now . . ."

"Yes, and now . . ."

"Now it is different. Now we are both grown up, now we can please ourselves, the world is ours."

"It's taken you a very long time to find that out." She turned on him furiously. "It's been so easy for you. You can travel the world, meet whom you like, go where you please, while I have been tied to that hateful mill."

"Have you? I doubt it," he smiled provocatively. "Oh come, don't let us waste time throwing accusations at each other. Life is far too short."

"You seem to forget," she said in a stifled voice, "I am married."

"Darling Sylvia, that's part of your charm. You can't seriously believe that a small thing like marriage is going to prevent me making love to you at the earliest opportunity."

His audacity took her breath away.

"It must."

"Nonsense, my sweet, there is no such word."

In an agony of indecision she urged her horse forward to try and escape from him but they had strayed from the path by now and she found herself galloping down a slope that led into a little copse. The low hanging branches brought her up short and then he was beside her, had slid from the saddle and was reaching up to her.

Helplessly she felt his arms around her as he lifted her to the ground. Then she was propped up against the tree, her hat thrown aside as he kissed her, gently at first and then with an increasing depth and passion so that she felt her very bones melt into ecstasy and desire. He tugged at her stock and kissed her throat. She had dreamed of it for years, lain awake at night imagining herself in his arms and now it was happening and she had no power to resist. Her arms went around his neck, her hands tangled themselves into the thick brown hair as he sank to the ground drawing her with him, his kisses becoming fiercer and more demanding. It seemed an eternity before she breathlessly pulled away, pushing back the heavy blonde hair.

"What are we going to do? Oh God, what are we going to do?"

He smiled, that damnable fascinating crooked smile that turned her blood to water.

"You know what we are going to do and it must be soon, very soon."

"But how? Papa is here with me," she murmured despairingly.

"Leave it to me. I will find a way."

He kissed her again expertly and lingeringly until she had to

121

use all her strength to push him away.

"We must not stay – the others – "

"No, you're right, we must not. We must ride back, cool and collected if tongues are not to wag. Your horse bolted and I was there to render assistance must be our story. What are you doing this evening?"

"I don't know." She sat up distractedly trying to pin up her hair and refasten her stock with trembling fingers. "Yes, I do, I am to be at the play."

"Then I shall be there too."

He helped her to her feet and found her hat while she brushed herself down. Then he fetched the horses and lifted her into the saddle.

They rode back quietly side by side and caught up with the rest of the party who looked at them curiously but made no comment.

Once, staring in front of her, she whispered, "I shouldn't be doing this. It is wicked."

"Of course it's wicked, that's why it is so delightful."

"What a devil you are and what do I do about Tom?"

"Tom can take care of himself."

Was he right? Were all men the same? Was Tom amusing himself with the schoolmistress for whom he had already shown such unusual partiality? He could have come to Harrogate with her but had deliberately stayed at Castlebridge. She did not want him, but he was still her husband. A wave of angry jealousy pounded through her at the very thought that his eyes might stray elsewhere and she let it grow as if in some measure it excused her own disloyalty.

When they had dismounted and the grooms had taken the horses away he stood looking down at her.

"Feeling pangs of conscience?"

She looked away. "I don't know . . ."

"Then don't. Don't let them torment you, my darling, it's such a devilish waste of precious time."

He took her hand, pushed back the cuff of her glove and kissed the slim wrist so that her pulse seemed to race and throb.

"Till tonight then."

"Till tonight."

Those strange eyes with their heavy lids flashed suddenly and she felt the hot blood rush through her so that she trembled, dizzy with anticipation of what the night could bring. Then he bowed formally and correctly before he strolled away.

9

The fête at Farley Grange had been held in September for so many years that no one could now remember when it had begun. Old Hacky Jones, who claimed to be over a hundred, quavered that he remembered being carried to it as a 'a babby' but no one was quite sure how reliable his memory was when he mumbled away after several tankards of strong ale. Originally intended for the tenant farmers and villagers over whom the Strattons had benevolently ruled for generations, it was now held on a Sunday and had become an uneasy mingling of country folk and mill hands from Castlebridge.

"It's a tradition," said Martha to Della, calling in on her way through the village. "I remember my father telling me once that his grandfather, who lived to a great age, remembered it being held the very year the Old Pretender landed in Scotland, German George shook in his shoes and everyone trembled at what might happen next. Sometimes I think it's about time we gave it up. Times have changed. Last year troublemakers came in a cart from Bradford and it ended in a pitched battle, with people badly hurt. But Bret won't hear of it and he can be very obstinate. You *will* come, won't you? We have a kind of informal garden party for our own friends and there'll be dancing in the evening. You can stay with us overnight."

"This is all so new to me. I'd love to come if you're sure I won't be in the way."

"On the contrary. Aunt Lavvy is growing very old. I shall probably be only too glad of any help you may care to give."

To her dismay, Della found that the schoolmistress was expected to organize the children's foot races. This was another age-old tradition with a substantial money prize for the winners. The whole school buzzed with it for a fortnight before and even the boys and girls who worked in the mill were eager to take part. She would have been lost if Tim Withers had not offered to help her out. He had picked up a fever during the hot August in the fetid slums of Bradford and had come to

123

Castlebridge for a few weeks of convalescence.

The day that was to be so momentous in so many different ways began very pleasantly. It was fine and warm for late September, one of those gentle mornings with a slight mist and a faint smell of autumn. Della walked up to the Grange very early with Tim and Abigail. They set out the markers for the races across the field, one for the elevens to fourteens and a shorter distance for the little ones.

A further field had been allotted to the hucksters who had been gathering for the past week. The races would take place in the early afternoon so, when their work was done, they walked up to take a look at the fair. People were already beginning to arrive in wagons, carts and on foot. Village bandsmen were trying out their instruments, a violin, a trumpet, a trombone and something that curved and writhed which Tim called a serpent and made Della laugh. She had never seen a country fair like this and was fascinated as they wandered from booth to booth, giggling at the lurid posters that advertised the attractions, the fat lady with a long black beard, a mermaid in a bottle, a cat with two heads, Punch with his Judy and a small sad dog in a frilled collar. There was bowling for a pink grunting pig, men conjuring, acrobats tumbling over one another and forming impossible pyramids of sweating human bodies, with giants that walked on stilts and even a big shambling brown bear who hopped from one painful foot to another to the tune of his master's tin whistle. Later it would become unbearably noisy and rowdy but in the early morning the dew-wet grass smelt fresh and the breeze blowing across the dale was cool and fragrant.

They had been joined by Mary Ann. The girl looked very pretty that morning, thought Della approvingly, in a clean cotton frock, her hair newly washed and tied up with the pink ribbon she had given her.

"Me Ma told me to come early 'cos last year I helped Miss Hutton with the little uns," she explained and beamed up at Tim who was obviously an old friend.

"How's that nasty rash coming along?" he asked.

"All gone," she tilted up her face for his inspection, "but I've still got me freckles," she went on ruefully.

"Can't do much about those unless I take my knife and cut them out," he teased pinching her nose so that she squealed. "Don't worry, they look very attractive."

"That's what you say. The other girls call me *spotty*!"

"Let 'em. They're not nearly so pretty as you."

She pouted and giggled as he put a brotherly arm around her waist.

They saw men leading long thin dogs that Tim said were whippets. Later they would be racing them. There were pigeons in crates by the dozen and a tent set rather apart from the others where men were slipping in and out with baskets from which there came muffled squawkings and angry scuffles.

"They are bringing in their cocks. They'll be matching them against one another later," said Tim. "That's where trouble started last year. The betting can be fierce and men come in from far and wide. They are deeply resented if their cocks turn out to be champions."

Della had never seen cockfighting but she had heard about it. "My father called it a cruel sport. Why doesn't Bret forbid it here?"

"He enjoys it as much as they do. Didn't you know that about him? Bret would gamble away Farley Grange and everything he possesses if Martha didn't keep tight hold over the purse strings and even then he sometimes escapes her clutches." There was a slight contempt in Tim's voice.

Mary Ann said resentfully, "Me Da has a cock. He thinks more of it than he does of us, me Ma says. We can go hungry so long as he can feed it with eggs and sherry and such like."

"Will he be here today?" asked Della.

"Aye, he will that *and* spoiling all the fun for me and me Mother."

There was a note of pure venom in the young voice that troubled Della but the next moment it had vanished in a squeal of sheer childish delight when she saw the man with the puppies. There were a dozen or so of them, all shapes, sizes and colours, squeaking and tumbling over one another as Mary Ann fell on her knees beside them. She picked one up and the little creature curled confidingly into her neck. She hugged it ecstatically as it licked her cheek.

"Would you like to keep it for yourself?" said Tim impulsively.

"Oh Dr Tim, could I?" she breathed and then her pretty face clouded. "But I don't know whether me Da will let me."

Tim muttered something uncomplimentary under his breath and handed over the money to the dealer who obligingly

125

supplied a piece of string so that Mary Ann ran ahead of them with an enraptured thank you, the puppy pulling her all ways.

"Was that wise?" murmured Della.

"Dan Carter is a brute. Let the poor lass have a bit of fun for once in a way. She has always been the one to miss out."

"Why? What have they against her?"

Tim shrugged his shoulders, avoiding a reply, and presently when Mary Ann had run away to show off her new possession to the other children, they saw Bret hurrying to meet them.

"Oh there you are. I've been hunting everywhere. Martha sent me to find you both. Luncheon is being served."

"I don't know as I'm dressed for such a grand occasion," said Della doubtfully looking down at her flowered cotton gown. "I think perhaps I'd better stay with the children."

"Nonsense. They don't need you nearly as much as I do. You've never seen such a lot of sour-faced frumps and dowds as Martha has seen fit to invite. I'm quite terrified so you must take pity on me." He drew her arm through his and grinned at Tim. "What have you done with your patients, my dear fellow, left them to die without you?"

"They are being cared for," said Tim gruffly.

He kept close at Della's other side so that she arrived at the house firmly escorted by the two young men and ran full tilt into Tom Clifford who had just arrived.

"You're late, Tom, and what the devil have you done with Sylvia?" exclaimed Bret. "Isn't she with you? She's not deserting us, I hope."

"She will be coming later," replied Tom curtly and turned to greet his hostess.

Bret raised his eyebrows with an expressive little shrug but made no comment and Della wondered what had happened between husband and wife that morning to make Tom look so angry.

It was the first time she had seen him not wearing the high stock and sober broadcloth of the business man. He must have ridden up from Rokeby Hall and the dark green riding coat and fawn breeches suited his tall figure. Ever since she had come back from Harrogate she had been deeply troubled. She told herself it was simply the natural concern anyone might feel for a man being deliberately deceived by his wife but in her heart she knew it was nothing of the kind. She had only seen him two or three times in the last few weeks: once when he called to ask her

126

if she would draw some more designs for him and stayed for an hour or so discussing them with her and then again when he brought her a basket with a pheasant shot by Rob, some fine fruit from the hothouse and a bottle of wine.

"My wife thought you would like a few additions to your larder," he said awkwardly, putting the basket on the table and accepting a cup of chocolate which she had just made for herself.

She was becoming only too well aware of the inquisitive eyes that followed his coming and going. She heard the note of sheer disbelief in Lil's voice when she unpacked the basket.

"Well, if that en't a living wonder! Her ladyship never concerned herself with Miss Hutton, never once in all the time she were here, nor the Master neither."

She must not fall in love with him, she told herself over and over again. She must not, it was wrong, it was sinful as well as being totally ridiculous, and she thought she had succeeded, despite the slight breathlessness when his hand accidentally touched hers and the pleasure she took in his company.

The three months of probation were past and she knew that she had not made a success of the school, try as she would. The sensible thing would be to resign, but she kept putting it off. She dreaded the day when he would say, no doubt kindly enough, that she had not come up to his expectations and regretfully he must find another, more suitable teacher.

She watched him move among the guests and was determined not to show disappointment because he had not singled her out, had not even greeted her. She let Bret lead her into the house, laughing with him and Tim as if she hadn't a care in the world.

The buffet luncheon was being served in the great hall, a magnificent spread laid out on the long oak tables, a giant salmon, roasted chickens, York hams, a quarter of lamb, duck with green peas, fruit pies and cream puddings, with a plentiful supply of burgundy, claret and champagne to drink the loyal toast.

"All this food for so few people and in the slums, where I work daily, they're starving on blue skimmed milk and crusts of mouldy bread," whispered Tim, looking with disgust at his loaded plate.

"If you wrapped it up and distributed it, what would it mean? Hardly a mouthful each," said Della practically.

"You have an uncomfortable way of cutting me down to size," he replied with a wry smile.

"Oh Dr Tim, you're such a good person. You make me feel guilty and that's not fair when I'm so hungry," and she put a hand on his.

His ability to laugh at himself was one of the qualities that had already endeared him to her.

The company was a mixed one, a good number of the local gentry who had ridden over with a sprinkling of the richer tenants with their comfortable wives and a few of the successful tradesmen, a little uneasy in this distinguished gathering, their wives and daughters showing off their wealth in rich silks and handsome shawls, in flowered and feathered bonnets and the flashing rings on their fingers. Della saw them whispering among themselves and was aware of curious glances. They were no doubt wondering who she was and what she was doing there in her simple cotton gown and chipstraw hat with its plain ribbon which she had thought suitable for such a country day. She had a feeling that Miss Hutton had never been invited to join this select luncheon party and wondered if it was Bret who had been behind Martha's invitation.

She thought it wisest to melt discreetly away as soon as she had eaten and Tim immediately decided to go with her.

"You don't have to come away now," she protested. "I can manage very well on my own."

"If I am obliged to stay and make inane conversation and look at their smug over-fed faces one moment longer, I shall do something desperate."

"Like what?"

"Oh I don't know — say what I really think about the disgusting way they indulge themselves and grind down their miserable employees to a wretched pittance."

"Be fair. They're not all like that. Tom isn't."

"No, he isn't, but then Tom is different." He glanced down at her. "You like him, don't you?"

"Any reason why I shouldn't?"

"No reason at all, only . . ."

"Only what?"

"Oh nothing. Come on, let's get these children sorted out. Where on earth has Abigail got to? She ought to be taking care of the little ones."

128

It was late afternoon by the time the heats had all been run and the final races took place. By that time a tremendous crowd had gathered. There was a good deal of shouting and cheering, bets were cheerfully being taken and lost, the children, crazy with excitement, were being spurred on by proud parents.

Bret had come down from the house to present the prizes, backed up by Martha and Aunt Lavinia resplendent in a purple silk gown and a black lace parasol. Other members of the house party came drifting up to watch the fun with well-bred indifference. The final of the little ones' competition was won by a thin, white-faced child whom Della had last seen crawling along the rows of looms on the factory floor. He stared at the golden guineas Bret put in his hand as if it was some wondrous gift come down from heaven, then he gave a wild whoop and bolted across to throw his arms around his mother.

The last race looked like being a trial of speed between Mary Ann and her brother, the detestable Jem. Tall and slim for her age, Mary Ann had won her heats easily. Now it was girl against boy and yet somehow more than that. It was only as they lined up that Della noticed Dan Carter. He had pushed himself to the front, stocky, self-assertive, with a tough group of his own cronies around him. His wife was standing just behind him, the two younger children clinging to her skirts. It was the first time Della had seen Jane Carter and she realized from whom the girl had inherited her looks. Jane's worn unhappy face still had the remnants of beauty.

The girl and boy were standing on their marks and suddenly there was a hush. In the distance the village band thumped away at their instruments. Then Tim gave the signal and they were off. It was a long distance to the end of the field and back again. For some reason Della found herself watching with a tense excitement which was absurd. What was it after all but a children's race, not a matter of life and death? At the turn they were side by side, then slowly Mary Ann began to gain. The girls, none of whom liked Jem, began to scream encouragement as she came racing down the course kilting up her long skirt to run more easily and showing slim legs in black stockings. She came past the winning post, Tim raised the flag shouting "Bravo!" and wild with triumph she flung her arms around his neck. He laughed and swung her round, skirts flying, then kissed her boisterously. The next moment he was flung to the ground as Dan Carter tore them apart with a vicious blow that

129

sent Mary Ann spinning to her knees. It had all happened so quickly that for a moment no one moved. Stunned, Mary Ann lay where she had fallen as Tim scrambled to his feet groping blindly in the grass for his spectacles. Dan had crossed to the girl and jerked her roughly to her feet.

"Git away from him, you bitch, d'ye hear me? Git you home and stay there!"

He would have hit her again if Della had not run to seize his arm. He flung her off so that she stumbled backwards.

Mary Ann was staring at him, the pretty face contorted with fury. "I hate you, I hate you!" she screamed.

He struck her savagely across the face and then Tom was there, thrusting him away from her.

"Let her be, damn you. What has she done?"

"Aye, you'd take her part, wouldn't you, Master? D'ye think I don't know whose git she is, whorin' after men like her mother before her. And now it seems you're like to do the same," he thrust his face forward ugly with passion. "Just like your father – d'ye think we don't know – you and your fancy piece up there at the school!"

The coarse abuse poured out and then Tom hit him. Taken by surprise he fell backwards. Slowly he got to his feet, blood running down his chin, his face murderous while Tom waited. It was scarcely more than a few seconds but to Della it seemed much longer. Then Mary Ann, sobbing wildly, snatched up the whining puppy and ran away from them across the fields. Into the sudden stir, coming lightly through the crowd who parted before her, came Sylvia in her cream silk gown, her wide leghorn hat with its rosepink ribbons, gaily swinging her lace parasol.

"They told me you were all here," she looked around her with wide eyes. "Have I interrupted something?"

"No, my dear, nothing." Tom thrust his bruised hand behind his back. "I apologize, Martha, if I've caused any disturbance."

Dan Carter's comrades had grabbed him by the arms and were dragging him away. The villagers thrilled with the drama began to disperse with backward looks, muttering among themselves.

"Have you been fighting, Tom, surely not?" remarked a cool amused voice. "Have we missed something exciting? How absolutely maddening."

And breaking into the circle of watchful faces, smiling, sardonic, came the man Della had last seen at Harrogate, elegant as ever and completely sure of himself.

"Oliver!" exclaimed Tom. "I'd no idea you were to be here."

"Neither had I." Bret had come forward holding out a hand in welcome. "My dear chap, I thought you were to be abroad all summer. Why didn't you let us know?"

"There's hardly been time. Martha, my dear . . . Miss Lavinia looking as handsome as ever." He was greeting them bending over their hands with charm and grace. "It's been a long time but I'm delighted to be back. And who is this?"

He had turned those strange heavy-lidded eyes on Della, a little smile playing about the thin lips.

Oliver Craven, her cousin, she might have guessed. It was obvious now, but stupidly she had never connected them in her mind, and he knew exactly who she was, she was certain of it.

All this flashed through her mind in a second. Then Sylvia was saying carelessly in her sweet silvery voice, "Oh that's only Miss Lismore, Tom's little schoolmistress at the school."

"Miss Lismore, your servant." He took her reluctant hand and raised it to his lips. "Surely we've met before somewhere – was it in London or was it Harrogate?"

"I'm afraid I don't remember."

"No? Maybe you will later. I'm sure we shall meet again and very soon."

"Perhaps."

Then Sylvia's hand was on his arm. "Oliver, do come. Martha is calling us to tea and Tom is waiting."

He bowed slightly and followed after the others leaving her alone.

Bret said hurriedly, "Make sure that poor child gets her prize, Della, will you?"

He put the guineas into her hand and went quickly after Oliver and Sylvia.

She was standing rather forlornly looking after them when Miss Lavinia gave her a little prod with her parasol.

"What you need after all that is a good bracing cup of tea," she said brusquely, "and so do I. You come along with me."

"I think perhaps I'd better go and find Mary Ann," she said slowly, "she was very upset."

"Dr Tim will see she comes to no harm. That young man has a passion for lame dogs, haven't you noticed? Now be a good girl and lend me your arm. I find I'm not so brisk as I used to be."

Della had an idea that the old lady was not nearly so helpless as she liked to pretend but she let her lean on her arm and together they walked slowly towards the house.

They were silent while they crossed the field, then Miss Lavinia gave her a quick sly look.

"Go on, my dear, ask your questions. I can see you are bursting with them."

"Oh I'm not. That's unfair – but I was just wondering – "

"Why that very unpleasant character, Dan Carter, behaved so abominably."

"It was all so innocent. Tim gave Mary Ann the puppy this morning. He has been nice to her all day and she was saying thank you, that's all. It was hateful of him to make it seem something else – something quite different," she ended lamely.

"Yes, well, you're probably right but it's not quite so simple as that. You need to go back a little further."

"How do you mean? Is it something to do with Tom?"

"She's not *his* daughter if that's what you are thinking. If you want it put plainly she is more likely to be his half-sister."

"Half-sister? But how?"

"It was common gossip at the time but maybe true for all that and Dan Carter must have guessed, though he likes to believe he was deliberately cheated."

Miss Lavinia stopped and plumped herself down on one of the garden seats set along the shrubbery.

"Do you mind, my dear? I could do with a moment's rest to catch my breath."

Della sat beside her. "Miss Lavinia, you can't get out of it like that. Now you've started, you must tell me the rest."

"Must I indeed? And what is it to do with you, Miss?"

The old lady smiled aggravatingly and then settled herself comfortably. "Very well. This is my own version of the story but I daresay it is near enough to the truth. Did you know that Jane Carter is Rob Hunt's daughter?"

"Rob who looks after Tom's horses?"

"That's right and his father's before that. Jane was only twelve years old when she went to the Hall as nursery maid just before Tom was born. She was always a very pretty girl, well brought up with nice manners. After his wife died in the cholera epidemic, John Clifford was a lonely man and in his own way a

132

handsome one. Do I need to go on? The inevitable happened."

"You mean he fell in love with Jane?"

"I don't think I'd call it love," said the old lady judicially, "not in the romantic fashion you're thinking of, but she gave him what he needed and I daresay the girl was dazzled by her master's attentions. Does it shock you?"

"No, no, of course not."

"I didn't think it would. You didn't grow up in a nunnery."

"Not since I was sixteen and even nuns can be worldly wise. You would be surprised."

"Would I? I doubt it, human nature being what it is," said Miss Lavinia dryly. "Now where was I?"

"You were going to tell me where Dan Carter came into it."

"Ah well, that's partly guesswork on my part, but it does seem that he had always wanted the girl. He had even approached her father about it. He had a good position at the mill and had already made advances which Jane had rejected. Then to everyone's surprise it was suddenly settled and a wedding planned with a handsome gift from John Clifford and a house in the new factory town he was building for his workers."

"Do you mean he sold her off when he knew she was pregnant?"

"Perhaps. No one knows for certain except Jane herself and maybe Dan Carter."

"But that's horribly callous."

"Perhaps it is but men do behave like that at times, even the best of them. No doubt he thought he was providing hand-somely for his little mistress and her by-blow by giving her a good husband and a good start in life and never realized for a moment that he was condemning her to years of misery and humiliation. I have sometimes wondered if the bullet that killed him was revenge for a private grievance rather than a blow for the cause of the factory workers."

"You mean it was Dan Carter who fired that shot?"

"I'm not accusing anyone but that doesn't mean that I don't have my opinion."

"Does Tom know?"

"About the girl? Perhaps not at first but he must have long guessed at it."

"Then why doesn't he do something for Mary Ann?"

"My dear child, Tom has his own troubles, both at the mill

133

and at home." She hoisted herself to her feet. "If we don't make haste I shall miss my cup of tea." Then she paused for an instant. "One word of warning. Don't encourage him to spend so much time with you."

"I don't encourage him," she said indignantly. "It's only because I'm doing some work for the mill which he asked me to do."

"Is that the only reason? I have heard differently."

"Then you have been listening to lies," she said fiercely.

"Now, now, don't be angry with me. Perhaps in London life is more free and easy but up here it is different. You heard what Dan Carter was saying. Tom's not his father but if anything should happen, it will be you they will blame not him."

"But why should they? I've done nothing wrong."

She was angry that such accusations should be levelled against her. Why shouldn't she see Tom when she liked? What was wrong with it? What harm were they doing? Why shouldn't she take pleasure in his company while his wife amused herself with another man – and then suddenly she stopped dead. She had forgotten that the man in question was Oliver Craven, her own cousin – Oh God, what a tangle everything was!

Miss Lavinia said testily, "Do come along, my dear, it's beginning to blow cold. I shall be glad to be back at the house."

"Yes, of course, I'm sorry." She took the old lady's arm. "Thank you for telling me what you did. I shan't forget it or your advice."

It had been arranged that she should sleep at the Grange that night.

"These parties sometimes go on till the small hours," Martha had said. "Lord knows what state Bret will be in by then and you must not walk home alone."

So she had brought a bag earlier, with a dress to change into and a few necessities. Now she thought it might be better to make her excuses and prepare to walk the five miles back to the schoolhouse through the cool September evening. The slur that Dan Carter had put upon her innocent meetings with Tom had been heard by many of the house party and whether they believed it or not she shrank from meeting them face to face and seeing the speculation in their eyes. It was a small incident that changed her mind.

She saw Miss Lavinia safely installed in her favourite

armchair, fetched her tea and cake and then stood for a moment undecided among the noisy chattering throng in the great hall. Logs were smouldering on the wide hearth and a group of young men were standing in front of it with Sylvia in their midst. She was laughing, colour in her cheeks, her eyes brilliant, holding something high above her pale gold head and Della saw it was the cluster of roses she had worn tucked into her waist. She threw the nosegay up into the air. They all reached for it but it was Oliver who caught it with an expert flick of the wrist that spun him round. Across the crowded room his eyes met Della's, cool and challenging with that same faint enigmatic smile and she knew at once that whatever game he was playing, whether or not he was choosing his moment to expose and humiliate her in front of all these people, she was not going to run away from it, not even if it meant being ignominiously dismissed, not even if it meant never seeing Tom Clifford again.

Oliver turned back to Sylvia and, released from those compelling eyes, Della shivered suddenly. A maid with a tray of teacups paused beside her but she shook her head and made her way through the hall and up the stairs to the small room that had been assigned to her. There she could gather herself together and face whatever the evening might bring.

Martha's maid had laid out her nightgown and hung up her dress. She looked at it critically. It had seemed just right for a country evening when she had decided to wear it but now she was not so sure. She had made it herself to her own design. Several skirts of pale green organza which Madame Ginette had not liked and had let her buy cheaply, fell over a stiff silk petticoat. Puffed sleeves to the elbow were trimmed with fine lace. She surveyed herself in the mirror when she was dressed. A few gold stars scattered here and there in the folds of the wide skirts shimmered as she moved. Was the neck cut too low for this prim and highly respectable society? She took up a gauzy scarf which Lucinda had passed on to her at Harrogate, draping it around her bare shoulders and then abruptly threw it aside. If they thought her a fancy piece up from London, then she would act the part and to hell with it as Papa would have said. She opened her little jewel box to find a necklet and the golden skull rolled from its tissue paper. On an impulse she could not have explained, she took it out, found the chain that held the simple locket with her mother's portrait and threaded it through the tiny gold ring. It fell just above the cleavage of her breasts. She had swept the black hair away from her ears into a simple knot at the back of her head. A few garden roses had been put in a vase on the dressing table. She chose a white one and fastened it into the dark hair. If those wives and daughters downstairs in their rich silks with their jewels and curls thought her a dowd, then let them. Tonight she was going to be herself – Delphine Craven, daughter of Paul Craven, and proud of it.

Unwittingly she could not have achieved anything more stunning. The great hall and the drawing room had been stripped of furniture and the rugs rolled up. The fiddlers and a base viol were already installed and were tuning up their instruments. The guests were lining up for the first set dance as she came down the stairs, the light from the many branched candelabra falling directly on her.

The women stared, wrinkling contemptuous noses and secretly envious. The sporting young men thought, "The schoolmarm mouse has turned into a Princess. Old Tom may be a stick-in-the-mud, but by Jingo, he knows how to pick 'em!" Sylvia, standing beside Oliver, saw his eyes widen, heard a quick intake of breath and decided there and then that her husband must be persuaded to get rid of this tiresome slut of a girl before she did any more damage.

Bret and Tom started forward together but Bret got there first and took her hand.

"You're just in time for the first dance – only country fashion I am afraid, but I hope you will do me the honour," and he led her to take her place opposite him.

She had made up her mind to enjoy herself and she did. In and out and up and down they danced to the merry sound of the music. Once she found herself hand in hand with Tom. He pressed her fingers and smiled at her and she smiled back warmly and happily. Then Bret was whirling her around again and when they stopped at last, panting a little, he found her a chair and stood looking down at her, his eyes on the ornament around her neck.

"It's very unusual," he said. "May I ask where it came from?"

"I don't know. It was given to me."

"I've only seen one like it once before."

"Really." She was at once intrigued. "Where was that?"

136

"I can't remember. Somewhere or other. You know how things are. They remain in the mind but you can't place them." But she had a queer feeling that he did know and was deliberately evading an answer. Then another dance was being set up and someone else came to claim her for it.

Up here in the north the robust customs of an earlier age still persisted. The decorum, the dull respectability that had begun to spread through the Court and London society with the accession of the youthful Queen Victoria had not yet reached Yorkshire. As the evening wore on and the wine circulated, the country dances became a good deal more boisterous and uninhibited. After one particularly energetic round she leaned against a pillar, hot and breathless, and hunting for an elusive handkerchief.

"Try this," said a cool voice.

She looked up to see Oliver Craven holding out a spotless square of linen and watching her quizzically.

"Thank you but I have my own."

She dabbed at her face with a wisp of lace-edged lawn.

"Do you find our way of amusing ourselves a little too vulgar for your taste, Miss Lismore?"

"Not at all. I'm enjoying myself immensely."

"Wonderful." He pushed back a curtain. Behind it the long window opened on to the terrace. "It's a delicious night. Shall we escape for a few minutes and sample it?"

She hesitated. "I'm not sure whether I should."

"Are you afraid to trust yourself to me?"

"Is there any reason why I should be?"

"None that I know of, but it's your choice." He smiled and held out his hand. "Come now. Be brave."

She put the tips of her fingers in his and let him lead her on to the terrace. The parapet ended in a flight of steps and a large stone urn in which late flowers still bloomed. In the distance there were flickering lights and the faint sound of music.

"The yokels are still making merry with the help of Martha's barrels of ale. There'll be some sore heads in Tom's mill tomorrow."

The cool night air was refreshing. A shaft of light from the window behind them lit his face into sharp sardonic angles as he leaned back against the stonework, his eyes on her.

"You puzzle me, Miss Lismore. What is a young woman like you doing up here teaching mill brats their ABC?"

"It's a way of earning a living, Mr Craven."

"And is that necessary?"

"Very necessary."

He put out a hand and lifted the gold skull, his fingers ice-cold on her bare skin.

"A strange adornment for such a pretty neck, isn't it?"

"That's what Bret said."

"Did he indeed?"

"He also said he'd seen it somewhere before but he couldn't remember where. Do you know?"

"I? Why should I?" He let it slip from his fingers. "Was it a gift?"

"Not exactly. It was found by someone whom I love dearly and given to me."

"Rather a macabre love token, if you will forgive my saying so.

> 'The grave's a fine and private place
> But none I think do there embrace.' "

A little shiver ran through her. He was playing with her of course, some game of his own which she did not understand, but if that was what he wanted, then she would play it with him.

"I prefer the poet's other lines –

> 'But at my back I always hear
> Time's winged chariot hurrying near,
> And yonder all before us lie
> Deserts of vast eternity.' "

He looked surprised. "You know the work of Andrew Marvell?"

He had thought to score over her and had failed. She knew a moment of triumph.

"My Belgian convent taught me very thoroughly."

"A learned lady I see."

"Isn't that what a schoolmistress should be?"

He stretched out a hand, lifted up her chin and unexpectedly kissed her. His lips were cool and had a kind of frightening fascination. After a startled moment she pulled herself free and ran away from him into the ballroom where the music still played, where there was warmth with laughter and people, and did not notice that Sylvia had come through a further door and had stood watching them.

She came swiftly up behind him. "Are you too falling under the spell of Tom's little schoolmistress?"

"A disturbing young woman," he said casually, "and not at all what she seems."

"Is that why you were making love to her?"

"Oh come, my dear," he went on airily, "hardly making love. What's a kiss here and there?"

"It may mean little to you but it means my whole life to me."

He frowned as he turned to face her. "No drama tonight, Sylvia, please. It's neither the time nor the place."

"How can you be so heartless?" she said passionately. "I've scarcely seen you alone all the evening."

"My dear love, one of us has to be sensible. Tom has old-fashioned notions of honour. Do you want him to call me out? Pistols for two on High Tor at dawn are not my idea of amusement."

"Don't make fun of me. Can't you be serious about anything?" She moved closer to him, putting a hand on his arm. "Oliver, what are we going to do?"

"Go on as we are. It's a very delightful and satisfactory arrangement."

"How *can* you say that? You're free – you can go where you like, do as you please, but I have to live with Tom, listen to Tom, sleep with Tom . . ."

"Do you?" he said sharply, "Do you sleep with Tom?"

She looked away from him. "Not since I came back from Harrogate. I couldn't – I couldn't bear him to touch me, not after . . . but there will come a time – there must – then what shall I do?"

"Let's not meet trouble halfway. You can manage Tom, you always could, poor devil – isn't that so?"

"It's not as easy as it was," she said sullenly. "Tom has changed." She slid an arm around his neck. "Oliver, take me away from here. We could go abroad – Paris, Florence, Rome – it would be wonderful. I've always longed to travel."

"You would cut yourself off from decent society."

"What does that matter? We would have each other."

He stirred restlessly. "One day perhaps we'll take the plunge, but not now."

"Why, why, why?" she said, fretful and impatient as a spoiled child.

"A great many reasons." He was evasive. "There is my

139

father for one – he is growing old and difficult. There is Larksghyll, there is a lamentable lack of cash. I'm in devilish low water just now. Lovers can't live on air."

"I have my jewellery, a great deal of it. Tom has always been very generous."

He made a gesture of distaste. "I may be all kinds of a rogue but I draw the line at living on your husband's gifts of love."

"You don't care, that's what it is," she said violently. "You don't care what happens to me. All you think of is your own pleasure."

"Keep your voice down, for God's sake. Do you want everyone to hear you?"

"Let them. I don't care any more – I tell you I don't care."

"Well, I do." He took a quick look around, then slipped an arm around her waist and drew her close to him.

"Dearest Sylvia, we've had some wonderful moments, haven't we? Don't spoil them all now. We'll find time to be together, you leave it to me. Larksghyll is not far away and you ride Sheba every morning, don't you?"

He stopped her protest with his mouth and after a moment she yielded to his kisses, surrendering herself to him utterly for a few blissful moments. Then he drew back.

"I'll go in first, you follow in a minute or two. Better not to be seen together."

She watched him leave, her hands pressed against her lips as if she were holding there the memory of his kisses. Ever since she had come back from Harrogate she had lived in a turmoil. The few hours they had spent together had been for her both devastating and ecstatic. Tom, fearful of hurting her, had sometimes treated her as if she were made of glass. Oliver had no such scruples. She thought back to that first night they had made love, the lies she had told her father, the terror of being discovered. Afterwards she had lain on the bed ravaged, her hair spread across the pillows, her body aching with fulfilment and hungry for more. To come back to Castlebridge, to become again wife and mother, had been torment to her reckless and undisciplined spirit. Ever since she was a child what she wanted she *must* have at whatever cost. It had been denied to her once but not again. She would not let him go this time. She was jealous of his every moment away from her, every look he gave another woman. She had never read Byron, never heard those wise and cynical words –

> 'Man's love is of man's life a thing apart
> 'Tis a woman's whole existence'

and if she had, she would have scorned them. For Sylvia it had always been all or nothing.

She tidied her hair with shaking fingers, pressed her handkerchief to her lips for an instant and went back to the ballroom. There she ran into Tom.

"Where have you been?" he asked. "I've been looking for you everywhere."

"Only outside for a breath of air. It's too hot in here."

"Were you with Oliver?"

"Why ask that?" she said with a quick burst of temper. "If you really want to know, he is flirting with your Miss Lismore."

Tom frowned. "I know Oliver in one of his moods. I hope he is not pestering her."

"Far from it. She looked to me as if she were enjoying his attentions," she said provokingly.

He looked annoyed but only said, "It's getting late. Shall we go?"

"Not yet. You know Bret expects us to stay till the end."

He sighed. "As you like, my dear."

Della had found it a very disturbing evening. That strange little conversation with Oliver troubled her. Did he know something about that fatal evening or was it all just an act, something to amuse a devious mind? She had been tempted to challenge him, say who she was and defy him to do his worst, only something about his chilling offhand manner daunted her.

The evening was not yet over. Later, very much later, she was dancing with Tom. She had been aware of his eyes on her more than once but it was the first time they had come together. It was long after midnight, most of the older guests had already left, their carriages bowling down the drive, only a few of the younger couples remained, with a sprinkling of the brighter spirits among Bret's friends.

"The last dance," announced Martha. The musicians, hot and sweating, heaved a sigh of relief. They ended with a final flourish, converting the sedate waltz into a crazy gallop. The men swung their partners round and round ending with a smacking kiss. Tom was in wild mood, quite unlike himself, his dark hair falling over his forehead. He lifted Della high so that

141

her wide skirts flew madly around her. His lips touched hers briefly, then suddenly she was crushed against him, his mouth hard on hers, fierce and demanding, while she felt her whole body surge forward to meet his. It lasted seconds only, then they had broken apart, were staring breathlessly at one another in a kind of amazement as if afraid of the discovery they had made. Then Tom straightened up, tossed back the disordered hair, spoke without looking at her.

"It's shockingly late. I must find my wife. What about you? Can we give you a lift back to Castlebridge?"

"I'm staying here. Martha is giving me a bed for the night." Her voice, cool and distant, did not seem to belong to her.

"I'll say goodnight, then." He turned away from her, catching Martha as she came past them. "Have you seen Sylvia?"

"She is in the library with Oliver. They are playing cards."

He muttered something under his breath and strode across the hall.

Martha said worriedly, "Bret and some of his cronies are gambling. I wish he wouldn't. Once the fever gets him, he never knows when to stop. You go to bed whenever you feel like it, Della. There are still people I must speak to."

She moved away to bid farewell to other guests who were on the point of leaving.

After a moment Della walked after Tom. The young men were lounging around a table, candles burning, glasses at their elbows, engrossed in their game. She guessed it might well go on all night and understood something of Martha's anxiety about her young brother.

Sylvia was perched on a stool just behind Oliver leaning over his shoulder watching the play of the cards.

Tom had paused just inside the room. He said, "It's past two o'clock, Sylvia. Time we went home."

She looked up defiantly. "Presently, when the game is finished."

"Now. Rob is bringing the carriage." There was a decided edge to his voice.

"Let him wait. I'm Oliver's luck, aren't I? While I'm here, he can't lose."

Oliver laid down his cards with a final gesture and Bret sat up with an exclamation.

"By Jupiter, it's deuced unfair. He's got Lady Luck beside

142

him."

Tom took a step into the room. "Sylvia, are you coming?"

"Not luck, dear boy, just skill." Oliver picked up the cards shuffling them between long thin fingers. "You had better go with your husband, Sylvia. He is waiting for you."

"Damn you!" she whispered under her breath. Then she picked up her silk shawl and slung it around her shoulders. "You can take your revenge now, Bret darling. Lady Luck is on her way out."

Della watched her as she sailed across the room and took Tom's arm. "You're right, dearest, you always are. It's high time we went home."

10

Sylvia said, "I'm sorry, Tom, but I'm not having one of those mill brats from Castlebridge in this house, not even as a scullery maid, and that's final."

"Mrs Fenton mentioned she could do with extra help in the nursery. After all Nanny Roberts is not so young," said Tom tentatively.

"She said nothing to me and in any case it's my decision, not hers."

It was the morning after the fête. Tom had breakfasted early and had come up to his wife's room before leaving for the mill. He stood in front of the fireplace, looking formidable and curiously out of place in this very feminine room with its frilled curtains and figured satin bed hangings. Sylvia leaned back against her lace-edged pillows, the white cat snuggled down beside her, and watched him through half-closed eyes.

He made an impatient gesture. "Mary Ann is a cut above the others. Her mother has brought her up well and she is intelligent. Della speaks highly of her."

"Oh it's Della now, is it? And what she says is gospel, I suppose."

"For heaven's sake, Sylvia! The girl has been here for five months, we have seen her frequently, surely there is no need to remain on such formal terms. There is something else I might mention," he went on awkwardly, "Mary Ann is different from the rest of the family and that has made her very unhappy at home."

"We all know the reason for that, don't we?" said Sylvia dryly. "After yesterday's affair I imagine the whole neighbourhood must know."

"It's an old scandal with no foundation."

"Oh Tom, don't be so naïve about it and don't think I don't know. Your father passed his pregnant mistress on to one of his millhands and whether he suspected or whether he found it out by accident, Dan Carter has punished her and the girl for it ever since. Don't think I'm blaming my father-in-law. I liked him. He was a hard man but he knew exactly what he wanted and made sure he got it. I respect that. In actual fact the morals of some of my Farringford ancestors have not been above reproach, but don't you see if you bring Mary Ann here, it will start up the gossip all over again. Tom Clifford's half-sister scullery maid at Rokeby Hall – that won't sound so good, will it?"

He had to admit that she was probably right for once, and for some reason it irritated him. He said shortly, "Well, if you won't, you won't. I shall have to think of something else."

"Why don't you dismiss Dan Carter? From what I hear he's always caused trouble."

"Because if I do, I shall probably have a strike on my hands. He's popular with some of the men particularly since the rioting in the other mill towns."

"Aren't you master in your own mill?" she asked sarcastically.

"Oh I'm master right enough but even I cannot run it singlehanded. If we're shut down for six months or more, you and I and all of us will feel the pinch. And you won't like that, will you? No more expensive pleasure trips whenever it takes your fancy."

He moved towards the door, then stopped and came back to the side of the bed.

"By the way, why didn't you tell me you and Oliver spent some time together at Harrogate?"

She looked up quickly. "Who has been talking to you? Was it your schoolmistress? I saw her there, you know, with that flashy actress friend of hers."

"No, it was not Della. It was one of Bret's friends last night."

"If you must know it was when Papa was taking his medicinal baths. I was left very much at a loose end and so I was glad of his company. It was all quite harmless. We went to the theatre, saw Macready in *Hamlet* actually, went driving together once or twice – it never occurred to me that you would object."

"Of course I don't object. Oliver is an old friend. I just thought it strange that you didn't mention it when it's so long since we have seen him up here in Yorkshire."

She shrugged her shoulders. "There was so much to do, so much to see to when I came home. I never once thought about it."

He looked down at the lovely face turned away from him, aware of uneasiness, only half believing her, then he said briskly, "Well, I must be going. I'm late already." He bent to kiss her cheek and the white cat arched its back and spat angrily. "Damn that animal! Do you have to keep it always with you?"

She laughed and fondled the cat's silky head. "It's not my fault that Duchess doesn't like you."

"It's mutual," he muttered, then patted her cheek lightly and went out shutting the door with a snap that betrayed his annoyance.

He would not permit himself to believe that his wife had been guilty of anything but indiscretion, but there had been an unpleasantly sly innuendo in the casual comments that had reached his ears and it riled him that she had not seen fit to confide in him, so that he had been taken by surprise.

There was Mary Ann too, a situation he had tried to ignore ever since he had guessed at it after his father's death. Now it was out in the open whether he liked it or not. Other men might shake it off as of no consequence but he was cursed with a feeling of responsibility for others. He stood at the bottom of the front steps waiting for his horse to be brought round and allowed himself to think for an instant of what he had resolutely put out of his mind ever since it had happened – that fierce elemental surge which had burned through him when he had held Della in his arms, the certainty that she felt the same, that something had fused between them from the first night he had seen her, a soot-smudged waif facing defiantly up to him – an immediate recognition – which he had refused to admit. Damn it, he was not a lovesick boy but a married man with a son and a mill that needed all his skill to keep steadily working . . .

"Your horse, sir."

The boy was gazing at him – how long had he been standing there, for God's sake, like some numskull!

"Thank 'ee," he took the bridle, vaulted into the saddle and went down the drive at a pace that set Rob and the stable boy wondering what had hit the Master that morning to send him off so recklessly.

Della thought much the same when she saw him ride by during school break. The first part of the morning had been unbearably tedious, the children half asleep and more than usually stupid. Mary Ann had not turned up and she felt worried about her. The shouting of the boys as they chased the shrieking girls about the yard made her head ache, until she could have screamed with them. She had lain awake half the night trying hard to concentrate on the curious conversation with Oliver Craven simply to prevent herself dwelling on Tom, but despite all her efforts her mind kept returning to it. Why? Why remember a kiss so vividly? Everyone was kissing at that moment, it was fun and meant nothing, except stupidly, idiotically, it mattered to her. It had brought her up with a jolt, made her realize with a frightening certainty how much he had begun to mean to her. And it must not be.

Wakeful and on edge, she had got up soon after six when all the rest of the house was sleeping, had an early cup of tea with Martha's cook in the kitchen and resolutely walked the five miles back to Castlebridge.

She had an unexpected visitor at midday. Tim came knocking at her door with the puppy he had given to Mary Ann.

She went to meet him apprehensively. "What happened? Is she all right?"

He nodded. "I found her in the end. She had hidden herself in a spinney down by the brook where the children sometimes go paddling in the summer. I persuaded her to go back home."

"Should you have done that?"

"I don't think he will touch her again. Her mother will protect her. But she is very afraid for the puppy. She says will you take care of him for her? If not, I daresay I can get my mother to look after the little fellow or Abbie."

"Of course I'll keep him for her. I'd like to. She can come here and see him whenever she wishes. She can take him out for walks."

"She'd like that if Dan doesn't send her into the mill."

"Would he, Tim?"

"I think he might simply because her mother has always stood out against it. She wants something better for the girl."

It was Tom who should do something, she thought, but could not bring herself to discuss with Tim what Miss Lavinia had told her.

"Is there anything we can do?" she asked.

"I don't know. There might be an opportunity for her in Bradford. There are one or two well-to-do families with children who might be willing to take her as under nursery-maid, but she is so young," he said doubtfully. "And in any case I must go now. I can't leave my superior to carry on alone any longer. I'm taking the afternoon coach."

He held out his hand and she took it.

"You're such a dear, Tim, you and your father and Abbie have all been so kind. I don't know what I would have done without you." She paused a moment then reached up and kissed his cheek. "Goodbye and good luck."

He blushed and grinned at her. "By the way, Mary Ann has christened the puppy Scamp. Goodbye for the present."

He left quickly under the interested gaze of twenty pairs of eyes lining up for afternoon school.

Sometimes a small incident, a promise only half-intended, a casual remark, can set off a chain of events that will alter lives and change destinies. Perhaps if Tim had not unwisely suggested that there might be an opening for Mary Ann in Bradford, things would have fallen out differently. But he had said so, meaning only to comfort her, and she flung it defiantly in her father's face when at the end of that week he came home from work and announced that she would be working in the mill as a comber on the following Monday.

Her mother said, "No, Dan, no. It's not right. She is not fit for work of that kind and you promised me . . ."

"Shut up, woman. She'll do as she's told and that's the end of it. What's so special about her, eh? High time she was workin' like Jem and the rest of 'em."

Mary Ann had been setting the table for supper. Her pretty face had sharpened and gone very white.

"I shan't go."

"You'll do what I say, Miss, or it will be the worse for you."

"I shan't go, I won't, and you can't make me. I hate the mill. Look at what it's doin' to our Ma. She don't ever stop coughing. She'll be spittin' blood soon and I'll not do the same. I won't, I swear I won't!"

"Now you listen to me, my girl." He advanced on her threateningly and she backed nervously away from him, her voice rising shrilly.

"I can do better than that, I know I can. Miss Lismore said so. She says I got brains and she'll go on teaching me if I want . . ."

"So it's that interferin' bitch from the school, is it, puttin' these grand ideas into your head. I'll not have it, d'ye hear? Perhaps that'll teach you to listen to her and not to your father," and he hit her so hard that she stumbled and clutched at the table to steady herself.

"Dan, don't! You'll hurt her!"

Her mother grabbed his arm and he flung her off roughly.

"You leave her to me. It en't none of your business."

Jane fell sideways and put out a hand to save herself. A boiling pan on the hot stove tilted and the scalding liquid spilled across her wrist.

Mary Ann heard the stifled cry. She snatched up the bread knife from the table and flew at him with it. He held her off easily, twisting her wrist so savagely that the knife fell to the floor.

"Murder me, would ye, ye little devil. Now you listen to me once and for all . . ."

"I'm never goin' into the mill, never, never," she screamed into his face. "I'll run away. I'll go to Bradford. There's work there. Dr Tim told me so. He will look after me."

"So that's it, is it? You'd be off with a man, would ye? That's what's at the bottom of it, and him calling himself a doctor, the dirty tyke!"

The pent-up fury that had smouldered in him ever since the fête, the burning humiliation when Tom had knocked him down, the jeers of his workmates as they dragged him away, burst into physical violence. He picked up the heavy buckled belt he had put on the table when he came in and beat her unmercifully about the head and shoulders. She screamed as the blows rained down on her, putting up her arms to try and protect her face. The two smallest children broke into noisy sobs as their father lashed out brutally at the cowering terrified girl. It was her mother who saved her. She opened the door behind Mary Ann so that she could thrust her through it and then slammed it in her husband's face, unflinchingly taking the last infuriated blows upon herself. She leaned back against the door, trembling, pale as death, nursing the reddened and blistered hand against her.

"Do you want to kill her?" she whispered. "If you do, then you must kill me first."

He stood panting, his rage slowly ebbing, colour fading from his face, leaving it stark and grim. Then he buckled the belt

149

around his waist, thrust her aside, flung open the door and stormed out. Her strength gone, Jane fell to her knees, praying that he would not find her, that Mary Ann would have had the sense to run and take refuge with one of their neighbours.

It was past nine when Della heard the frantic knocking at the door and went to open it. Mary Ann was crouched on the step.

"May I come in?" she whispered. "Please, Miss Della."

"Yes of course. Come in quickly."

The girl looked fearfully around her before she slid through the door which Della shut and bolted. It had been raining outside and she gasped as the lamplight fell on the hair hanging lankly around the girl's bruised white face. One eye was half closed, red angry wheals showed up clearly on her neck and shoulders, blood oozed where the buckled belt had torn away the thin cotton blouse.

"My dear child, whatever has happened to you? You're soaked to the skin."

"I've been hidin'."

"Who did this to you?"

"It were my father. He wants me to go into the mill but I won't, I won't, so then he beat me."

She was trembling so much that the words jerked out through choking sobs and Della put an arm around her.

"Come and sit down. Try to tell me quietly from the beginning."

The evening had turned chilly and she had lit a fire. She poked it into a blaze and drew the girl into the warmth as she sobbed out her story and then fell silent.

"Quite a number of girls *do* work at the mill," said Della gently. "Why do you hate it so much?"

"You wouldn't understand, Miss. 'Tis the combers. They tease the wool and then the air is filled with fluff. It's like being suffocated, my Ma says. He makes her work there, though her lungs are weak, and old Dr Withers says she will die if she goes on. I've seen her gettin' weaker and weaker and coughin' and coughin' till she can't breathe. I'm frightened – I don't want to die like her, Miss," she went on passionately. "I don't want to spit blood and die like she will."

"Ssh, quiet now," said Della soothingly. "We'll think of something. Does your father know you have come here?"

"Nay, I don't think so. I hid till I saw him come out. He'll

150

have gone drinkin' with the other men but I don't want to go back there. You won't make me go, will you?'' She clung to Della's hands falling on her knees, beseeching her, close to hysteria. "He'll kill me if I do, I know he will. You don't know what he is like when the drink is in him.''

"No, I won't make you go back. Don't be afraid, but your mother will have to know. She will be worrying about you.''

"Aye, she will. I didn't think o' that. Poor Ma.''

"Somehow I'll have to let her know and then we must think what best to do. First you must take off those wet clothes. Then I'm going to bathe those bruises and put something soothing on your face and eye. After that you must go to bed. Tomorrow I'll speak to Mr Clifford.''

"What can the Master do?'' said Mary Ann, sinking back on her heels hopelessly.

"He'll think of something.''

The girl had turned away her head. Nervous fingers plucked at her cotton skirt. "You've heard what they say about him – and about me?''

"Yes, I've heard.''

"My mother told me it was all a stupid made-up tale and I shouldn't take no notice, that Dan were my father and I were never to think on it, never . . .''

"And do you?''

"Aye, I do sometimes.'' She stared in front of her. "It's like a story – like something you read in a book, something you know can never come true, but 'tis nice to dream about.''

Della could see the child's starved imagination fixing on it like a fairy tale. She said gently, "We all like to dream and sometimes dreams come true in a way we don't expect, you know. Now come along with you upstairs.''

Mary Ann struggled to her feet and as Della went to the fire to fetch a kettle of warm water, there was another knock at the door. They froze turning to one another in alarm.

"Go into the kitchen, Mary Ann, and stay there until I see who it is.''

She waited until the girl had gone before she opened the door a crack and peered out into the darkness. A small boy not more than six or seven stood on the step outside.

"Me Ma sez I was to ask if our Mary Ann were here and if she were could she stay 'cos it'll be safer and later on she could go to our Auntie who lives t'other side of Castlebridge,'' he said in

151

one long breath as if learnt by heart but Della got the gist of it.

"You tell your mother Mary Ann *is* here and quite safe for the time being. Has your father come home?"

"Nay, an' he won't, not till he has a skinful, that's what Jem sez," he went on still in one long stream. "It were awful, Miss, Mary Ann went for our Da with cookin' knife and Dolly – that's me sister – an' me, we thought he would kill her," his eyes were shining with a mixture of excitement and fear.

"Yes, well, it will be all right now. You go back home and tell your mother I'll try to come and see her tomorrow."

She gave him a gentle nudge in the right direction, then went in, closing the door and bolting it. If Dan Carter came storming round the schoolhouse she wanted to be prepared.

"Was that our Jimmy?" asked Mary Ann, coming in from the kitchen.

"I think it probably was. He'll take a message to your mother. Now let's go upstairs and do something about those bruises."

She dealt as best she could with the girl's injuries. Here and there the heavy buckle had torn the skin badly. She bathed the sore places and put on a healing ointment. She lent Mary Ann one of her own nightgowns and, there being no second bedroom in the schoolhouse, she took some blankets to make up the couch downstairs for herself.

"I can't take your bed," protested Mary Ann. "'Twouldn't be right, 'twouldn't be proper."

"Now you get under those blankets," she said firmly. "You're going to feel those bruises presently. I'll bring you up a cup of hot milk to help you sleep."

"Can Scamp come up here?" whispered the girl tentatively when Della came up with the milk. "It would be company like."

She had probably never slept alone in her life, thought Della, and found the prospect terrifying.

"I'll bring him," she said. "He can stay up here but not on the bed please."

Later she settled herself on the sofa in front of the dying fire, not a little apprehensive at what she had taken on, but borne up by strong indignation and a firm determination to talk to Tom Clifford about it as soon as she could on the next day.

Stiff and uncomfortable, she woke very early and heard the clang of the great bell summoning the millhands to work while she made some tea. She went up to Mary Ann and found her still asleep, the puppy snuggled down beside her. Her face was very swollen, the bruises beginning to darken. She stirred restlessly and Della putting a hand on her forehead, felt it hot and feverish. She made up her mind there and then. Better to catch Tom as soon as he reached the mill. She had watched him ride by so often she knew his times almost better than he did himself. She was writing a note for Abbie to say where she had gone when Lil arrived and began to bustle about the kitchen. Presently she came in and knelt down by the hearth with a great clatter of dustpan and broom.

"What's that Mary Ann doin' sittin' up in your bed large as life?" she said with strong disapproval.

"Her father turned her out so she's staying here for the moment."

"Fine goings-on, I must say!" Lil pursed her lips. "And what do I do if that Dan Carter comes round here demandin' his girl back?"

"Shut the door in his face."

"Aye, I'll do that all right, don't you worry, but supposin' he kicks it down?"

"He won't," said Della and wished she felt more confident. Dan Carter seemed capable of any violence. "I'm going to see Mr Clifford at the mill. Give this note to Miss Withers, Lil, and tell Mary Ann that she is to stay in bed till I come back."

"Quite the fine lady, en't she?" Then Lil grinned. "Don't 'ee fret, Miss Della, her Da won't get past me. Never did like him, the great bully. I'll have a pan of boiling water at the ready."

"We're not being besieged," said Della with a smile.

"Not yet but you never know," muttered Lil darkly. "Best be prepared. He's a dirty fighter, my Da sez, even at t'mill."

In the fresh morning light the whole drama had somehow become faintly ridiculous and yet somehow she knew it was not. It had gone on far too long. If something weren't done soon it could end in tragedy and it was up to her to make sure that it didn't. She put on her cloak and walked briskly into Castle-bridge.

The day had started badly for Tom Clifford. A new and expensive machine which had recently been installed for the purpose of producing the fine textured cloth he had shown to Della all those weeks ago had mysteriously broken down and a large quantity of valuable material was irretrievably ruined.

"What has caused it?" he demanded with justifiable anger. "Is it the machine or is it the men who are at fault?"

"Not being an expert I couldn't say, sir," said his chief clerk woodenly. "But I do know that the hands were very unhappy about it from the start."

"Because some of them are afraid of losing their jobs, is that it?" he said with exasperation. "I've already told them that I would do what I could to provide other work."

"They don't believe you, Mr Clifford. In Bradford a great many men have been thrown out on to the scrapheap and are starving. Dan Carter has been talking to them about it."

"That damned troublemaker abusing his position again! Where is he? Send him in to me and I'll have something to say."

"He's not in yet."

"My God!" exploded Tom. "Who would run a mill in these days! Does he think he can do as he pleases because up to now I have allowed the men a certain freedom to express their views? From now on it will have to stop. I'm not going to be dictated to by him or by anyone, Barker, and that's final. I'll tell him so when he comes in."

"It's as you wish, sir, of course, but you could regret it."

"Are you on his side too?" exclaimed Tom and brought his fist down angrily on the desk. "Once and for all am I master here or aren't I?"

"I'm sorry, sir, but I was only expressing an opinion."

"Then I would be obliged if you would keep it to yourself in future."

"I *am* your confidential clerk, sir," said Barker stiffly.

And because he was an old man who had served his father loyally, Tom let his anger ebb away.

"Yes, I know that. Now is there anything else?"

"There is a young lady who has been asking to see you."

"A young lady? Who for heaven's sake, at this hour?"

"Miss Lismore – from the school, sir."

"Della? What the devil does she want?"

"She didn't say, sir. Shall I tell her it is inconvenient?"

"No, no. It's all right. Let her come in, Barker."

The clerk went out and he got up from behind the desk and crossed restlessly to the window. He was fresh from a battle with Sylvia, still smarting from her last barbed remark. She had come down to the dining room dressed for riding while he was still finishing breakfast.

"Where are you off to so early?" he had asked mildly. "It's becoming quite a habit with you these days."

"Is that a crime?" she had snapped at him.

"Not that I know of, my dear," he went on, determined not to be provoked into a useless quarrel. He went with her to the front steps where the stable boy held Sheba for her. When she was settled in the saddle, he put a hand on the bridle.

"I do wish you wouldn't ride out alone, Sylvia. It worries me. Anything could happen out on the moors. You should take Rob with you or one of the lads."

"Why? Don't you trust me? Do you want to send a spy to make sure I don't go to meet a lover?"

"If that's meant to be a joke, it's in very poor taste," he replied dryly.

She slapped the neck of the mare so that she jerked forward and he stepped back quickly just in time to see the grin on the boy's face wiped off when he saw his master's glare.

That tiny incident, coupled with the trouble at the mill, had set him on edge but he was unprepared for his reaction when he turned to Della as she came in.

In her haste she had not stopped to put on her bonnet. The dark hair clung around her forehead and the keen wind had whipped colour into her face. In his eyes she looked as fresh as the morning and the sudden rush of sheer pleasure at the sight of her had the effect of making him even more angry with himself.

He said more harshly than he intended. "Well, Miss Lismore, and what can I do for you?"

She hesitated, intimidated by the touch of ice in his manner and she glanced at the clerk who had come in with her.

"May I speak to you alone?"

He frowned. "If you wish." He nodded to Barker who went out, shutting the door behind him. "I'd be grateful if you would be brief," he went on. "I'm extremely busy this morning."

"It's something that happened last night – about Mary Ann."

"What about Mary Ann?"

She told him as shortly and graphically as she could and he listened in silence. When she had faltered to an end, he turned his head to look at her.

"And what do you expect me to do?"

"I don't know – I thought – she can't go back, that's obvious. It's not the first time she has been brutally treated. I've seen it ever since I've been here."

"So you once told me." He came back to his desk and she faced him across it. "I still don't see how I can interfere. Dan Carter is her father."

"Is he?"

He looked at her sharply. "You have been listening to local gossip. In law he certainly is."

"Law!" she repeated scornfully. "What has the law got to do with it? Suppose next time he kills her, what would the law do then?"

"Hang him, perhaps."

"How *can* you be so indifferent? So callous? This man works for you, doesn't he?"

"He does and he is a good workman so far as the mill is concerned. I have no right to dismiss him because of his treatment of a disobedient child."

"Oh!" she exclaimed on a long breath. Indignation, disappointment in him, sweeping through her. "I thought you were different. I thought people mattered to you but I see I was wrong. You're like everyone else. You care only about yourself. Are you so afraid of scandal? Or is it your wife who objects?"

That touched him on the quick. He said stiffly, "Please don't criticize my wife."

"I'm not criticizing her but I know what I think and that's something you can't prevent."

"And what the devil do you mean by that?"

His sudden anger surprised her. She had spoken thoughtlessly, remembering Harrogate and what she had seen there. Now she knew she could not explain.

"What should I mean?"

"That's what I want to know." He came round the desk to her taking her by the shoulders, his grip hard. "What is it you are trying to tell me?"

She shook herself free. "Nothing. And if you won't help me with Mary Ann, then I must do something myself."

"And what can you do?"

"I don't know yet but I'm not willing to stand aside and let a child be brutally victimized."

She started for the door and he stopped her. "Don't do anything rash. Dan Carter can be dangerous."

156

"Isn't that what I've been telling you? Don't be afraid, Mr Clifford, you won't be blamed. I assure you that I can look after myself."

She went out quickly and he went after her only to collide with Barker coming back along the passage.

"Dan Carter is here to see you, sir."

Tom hesitated and then went back into his office. "So I see. Let him come in."

The man stood just inside the door as Barker closed it behind him. He looked terrible, his face puffy and swollen, dark with a stubble of beard, one eye raw and half closed.

For an instant they stared at one another, then Tom said crisply, "You're very late. Work at this mill starts at seven o'clock, and not at ten."

"I know that," he muttered sullenly.

"What were you doing last night, drinking or fighting?"

"None of your business," said Dan truculently.

The studied insolence caught Tom on the raw but he controlled his anger.

"Some time ago I placed you in a position of responsibility and you have abused it abominably. What the devil do you mean by inciting the men to wreck a valuble machine?"

"That's a bluddy lie," he blurted out. He crossed to the table glaring at Tom across it. "All I did was to tell the men what they could expect from you and others like you. When it suits your pocket, out they can go and die in the filth of the gutter, their wives and children an' all."

"I've not sacked a man yet without good reason but I will and I swear I'll start with you, Dan Carter, if there is any more trouble and if you don't keep your mouth shut in future. I'll have no more secret meetings, no more of this Chartist rubbish spoken of inside this building, do you understand?"

"A man has a right to be heard."

"Not in my mill he doesn't, not any longer."

Dan leaned across the desk, his face ugly. "You think you can do as you please with men's lives, you and your father before you, but he learned his lesson and so will you, Tom Clifford, same as others are doing all over Yorkshire."

"Are you threatening me?" said Tom dangerously.

"Take it how you like, Master. If I go, then t'others will go with me. Then what'll you do for her ladyship's silks and satins," he went on mincingly, "for your fancy school up the

157

road there and the little piece you've brought in, showing off her airs and graces, teaching our children to turn against us, entertaining her gentlemen friends? You en't the only one making his way up there, you know, not by a long chalk."

But this time he had gone too far. The anger boiled up. For a long time Tom had put up with Dan Carter because of an uneasy feeling that in some way he owed him something on account of his father, but not any longer. He would have liked to have smashed his fist into the hateful swollen face but he would not brawl, not here on his own ground. With a tremendous effort he kept his voice cool and steady.

"That's enough. You can go now, Carter."

"Go?" he stammered, brought up short. "Go?"

"That's what I said. I'm sacking you. You can leave now and don't come back. If you show your face inside this mill just once again, you'll be turned out. Understand?"

"You can't do that."

"Oh yes I can. The law is on my side. I can dismiss you without a penny for what you have done. I could have you brought up before the court, but you've a wife and children, God help them, so my clerk will give you a week's money. Now get out."

"Damn you! 'Tisn't fair, 'tisn't just."

"Don't waste your breath cursing me. Go before I call someone and have you thrown out."

For a moment Dan Carter still faced him, then he threw up his head truculently, swung round and strode to the door. He had flung it open before he turned back.

"And what about my girl?"

"What girl?"

"You damn well know who I mean. My Mary Ann."

"Is she yours? It's the first I've heard of it. You've been very fond of boasting that she should be my responsibility so I'm taking her off your hands. I'll look after Mary Ann."

"You – you'll what?"

"You heard me. You'll never again have the pleasure of beating her insensible, not if I can help it."

Dan's face turned a dull red and seemed to swell with baffled rage. Tom had a feeling that if there had been a knife handy he would have hurled it at him. As it was, with the wind taken out of his bluster, there was nothing more he could say. He went out, slamming the door after him.

For the first time that morning Tom drew a breath of relief. For far too long Dan Carter had been a thorn in his side. Now he had got rid of him and be damned to the consequences. He still had to settle the question of the girl. He regretted his harshness to Della. She had caught him at the wrong moment when some perverse contrary spirit had taken possession of him. She had every reason to despise him for it. As soon as the day's work was done with he would put into practice a plan that had already suggested itself to him as a possible solution. Then perhaps she might think differently of him.

The first that Della heard of it was the following afternoon. She had spent a wretched day half afraid that Dan Carter would turn up noisily demanding his daughter's return, hating Tom because in some obscure way he had made her feel foolish in running to him for help as she had done, and despite her proud boast, very uncertain in her mind as to what steps she could take. After all Tom was right. The law was most definitely *not* on her side. Fathers could beat their children to within an inch of their lives if they wished and frequently did so. There was no law against it and never had been. She was saved in some measure because during the whole of that day the girl had suffered a severe reaction. She was sick and feverish as well as in great pain and could be safely kept in bed.

She had heard in a roundabout way, through the children, of Dan Carter's dismissal. It had spread through the village like wildfire. For a long time he had dominated the community, big, powerful, hectoring, a man who could fight and hold his liquor, a man who had spoken his views boldly and yet kept his job, a man who liked to boast to his cronies that the Master for all his authority still couldn't do without him at his back. And now like the rest of them he was down on his luck, thrown out, left to rot for all his fine talk. There were some who regretted it, those who had liked to hide behind the big bully mouthing the abuse they had not the courage to express themselves, but there were also a great number who were secretly pleased. As for Dan himself, he was possessed with a black rage, cursing his hapless wife, cuffing his children into terrified silence and brooding over his revenge.

It was after school and Della was sitting down to a welcome cup of tea when the carriage stopped outside the schoolhouse. Abbie, who was just leaving, peered out of the window.

"Goodness," she exclaimed, "it's Miss Lavinia and she is coming here."

She ran to open the door as the old lady stepped down in a rustle of grey silk and lavender paisley shawl and sailed up the path. She nodded an acknowledgement of Abbie's greeting.

"How are you, my dear, in good health I hope? Give my regards to your mother. It's Miss Lismore I wish to have a word with."

"Good afternoon, Miss Lavinia," Della had come to meet her. "This is a very unexpected pleasure."

"Well, I hope it is," said the old lady, marching in and looking around her, while Della exchanged a look with Abbie who discreetly slipped out and closed the door.

"Won't you sit down? May I offer you a cup of tea?"

"Thank you. Very little milk and no sugar." She settled herself comfortably in the best chair by the fire. "You've done wonders with this place, I must say, made it look a little less like a prison." She accepted the cup of tea, took a sip or two and then put it on the table at her side.

"I presume you know why I am here."

"No, I'm afraid I don't."

"Tom Clifford hasn't told you?"

"No."

"This girl – this Mary Ann – she is still with you?"

"Yes, she is upstairs. She's not been at all well and though she is better today, I have made her keep to the bedroom."

"Very sensible."

"Shall I call her?"

"No, not for the moment. I believe you went to Tom yesterday morning asking for his help in protecting the girl from that unpleasant brute, Dan Carter."

"Yes, I did," said Della ruefully, "and I failed completely."

"On the contrary, my dear, you succeeded, rather too well, I fear," remarked the old lady dryly.

"I don't understand."

"Don't you? Dan Carter has been dismissed from the mill and what may come out of that is anybody's guess. I rather think Tom has raised the devil and will have to face some unpleasant consequences. However, I don't think anyone can make a scandal about Bret Stratton's respectable Great Aunt taking pity on a village girl and bringing her up to decent service as a lady's maid."

"You mean that Mary Ann is to go to Farley Grange?"

"Exactly. Tom came to me yesterday evening, since it seems his wife is unwilling to help him in the matter. Sylvia shows a little common sense for once."

"But doesn't Martha mind?"

"Why should she? I'm growing old. I can't run about as I did. I can do with a pair of stout young legs to fetch and carry for me. Is she neat and clean? Can she read and write?"

"Oh yes, very well, and she's very eager to learn. Dear Miss Lavinia, it is really very good of you."

"Don't thank me, thank Tom Clifford. It was his idea. And now perhaps you had better fetch her down."

And so it was arranged. Mary Ann, still bruised and in pain, but her hair washed and clean and wearing an old blouse Della had given her to replace the torn one, curtseyed shyly to Miss Lavinia.

"Well, child," said the old lady brusquely looking her up and down, "Mr Clifford tells me that you don't care for the idea of working in his mill. Is that true?"

"Aye, ma'am, it was that what made my father so angry, but I couldn't help it, really I couldn't," she said faintly, not a little scared of this formidable figure she had only glimpsed from a safe distance.

"A young woman who knows what she wants and can speak up for herself, I see," remarked Miss Lavinia a little tartly. "How would you like to come and work for me?"

"For you, ma'am?" The girl gasped and looked at Della who smiled back encouragingly.

"That's right. I'll expect you to work hard. I can be quite a tyrant as you'll soon find out. You'll be run off your feet, I shouldn't wonder and how will you like that?"

"Oh very much, ma'am. I don't mind hard work. I've always helped my Ma with the little ones."

"Good. Then that's settled. Come along now. You can make a start by giving me your arm. We'd better not keep the carriage waiting too long."

The only objection Miss Lavinia made was about the puppy.

"I really can't be doing with a young dog," she said firmly. "Martha's monsters would eat him alive."

"I'll take care of him for you," said Della quickly seeing the tears spring to Mary Ann's eyes. "He can come with me when I visit the Grange."

161

She watched the carriage drive away, holding Scamp in her arms and immensely cheered because after all it was Tom who had solved the problem. It gave her a warm feeling to know that she had not misjudged him and she made up her mind to thank him at the very first opportunity.

11

Lil came tearing in next morning, bursting with the latest news.

"You'll never believe, Miss, but they're out on strike, all the lot of 'em, 'cept the girls on the looms. They've got more sense."

Della stared at her. "Why, Lil, why? What has happened?"

"The master has sent Dan Carter off with a flea in his ear," she went on gleefully, "and they've all walked out with him and they're not goin' back in t'mill again, not till he's taken on again."

"I don't think Mr Clifford will go back on his word," said Della doubtfully.

"That's what me Da sez. 'Tis a matter of pride, see. Me Da sez he's never known the like, not since five years gone when old Mr Clifford was shot dead."

"They'll never go so far as that!"

"Me Da sez there's no tellin' what they'll do, not with the riotin' and burnin' all over t' country," went on Lil, with a kind of gloomy relish.

Rumour had exaggerated. Only about a third of the workers had walked out with Dan, but it could be serious for the mill. Tim had been right after all, thought Della, and it had only needed a spark to set the fire alight. Maybe it was she who had inadvertently provided that very spark.

It was a difficult day. The infection had spread to the school. Some of the children had not come in at all and those who had were exasperatingly slow and only stared back at her dumbly when she rebuked them. She was thankful when the afternoon was over and the last of them had gone racing out of the yard. It was then that she made up her mind to go and see for herself what was happening. She did not know what she could do or even if she would be able to see Tom, but she felt somehow responsible and was too restless to stay quietly at home and do nothing.

She had never before found herself among a hostile crowd

and it was an unnerving experience. The millgates were closed and more than a hundred men surged up and down waiting for the factory bell to sound, ready to hurl stones and abuse as the hands still at work came filing out. All around her were sullen angry faces as she pushed her way through them until she could reach the iron railings and could see where the big drays that carried the rolls of woollen cloth to market were standing idle. She realized then how foolish it had been to think she could get to Tom and what could she say to him even if she did? She turned to go and found herself facing a little semi-circle of women silently watching her.

She saw the hatred in their faces. She was a foreigner, the alien from outside their limited lives, a victim, a scapegoat, on whom they could spend their frustration and anger. For an instant no one moved, then a big woman, obviously the leader, her shawl tightly wrapped around her, took a step forward and peered into her face.

"D'ye see who this is, 'tis her ladyship, the schoolmarm," she said jeeringly, "and what would she be doin' here, d'ye think?"

The others began to move in closer backing her up.

"Runnin' after the Master!"

"Can't keep her hands off him!"

"Nor his off her!"

The ribald laughter that greeted that sally made her shiver. She said, "Will you please let me pass?"

"Will you please let me pass?" mimicked the leader in a high mincing voice. "Did ye hear that?"

"Waitin' for him, are ye?"

"He's somethin' else to worry about than hoppin' into bed with his fancy piece!"

"Let's take a closer look at her, shall we?"

"Find out what she's made of."

"Sugar and spice maybe," shouted one of the men from the back and again came that bellow of coarse laughter.

The women began to close in on her. It was frightening and she backed away. For the first time she began to feel fear. Some of the men had drawn nearer, prepared to enjoy the spectacle of her baiting, and she knew it would be useless to appeal to them for help.

"Let me go," she said struggling to push them away from her. "What harm have I ever done to you?"

"Plenty. Ye're not wanted up here. Get back to where you

come from."

And that was like a signal. Someone coming up behind her grabbed at her hair so that the pins came loose and it fell around her neck.

"Dark as a gypsy," the big woman crowed.

"Black as the devil himself!"

"Let's take a look at the rest of her. Find out what he sees in her!"

There was something obscene about the glee with which they now set about her. They were all around her, one plucking at her lace collar, another snatching at the brooch at her throat. A hand tore violently at the tiny gold stud in her ear and involuntarily she cried out with the sudden pain. The men were laughing and cheering them on and she backed against the railings, clinging to them desperately, terrified that if she lost her footing they would be on her in a kind of frenzy, stripping the clothes off her, tearing at her like wild beasts.

The end came so swiftly it was almost unbelievable. Her head was swimming, her hand slipping helplessly down the iron railing when she heard the gate open, heard a powerful voice shout, "What the devil is going on?" and a sudden silence, a shuffling of feet as the women drew back and she was staring up at Tom on his big black horse thrusting his way towards her.

He did not waste time in asking what she was doing there nor did he risk dismounting. He simply bent down to her, whispered, "Take hold of me," and with a powerful heave had lifted her up in front of him and urged the horse forward. Despite their anger and frustration, the habit of authority was still strong. They parted to let him through. She was crushed against him, one arm round his neck as he set his horse to an easy canter and then they were free of them, had left even the stragglers behind and were out on the high road.

He said nothing until they reached the schoolhouse when he let her slip to the ground and followed himself.

"What on earth were you doing there on a day like this?" he demanded. "God knows what they might have done to you if I'd not been there."

"It was horrible," she put both hands up to her face still trembling. "I didn't know . . . I never dreamed . . ."

He looked down at her, white-faced, dishevelled, blood trickling from her ear, her blouse shamefully torn, bonnet and shawl lost.

"Thank God, it wasn't worse," he said more gently. "Are you hurt? Shall I fetch Dr Withers to you?"

"No, I'm all right. I . . . I wanted to see you, to thank you for what you have done for Mary Ann. I didn't realize . . ."

"That I'm not precisely popular at the moment," he went on dryly, "nor you either it would seem. It was a kind thought, since we didn't exactly part friends the last time we met, did we?"

"That's why I wanted to see you. I felt guilty."

"No need for that. Dan Carter has had this coming to him for some time."

She shivered. "Why do they hate me so much?"

"You must try to understand. They are blaming you because you're a stranger and you attacked one of their own in defending Mary Ann. They may not like Dan very much but he still belongs to them. I did warn you, didn't I?"

"Yes, you did," she said, a little forlornly.

"It will blow over and they will forget soon enough. Now go in and make sure you bolt the door. There may be trouble brewing but don't be afraid. It is nothing that we cannot overcome."

She thought of his father brutally struck down out on the moor and shuddered. She put a hand on his arm.

"They won't attack you, will they?"

He smiled grimly. "I'd like to see them try."

And quite suddenly she couldn't bear it. She was clinging to him.

"Take care, Tom, please, please take care."

His arms went around her, he was holding her close, his mouth against her hair murmuring words of reassurance. It was a minute before she could pull herself together and draw away in some confusion.

"I'm sorry – you must think me very stupid – I don't know what came over me."

"Are you sure you're all right? Would you like to come back to the Hall with me?"

"No, no. I'm not frightened, not for myself. What happened was just foolishness and in a way I asked for it by going down there."

He frowned. "It was outrageous. I shall make sure they pay for it."

"No, don't, please don't. You have enough to worry about."

He hesitated and then touched her face with a gentle finger. "You're what my father would have called 'a gradely lass.' Now go inside and take care of yourself. Remember what I've told you. Don't always feel you must fight other people's battles for them."

"I'll try not to," she murmured tremulously.

"Mind you do."

He waited until she was inside and the door closed before he remounted and rode home, a good deal more disturbed than he had revealed to Della. The infection of revolt had spread further than he had expected but he was determined not to give way to weakness. He had always shown more consideration for his workers than was usual among the millowners and it angered him that at a time like this so many of them had listened to Dan Carter and turned against him. The stupid mindless attack on Della sickened him and strengthened his decision. Tomorrow he would issue an ultimatum. Either the strikers returned to work by the following Monday or they would be summarily dismissed and if they suffered for it, then so much the worse for them. It would be by their own choice.

At the house the boy took his horse and he went through the hall and up the stairs with the intention of washing and changing before they sat down to eat. Sylvia was fond of complaining that he brought the greasy smell of the fleeces back with him from the mill. As he passed the drawing room on the first floor he heard the sound of voices and he opened the door. Sylvia was lying back on the sofa with Oliver lounging close beside her and the odd thought struck him how alike these two were, both of them slim, long-limbed and elegant, like overbred aristocratic greyhounds. It had the uncomfortable effect of making him feel awkward and clumsy. He shook it off angrily and walked into the room.

Oliver straightened up and said lazily, "So you're back, my dear fellow, still thankfully all in one piece. I heard you were having a spot of trouble and I thought I'd drop in and find out exactly what was going on."

"Very kind of you," said Tom dryly, "there was no need. It's nothing I can't deal with."

"You'll never believe it but Tom has at last plucked up courage to rid himself of that trouble-maker, Dan Carter," said Sylvia carelessly, "and now of course half the men have walked out of the mill with him."

"Isn't that dangerous?"

"It could be if they remain out and I can't fulfil my orders, but that's my worry." Tom had come to stand on the hearthrug looking down at them. "Are you staying to sup with us?"

"No, I'm afraid not." Oliver got to his feet. "I just called in on my way home to say goodbye. I'm off to London very soon."

"London?" Sylvia sat up. "You never told me."

"Didn't I?" he went on lightly. "Some business has turned up. Such a bore but money's tight as usual and Father is selling some land. You know how things are with him. He prefers me to deal with these things."

"How long will you be away?"

He shrugged his shoulders. "A month or two perhaps. I'll be back by Christmas. We'll have a party, shall we? It's time Larksghyll put on a show. Will you loan me Sylvia, Tom, to do the honours for me?"

"That will be for her to decide," he said stiffly.

"That's settled then. Hope all goes well at the factory, old man. Don't go and get yourself knocked off. Shoot first and think afterwards is my motto when dealing with wretches of that kind."

"I hardly think that will be necessary. Some of these men and their families go back to my grandfather's time."

"Oh Tom, for heaven's sake," said Sylvia impatiently. "Why worry about them? What have they ever done for you? Think of yourself for once, think of me and your son."

"I'm hardly likely to forget, am I?"

Oliver glanced from one to the other with his ironic smile before he moved to the door. "Well, I must be off."

"I'll see you out," said Sylvia hurriedly and went with him.

The door closed behind them and Tom remained staring into the fire. There had been nothing he could put a finger on and yet he sensed a current of feeling between those two, an intimacy from which he was excluded.

"Tell me," he said when Sylvia came back, "does Oliver make a habit of calling on you when I'm out of the house?"

"Good heavens, what a peculiar question! He has come once or twice. Is there any reason why he shouldn't? I thought he was a friend of yours."

"Of mine, yes. I never thought you cared very much for him." He suddenly swung round on her. "All those early

168

morning rides of yours, do you go to meet him?"

"Why all these questions suddenly? What have I done wrong? Don't you trust me?"

"I thought I did. Now I don't know . . ."

"And what does that mean?"

"I'm not sure."

He was torn between a desire to shake the truth out of her and an uneasy feeling that he didn't want to know because if he did, if Oliver *was* her lover, then he would be faced with chaos. He could not accept it tamely, he would be forced into action.

She was staring at him curiously. "What's the matter, Tom? Has something more happened at the mill today?"

"No, nothing further," he muttered and moved towards the door. "I must go and get changed."

"Peter was asking for you. Will you say goodnight to him before we have supper?"

"Yes, yes, of course." He went out quickly shutting the door.

She looked after him frowning. Did he suspect? She had always felt so sure of being able to sway Tom to her side in any argument, but he had been different lately, more withdrawn into himself, not so easily teased and cajoled. Then she forgot Tom in her rage against Oliver. How dare he announce so cavalierly that he was going away? The hidden meetings out on the moors, the secret hours she had spent with him at Larksghyll were like a drug of which the need grew ever more urgent. How easy it was for him and how damnable for her. In a riot of turbulent emotion, she never gave a single thought to the fury outside that was building up against her husband.

Tom held firmly to his decision despite the plain fact that work at the mill would be severely held up if the men did not return. It would be well nigh impossible to fulfil his many overseas orders, which could be damaging at a time when competition was particularly fierce.

The ultimatum was issued and the rest of the week crept slowly by. On the following Monday some dozen or so of the strikers trickled back urged by wives who had a home to keep and children to feed. A wage of fifteen shillings a week left little margin for savings. A hard core obstinately still stayed away and Barker, who had an ear to the ground, reported to his Master that meetings were being held and certain fiery spirits who had aroused the rabble in other places were said to have joined them. Tom took what precautions he could, put a guard on the mill each night and made a point of himself going around the workrooms with a calm and confident manner as if nothing had happened. They can't hold out, he told himself. When hunger begins to bite, they will realize the folly of losing everything for the sake of one man who has never had any thought except for himself. He miscalculated, as a great many people had done even in London where riots in the far north were more often than not cause for laughter rather than questions being asked in Parliament. The days passed quietly. Men walked the streets or gathered in uneasy groups at corners. Della took to handing out bread and cheese to some of the children whose dinner boxes were distressingly empty. So when the attack did come, it was totally unexpected and it went very much further than the rebels had ever intended.

It was October, the days were drawing in and they had been plagued by rainstorms and bitter winds. Della, walking up on the moors and facing a personal crisis of her own, found a certain satisfaction in breasting the gale that swept across Wharfedale and whipped the river along by Bolton Abbey into a foam-flecked frenzy.

"We shall have snow soon," predicted Lil gloomily one morning. "Can't you smell it, Miss, it comes on the wind."

It was more than a fortnight since she had seen Tom and one night when she was sitting close beside the fire, listening to the wind that went storming and howling across the high limestone ridges beyond Castlebridge, she knew that the time had come when she must leave. Bret had called earlier that evening. He was driving the dogcart and urged her to go back with him to the Grange.

"Do come. I'm wearied to death with only my sister and Aunt Lavinia for company." He was in a strange restless mood, wandering around the room, picking up a book or an ornament and then putting it down again. "Don't you ever feel stifled up here as if you can't breathe? Don't you long to go back to London, to people around you and life."

"I find plenty of life going on up here," said Della, smiling at his boyish intensity, "and a big city can be the loneliest place on earth. I have experienced it."

"Have you?" He was staring at her. "I was with Oliver not so long ago. He comes and goes as he wishes, lucky devil. I'd have given anything to be going off with him."

"Why didn't you?"

"Oliver's a high flyer, as Martha says, and money is not too flush with us at the moment, as she keeps telling me."

"Have you been gambling again?"

He swung round on her. "What do you mean by that?"

"Nothing." She was taken aback. "It was only something Martha said once."

"Anyone listening to my sister would think I'd staked Farley Grange on the luck of the cards and then lost it." He walked away from her and went on in a stifled voice. "I did do that once."

"Oh Bret, you must be joking." she said incredulously. "Whatever happened?"

"I won it back again."

"How, for goodness sake?"

"Oh I don't know. The luck changed. It does, you know. That's what grips you. You're certain that it's waiting for you just around the corner and you must go after it!" His eyes were shining, his body tensed, then he gave her a quick, half-ashamed glance. "You probably think me crazy like Martha does sometimes. Do come back with me, Della. I promise I'll drive you back in the morning in time for school."

"No, Bret, no."

She would not go with him for all his urging, but went out to see him drive away and then came back to the house, forgetting him almost immediately as her thoughts flew back to Tom and the decision that must soon be made.

She had never wanted to fall in love with him, had never realized how it can take hold of you, not with a lightning strike but with a slow devastating fire. What magic did he possess that she should be filled with this aching hunger just to see him, feel the touch of his hand, hear his voice with its rough tenderness? That moment when he had held her in his arms after the brutal handling by the women, she had known by some subtle affinity between them that he too was gripped by the same magic. Della had not grown up protected from the world. In that ramshackle society she had learned a great deal about men and women too. She had known that it lay within her power to draw him to her and she had pulled back, frightened at what she could do. Some inner knowledge told her it would not work with Tom. He was not like Oliver. It had been easy to judge him – off with the old and on with the new –

but that was not Tom. He would not easily forget or put aside a woman he had once loved. So the sooner she went away the better. She had saved a little money. She would return to London, go and see Madame Ginette, and if there was no opening there, then there would be other work. Lucinda had said once that Mr Kean, unlike other theatre managers, had conceived the revolutionary notion to dress his plays in the period in which they were set and there was scope for someone who could study and design historical costumes and teach others to make them. Perhaps there would be a chance for her there.

Before she went to bed that night she looked from the window. The wind seemed to have gathered in strength. It whined around the rooftops like some shrieking banshee from the old Irish tales she still dimly remembered her mother reciting to her, tales of the High Kings of Tara and Deirdre, the beautiful, the tragic –

> Beauty is like a flower
> Which wrinkles will devour
> Brightness falls from the air,
> Queens have died young and fair –

She shivered violently. Something heavy, a fence post or an iron lid went bouncing and crashing down the road and she drew the curtains quickly to shut it out.

Sleep came surprisingly soon. She had often dreamed of her father, as happens when someone beloved is lost or dead – happy dreams when he would be there so alive, so real that she could smell the faint odour of expensive cigars that had always clung to him – dreams from which it had been misery to wake and know the sharpness of loss all over again. But this night it was different.

She was on a ship with him, a ship that was being buffeted by great waves. She was staring across a grey heaving sea swept by storms of wind and rain. Then in the way of dreams the scene abruptly changed. It was hot and dark, so stifling that she could scarcely breathe. One part of her knew quite well that it was the convict ship. There was a confusion of people, men, women and children too – there were shouts, screams and a wild agonized weeping. She was clinging to her father's arm, surrounded by a kind of miasma of terror. They were both of them fighting to free themselves from it and then frighteningly her father was

172

torn away from her and she seemed to run down endless dark passages, calling and calling his name as it grew hotter and hotter. There was smoke suddenly, thick black smoke and her mouth was so dry she could not shout any longer. She was suffocating, struggling to emerge from a smothering blanketing darkness.

It was Scamp who roused her. Ever since Mary Ann had gone he had slept in his box close beside her bed and he was running backwards and forwards, barking frantically and pawing excitedly at the bed coverings.

Suddenly she broke out of the nightmare. She was sitting bolt upright, sweating and gasping. The dreams had become reality. The room was filled with choking smoke. She coughed and found it almost impossible to breathe. She scrambled out of bed and ran to the door. As she opened it, she was met by a sheet of flame pouring up the staircase and in panic she slammed it shut again. She snatched up the terrified little dog and raced to the window. Outside she could glimpse figures moving about with torches. She banged on the glass but no one looked up to see her. She tugged at the iron clasp but it had rusted in and she could not budge it. It had never been opened since she had been in the house. More smoke billowed into the room. There was a crash as part of the staircase collapsed and flames were licking around the badly fitting door. She was suffocating and her head began to swim. She fought with the bolt again but the small-paned lattice window remained obstinately closed. Frantically she beat her hands against it as the heat grew. One of the panes broke gashing her hand. Someone outside shouted but she felt her strength go as pain and terror engulfed her. Nothing could save her now – nothing – nothing – her hand slid helplessly down the wall, leaving a trail of blood as she fell.

It was Rob Hunt who saw the fire and gave the alarm. One of the horses was sick and he had been up with it until nearly four o'clock in the morning by which time the fire had taken a good hold on the school and the house beside it. When he came out of the stable and saw the flames shooting up into the sky his first thought was of the mill and he ran to the house, hammering on the door and bringing Mrs Fenton down in her dressing gown demanding to know what the trouble was. By the time Tom was roused, had dressed hurriedly, seized the horse waiting for him

173

and arrived outside the school, a number of people were already gathered, milling about uselessly or staring in helpless fascination at the fire. Perhaps if it had not been for the fierce gale it would not have spread so far so quickly. Afterwards the men were to swear to God that all they intended was to make a protest to the Master about the injustice of their treatment. But that did not explain how books and anything else inflammable had been piled together and soaked in kerosene nor why the kitchen window had been ruthlessly smashed and a thick bundle of burning straw hurled in to land at the foot of the staircase.

Tom's first anxiety was for Della. "Where is Miss Lismore?" he demanded, thrusting through them half-blinded by the smoke and the flaring torches.

"She en't there, Master," said a glib voice at his elbow. "Saw her ride off with t'squire. 'Bout six it were. She'll be away with him up at Farley Grange."

"Are you sure of that, man?"

"Aye, sir, sure as I'm standin' here."

"Thank God for that."

He galvanized the men into action, organizing a fire-fighting team. Equipment was pitifully inadequate, but he formed a chain of hands carrying buckets of water from the well at the back and had others handling the giant iron rakes to pull down some of the already smouldering roof and at least prevent it from spreading further. So it was not until later that Lil, who was standing with some of the other women, gave a piercing shriek, pointing to the window and he saw the desperate white face eerily lit by the flickering light.

"My God, she's up there! She's trapped!"

He made a dash for the door and was driven back by the fierceness of the raging fire. There was no possibility of reaching her that way.

"A ladder!" he shouted. "Bring me a ladder – quickly!"

Rob and another man raced away but even then it took time and he cursed himself for believing the lying assurance that she had left the house. He grabbed hold of one of the iron rakes, yelled, "Stand back!" and swung it with all his strength at the window smashing in the panes and frail wooden surround. Then the ladder was there, someone handed him a wet rag. He wrapped it around his mouth and began to climb up it.

He was a big man and the opening was small but he

scrambled through it somehow, recklessly tearing clothes and hands on the jagged glass. The flames had reached the bed by now and were licking up the curtains. The smoke was so thick that for a moment he could see nothing. Then the dog gave a yelp as he tripped over it and he saw that she had fallen to the floor in a welter of broken glass. He picked her up in his arms and staggered to the window. Rob had come up after him, a muscular wiry man. He took the girl from his master, holding her with one arm across his shoulder.

"The dog!" she was muttering, "I can't leave the dog!"

Tom watched Rob move cautiously down rung by rung, willing arms stretching up to receive him and his burden, then he turned back into the room. The puppy, terrified out of its wits, had run to take refuge under the bed. A blazing curtain pole fell on Tom as he snatched at its scruff. He thrust it aside but not before it had scorched across his hands and down the side of his face. Then he was back at the window. He squeezed himself through the narrow opening, one hand clutching the squealing dog, and climbed down the ladder just in time, as part of the roof caved in with a deafening roar and a shower of sparks and billowing smoke.

Someone had wrapped Della in a blanket and Dr Withers was on his knees beside her. Tom pushed the little dog into Lil's hands and came to her other side.

"How is she?"

"Shocked and nearly suffocated by the smoke. There are some superficial cuts from the broken glass," said the doctor, "but I don't think she is badly hurt. It looks as if you got her out just in time."

Tom couldn't speak. For a paralysing moment he had believed her dead and was still shaken by it.

Della's eyes flickered open. She seemed to emerge from a horrifying nightmare daze of fire and smoke and the terror still remained.

"Tom!" she muttered. "Tom!" and would have started up.

He pushed her gently back. "You're quite safe now and the little dog."

She saw the blackened face and the blood where the glass had torn his hands.

"Are you . . . hurt?"

"Never mind about that. It's all over now. I'll be taking you up to the Hall."

"Better let me take a look at you," said the doctor briskly.

"Those are nasty burns."

"Presently. I'll tell Rob to fetch the carriage and take both of you to the house. I'll follow as soon as I've done all I can here."

"How did it start? Accident or design?"

"I don't know yet," he said grimly, "but, by God, I mean to find out."

When he got back to the Hall at last, it was to find the whole house up and agog with excitement down to the smallest scullery maid and bootboy. Mrs Fenton came to tell him that Della had been put to bed in one of the spare rooms and the doctor was now with her.

"And my wife?" he asked.

"Madam is in her room, sir. She told me to see to this young person."

"Thank you, Mrs Fenton."

He went bounding up the stairs and met Dr Withers on the landing as he came out of the room.

"She's a strong healthy lass," he said calmly. "She'll suffer a reaction of course, but a few days in bed and she'll be as well as ever. I've given her a sedative to help her sleep so I shouldn't disturb her. Now, Tom, what about you? I don't like the look of those hands of yours."

"I had better see my wife first."

He went past him but did not go immediately to Sylvia. Instead he opened the door of the room to which Della had been taken. A lamp turned low gave a warm glow. He crossed to the bed. She was already drowsy and opened heavy eyes when he looked down at her.

"You saved me," she murmured. "The sea, that terrible sea – and the flames! I would have drowned."

"You're dreaming," he said gently and touched her hair. "All is well now. Try to sleep."

He went out closing the door quietly. In her bedroom Sylvia was standing by the window in her dressing gown and she swung round as he came in.

"Tom!" Her hands flew to her mouth. "I thought – they told me – "

"That I was burned to a cinder, I suppose. Nothing of the kind, my dear. You can't get rid of me as easily as all that."

"Don't! Don't joke about it. It's too horrible."

"I'm sorry. It's not been so easy. Thank God, no one has been seriously hurt."

"Oh Tom!" she would have gone to him but he motioned her back.

"Better not touch me. I'm filthy."

The handkerchief he had wrapped around his hands was soaked in blood. One side of his face was raw and blackened and she shrank away from it.

"You're hurt."

"Nothing much. We had to smash the glass of the window to get in."

"You could have been killed. You risked your life just for that girl."

"I would have done it for anyone."

"You didn't think of me."

"There wasn't time to think of anything but the urgent need to get her out. Don't distress yourself. It's over and all we've lost is the school."

"I can't say I'm sorry about that."

"You never approved of it, did you?" he said dryly. "Well, I don't see myself rebuilding, not at the present time at any rate. You know I brought Della here. She must stay until this whole business is cleared up."

"It's your house, Tom."

"Isn't it yours too?"

"I'm sorry – I've been so – so upset, I don't know what I'm saying."

He felt the constraint between them and did not know how to break it down.

"I'll tell Mrs Fenton to bring you a hot drink. We're all going to need something. Then I'd better let Alec Withers get on with the good work. Can't stand here dripping blood on your carpet."

"Take care of yourself, Tom."

She stretched out a hand and he leaned forward and kissed it without touching her.

"Don't worry about me. I'll be all right."

When he had gone she sank down on the bed, burying her face in her hands. For one dreadful moment when a frightened stable boy had come racing from the school gasping out that the Master had gone plunging recklessly into the fire, the appalling thought had flashed through her mind. If anything happened to him, then her problem would be solved, she would be free, free to go to Oliver, free to live her own life far away from this hateful place, and the next moment she had been filled with sick revulsion at her own ruthlessness.

12

Della felt the effects of the fire far more severely than she had expected. She woke later in the day with a dry mouth, an aching feverish head and a most unpleasant choking sensation which Dr Withers said was due to the poisonous fumes she had swallowed.

"You stay where you are, my lass," he went on in his forthright way, when he called that afternoon. "Shock can take all the stuffing out of you and there are some very nasty cuts and burns. They're not going to vanish overnight, you know."

"But I can't stay in this house, it's not right. It's imposing on Mrs Clifford," and *I know very well she doesn't like me* was on the tip of her tongue, but remained unsaid.

"As to that, my dear, Tom Clifford is master of the house not his wife," remarked the doctor dryly, "and in any case where would you go just now? The school and most of your possessions, I'm sorry to say, have gone up in smoke."

She had not thought of that and it made her feel lost and very vulnerable but she still persisted a little feverishly. "If the school is lost, then I shall no longer be needed here. It will be time for me to go."

"That will be for Tom Clifford to decide. He is your employer, after all. For the present you remain where you are, young lady, and that's an order. I'm not letting a patient of mine out of my clutches till I say the word." He smiled, patted her hand and moved to the door. "Now I must take a look at my other patient."

"Is Mr Clifford badly hurt?"

"He'll survive if only I can prevent him charging down to Castlebridge and taking personal vengeance on those who committed this outrage."

"Wasn't it an accident?"

"That's something we have to find out, don't we, but I must say I doubt it, I doubt it very much."

She found the suggestion that the fire had been deliberately planned and that she could have died in it more than a little frightening and she lay very still after the doctor had gone, feeling too exhausted and drained to make any effort and only thankful that the decision had been taken out of her hands. It was a queer sensation to be lying in a strange bed without even a nightdress to call her own, like someone thrown up on a desert island. With a shudder she remembered the horror of the nightmare from which she had woken into the panic of the fire.

She stayed in her room for two whole days, forbidden any visitors and seeing only the doctor, Mrs Fenton, who looked in each morning and frowningly asked her if there was anything she needed, and Rose, the maid, who lit the fire, brought her food and hot water and also a dressing gown in fine soft blue wool with a wide satin sash.

"The mistress thought you might be needin' it, Miss" she said laying it carefully over a chair.

"It is very good of her."

"Lor' Miss, you don't want to worry your head about that. It don't mean nothin' to her. She has a cupboard full of 'em."

On the third day she was determined to get up immediately after she had drunk the tea and eaten the boiled egg and thin bread and butter sent up from the kitchen. Messages had come from Abbie and a basket of flowers out of the hothouses from Martha but that was the day she had two visitors.

The first was Lil, very neatly dressed in her Sunday mantle and bonnet and with her usual exuberance a little damped by awe as she looked around her. With her came Scamp pulling at his lead and jumping up at Della excitedly, despite the loss of half his coat scorched off by the fire.

"I've been puttin' goose grease on his back," said Lil. "Me Ma says you're not to worry, it'll grow again in no time."

She was followed by Rob and one of the boys, manhandling her large tin trunk – considerably scorched and blackened by the fire but still miraculously intact. Della exclaimed joyously when she saw it.

"I thought I had lost everything."

"There weren't much we could save," explained Lil regretfully, "but one of the men dragged the trunk out when it were still smoulderin' and my Da took charge of it."

"I'm so grateful."

How lucky that there had been no suitable cupboard or wardrobe and she had been obliged to keep most of her clothes laid between sheets of paper in the trunk. How hateful to have been obliged to beg cast-offs from Sylvia before she could even make an appearance downstairs.

"I've never been here before," said Lil, looking admiringly around the room with its fine bed and handsome furniture, the thick rugs on the polished floor and the heavy damask curtains. "Is that one of her ladyship's bedgowns?" she leaned forward fingering the soft blue wool wonderingly.

"So Rose tells me, but I've not seen her since I've been here, not once. Lil, what is happening in Castlebridge? Nobody has told me anything."

"There has been a fair old rumpus goin' on. All the men on strike have been questioned over and over. They're sayin' now as it were Dan Carter as started it but they can't find him nowhere. His wife swears he'd gone off to look for work at one of t'other mills before that night but there are others as says different. It was me who saw you up at the window, Miss Della, it gave me such a turn as I'll never forget and then when the Master went up that ladder . . . I thought my heart would stop," she paused still shaken by the thrill of it though the danger was past.

"I know what he did, Lil. If it hadn't been for him I wouldn't be here."

"Nor Scamp neither. Eh, it were a night an' no mistake. When he went back into the fire, we thought he was gone once and for all and someone gave a cheer when he came out with the pup." She got to her feet. "I mustn't stay long. That Mrs Fenton gave me such a funny look 'cos I came knockin' at front door. I thought she was goin' to send me packin' but the Master poked his head out and she didn't dare say nay to him. Shall I leave Scamp with you?"

And suddenly she felt as if there was nothing she wanted more than the company of a little dog, warm, alive and unquestioning, to take her mind off her feeling of desolation.

"Yes, do. I'm up now. I shall be able to look after him."

It was a wonderful relief to find so much still undamaged in her battered trunk. On the top was a big book, curling at the edges from the heat, but with the animal pictures still intact. She had meant to hand it over to Abbie for the little ones and had forgotten. The money she had put on one side, little enough, was still there in a blackened silver mesh purse but the small casket in which she had hidden the golden skull was not to be found. She searched frantically before she remembered she had put it in a drawer of the dressing table and that, with so much else, had gone, devoured by the hungry flames. So her only clue had vanished, not that it would ever have proved anything, yet she felt its loss acutely. For some reason it swept her back to the nightmare, the ship, the heaving grey sea and her father torn away from her. The sense of loss, the heat and the choking smoke seemed to swirl all about her once more and she sat back on her heels, her hands pressed against her smarting eyes.

A muffled growl from Scamp roused her. She looked up to see the small golden-haired boy standing in the doorway with the big brown dog as usual beside him.

"What are you doing?" he demanded, staring at her curiously. "Are you crying?"

"No, no, of course not. I was looking for something," she scrambled to her feet and picked up Scamp who was putting up a brave show of defending her against possible enemies.

"You needn't be afraid," said Peter loftily. "Rusty won't eat him."

"It might be the other way round," she said smiling.

"That's silly."

The boy came into the room and Rusty came with him. A little apprehensively she put the puppy down. The two dogs eyed each other for an instant, backs bristling, then Rusty pushed the baby with his nose, Scamp gave a sharp yelp and butted him back. Formalities over, Rusty sank down, putting up with the puppy's little squeaks and nips with a bored resignation.

Peter had come to stare at the trunk. "It's all black."

"Yes, Don't touch it, it will make you dirty."

"Was it in the fire?"

"Yes."

"Nanny says you would have been all burnt up if my Papa hadn't rescued you."

"That's right."

"Are you going to stay here now?"

"Not for long. You see there's no school any more."

He had picked up the book and was looking at the pictures. "Is it yours?"

"Would you like it? Can you read what it says?" He shook his head. "You should be able to, a big boy like you. Would you like me to teach you?"

"Now?"

She laughed. "Why not?"

She sat on the rug by the fire and held out her hand. The boy hesitated and then ran to nestle beside her following her finger as she spelled out the words.

She had put an arm around him pulling him close and they were laughing together at the antics of a ginger cat called Penny when Sylvia opened the door and was immediately seized with an unreasonable jealousy.

She said sharply, "Peter, what are you doing here? Go to Nanny at once."

"Don't want to," he replied sulkily.

"Did you hear what I said? Do as you're told."

"No. I want to stay with Della."

"Miss Lismore doesn't want you here."

"Yes, she does, don't you?"

The eyes that were turned to her were singularly like his father's.

"Yes, of course I do," she whispered. "But perhaps just now you should do as your Mamma says."

"All right, but I shall come back."

He looked from his mother to her and grinned, then gripped Rusty's collar and marched out defiantly.

"I'm afraid he is very self willed," said Sylvia. "Now you are feeling better, I came to see if there is anything else you need."

"Thank you but, as you see, my trunk had been rescued so I can at least dress myself now."

"Good. No doubt you will be leaving us very soon. My husband will arrange all that for you."

Scamp skidded across the floor chasing a fugitive flicker of the sun and Sylvia looked down at him.

"Is that the little mongrel Tom brought out of the fire?"

"Yes. It was wonderfully brave of him.

"It's just the kind of senseless thing he would do. It could have cost him his life," said Sylvia scathingly. "If you feel well enough, perhaps you would care to join us for the evening meal today."

The invitation came so grudgingly that she felt the wave of hostility like an icy wind blowing between then and had no clue to the secret anxiety that had begun to fret Sylvia's nerves beyond endurance.

"Thank you, no. I would prefer to stay here if it does not cause too much inconvenience."

"As you wish." She scanned Della from top to toe before she said slightingly, "That blue suits you. Keep it. I've no further use for it."

Deliberate or not, it made Della feel like a servant being condescendingly given her mistress's cast-off and she could willingly have stripped it off and thrown it back at her except that Sylvia had already gone, shutting the door behind her and in any case it was a stupid and useless gesture. It did, however, strengthen her decision to go away as soon as it could be arranged.

With this resolution in mind she got up early the next morning and was washed and dressed by eight o'clock.

"Is Mr Clifford still in the house?" she asked when Rose came to fetch her tray.

"He is taking his breakfast, Miss."

"Thank you."

She still felt a little unsteady and the high-necked blouse chafed the sore patches on her shoulders, but when the maid had gone, she went slowly down the stairs, holding on to the balustrade until she had reached the hall, and found her way to the dining room. It was rich and sombre, with massive dark furniture and red silk damask walls. Tom was seated at one end of the long table and rose to his feet when she came in.

"Della! Should you be out of bed? The doctor told me you should take things very quietly."

"I am perfectly recovered now. May I have a word with you?"

"Of course, come and sit down." He pulled out a chair for her. "Have you had breakfast?"

"Yes, thank you."

"Let me pour you some coffee."

He fetched a cup from the sideboard and filled it from the silver pot, putting cream and sugar beside her before he sat down again.

One side of his face was raw and angry from the scorch of the falling beam and his left hand was still bandaged. Almost without realizing it, their eyes were devouring one another, the bond that had grown between them deepened and strengthened by the knowledge that he had saved her from a terrible death.

She sipped the coffee before she whispered, "I have wanted so much to thank you . . ."

"There is no need . . ."

Involuntarily he stretched out a hand and clasped hers. It was unexpectedly warm and comforting.

Then she braced herself. She must not give way to her feelings for him. She gently withdrew her hand.

"I understand that the school has been totally destroyed."

"Yes, unfortunately, and at the present time I can't see my way to rebuilding."

"In that case you will no longer be needing a teacher."

"We needn't worry about that for the time being."

"But we must," she went on firmly. "I'm very aware that I have not come up to your expectations, but I have tried, and I think a few, just a few of the children, may have learned something."

"You mustn't belittle yourself. You have done very well."

She met his eyes and smiled. "That's kind but let's be honest with one another. I'm simply not the stuff of which teachers are made. I should never have come here."

"Don't say that. I'll tell you one thing and I mean it. To some of them, and Mary Ann is one, you've opened the door to a knowledge of gentleness, sensitivity and beauty and that's something that I'm pretty sure your predecessor, Miss Hutton, never did."

"Oh that's a lovely thing to say. I only wish it were true."

"It is true. I'm a blunt man, I can't make fine speeches, but that's the truth as I see it."

"I hope it is. It makes up for a lot, but now it is time for me to leave."

"No!" Everything in him rose up against it. He didn't want her to go. The thought that she might be lost to him for ever was so unbearable that he went on quickly. "No, you can't go, not yet, not for a few days at any rate. There is an enquiry into the causes of the fire – you may be needed."

"But I know nothing about it."

"You know about Dan Carter and Mary Ann – it would help me considerably if you were to stay – besides there is something else. I owe you compensation for what you must have lost, so much has been destroyed."

"Lil has brought my trunk. There are several articles of clothing in it."

"That's nothing. I can't allow you to go from here penniless and robbed of everything you possess."

"It's very kind of you. I could stay on for a while, I suppose. I could take some lodgings in the village."

"You'll do nothing of the kind," he interrupted vehemently. "You will stay here. The house is large enough, God knows."

"I don't think your wife would care for that."

"Sylvia will understand the necessity."

She had the queerest feeling that all they were actually saying to one another, the polite stilted phrases, meant nothing at all. Beneath them there was an urgency that was sweeping them along and they were helpless against it.

She said at last reluctantly, "For a few more days then."

He heaved a sigh of relief. "Thank you. I'm very grateful."

She went back to her room with mixed feelings. She wanted to stay, there was no doubt about that, but was it wise, was it sensible? Then suddenly in reckless mood she cast aside her misgivings. Fate had brought her here, Fate had decided for her and in any case what difference could a few days make? She could always keep out of Sylvia's way as much as possible.

In the meantime there was a great deal to be done. She could not travel the two hundred miles to London in what she had on. She needed a warm cloak, new boots and a bonnet, all destroyed on that disastrous night. She must ask Tom if Rob could drive her into Skipton or even Bradford where there must be a dressmaking establishment.

It all took much longer than she had expected. Up here in the north there were no large shops and the dressmakers recommended by Sylvia took their time. The days lengthened into a week and she took to breakfasting early with Tom, a meal at which his wife never made an appearance. It was he who told her what was happening in Castlebridge. The enquiry was fizzling out from lack of any real evidence, and most of the strikers had already begun to drift back to work.

"I could have pressed for severe punishments," Tom told her. "We're not the first to suffer an attack of this kind and the magistrates have been urging me to make examples. If it had been Dan Carter I might have been tempted, but most of them are no more than sheep, listening to anyone with the gift of the gab. They can't see beyond the end of their noses. I can't let them starve even if I'd like to knock their silly heads together. Besides I have a mill to run and orders to fulfil. There is only one thing I regret."

185

"What is that?"

"My father had an easy-going relationship with his work-people. He was a stern man and indubitably always the master, but he had once been one of them and it makes a difference. I have tried to keep that going and I thought I had succeeded. I persuaded Alec Withers to undertake a medical clinic and I gave them the school, but somehow they've never trusted me as they did him and always there has been Dan Carter with his poisonous tongue. I can do nothing to remedy that."

"Now he's gone, it will be easier I'm sure."

"I doubt it," he sighed.

Without consciously realizing it, he found himself telling her about the day's work, something he had never done with Sylvia, and Della listened and responded, sometimes making shrewd comments from her own limited experience in London.

During the day she went for walks in the gardens or up on the moors, forced to borrow a pair of stout boots and one of Nanny Roberts' thick mantles until such time as the new ones she had ordered were ready for her. One day Bret called and drove her over to the Grange where Martha made a great fuss of her and Mary Ann regarded her with shining eyes as something of a heroine.

"Are you happy here?" she asked the girl.

"Aye, I am that, 'cept I miss the little uns sometimes. Miss Lavinia says I can visit there once a fortnight now my father is not there."

"How is your mother managing now he's gone?" But Mary Ann shook her head.

"She didn't say, Miss."

It was Miss Lavinia who told her. "Can't you guess? Tom is paying her that wretched man's wage each week of course. He's never been one to evade his responsibilities. It'll lead to trouble one of these days, you mark my words."

In between times Della made friends with Peter. He was a lonely child with no brothers or sisters and no other boy with whom his mother would allow him to associate. So when he could escape from Nanny Roberts, he was to found in the kitchens driving Cook to distraction or with Rob in the tack room or plaguing Tod, the groom who looked after his pony, which he very soon dragged Della to see and admire.

"Papa gave him to me for my birthday," he announced proudly, "and he's called Nutmeg because of his colour."

"Who is teaching you to ride him?"

"Mamma did at first but she got cross with me because I didn't do it right and Nanny says I'm not to worry her now because she isn't very well. Would you come out with Rob and me?"

"I don't know. You must ask your Papa about that," and thought she must not let him grow too fond of her, that would be a mistake, and yet she was finding the child very difficult to resist.

She spent a lot of the day in her room and the boy started to come to her there, bringing his games and toys to show her and asking her to read to him. Nanny Roberts, suspicious at first, gave in after a few days, glad of the opportunity to slip downstairs for a cup of tea and a gossip with Mrs Fenton, the only one among the staff who still looked at Della with strong disapproval.

She had been at the Hall for a fortnight when the weather turned a great deal colder. A thick fog spread across the moors and persisted day after day. One day when she came down earlier than usual, she found the dining room empty, the fire burning sulkily and a heavy white mist that seemed to press against the windows and penetrate into the room so that the lamps had to be lit and burned with a kind of yellow halo.

The Times lay neatly folded beside Tom's plate. It usually reached them several days later than publication. As a rule no one touched it before the master of the house and she did not know what induced her to pick it up that morning. She opened it casually and the thick black headline to one of the shorter paragraphs caught her eye.

Tom coming in a moment later saw her staring down at it, the colour fled from her cheeks, her hands clutching the printed pages.

"It's not true, it can't be true!" she was muttering.

"What is it? What can't be true?"

"There, look there!"

She dropped the paper on the table pointing at it with a shaking hand.

He bent down to read the paragraph. It stated briefly that Her Majesty's ship *Panther* bound for Botany Bay with a cargo of convicts, men, women and children, had encountered mountainous seas somewhere off the coast of South America and had sunk with apparently the loss of all on board. So far no survivors had been reported, though there were unconfirmed rumours that a small vessel trading among the Pacific islands had seen a raft, but whether anyone on it was still alive was in very serious doubt. He looked up and met her eyes.

"My father was on that ship," she said wildly, "do you understand? My father! Oh you may as well know now. What does it matter any longer? Lismore is my mother's name. My father was Paul Craven, convicted of murder and transported to Australia for seven years, seven long hellish years, for a crime he did not commit." Her voice choked into a stifled sob. "I lied to you when I came up here. I lied because I was afraid you would not accept me if you knew and I needed the work." She dropped into the chair, burying her face in her hands.

He said gently, "You mustn't distress yourself on that account. I know who your father was, I've known for some time."

"You know?" Astonishment for a moment banished her grief. "You know, but how?"

"Bret told me."

"Bret!"

"Yes. It seems he saw you at the trial in London and made enquiries as to who you were. He thought I ought to know."

"But he has said nothing."

"When he told me, I asked him to keep silent. If you chose to hide your identity from us, that was your decision."

"And it made no difference?"

"Not to me. Why should it? You are not responsible for your father's actions."

"It was not because I was ashamed of him," she said fiercely. "You must not believe that. I know he was never what people like you would call respectable. We lived as we could, sometimes working, sometimes by gambling, flush when the horses won or the cards were right, in debt when they lost. He may have done all kinds of foolish things, but he never willingly harmed anyone. He was the dearest kindest person in the world and I loved him. And now I can never hope to see him again, never, never, and I don't know how to bear it." She struggled to her feet. "I must write – I must try to find out what really happened."

"If there is anything I can do . . ."

"How could there be? What I want more than anything, what I've always wanted, is to find out who was the real

188

murderer and clear his name."

"That won't bring him back."

She turned on him. "How do you know? There is a chance, just a chance that he has survived. There is, isn't there?"

"Perhaps."

"I'm a fool, aren't I? That is what you're telling me. I'm a fool even to hope, but I feel so very alone."

"You mustn't feel like that." He had taken her hand, holding it firmly in both of his as if to give her strength. "Forgive me for suggesting it but I gathered from Bret that Oliver is related to you in some way. Isn't it he who could help you now with enquiries?"

"Oliver!" she exclaimed and drew away from him. "Oliver is my cousin but he has never acknowledged the relationship, never once."

"Perhaps he respected your wish to conceal your identity," he said gently.

"No, no, that's not the reason. There's something more than that. I saw him at my father's trial, though then I didn't know who he was. He made no move to help him in any way and when I went to Larksghyll, my uncle drove me from his garden as if he hated me."

"Why? For what reason?"

"I don't know. I've never known, only that sometimes it frightens me." She looked up at him suddenly. "Tom, I know that Oliver is a friend of yours, but don't trust him, don't ever trust him." She would have said more, the words trembled on her lips – "Haven't you guessed yet that he and your wife are lovers?" – but then the door opened and Rose came in carrying a loaded tray and she knew she could not say it, could never say it. With a muttered "Excuse me" she hurried from the room.

Safely back upstairs, she walked up and down the bedroom restlessly. The blow had been so sudden and unexpected, she still found it hard to take it in. Always she had cherished the hope that somehow he would be reprieved, that one day they would be together again, and now the hope had vanished. Her mind flew back to her dream on the night of the fire. Could that have been the moment when the ship went down? Had she in some strange way suffered with him at that terrible time? She could not bear the thought of him dying alone, swallowed up in the cruel black waters. The fog seemed to have crept into the room and she shivered. She stopped for an instant to stare into

189

the mirror. Her face looked white and blurred as if she too were drowning. She shuddered away from it and began to walk up and down again.

Perhaps Tom had been right. There *was* her uncle at Larksghyll, there *was* Oliver. Perhaps they could find out far more than she could alone. They had been estranged, but surely her father, whatever he might have done in the past, had suffered enough? What grudge could they hold against him now? She would go to them as soon as she could. Now, this very day; it was still early. One glance from the window told her it was impossible. The fog had grown thicker than ever. To attempt to ride across the open moorland would be madness. She leaned her forehead against the cold glass in frustration and thought how very odd it was that Bret, apparently so open, so ingenuous, had known all this time who she was and yet had given her no hint. And it was Bret who had recognized the golden skull and Oliver too – she shivered at the memory of his cold fingers on her neck as he picked it up. Why? Did it mean anything or was it pure coincidence? If she went away from Castlebridge as she had fully intended perhaps she would never know and yet how could she stay any longer?

Oh Tom, Tom, she thought despairingly, why did I have to fall in love with you and complicate my life in this way? And yet there was comfort in knowing that now she need hide nothing from him. The fact that he had known and still accepted her without questioning warmed her heart.

She remained in her room all that day, refusing food until in the late afternoon Rose brought her a tray of tea with thin bread and butter and put it down firmly on the small table.

"You must take something, Miss, or you'll be making yourself poorly again. Cook says would you like a lightly boiled egg or a slice of nice chicken?"

"No, thank you, Rose. It's kind of Cook but this will be all I need."

Peter, poking his head around the door, said in a penetrating whisper, "Have you the headache like Mamma when Nanny says I must be very very quiet."

"Yes, I have. I'm sorry."

"Poor Della. Shall I make it better?"

He darted across to her, planted a cold wet kiss on her cheek, and went away on tiptoe.

That evening after husband and wife had supped alone together and were sitting in the drawing room, Tom looked up from the paper he had been scanning and said suddenly, "I have been thinking. Peter is really growing out of Nanny. It is high time we thought of a governess for him."

"He's only just five," objected Sylvia.

"Quite old enough to begin learning to read and write. It occured to me that if she would consent to undertake it, Miss Lismore would be a very suitable person."

Sylvia sat up. "Why that girl of all people?"

"She is here on the spot for one thing. She is well bred, well educated and has had experience of teaching."

"She didn't manage all that well at the school, did she?"

"I think teaching our son will be a rather different proposition. Besides he appears to have taken a liking to her, which is a good start surely?"

Sylvia looked across at him curiously. "What has made you bring this up today particularly?"

"Oh for various reasons." He got up and crossed to the fire, bending down to put on more coal and stirring it to spark and flame. "I owe her some sort of compensation for one thing. Then it seems that she has just lost her father who was on board a ship bound for Australia and which sank with the loss of crew and passengers."

"How can you possibly know that?"

"The news was in *The Times* this morning."

"How can you be sure it isn't just an invention on her part to win your sympathy now she's lost her post of schoolmistress here?"

He made an impatient gesture. "Why are you always so much against her? It so happens that I know her distress when she read the announcement was perfectly genuine."

"And that of course made you feel sorry for her." She got up from the sofa and walked across to him with something of her old seductive grace. "Tell me, Tom, you are not by any chance falling in love with this girl, are you?"

"Because I occasionally take pleasure in her company? My dear Sylvia, I might as well ask you if you're in love with Oliver because you appear to find him more amusing than your dull husband."

If she was startled, she didn't show it. She said lightly, "And what exactly do you mean by that?"

191

"Just what I said. Isn't it true?"

"Of course it isn't. You're talking nonsense."

"Am I?" He laughed. "Perhaps I am. To return to Peter. He is already receiving far too much attention from the servants. I don't want him to grow up spoiled. After all he is our only one."

She had her back to him, nervously rearranging the position of a bowl of flowers on the side table. "Perhaps he needn't be our only one."

For a moment he said nothing, his eyes on the pale gold hair, the slender white neck rising from the lace of her low-cut gown. "My dear, you seem to forget that you have closed your door against me very effectively for the last few months."

"It could be opened again," she said breathlessly. "You are my husband after all. You have the right."

He reached out and turned her round to face him, letting his hands slide over her bare shoulders and feeling the involuntary shrinking away at his touch. He let his hands fall.

"I don't find any pleasure in exercising my right as you call it when you are obviously so unwilling."

"I suppose you'd rather make love to your schoolmistress," the words burst out of her before she could bite them back.

"That's quite unforgiveable," he said coldly. "When have I ever given you cause to say such a thing?"

She put a hand distractedly against her forehead. "I'm sorry. My head aches so much that I hardly know what I'm saying."

"You've not been well all this last week," he said with real concern. "I wish you would let me send for Dr Withers."

"That old fool! I know what he'd say." She suddenly turned to him. "Would you mind if I went to London for a few days? Papa is there. I could stay with him and perhaps consult his physician."

"It's hardly suitable weather for making such a long journey," he objected.

"As soon as the fog clears then. Please, Tom."

"I'd rather you waited a little. God knows I don't want to put difficulties in your way but we've come through a bad patch and you know how people talk. I don't want it said that my wife is deserting me."

"Oh the mill, the mill, always the mill!" she exclaimed. "You must always be so respectable, so above reproach – your father wasn't like that. He went his own way and be damned to what people might say of him."

192

"And left a legacy for me to deal with which they murdered him for. Do you want that to happen to me, Sylvia?"

"Oh you always twist everything I say."

"That's not true," he said stiffly, "but I do expect a certain loyalty and co-operation from my wife."

"Haven't I always given you that?"

"Up to now." For a moment their eyes were locked together. Then he went on more gently, "It will be Christmas in a couple of months. Leave it till the New Year, then perhaps I will be able to go with you."

"As you wish." She sighed and turned away from him. "I'm exhausted. I think I shall go to bed. Goodnight."

"Goodnight, my dear."

He watched her go and then turned back to the fire, stirring it with his foot seeing it flare up and wondering at himself. A year ago and he would have gone after her, yielding to her wish, letting himself be persuaded against his own better judgment. What had happened to that passionate infatuation with her beauty that might have so easily deepened into a lasting love if it had not been so persistently damped by her utter indifference? All this last year and longer he had striven to keep it alive, finding excuses for her, blaming himself for their quarrels, and now it had vanished and left only pity, a certain tenderness, regret for what had once been so important to him.

He still refused to believe that she was being deliberately unfaithful to him. Such a thing was surely unthinkable. That she liked to keep Oliver at her beck and call was understandable. She had always had men at her command, men who desired her, and in the very early days they had laughed about it. If it went any deeper then he pitied her. He knew Oliver better than she did. With all that sardonic charm, a devil lived within him, a restless demon never satisfied that had already once or twice nearly brought him to ruin. If he had laid hands on his wife – he clenched his fists together, surprised at the hot surge of anger which raced through him.

And then there was Della. He walked up and down the drawing room much as she had done earlier that day, trying to make up his mind. The idea of asking her to stay on as governess to his little son had sprung unbidden into his mind. Outwardly it was eminently suitable. It enabled him to pay his debt by offering a livelihood, it satisfied his natural generosity of spirit towards her helpless plight, but in all honesty he knew that neither of these reasons was the true one. He wanted her to stay even if it meant asking for trouble, even if he was well aware it was playing with fire. His father's strong spirit that had never brooked interference, that had created the mill against all odds, lived in his son though it had never yet had outlet.

"Be damned to it!" he exclaimed aloud, standing still and clapping one hand against the other, "I'll ask her and if she refuses, then I'll abide by it, but if she consents . . ." but he would not pursue that. She had come into his life like a waif from another world than his, with a mystery about her only partly explained and he had no intention of letting her go, come what may.

13

It seemed to Della that while the fog lasted it had a peculiar claustrophobic effect. Tom rode down to the mill as usual, the members of the household went about their normal duties but no one came in from outside. There were no visitors, no newpapers, no letters. It was as if they were shut into a cold, wet, clammy prison that isolated them from the rest of the world. Tempers tended to fray a little. Peter, unable to play in the garden or go out for his usual walks, charged up and down the passages, bellowing and shouting while pretending to be a horse until Nanny Roberts lost her temper and slapped him hard. Sylvia, nerves fretted beyond endurance, reacted by quarrelling violently with her, then burst into tears and retired to bed with a splitting headache while Della kept discreetly out of the way. After nearly a week, the fog in its own inexplicable way vanished.

Della woke that morning aware of light. She looked from her window on to a changed landscape, sparklingly clear and touched with a slight frosting on grass and trees that a pale sun turned to silver. She dressed quickly with a great longing to escape out of the house, to breathe pure keen air after what seemed like a miasma of misery and frustration. The post that had been heavily delayed arrived in a satchel of mail. Tom was deep in it when she came down to the dining room. He greeted her with an absent-minded smile and handed her two letters. One, sent on by Mrs Frant from her old lodgings in London, was from the authorities informing her briefly in cold official language of the death of her father at sea. The other was from Lucinda, pages and pages of it in her dashing scrawl, from which Della, scanning it quickly, gathered that she had been invited to join a distinguished company who were taking a Shakespearian season to Paris in the very near future. It was the last paragraph obviously added as a postscript just before the letter was sealed that startled an exclamation from her and Tom looked up.

"Not further bad news, I hope?"

"No, rather the contrary. It seems that my father's case is to be reopened."

"For what reason?"

"Lucinda writes that she has met a man closely connected with the new London Constabulary. He told her that fresh evidence has come forward but he could not say more than that."

"It must make you very happy."

"It might have done," she said with some bitterness, "if the same post had not brought me official confirmation of his death." She rose to her feet. "Will you excuse me? I would like to write off at once and ask for further information."

The news had filled her with a tremendous restlessness. Could it be true? She read the letter again, trying to extract more from the few brief lines. The house seemed to stifle her. She would have liked to have taken Tansy and ridden out into the fresh morning. She needed air in which to breathe and think but her new riding habit had not yet come from the dressmakers. She put on a warm cloak, tied a scarf over her hair and went out of the house making her way first to the stables with a handful of sugar for Tansy and Nutmeg. She had not expected to see Tom there. He was talking to Rob while his horse was being saddled. She fed the sugar to the mare and fondled Nutmeg who was pushing his nose against her asking for more.

"All gone, Mr Greedy," she said and would have walked on, but Tom caught her up.

"It feels good to breathe clean air again, doesn't it?"

"Wonderful. It has made me long to walk up on to the moors."

"I wish I could come with you." He glanced down at her. "Is the news you received this morning going to carry you away from us?"

"I don't know. I've hardly taken it in yet but in any case I can't stay any longer. You have been very kind, very generous, but everything is settled now. It is time I moved on. I'm a working woman, you know, not a lady of leisure. I must find another post – and quickly."

The wind had whipped colour into her face. The brave defiance with which she was facing a bleak future touched him and he abruptly made up his mind.

"Before you make any decision," he said, "I have a

suggestion to make. It has been in my mind for some days now. Since the school is wrecked and there is no possibility of reopening it for the time being, would you consider staying on and teaching my son?"

He had taken her by surprise. She stood still taking a deep breath before she said slowly, "What does Peter's mother have to say about it?"

"Sylvia and I have already talked it over. She agrees with me that the boy has outgrown Nanny. He badly needs a certain amount of discipline." He smiled a little. "It's time he began to learn that life is not all play. Would you undertake that for us?"

She looked at him. The breeze that had blown away the fog was ruffling the thick brown hair. The scars on his face left by the fire had begun to fade but were still visible. Oh, she wanted to stay, no doubt at all about that, but she still hesitated.

He reached out and took her gloved hand. "What do you say?"

"I don't know. It is so unexpected. I'd like to think about it."

"Of course. Take as long as you like." The boy had brought his horse and stood waiting. He pressed her hand. "Tell me this evening how you feel about it. Enjoy your walk."

She watched him ride away, then went back to the house, fetched Scamp and took a path through the gardens that led up on to the open moor.

Over the months she had learned to love the sense of distance, the feeling of space, the clean smell of the wind, the turf springy underfoot and now crisped by the frost.

She walked quickly, the little dog gambolling ahead, her thoughts going round and round. She had not realized how much she had counted on Lucinda being in London when she returned. With her away in Paris possibly for months, the city would be like a desert. She shivered at the prospect of the lonely lodgings, the hunt for work, the hard rejecting faces of employers, the utter bleakness of crowded streets where everyone was too much concerned with his own life and problems to spare time or thought for anyone else. She would have faced it if there had been no alternative but now suddenly there was. She tried to look at it dispassionately. She liked the child and he liked her. She saw no difficulty there and it would give her breathing space while she reconciled herself to the loss of her father.

On the surface of course it was eminently suitable. She could

197

almost hear Mrs Barnet saying smugly, "How fortunate you are! You have lost a good post through no fault of your own and have now been offered another one even better. Snap it up, my dear, well paid positions for penniless young women are hard to come by."

It was all perfectly true but then Mrs Barnet would never dream of looking below the surface. She would know nothing about the grim reality of loving a man, of seeing him daily, eating with him, talking with him, and knowing him to be as far away from her as the moon. Why had Tom asked her to stay? She couldn't believe that Sylvia had agreed willingly. Round and round went her thoughts like mice scurrying round in a cage and still she couldn't decide one way or the other. She was walking faster and faster, head up, facing the wind, not looking where she was going when she tripped suddenly, one foot going down a deep hole and pitching her forward. Temporarily winded she heard Scamp barking furiously, a shadow came between her and the sun and she looked up to see Bret smiling down at her from what seemed a great height. Then he slid from the saddle and knelt down.

"I saw you coming across the field and then you fell. Are you hurt?"

"No, no, I'm all right." She began to scramble up.

"Have you twisted your ankle?"

"No, I don't think so." He helped her to her feet and she tried it tentatively. "It's a little bruised, that's all."

"Have you far to go?"

"I'm not going anywhere. I'm just walking."

"Glad to be out after that filthy fog like I am. Come on, you ride Brutus and I'll lead him."

"No, I'd rather walk, really I would. It will be better."

"Very well if you're sure. I'll walk with you and see you safely back."

He took hold of the bridle and drew her arm through his. "That's better. Forward march. Now tell me, are you really quite recovered from the effects of that hideous fire?"

"Yes, of course I am." Her ankle pained rather more than she had expected but she valiantly limped on. After a moment or two she said, "Bret, may I ask you something?"

"Of course you can," he said gaily. "Fire away."

"Why did you tell Tom you knew who I was and yet say nothing to me about it?"

"So he has told you, has he? I thought, like he did, that if you wanted it that way, then it was up to me to keep silent."

"Why did you come to the trial?"

He shrugged his shoulders. "Why does one do anything? No particular reason."

She gave him a quick look not sure she quite believed him. "It wasn't because you happened to know any of the men who gambled with my father on that night?"

His reply was almost too vehement. "Know them? Of course not. Why the devil should I?"

"Don't be angry. It's just that Martha did say once that you occasionally went around with that kind of set and the little golden skull I wore on the evening of your fête – that came from someone who was there and you did recognize it immediately."

"If you listen to Martha, you'd think I spend my life in gambling hells," he said with a touch of anger. "As for the skull, it was chance, pure chance. Articles of that kind are not so rare. I must have seen one like it somewhere." He swung round to look at her. "Why are you asking all these questions?"

"Because it is very much in my mind just now. I heard today that the case against him may be reopened."

"But that's not possible!" He spoke with so much emphasis that she looked at him in surprise and he quickly recovered himself. "Surely that's very unusual. Why? For what reason?"

"I don't know yet, only that some fresh evidence has apparently come forward."

"What possible proof can they find now after all these months?"

"Who knows? The irony of it is that whatever happens, it has been too late. The ship carrying him to Australia has sunk with no survivors," she said bleakly.

"Oh God, not that! Are you sure? Is there no hope?"

"Not as far as I know." She stopped, partly to rest her foot. "I suppose I should tell myself that it is better than seven years of hell in a convict settlement but I can't, Bret, I can't. I loved him too much." She turned to face him. "All I long for, all I hope for, is to see the man who sent him there punished for what he did."

"I wish there was something I could do."

"There is nothing, except help me to find the murderer."

"Believe me, I would if I could, but it is surely too late for that."

199

He had taken her hand, gripping it tightly, and she thought how strange it was that, though the day was cold, there was sweat on his face. Then he released her.

"Come along, what are we standing here for? It's freezing and you're shivering. Up on to Brutus with you."

He swung her up on to the horse and they walked on together as far as the gardens where she begged to be set down.

"Will you come in?"

"No," he said. "I'm due back at the Grange. Take care of yourself."

Then with a wave of his hand he was in the saddle and riding away at a sharp trot.

It was that meeting with Bret that made up her mind for her. When she got back to the house, had shed her cloak and was putting a cold compress on her bruised ankle, she knew she had decided to accept Tom's offer. She was going to stay in Yorkshire. Bret had not been his usual light-hearted self and it worried her. She wondered if he knew more than he was willing to admit. The mystery of Larksghyll still remained unsolved and now more than ever she wanted to know what had happened all those years ago. What it was that had driven her father from his old home and had never been completely banished from his mind. Now it would be easier. Now that Tom knew who she was and had accepted her, she felt as if a dark cloud had lifted. She was free to be herself, free to claim kinship if she wished and when Oliver came back from London, she would tackle him and her uncle together, making it quite clear that she wanted nothing from them, nothing at all, only the truth.

So when that evening Tom asked her if she had come to a decision, she was able to say frankly, "I've never undertaken to teach a little boy before but if you really want me, I'd like to try. We have already started to read together and he is very eager to learn."

"So you *will* stay with us?"

"If Mrs Clifford agrees."

Sylvia looked up from the sofa. "Don't ask me. My husband decides these matters, not I."

Tom said quickly, "My dear, you know you agreed with me that the child needs taking in hand."

"And you think Miss Lismore the right person to carry it out. I only hope you're right."

Across the room Della met the large violet eyes with their dark silky lashes and for the life of her could not read their expression. Was she simply indifferent about her son? Or was there something troubling her beside which everything else paled to insignificance? It worried her a little and with a tiny shiver, she suddenly had a queer feeling that all three of them were standing on the brink of something unimaginable, something dark and fearful from which there would be no escape. Then it had vanished, leaving her shaken but still determined. The die was cast. There could be no drawing back now and later in the evening she knew she was right when she saw the pleasure on Tom's face as they talked about what she would need to transform the nursery into a schoolroom. Sylvia said little, lying back on the sofa staring into the fire as if lost in a dream of her own.

The next morning it felt good to have something to occupy her mind and she went down to talk it over with Abbie Withers, who had been teaching small children for two years.

"I don't want to force him," said Della earnestly. "I'd like him to learn to read and write and draw because he enjoys doing it."

"No one can be as obstinate as a five-year-old determined to play and *not* work," said Abbie speaking from experience.

"Then I'll turn his play into work," said Della boldly and they sat down to make lists of books, instructive games, crayons, coloured sheets of paper, pictures and maps, spending a day in Bradford with Tim, who laughed at Della's earnest insistence on carrying out her own ideas.

"Is this how you tried to teach the children at the school?" he asked with a sly grin at his sister. "If so, I don't wonder young Jem turned into a rebel."

"What a perfectly beastly thing to say! As a matter of fact it wasn't," she admitted ruefully. "I tried hard, but in the end I had to stick to the old fashioned methods and reinforce them with the cane. Peter is different."

"That remains to be seen," commented Tim cynically. "All young children are demons till they learn to be angels."

Afterwards Della was to think of this time as very happy, a lull before the storm broke and threw them all into chaos, but of course it was not all easy-going. Peter was a much-indulged little boy with a will of his own. At the start there were some fiery battles when at nine-thirty his nursery turned into a

201

schoolroom and for two hours he was set down at a table with a book or a slate or a box of crayons and a big map, when he had made up his mind to ride his pony, or race around the lawns with Rusty or plague the life out of Rob or Cook. Mostly she was able to deal with his tantrums, until one morning at the end of the first week when everything went wrong, when out of sheer temper he tore his new book in half, stamped on his slate, kicked Nanny Roberts when she spoke sharply to him and because Scamp objected to having his long ears pinned on top of his head, hurled the little dog across the room so that he hit the wall with a crack and a loud yelp of pain. Della out of all patience slapped the boy hard. He stared at her, his face scarlet, and then ran screaming to his mother.

Sylvia, holding the wildly sobbing child tightly against her, was scathing.

"You may have used the cane on the brats at the school but you'll not use physical violence on my son."

"He deserved it," said Della shaken but stubborn. "No child should be allowed to treat a defenceless creature as he did simply because he couldn't have his own way. He needed to be taught a sharp lesson."

"He is far too young to understand."

"He's not a baby. He knew very well what he was doing."

Sylvia's eyes flashed. "Do you presume to teach me about my own child? God knows what harm you may have done. It was against my wish that my husband engaged you in the first place and I'll make absolutely sure he knows exactly what has happened when he comes home. You will kindly leave Peter to Nanny and me for the rest of the day."

There was a brief battle of wills, then Della bit her lip and went back to her own room, blaming herself because she had not foreseen it and yet knowing that sooner or later the clash was bound to come.

When Tom returned that evening Sylvia poured out the whole story and he went up to the night nursery where a much-chastened little boy had been firmly tucked into bed by Nanny Roberts.

"What is this I've been hearing about you?" he said, sitting on the side of the bed.

"I didn't mean to hurt him," said a muffled voice from the depths of the pillow.

"Maybe you didn't but suppose you had killed him. How

would you be feeling then?"

"Mamma said he is only a little mongrel."

"That has got nothing whatsoever to do with it," said Tom sternly. "Now sit up and look at me."

A small tousled head turned round and two eyes puffy with crying stared up at his father. He was moved with tenderness. Maybe the boy *was* too young to understand but he must still try.

"Now listen to me, Peter. Never at any time strike and injure someone small and defenceless simply because you're angry with yourself. Do you know what I mean? I think you do and you won't do it again." He smiled suddenly and ruffled the pale golden hair. "You're in luck, my lad. At your age my father would have given me a sound beating."

"Are you going to beat me?" There was a faint quaver in the voice.

"Maybe not this time, not if you say you're sorry to Della and to Nanny."

"And to Scamp?"

"Most particularly to poor Scamp."

The boy gave a gulp and then stretched up to put his arms around his father's neck, burying his head against him. Tom hugged him tightly before gently freeing himself.

"It's all over, son. Go to sleep now."

He tucked the blankets around him and dropped a kiss on the flushed forehead. When he came out of the room he found Della waiting for him.

"Do you want me to go?" she asked bluntly.

"Good God, no. Whatever put that idea into your head?"

"Your wife was very angry with me."

"Don't take too much notice of that. She was very upset and she has not been well lately."

"If she feels so strongly about it perhaps it is better that I don't stay."

"Oh come now. I thought you were ready to face any challenge head on. Isn't that what you told me once? This was a very small storm, wasn't it?"

"If Peter hadn't run to his mother, I would not have told you anything about it."

"I thought so. So let's put it behind us, shall we? I'm pretty sure it will not happen again."

She smiled a little tremulously. "I shall try and make sure it doesn't."

"Good. Now come down to the drawing room with me and forget all about it."

"No . . . thank you. It's been a long day. I'd prefer to make sure that Peter is asleep and then I think I shall go to bed. Goodnight."

"Goodnight."

It was a small incident but it had made him realize sharply how much it meant to him to have her here in his house and thinking of that he was unprepared for the storm that met him when he went downstairs.

"I hope you've told that wretched young woman to pack her trunk and go," said Sylvia as soon as he entered the room.

"I've done no such thing, nor do I intend to do so. In a way I expected something like this. It's exactly what the boy needs."

"How can you say that? You were not here. You didn't see the terrible state Peter was in. He cried himself sick. I very nearly sent for Dr Withers."

"I'm very glad you didn't. A fine pair of fools we'd have looked sending for a doctor to cure a fit of temper." He came to sit beside her on the sofa. "There's nothing at all wrong with the boy except that he has been forced to learn painfully that he cannot always have his own way."

"You're so hard on him."

"Am I? Not nearly so hard as my father was with me." He put a hand on hers. "Don't fret about it, my dear. I think perhaps I view it a little more impartially than you do."

"If you say so, then nothing I say will change your mind. I must accept it, I suppose." She pushed his hand away and got up, moving restlessly across the room. "Tom, I must get away from here."

"I thought we'd settled all that. If things go on as they are now, we'll take a holiday in the New Year, to London perhaps or even further if you would like that."

"But that's weeks and weeks away." She turned round on him. "You don't know what it is like bottled up here all day. It's like being in prison. I feel as though I shall run mad."

"Aren't you exaggerating?"

"You don't understand, you never have," she went on feverishly. "I can stay with Papa. I can go about with him, meet people, buy some new clothes, look for Christmas gifts. If you can't come with me, then I'll go alone."

He looked at her for a long moment, the brilliant eyes, the pale hair falling in curls on the white neck. "You could do all these things in Leeds or Manchester. Why are you so anxious to go to London? Is it because you know that Oliver is there?"

He had taken her aback. She licked dry lips. "That's a crazy thing to say."

"Is it?"

"You know very well that's not the reason. If you must know I'm beginning to detest Oliver."

"That's a very sudden change of heart, isn't it?"

"He behaved badly, very badly, before he went away."

Tom frowned. "Badly? How do you mean? In what way? You didn't tell me."

"Oh I don't want to talk about it now. There was so much else – all the trouble of the fire – and I thought it would make you angry but if he were not a friend of yours, I wouldn't care if I were never to see Oliver again."

He looked at her flushed face, heard the vehemence in her voice and was puzzled by it. In her peacock blue gown she made him think of a beautiful exotic bird caught in a net and thrashing wildly and helplessly in an effort to free itself and he felt a stir of pity for her. He sighed.

"God knows, I've never wanted you to feel imprisoned. If you must go, I will make arrangements for you to travel by post horses. It will be a long cold journey, I'm afraid, and you had better take Rose with you."

"Thank you, Tom, thank you. It won't be for long. I will be back at Christmas." Impulsively she ran across to him putting her arms round his neck and kissing him like a grateful child. Her lips were dry and feverish. His arm went around her, but she drew quickly away. "It's late already. I think I'll tell Rose to start packing now."

Some time later she stood in the middle of her room looking at the bed piled high with the clothes she had pulled almost frantically from her drawers and wardrobe, skirts and finely tucked blouses, rich silk ballgowns and lacy underwear, fine silk stockings, bronze slippers for dancing, fur mantle and elegant small boots for travelling.

"You'll never be wantin' all these just for a week or two, ma'am," said Rose doubtfully.

"No, I won't, will I?" She felt suddenly exhausted, the hectic excitement fading. She ran her eye over them, picking gowns out at random. "Pack that and that and that – as for the rest, put in whatever you think may be necessary."

"Very good, Madam."

The maid began methodically placing aside the chosen garments and then carefully tidying away the rest to chests and drawers. She had never known her mistress to be so careless about the clothes she chose. Usually she changed her mind a dozen times so that a bag could be packed and repacked bringing Rose almost to tears of exasperation before she was satisfied.

Presently when the last dress had been hung up, Sylvia said impatiently, "Leave all the rest, Rose. You can finish in the morning. We shall be leaving just as soon as Mr Clifford can make the travelling arrangements. You had better put your own things together. You will be coming with me."

"Very well, Madam. Is there anything more?"

"No, nothing more tonight, but make sure I have an early call."

"Goodnight, Madam."

And Rose went off downstairs to drink a late cup of tea with Cook in the kitchen. She usually considered herself a cut above kitchen staff but she sometimes enjoyed these late evening gossips which Mrs Fenton thought herself too grand to attend. It was intriguing to speculate on what had happened between husband and wife that evening to send their mistress rushing off to London at a moment's notice.

"I reckon as it's that Miss Lismore staying on as governess which has got up her nose," said Cook pouring more tea and ladling in the sugar. "I was sure after the rumpus today that she'd be sent packing."

"Master wouldn't hear of it," said Rose. "I heard him say so when I fetched the tea tray from the drawing room. She didn't half like it, I could see that, but when he makes up his mind, then that's the end of it. She couldn't budge him."

"If you asks me," ventured the kitchen maid who was occasionally as a great privilege permitted to join them, "I think the Master's got his eye on the schoolmarm. Me Mum says as he was always in and out of the schoolhouse and look at what he did at that there fire."

"Nobody asked your opinion, Miss Impudence, so you keep your mouth shut," said Cook crushingly. "Master's not that kind of a man, never has been, not like his poor Pa. It's her ladyship as is the flighty one, that's what I've always thought and I'm sticking to it. What do you say, Rose?"

"I'm not sayin' anythin', 'tisn't my place," said Rose virtuously putting down her emptied cup, "except for one thing." She leaned forward whispering conspiratorially, "You-know-who is still in London by all accounts and you can make what you like of that!"

While the servants gossiped in the kitchen Sylvia slowly undressed. Naked she stood in front of the handsome pier glass running her hands over full breasts, slim waist, rounded hips. She was certain now that she was pregnant and it was with Oliver's child. There was no doubt about that, no doubt at all, and Tom would know, he could not fail to know. She had not slept with him since before she went to Harrogate. She had kept herself away from him, making a hundred excuses, until at last he had let her alone and her own attempt to draw him back to her in the first terror of suspecting herself with child had failed dismally.

She shivered violently, pulled her nightgown over her head and huddled her dressing gown around her. What she had told him that evening was true in a way. There were moments when she hated Oliver, hated the hold he had over her and yet – oh God how true it was that hate and love were part of the same thing. Even though the room was icy cold she burned with a fever of longing for him. He had gone, leaving her without a word, and yet the very thought that she would be seeing him soon, that he would hold her in his arms, conquer her with his devilish charm, laugh and make love to her until her body ached and was still hungry for more made her tremble with desire. This trip to London was a journey into the unknown but this time he must listen to her, he must take her away, he must understand the necessity. She cared nothing about the scandal, nothing about society, nothing about anything but the over-whelming wish to be with him.

If he refused – she pressed her hands against her hot cheeks – but he couldn't, not now, she would not contemplate such a frightening end to her dream. She did not dare to think what Tom might do when he found out – once she had believed he was totally in her power, but not any longer. There was an unexpectedly hard streak in him which might react violently to her infidelity – to the callous betrayal by a man whom he had called friend.

She climbed into bed with all these thoughts still surging through her mind. Presently she heard Tom come up the stairs and pass her door on the way to his own room. A fleeting regret for the love she had wantonly thrown away flashed through her self-absorption. It was one of the reasons why she had not objected more strongly to Della remaining in the house. If he felt some kind of liking for the girl he might let her go more easily. It could provide a weapon, something with which she could strike back at him if the necessity arose.

She fell asleep at last lost in an utterly impossible dream and quite unable to realize the grim reality that awaited her.

Part Three

OCTOBER TO JANUARY
1840–1841

14

With Sylvia gone the house seemed to settle into a quiet routine. Mrs Fenton had always run the household very efficiently, though she scrupulously deferred to her mistress for orders and was more often than not dismissed with a careless wave of the hand.

"You carry on as you like, Fenny, you always know best."

Now she duly presented herself to Tom at breakfast time, asking for any new instructions.

"I leave it to you, Mrs Fenton," he said. "If Miss Lismore requires any change in the nursery routine, then no doubt she will let you know."

Mrs Fenton stiffened. "I'm sure I shall always do my best, sir."

She treated Della to such an icy stare that it intimidated her and she said quickly, "Oh no, there's nothing, nothing at all. I'm very happy with the way things are."

"Very good, Miss. Is that all, sir?"

"Yes, thank you, Mrs Fenton."

She left the room with an air of such rigid disapproval that Tom sat back in his chair with an amused grimace.

"That woman has always made me feel I am still ten years old with something disgraceful to hide. She came with Sylvia from Sterndale and has never forgiven me for not living in a castle with powdered footman to serve at table and the innumerable flunkeys that sooner or later are going to drive my father-in-law into bankruptcy."

For those weeks running up to Christmas it seemed to Della that even the weather was magical. Cold but very clear, there were days when frost and a thin brilliant sun turned the dales to a glory of russet and silver. Almost every afternoon she would ride Tansy up on to the moors with Peter trotting beside her on Nutmeg and they would come home with simple treasures, a branch of berried holly or a coloured stone with curious serpentine lines from some ancient evolution of time. Once they found a sheep's skull quite intact and bleached to ivory.

Sometimes Tom would look into the schoolroom before he left for the mill, sitting down at the table beside his son, picking up a book and reading from it or drawing absurd pictures with the coloured crayons that sent the boy into gales of laughter until Della ordered him from the room before he completely destroyed her carefully planned discipline.

In the evenings after they had supped, she would sit with him in the drawing room for an hour or so and he would tell her about the day at the mill or talk of his plans for the future. Once after a day at the Bradford Exchange he came home in great excitement.

"I met a man whom I greatly admire for the first time today. Titus Salt employs three times the number I do but we found we shared some of the same ideas, one of them being the plain fact that you can get far more out of people if you provide them with better living conditions, something my father had always advocated and I have tried in a small way to put into practice. But this is what was really interesting." He produced two small samples of wool and showed them to her. "Do you know what these are?" She shook her head and he went on with growing enthusiasm. "This one is called Angora and it comes from a kind of Asiatic goat with long fine hair, soft as silk. He is having it shipped from Constantinople and experimenting with turning it into cloth, and the other is Alpaca. Some time ago, he told me, he saw the bales of wool being shipped from Peru and sent one of his men to investigate. It comes from an animal like a llama. That is what I'd like to do. Experiment with new raw material, create better machines, broaden the market." He paused and grinned disarmingly. "You think I'm being recklessly ambitious, I daresay."

"No, I don't. Why should I?"

"Some people do," he said ruefully.

At other times she related some of the adventures she had shared with her father, laughing at the shifts they had occasionally been put to in order to live.

"One of the worst was when we were living in Rome. We had an apartment looking out on a narrow alley and one night I was preparing for bed when I heard a scuffle under my window. When I looked out I saw my father being attacked by a couple of ruffians and getting the worst of it. The only weapon I could think of was the poker so I snatched it up and flew down the

212

stairs. Quite by chance I hit one of them such a crack on the head that he collapsed into the gutter. I forgot that I was wearing my red dressing gown and the other must have thought I was some kind of an avenging fury because he fled. I managed to get Papa up the stairs and it was not until I had washed away the blood and bathed his cuts and bruises that I remembered what I'd done. I thought I must have killed him and it was the most dreadful feeling. I couldn't rest till I had crept downstairs again and peered out. There was blood all over the pavement but no body, so he must have lived after all."

"I'd no idea I was living with such a doughty female," he said teasingly. "Was it robbery?"

"They didn't get time to steal his purse but politics at that time in Italy were very divided and my father was never one to hold back if he saw injustice being done. I used to worry about what he might say next so I wasn't sorry when we packed up and came back to England."

And Tom, looking at her so demure in her simple gown with its lace collar, the silky black hair swept back from the small ears, the large blue eyes smiling serenely at him, wondered that any young woman living such a life, so different from the usual carefully guarded young girl, could still have preserved such a quiet air of purity and innocence.

The intimacy grew between them born of shared interests, of laughter and an increasing joy in each other's company, constantly aware of one another even though he never so much as touched her hand. And during this time of peaceful happiness it did not strike her that there might be others who could misinterpret it and be only too ready to condemn.

No further news of the reopening of her father's case had yet come through from London, but she was reminded of it when one afternoon she rode up to Farley Grange to take tea with Martha and Miss Lavinia.

"Bret has gone to London," said his sister in answer to her question. "He had a letter from Oliver and was off the very same day."

"Did he tell you why?"

"No, except that I think it had something to do with that queer business of Oliver's uncle."

Was now the time to tell Martha of her own close relationship with Oliver and Larksghyll? She hesitated, the words already on her lips, then she drew back, thinking it better to

213

wait until the whole matter had been cleared up once and for all and she had found out the truth.

When Martha was out of the room Miss Lavinia said in her blunt way, "I hear her ladyship has taken herself off again leaving you and her husband alone together. Is that wise?"

"I don't know what you mean. Now the school is closed, Mr Clifford has asked me to stay on as governess to his son. Is there anything wrong in that?"

"So it's *Mr* Clifford now, is it?" said the old lady dryly. "Oh come, my dear, you are a very attractive young woman and Tom is a man like other men."

"If you are implying there is anything wrong between us, then you are quite mistaken."

"Now, now, don't get on your high horse with me. I didn't say I believed in any such thing but there are a good many people who might, people who take pleasure in creating scandal and vilifying the innocent. I'm warning you, that's all. Be careful."

All the way home across the moor Della fumed with strong indignation, but all the same that evening, instead of going to the drawing room as usual and waiting for Tom to join her, she went back to the schoolroom and she was there sorting articles for use on the next day when he came knocking at the door.

"What's wrong, Della? Aren't you well? Have I done something to upset you in any way?"

"No, it's not that." She found it difficult to explain. "It's just that – it was something Miss Lavinia said – well, I don't want to give anyone the opportunity to talk about us."

"Is that all? Do you think I care a rap what a parcel of silly chattering women may say? It's always been the same. If I so much as smile at one of the girls in the weaving sheds, then I am her lover. When poor simple Peg had her baby and I gave her a few guineas to help her through a bad time, there were some ready to swear that I was the father."

And because she had led so different a life, far from the petty narrowmindedness of a small community, she let herself be persuaded, the days passed and they went on as usual till the letter came.

It was one morning in December with only a short time to go before Christmas. They had been expecting Sylvia to return for the past week but she had not come and secretly Della was glad of it. As if by mutual consent they rarely spoke of her, Tom because out of loyalty he would not criticize the woman he had loved and married to anyone and Della because she could not bring herself to voice her belief in Sylvia's liaison with Oliver to her husband.

He glanced at one of the letters and handed it to her with a smile. "Which one of them is it from this time, do you think?"

It had been addressed in badly formed capitals and must have been delivered by hand. After the fire one or two of the children had shown off their hard-earned skill by writing her little ill-spelled notes. This was no doubt one of them rather delayed, but probably inspired by the replies she had sent to the others. She unfolded the sheet of thin paper and then stared down at it with growing horror. It stated in basic farmyard terms exactly what she and Tom were presumably doing together.

It was like the writing on the wall all those months ago only worse, far worse. It turned her sick with disgust.

"Oh how vile! How could they!"

The words were forced out of her and she crumpled the paper fiercely into a ball.

Tom looked up in some concern. "You're white as a sheet. What is it? Let me see."

"No!"

She wanted to destroy it, wipe it away, forget it, but he had taken the paper out of her hand and was carefully smoothing it out.

He ran his eye over it quickly, then got up, crossed to the fire and stood watching it burn to ashes.

"That's the only way to deal with filthy things like that."

"But whoever it is who has written it is threatening to tell your wife these lies, to make it seem as if – as if we – " she choked and got to her feet. "Miss Lavinia was right. I should never have agreed to stay here. I can't bear that they should think such things of you. I will leave today – now – "

"You'll do no such thing. That is what they want – to drive you away. Can't you see that to go now would be an admission of guilt, it would be playing into their hands. We carry on as usual as if it had never been received."

"But who is it, Tom? Who would do such a thing?"

"I'm not sure," he said thoughtfully, "but I *have* heard that Dan Carter has been active again. I've friends who have warned me we could have more trouble with the Chartists, more riots, more burnings perhaps."

"You didn't tell me."

"So far they are only rumours. It is hard to persuade men to strike in the winter months when food is scarce and expensive. Unless something happens to bring it to a head, it will come in the spring."

"But would Dan Carter stoop to this – this petty spite?"

"He might. He's not yet paid me back for what my father did. It would seem that even the fire has not satisfied his lust for revenge."

She stared at him. "Does it worry you?"

"No. If it comes then I will deal with it and in the meantime life must be lived. I'm losing no sleep over it." He gave her a wry amused smile. "Isn't that what your redoubtable father would have done?"

"Yes, yes, it is and don't you dare to make fun of me! If you do I shall never tell you anything about him again. But Tom, all the same it still troubles me, it troubles me deeply."

"Now listen to me, Delphine Craven, here you are and here you stay until *we* decide otherwise and no one else." He had taken her by the shoulders, his eyes on her face. "Understand?"

"Yes, yes, I suppose so."

"Good. Now something I had in mind to bring up this morning. The trip we were planning for next Sunday. This remarkably good weather can't last much longer. The snow has held off this year but if it comes we may be boxed up here for weeks and there is one particular spot in our moorland I've long wanted to show you. You make all the arrangements, will you?"

So she went ahead, asking Mrs Fenton to pack a small luncheon basket for them and smiling a little at the housekeeper's silent disapproval. She was pretty sure she was being condemned as a wanton hussy who had tempted the Master into behaving like a heathen and riding out on a pleasure trip instead of attending the church service, but she felt she didn't care. The days were going by so quickly. Soon Sylvia would be home and it must all come to an end. The very thought made her heart contract painfully but she tried to push it away from her. There were still these hours to be enjoyed.

At the very last moment Peter begged to be allowed to go with them.

"No, son, it's too far for you to ride," said Tom.

"But I've been as far as that with Della. I have, haven't I? Oh please, please, Papa."

He danced up and down hanging on to his father's hand and gazing up at Della imploringly. Above his head their eyes met and she nodded.

"All right," said Tom, "but only if you do exactly as you're told. Tell Nanny to dress you warmly and Rob shall saddle the horses. If he tires," he went on to Della, as the boy ran off jubilantly, "I'll take him up in front of me and we can lead the pony."

It was one of those mornings which only come rarely in winter, so cold that the horses' breath hung in the air like steam, but brilliantly sunny, shrubs and grass tipped with frost, the black spectral branches of the trees edged with silver. The air smelled of bracken and dead leaves and here and there as they passed a lone farmhouse came the warm rich smell of woodsmoke.

Under Tom's guidance she was seeing a part of the moor she had not yet explored. The fells seemed to sweep up and dip down in great frozen waves that reminded Della of the sea, mile upon mile of grey brown moorland with no sound but the tinkling of some mountain brook, the cry of a snipe or curlew far above and the distant bleating of the black-headed curly-horned sheep with their thick woolly coats bred for these bleak uplands. They rode on with Rusty bounding ahead until after a time they scaled a small hillock and Tom pulled up.

"This is what I brought you to see," he said.

She was looking up at a magnificent curving wall of solid limestone jagged and streaked like a frozen cataract of water rising up from an enormous mountain lake. The sheer grandeur of it mirrored in the still water took her breath away.

She said wonderingly, "It looks like a castle built by giants in the very beginning of the world."

"Perhaps it was. Once or twice in my life when things have for some reason become intolerable I have come up here. In this place one can be entirely alone and it somehow helps to realize how small and insignificant are one's worries in the vastness of nature and time. It makes me think of some lines I read once." He paused, eyes half-closed. "They went something like this – if I can remember them –

'To see a world in a grain of sand
And a heaven in a wild flower

Hold infinity in the palm of your hand
And eternity in an hour.' "

"I thought you never read poetry," she said with a little smile.

"Neither do I, but those lines stuck somehow. I don't even remember who wrote them."

"It was a man called William Blake, a visionary, mystic perhaps."

He looked almost shamefaced. "I've never confessed that to anyone before. It doesn't exactly belong to a hardheaded manufacturer of woollen cloth, does it?"

"I don't see why not," she said sturdily. "There's poetry everywhere if you look for it. This is a wonderful place. Thank you for sharing it with me."

Impulsively she stretched out her hand and he took it in his. For a moment they were lost in one another, closely united without a word being said.

Then Peter said plaintively, "It's cold up here, Papa, and I'm terribly hungry," and the spell was broken.

Tom laughed. "This wind certainly whips up an appetite. Let's find a sheltered spot and find out what Mrs Fenton has packed up for us."

It was a merry picnic with crusty newly baked bread and slices of chicken, hard boiled eggs and Cook's special apple pasty plump with fruit and flavoured with cinnamon. There was a bottle of milk for the boy and a sip of the fiery brandy from Tom's silver flask for Della. When they had eaten their fill and repacked the basket she thought, "This has been my perfect day – one I shall remember all my life. Nothing can ever spoil it."

They remounted and started happily on the journey home with no thought of what was to come.

It happened when they were only a few miles from the Hall and began with a sheep. Rusty was a country dog, far too well trained to chase sheep, but the silly creature had strayed across their path. He gave a warning bark and it began to run straight ahead while his instinct told him it must be sent back to rejoin the flock. He darted about chivying at its heels and then raced after it. Nutmeg, bored with the slow ride home and scenting stable and supper, started forward to join the hunt. The path crossed a little brook with a plank bridge. The sheep went over it, closely followed by Rusty barking joyously. Then Nutmeg decided to jump. Peter already tired was not strong enough to hold him. He shot over the pony's head and struck his head against a large jagged boulder by the side of the stream.

Tom, riding beside Della, saw what was going to happen a fraction too late. He spurred forward, flung himself from the horse and was kneeling by the boy when Della reached him. Breathless she slid from the saddle and went down on her knees beside him.

"Is he hurt badly?"

"I don't know." Tom lifted the child very gently. The boy's head fell back against his shoulder, the colour gone from his face. "He's unconscious. We must get him home as quickly as we can. Can you help me with him?"

She took the boy from him while he caught the horse and remounted. Then with some difficulty she hoisted the boy up and Tom took him in front of him, wrapping his riding cloak warmly around him. Somehow she managed to scramble back into the saddle. The sun was sinking, a great red ball staining the sky crimson and the warmth had gone out of the day with the fading light. They dare not ride fast fearing the jolting might do more damage and it was very cold and almost dark by the time they reached the Hall.

Tom carried his son to his bedroom and left Della and Nanny to undress him and wrap him in warm blankets while he went downstairs to send Rob urgently for Dr Withers.

When he came upstairs again it was to see the child still lying apparently lifeless, his face very pale and a blueish look to his lips though there was no other damage to be seen except a slight graze on his temple where he had struck the stone. There was nothing they could do while they waited, except pile on more blankets and put a hot brick wrapped in flannel at his feet.

The doctor, fetched out of the church where he had been attending evening service with his wife and daughter, arrived half an hour later.

He came bustling in, his usual cheerful self. "Now what's happened? Rob said Peter has met with an accident. What's the young rascal been up to, eh?"

But his manner changed abruptly when he saw Tom's face and turned to look at the child. He examined him very carefully, testing reactions, checking his pulse, deliberately taking his time before he straightened up, his face very grave.

"Well," said Tom, "how bad is he?"

"Tell me exactly what happened."

"There's nothing to tell. The damned pony threw him. He hit his head. That's all we know."

"As far as I can see it's a serious concussion. There has been bad bruising and he is in a coma. How much damage has been done and how long it will last neither I nor anyone else can foretell at this stage. It could last a few hours or even a few days."

"But can't you do anything to help him?" demanded Tom. "Surely there must be something."

"No, there is nothing we can do except keep him warm and quiet and watch him constantly. There is a danger that he could turn on his face and suffocate. He is in God's hands, my friend, not in mine or yours."

"That's so damnably easy to say," said Tom bluntly. "Do you mean that he could die?"

"We don't need to think about such an outcome at this stage."

"But he could, isn't that so?" insisted Tom and closed his eyes for an instant as the horror of it swept over him. "Oh my God, and it was all my fault. I should have seen what was happening, I should have insisted on taking him up in front of me. It was too far for the boy to ride. He was tired and that's why he was thrown. I blame myself. I should have realized it."

"It's no use thinking of that now," said the doctor forthrightly. "It has happened. It was an unfortunate accident. Now we must give him what help we can."

Della had been silent all this time, watching Tom's face, knowing how bitterly he was accusing himself and perhaps her too. They were both guilty.

She said quietly, "Doctor, is there anything I can do, anything at all that may be of some use?"

"Very little, I'm afraid, except as I said, stay with him." He paused a moment and then went on thoughtfully, "You could try talking to him even if there is no response. Not all the time but at frequent intervals. I have known cases where it has penetrated the brain if the damage is not too extensive. If there should be the slightest change, call me at once. Otherwise I will be back tomorrow morning to see how he is." He took Tom's arm. "Try not to worry too much. Sometimes these things look worse than they are."

"I hope to God you are right."

They went out together and Nanny Roberts, deeply shocked,

tears running down her face, turned to Della.

"What a terrible thing to happen, Miss, and her ladyship so far away from us in London. She will be near out of her mind when she hears of it."

"Mr Clifford will send a message to her and you never know, he may be quite better before she can get back here," said Della, trying to sound cheerful and practical. "Will you stay with him while I change out of these clothes? Then I will be back to take over. We must share the nursing, Nanny."

All that night the boy lay in the death-like coma and Tom shared the lonely vigil sitting motionless by the bed, the room filled with shadows from the flickering fire. She knew he suffered intensely, all the more because he blamed himself so severely. The next morning he sent Rob into Bradford to despatch a message by the fastest mailcoach to his wife, but it would be some days before she could be expected to return.

Della went down to the dining room to try and persuade him to go to the mill as usual.

"How can I?" he said pushing aside the scarcely touched plate of food. "How can I think of anything with the child lying up there, perhaps close to death."

"It will be better," she said. "You will only torment yourself uselessly if you stay here and there is nothing you can do. Nanny and I will be with him continually and the instant I see any change, I will send word to you." He looked at her uncertainly and she put a hand on his arm. "I promise you, Tom. I love him too. Who knows? By the time you come home this evening he may be sitting up and laughing about it."

But she was too hopeful. All that day Peter lay motionless. Dr Withers came, examined him again and said little but she saw his face and drew no comfort from it. He suggested sending a nurse from the village to share the nursing, but both she and Nanny were firm in refusing the offer. No one but themselves should care for the boy.

All day she tried to do what the doctor had suggested. She held the child's hand in hers trying to convey her own warmth and strength to the limp fingers, talking to him in a slow clear voice. Rusty had obstinately refused to leave the bedroom and she let him come close to the bed pushing his rough brown head against Peter's hand. She brought Scamp hoping the puppy's shrill barking might rouse him but all to no avail. When Tom came back that evening, the hopeless look she gave him as he entered the room told him what to expect.

It was like a hideous nightmare from which there was no waking. Another day and night followed and she scarcely stirred from the room except to eat a hasty meal or snatch an hour or two of rest. The whole household seemed to be waiting in hushed anticipation of the worst. In the kitchen Cook, following the doctor's instructions, took infinite pains to prepare a thin nourishing broth, stopping now and again to brush away the tears from her red perspiring face.

"And to think 'twas only t'other day that I slapped the little dear for stealin' my hot cakes and pokin' his finger into the cream," she mourned.

It was on the third morning that the snow came. Della had gone back to her own room to wash away the trauma of the long night and change into fresh clothes. She drew aside the curtains and caught her breath in sheer wonder. She was looking out on a white world. Everywhere it lay on tree and shrub, on paths and lawns, and still it came down as she watched, huge feathery flakes driven by the wind in great gusts blotting out the landscape.

When she went back to the sickroom Tom was there alone.

"I've sent Nanny to get some breakfast," he said. "She looks worn out. I'm not going to the mill today."

"Because of the snow?"

"No, not the snow. Look at him. I can't leave him, I daren't."

He was standing by the bed and she crossed to join him. Together they gazed down at the child. He seemed to have grown smaller, become more frail, more vulnerable, the pale cheeks sunken, the golden hair lustreless and damp. The courage and determination that had sustained her till then seemed to drain away. She groped for Tom's hand and felt his fingers clutch hers convulsively in a painful grip.

"If only there was something I could do, Della," he murmured despairingly. "I feel so damnably helpless."

She took a deep breath. Somehow she must find strength for both of them. She braced herself in an effort to buoy him up.

"We must continue to do what Dr Withers said. We will work together. We'll talk to him. We'll bring the dogs, we'll do everthing we can to rouse him. We must. We can't let him slip away from us like this without a fight. We won't *let* him die."

222

She thought of that day afterwards as one of the worst she had ever lived through. They talked until they were hoarse and could never afterwards remember anything of what they said. She read him a favourite story, recited nursery rhymes, sang a little song, brought the dogs and his toys, fetched Rob from the stable who came walking on tiptoe, subduing his voice, touching the boy's face gently.

"Eh, Master Peter, you must rouse up now. Nutmeg's frettin' after you somethin' cruel. You'd not want him to be taken sick now, would ye?" and he turned away rubbing a rough hand across his eyes, not willing to show how much he was moved.

In the late afternoon exhausted and spent they fell silent and Tom suddenly sprang to his feet.

"I can't go on with this, Della, I can't. Why carry on talking, talking, when it is all totally useless? If it has to come, then it must, but this – this – it's unbearable – it's like flogging a dead horse!"

He stumbled across the room to the window flinging back the curtains, staring out, leaning his forehead against the icy glass. Outside the snow had drifted into gigantic piles, five feet high in places.

"Sylvia will never be able to come through this. There's not a coach that will risk venturing out in such weather. It would be madness."

"Does it distress you?"

"I don't know. I just don't know any more." He beat a futile fist against the window pane. "Sometimes I have wondered how much she cares for the boy."

The long hours passed at last and late in the evening Della persuaded Tom to eat something and rest for a while. Then she went to her own room to change. It was easier to get through the night if she took off the heavy winter gown, the petticoats and corset and wrapped herself in a warm dressing gown. When she went back to the nursery she dismissed Nanny Roberts to her bed.

"You must sleep for a few hours, Nanny, you're not as young as you were and it's wearing you out. I'll call you if I need you."

The old woman was reluctant but she went at last and Della settled down in the big armchair drawn close to the fire. She found that she dozed very lightly, getting up every half hour or

223

so to look at the boy and feeling her heart sink when there was still no stir, no sign of life.

It must have been about two o'clock, that dead hour of the night when everything seems at its lowest ebb, that she roused herself to make up the fire and then crossed to the window. She pulled the curtain aside. Outside the garden had turned to magic. The snow had stopped and moonlight flooded a world of unbelievable purity and enchantment.

She opened the casement a crack feeling the air icy and invigorating after the stuffy warmth of the sickroom. A flake or two of snow fell into her hand and she stared down at them.

"To hold infinity in the palm of your hand – "

The words came back to her and with them such a surge of love for Tom that she held her breath, so shaken by it that for an instant she could not move. Then the wind tugged at the opened casement making her shiver and she pulled it in fastening the latch securely. She was about to draw the curtain when behind her in the room there came a thread of sound. She turned her head hardly daring to move and it came again.

"Mamma," murmured a tiny voice, "I want Mamma."

She flew towards the bed turning the lamp a little so that the light fell on the child's face. The eyes were wide open, staring blankly up at her.

"Mamma," he said again in a voice that seemed to come out of a dream.

"Mamma will be here soon, dearest. This is Della. You remember Della?"

"Della," he repeated and very slowly recognition came into the eyes. He put a hand to his face. "My head hurts."

"It will be better soon." She picked up a cool damp towel that lay beside the bed and pressed it against his forehead.

"Am I ill?" he mumbled.

"You had a bad fall but you are going to be quite well soon."

"Was Papa here?"

So something must have got through to him after all. "Yes, he was, darling."

She could have wept with the intensity of her relief but she must fetch Tom now. She must let him share in the miracle. She raced along the passage and knocked at his door. There was no answer and the bed was empty when she looked in so, she flew down the stairs and found him in the dining room, crouched

224

before the dying fire in his dressing gown, a glass in his hand.

"I couldn't sleep," he said as she came in and then got to his feet. "What's happened? Is he . . .?"

"He has opened his eyes, Tom, he is awake. He is asking for you."

He put the glass down and went past her and up the stairs two at a time. She followed after him wanting to say, "Be careful. Don't pick him out of his bed, he is still very fragile," but she need not have worried. By the time she had reached them he was bending over his son, his face filled with such tenderness that it moved her inexpressibly.

"Hallo, son."

"Hallo, Papa."

"How do you feel?"

The boy wrinkled his nose. "Funny. My head buzzes."

"You took a nasty knock."

"Did I?" One small hand crept up and touched his father's cheek. "Why are you crying, Papa?"

"Nonsense, I'm doing nothing of the sort." He captured the boy's hand, finding it difficult to speak.

Peter stirred restlessly. "I'm hungry."

Tom looked at Della and she said quickly. "He can have a few spoonfuls of broth. We have kept it warm and ready by the fire just in case."

She brought it and Tom raised the child a little and obediently he swallowed the soup prepared by Cook with such loving care.

The wonder and relief of it remained with them, drawing them very close together as they stayed beside the little boy, talking to him gently and making him comfortable. At length he fell into a sound refreshing sleep and they sat there for a while longer watching him, exhausted but at peace, Della leaning wearily against Tom's shoulder, his arm around her waist, pulling her close to him.

They were surprised by Nanny hurrying into the room in great agitation, a shawl huddled around her shoulders.

"You ought to have woken me, Miss. It's past four and such a bitter cold night," and they both turned to her with the joyful news.

"Thanks to the blessed God," she said fervently, coming to look down at the boy and still finding it hard to believe that the worst was over. "And there was I beginning to think I'd never be able to face her ladyship again. It's like a gift from heaven. Now you go and take your rest, sir, and Miss Della too. You look tired out. He'll be safe with me till morning. You don't need to fret."

"I know he will, Nanny, and I'm grateful," said Tom, "and I'm sure Mrs Clifford will feel the same when she comes home."

"It weren't only me, sir," said Nanny fairly, "Miss Della took her share. Now you go off, the pair of you, or you'll be fit for nowt come morning."

"I tell you one thing," said Tom stopping suddenly on the landing outside the door. "I'm starving. I don't seem to have touched a thing for days. I could eat a horse."

"I don't know as I can supply a horse," said Della in the same mood of relief and elation, "but I could forage for something in the kitchen."

"What a wonderful idea! I'll come and forage with you."

They stole down to Cook's kingdom like guilty children and hunted through the larder and while Della cut slices of bread, Tom carved recklessly thick slices of York ham, looking up boyishly to say, "Cook will probably have my blood for this."

Della blew up the fire under the kettle and made mugs of boiling chocolate, then they piled it all on a tray and carried it up to the dining room where Tom went down on his knees using the bellows and coaxing the embers to a glow before expertly building up small pieces of coal.

"It reminds me of the first day I came here," said Della bringing the tray and putting it between them. "I thought you were the most overbearing man I'd ever met and I hated you for getting the fire to burn when I had dismally failed."

"And I was horrified to discover that instead of engaging a respectable middle-aged schoolteacher, I'd been landed with a waif who looked like a chimney-sweep and turned out to be a very obstinate and self-willed chit into the bargain."

How long ago it seemed and yet it was barely eight months. They laughed over it and tackled the food hungrily. Presently Tom got up and fetched the decanter of brandy. He looked at Della questioningly but she shook her head so he added a little to his own mug and replaced it coming back to sit on the rug beside her. The rest of the big room had become very cold but in the small circle of firelight it was warm and relaxing. She sat with her knees drawn up and her back against an armchair holding the mug between her two hands too tired even to talk.

Presently Tom stirred and yawned. "It's no good. Like good children we must do what Nanny says and go to bed." He took the emptied mug from her and put it with his own in the hearth, then turned back to her.

"You know, Della, I don't think I could have got through this but for you."

"I only did what anyone would have done."

"No, not anyone. We owe you a very big debt, my son and I."

He leaned across and kissed her cheek. At any other time she would have steeled herself against him but too much had happened. For weeks they had lived side by side, close in spirit, but never touching. They had fought together for the boy's life and won through.

"Oh Tom," she breathed, "dear Tom," and swayed towards him stretching out a hand to caress his cheek.

He held back only for an instant, then he had seized the hand and pulled her to him crushing her against him. He was kissing her hungrily and she had no will to resist. For a few minutes the sweet painful madness possessed them both. They were clinging together fiercely. She yielded her mouth to him feeling his hands everywhere, tangled in her hair, slipping down her neck, over her shoulders, thrusting aside her dressing gown to close over her breast.

It was several minutes before sanity returned, coldly, hatefully, blightingly. As if in letters of fire she seemed to see the vile accusation in that filthy anonymous letter and knew that she must be the stronger. If she let this moment carry them away as she longed passionately to do, it could destroy everything between them. Being the man he was, Tom would regret it to the end of his days and that was something she could not endure.

It took all her strength to thrust him away from her and he was staring at her, his eyes wild with baffled anger.

"Why, Della, why!"

"Because," she breathed, "because we're not as the liars outside would have everyone believe."

"Be damned to them!"

"But we still can't damn ourselves."

She was trembling. If he seized her now, she would be lost, she would refuse him nothing, and she felt herself hopelessly torn between longing and fear.

For a moment he did not move, then he stumbled to his feet

227

and stood leaning on the mantel, his face hidden from her.

"I love you, Della," he muttered and suddenly raised his head, shouting it aloud. "I love you."

"And I love you too," there was a painful relief in admitting it at last, "but there is your wife."

"Yes," he said with infinite weariness, "there is my wife. Why did you have to remind me of her?"

"It's better now than afterwards."

"Is it?"

"Tom, do you love her still?"

"I don't know. For God's sake, why ask me that now?" He began to walk up and down the room as if he sought release by putting his feelings into words. "I loved her once, crazily, blindingly. She was seventeen and seemed to me so beautiful, so rare, that when her father agreed to our marriage against all odds, I believed myself the most fortunate man on earth. I did not realize till afterwards that she had been forced into a marriage she loathed with a man she despised and even then, in my arrogance, I believed I could win her, that if I lavished on her everything she had ever wanted, she must love me in return. What a fool I was, what an utter God-damned fool! Gratitude doesn't bring love, it breeds contempt and hatred."

"Was there someone else?"

He stopped his pacing to look down at her. "What makes you say that?"

"Young girls do form strong attachments."

"Did you?"

She smiled wearily. How like a man to pour out his love for another woman and at the same time be unable to endure that she would ever have loved anyone but him.

"Nothing of any importance." She got to her feet. "Tom, you realize I can't stay here any longer. This time I must go."

"No. I won't allow it."

"You must," she went on steadily. "When your wife comes home, when Peter is strong again, then I will leave."

"Don't you understand anything? Haven't you listened to what I have been saying?" he said violently. "My marriage has been a sham from the very beginning. I know that now. It ended years ago soon after Peter was born when she told me brutally, 'We made a contract, you and I, and I've fulfilled my part of it. You have your son and now no more.' But I still wouldn't believe it. I tried to keep it alive and I ended up by deceiving myself . . . and then you came."

He crossed swiftly to her, putting his hands on her shoulders in a painful grip, his eyes burning down into hers.

"I'm to blame for all this. I should have sent you away at the very start – in those first few weeks – but I couldn't. I couldn't because I was learning what love can be – not a boyish infatuation, not a frantic desire to conquer and possess, but something true and lasting, a durable love, and I could not bear to let it slip from me . . ."

"Tom, don't please please don't!"

The gentleness, the longing in his voice nearly overwhelmed her. If she listened to him a moment longer, she knew she would be lost. She could not fight against him any longer. A sob caught in her throat and she broke away from him and ran from the room.

Already the household was astir. A tuneless song came from the kitchen where Cook stoked the fire into a blaze. There was a clatter of dishes, doors opened and shut, someone laughed and was slapped for it, and one of the housemaids, bucket in hand, stared at her in surprise as she stumbled up the stairs.

In her own room Della threw herself on the bed, racked by great dry sobs born of fatigue, reaction and a tearing wretchedness. Had she done right or wrong? Her body felt drained and yet restless tormented by an unfulfilled ache of love and regret. If only it had not happened. If only they had been able to keep the loving friendship of the past few weeks. She knew she was asking the impossible. No relationship such as theirs stood still and she should have realized it. And there was no solution. Whatever happened in London society, up here in this narrow community, divorce for any reason was unthinkable, unheard of, damning a woman, shutting her out for ever from all decent people, damaging a man with the label of unreliability, quite unsuitable for the conduct of weighty affairs of business, and what alternative was there? To become his mistress, hidden away with all that meant in furtive shameful secrecy, bearing children who would be tainted with the stigma of bastardy, the ever-constant dread of being found out, the fear of love turning to bitterness and recrimination. Tom was not a man to accept such a situation lightly. No, she thought drearily, no, better to finish it now with a clean break however painful, however hard to face.

She fell at last into an uneasy doze to wake, unrefreshed and

229

find a thaw had set in with the dawn. Outside under a sullen weeping sky the snow had slowly begun to melt into great heaps of grey slush and it was bitingly, cruelly cold with a persistent icy damp that crept into every bone.

When she was dressed she paused for a moment to look into the mirror. Soon it would be Christmas. During the last few fraught days she had lost all count of time. Now the snow was going there was nothing to hinder Sylvia's return. Tonight or tomorrow she would surely be here. Her face, unusually pale, stared back at her, dark shadows under her eyes, her hair lank and without lustre. What had she to offer against that radiant golden beauty?

Unbidden some lines her father had once quoted to her came back into her mind –

> True love is a durable fire
> In the mind ever burning;
> Never sick, never old, never dead,
> From itself never turning.

She had believed they referred to the love he bore her dead mother and now they came back to haunt her, a love she would never know nor be allowed to prove. Her thoughts entangled her like cobwebs and she thrust them away from her angrily as a knock came at the door. The youngest parlourmaid looked in timidly.

"Master says Dr Withers is here and would you come, Miss?"

"Very well."

She followed the girl out of the room. Whatever the agony of the night, the burden of the day had still to be taken up.

15

Dr Withers was delighted with the improvement in the boy's condition, but also very cautious.

"It's an excellent sign but he is going to need the greatest care. There is still that extensive bruising even though the pressure on the brain has apparently been lifted," he said warningly. "Keep him in bed, no excitement, no noisy games, no romping and very light food. Do you understand?" He looked from Tom to Della with his warm smile. "You've come through an ordeal, I know, but we're not quite out of the wood yet."

"I'll do my best, doctor."

"I'm sure you will, my dear. You're a lucky fellow, Tom, to have had this girl at your side this past week."

"I know I am."

"When do you expect Sylvia?"

"It depends how far she had reached before the snow came down," said Tom with an effort. "Perhaps by tomorrow evening if she's lucky and provided the roads are not flooded."

"If it's not one damned thing, then it's another," went on the doctor cheerfully. "I've had enough cracked arms and legs, sprains and contusions, during the last few days to last me a lifetime and if this thaw doesn't produce a sorry collection of colds, coughs and congestions of the lung, then I'm a Dutchman!" He bent over the bed. "Now you be a good lad, do just as your nurse tells you and we'll have you up and about again in no time."

He pinched the boy's cheek and bustled away. Tom gave Della a quick look and followed after him.

After the hours of anxiety, and the high elation of the previous night that had flung them together with results she could not yet foresee, it seemed a long and wearying day. To deal gently but firmly with a fretful partly convalescent child took all her patience, not helped by Nanny who, in relief that her charge was not to die after all, was greatly inclined to give in to his slightest whim. It required tact and persuasion to make her see that sweet cakes and chocolate were not the best foods for a finicky appetite and demands to be allowed to get up for a ride on his rocking horse had to be quietly resisted and his attention diverted to something else.

There were other matters to be dealt with. Mrs Fenton came in the mistress's absence, asking about preparations for Christmas with a sly politeness she didn't trust at all and she referred her coldly to Mr Clifford. Abbie Withers turned up, splashing through the puddles, her skirts held high, asking if she could do anything and then staying on and on to chat until Della, her head now aching viciously, could have screamed at her. A messenger came hotfoot from Farley Grange, mud to the eyebrows, and carrying an anxious note from Martha so that a letter of reassurance had to be written at once while the groom waited.

She had thought to find time to retreat to her room and think seriously about her own future but there was no opportunity and by the time Tom returned from the mill, she felt as if her nerves were worn to shreds.

He did not come upstairs until after he had dined alone. He too had suffered a troublesome day. One of the new machines had inexplicably gone wrong as they did on occasions and the man who usually dealt with these teething troubles had fallen from his horse on the ice and broken his leg in three places. The delivery of goods both in and out had been hopelessly delayed and there were letters of complaint from customers, all trivialities that on other days he would have taken in his stride but coming on top of sleepless nights and emotional disturbance irritated him beyond endurance. He came home to an empty dining room, no sympathetic listener waiting for him, the house cold and unfriendly, the vast table elaborately laid for one.

He poured himself a generous measure of brandy, something he did very rarely, and asked the servant who came hurrying in where Miss Lismore was.

"She is with Master Peter, sir, and is taking all her meals upstairs. Shall I serve your dinner now?"

He waved his hand irritably and swallowed the fiery spirit at a gulp. "As soon as you like."

After the meal was finished, still on edge, he went up to his son's room, the door slipping from his impatient fingers so that it hit the wall with a crash.

"For heaven's sake, do you have to come in like that?" exclaimed Della. "I've spent over an hour getting Peter to sleep and now look at what you have done."

He was ready with a sharp answer when he was forestalled by a small sleepy voice.

"Is that you, Papa?"

"Yes, it is." He moved guiltily to the bed. The eyes looked enormous in the pale face with its dark bruise. "Did I wake you up, old son? I'm sorry."

"I wasn't really asleep. Have you come to tell me a story like Della does?"

"If that's what you want?"

He pulled up a chair and obediently began on the current favourite. "There was once a little boy – "

"Like me?"

"Just like you and he lived with his mother who was very very poor. One day she sent him to market to sell their cow and . . ."

But the boy had been only partly roused. His eyes closed as he snuggled down into the pillow still clinging to his father's hand.

Della had retreated to the fire and stood watching them with a strange detachment born of extreme weariness. What was there about this man to cause her such havoc? Why did that lean face with its high cheekbones, forceful chin, expressive mouth, cause her to tremble with a mingled love and despair? She could find no satisfactory answer, only knew it for a damnable fact.

Presently he cautiously withdrew his hand and came to stand beside her.

"I'm sorry," he began tentatively, "I didn't realize . . ."

"It doesn't matter," she replied brusquely. "It's just that it has been a very long day."

"It's been a long day for me too," he said wryly. "Have you eaten?"

"I'm not hungry. Presently I'll fetch something on a tray."

They were speaking in whispers and he said irritably, "We can't talk here with the boy sleeping. Come into the other room."

He took her arm obliging her to go with him into the adjoining nursery and pulling the door to after them.

233

"Now – why are you shunning me?" he demanded bluntly.

"I'm doing no such thing."

"Oh yes, you are. There was no need for you to shut yourself away up here. There is Nanny. She can take care of the boy for an hour or two."

"If you knew what trouble I've had with Nanny all day, you'd be more sympathetic," she flashed at him.

"Don't make excuses. I meant what I said last night. I've been thinking about it all day. I'm not going to let you go from me, Della. I can't go on with my life as it is. I can't stand the emptiness, the utter futility – not any longer."

His peremptory tone, the way in which he seemed to be taking her consent for granted, aroused fretted nerves to anger. She said sharply, "If that means that you are asking me to become your mistress, then the answer is no. No, no, no!"

But he went on as if she had not spoken, brushing her protest aside, pouring out what had been growing in his mind during the hours at the mill.

"It has become quite clear to me. I'll arrange a separation. It can be done. Sylvia can live in London. It is what she has always wanted. She has hated the mill, loathed everything about this house, about my work and the life we lead here. She will agree, I'm sure of it . . ."

"And Peter? What about your son? Will you let him go too?"

That pulled him up short. "Peter stays with me."

"Oh no, he won't. I don't know much about the law but I do know that in any legal separation a child goes with its mother and not with a father who is living with another woman. In the end you would hate me for it. No, Tom, no, I could never agree to such a situation, never, never!"

She had turned away from him, shaken and confused, burying her face in her hands and he came after her, swinging her round to face him, taking her hands away and holding them tightly in his own.

"I thought you cared for me."

"I do care, I care too much to let you ruin your life," she went on passionately. "Do you imagine I don't know how it would be, what it would do to both of us, a life of deceit and lies and misery? I've seen what the people up here can do. Do you think for one moment that it could be hidden from them? They would condemn you for it. You would be pilloried, despised, the work you do that means so much to you brought to ruin. I'm not going to let that happen. It would destroy you, it would destroy us both."

"You will be doing that in any case if you go away and leave me."

"And there is your wife," she went on wearily, "she would be for ever between us. I know how you feel about her still. If she needed you, you would go to her."

"No, no, you're quite wrong. It's all over between us."

"Is it? I don't think so. Perhaps it never will be. You're blind where she is concerned. Have you any idea even now what she is doing to you?"

"Let's forget Sylvia for the time being."

"We can't – we can't ever forget her," she cried out vehemently and suddenly the tension broke and they were flaring at one another saying cruel hurtful things which they neither meant nor intended until at last she could stand it no longer.

"Go away, Tom, go away, please, please!"

And he stood silent for a moment, his mind in a whirl, knowing she was right and refusing to admit it, hating himself for what he had said. Then without another word he turned and went out of the room, the door shutting with a snap that had something final about it.

She dropped into a chair shivering in the cold room where the fire had long since died feeling more desperately alone, more bereft even than when her father had abandoned her. She stayed there for a long time, sick waves of fatigue, hunger and wretchedness shuddering through her until she was roused by a knock at the door.

The maid who came in was carrying a covered tray.

"Master said I was to bring you this, Miss." She looked around her. "Will you take it here or by fire in t'other room?"

"You can leave it," she said and when the girl had gone lifted the linen napkin that covered it. Tea and toast and a lightly cooked omelette – she began to laugh and cry at the same time because even in his anger he had thought of her, because it was so much part of the man she had seen and loved from that very first day.

It was about eight o'clock the next evening when Sylvia returned. Della, who had just got Peter to sleep, heard the horses clattering up the drive, the commotion of arrival, the sound of voices. She opened the door quietly and went to the head of the stairs. She saw her come in, the long furred mantle trailing behind her, Rose and the servants following, their arms filled with luggage and parcels. Tom was in the hall to meet her. She went to him with outstretched hands and he took them, kissing first one, then the other. Her voice floated up, quivering, agitated.

"What a terrible terrible journey! I thought I'd never get here. My baby – how is he? All these days, every step of the way, I've been in agony."

And Tom with his arm around her was kind and reassuring. "Don't upset yourself, my dear. He is better, much better, not quite well yet, but on the mend."

"I must see him."

"It's late. Wouldn't it be better to wait for a little? He will be asleep."

"How can I wait?"

She tossed aside cloak and bonnet and came up the stairs as Della retreated back into the nursery. She swept in, the skirt of her velvet travelling costume soiled and muddy, the pale gold hair tumbled about her shoulders.

"He is sleeping, Mrs Clifford," said Della tentatively but Sylvia took no heed.

She scooped up the startled child, hugging him against her, smothering him with kisses.

"My darling, my baby, I thought I'd lost you."

He struggled a little in her arms, still half asleep. "Is it really you, Mamma?"

"Yes, it's your Mamma. I'm here now to love you and care for you."

Then Tom was in the room with them. He said gently, "Don't excite him too much, my dear. The doctor has warned us against it."

"He's so thin and pale," she exclaimed. "Are you sure . . .?"

"Believe me, he has had every possible care." He put a hand on her shoulder. "Come and change out of those damp clothes or you will be ill yourself."

"Later, later," she said impatiently.

"No, now, you must be exhausted."

She released the child to him reluctantly. "Oh very well, if you say so."

"I do say so."

She bent over the boy as Tom settled him back against the pillows. "Don't fret, darling. Mamma will be back soon."

Then she got up, letting her husband put his arm around her and lead her from the room.

It was left to Della to soothe and quieten a wildly excited child, sitting up in his bed, his face flushed, question after question tumbling out.

"Yes, you will see your Mamma tomorrow, she's not going away again and it will be Christmas and I'm sure she will have brought presents for you. Go to sleep now and the day will come all the sooner."

When at last he had dozed off she remained sitting by the fire refusing to let her mind dwell on husband and wife closely reunited downstairs until very much later Sylvia came in again, quietly this time. She had changed into something soft and clinging, a bedgown of sapphire blue trimmed with swansdown, the gold hair tied back with a ribbon. In the light of the shaded lamp Della thought she looked thinner. There were faint hollows in the pale face and dark shadows under the eyes. They seemed only to enhance her beauty.

She looked down at the sleeping boy touching his cheek with one caressing finger before she turned to Della.

"My husband tells me we owe you a great debt for all you have done."

"That's what I am here for."

"Yes, well, we must make sure you have some fitting recompense."

"There is no need for any recompense, Mrs Clifford. Anything I have done has been out of love."

"Love of my boy or love of my husband?" trembled between them but the question remained unasked and for the space of a heartbeat their eyes measured one another, then Sylvia shrugged her shoulders.

"Well, we shall have to think about it, won't we? Goodnight, Miss Lismore," and she went out, closing the door quietly behind her.

When Sylvia came into her bedroom that night Rose was still there unpacking the luggage, hanging up gowns and laying underwear in drawers. She watched her for a moment before she said impatiently, "Leave that now, Rose. You can finish the rest in the morning."

237

"If you say so, Madam. Is there anything else? Shall I brush your hair for you?"

"No, not tonight. You'd best get to bed. You must be tired too."

"Well, it has all been a bit of an experience, hasn't it, Madam? All that water everywhere – when the carriage rolled into it I thought our end had come and we'd be washed away."

Sylvia smiled faintly. "So did I but it wasn't to be. It's over now. Goodnight, Rose."

"Goodnight, Madam."

And the maid went off downstairs to spend a comfortable hour with Cook recounting over a strengthening cup of cocoa how they had set out from London against all good advice, had been caught in a blinding snowstorm that sent the coach into a ditch and had been holed up for more than two days in a very indifferent inn.

"Somewhere near Derby they said it were with the mistress frettin' somethin' terrible," she went on feelingly. "Never seen her in such a state, couldn't rest and goin' on and on at the coachman till at last he agreed to start out again through such floods as you never saw. I'm not tellin' a lie but I said a prayer of thankfulness when I saw the lights of the Hall."

"We've had our ups and downs too what with the boy took so sick, the Master near out of his mind over it and that Mrs Fenton pokin' her long nose into where it weren't wanted," and Cook pulled her chair closer prepared for a long cosy chat.

Despite the hastily lit fire now burning brightly, the room was still very cold and Sylvia shuddered with chill, fatigue and some deeper malaise. She pulled a stool close to the hearth and sat down gazing into the flames, her mind flying back over the last few weeks.

Whatever she had hoped from that precipitate flight to London had not been fulfilled. At first she had been almost deliriously happy. Her father had been surprised to see her but gave her a hearty welcome in his easy-going way. She was plunged into all the joys of the winter season. As his daughter, as the former Lady Sylvia Farringford, she was invited everywhere, the husband in trade left behind in Yorkshire and discreetly forgotten. Tom had been generous with money. She spent it lavishly. Then one morning she swallowed her pride, hailed a hackney carriage and drove to the Albany where

Oliver had his bachelor apartment.

He opened the door himself still in his dressing gown, frowning heavily at first and then laughing as he drew her quickly into the narrow hall.

"My God, my love, of all the wide-eyed innocents! Didn't you realize this is a monastic enclave? No women welcome. Oh we entertain our little bits of muslin but no respectably married woman would imperil her reputation. My neighbours will be all eyes and speculation!"

"Who cares about that?" she exclaimed defiantly throwing back her veil. "Oliver, how could you leave me as you did? I had to see you."

He tilted up her chin. "So you've torn yourself away from Tom just for this. I'm immensely flattered and enchanted."

He bent his head to kiss her so that reproaches, anger, all vanished in relief and pleasure.

"You *are* glad I've come."

"Of course I'm glad. How could I be otherwise? Where are you staying?"

"With my father." She looked away, blushing a little. "It's so difficult – I don't know where we can meet."

"Where indeed, shameless one?" He shook his head over her with his teasing smile. "Suppose you leave that to me."

In some ways for all her boldness she was an innocent, not nearly so worldly wise as she liked to believe. She knew nothing of the houses of assignation where lovers could meet discreetly safe from jealous husbands or outraged fathers until Oliver took her to one in a closed carriage one bleak winter's afternoon. To her fastidious taste the well-furnished room had a used look, something like a third-rate hotel, but when he had quenched the candles, the firelight lent it a spurious glow and she forgot it as slowly and sensuously he began to undress her. After they had made love together her body relaxed into languor and peace. She lay and watched him through half-closed eyes and knew that this was her destiny and she could never escape it.

They could not meet often, but there was a secret pleasure in smiling into those slanting sleepy eyes at some ball or evening party and sharing the knowledge of those hidden afternoons. She heard odd rumours about him, vague disquieting comments. Someone remarked in her hearing, "Oliver was always a high flyer, but he's riding for a fall and it's a damnably long way from the heights."

Lord Sterndale said one morning over his dish of devilled kidneys, "Don't encourage that fellow Craven too much, Sylvia, there's a deuced ugly story going the rounds."

"What kind of story?"

"Never you mind, but I don't like the man, never did. You know that well enough."

He frowned at her. That discreditable episode in the past was far behind her but he did not altogether trust this wayward daughter even now. That husband of hers was too soft. Why the devil didn't he keep her on a tighter rein?

She ignored it all, concerned only with her own personal problem.

She leaned forward on her stool staring into the fire, her hands tightly clasped together, remembering the last time they had met barely a week before she had left to return home.

He had made love to her that afternoon, with a slow deliberation that raised her to a breath-taking ecstasy, and afterwards she was lying on the bed still only in her petticoats, watching him as he carefully arranged his starched neckcloth in the mirror.

She said tentatively, "Oliver, what are we going to do?"

"Do?" he replied lazily without turning round. "Why should we *do* anything?"

"It's nearly Christmas. I shall have to go back to Castle-bridge soon." She sat up, her heart beating. It was now or never. She took a deep breath. "Oliver, I'm going to have a baby."

His hands were suddenly very still. "Tom will be pleased."

"It's not Tom's child. It is yours."

"Are you sure?"

"Absolutely sure."

"How long have you known?"

"For certain, only for the last month."

"Have you told Tom?"

"No, no, how could I? He would know . . ."

"That the child wasn't his."

"Yes. We've not been together, not since – not since the summer."

"Oh God," he exclaimed suddenly, "of all the damned stupid things to happen!"

"Why, Oliver, why?" She was off the bed, coming close behind him, leaning her head against him. "We could go away, be together for always."

"Don't talk like a fool. It's not possible."

"Why? Why isn't it possible?"

"Never mind why. Just believe me. It's out of the question." He turned to her, his face bleak, studying her before he said quietly, "You could get rid of it."

The colour flushed into her face. "Oh no, no, that's horrible, disgusting."

"A number of women do. It's easy enough to arrange. It only needs money, I'm told."

She shrank away from him, her eyes terrified. "I couldn't, I couldn't. How can you suggest such a thing?"

"Because, my dear innocent, the only other alternative is to go back to Tom, persuade him into your bed and choose a moment to tell him. There are such things as babies born prematurely and he is so damned trusting, he would never question."

She stared at him chilled by the brutally practical voice speaking of something so intimate to them both, bitterly resenting the implication that she was in some way to blame, and inwardly shaking with a terrible gnawing anxiety that had tormented her for the last month.

She was too numbed to argue. She let him obtain the address of a convenient doctor from the proprietor of the house where they met. She saw the hard eyes look at her with contempt when they passed her in the hall on their way out and wondered to how many others she had given that same address. She put the paper carefully away and then a few days later after hours of sleepless argument with herself swaying first one way and then the other, she put the money Oliver had given her into her reticule, looked again at the address and took a hackney carriage to a dingy street in Soho.

She stood on the dirty doorstep of the tall narrow house and raised the knocker. A woman opened the door, middle-aged, nondescript, but with eyes that pierced through the silk and velvet, the camouflage of wealth and position to the shivering naked body within.

"Come in. What are you waiting for?" she said and smiled and it was at that moment that Sylvia knew she could not do it. Every decent instinct in her revolted against it.

She ran down the steps and along the street, and then walked and walked until at last she had brought herself to some degree of calm before returning to her father's house. The next day the letter came from Tom and almost in relief she set out on the journey home.

Perhaps, she thought, wearily getting to her feet, it would have been better if she had been swept away in the flood that had nearly engulfed the carriage. She threw off her dressing gown and climbed into the big bed. The sheets struck icy cold though the warming pan had been used and a hot brick placed at the foot. She felt very alone. Even Duchess had abandoned her. In her mistress's absence the white cat had been seduced by the warmth of the night nursery fire burning night and day and had transferred her allegiance.

Tom had greeted her kindly, had enquired solicitously how she felt, had asked what she had done, whom she had met and whether she had enjoyed herself, but the fire, the passion that had once been there was notably absent. It was that girl of course, standing looking at her with her direct gaze. Something had fused between those two, she was sure of it and an angry fire of jealousy ran through her and then died into futility.

It was near to midnight when she heard him come up the stairs. She heard him pause outside as he had done so often in the past. "Persuade him into your bed," had been Oliver's advice. The very thought of it revolted her but it must be tried. With a dry mouth she called "Tom!" and then waited. He opened the door quietly.

"Did you want me? I didn't come in. I thought you would be asleep." He crossed to the bed and stood looking down at her. "Can I get you something? A hot drink?"

"No, thank you. Are you glad to see me back home again?"

"Of course. The boy has been asking for you every day."

"I have brought Christmas gifts for him, for everyone." She was talking at random. "We will have them tomorrow."

"That was thoughtful of you. You look a little pale still. Are you sure you are quite well?"

"Yes, quite well."

"Then I'll say goodnight, my dear." He bent down to kiss her cheek and she caught at his hand.

"Tom, stay with me."

For a moment he did not move, then he gently withdrew his hand. "Better not, Sylvia. I've not been sleeping well lately – the boy, trouble at the mill, one thing and another. I shall only disturb you."

"I might prefer to be disturbed."

"Now that's talking nonsense. You need all the rest you can get after what you've been through. You'll feel much better tomorrow after a good night's rest."

He smiled, pressed her hand and went. She did not know whether to laugh or cry. So much for Oliver's confident alternative plan.

She knew she had lost him, that the hold she had once held over him was gone for ever, and even then in her blind self-absorption never understood how much of the blame lay in herself. It was much later in the night that the idea came to her, wild and daring, an idea that appealed to her by its very audacity. She lay and thought about it. If all else failed, then what had she to lose? She hugged it to her until she fell asleep at last.

16

Christmas Day passed very quietly. The carriage took them to church for the morning service, Tom standing beside Sylvia in the front pew, Della careful to place herself behind them with Mrs Fenton, Nanny and the upper servants.

Outside afterwards acquaintances greeted them, Martha and Bret with them.

"Aunt Lavvy says her rheumatism is feeling this damp cold so she has stayed at home and hopes the Christ Child will forgive her old bones," said Martha, laughing.

The servants set off to trudge back to the Hall and Della would have gone with them if Tom had not stopped her with an impatient gesture.

"No need for that. You can come with us in the carriage."

To argue would make too much of it so she stood waiting while Martha tried to persuade them to spend the New Year with them at Farley Grange.

"Better not," said Tom. "We've come through a very trying time and the boy is hardly recovered yet. I'm sure Sylvia agrees with me."

Bret stood at one side saying nothing huddled in his caped greatcoat and moodily swinging his stick.

To break the silence Della said, "Martha told me you'd been in London. When did you return?"

"A day or so ago."

"Did you hear anything about my father's case?" she asked quietly.

He looked quickly at her and then away. "I believe you may hear news soon."

"What news? Good or bad?"

"I don't know. It's not my concern. You must ask Oliver," he said irritably. In the cold frosty air his face looked white and pinched.

She could not understand why he should seem so ill at ease. Sylvia had looked up.

"Is Oliver back at Larksghyll?"

"So I understand. Oh do come along, Martha, for heaven's sake. It's freezing standing here."

"Impatient boy." Martha took his arm smiling back at them. "Happy Christmas to you both and to Della," and they moved away.

"We must be going too," said Tom.

In the carriage Della took her place awkwardly beside Sylvia while her husband sat opposite them.

Peter was allowed to get up for an hour or so during the afternoon and was surrounded with gifts – new games, books with splendid pictures, a horse on wheels looking remarkably like Nutmeg, a brightly coloured spinning top, a Noah's Ark with a long procession of animals which he set out two by two – Sylvia had bought extravagantly. There was something new too which Tom produced looking mysterious, a kind of lantern which with the help of a light and coloured glass plates enabled him to project pictures on a white sheet hung up against the wall – *Jack and the Beanstalk*, *Red Riding Hood and the Wolf*, *Sinbad the Sailor* and *Robinson Crusoe* – making the boy squeal with delighted wonder. But he tired very quickly and Della went with him when Nanny carried him off to bed.

Sylvia coming up to kiss her son goodnight met her outside the nursery door.

"Perhaps you would care to join us in the drawing room this evening, Miss Lismore," she said. Anything was better than the long evening alone with Tom and the widening gulf which seemed to have opened up between them.

"Thank you. It is very kind of you."

Della found it difficult to refuse without causing comment. She too had received gifts. She looked at them in her room before she went downstairs, a pair of knitted mittens from Nanny, a dozen finely embroidered handkerchiefs from Sylvia, a Paisley shawl in finest cashmere from Tom. She hid her face for a moment in its soft folds and then with a defiant gesture threw it around her shoulders. The dark rich colours set off the black hair and she saw Tom's eyes light up as she entered the drawing room, then he rose to place a chair for her so that she should have the benefit of the fire. She thanked him with a word and thought with a kind of desperate hunger that only a few nights ago here in this very house they had been in each other's arms and could never be again, never. It laid a constraint on the evening that was difficult to break down.

Sylvia, half-reclining on the sofa, the lovely face still shadowed with fatigue, looked from her husband to Della and wondered how much truth there had been in Mrs Fenton's sly insinuations that morning.

The servants had all been given their presents and she had come in asking for orders as usual when Sylvia was seated at her dressing table.

"There have been certain problems due to the weather, your ladyship being away in London and Master Peter almost at death's door but I hope you will be satisfied with what has been planned."

"Since we shall be very quiet over the holiday with no guests," said Sylvia indifferently, "I'm sure you and Cook will have already made all the necessary preparations."

"We always endeavour to do our best."

"I'm sure you do." Sylvia looked up as the housekeeper still hovered. "Is there anything further, Mrs Fenton?"

"There is just one other thing, your ladyship. I don't care to say it but since I have been in your service and that of Lord Sterndale all my life, I feel it is my bounden duty."

"Good heavens, what is all this about? Your duty to what may I ask?"

"I feel I must mention the undue familiarity between Mr Clifford and Miss Lismore since you have been away."

Sylvia, whatever she might think herself, had an aristocratic distaste for servants' spiteful gossip. She said freezingly, "And what do you mean by familiarity, Mrs Fenton? Are you trying to tell me that as soon as my back is turned, my husband takes the governess to his bed?"

Mrs Fenton, shocked at her appalling frankness, drew back hastily. "I wouldn't like to go so far as to say that," she stammered.

Sylvia turned to look at her with an icy hauteur. "I should think not indeed. My husband and Miss Lismore have been drawn together in a fight to save my son's life. For that I'm deeply grateful to them both and that's an end of it. I'd be glad if you would remember it. It's surely your place to silence any foolish tittle-tattle of that kind, if indeed there has been any, and certainly not encourage it. Is that understood?"

"Yes, yes, your ladyship, of course. I would never have

246

mentioned it but I thought that you should know . . ."

"I am not interested in your conjectures," said Sylvia cutting her short. "That will do, Mrs Fenton, you may go," and the housekeeper, considerably abashed, scuttled away.

Now she looked across at Tom lying back in his chair glancing through the latest novel by the clever Mr Dickens which was one of her gifts to him and doubted if there had been any real truth in the suggestion that lay behind Mrs Fenton's allegations. He was too transparent, she would have known if he had been guilty of sleeping with Della. He was not as clever at hiding his feelings as Oliver was and for a moment she was filled with regret and a kind of despair. Why was it that she could have lived with him for six years, borne him a child, and yet could still feel absolutely nothing, yet one glance from Oliver, one touch of his hand, and she was torn by such a tangled mingling of love, desire and anger that she could find no peace?

Those few days between Christmas and the New Year were a breathing space during which Della slowly made up her mind. There was a kind of brooding quietness in the house as if each one of them was absorbed in their particular problem, waiting for something to happen that would provide a solution. The half thaw persisted and with slush underfoot and wind-driven rain, it became impossible to walk or ride outside. The mill had closed for Christmas Day only and Tom splashed his way down through the melting snow and showers of sleet chiefly, thought Della, as a means of escape.

At the end of the week the weather began to improve. The floods receded, it grew colder and crisper, a pale sun fitfully shone and one morning Della asked Rob to saddle Tansy and rode out and up on the path that led from Bolton Abbey along the bank of the Wharfe. It was heaven to be free from the house for a little, free from the long days in the nursery inventing ways to amuse Peter who was growing stronger each day but still on doctor's orders forbidden to take any kind of exercise except of the gentlest kind.

She knew now exactly what she was intending to do. She was going to Larksghyll to confront Oliver and her uncle. They were the only relatives she had in the world and the rift between them and her father must be explained and healed. After that, with her mind clear, she must leave Castlebridge, go back to

London and look for work. There must be something she could do. Mrs Barnet had once spoken of young women going as governesses to foreign countries, even as far as Russia. Her experience of travelling with her father might stand her in good stead for such a post. Hearts are tougher than you think, she told herself. They don't break, though sometimes during these last few days, seeing Tom, talking to him, so close and yet so many miles apart, the pain was so sharp as to be almost physical, like an open wound that would not heal.

She climbed up till she reached the Strid where the river, swollen by the melting of the snow, came pounding down between the narrow chasm with a deafening roar, sending up fountains of ice-cold water. It was terrifying yet exhilarating and she was standing there almost on the edge with the wind-blown spray in her face when she saw another rider coming down from the upper path and recognized Sheba first and then Sylvia.

They drew up beside her, the nervous mare tossing her head a little as the spume burst and showered over them both. Sylvia gentled her with a soothing hand.

"This is one of my favourite places," she said. "How wild it is today, how thrillingly stormy with the river in spate."

"A little too wild. Hadn't we better move back a little from the edge?"

"Are you afraid? There is no danger. I used to think I would like to try that leap for myself."

"The last one who did drowned in the flood."

"So legend says. Sheba could do it, you know. Oliver dared me once. It was summer then but Tom forbade it." She sounded regretful.

"So I should think. It would be madness," exclaimed Della with a shiver.

The water, creaming and sparkling, came leaping and hurtling down, bouncing from rock to rock with an almost demonic force.

"Yes, but then madness is tempting sometimes, don't you think?" Sylvia gave her a sideways glance. "No, perhaps you don't. You've never wanted to toss everything overboard, to cut away from your dull life and do something new, something outrageous – or have you?"

"Perhaps we all feel like that occasionally but we might

throw away the good with the bad and then where does it land us?"

"Does it matter? That's the most exciting part, isn't it? Not to be sure, to plunge into the unknown."

It was queer but Della had a feeling that for the very first time they were talking together woman to woman without any barriers.

Sylvia was looking at her with narrowed eyes. "I don't think I've ever quite understood you. I knew it the first time we met. There was something different about you, something danger-ous to all of us. I told Tom that he ought to send you away."

Della lifted her head proudly. "But he didn't."

"No, he didn't and I think he was wrong." She paused and then said bluntly, "Are you in love with my husband?"

The suddenness of the question took her aback. "I don't think you can expect any answer to that question."

"That means you are. Is he in love with you?"

"Why don't you ask him?"

"Perhaps because I don't want to know the answer." She stared moodily across the flying white spray. "I'm going to have a child."

It struck Della like a blow. "Does Tom know?"

"Not yet. I wasn't sure myself till I consulted a doctor in London."

Was it true or was she lying? Was it Tom's child or was Oliver the father? If it *was* true, then she and Tom . . . she shied away from that thought.

She said in a stifled voice. "It will make him very happy."

"Will it? I wonder."

Sylvia jerked Sheba's head round so suddenly that the mare's hoof slipped on the wet rock. For one perilous moment they teetered on the edge while Della held her breath, not daring to move, then the horse righted herself and they went trotting up the steep path and away.

What had made her say that? Sylvia's mind was in a whirl of indecision. Perhaps because it was a relief to admit it and partly out of sheer malice because if that girl believed she had captured Tom, heart and soul, this would give her cause to doubt and question.

And she was right. Della taking the downward path more soberly knew without a shadow of doubt that the sooner she left Rokeby Hall the better. If Sylvia was to bear what he believed

249

to be his child, then Tom would never bring himself to abandon her.

She got up early the following morning with the firm resolution to go to Larksghyll that very day and knew as she dressed how much she dreaded it. She told herself over and over again that there was nothing to fear and yet it made no difference. The strangeness of that first encounter, her uncle's rebuff, had never vanished from her memory but it had to be faced.

It was not a promising day. There was a grey chill in the sky that could mean more rain or even snow. Tom had gone early to the mill that morning and Sylvia had not yet left her room when she came downstairs. She had told no one where she was going, only mentioning to Nanny that she felt the need for a day away from the house and implying that she might pay a long promised call at Farley Grange. Rob had Tansy ready for her and she set out bravely to ride the miles to Larksghyll.

It was too bleak a day for loiterers so she saw very few people on the road across the moor, only a shepherd with his dog and an occasional farm wagon, the carter calling her a cheery greeting. It was not a coach road and she was surprised to be passed by a black closed carriage with royal arms on the door which reminded her of the police detective who had come to fetch her for questioning at the time of her father's trial and she wondered what it was doing there and if some unhappy person was to be arrested.

The village was very quiet when she passed through it and came at last to the gateposts and the long-neglected drive she remembered so well. She paused there undecided. There was still time to draw back. She was not required to go on. She could put the whole situation behind her and forget it, except that to do such a thing would be the act of a coward and she knew she would regret it for the rest of her life. If only she was not so alone. If only her father could have been there beside her laughing at her fears, saying, "It was my home. I grew up there as a boy. Come and share it with me."

But he was dead, his body picked clean to the bone lying at the bottom of that distant sea unmarked and forgotten. So there was nothing left but to take up the challenging inheritance he had left to her and never explained. She drew a deep breath and resolutely trotted up the moss-grown avenue.

The house lay sombre and mysterious as she had remembered it, but there was more life about it than on that previous day. A window was open and as she skirted the pond with its broken fountain and whispering reeds a maidservant leaned out to shake a duster and then withdrew quickly. A boy appeared from what must be the stables, whistling, hands in pockets, and then stopped abruptly, staring at her as she reached the steps and dismounted. She beckoned him and he came slowly towards her.

"I'm not sure how long I shall be," she said crisply. "Will you take my horse?"

"Aye, Miss, I'll do that," he took the bridle but still stared as if he had expected her to be someone else.

"Is Mr Craven at home, do you know?"

"Aye, Master be there and Mr Oliver."

"Thank you."

He led the horse away as she went up the steps and raised the heavy iron knocker.

The elderly manservant who opened the door gave an audible gasp and stared at her so hard that she thought, "What's wrong with me? Why do they look at me as if I were a ghost?"

But the shock, if it were one, was only momentary. He said courteously, "Beg pardon, Miss, but just for a minute I thought . . . What can I do for you?"

"I would like to see Mr Craven, Mr George Craven, if that is possible."

He looked doubtful. "The Master does not see many visitors."

"I think he will see me," she went on steadily. "My name is Delphine Craven. He is my uncle."

If she had surprised him, he did not show it. He moved back. "In that case please step inside, Miss Craven. I will find out if he will receive you."

He left her standing in the hall and she glanced around her with an uneasy feeling that she was now trapped in the lion's den and there was no escape. It was large and heavily panelled in some dark wood, handsomely furnished in an old fashioned way but there was no welcoming fire in the great hearth and it had a dusty unloved look from the worn rugs on the marble floor to the sombre portrait of some forgotten ancestor above the mantel.

She was there for some minutes becoming more and more

chilled and apprehensive before the butler returned.

"Will you come this way, Miss?" he said austerely and she followed him up the staircase at the far end of the hall.

The room to which he led her was long and narrow running across the front of the house with windows all down one side and on the other a wide hearth where a few giant logs smouldered sulkily on a mound of grey ash. Portraits alternating with tall bookcases stretched on either side.

"Mr Craven will be with you immediately," he said. "Would you care for some refreshment?"

"Thank you, no."

"Very good, Miss."

He left the room quietly closing the door behind him leaving her very unsure of herself and now that the moment had come still uncertain of what she was going to say when her uncle appeared.

She was too restless to sit down and began to walk up and down the room looking up at the portraits. After all these were presumably her ancestors too. They were for the most part indifferent paintings with nothing to engage her particular interest till she reached the one hung at at the far end and stood still caught by the likeness. It was a young man in the riding dress of perhaps a hundred years earlier and except for the long curled hair might have been her father at twenty, handsome, dashing and not altogether to be trusted. He stood hand on hip, looking at her, it seemed, with an impudent charm and as her eyes moved from his face, her attention was caught by something else, a jewel worn foppishly in the lace-edged stock, a golden skull meticulously captured by the artist so that even the diamond eyes had a painted sparkle, a favourite ornament perhaps, a family heirloom. Had it then belonged to her father after all? But if so why in all the years they had spent together had she never seen it? Or was it Oliver who had worn and lost it? Had he been there on that fatal night? A dozen tiny clues seemed to rush together. She moved nearer to examine it more closely when a voice spoke behind her.

"Handsome devil, isn't he? A rascal of course but an engaging one wouldn't you say? Just such a one as your late Papa, my dear cousin."

She swung round to find Oliver standing just behind her, smiling down at her with half-closed eyes and the blood seemed to pound in her temples so that it took a great effort to keep her voice calm and steady.

"It was not you I came to see but my uncle."

"My father suffers from poor health. He has asked me to deputize for him." He was studying her questioningly, his head on one side, that devilish smile of his playing about his mouth. "So you've decided to drop your anonymity, you're not ashamed of the name of Craven any longer. I wonder why. Can it be that you'd like to dip your pretty fingers into the pie? That you believe you have some claim on the family fortunes? If so, my fair coz, I fear you are going to be disappointed."

The contempt in his voice infuriated her. "That is not the reason I came here. I want nothing from you, or from my uncle, only the truth."

"That's a tall order," he said mockingly. "What truth?"

"To start with the truth about that," she pointed a shaking finger at the portrait, "that jewel, that golden skull. You recognized it so quickly that evening at Farley Grange, but it never belonged to my father. It was yours, wasn't it, and you lost it? You were there that night."

He paused for a moment and then shrugged his shoulders. "Yes, I was there. What of it?" and he walked away from her towards the hearth stretching out his hands to the heat as if he were cold.

She followed after him. "If you were there, then you must have known what happened. Why didn't you speak out? Why didn't you try to save him?"

"It was impossible."

"Why? Why was it impossible?" Then suddenly the truth seemed to hit her in the face like a physical blow. "I know why. It was you, wasn't it? It was you who fired that shot."

He stood quite still, hands still outstretched to the blaze, before he said slowly, almost indifferently, "Yes, I shot him, a detestable fellow who only got what was coming to him. He had been cheating us left and right for most of the night."

"And you deliberately let *my* father take the blame. You let him suffer for what you had done. You watched the trial. I saw you there and you did nothing. How could you be so heartless, so utterly callous?"

The face he turned to her had lost its casual charm, its look of amused indifference. The lines around eyes and mouth had deepened, the eyes blazed.

He said savagely, "Wasn't it high time he paid some of the

253

debt he owed to us?"

She stared at him bewildered. "What debt? I don't understand."

"Didn't you ask him why he played the martyr – why he nobly let himself be pilloried for another man's sin?" he said with a bitter angry sarcasm. "Don't play the innocent with me."

"I did ask him but he would tell me nothing."

"No, that wouldn't be his style at all, would it? He wouldn't want his little daughter to be disillusioned, to find out her idol was a hollow sham." He suddenly moved to her seizing her shoulders in a grip of iron. "Did he never tell you how he brutally broke my father's heart, destroyed his health, condemned him to live in a twilight world and turned my childhood into a lonely hell?"

"I don't know what you mean," she faltered.

"Then it's about time you did. You wanted the truth, you shall have it. Come with me. I've something to show you."

He took her hand pulling her with him out of the room, up another flight of stairs and along a passage. He flung open a door into a bedroom no longer used, a place where odd pieces of discarded furniture had been carelessly stacked. He opened the shutters so that wintry light fell on a picture propped against the opposite wall.

"Look at that," he commanded. "Look at it closely and tell me what you see."

It was queer but it might have been a mirror into which she was staring, the black hair falling on the slim shoulders, the wide blue eyes, except that this girl was very young, hardly yet a woman, absurdly innocent, shyly smiling, and the long cream muslin dress was the fashion of more than twenty years before.

"It's my mother," she breathed.

"Yes, it is Olivia O'Dowd Lismore – your mother . . . and mine."

"Yours?" she turned to him incredulously.

"Yes, mine. You're not my cousin, but my half sister." He laughed briefly and mirthlessly. "I wondered how long it would be before you guessed it."

The questions crowded in on her so that she could scarcely breathe. "But how? Why?"

He looked at her for a moment. "Did he really tell you nothing?" She shook her head dumbly not yet able to take it in,

254

shivering in the intense cold of the unused room. "In that case you'd better hear it but not here. It's not a pretty story but there's no need to freeze in the telling."

When they were back in the long gallery, he said abruptly, "You're looking pale. Would you like coffee or brandy perhaps?"

"No, no, nothing."

"As you please." He turned to the fire, kicking the logs so that they flared into a wave of heat. Then he stood looking down into it and the flames lit strange angles of jaw and cheekbones, giving an odd twist to the pale narrow face while she waited full of dread, not wanting to hear and yet knowing that she must.

"Think of two brothers," he said at last wearily, "twins as it happens, one of them, the older by a few hours, was very frail, delicate in health, hardly expected to live."

"My Uncle George?"

"Your uncle and my father. As he grew up he was always striving to match up with his adored brother, only an hour or so younger, but handsome, strong, always the favourite with everyone, the apple of his father's eye who could never forgive his heir for being so disappointing, so totally unable to take a full part in the boisterous, hunting, drinking society that was part of life up here in the dales then."

He stopped, bending down to put another log on the fire. Then he straightened up and went on briskly as if he wanted to get it over and done with.

"They grew up and there came a time when your father went to university and George whose health would not permit him to join in the rough and tumble of student life was sent to Ireland on some business connected with a family estate and there he fell helplessly and passionately in love. She was the daughter of a feckless Irish peer who had wasted almost all his fortune on the racecourse and was as pleased to sell his sixteen-year-old daughter into marriage as she was to escape the crumbling debt-laden castle in County Wicklow. They were married and he brought her to Larksghyll and perhaps she was happy when a year later their son was born."

"And that son was you?"

"Yes. I was six when my Uncle Paul came home. He had followed the years at Cambridge with travelling abroad and he returned with all the glamour and good looks, all the expertise

255

and practised charm of a man of the world. I don't need to tell you about that, do I?"

She shook her head. She could see her father bursting into this quiet dull household like some radiant visitor from another planet, charming everyone with his many gifts and dazzling the unsophisticated lonely young girl from County Wicklow.

"You can guess what happened. Quite heartlessly he set out to capture his brother's wife, knowing full well what she must have meant to him."

"That's a brutal thing to say," she exclaimed indignantly.

"Perhaps, who knows? The point is that it happened. She fell hopelessly in love with him and for a long time my father, trapped like everyone else by his brother's magic, wilfully blinded himself."

She sensed his angry bitterness that must have festered throughout the years, but thought she saw it more clearly than he did. How can you prevent the lightning stroke of love that takes possession of you before you can learn to resist? She had never meant to fall in love with Tom and yet here she was caught up in the snare.

She said, "Perhaps they could not help themselves."

"That's so easy to say. He could have gone away, couldn't he, before it was too late? But he didn't. Maybe it was envy. He was the younger son and his sickly brother would inherit everything. Whatever it was, he remained until the truth came out at last with grief and rage and a blazing quarrel. He was ordered from the house and went, taking her with him. My father followed them." Oliver turned to her with a twisted smile. "Like a page from a cheap melodrama, isn't it? He drove himself but he was not a horseman like his brother and it was winter already, ice and snow everywhere. The carriage crashed into a ditch. The lovers never paused, they fled on their way escaping from England, taking refuge in Italy, leaving him horribly mangled in tangled wreckage to be picked up later by a passing wagoner."

"Wouldn't it be kinder to believe that they didn't know?"

"Perhaps, but far more likely to assume they were concerned only with themselves. It broke him not only physically but mentally. He divorced her, a long and wretched proceeding which brought him not sympathy but condemnation. A gentleman should take the blame, not shame his erring wife," he went on with savage irony, "and then he retreated into a world of his own, shielding himself from the pain of all personal contacts."

"You could have been only a child, how can you know all this?"

"I grew up with it. They told me my mother was dead but I knew that to be a lie. A child sees and knows far more than you think and I too had been entranced by my uncle's glamour. Servants talked pityingly. I hated them for that. I saw my father turn from me in dislike because, though I was her son, I could never take her place. It cured me once and for all of ever putting my trust in any woman."

Della was silent. Her mind in a turmoil, her image of her father tarnished but not broken. She knew now that he had regretted it all his life but characteristically put it behind him as he put all painful things, living heedlessly from day to day, until that moment came when he found he could not inflict that last cruelty on his brother. He could not let Olivia's son be branded as a murderer.

"Supposing the verdict had been hanging and not transportation, what would you have done then?"

"I wonder. As it was, I thought seven years in a convict settlement was a just punishment for my father's long agony. I did not foresee death by drowning."

"Would you have cared if you had?"

He let his eyes dwell on her for a moment. "You ask too many questions."

"I was told that the case against him has been reopened."

His face went suddenly very bleak. "I have heard that too."

"Will it affect you?"

"Are you hoping that retribution will fall on me at last?"

"No," she said seriously. "I don't think I do. He is gone. Nothing will now bring him back."

"That's true." He paused and then went on in a gentler tone than she had ever heard from him. "I'm going away almost immediately, far away, maybe to India or even further, and it could be for a very long time. Will you come and see my father, talk to him, be kind to him?"

"The last time we met he drove me out of the garden."

"He told me about that. It was the shock of recognition, but now I think he will feel differently. I believe it would give him peace of mind to meet Olivia's daughter in friendship."

"I don't intend to stay in Yorkshire but I will come before I

257

leave."

"Thank you. You're a strange young woman, Delphine Craven, something reckless from your Irish mother with a good dose of your father's gift of charm. When I first saw you at Farley that night, I thought it might be amusing to make love to you, to my cousin, my half-sister. That was something different, something I had never tried before."

She was not sure if he were serious or saying it jestingly merely to shock her. She got to her feet.

"You wouldn't have succeeded."

"Wouldn't I? Since this is the last time we shall meet, I'm tempted to try."

With a movement that took her by surprise he pulled her into his arms and kissed her hard on the mouth. In some terrifying way it had a desperation about it almost as if he sought some kind of comfort. She struggled to free herself.

"Oliver! No!"

"Yes," he said and laughed. "A brotherly kiss this time."

As his lips touched her cheek they were interrupted.

A sharp voice exclaimed, "Oliver!"

The door had been flung open and Sylvia stood there, surprise and anger on her face.

He did not move away, his arm was still loosely around Della's shoulders.

"What the devil are you doing here, Sylvia?" he said coolly.

"Am I disturbing you? Do you usually make love to the servants?" she said with a scalding contempt.

"She's not a servant, my dear, very far from it. She's my cousin, we are very closely related indeed. Didn't you know? Did Tom never tell you?"

She had come into the room looking at Della accusingly. "Is this true?"

"Yes, quite true. Oliver, it is better if I go now. I'll not forget anything. I could never forget."

"Never is a long time, cousin, but it seems that regrettably we must say goodbye."

Deliberately he raised her hand and kissed it. For a moment she looked deep into his eyes and then went quickly from the room.

"What does that little masquerade mean?" said Sylvia.

"Exactly what it looked like," he said wearily. "I'm going away and we were saying goodbye."

"Going away? When?"

"Very soon. Why are you here?"

"I had to talk to you. What was that girl doing in this house?"

"Not at all what you appear to think," he said ironically. "There were certain family matters to be discussed."

"What has she been hiding from us?"

"Nothing of the least importance."

"I wish I could believe you."

"Well, you can. Contrary to what some people think, I usually tell the truth." He dropped into a chair close beside the hearth. "Now for pity's sake, be reasonable. I'm not in the mood for hysteria."

"How can you be so cruel?"

She sank down on the footstool and put both her hands on his knee looking up into his face. "Oliver, I love you so much. I can't go on living without you."

He stirred a little restlessly. "So you told me. We spoke of all this in London, my dear, have you forgotten already? Have you settled that – that small difficulty that was troubling you so much?"

"How can you speak of it like that? It's your child as well as mine." She drew away from him shrinking into herself, her arms round her knees. "It was a vile filthy place. I could not allow such people to touch me." She shuddered. "I would have felt degraded."

"And Tom?"

"Tom is estranged from me. I think that girl has made up her mind to steal him from me."

"I doubt that," he said dryly. He got up abruptly, pushing her to one side. "So now what's to be done?"

"You said you were going away. Couldn't you take me with you?"

"No. I told you before. It is not possible."

"Why? Why?"

He turned round to face her. "If you must know because I shall be a hunted man. I shall have the dogs after me wherever I go and I can't run with a woman and child hanging on to my coat tails."

She struggled to her feet, her eyes wide, staring at him. "Hunted? For what? What have you done?"

"Never mind about that. The fact remains. I can't take you

259

with me and that's final."

"I don't believe you," she said slowly. "This is just a trick to escape. You're tired of me, you don't care any longer. It's like it was before and I wouldn't believe it. I thought this time . . ." her voice broke into a sob.

He came to her then putting his hands gently on her shoulders. "Now listen to me, Sylvia. We've had a wonderful few months together but in your heart you knew it had to end some time as I did."

"No, no, no!" she sobbed helplessly.

"Be sensible. Of course you did. I'm fond of you, I always shall be but now the time has come. Go back to Tom, persuade him, confess to him if you like. He's a good man. He will never leave you, he will be kind."

She dragged herself away from him, her eyes wild. "You don't care at all, do you? You're utterly heartless. I've never been anything more than a plaything, a silly adoring woman to pick up and toss away whenever you felt inclined. I hate and despise you for it . . ." her voice choked and she turned running from the room.

She looked so distraught that he went after her, calling her name, but she took no heed. Outside in the courtyard the boy was walking Sheba up and down. She snatched the bridle from him, he gave her a leg up and by the time Oliver reached the steps she had given the mare her head and was galloping down the drive at a breakneck speed, only one thought in her mind, that wild audacious idea that she had been nursing for days. He could not be allowed to treat her as he treated other women, a cast-off mistress, some cheap whore who had lost the power to charm. Lord Sterndale's daughter was different and by God, she was going to prove it to him.

17

When she left Larksghyll Della did not return to the Hall immediately. There it was so difficult to be alone. There were too many demands made on her and she had to have time to reconcile her own memories with the grim story that Oliver had related with a savage bitterness that had surprised her. He had always seemed a man so entirely self-sufficient, so confident of himself. That early experience of betrayal, that loss of his mother, must have bitten deep into a sensitive child and left him permanently scarred. She had thought once that nothing could give her greater satisfaction than to see the man responsible for sending her father to his death suffer in his turn, but now in her heart she found a reluctant understanding of Oliver's motive. Her own memories of her mother were precious childish ones, a cloud of soft dark hair, a gentle lilting voice that sang sweet Irish melodies to her as she drowsed into sleep. She remembered being held in loving arms, filled with a sense of warmth and security that was abruptly snatched away when she died so suddenly and left her bereft and clinging to her father, the only anchor in a sea of desolation.

Did her mother ever regret the small boy she had left behind, did she ever pity the gentle shy man she had abandoned sick and broken-hearted? Or was it that she had felt passionate love for the first time and was completely overwhelmed by it so that nothing and no one mattered any longer but the beloved? These were questions only her father could have answered and he was gone.

Unwittingly she had taken the path that led up to the Strid and she paused there for a few minutes shuddering as the cold grey winter's day began to close in around her. She thought of Sylvia. What had brought her to Larksghyll? Was she still so crazily in love with Oliver that she could risk so much and if he went away as he had said, would she turn back to Tom in her despair, sure of his loyalty if not of his love?

She turned Tansy and took the downward path knowing

261

with a sick certainty that she did not possess her father's ruthlessness. After what she had heard that day she could not come between husband and wife when the happiness of a child was at stake. She could not rip apart the secure world of a small boy and create another Oliver.

It was only four o'clock but already it was dark under the trees as she rode up the drive and dismounted. Tansy was thick with mud and feeling guilty she offered to rub her down herself when she led her to the stables.

"Nay, Miss, you look right perished wi' the cold," said Rob, coming to take the bridle. "You get yourself inside. I'll see to the mare."

Thankfully she let him take charge, realizing suddenly that she was chilled to the bone and faint with hunger having eaten nothing since the early morning tea and toast.

As she turned to go she saw that Sheba was back in her stall and said unthinkingly, "I see that Mrs Clifford has returned already."

"Aye, and ridden the poor beast into a fair lather, sweatin' and shakin' all over she were," said Rob disapprovingly. "'Tain't like her ladyship. She usually has more thought for the mare."

It gave Della a feeling of uneasiness as if everything that day was building up to some kind of climax and yet after she had changed out of her riding dress and gone along to the nursery it all seemed so much as usual that she told herself she was giving way to imaginary fears. The room was filled with light and warmth from a briskly burning fire and Nanny was presiding over the tea laid out invitingly on the table. Peter whooped with pleasure as she came in and Nanny looked up half-scolding, half-pleased.

"You're very late, Miss, and you look pinched with the cold. Tea's just made. Will you take a cup?"

"I'd love one." She sat down beside the little boy. "What have you been doing today?"

"We played some of my new games but Nanny gets them all wrong and then she cheats." He smiled up at her winningly, his face smeared with chocolate. "Will *you* play with me after tea and may I have another cake?"

"How many have you had already?"

"Only one and it was a very little one."

She exchanged a glance with Nanny. "Just one more then as

262

a special treat."

She sipped the hot tea gratefully and ate some of Cook's scones that were light as a feather and drenched in butter and strawberry jam, and thought how sane and ordinary and welcoming it all was after the fraught hours of the morning.

The games board came out after tea and after a hectic and noisy session the toy theatre was set up and Peter's favourite, *Jack and the Beanstalk*, with painted scenes and a most effective and frightening giant, was played through with a great deal of gusto and laughter.

Then Nanny came back saying, "Time for bed, young man," and Della went down to fetch a cup of chocolate and some biscuits for the boy's supper. As she went through the hall she saw the door to Tom's study was open and she paused for a moment. He was standing in front of his desk, a pistol in his hand, which he was carefully reloading.

He glanced up, saw her and smiled. "You look surprised. I'm not intending to shoot anyone."

"I did wonder." She took a step into the room. "It's a very handsome weapon."

"Yes, the latest model made in London for my father. He had his name engraved on the silver plate. Ever since the trouble in the summer I have kept it oiled and loaded just as a precaution. Have you ever fired a gun?"

"No, never."

"Oddly enough, Sylvia is quite proficient. Lord Sterndale apparently enjoyed taking pot shots out of his window shooting at crows and squirrels so she tried her hand at it. She fired this once out of the drawing room window of all places. Fortunately she did not hit anything."

"I don't think I should dare. I must go. I'm on my way to fetch Peter's bedtime chocolate."

He put the pistol in a drawer and closed it. "Nanny said you'd been out all day. Did you go to Farley Grange?"

"No. I went to Larksghyll."

"Was Oliver there?"

"Yes. I must go."

He moved towards her. "No, not yet. Won't you tell me about it? Ever since Sylvia came back you have kept away from me."

"Only because I must."

"I don't think I can stand it much longer," and he reached

263

out and captured her hand.

"Tom please, please. You must let me go."

"I love you."

"Don't, please don't. I can't bear it, not now, not today."

"Why not today?"

"I'll tell you about it sometime, but not now."

She pulled her hand away and went quickly, hurrying down the stairs to the kitchen, all the events of the day crowding in on her again. She paused outside the door to recover her breath, to force herself to go in quietly, respond cheerfully to Cook's chatter as she poured the chocolate into the silver cup, adding three of her own special biscuits to the saucer.

When she got back to the nursery she found Sylvia was there. The big armchair had been pulled in close to the fire and Peter, already in his nightshirt, was on his mother's lap. She was nursing him almost as if he were a baby again while the white cat was curled luxuriously on the rug at her feet. It reminded Della forcibly of that very first meeting, of the picture they had painted, the beautiful young wife with the golden haired boy, and yet there was something strained about it, something almost desperate in the eyes that turned towards her.

"Put the chocolate in the hearth. I'll see Peter into bed tonight."

"Very well." She put the tray down and stooped to touch the boy's touzled head.

"Goodnight, Peter. Goodnight, Mrs Clifford."

"Goodnight."

Not a word about the meeting at Larksghyll, none of the questions she had expected. It was almost as if it had never happened, as if something else far more important had blotted it from her memory.

Della closed the door behind her and then not wanting to face Tom again, went down to the kitchen once more and asked if she might have her supper alone in her own room that evening.

It was some time later that same night that the youngest parlourmaid was sent upstairs to fetch the tray from the drawing room and came back quite pink with subdued excitement.

"Master's in such a temper as never was," she reported breathlessly. "He glared at me when I went in. 'Get out,' he roared, 'and be quick about it!' I was that scared, I picked it up

264

and ran." She dumped the tray down on the table so that everything rattled.

"Rubbish!" said Cook forthrightly. "Master's not like that and take care what you're doin' with that tray. It's the best china and Mrs Fenton will stop it out of your wages if you break one of them cups."

"Well, he was then," went on the girl defiantly, "never saw him in such a state and her ladyship white as a sheet and glarin' back at him somethin' awful. Do you think she's guessed about you know what?"

"You keep your mouth shut, my girl, or I'll have it washed out with soap and water," said Cook threateningly. "Talkin' about your betters in that way! I never heard of such a thing! You take those things out to the scullery and wash them up — careful mind — and after you've put them away you can get off to bed."

But after the girl had flounced off, she and Rose exchanged significant glances. It is well nigh impossible to keep anything from servants and they had always been on Tom's side, and Della's too after the way she had cared for the young master, while deeply resenting Mrs Fenton's high-handed methods and regarding her ladyship with suspicion as a flighty piece, not honest down-to-earth Castlebridge stock.

After Sylvia had put Peter to bed she had stayed for a while watching him as he drowsed into sleep. When she was in London she had faced the fact that to go away with Oliver meant leaving her little son but the baby growing within her had left her no other choice. She could still hear Oliver's brutal words, "I can't run with a woman and child hanging on to my coat tails." She didn't believe for one moment that he was in any danger. That was just an excuse to escape and once again the anger boiled up within her. She went down to the drawing room to find her husband sitting beside the fire, a book in his hand, a square solid reliable man, decent and honourable, and in her unhappiness she was seized with a violent desire to hit out, to hurt, to make him suffer as she was suffering.

She said with a fine show of anger, "Why didn't you tell me that the wonderful Miss Lismore you admire so much is Oliver's cousin, the daughter of that infamous uncle of his?"

Tom looked up. "Where did you hear that?"

"Does it matter? It's true, isn't it?"

"Yes, it's true."

"And you knew?"

"Almost from the start."

"And said nothing to me or to anyone."

"I saw no reason why she should suffer for what her father did."

"As a teacher at that wretched school of yours, perhaps not, but to bring her here, to live in close contact with our child. How could you do such a thing and hide it from me?"

"I don't think she is likely to teach him to gamble or to shoot anyone dead," he said ironically.

"Don't joke about it." Recklessly she allowed her restless unhappy mood to strike out at him. "You wanted her here in this house because you were already in love with her."

"Sylvia please," he said wearily. "We've spoken of this before. You're talking nonsense and I don't want to discuss it any further."

"No, because it's true, isn't it, it's true?" She leaned forward spitting the words at him, "If you don't send her away, I shall leave you, Tom. I shall go away from here and I shall take Peter with me."

"No." He got up and threw down the book. "I'll never permit it. Go if you must. Perhaps it might be better for both of us to live apart, but you shall not take my son from me."

She had hit out at random and he had taken her by surprise. She said slowly, "You've already thought about it. You've discussed it with that girl."

He turned away to the fire so that she could not see his face. "What I may have done or not done is of no consequence. The fact is that our marriage came to an end a long time ago even if it ever began," he said with extreme bitterness. "God knows I've done my best but I think we've both realized it all this past year."

But she was not listening to him. "So it is true. You *are* her lover, have been all the time I've been away, perhaps even before that. Mrs Fenton told me but I wouldn't believe her." Her voice rose. "I knew that girl was a slut, I knew it from the beginning, but I didn't realize she was also a liar and a cheat."

He swung round. "Don't dare to speak of Della like that."

"I shall say what I like."

"Oh no, you won't, nor Mrs Fenton either. She's a damned liar. Did you ask her to spy on me while you were in London?"

"And what if I did?" she said tauntingly.

"By God, if I thought that were true . . ."

He took a step towards her and she faced up to him defiantly, the memory of the afternoon sweeping through her unbearably, "And don't think you're the only one. She spent the day in Oliver's arms."

He checked, not for the reason she imagined. "And what the devil were you doing at Larksghyll may I ask?"

He was looking at her so strangely that she was suddenly frightened, realizing that she had gone too far and it was at that moment that the maid knocked and came in and was ordered peremptorily from the room. It gave Tom time to control himself.

"I'm sorry," he said when she had gone. "I should not have spoken like that. We're both of us upset and saying things we don't mean. Let's leave it till the morning. If we have to continue living together, at least let's try to do it decently."

He was not nearly so calm as he appeared on the surface. Ever since Sylvia had come back he had been torn in two. To ask her for a divorce would involve Della. There was no hiding anything in this closed community. He was not a wealthy aristocrat. He could not take her abroad and live the scandal down as they did in high society. His livelihood, his deepest interest lay here in this narrow Yorkshire town that would unhesitatingly condemn them both. And how could he divorce Sylvia? Even if he could prove a liaison with Oliver he shrank from exposing her to the shame and disgrace.

Watching him, Sylvia had a sudden enormous desire to confess, to tell him everything, to throw herself upon his mercy. She stopped him as he moved towards the door.

"Tom!"

"Yes." He paused reluctantly. "What is it? I have some work to do. Things have been going badly and the mill doesn't run itself."

"The mill, the mill, always the mill!" she exclaimed in exasperation. "What is wrong now?"

"It's not so much that things are wrong with us as with the whole country. Did you hear nothing of it in London? Didn't your father tell you?"

"Papa doesn't concern himself with such people."

"Then he should. The unrest has been spreading and spreading all this autumn and winter. So far we've escaped but

267

I don't know for how long or how it will ultimately affect us."

The momentum that had carried her towards him was checked. She felt a great wave of hopelessness sweep over her.

"I see," she said dully. "I didn't realize . . ."

"You never have, have you, my dear, and never cared either. My fault perhaps as much as yours. You look tired," he went on more gently. "Why not make sure of a good night's rest?"

"Yes, perhaps I should. Goodnight, Tom.

"Goodnight, my dear."

She waited for a little after he had gone, then rang for Rose. She gave her some brief instructions and then went up to her own room.

It was some time after midnight that Della got up and slipped on a dressing gown. She had gone to bed early, feeling unutterably weary, but sleep was far away. After hours of lying wide awake, staring into the blackness of the night and seeing over and over again the stark events related to her that day, she wondered if a warm drink from the kitchen might help to soothe her jangled nerves. She stole quietly down the stairs. She was on her way back when the creak of a door stopped her. The hall was only lit by a lamp turned very low and a white wraith floated across it, paused and then went on up the main staircase. Perhaps Sylvia like herself was unable to sleep and had come down seeking a remedy. She waited until she had vanished before going on her way. After sipping the warm milk she fell asleep at last.

Some unidentifiable sound roused her and she started up in alarm and then thought it must have been a dream. The room was very dark and, still vaguely troubled, she slid out of bed and crossed to the window. Outside it was only just light and everywhere was thick with a heavy frost while shreds of freezing mist hung among the trees blown by a restless wind.

She shivered and looked at her watch. It was just after seven and the house was already alive. There was a clashing of milk pails and a boy whistled cheerily as he made his way to the stables. She washed quickly in the ice-cold water and began to dress.

As she came down the stairs she saw Tom emerge from his study frowning impatiently as Mrs Fenton came bustling through the service door.

"Did you ring for me, sir?"

"Yes, I did. Has any of the servants been in my study this morning?"

"Not so far as I know, sir. That room is not usually cleaned until after you have left for the mill and the fire is not lit till the afternoon."

"Find out if anyone at all has been in there since yesterday evening, will you? It's important."

"Very good, sir."

She hurried away looking mystified and Della came down the last few stairs.

"What is it? What has happened?"

He turned back and saw her. "When I went in just now I saw the desk drawer was half open. My pistol has been taken. I usually lock it. I must have forgotten it yesterday."

The white ghost of the night before flitted through her mind. She said involuntarily, "Sylvia!"

"Sylvia?" he repeated. "*Sylvia*! What makes you say that?"

"I'm not sure," she faltered, "only I thought I saw her down here late last night."

"You saw Sylvia? We'll soon find out about that."

He pushed her aside and bounded up the stairs. She followed after him.

He flung open the bedroom door. The room was empty except for Rose busily tidying away scattered garments.

"Where is my wife?" he demanded.

"She went out early, sir, before even it was light. She asked me to call her and tell Rob to have Sheba ready saddled for her."

"Riding? At this hour and in this weather! Where, for God's sake?"

"I don't know, sir, she didn't say." Rose looked scared. "I only did as I was ordered, sir."

"Yes, yes, of course. It's all right, Rose. You can go. Finish this later."

"Very good, sir."

She gave them a quick glance as she passed them and Della waited till she had gone and then pushed the door to before she spoke.

"I think she has gone to Larksghyll."

"Why? Why should she go there again at this hour?"

"She came while I was there yesterday. I left her with Oliver and he had told me that he was intending to leave England

269

today."

He was very still. All this time he had deliberately shut his eyes to it but now it must be faced.

"Are you saying that they are lovers?"

"Ever since the summer. You did know, didn't you, Tom?"

"I knew and yet refused to believe. Oh my God, how could she be such a fool as to put her trust in him – in Oliver of all people!" He swung round on her. "How long have you known this?"

"I saw them together at Harrogate."

"And never told me."

"How could I?"

Then suddenly he hit one fist against the other. "What a damnable fool I've been! Why didn't I realize it last night? She has taken that gun but why? She must be out of her mind. I must stop her. I must get it back from her."

He went down the stairs two at a time and through the hall, shouting for Rob to bring his horse. Della did not hesitate. She fled to her own room, unbuttoning her dress as she went, tearing it off and scrambling into her riding skirt. She tied a scarf over her head and ran down the stairs. Oliver was her cousin and his father was her uncle. Whatever happened at Larksghyll today concerned her just as much as it concerned Tom.

Rob was grumbling as he saddled Tansy. "First there's her ladyship riding off like some danged madwoman, then the Master away like the North wind and now you, Miss. What's happening, eh? You tell me that."

She did not listen, only urged him to hurry. Then he had given her a leg up, his last words following her as she cantered down the drive.

"You go easy, Miss, roads are hard as iron out there. You'll lame her sure as I'm standin' here if you don't watch out," but she took no notice, only urging Tansy forward, not daring to think of what she might find at journey's end.

It was still early by the time Sylvia reached Larksghyll, her face whipped by the icy wind, her hands frozen to the reins. She had ridden at such a pace that Sheba was sweating and shaking as she dismounted. The house was already astir, a travelling carriage in the drive, horses being led out for harnessing, the front door wide open.

She beckoned one of the stable lads. "Take my horse," she commanded, "and look after her. She's had a hard ride."

"Master said . . ."

"Never mind that now. You do as I say and hold her ready. I may want her soon."

He was silenced by her imperious manner and only gaped as she ran up the steps. Luggage stood ready in the hall. Someone shouted in the depths of the house and she stood for a moment uncertain what to do next. Then Oliver came down the stairs, impeccably dressed as always, his caped coat over his arm. He checked when he saw Sylvia and then came steadily on.

Breathlessly she waited for him.

"What the hell do you think you're doing coming here at this time?" he muttered savagely under his breath.

She licked dry lips. "Oliver, I – I could not let you go – "

"Wait," he commanded taking her roughly by the arm and propelling her through the door and into a small panelled dining room that led off from the hall. He released her, threw his greatcoat over a chair and turned round to face her.

"Didn't I make myself perfectly clear yesterday," he said icily. "I have no intention of taking you with me and nothing you can say or do will change my mind."

She had reached a sort of calm from nerves stretched to the uttermost, all her mind concentrated on achieving one object.

"You can't stop me," she said. "I won't let you leave without me. I shall follow after you."

"Oh no, you won't. I shall make sure of that. I shall order my servants to lock you in a room till a message to your husband brings him here to fetch you."

"You wouldn't dare do that."

"Indeed I would. I think you know me well enough for that, but it won't be necessary, will it?" He could see how she held herself, how taut she was, like a harp string wound to the highest point before it snaps. He went on more gently, "Aren't you being a little foolish, my dear? Go back to Tom, wait a little and when I can see my way more clearly, then I will send for you."

"No. You said that once before and it meant nothing, nothing. You let my father sell me to the highest bidder, but I'm not a child any longer and it's not going to happen again. Perhaps this will make you change your mind."

Adroitly she pulled the pistol from the leather saddle bag she had slung across her shoulder.

His voice changed. "Good God, Sylvia, are you crazy? Don't play about with things of that kind. It's dangerous."

"I'm not playing, Oliver, and you needn't be afraid. I know how to handle it. Papa taught me."

"Now listen," he said persuasively, "this is ridiculous. You can't threaten me like that. Put that gun down and let's talk sensibly. I haven't much time but I'll try and explain."

"We've talked and talked all these months and it has got us nowhere. This time I'm the one who is telling you. Either you take me with you or I turn this pistol on myself."

"Sylvia, for God's sake . . ."

"I mean it, Oliver. I'm not afraid. Without you I don't care what happens to me."

There was the suspicion of a quiver in her voice and he thought she might well be cracking. The damned pistol probably wasn't loaded but she was holding it steadily enough. Somehow he had to get it away from her. He edged nearer and then made a sudden dive to wrest it from her. They struggled for a few minutes with him unwilling to hurt her too much. Then she jerked away and pulled the trigger. The impact hit him full in the chest. Shaken by the recoil, deafened by the explosion, both hands still clutching the pistol, she saw him stagger, an almost ludicrous look of surprise on his face, saw him lose balance, grab at a chair for support and then crash to the floor. She saw him struggle to sit up again and fall back with a groan before realization of what she had done hit her. She dropped the gun as if it burned her fingers. She knew she ought to summon help but she was so paralysed with horror that she could not move, her throat closed up, unable to utter a sound.

He tried to raise himself. "You fool," he muttered thickly, "you've done for me – and for yourself. I – I – meant . . ."

He choked on a gush of blood, it trickled from his mouth and spread across the white shirt. She shuddered violently and with a strangled cry she ran out of the room, across the hall and out of the front door. The boy was still walking her horse up and down. She snatched the bridle from him, scrambled into the saddle and tore away down the drive.

The thick walls of the ancient house had muffled the sound and it was some minutes before one of the servants came into the hall to fetch the baggage and saw the door to the dining room half open.

He said tentatively, "Are you there, Mr Oliver? Horses are harnessed and all's ready to go."

Getting no answer, he pushed open the door and went in. The next moment, shaking all over with shock, he was back in the hall shouting for help.

By the time Tom arrived about an hour later the whole household, shocked and horrified, knew that the young master lay weltering in his blood, shot down by Sylvia Clifford, beautiful as an angel and wild as a hawk. In the kitchens and stables they had been talking of the affair for months, speculating about those secret visits of hers and now, they told one another, because he had tired of her tantrums, she had taken a dramatic revenge. The boy who had held her horse and seen her coming and going was the hero of the hour, telling it over and over again. To give added spice, here was her husband coming up the drive at breakneck speed, dismounting and striding up the steps with a face like stone and with him the young woman, who gossip said was his mistress, and who bore such an uncanny resemblance to the portrait in the attic which no one ever mentioned.

In the hall Tom was met by Crosby, the old manservant.

"I have reason to believe that my wife is here," he said abruptly.

"No, she is not here now, sir. She left some time ago."

"And Mr Oliver?"

The old man paused before he said quietly, "You had better come in here, Mr Clifford."

In the small room they had laid Oliver on the sofa. The butler drew back the caped coat that had been spread over him. Della drew a sharp breath. The shock turned her giddy. She clung to a chair determined not to give way. Even in death Oliver's face bore traces of that faint sardonic smile of his.

"We've sent for the doctor," went on the old man, "though it is obvious there is nothing he can do."

"What happened, Crosby?"

"I don't know precisely, sir. Mr Oliver was preparing to leave for an extensive trip abroad when it seems Mrs Clifford arrived asking for him. I was upstairs at the time but it appears there was some kind of an accident. She left the house very hurriedly and it was not until some minutes later that we found Mr Oliver lying there." He pointed a shaking hand at the stained carpet.

"And the gun?"

"It was lying nearer the door. It is there on the table. It is yours, I understand, sir," he went on in a neutral voice.

"Yes, it is mine. Have you sent for the magistrate?"

"Sir Anthony Hunter is celebrating the New Year in London, I believe, and is not returning until tomorrow, and since this must surely have been the result of some kind of an accident . . ."

They exchanged glances. There were no police nearer than Bradford. Avoid scandal at all costs was in both their minds.

Tom said heavily, "Yes, an accident of course. I am afraid my wife has not been well for some time. Do you know where she went when she left here? I must go after her. In the present circumstances she may not be responsible for her actions."

"I understand, sir. The boy saw her leave. He will tell you."

"Where is Oliver's father? Should I see him?"

"Mr George is very shocked and distressed, sir. I don't think he will be willing to see anyone just now."

"Very well. I will come back as soon as I have found my wife and know her to be in safe hands."

In the hall he seemed to see Della for the first time.

She said, "Tom, I will stay here. There may be something I can do."

"Thank you."

He gripped her shoulder hard and she was shocked by the look on his face. However they might try to hush it up, it was his wife who had murdered her lover, the man he had called friend, and she guessed he felt deeply the responsibility. He should have known. He should have prevented it.

The old servant stood looking after him as he rode away with a certain pity. He said sombrely, "He won't be the first or indeed the last to suffer a woman's betrayal," and she realized that Crosby must have known her mother well, must have been here all through the trauma of the elopement and what followed it.

Then he had turned to her saying gravely, "I'm sorry, Miss. These are times when one forgets one's duties. May I show you to a room where you can rest? Have you breakfasted? Shall I bring you something?"

"No food please but I would dearly like some coffee if that is possible."

"Of course. Come this way and then I will speak to Cook."

The room to which he took her was plainly furnished and very cold, a guest bedroom that looked as if it had not been occupied for many years, but it did give her breathing space, a few minutes in private to pull herself together. To see Oliver lying dead had been a shock which only now was beginning to make itself felt and with it a sense of loss, a deep regret which she had not expected to feel. She was shaking with cold and reaction. She pulled off the scarf and began to pin up her windblown hair with trembling fingers. She had told Tom she would stay on the spur of the moment and now scarcely knew how she was going to deal with the uncle who had rejected her so forthrightly. A knock at the door startled her and a young maidservant whose eyes looked puffy with crying came in carrying a tray with a silver coffee pot and a plate of freshly buttered toast.

The girl bobbed a curtsey, put the tray down and would have gone if Della had not stopped her.

"Can you tell me which is Mr Craven's room, Mr George Craven?"

"Master has the one at the end of the passage. Poor gentleman, he were that upset . . ." she gulped, bobbed another curtsey and ran from the room.

The coffee was hot and strong and Della drank it gratefully. She had eaten nothing that morning and needed strength to face what the day might bring. She did her best to swallow a mouthful of the toast but it stuck in her throat and she pushed the plate away. Now the time had come and had to be faced, she plucked up her courage and went along the landing to the door at the end. She knocked but there was no sound from within so she knocked again more loudly. There was still no reply so she resolutely opened the door and went in. The curtains had been drawn and the room was shadowed to a kind of twilight. It took a minute before she saw that her uncle was sitting in a chair beside a fire that had almost burned to ash.

He said tonelessly, "I've already told you, Crosby, I want nothing only to be left alone."

There was something so unbearably lonely about the hunched figure, the bowed head with the untidy grey hair, that she did not stop to think. She ran across the room and went down on her knees in front of him.

"It's not Crosby, Uncle George, it's Della, your niece Della."

He stared at her for an instant as if dazed. Then he said in a harsh whisper, "You're Olivia's girl."

"Yes, Paul's daughter."

"You came here once before."

"Yes."

"It was Oliver who told me who you were – Oliver – "

And then it was as if something cracked inside him. He began to weep, painful wrenching dry sobs. After a moment's hesitation she put her arms around him and held him close. It did not last long. In a few minutes the shaking stopped. He drew himself up in the chair and she sat back on her heels still holding one of his hands.

"I'm sorry," he murmured. "It's not the way I would have wished to welcome Olivia's child to Larksghyll."

She had expected anger, recrimination, bitterness, and this weary acceptance left her almost speechless.

"Never mind. I'm here," she whispered at last, "that is what is important."

His eyes moved slowly over her face. "You are so like her."

"Did you hate her very much for what she did to you?"

"I could never hate her. It would have been so much easier if I had."

His temporary breakdown had somehow broken the ice between them. She left him to recover while she rebuilt the fire and then drew back the curtains to let in the wintry light. The room was part bedroom, part sitting room, with a large curtained bed, but also a desk laden with papers and book-shelves against one wall.

She came back to sit close beside him and as if by mutual consent they did not talk of the past but only of what must be done in the present crisis. Contrary to what she had believed, she found that her uncle might have withdrawn from society and lived the life of a recluse but he also managed his estate efficiently and was perfectly aware of what was happening around her.

"Oliver and I have never been close," he confessed at one point, "my fault maybe. He had a wildness I found difficult to understand. He should have been your father's son, not mine," he went on dryly. "I knew he lived recklessly but I felt I had no right to interfere – but to die like that – so uselessly . . ."

It was difficult to find words of comfort when time was racing by and she found it impossible to stop her thoughts flying after

Tom. Where was he now? Had he found Sylvia yet? What would he do if she were accused of murder?

Any hope that they might have cherished of the situation escaping police investigation was destroyed almost immediately.

It was about eleven o'clock when the doctor came, not a genial friend like Dr Withers but an abrupt uncouth stranger. He had been out on a case when the messenger reached him, had come a long tiresome journey and was in a bad temper.

Della saw him in place of her uncle and he eyed her up and down.

"Who the devil are you?"

"I'm Delphine Craven, Mr Craven's niece."

"Never knew he had any close kin. On a visit, are you? A pretty kettle of fish I must say. Nothing I can do for the poor fellow, dead as a doornail. Who shot him?"

"It was an accident."

"Maybe," he snorted, "but I beg leave to doubt that. I can't sign any death certificate, you know, without informing the police. He was never one of my patients, preferred one of those smart London quacks. How's the old man taking it? I've been called in to him once or twice."

"He is shocked but bearing up remarkably well," she replied, disliking him more and more every minute.

"In that case I'll be off. I've a busy round, you know. You will be hearing further very soon."

He was right. It was far sooner than even he had expected. She was attempting to eat a little of the hastily prepared luncheon of bread and cold meat when Crosby came in looking worried.

"There is a person asking for Mr Oliver, Miss. I don't like to trouble the Master."

"Who is he? Have you any idea?"

He drew a little nearer. "Not quite a gentlemen, Miss, if I may say so. I fear he may be someone to do with the law."

"The law? Do you mean the police?" He nodded. They both knew it had to be faced. She pushed aside her plate. "Very well, Crosby, I will see him. Show him in here please."

The man who came in was dressed soberly in black and might have been a lawyer's clerk except that there was nothing in the least ordinary about the thin-lipped mouth, the authoritative air and the pale eyes that probed and missed nothing.

He said at once, "It is Mr Oliver Craven I wish to see."

"So I understand. I am his cousin. May I ask why you wish to see him?"

"I am Detective Inspector Becket of Her Majesty's Metropolitan Constabulary and I hold a warrant for his arrest."

That startled her. She said the first thing that came into her head.

"For debt?"

"For murder."

So it *was* true. They had caught up with him at last and that was why Oliver had been leaving the country so hurriedly. The policeman was eyeing her narrowly and she guessed he knew who she was and was waiting for her reaction.

She said in a stifled voice, "That's a terrible thing to say, Inspector."

"The worst there is. You should know that well enough, Miss Craven, if I may say so. If you are hiding him or withholding information as to his present whereabouts, then I am afraid you will be judged accessory and charged with obstructing the duty of the police."

There was the faintest possible smile on his face and she hated him for it.

"I am doing neither. I fear you have come too late. My cousin is dead."

"Dead!" The smile vanished. The thin mouth shut like a trap. "When did he die?"

"A few hours ago."

"By his own hand?"

Almost she wished she could say yes and that would be the end of it and the next instant knew it was impossible. Too many people knew the truth. She parried the question.

"What makes you say that?"

"Knowing the kind of gentleman he was," he said dryly, "I think he may have seen it as a way of escaping justice. Don't evade the question. How did he die?"

"It was an accident."

"Did it happen here?"

"Yes."

"May I see the body if you please?"

"If you must."

"Indeed I must and I must also interview and question everyone here in this house. Is that understood?"

There was no help for it. He summoned his colleague from the carriage waiting outside and let her lead him to the room where Oliver lay stiffening in the rigour of death. Then she went to tell Crosby what had happened. They looked at one another in despair. Now that the majesty of the law had taken over, there was no certainty as to what the consequences might be for them, for Tom or for Sylvia.

The afternoon wore through and seemed to last for ever. The questioning went on and on. Laboriously everything was taken down, read over and signed except for the smallest scullery maid and the boot boy who made their mark, some of it frankly garbled and distorted, but the truth emerged clearly to any astute mind and it was obvious that Inspector Becket possessed that quality. He was, however, remarkably gentle with her uncle for which Della was grateful.

Her turn came at last and when she entered the room, the policeman had walked across to the window stretching himself as if weary of the long sitting. The winter day was already darkening and candles had been lit. He turned and eyed her thoughtfully.

"And what part did you play in this sordid little drama?" he asked dryly.

"What are you implying, Inspector?"

He came back to the table and glanced at his notes. "I understand that you are at present employed as governess to the son of Mr Thomas Clifford of Rokeby Hall."

"Yes."

"And it seems hiding under a false name. Why, may I ask?"

"I should have thought that obvious to someone of your intelligence," she replied coolly. "I had been advised that the daughter of a condemned criminal might find his name a disadvantage when seeking a post and I needed one very badly."

"And your cousin here did not give your identity away?"

"No, but my employer Mr Clifford knew of it."

"And kept silent? Very unusual if I may say so." He leaned suddenly across the table. "Are you and Thomas Clifford lovers?"

The question was rapped at her so abruptly that she needed a moment before she could steady her voice.

"If it were true, which it is not, what has that to do with your case against Oliver Craven?"

"Very little except that it may very well explain why Mrs Clifford was driven to take the desperate measures she did. You and your father before you, Miss Craven, would appear to have the habit of becoming embroiled in some very unsavoury affairs."

She realized then with a feeling of sickness that every tiny detail was going to be dragged out, commented upon and misinterpreted, that there would be no hiding anything however innocent it was. The Inspector's pale eyes held hers across the table.

He said, "Did you never have a moment when you would have been pleased to pull that trigger yourself, Miss Craven?"

"And if I did," she replied fiercely, "what has that to do with you or with this case?"

"Nothing at all, simply curiosity on my part. There is plenty of evidence as to how your cousin died, but whether accidentally or deliberately, it will be for the Coroner's jury to decide."

He led her through the routine questioning, how Tom had found that his pistol was missing, how she had come with him because she was worried about his wife's state of mind, how he had gone at once in search of her.

"And she has not yet been found?"

"Not as far as I know but Larksghyll is very isolated."

He rose to his feet. "I shall have to take the body into custody until after the inquest and the removal will take place early tomorrow. After that his father will doubtless wish to arrange burial." He gathered his papers together and put them in the leather satchel he had brought with him and then nodded to his colleague. "Have the carriage brought round immediately."

"Very good, sir."

When the man had gone, he looked again at Della, his voice more human than it had been all that long dreary afternoon.

"These things take time but you will be hearing in due course that your father has been granted a pardon. I regret that it has come too late."

"So do I," she breathed, "so do I. Is there absolutely no hope?"

"So far as we are aware nobody survived and it is now some months since the ship was lost. I would not care to hold out any hope except that the sea is unpredictable. Stranger things have happened."

"But are unlikely?"

"Very unlikely, I am afraid."

She went with him to the door and saw him leave with relief. The black closed carriage was the one she had passed on the previous day and thought of little significance. It now seemed very far away.

She went up to tell her uncle of the Inspector's departure and found him calmer and more composed than she had anticipated. Beneath that diffident manner there was a hidden strength only waiting for necessity to call it into being.

When she came down again Crosby was waiting for her, asking about the serving of the evening meal.

"The Master eats very plainly, Miss, and Cook has been greatly upset and disturbed."

"Then I shall eat very plainly too. Do whatever you think best," she said wearily.

"I have taken the liberty of lighting the fire in the small sitting room. I thought you would prefer that to the dining room."

"Oh yes please." She felt as if nothing could persuade her to enter that room of death again.

It was a pretty room on the first floor unlike the rest of the house, with light graceful furniture of an earlier time, but it had a forlorn unused look as if no one entered it except the maids to wipe a hasty duster over the furniture. The chill seemed to have eaten into her as if she would never be warm again. She crouched as close to the fire as she could and wondered if this could have been her mother's room where she had sat and dreamed of the man who had stolen her heart until the time came when she had abandoned it for ever. There was a book on the low table as if left there by the last occupant, a slim book in finely tooled leather. They were poems of love and she turned the pages at random until her eye was caught by one of her father's favourites –

> 'Know that love is a careless child
> And forgets promise past . . .
>
> He is won with a world of despair
> And is lost with a toy . . .'

Walter Ralegh, that other passionate adventurer, had known all about the pain and ecstasy of love three hundred years ago, just as her father had, and now she herself.

A tray of food was brought and she forced herself to eat a little and drink the glass of wine that had been thoughtfully provided by Crosby and then she sat on, unwilling to leave the fire for the cold and unwelcoming bedroom. She was half dozing in the warmth when she was roused by a hammering at the door downstairs. Tom, she thought, it must be Tom, come back as he had promised. She dreaded what he might have to tell her but could not stop herself flying down the stairs ahead of Crosby whose stiff bones could not move so quickly.

She stared at the cloaked figure sprinkled with light snow and the joyous exclamation died on her lips.

It was not Tom who stood there, but Bret, his face in shadow looking ten years older. She stepped back to let him enter and then slammed the door against the dark cold night.

"What is it? You look . . . what has happened?"

"Tom asked me to come. He thought you would want to know."

"Know what?"

"He has found Sylvia."

"Found her?"

"He took her out of the Wharfe down below the Strid. She was caught against some rocks otherwise her body might never have been discovered. The police must already have been alerted. They were waiting to question Tom and Sylvia about Oliver when we got back to Rokeby Hall."

He paused and she watched his face. It seemed as if moment by moment the hideous shadows gathered and lengthened about the events of the day.

"Go on," she whispered. "There's more, isn't there?"

"Yes. She had suffered a heavy blow on the back of the head. The water had washed away the blood of course but Dr Withers found it when he was called in to examine the body."

She was staring at him. "And they think – that it could be Tom – no, no, no! I will never believe it."

"Nor I but all he could say was that he searched for her till it was dark and it was not until Sheba came home, bruised, bloody and soaking wet that he went out again to the river and found her."

"Oh my God, poor Sylvia!" For a moment she was so shaken she could hardly speak. Was it possible that in wild panic she had ridden away and made that crazy leap across the Strid? She said slowly, "She was always fascinated by that rocky chasm.

She told me once. She could have slipped and fallen. It will be icy there now. It could have been accidental."

"That's what we thought but those others – even Dr Withers – "

"They believe Tom followed after her and when he came up with her at last, killed her and threw her body into the river. Is that what they think?"

"They didn't say so but I could see the doubt in their faces and so could Tom."

"I must go to him."

"No, Della, no. He doesn't want that, not now, not yet, and in any case it's very late and beginning to snow. We could never get through."

"Tomorrow then, I'm going tomorrow whatever happens. There's the child, Bret, you must understand that, a small boy suffering from the shock of his mother's death and Nanny Roberts half crazy with grief."

"Very well, we will go tomorrow. I'll take you back myself if I can stay here for the night. I don't want any bed, just somewhere warm to rest for a few hours."

"Yes, of course. You must be frozen. My uncle would wish you to stay."

She took the heavy cloak from him and gave it to Crosby. "Find some food please and hot coffee and then take it with the brandy to the small sitting room."

"Yes, Miss. It is a sad day for all of us, Mr Bret."

"Yes, Crosby, a terrible day."

When the old man had left them, Della said hesitantly, "Oliver is still here. The police have not taken him away yet. Do you want to see him?"

A spasm crossed his face and he shivered. "No, no, I couldn't. I've always hated death – even if it is only one of the dogs." He looked appealingly at her like a small boy yearning to be comforted. "You do understand, Della?"

"Yes, I understand."

She sat with him in that quiet room, talking very little while he drank the coffee and poured himself a generous measure of brandy.

"I can't believe that Oliver is dead," he said leaning forward nursing the glass in both hands and staring into the fire. "I've known him ever since I was at school. He was years older than me, one of the bloods along with Tom. Once he knocked down

283

some great brute who was bullying me – youngsters always go through hell for the first few terms – and after that he became a kind of hero."

"And went on being something of a hero after school," she said with a smile.

"Yes, I suppose he did. That's why I could never tell you . . . Oh God, Della, if you knew what a load it's been on my mind ever since you came up here." He put down the glass and got up, taking a few steps across the room and then swinging round to face her. "I can't keep it back any longer. It's about that night . . ."

She guessed at once what he was going to say. "It's all right, Bret. I know what happened now. Oliver told me himself and I know that the police have reopened the case and were tracking him down. That's why he was going abroad. Even if Sylvia had not done what she did, he might not have escaped. The Detective Inspector was here this afternoon with a warrant for his arrest."

A tremor of alarm crossed his face. "He was here already. Did he say what they intend to do? Will it all have to come out?"

"I don't know. I hope not for my uncle's sake. If he is dead, they can't bring him to trial."

"No, I suppose not." He paused uncertainly and then went on with an effort. "Did Oliver tell you everything? Did he tell you about me?"

"You? Why should he say anything about you?"

"I was there. It was my fault that it all happened."

She looked up at him and quite suddenly it was as if everything fell into place, Bret's recognition of the jewelled skull, his evasions, Martha's anxiety about her wayward brother's obsessive gambling.

She said quietly, "I think you'd better tell me everything, all the things Oliver left out. What really happened?"

He came to sit down again, the firelight playing on the boyish face with its look of fatigue and strain. The words began to pour out as if it was a relief to unburden himself and the picture grew as she listened.

"It was Jack Hughes who began it. None of us liked him and he'd been losing night after night all that week. He was mad keen for a chance to win something back. Oliver said 'Why not?' and fixed it up, just the four of us. Your father wasn't in it to start with. I didn't know him at all. Then one of the four

284

backed out and Oliver said, 'I know the very fellow. He's a relative of mine and game for anything,' and so it was arranged."

He paused and she wondered if Oliver, with that sardonic twist of his, had deliberately engineered that meeting.

"It was the worst night I've ever lived through," whispered Bret. "Nothing went right for me yet I kept on hoping and hoping. Can you understand that, Della, can you? You are so certain that the luck must change and it does sometimes, but not that night, and yet I couldn't stop myself going on and on. It's like a fever when it takes you. You can think of nothing else. I lost everything, I put myself hopelessly in debt, and at last in a kind of crazy desperation I staked Farley Grange and when I lost that too, that sneering devil Jack Hughes, whose banker father could have paid all *his* debts ten times over, began to laugh. I realized then what I'd done. I'd ruined not only myself but Martha and the home she loved above all things. I'd left Aunt Lavvy penniless and all our dependants. I think for a moment I lost my wits entirely. All I could see was that hateful grinning face gloating over my folly. The pistol was there to my hand and loaded because that afternoon Oliver and I had spent at the shooting gallery. I cocked it. Oliver shouted, 'Stop, you damed fool!' and made a grab to take the pistol from me and his finger must have slipped. The next thing I knew Jack Hughes was lying on the floor, blood all over the place and your father kneeling beside him. He was saying, 'We must get a doctor.' I couldn't think what to do and it was Oliver who silenced him. He arranged everything and to my shame I let him do it. He shut up my protest saying, 'Don't worry about my uncle. He's a damned clever fellow. He can get himself out of anything far easier than we can.' Afterwards, when it came to the trial, I knew I ought to speak out and I couldn't. I wrote a letter to the police and tore it up. I was afraid, not only for myself, but for Oliver and for Martha too. I could see her face condemning me and did not know how I could bear it. You do see that, don't you?"

She did not answer. It had been too sudden and too unexpected and he buried his face in his hands with a half sob.

She sat for a long moment staring in front of her and seeing it all so clearly: the boy with the fatal weakness, so easily influenced by Oliver who had always been the stronger of the two, who had always befriended him even in this last extremity, but who saw it as a heaven-sent chance to satisfy the need for revenge that he had nursed inside him for almost all his life; and her father, accepting it as payment for that nagging debt, that redemption of honour that perhaps had dogged him ever since he and her mother had fled from Larksghyll. What a tangle of motives and how obvious it all seemed, now she knew the whole story.

Bret raised his head. "Can you ever forgive me?"

"Forgive? I don't know. When it first happened, I thought there could be nothing bad enough to punish those responsible for my father's misery but you can't go on letting hate and vengeance fester for ever."

"When you came here, it seemed like destiny taking a hand in our lives," said Bret with pathetic eagerness. "I thought now I can make reparation. There has only been one thing holding me back from asking you to be my wife and that was knowing that I would have to tell you the truth first and until now I could not bring myself to do that. Now I have." He paused, his eyes on her face. "What would you have said if I had asked you to marry me?"

"I think you know, don't you? I like Martha and Aunt Lavinia, and Farley Grange is the most beautiful house I've ever seen, but that's not enough, is it?"

"I have thought of it over and over again," he said earnestly. "I could make it enough, Della, I know I could."

"No, Bret, no. Not for me."

He turned away his head. "It's Tom, isn't it?"

"I'm not answering that." She got up then and put a hand on his shoulder. "It must have been painful for you but I'm glad you've told me. I'm going to leave you now. We must have a few hours rest before we go back to Castlebridge."

He seized her hand and kissed it. "I wish you'd stay. I feel so – so lost." He shivered. "I've never liked this house, ever since Oliver first invited me here."

He was like a child crying in the night begging to be reassured but the day had lasted too long. She could endure no more. She shook her head and went quickly.

Crosby must have ordered a fire to be lit in the room that had been allotted to her and a lamp glowed softly on the dressing table. For the first time she felt that Larksghyll had accepted her and she was no longer an unwelcome stranger. It was strangely comforting.

She did not undress, only took off her riding skirt and lay down on the bed, pulling the blankets over her. The events of the day, the horror of Oliver's death, even the revelation of Bret's part in her father's condemnation, were all swallowed up in her anxiety about Tom. Where was he now? How was he feeling? She tried to reach out to him and couldn't. It was as if the drowned body of his wife lay between them. She thought she would lie awake till morning, but after a while fatigue swept up in a black tide and thankfully carried her with it into oblivion.

18

It was noon by the time they reached Rokeby Hall and a light snow was still falling when they rode up the drive. The curtains had been drawn and the house had a blind look, as if it was shut up with its secrets against the outside world. A carriage stood outside, the same small black carriage with the arms on the door that had come to Larksghyll. Rob came to take the horses as Della slid from the saddle.

Bret said, "I won't stay. Martha will be anxious. Tell Tom we will be with him if he needs us."

Della nodded and ran up the steps. Mrs Fenton must have been in the hall. She opened the door, her face chalk white, her eyes bitterly hostile. Della pushed past her. Tom was coming out of his study. She could not stop herself. She ran to him with outstretched hands.

"I'm so desperately sorry . . ." and then she paused checked by the frozen look on his face. Too late she saw Detective Inspector Becket behind him with another man.

"I'm glad you've come back, Miss Lismore," Tom was speaking formally, "I'm sure that Nanny will be pleased to have your help with Peter."

"Yes, of course." She matched his tone. "I hoped to have been here earlier but the snow made the roads difficult."

Both policemen were regarding her gravely.

"Miss Lismore is my son's governess, gentlemen," went on Tom in the same neutral tone.

Inspector Becket nodded. "We met yesterday in rather difficult circumstances. Good morning, Miss Lismore."

"Good morning, Inspector."

She wondered if he was playing a game with her, when he knew perfectly well who she was but she said nothing more, only turned away and went quietly up the stairs.

It was a relief to strip off soiled clothes. She washed in cold water, unwilling to ring and face the servants yet. Dressed in her darkest dress, her hair neatly combed, every inch the humble governess, she went to the nursery. Nanny, her eyes swollen with weeping, was sitting by the fire while Peter sprawled on the rug surrounded by his boxes of coloured bricks listlessly piling one on top of the other.

He looked up as she opened the door, then silently scrambled to his feet, raced across the room and buried his head against her skirt. She put her arms around him, holding him tightly.

"I can't do nothing with him," whispered Nanny distractedly, "ever since they brought her ladyship home. He won't speak, won't utter a single word."

"It's shock, I expect. Did he actually see her?"

"Aye, he did. We happened to be going up the stairs and he ran back as they brought her in."

"Mamma was drownded," said a tiny muffled voice, "she was all wet . . ." and the small hands clutched at her.

"I know, darling, I know." She stroked his hair gently. "We must try not to think about it."

"Such a terrible, terrible thing to have happened," went on Nanny, "I can't hardly believe it even now. She was so beautiful, so full of life. When I see her lying there it doesn't seem true that she should be gone from us. Why should she do such a thing, why, why? It doesn't seem right." She lowered her voice. "And some of 'em are saying such wicked things, Miss, about her ladyship – and about the Master . . ."

"I have heard a great many rumours already, none of them true," she said crisply. "Nanny dear, why don't you go and rest? You look worn out. We'll have a talk about it later."

"I don't know as I ought, though it is true that I've been up best part of the night."

"I'm sure you have. You go now and have a nice lie down. I'll look after the boy."

All the rest of that day there were constant comings and goings in the house, but she was left alone in the nursery and no one called her for questioning. She knew that in the servants' quarters there was endless speculation hushed the instant she entered the kitchen and she guessed that this was merely a respite. Very soon she and Tom would be plunged into the midst of it and she dreaded to think what the consequences might be.

She had the greatest difficulty in getting Peter to sleep that evening. Usually so talkative and full of life, he had hardly spoken a word all day, only clinging to her obsessively and refusing to be left alone even for a few minutes. She could not persuade him to eat more than a mouthful of food and even his favourite chocolate cake did not tempt him.

The house was very silent when she came quietly out of the room at last with a sigh of relief. The police had not yet taken Sylvia's body to the mortuary and in some queer way the whole house seemed full of her presence, with the servants creeping about on tiptoe through the darkened rooms. There had been no opportunity to speak to Tom alone and, though she yearned to go to him, she thought it was wiser to keep a distance between them. The strain of the last two days was beginning to tell and she shivered with chill and an intense weariness. She went to bed early after a light supper in her own room and to her own surprise fell asleep almost immediately.

It must have been after midnight when something woke her. The room was very dark and she sat up alarmed as the door slowly opened. Then she saw the tiny figure in the long white nightshirt and was scrambling out of bed and gathering the child up in her arms. He was holding on to her, shaken by long heartbroken sobs. She wrapped a blanket around him and cradled him in her arms until at last the sobs died away and the shivering stopped. Presently she carried him back to the nursery and tucked him into bed, holding his hand and talking to him soothingly until he drowsed into sleep and she could gently free herself. She made up the dying fire as quietly as she could and was taking one last look at the sleeping boy when someone whispered her name.

In his dark dressing gown Tom was only a shadow in the doorway.

He said, "What's the trouble? I thought I heard someone moving about."

She put a finger to her lips and joined him outside, pulling the door to quietly.

"Peter had a bad nightmare. He saw his mother brought home and he has heard the servants talking."

"Oh God, I tried to keep it from him. I didn't know how to tell him. How can a child understand such a thing?"

"I think he may sleep now but it will take time and we shall need to be very patient with him."

She had not stopped to do more than throw a woollen shawl around her shoulders and she shivered in the draughty passage.

He said, "You're cold. You must go back to bed."

290

"Yes," but she did not want to leave him yet. It was the first contact they had had since everything had crashed around them. "Tom, what is going to happen?"

"Your guess is as good as mine. I can't seem to take it in, even now." He passed a hand over his face. "What could have happened between her and Oliver? She must have been terrified when she saw what she had done."

"Did she fall into the river, Tom, or did she kill herself?"

"That's something we shall never know and was it I who drove her to it? That's what is haunting me. I never even thought of the river till Rob came to tell me that Sheba had come back to the stable. The mare must have fought her way to the bank, leaving Sylvia to drown." He paused. "I keep thinking of that over and over again. You know what they are hinting at, don't you?"

"Bret told me."

"It's so damnably plausible. I can see how their minds work. Husband kills wife in jealous rage – you can read the headline, can't you? And the night before we had quarrelled stupidly, over nothing important, but the servants may well have overheard it."

"They can't prove anything against you."

"Maybe not, but mud sticks. You must go away from here, Della, go now before any of it clings to you."

"I'm not afraid and I'm not going to be driven away by scandalmongers," she said bravely.

He was looking down at her, the dim light of the shaded lamp casting queer shadows across his face and she was suddenly afraid.

"I love you, Tom," she whispered urgently. "You do know that, don't you?"

"Yes, I know, but I wish . . ."

"And I'm with you all the way."

She reached up and kissed him, no passion, only longing to give comfort. He pulled her against him holding her tightly, both of them so badly in need of reassurance that it might have gone further if it had not been for a whimpering cry from the room behind them.

Della freed herself. "I'll go to him."

"No, you must have your rest. I'll stay with him for a while."

Tom cupped her face between his two hands and kissed her gently, then watched her go quickly to her room before he turned into the nursery.

Mrs Fenton from the floor above had seen the two figures meet and embrace. She had always known it, she had warned her, hadn't she, and a bitter jealousy on behalf of her dead mistress rose up in her throat like gall.

Della was up early the next morning and after breakfast she saw the horsedrawn police ambulance outside. Tom had gone out to the men and she nerved herself to go into the bedroom. It seemed somehow heartless to let Sylvia be carried out of the house without another woman to share the indignity. The curtains had been closely drawn and the room was very dark. Two candles had been lit beside the bed and had burned into long shrouds of wax. The embroidered sheet had been turned back so that only the face was visible, marble white framed by the pale gold hair, incredibly innocent and beautiful. She stood looking down at her, stirred by pity. "He is won with a world of despair" – how true that had been of Sylvia's love for Oliver. She thought of the night she had come to Rokeby Hall and seen her for the first time, fragile and lovely. Something had flared between them then and now it was finished – or was it? She had gone out of Tom's life but the shadow was there still. She was just about to replace the sheet over the quiet face when a hand gripped her wrist like a vice.

"Don't dare to touch her!"

She looked up to see Mrs Fenton standing close beside her.

"What are you doing here?" she went on in a harsh whisper. "Have you come to gloat over what you have done?"

"I came because the police are here already."

"The cruelty of it that she should be lying there dead and cold and all because of you." There was a hint of obsession in the eyes glittering in the flickering light of the candles and she still held Della's wrist in a painful grip. "You think he is yours, don't you? You believe you've won, but I'll see you pay for it. I'll make sure they know, that everyone knows, what wickedness has been going on in this house and how much he wanted to be rid of her."

"You're crazy. Nothing has been going on, nothing at all," said Della sharply, wrenching her wrist away. "You had better be careful what you say."

"Oh I'll be careful, don't you worry." She thrust her face close. "I'm not a soft fool like that Nanny Roberts toadying up to you. He was never worthy of her, never. I saw that from the very start and I told her so. He is beginning to realize it now. He'll find out how much he has been tricked and he'll suffer for it, he'll *suffer* for it!"

Her voice rose and then broke off abruptly as the door opened and she shrank back as Tom came in.

He said curtly, "What are you doing here, Mrs Fenton?"

"I came to see that all was ready, sir."

"Very well. You may go now."

She raised her head. "I'd like to give in my notice, sir."

"If you must, Mrs Fenton, but this is hardly the time. Come to me later."

"I'd like to go now, today."

"Whenever you wish, but please leave me now."

It seemed as if she would defy him but his stony face daunted her and she went reluctantly out of the room. After a moment Della followed her, guessing that at this time he wanted to be alone with his dead.

She had always been aware of Mrs Fenton's dislike but had not realized how deep and prejudiced her devotion to Sylvia was, and it troubled her. She wondered if perhaps the housekeeper had spoken rashly out of a rush of emotion for her dead mistress, but she was wrong. Mrs Fenton stuck to her decision. Tom was shut away for most of the day but Della heard it from Rose when she brought up nursery tea.

"That Mrs Fenton has packed her traps and gone off, Miss, and I can't say I'm sorry. If you ask me, Master was glad to see her go an' all. Paid her off, he did, and didn't even ask that she serve out her notice."

"How will you manage?"

"We did well enough in old Mr Clifford's time and we'll carry on now," said Rose sturdily. "Cook's been in service here since the Master were born, then that Mrs Fenton comes along with her ladyship and tries to change everything. Never did care for her grand airs. She were always on about how much better things were done at Sterndale Castle till we were fair sick and tired of hearing about it. It'll be a right treat to be rid of her."

That might be true of the servants but the abrupt departure of the housekeeper so closely connected with Sylvia was bound to cause unpleasant comment. Tom was curt when Della spoke to him about it that evening.

"The woman was insolent," he said briefly. "I would have dismissed her in any case and since she chose to leave at once, I let her go and was glad of it."

It was Martha who brought it up again the very next afternoon. Tom had gone off to the mill and Nanny was with Peter, so Della received her alone. Rose brought tea and biscuits and Martha waited until the door was shut and then stopped Della as she prepared to pour the tea.

"Before you do that there is something I must say to you." Martha, who was always so calm and matter of fact, was looking down at her hands knotted together in her lap before she went on hesitantly. "I don't find this easy to say but Bret has confessed everything. I need hardly tell you how badly I feel about it. That *my* brother should allow himself to become mixed up in such a – such a shocking affair and that it should be your father – it has upset me terribly. I've always been aware of his weakness; I've warned him about it again and again. I've always felt that Oliver's influence was far too strong – I suppose I shouldn't say that to you seeing that he was your cousin – but he was well able to take care of himself whereas Bret . . ." She looked up. "It's been so difficult to go on preaching and preaching and I know only too well how Bret has resented it."

Della had never seen her so greatly agitated. It was so easy to understand how the young man had rebelled against the elder sister who could be so hard and was yet so well meaning.

"Don't distress yourself," she said gently. "It is over now. Oliver is dead and it is finished. Nothing can now bring my father back."

"But you must feel so bitter against Bret, against them both."

"No, I did once, but not any longer and in Oliver's case there were family circumstances – " she paused, unable to speak yet of a past that was still so raw in her memory. "I can't explain now, Martha, perhaps one day I will be able to tell you. I only hope that Bret's part in it will never have to be made known."

"You could have told the Detective Inspector everything."

"I could but what good would it have done?"

It was queer, she thought, how something that had been of such vital importance now seemed to have become strangely remote compared with what was happening between herself and Tom.

"I'm grateful," breathed Martha, "truly grateful. Bret has

always been my little brother. Ever since our parents died I've known that I must look after him and it has not always been easy. This – this horrible affair has made me feel that I have failed completely in everything that I've tried so hard to do."

"No, Martha, no, you mustn't think that. You have been splendid. Nobody can be totally responsible for another's actions. Perhaps he will have learned something from it."

"Perhaps, we must hope so." Martha managed a faint smile. "I've not dared to tell Aunt Lavinia. She has such strict notions of truth and honour I think she might have insisted on a public confession."

"In the present circumstances I think that would be a little too much, don't you?"

Martha accepted a cup of tea and sipped it slowly before she said, "I hear that Mrs Fenton has left very suddenly."

"Yes. She was devoted to Mrs Clifford and is naturally very distressed."

"Did you know that she has not gone from Castlebridge? She is staying in the town and making some absurd allegations about Sylvia's death."

"How do you know?"

"Mary Ann was visiting her mother and came home full of it." She put down her cup. "Did you know that Sylvia was pregnant? Dr Withers had it from the police surgeon."

"Yes, I did know. She told me."

"It will have to come out at the inquest." Martha lowered her voice to a whisper. "If it wasn't Tom's child, it could go against him."

"Yes."

"Was it?"

"I don't know."

"Della," Martha went on urgently, "you shouldn't stay here now that Mrs Fenton has left. There will be talk, scandalous talk, that could affect both you and Tom. You don't know what it is like in a shut-in community like this."

"Oh yes, I do, Martha. I've experienced it already and I'm not going to be intimidated by it. Is this a time to desert Tom, to abandon his child? Peter has been greatly disturbed. He saw his mother carried into the house. He doesn't understand what has happened but it haunts him and for some reason he has more trust in me than in Nanny Roberts."

"I was going to suggest that you come to us at Farley Grange.

Bret admires you so much and Aunt Lavvy is fond of you."

"It's kind of you. I appreciate it, but I've made up my mind. I'm not running away with my tail between my legs when I am guilty of nothing. As long as I can be of use to Tom then I intend to stay. If he wants to be rid of me, then it will be time for me to go."

She refused obstinately to be persuaded, but, after Martha had left, she wondered if she had been right. Was she determined to stay because of Peter or was it Tom that mattered so desperately? A huge gulf seemed to have opened up between them which she could not bridge.

She did not realize that a man normally as open, straight-forward and honest as Tom had been plunged into a turmoil of conflicting emotions that he found hard to cope with. The discovery of his love for Della had been followed so swiftly by the certainty of his wife's infidelity – two months pregnant, the doctor had said, and it was Oliver's child, it had to be – it must have been fear that sent her running frantically to Larksghyll, that had led to her cruel death among the rocks of the river – more and more he became convinced that the guilt lay in him. By his own blindness he had brought Oliver to death and his wife to an agony of mind that made him sick to contemplate. He felt as guilty as if he had actually struck that blow and thrown her body into the black water. He needed time to steady his mind against his whirling thoughts and he was not being given time.

In the next week or two events moved very swiftly, following one another with a frightening inevitability. For months now Della had lived in the closed atmosphere of Rokeby Hall absorbed in Tom, in the little boy, in Sylvia's reaction and her own tormented feelings, so that she was unaware of what had been happening in the outside world and how it might affect them.

It was only a day or so after Martha's visit that she took a walk down to Castlebridge to fetch a draught from Dr Withers which he had strongly recommended to calm Peter's nervous fits of crying and persistent nightmares. One of the servants could have easily gone but she welcomed the walk. It was a grey day, bitingly cold but dry, and she walked briskly. She collected the medicine and stopped to have a few words with Abbie. On the way back she ran into a party of women coming out of the mill gates from the early shift. They blocked her path staring at her with undisguised hostility. She paused uncertainly with unpleasant memories of that last encounter some months before. It was a long moment before they parted silently and let her through and it took courage not to run but to walk steadily with head held high.

Once past them she quickened her steps and turned down a side lane before she became aware that one of the women had separated herself from the others and had come up beside her, plucking at her arm. Nervously she tried to pull away and then saw that it was Jane Carter.

"Miss Lismore, may I speak to you for a minute?" she said in an urgent whisper. "Not here," she gave a quick look behind her, "in my place. It's close by."

She pulled Della along and into the door of one of the small houses running like a ribbon down the narrow road. It was a poorly furnished place but neat and clean enough. Once inside she pushed the door shut.

She said breathlessly, "I didn't like to come up to the Hall with her ladyship gone and all the trouble but I thought I must warn the Master."

"Warn Mr Clifford? What do you mean?"

"It's about Dan, Miss. He were here t'other night."

"Your husband?"

"Aye and he were right pleased with himself. He's been behind all that's been happening at t'mill this past week."

"What has been happening?"

"Didn't you know? Didn't Master tell you? One of them big machines was smashed two nights ago – and seemingly no one there so they couldn't prove owt, try as they would and now he's planning something else against t'Master. You see he en't never forgiven him for dismissing him and taking Mary Ann away – not that he ever wanted her but he just hated to let her go – he goes on and on about it till sometimes I think he's not quite right in the head but he's my husband and I can't let him go on to commit murder."

"Murder?"

"Aye, it could come to that. Some time soon there's to be a big rally of men from all parts out on moor and then they'll be marching on Castlebridge and the mill. He'd kill me if he knew what I was saying but Master has been good to me and Mary Ann – I've known him since he were a little lad and I were right

297

fond of his father – I'd not see harm come to him 'cos of Dan. I thought if you were to tell him, then he would be prepared, see?"

"Yes, I do see, Mrs Carter. I'd better go now and thank you for telling me. I'll make sure that Mr Clifford knows."

"Take care how you go now. I'd not let them others think as I was giving anything away."

They looked carefully up and down the road before she slipped out. She thought about it all the way home and went resolutely down to speak to Tom as soon as he returned from the mill. He was in his study where he had taken to sitting each evening, even having his meals served there, and he listened quietly, almost indifferently, to what she was saying.

"You didn't tell me you'd had all this trouble with the mill," she said reproachfully.

"I didn't see why you should be worried."

"But I want to share it with you, Tom."

He swung around to face her. "Della, you should go away from here."

"Do you want me to go?"

"That has nothing to do with it. I am concerned for your safety."

"Safety?"

"There's a queer feeling running through Castlebridge," he said with a twisted smile. "It seems that I have become something of a monster, conniving with my mistress to murder my wife."

"But that's sheer nonsense. Nobody could believe such a thing of you."

"No one with any sense, but unfortunately mobs take little heed of sense."

"All the more reason why I shouldn't run away. You said that yourself, don't you remember, when we received that filthy letter."

"That was different. My wife was still alive."

And still stood between them more powerful in death than she had been in life.

She said quietly, "In any case I cannot go from here until the business with Oliver is brought to a conclusion."

"I'd almost forgotten about that," he said wearily. "Inspector Becket told me something of it. It must have been a bitter discovery for you to find your own cousin had been the

298

cause of your father's ruin."

"There were reasons."

One day she must tell him exactly what had happened but not now, he had troubles enough of his own.

He turned away from her, leaning one hand against the mantel. "I'm beginning to believe I never really knew Oliver or my wife. I've lived in some kind of an idiot's paradise."

"You will remember what Jane Carter told me. You will take care."

"There's not a great deal one can do," he said wryly. "I've been expecting something of the sort for months now. In Leeds and Bradford the police have proved quite inadequate to control the rioters and they've been obliged to call in the military. I had thought it might have been in the spring but I was wrong. The hard winter is bringing matters to a head and Castlebridge won't escape."

She thought he sounded almost glad as if it was easier to fight his way out of that kind of battle than deal with the miasma of personal betrayal and suspicion that dogged him now.

He looked desperately strained and tired so that she longed to put her arms around him and comfort him as she comforted his son but sensed that now was not the time but when all this was over . . . she dared not let her thoughts run ahead, it was best to take each day as it came.

The trial of a man already dead, the pardon of a prisoner unjustly condemned and unfortunately perished at sea all took place in London and made very little impact on the people of Castlebridge to whom anyone living only five miles away was a foreigner. Even the enquiry into the shooting which took place in Bradford and resulted in a verdict of accidental death aroused small interest. What was being waited for with the utmost anticipation was the inquest on the Master's wife, the lovely Lady Sylvia. In one of those queer switches of public opinion, her arrogance, her high-handed ways, even her contempt for the mill folk, were all forgotten. She had become a tragic victim. What could the Master have done to force her to run to his friend begging for help and send all that frail beauty to a savage death in the rockstrewn waters of the river? In the mill, at street corners and by cottage fires, it was talked over endlessly and grew in the telling, especially among the women. Only one or two sturdy souls among husbands and fathers said

299

obstinately, "Stop yapping about it, you silly bitch. T'Master's decent enough, always has been, he wouldn't never do a thing like that and as for her ladyship, pretty as a picture maybe, but flighty as they come, you mark my words!"

Oliver's funeral took place a week before the inquest on Sylvia was to be held and Della knew she could not leave her uncle to face it alone.

Tom said, "I shall not attend myself but you must take the carriage. I am not too well acquainted with your uncle but I would like to show respect."

So Rob drove her over to the small church close beside Larksghyll and she stood beside her uncle, feeling as remote as if it were all happening to someone else, and it was not her enigmatic sardonic cousin who lay in the narrow box they were lowering into the earth. There was not a great number of carriages and most of them came out of respect for George Craven. Oliver had spent very little time in his family home since he had grown up.

Martha was there with Bret, who looked pale and drawn. He gazed beseechingly at Della, but she shook her head silently and he followed his sister to the carriage.

When they were walking away from the church she glanced back once to the lonely grave and saw a tall bearded man who stood bareheaded, looking down at it and wondered who he was. He didn't come back to Larksghyll where she had to stand with her uncle greeting men and women she didn't know who eyed her with avid curiosity, sipping Madeira and speaking together in suitably hushed voices.

She thought for one moment that it would have been a relief to stay on in the old house and escape for a few days from the fraught atmosphere of the Hall, but that would have been cowardice. She kissed her uncle, promised to come again soon and let Rob drive her back to face whatever was to come. She had made her choice and she would see it through whatever the cost.

19

The inquest on Sylvia Clifford was held in the Castlebridge inn which was the largest room available and was crammed to the doors, even spilling outside into the yard. Lord Sterndale was not there. He had been in Paris when the news reached him and the shock and distress at his daughter's death brought on a fever which made his return to England out of the question. Della thought Tom was relieved at not having to cope with his father-in-law at this wretched moment. The Coroner was Sir Anthony Hunter, the local Justice of the Peace, one of the landed gentry who had a vast contempt for those in trade, knew Sylvia's father personally and was aware of a strong distaste for the whole unsavoury affair. After all Lady Sylvia Farringford was one of his own class even if she had married beneath her – no doubt that millowning fellow had driven the poor girl to desperation – and he was extremely anxious to avoid a verdict of suicide. He questioned witnesses relentlessly and the servants, bewildered and slow-witted, unintentionally gave a false impression of a beautiful young woman tied into an unhappy marriage with a husband who neglected her and showed a marked preference for a young woman in his employ whom he deliberately and callously introduced into his own household.

Only one or two snatches of the questioning stood out in Della's memory during that long day. It was Mrs Fenton who drew the most damning picture. She spoke out calmly and clearly, every inch the loyal family servant.

"I warned her ladyship," she went on, "of what was going on while she was away in London, but she would not believe me. She trusted her husband implicitly."

"And yet it seems she ran away to take refuge with a neighbour and friend where a most unfortunate accident took place."

"To my certain knowledge, sir," she continued with every appearance of honesty, "she quarrelled bitterly with her

301

husband the night before and in despair she took the pistol with the intention of taking her own life. Mr Craven tried to prevent her with tragic results. Mr Clifford followed after her with what motive I cannot imagine and *that* girl went with him."

"You mean the young woman who is acting as his son's governess?"

"A young person who knows exactly what she wants and is quite ruthless in pursuing it," said Mrs Fenton vindictively.

"Are you suggesting that Mr Clifford and this – this young person may have had the intention of getting rid of her once and for all? I am afraid there is no proof of any such motive but the doubts must remain. Thank you, Mrs Fenton. You have helped us considerably. You may step down."

She threw Della a triumphant glance as she passed her. It had been a clever combination of half-truths and all the more damning for that.

Sir Anthony treated Tom with the condescending manner he might have used towards one of the tradesmen who supplied him with groceries. Della could see how furiously he resented it. He answered the questions put to him as curtly as possible.

"It would appear that your wife felt that you neglected her. I understand you never accompanied her on her journeys away from Castlebridge."

"A mill does not run itself and it provides us with the means to live. I could not afford to be away for weeks at a time but I was always willing to allow her freedom to come and go as she wished."

"And maybe it gave you the opportunity to indulge your preference for the pretty governess you had engaged to teach your son."

"I deny that – I deny it absolutely."

A rustle of sound ran all round the court and Sir Anthony glanced down at the papers before him.

"Very well. It has been implied by some of the witnesses that there may have been familiarity between your wife and a certain Oliver Craven who was a personal friend to you both. Did you know of this?"

"I knew she was fond of Oliver but then we both were. I have known him most of my life."

"It would appear from the doctor's report that your wife was pregnant at the time of her death. Were you aware of this?"

"No."

"Was this child yours?"

Tom hesitated. He was under oath and yet to speak the truth would shame Sylvia before all these listeners greedily looking for scandal. He could not do it. He could not blacken her when she was beyond all help. He compromised.

"I had no reason to think otherwise."

"It is not within the power of this court to make accusations but I feel obliged to put the question to you. Did you on that fatal day either accidentally or deliberately strike your wife in such a way as to cause her to fall to her death in the river?"

Tom raised his head, his eyes going challengingly all round the silent court from jury to avidly listening public.

"No, I did not."

The questioning went on painstakingly for another hour or so but the jury, firmly led by Sir Anthony and in the absence of any kind of proof one way or the other, brought in a verdict of accidental death.

Della, pushing her way out through the crowded court, was thankful that Dr Withers had come to her side. She could see Tom ahead of them thrusting his way forward looking neither to right nor left. There was a bunch of ruffians gathered at the gates who shouted, "Murderer!" accompanying it with other words of abuse which she hardly understood but of which the meaning was plain. He took absolutely no notice but reached the carriage that Rob had brought around and stepped into it. As it moved forward someone threw a large stone. It smashed through the window and one of the horses whinneyed and tried to rear. Rob, swearing under his breath, brought them under control and started forward so that the mob still muttering threatening abuse were obliged to scatter in front of them.

"How can they be so vile!" exclaimed Della. "It's so brutal, so unjust."

"Tom will weather it. He's a good deal tougher than some of them," said Dr Withers. "How did you come here, my dear? You ought not to walk home alone."

Bret had come up on her other side. "I've got the dog cart. I'll take Della back to the Hall."

"Mind you take care of her," said the doctor. "There's an ugly temper amongst these wretched layabouts."

It took time to get through the yard to where he had left the dog cart but Bret, young as he was, was still the squire of Farley Grange and his sister was greatly respected. They might mutter

303

and stare but they fell back grudgingly and let them through. He tossed a shilling to the boy holding the horse and helped her into the cart. Then he took the reins and they set off.

"I'm so thankful you and Dr Withers were there," she said, breaking the silence between them as they drew away from the crowd.

"I suppose you've a pretty low opinion of me," he said gloomily staring straight ahead. "I know Martha has. She has made that very plain."

"Oh Bret," she said with exasperation, "for heaven's sake stop being sorry for yourself! Just be thankful that it's not been worse for you." Then because he looked so hangdog, so boyishly woebegone, she felt sorry for him. "Don't take it so much to heart. I daresay every one of us has something to be ashamed of if the truth were known."

"That ought to make me feel better but it doesn't," he gave the horse an impatient flick with his whip. "I suppose you'll be leaving Castlebridge very soon now."

Would she? The prospect suddenly became very bleak. She didn't reply and he went on eagerly. "Before you go I wish you would come and stay with us at the Grange. Martha would like it very much and so would I."

She knew he was looking for a prop, someone who would give him back the self-esteem so badly bruised by Oliver's death but Bret must learn to stand on his own feet.

"No, Bret, no. I'm grateful but it's not possible."

If she went anywhere it would be to her uncle at Larksghyll, but better to make a clean break, no half-measures, no hanging on to something that seemed to have died between her and Tom.

He left her at the door of the Hall.

"Martha will be anxious to hear the results of the inquest. She would have come but Aunt Lavvy is not so well."

"Remember me to them both."

"I will."

She watched him for a moment and then sighed as she went into the house. Nanny would be eager to hear every detail and she did not relish going over and over all the events of that long tiring day.

As she entered the Hall, Tom was coming down the stairs.

"Oh there you are," he said, "I was worried about you. You should have come with me in the carriage."

"Far better not. Dr Withers was there, so I was not alone and Bret brought me home, but he wouldn't stay." She went to pass him. "Excuse me. I must go to Peter."

"No, don't go, not yet." He caught at her arm. "I want to speak to you."

"Now?"

"If you don't mind."

She followed him into the study, untying the ribbons of her bonnet. A fire was burning brightly on the hearth and a lamp had been lit and glowed on his desk. When he turned she saw that there was an oozing cut on his cheek where the smashed glass must have struck him.

He said, "Come to the fire. You must be cold. I think we shall have more snow soon."

She let the heavy cloak fall from her shoulders, looking very slim and young in the simple black gown she had made for herself in these last weeks. She crossed to the hearthrug and spread her hands to the warmth.

"I'm so thankful the jury brought in the verdict they did."

"Yes, it was a relief. I hardly knew what to expect – suicide perhaps or murder by person or persons unknown."

"That would have been impossible."

"It's what everyone in that court seemed to expect," he said dryly.

"That's how you feel today but it will pass, Tom, I'm sure it will. No one could possibly believe such a thing of you. They will forget very soon."

"They may but I won't."

He sighed bending down to put another log on the fire and then stirring it with his foot so that it flared up.

"Della, why didn't you tell me that Sylvia was pregnant?"

The question took her by surprise. "How did you know that?"

"Never mind how. Why did you say nothing?"

She paused to find the right words. "It was not for me to tell you. It was surely something between you and her."

"Even when it was not my child?"

"How could I know that? I thought – I believed that you and she . . ."

"How could you think that after you and I had been – had been so close? You must have realized how it had been for months between Sylvia and me."

305

And because she *had* doubted, because the very thought had been so painful, she turned on him.

"What difference would it have made if I had told you?"

"All the difference in the world. Can't you see that? I know now what was driving her crazy. She trusted Oliver and he betrayed her trust. Can't you realize that telling you must have been a cry for help?"

"It was nothing of the kind. She wanted nothing from me."

She thought of that day beside the Strid. It had been meant to hurt, to make her doubt him, she was certain of that, but she could not bring herself to say it to him.

"What would you have done if you *had* known?" she went on. "Kept her beside you, fathered Oliver's child?"

"How do I know now, but I could have done something. It tortures me to think that she dare not come to me for help, that I left her to the mercy of a man who used her like a plaything and then when it pleased him threw her aside. My God, if you knew how I felt when I took her out of the water, when I saw all that beauty battered and broken by those damned rocks, the very thought that she had ridden the mare into that chasm, what she must have suffered in those last moments . . ." he could not go on. He turned away so that she could not see his face.

And she did know, she saw it very clearly, saw him weeping over Sylvia, all the love he had once felt for her must have come flooding back and Della felt a chill run through her because the dead have a power stronger than the living over a sensitive man, shocked and distraught.

In the silence a log fell with a small crash. He took out a handkerchief and dabbed at the oozing blood on his cheek. When he turned back again to face her, he was calmer, his voice steadier.

"I know now how it must have been. That bitch of a woman, Mrs Fenton, must have fed her with lies, pouring poison into her ears about you and me so that she must have felt in despair that there was no hope anywhere, no one she could turn to for help and sympathy. Do you realize how that has made me feel? Can you understand?"

He was asking a great deal of her and suddenly all the doubts, all the nagging agonies and uncertainties of the last few weeks seemed to come to a head and she could not hold it back.

"Oh yes, I understand very well. I knew it from the very beginning. You talked to me of love but the moment she needed you, you would have gone to her forgetting me. How right I was not to believe you, not to trust a word you said."

"That is not true. I was trying to find a way for us that would hurt no one."

But now she could not stem the flood. It poured out, all the mingled pain and lost happiness of the last few months.

"No one achieves anything without being hurt. She was not a saint, not a martyr. For God's sake, face up to it, see her as she really was. She thought only of herself. She cared nothing about what she was doing to you. She had been Oliver's mistress at Harrogate, at Larksghyll, perhaps even in this house, in your own bed. She would have wilfully abandoned her child and gone with him without a single thought of you or of Peter."

"That's a brutal thing to say."

"It's the truth and you must accept it, not hide behind a tissue of sentimental lies."

Then they were both of them tearing at one another, saying cruel hurtful things coming out of the tension and stress of the last few days until suddenly she stopped. She saw the stony look on his face and was aghast at what she had done. She had lost him completely. Now he must see her as the scheming creature they all believed her to be who had plotted to capture him and so nearly succeeded, a selfish heartless monster like Oliver, like the man who had paid for it with his life and lay in his grave at Larksghyll.

They stood silent for a moment. Perhaps if either of them had yielded an inch, they would have been in each other's arms, but pride held them rigid.

Then she caught her breath in a half-sob. "If that's how you feel about me, then the sooner I walk out of here the better," and she ran away from him, snatching up cloak and bonnet as she went out into the hall, stumbling up the stairs and into her own room to collapse on the bed in a misery far too deep for the easy relief of tears.

She was facing a dreadful realization that her world had fallen into ruins about her and it was her own fault. If only she had been more patient and understanding, if only she had listened and sympathized – but now it was too late, hopelessly too late.

But even when everything is at its worst, you still have to go on from day to day, she thought wearily, getting up off the bed cold and stiff, splashing water on her face and combing her

307

hair. It was all very well to say "the sooner I walk out of here the better" and stalk out of the house, head held high. That's what happened in romantic novels when the heroine rides out into the storm, but real life was not like that, it had a pressing practical side.

To start with Tom had been right. It had begun to snow and continued all the evening. To travel from Castlebridge was an undertaking. Seats had to be booked on the stagecoach, somehow she had to get to Skipton – she could not walk ten miles dragging her trunk behind her. Even to escape to Larksghyll presented problems, a long long walk unless she borrowed Tansy – difficulties multiplied and she sighed. And that was not all. There was a little boy who ran to her confidingly in the nursery, demanding where she had been all day; Nanny was looking at her expectantly and there was Scamp who had grown into a fat round little dog of doubtful ancestry but who still had to be provided for. Above all there was the grim fact that Sylvia's body was to be returned tomorrow and buried on the following day. After that she would feel free to go. To ease her mind and take the first step, she turned out her trunk that very night and began to pack it with the garments not immediately in use.

When the funeral carriages lined up outside and the coffin was carried down, huge flakes of snow hung on the black plumes blowing on the horses' heads and lay thick underfoot. Nanny had dressed Peter very warmly with a thick muffler to guard against chill. Della was appalled that so young a child should be expected to go with his father, but here in the north it seemed that a boy must face the grim realities as early as possible. Nanny certainly expected it as did all the servants and even Tom himself.

She came down into the hall holding the little boy's hand tightly in hers. Tom lifted him into the carriage, then turned to Della.

"Get in," he said briefly.

"No."

"Don't argue please."

At such a moment a quarrel would have been unthinkable. Against her will she got in. He followed after her and lifted the boy on to his knee.

"Where are we going, Papa?" he asked, scared by the

solemnity. When his father didn't answer immediately, he pointed to the handsome glass hearse lavishly covered with flowers that preceded them. "Is Mamma in there?"

"Ssh, darling," whispered Della. "You will see presently," and she took one of the small black-gloved hands in hers.

In the graveyard after the service she drew back as far as possible out of sight among the upper servants. Peter, after one anxious look behind him, stood beside his father, a tiny figure trying very hard to be brave. At Tom's whisper he took a step forward and dropped the flowers in his hand on to the coffin.

There were a great number of people there, men and women, mostly strangers, and afterwards they paused to speak a word to Tom before they moved to their carriages. Martha had bent down to talk to the little boy and Aunt Lavinia leaned heavily on Bret's arm. Della drew back behind one of the giant yews that bordered the path and watched them walk slowly towards the lychgate. They would assume she had left with the others. Maybe it was no more than foolish pride, but she did not want to go back with them, didn't want to stand in the drawing room while the guests stared at her, wondering, and then glanced at one another significantly. By the time she had made her slow journey back they would doubtless have all gone.

What she had not reckoned with was the number of people who hung about the road outside. The mill had been closed for the morning and everyone it seemed, all the men and women of Castlebridge, had come out along the road to watch the cortège pass by. Afterwards many of them still stood outside the churchyard. They turned to stare at her as she came out. It was unusual to see so many men idle. They stood in uneasy groups on street corners and there was a queer atmosphere as if some deep unrest were brewing and it only needed some small incident to set off the explosion. She told herself she was being fanciful, but once years ago when she and her father had been in Italy she had seen revolution break out and sweep away everyone in its path, innocent and guilty alike. She did not realize that it was she herself who would provide the impetus that would set the ball rolling.

The heavy snow had now piled up on the roadways and walking was very difficult. It was impossible to hurry and after a little she began to regret the pride that had led to such foolhardiness. She was not sure when she began to realize that she was being followed. She was picking her way with some care when she happened to look up and saw that a bunch of slatternly women, black shawls tied tightly around them, clogs on their feet, were closing in on her. This time, with a tremor of fear, she knew she was not going to escape.

The funeral procession had stirred an emotional reaction. They were blaming her for everything that had happened. A couple of hundred years earlier and it would have been a witch hunt. Now it was a mindless attack on the stranger, the foreigner. She started to run and it was a mistake. They scented fear and were after her like animals, closing in upon her, plucking at her clothes. One of them snatched at her bonnet and another dragged at the shawl around her shoulders. They forced her up against a wall, jeering faces thrusting at her, calling her filthy obscene names. She tried to push her way out and only made it worse. She managed to run a few steps, slipped on the frozen snow and fell to her knees. Someone grabbed at her hair dragging her head back so that she cried out with the pain. She jerked herself free, tried to scramble up and was thrust forward falling on her face and striking her head against a piece of stone coping.

Dimly she was aware of shouts. She heard the startled neighing of a horse and a man's voice saying, "Great God, it's a woman they're attacking! Out of my way, damn you!" And suddenly they had drawn back and left her there a crumpled heap on a patch of dirty churned up snow. She tried to sit up and failed. A man's strong arms lifted her, another voice was saying, "She's hurt, sir. Bring her in here."

Her face was pressed against a rough frieze cloak, then she was being placed very gently in a chair and a cushion was put behind her head.

"She's coming round," said that same voice as she opened her eyes.

The first thing she saw was Lil's plain little face with the absurd topknot of hair and then slowly because her head hurt as she turned to the other side, she saw a man with a short beard, with thick brown hair flecked with grey, a face she knew but which couldn't be there because its owner was dead, drowned at the bottom of a distant sea. Did that mean that she was dead too?

"Father!" she gasped weakly. She closed her eyes and opened them again but he was still there. It wasn't a dream. "Papa, is it really you?"

310

"Don't talk. Drink this first. You'll feel better then."

He was holding a cup to her lips. She drank a little. It burned her tongue and ran down her throat like fire, but it was remarkably effective. In a few minutes her head began to clear. She could think again, could sit up and look around her. She was in a small cold room stuffed with furniture, an overmantel covered with cheap ornaments, someone's highly prized front parlour.

"What happened? Where am I?"

Lil said angrily, "It were those savages out there fallin' on you like a pack of wolves. I'd just come back from the buryin' when I saw they were after someone. Tried to stop 'em but they didn't take no notice till the gentleman come along and he soon had 'em on the run. Are you sure you're not injured, Miss?"

"No, I don't think so, only bruised." Della managed a faint smile.

"Our Benjy's got your horse, sir. He's a good boy, he'll see he don't come to no harm. I know Miss Della, see. I used to work for her up at schoolhouse. Just look what they've done to her," and she began to brush the snow and mud from Della's skirts.

"Never mind about that," she murmured feebly.

"I tell you what, Miss. I'll go and make you a nice cup o' tea. That'll make you feel more like yourself."

"Thank you, Lil. I'd like that."

Then she had bustled away and Della was gazing up at the man beside her, still finding it hard to believe the truth of what she saw.

She said again wonderingly, "Is it really you?"

He smiled. "Feel me, no ghost." His hand was holding hers warm and strong. "I was on my way to see you. Lucinda told me all about Rokeby Hall and when I called there, the stable boy told me everyone was at the funeral of the Master's wife so I came to the church but hardly liked to intrude. I thought I'd wait for a while and then come back later. I saw something happening right in front of me but had no idea that it was you. I couldn't believe my eyes. What on earth have you been doing, my love, to provoke an attack like that?"

"It's a long story. It still seems impossible that you should be here at all. How? Why? What happened?"

"That's a long story too. Shall we postpone it for a little and just be glad we've found one another again? We seem to have a genius for getting into awkward situations, you and I," he went

311

on with a wry smile.

Then Lil came back with a tray of tea, a bowl of warm water and a towel. She began to wipe the mud from Della's face and hands and dabbed ineffectively at her stained skirt.

"They've fair spoiled your nice gown, Miss. I sent one of the children to look for your shawl but it's that filthy, I'll have to wash it through for you."

"Don't trouble. It doesn't matter now, Lil," she said a little awkwardly, "I want to tell you. This gentleman is my father."

The girl's eyes grew big as saucers. Vague rumours about Della had spread around but nowhere near the truth.

"You don't say, Miss. Your very own Pa comin' to the rescue! If that don't beat all! Wait till I tell me Ma. She's on afternoon shift at t'mill but she'll be that pleased." Then belatedly she remembered her manners. "Pleased to meet you, sir, I'm sure," and she bobbed a curtsey.

"And I'm more than delighted to meet a friend of my daughter," he said with one of his heart-turning smiles and Della, with stiffening bruises and the beginnings of a powerful headache, knew with amusement that despite a convicts' prison and being drowned and come to life again, her father had lost none of his ability to charm.

A small boy came in from the kitchen, carefully guarding a lighted spill. Lil took it from him and knelt down to put it to the fire already laid but obviously very seldom lit, maybe only for christenings, marriages and burials. It was a rare privilege and Della protested that it wasn't necessary.

"Nay, but it is then and you're to stay here till you're rested. Me Ma would want it," said Lil very firmly, "and the gentleman too. If you en't seen one another in a long while, you'll be wantin' to have a nice quiet talk."

She shepherded the gaping small boy out of the room in front of her and closed the door.

The fire burned up and smoked and gave very little heat but the kind intention was there and they drank the hot tea, though her father wrinkled his nose at the powerful brown taste. Listening to him, she forgot for a little what might be happening outside in Castlebridge.

At her urging he began to tell her something of his adventures, minimizing the horrors of the convict ship, the filth, the sickness, the brutality, the appalling terror of the moment when they knew it was doomed, with men, women and

312

children locked below decks with no hope of escape. Fourteen days on a raft had reduced eleven men to only three near-skeletons who were picked up by a coastal trader carrying cargo between the Pacific islands. The Captain was not in the least interested in the law nor in whom they were. He gave them food, rough medical treatment and landed them on one of the bigger islands as soon as he could.

"By this time I had assumed another identity," went on her father.

"How do you mean?"

"There was a man on the ship who was not a convict, a man who was travelling alone and who had devoted his life to prison reform."

"A preacher, do you mean?"

"No, not a preacher. He was not concerned with God nor with religion as such. He was sailing with the convicts with the sole purpose of easing the cruel conditions, fighting for their rights and giving them hope, work he intended to pursue in the penal settlements when we should reach them. A good man, Della, not my style at all, you would say," went on her father with a twisted smile, "yet he and I spoke much during those hellish months and he opened my eyes to a great deal, I can tell you, while we battled through mountainous seas but mostly flat calm which was even worse. When the ship went down I managed to drag him out of the water and on to the raft. Without his spirit I doubt if we would have survived as long as we did and he was the last to die."

He paused and she saw that the memory was still raw and had power to move him deeply. She leaned forward to put a hand on his and he returned the pressure.

"I think I despaired for the first time that day. He knew he couldn't last much longer and he took out his own papers and what money he had been able to snatch up in the last frantic moments on the ship. He put them in my hands, an oiled silk packet stained with water and blood. 'They'll be more use to you than to me,' was all he said, but I knew what he meant. He was giving me back freedom of a kind. He died that night and when we let his body go overboard I was tempted to go with him. But the instinct to live is stronger than you think and can survive all kinds of misery. It kept all three of us going for another two days, I hardly know how, and when we landed at last in pretty poor shape, I took a passage home to England as honest John Westcot of Bermondsey, London."

"And found that the truth had been discovered and you were to be granted a pardon."

"Yes, but not immediately. I had it from Lucinda and would not believe it, still keeping to my disguise. It is a queer thing," he added, musingly, "I had accepted my fate in order to spare my brother. It seemed to me that I'd done him enough harm, and now it was being taken out of my hands and there was nothing I could do to avert it."

"Was it you I saw at Larksghyll the day Oliver was buried?"

"Yes." He turned to look at her. "How much do you know, Della?"

"Almost everything, I believe. Oliver told me the day before he died."

"About me and your mother?"

"Yes, that too. Why did you never tell me?"

"Maybe because I was ashamed."

"Did you realize how much your brother loved her?"

"It must be difficult for you to understand." He got up and moved restlessly to the fire looking down into the sulkily burning coal. "George and I had never been close. We were too different, I suppose. Strangely enough I had more in common with Oliver, though I only knew him slightly."

"My uncle said he should have been your son."

"He was Olivia's son. I never forgot that." He was silent for a moment and then went on briskly as if to get it over. "She was fond of George but I think she had married him to escape from her father and then found she had only exchanged one prison for another. I saw she was unhappy and I was sorry for her. I swear to God I never meant it to be any more than a summer flirtation. Then suddenly before we were even aware of it we were so deep in love that the whole world could go hang so long as we could be together."

> " 'Know that love is a careless child
> And forgets promise past,' "

she quoted softly.

"Damnably cruel, but only too true. What made you say that?"

"It was in a book she left behind her."

"Sounds trite and sentimental, doesn't it, but we used to read poetry together. It never seemed to occur to George that she

314

hungered for more than her child and the dull family round."

"And that's what you gave her?"

"I hope I did. I took her away with me but we only had five years, five short blissful years together, and I've thought many times since that if I'd left her with George, she might still be alive with a family of children around her. So you see I had my punishment. What you have done, you have to live with. There is no escape."

And she thought that perhaps for the first time she was seeing the depths that lay beneath that easy charm, that light-hearted acceptance of life that had aways characterized him.

She said, "Papa, do you remember the jewelled skull?"

"Oh Lord, yes. Oliver was wearing it that night and it must have been ripped off when he struggled with Bret. It had been in the family for a hundred years or more. I'd seen my father wear it and then George. That's why I picked it up."

"Lucinda gave it to me. It was a kind of clue that led me to Oliver. Then it was lost in the fire at the school."

"Perhaps it was a good thing. The first Craven to wear it was a devil of a fellow by all accounts and died in a duel over some woman he fancied, so maybe it brought bad luck."

For a moment she saw again that dashing young man in the portrait flaunting his jewelled bauble. Then she said, "Did you go to Larksghyll after the funeral?"

"Yes, later that same day. It was strange after so many years and the old place looked sadly neglected. Poor George. I think in a way he was glad to see me. We talked long and he told me as much as he knew. I would have come to you then but I'm still not entirely a free man. There are formalities to be gone through and I am, as it were, on parole till all is signed and sealed." He turned to look at her. "And that's quite enough about me." He came back to sit beside her. "Now I want to hear everything about you."

"There is very little to tell. You will have heard most of it from Lucinda. Kitty came back so Madame Ginette no longer wanted me at the salon. I had to find work somewhere so I came up here to teach in the little school."

"Under your mother's name?"

"I didn't want to do that, Papa. It was Mrs Barnet who insisted on it."

"Very wise of the old girl under the circumstances," he said dryly.

"Then the school was burned down and Tom asked me to stay on as governess to his little son."

"Tom?" queried her father with raised eyebrows.

"Tom Clifford. He owns the mill."

"And it is he who has just lost his wife in a drowning tragedy."

"Yes."

"Is he in love with you?"

"Oh Papa really, this is not the time to talk about things like that."

"Or what's more to the point perhaps – are you in love with him?" Then he saw the colour creep into her pale cheeks and added quickly, "It's classic romance, isn't it, governess falls in love with employer? I was only jesting."

"Actually it is not a jest."

"You don't mean – ?"

"You and I do seem to make the most awful mistakes when we fall in love, don't we?" she said wryly.

"Good God, is that why those abominable harridans out there were attacking you?"

"Partly. You see . . ."

But she got no further with her explanation. They had all along been vaguely aware of a certain hum of noise in the background but it now exploded into a terrific commotion. There was shouting, the sound of feet racing along the cobbles and a boy, his hands and face grimed with smoke, came bursting into the room, closely followed by Lil.

"They're settin' fire to the mill, Miss," she said shrilly. "Dick's just come from there and me Ma's in there with all the other women in the weaving sheds . . ."

"Setting fire to it?" Paul Craven was on his feet. "Are you sure, boy? Who are these people?"

"There's hundreds of 'em, sir, not all Castlebridge folk neither, most of 'em are from other parts."

These must be the men from the rally Jane Carter had spoken of, thought Della, pouring into the town and Dan Carter urging them on with murder in his heart.

"Is Mr Clifford there?" she asked.

"Aye, Miss, he is now. They sent him word and he came at once. They were breakin' windows and tryin' to batter down door so he came in back way through the goods entrance. He tried to speak to 'em but they shouted him down."

"Have you sent for the police?" put in her father.

"Aye, Master let me out through the back window and I went there first but there were only Sergeant Jones and a couple of his men. They can't do much. They've sent for militia, they told me, but they won't be here yet."

The boy was obviously scared, but enjoying the drama too.

"I'll come. God knows what I can do but there may be something. Can you show me the way?"

"Aye, sir, 'tain't far but we'll have to go by back lanes or we'll never get through."

Della had forgotten her bruises. She could only think of Tom.

"I'm coming with you."

"No, my dear, not you, you're not fit and there's nothing you can do."

"There may be people hurt."

"I'll come with you, Miss. I'm not standing by while those tykes out there try to burn up my Ma, but you can't go out like that, you'll catch your death, best have somethin' to put round you."

Lil fetched a couple of thick black shawls and they wrapped them around head and shoulders as they followed the boy out into the street.

Even the back lanes were crowded but they pushed their way through staring frightened women and excited children. By the time they reached the mill, they could see there was no hope of getting around to the back entrance. A vast crowd was milling backwards and forwards and had already smashed windows in the ground floor, though the front door, firmly barred, still held firm. A sort of fury seemed to possess the whole jeering, shouting, jostling mob, egged on by agitators who must have come on from the rally and were urging them on to more and more violence.

Paul Craven was a tall powerful man. He elbowed his way through and they followed in his wake until they could see where bales of hay and oil-soaked straw were being brought up and piled around the walls ready to be hurled through the smashed windows of the lower floors. It was easy to see the danger once those flaming bundles set fire to the inflammable materials inside. They stood for a moment, uncertain what to do, the crowd eddying around them, and then Della saw him. Dan Carter had leaped up on to the lower steps to the great front door. The wind carried his words away but she knew he must be yelling defiance, urging them on to light the fires and smoke out the owner with the scabs of workers who were barricading the mill against them.

"We must reach him. He is the ringleader," she gasped to her father. "If only we could silence him."

"That's not so easy."

He was looking around him to see if there was any way in which he could get into the building. Surely the more they had to help in the defence the better.

Then the door opened and a man came out on to the top step, a tall figure, still in the heavy black of mourning, who stood silent for an instant. An enormous yell greeted his appearance and then as he lifted his hand and waited an unexpected hush fell over the crowd.

"It's Tom," she breathed.

He was speaking, broadening his voice to the accent they all knew and understood, but it was difficult to catch all the words.

"You can strike me down if you like but if I go, then t'mill will go with me and after that who will give you work, who will keep your wives and children from starvation? Don't listen to those who come from outside – they're not thinking of Castlebridge folk but only of themselves and if trouble comes they'll be off sooner than you can blink. Soldiers are on their way and what good do you hope to gain out of it then? It'll be all of you who will hang for it, or rot in gaol or be sent overseas, leaving family to the workhouse. If that's what you want, then good luck to you. I'll be among the first to light the fire for I tell you now I've had my bellyfull of you these last weeks and I don't care one way or t'other!"

His utter contempt had taken them by surprise. A good many of them were listening now and some of the more sensible began to stir uneasily. The first fury had cooled. When the soldiers came there could be bloodshed. Some of them had seen it happen before and none but a few hotheads wanted to see it again.

They had not reckoned with Dan Carter. It was Della who saw him. He had drawn back to one side, partly hidden, but she glimpsed the gun in his hands. Not right in the head, his wife had said, eaten up with the lust for revenge, crazy enough to do murder.

She screamed out a warning and went plunging and stumbling towards Tom. After that it all happened so swiftly

318

that no one could have prevented it.

Dan fired, but by some miracle missed his aim and only winged Tom so that momentarily he staggered clutching at his shoulder.

Della, a little light-headed still, oblivious of danger, could only remember that they had quarrelled and could not bear to see him shot down still with that bitter anger between them. She ran and ran, the shawl falling from her, long black hair streaming behind her and, almost in awe of this wild figure, the crowd opened to let her through. She reached the steps and began to go up them to Tom.

Her father, going after her, grasped what was happening and reached Dan as he raised the gun again. He hurled himself at him but was fractionally too late, the gun went off and he saw Della waver and hold out her hands. He saw Tom catch her as she fell, then he had torn the gun out of Dan's hand and clubbed him with it. The boy Dick had followed him, wild with the thrill of it, and he thrust the dazed Dan towards him.

"Get something to tie him up," he said, "and don't let him escape whatever you do," and then he ran to his daughter.

By the time he reached the steps Tom was carrying Della inside. Blood was dripping from his sleeve but he took no heed of it. Willing hands made a couch of soft wool and he laid her gently on it.

Her father, following after him, pushed him aside and went down on his knees. He began to unbutton the close-fitting black dress already soaked with blood.

"Who the devil are you?" exclaimed Tom.

"Never mind who I am. For Christ's sake, get a doctor. Can't you see how she's bleeding?"

He pulled out a handkerchief, made it into a pad and thrust it inside the bodice against her breast.

"Go, one of you, quickly," said Tom and then was glaring angrily at the stranger. "Who are you? What are you doing here?"

"If you must know I'm her father."

"Isn't he dead?"

"Very far from it. Stop asking questions and give me another handkerchief. Now raise her a little. Gently, man, gently."

Della opened her eyes, only half-conscious. She murmured, "Tom! Where's Tom?"

"I'm here."

"Are you hurt?"

"Nothing to speak of."

"I wanted – I wanted to tell you – I'm sorry – "

"Ssh, don't talk." He was holding her hand in both of his and raised it to his lips. He turned an agonized face towards her father. "You don't think . . .?"

"She's not dying," he said brusquely, "not yet. Where the hell is that damned doctor?"

An anxious little group had gathered around them. Someone brought a blanket. Tom put it gently over her.

"Can't we do something?" he said helplessly.

"We'd better not move her. It could make the bleeding worse."

It seemed an hour but was actually only a few minutes and then Dr Withers was there.

"I was on my way," he said breathlessly. "I guessed there would be trouble when you left the Hall in such a tearing hurry. They're quietening down out there. Now where's the damage? Better let me look at that shoulder of yours, Tom."

"That's nothing."

"Worse than that, is it?" Then he saw where Della was lying and his voice changed. "Stand back all of you and let me come to her."

He knelt down and they stood silently watching while he made his examination. When he looked up, his face was grave.

"Can't do much here," he said gruffly. "We'd better get her back to the Hall."

"I've sent for the carriage."

They began to improvise a stretcher and when Rob came, they carried it slowly down the steps watched by silent groups. Some of the women from the looms overcome by the stress of the day were openly weeping.

The shooting had had the opposite effect to what Dan Carter, in his rage against Tom, had hoped. Instead of inflaming them it had shocked them. Most of them had come ready to shout and yell, noisily demanding their rights, even set the place alight and watch it burn, but they had not bargained for what could be murder. A man could be hanged for that. One or two of them lent willing hands to tie up the semi-conscious Dan. He had brought them to this, so let him bear the brunt of it. By the time the militia came galloping up with Sergeant Jones and his two subordinates some of them had already begun to slink home. The soldiers roughly rounded up the rest, riding through them with drawn sabres, until they fled in fear before the trampling horses. The riot was over. Now they would have to pay the reckoning.

For the next few days Della lived in a fevered twilight world where people came and went, where shadows swelled and then diminished, floated near and receded, where she seemed to hear the doctor say, "An inch nearer the heart and we'd have lost her," and in a vague way realized he must be speaking of her when she had no intention of dying. Fevered dreams when the father she believed dead was alive again, holding her hands, speaking her name, calling her back to him; an anxious little voice that said, "Della is not drownded like Mamma, is she?" and Tom's voice deep and fervent, "No, thank God!"

Then there came hours when the fog began to clear away, when the room assumed its right proportions and, despite pain when she moved and restricting bandages, new life began to surge through her.

One morning she opened her eyes to see Lil standing by the bed, a beaming smile on her face, dressed in the dark blue cotton gown and white starched apron worn by all the servants at the Hall. The frilled cap perched on the topknot of hair was absurdly endearing.

"I've brought you a cup o' tea and Cook says to ask if you would fancy a bite of somethin' to your breakfast, Miss," she said all in one breath.

"Lil, what are you doing here?"

"Master asked me Ma if I'd come as nurserymaid to Nanny Roberts and the new governess when she comes."

"New governess?"

Lil clapped a hand to her mouth. "Oh Lordy, I didn't ought to have said that. Nothin' is settled o' course but now your Pa has come home, Master did say as you'd be leavin' like."

So nothing had changed. He still did not want her, had still not forgiven her. She lay back, feeling suddenly very tired, the pain came back redoubled and the new life began to ebb away from her.

"You're not feelin' bad again, are you, Miss?" enquired Lil anxiously.

"No, much much better and tell Cook I think I could eat some of her milk toast with my tea."

"Aye, Miss, I will that and be back with it in two shakes," said Lil, forgetting her new dignity and running joyfully from the room.

There was so much she wanted to know and, maddeningly, no one would tell her anything. Even Dr Withers when he called was uninformative.

"Tom and your father have been summoned to Bradford," he said in answer to her questions. "There's an enquiry into the case of Dan Carter. It seems this is not the first riot he has been responsible for. They've been after him for some time."

"What will happen to him?" she went on, aware of uneasy pity for Jane Carter.

"God knows. Now don't start worrying your head about that rascal. Lie back and don't talk, there's a good girl."

"May I get up?" she asked when he had completed his routine examination.

"No, you may not, young lady. I had a great deal of trouble in extracting the bullet and I'm not going to have my neat handiwork go to waste. You will stay where you are for a few days yet." He stood up and replaced the blankets over her. "A fine dance you've been leading us with your little masquerade."

"I'm sorry. You must think me very deceitful but I never meant to be. Tom knew all about it and Bret."

"So I understand. Couldn't you have trusted Abbie and me with your shocking secret?"

The twinkle in his eye belied the severity in his tone.

"I could now but I didn't know you then."

"Never mind. All's well that ends well as someone once said, and now I must be off. You're not my only patient," and he bustled away.

The day wore on in the most irritating manner. Nanny looked in but only to ask how she felt, saying that she couldn't bring Peter and the dogs since the doctor had forbidden any kind of excitement. By the end of the afternoon she was bursting with frustration and it exploded when after a very light supper had been eaten and the tray taken away, her father strolled in.

"Wherever have you been all day?" she exclaimed as soon as he was inside the door.

"Answering damnfool police questions about Dan Carter. What the devil do I know about him?"

"And Tom?"

"He was there too, a lot more informative than I could be."

322

"What will they do to him?"

"There are a number of charges being brought against him. He'll be lucky if he escapes hanging."

Poor Jane Carter. It would be she who would suffer. "What about the mill?" she went on.

"I understand they are creeping back, cap in hand, most of them, and your Tom is Master all right. He is taking a tough line with them and I can't say I blame him. I honestly believe, my pet, that if you had not made such a good recovery, he'd have willingly seen them strung up, the whole bunch of them."

It should not have pleased her, but it did. Her father was looking down at her quizzically.

"How would you like to come to Australia with me?"

"Australia!" her voice rose to a squeak of surprise. "You're never going back there!"

"I thought I might," he said airily. "I've been talking it over with your Tom."

"Don't call him *my* Tom."

He cocked an eyebrow at her. "I rather thought he was. In any case after you've been through life and death with a man, formalities seem rather absurd. He's been having trouble with his supply of fleeces. I thought I could look into it for him and at the same time cast an eye over the convict settlements."

"But why?"

She was staring up at him in utter amazement and he turned away, hands in pockets, almost shamefaced.

"God knows, but the plain fact is that I did accept help from a man who died so I owe him a kind of debt. I couldn't do what he was intending to do in a month of Sundays, but I could take a look, I could perhaps put a voice to grievances, I could come back and bear witness to the frightful conditions. It probably won't do a damned bit of good but a least I will have tried. What do you think? Am I crazy?"

"No, not crazy," she said gently. "What does Lucinda say?"

"She may come with me. Actually she talked about taking a theatrical company out there one day."

"Papa, are you going to marry Lucinda?"

He swung round to face her. "Now don't start trying to make an honest man out of me. Lucinda is like me, she prefers her independence. Footloose and fancy free – that about describes us. Only one woman could have turned me into a family man and that was not to be."

323

"I like you as you are."

"Good, because I don't intend to change. But one thing I *am* going to do and that is to take you away from here just as soon as you can be moved."

"And supposing I don't want to go?"

"Then for once I'm going to play the heavy father and insist on carrying you off. Heaven knows I'm not a conventional man, but the situation up here, as far as I can see, between Master Tom and you, his dead wife and this whole place teeming with scandalmongering busybodies, has got completely out of hand. I'm lifting my daughter right out of it, and I may say that your Tom agrees with me."

"Did he say so?"

"He did – most emphatically."

"I won't go," she said rebelliously.

"We'll see about that. Now don't argue, my mind is made up, so you lie back and go to sleep like a good little girl while I go down and eat my supper."

He bent down and kissed her on the forehead. "Goodnight, my love."

"Papa, listen . . ."

"Not another word."

He smiled aggravatingly, shook his head at her and went out of the room closing the door behind him.

She lay for a while thinking about her father. Despite what he had said, he *had* changed, or perhaps not changed so much as just another part of him, hitherto rigorously held down, had come to the surface. But Australia! The thought of going all those thousands of miles away was altogether too daunting. She did not think he was right about Lucinda either. For all her independence, she loved him dearly and, successful actress or not, what woman does not long to be married?

She lay and fretted about Tom for another long day. She knew he had been beside her bed when she was in a high fever but now she was herself again he contented himself with sending messages through her father. It was not good enough. If he wanted her to go, then he must tell her face to face.

The late afternoon had brought Abbie with the gift of a thick white shawl crocheted by her mother and reporting that the children had begun to regard Della as something of a heroine.

"They didn't think that when they hurled me to the ground," she said tartly.

"But it's different now," went on Abbie warmly. "They all saw what you did and they're having second thoughts."

But Della only smiled and shook her head.

Nanny came with Peter, who presented her solemnly with a portrait of Scamp in red crayon chasing a ball as big as himself.

"It's for you," he said, putting it on the bed for her inspection and looking up at her anxiously. "Nanny says you're going away."

"For a little while."

"Not to Heaven like Mamma?"

"No, Peter, not to Heaven, not yet."

The only one who didn't come was Tom and by evening she could stand it no longer. She had been out of bed once or twice, taking a few shaky steps earlier in the day, but this was going to be an altogether more momentous undertaking.

When Lil came to fetch her supper tray she said casually, "Is Mr Clifford at home this evening?"

"Aye, Master's working in his study since your Pa is away for the night. He's not himself yet," she went on nodding her head wisely, "'tis only natural, I suppose. He's quiet like, don't hardly say a word, keeps himself close."

When she had gone, Della got up. She was obliged to sit on the edge of the bed for a minute or two combatting an infuriating giddiness and when she stood up, her legs felt so much like jelly that she clutched wildly at the bedpost but she was quite determined. Trying to put on a dressing gown over bandages proved far too much of a battle so in the end she gave it up, took the huge fleecy shawl that Abbie had brought, wrapped it closely around her over her nightgown and ventured outside.

The stairs presented a formidable obstacle and took some negotiating but she managed it by taking it step by step. Laughter floated up from the servants' quarters as she paused at the foot to recover breath. Then she moved across the hall, drew a deep breath and opened the study door.

"You can take the tray, Rose, I'm finished with it," said Tom without looking up from his desk.

Her first thought was that he had grown thinner, the high cheekbones were more apparent, there were dark shadows under his eyes and his arm was in a leather sling to ease the drag on the wounded shoulder.

"It's not Rose," she breathed.

He looked up and their eyes met. That last painful meeting seemed suddenly weeks away; days of sickness had swept away all differences, all agonies and they were gazing at one another hungrily. She had a sudden frantic wish that she had taken more trouble with herself and did not realize how hauntingly appealing she seemed to him, the dark hair falling in tousled ringlets around her pale face, the simple nightgown with its high frilled collar, the fleecy white shawl she hugged around her trailing on the floor.

Then he was on his feet, had moved to her side, his voice sharp with anxiety.

"Della, you should not be here. What are you doing out of bed?"

He put an arm around her as she swayed towards him, her strength beginning to desert her, and he half-supported, half-carried her to the big armchair beside the fire. She sank into it gratefully.

"You wouldn't come to me so I had to come to you," she said weakly, between tears and laughter.

He stood looking down at her. "Once I knew you were out of danger I thought it better not and your father agreed with me. He intends to take you away as soon as you are fit to travel."

"I know. He told me but I'm not going."

"He is right, Della, absolutely right. You must go."

She had tried to prepare herself for it and yet now sickeningly she felt as if the bottom had fallen out of her world.

"You mean you don't want me here any longer?"

"It's not a question of what I want, it is what is best for both of us."

She was not going to give in without a fight. "How can you judge what is best for me?"

He took a restless step away and then came back to her. "Listen to me. If I could throw everything aside I'd carry you off somewhere far away from here and we'd be married tomorrow but I can't. I'm not like your father. I haven't his free spirit. I am bound to the one thing I know and understand, the one thing that beside you has any importance for me – the damned mill."

"But I don't mind that," she said eagerly. "I will stay and work with you. Lying upstairs, I've been thinking about it. We could start the school again, we could set up a kind of meeting place where the young women could come with their babies – I

326

talked about it once with Abbie and Tim. Of course it would all take time and they would have to be persuaded to come but it is what they need."

He was looking down at her in astonishment. "You would want to do that after the way they treated you?"

"That was because they don't really know me. It is something that will pass."

For a moment he hesitated moved by her courage, her tenacity, then he spoke out vehemently.

"No, no, it's no use. I know what would happen. I have to think for both of us. If you were to stay here beside me, God knows where it would end. You'd be my mistress in a week, everyone would be pointing an accusing finger, tearing at you, blackening your name. Do you think I would allow you to be exposed to such insults or let such a slur be put upon our life together. Never!"

A chilling thought had struck her and it had to be brought out into the open before any decision could be reached.

"Tom, do you really mean all that or are you hiding behind it? Is it Sylvia who stands between us?"

It cut him short and for a moment he did not answer. Then he said slowly, "Perhaps you're right. I can't forget her entirely. I can't put her on one side as if she never existed. What she did in life and in death still disturbs me greatly. I still feel desperately responsible. Can you understand that, Della, can you?" and when she did not reply immediately, he went on. "Because if you can't – and it is a great deal to ask of you – then my life will be empty indeed."

She looked at him, saw the pain in his eyes and said quietly, "I had another idea this afternoon. I had meant to talk it over with my father first but maybe now is the right time. I don't care what you or Papa say but I'm not going to Australia with him or indeed to anywhere else. I love him as much as I ever did, perhaps even more now that he has come back to me from the dead, but I think I've grown up. I don't *need* him any longer, not like I once did. And so I'm going to Larksghyll. I'm going to stay with my uncle and try to give him back a little of what he lost. I believe my father will be pleased with that. And there when it is time, you will come to me."

She pushed herself up out of the chair and held out her hand. "Will you come?"

"Oh my love!"

He slipped his arm out of the sling so that he could draw her close to him. She leaned against him, relief bringing a mingling of tears and laughter.

"Careful!" he said warningly. "No excitement the doctor told me. I'm going to carry you straight back to bed."

"Not yet, and it isn't excitement, it is peace to know that I am forgiven."

"For what?" he smiled. "For saving my life?"

"For all the hateful things I said to you in this very room."

"Oh that. Perhaps we need to forgive each other."

"You know," she said contentedly, as his arm tightened around her, both of them conscious of pain but not caring a rap about it, "all the best fairy tales end with the lovers being happy together for ever and ever."

"And we must end with a parting."

"But not for long."

"No, please God, not for long."

Joan Aiken

LAST MOVEMENT

WARNER BOOKS

A Warner Communications Company

WARNER BOOKS EDITION

Copyright © 1977 by Joan Aiken
All rights reserved

Library of Congress Catalog Card Number 76-42055

ISBN 0-446-89681-0

This Warner Books Edition is published by
arrangement with Doubleday & Company, Inc.

Cover art by Jim Dietz

Warner Books, Inc., 75 Rockefeller Plaza, New York, N.Y. 10019

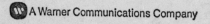 A Warner Communications Company

Printed in the United States of America

Not associated with Warner Press, Inc. of Anderson, Indiana

First Printing: June, 1978

10 9 8 7 6 5 4 3 2 1

All the characters in this book are fictitious, and any resemblance to actual persons, living or dead, is purely coincidental.

LAST
MOVEMENT

❧ 1 ❧

PRELUDE

The soft, hollow clunk and thomp of tennis balls, and voices calling scores, came echoing faintly across Crowbridge Park as I walked back to my flat. Evening sun sat comfortably on my shoulders. The birds were all singing like crazy creatures, because it was April and the apple trees were in bud and everything out of doors smelled new, cool, sharp, tingling with promise. I felt the same as the birds, could have sung like a crazy creature myself. I was going home for a bath and a cat nap—having been up since five that morning; then back to the Crowbridge Theatre Royal for a last couple of hours' work on the sets and costumes of *The Cherry Orchard* before the curtain rose on the first-night performance. It was going to be a terrific evening, I felt in my bones. For once, the parts had all fitted like gloves over the mixed members of the Crowbridge

9

Repertory Company; everybody, inspired with enthusiasm, had shelved feuds, forgotten differences, and worked in harmony, and the result was tight, coherent, animated, and heartbreaking. Further, it was the first time I'd been in sole charge of the scenery and costumes; fired by pride, I had worked till I was half dead. My sleep average during the past month had been about three hours per night, in spite of which I felt marvelous. For the first time in my life, I was completely fulfilled—happy—truly part of the professional group I belonged to, and, what was more, almost satisfied with the work I had done. Not *quite,* of course; the resources of the Crowbridge Rep were limited; but still, considering the costumes were made from all the cheapest materials we could get, polythene to hessian, and the scenery was painted on offcuts from the local do-it-yourself-furniture-kit factory, I considered the result a triumph. And so, in fact, did the rest of the company. At intervals during my three-hours-nightly sleeps, I couldn't help waking to think adoringly of my painted cherry orchard, with its greens, grays, and whites, which exquisitely offset the black, dove-colored, and mahogany tones of the costumes (luckily, there was also a dye factory in Crowbridge, and Rose Drew, the manager's daughter, was our Varya). I feared that after the play had ended I would never be able to bring myself to throw out those beautiful sets, and I foresaw they'd be furnishing my flat for the next five years.

The flat was another happiness. One room, semi-basement—true; but it faced out across the park toward the golden, peeling dome of the Theatre Royal, and I had been able to afford it only since my elevation to the status of Stage-Manager-plus-props (with concomitant raise of four pounds a week); one month, to be precise. Before that, I'd shared a room and use of kitchen with Rose Drew. Now I possessed a kitchen of my own, and even a bathroom with a brass geyser and mildew on the walls. No matter; it was mine; in time I'd cover or replace the landlord's hideous furniture with items chosen from junk shops and painted to suit my own taste. All that pleasure lay ahead! And meanwhile I could enjoy the evening sun sliding through my front window, my view of the park, and the privacy of my own dank bathroom.

I crossed the little front garden full of languidly sprouting hydrangeas (my landlord's; chosen presumably because they gave the least trouble, that being his line in all other departments), walked down the narrow, concreted alley at the side of the house, which led to my own front door, found my key, unlocked the door, and went in.

On the red tiles of the small entrance hall a telegram was lying.

I can remember exactly the way its rough yellow envelope picked up a touch of reflected light from the open, glass-paned door which led through into the living room.

It was addressed to Priscilla Graffin, which is my name, but which startled me a good deal because, when my father died, thirteen years before, and Mother went back to using her maiden name of Meiklejohn, changing by deed poll, I had followed suit. And nobody, either at my school or in the Crowbridge Rep, had ever used my first name, which is suitable only for tombstones. Everybody called me Mike. So it brought me up sharp just to see the words, formal and frightening, on the envelope, and I picked it up with hands

11

grown suddenly cold and sweaty, aware, too, at the same time, that the evening's sunshine was only a trailer for spring and that my flat felt as arctic as the inside of a Deepfreeze.

PLEASE COME TO STRETFORD HOSPITAL AT ONCE YOUR MOTHER SERIOUSLY INJURED said the impersonal, computerized letters on the rough buff paper they use for telegrams.

It was the kind of message that, deep down, we all know that we are going to get someday—because, however much we play about with lights and furnishing materials and words of powerful dramatic significance, the world is, in fact, a nasty and ruthless place, not intended for the welfare of humans.

I laid the telegram down on the ugly, unfunctional, varnished sideboard and began wandering about, mechanically putting things into a small overnight bag— slippers, toothbrush, money, sweater. If only I had a telephone. Engineers were coming to install one—but, knowing the G.P.O., another sixteen weeks would elapse before they arrived.

Sixteen weeks—what would have happened by then?

Luckily at that point it occurred to me that I might phone from my landlord's flat upstairs. His wife was not normally accommodating, but this was an emergency, after all. So I walked out, around, and up the steps to her front door. Besides, I ought to tell her that I was going away, and leave messages about laundry, the gas-meter man, the window cleaner. . . . As my brain clicked automatically through these patterns I saw the tall, coffin-shaped figure of Mrs. Charm appear behind the reeded-glass door.

Charm: never was such an inappropriate name applied to anyone so signally lacking in it. Her pale

12

mauve face was like an unsuccessful cake camouflaged with icing. Her damp eyes wept all the time behind gold-rimmed glasses, and her straw hair was nagged up into an inefficient, hassock-shaped pile.

"Eh, Miss Meeklejohn?" she said in a Belfast accent you could have bent into a coat hanger. "Was it abewt the telegram, then? The boy came heerr furrst, but I tawld him ye werr the grround-floor—"

"Yes, that's it," I cut in quickly—she was capable of going on for a long time yet—"It said that my mother's been injured in an accident, and I have to go to Stretford Hospital—I was wondering if I could use your phone?"

"Oh, how tairrible!" she was all fussy solicitude at once, very self-important with it. She ushered me to the phone, which perched precariously on a gruesome little glass occasional table among their tight-packed furniture. "Was it a car crash, then?"

I hadn't got as far as wondering about this. "Do you know where Stretford is?" I asked while waiting for Directory Inquiries to answer. Mrs. Charm had never even heard of Stretford. "I dew hope it's not tew far," she said unctuously.

As my mother was headmistress of a large comprehensive school in the Midlands, where the accident had presumably taken place, and as Crowbridge is on the south coast, I thought her hope was probably vain.

Directory Inquiries answered at last and found me the number of the hospital. I got through to them after the usual interminable delays filled with clicks and warblings and long periods of total silence.

"Is that Stretford Hospital? May I have the casualty ward, please?"

Connected with Casualties after another lengthy

13

wait, I was lucky enough to get an intelligent-sounding, clear-spoken voice.

"Sister Crouch here, Casualty? What do you wish to know?"

I said, "M-my name is Meiklejohn. I had a telegram about my mother, Mrs. Barbara Meiklejohn—"

"Meiklejohn? Thought your name was Graffin. Sorry about the slip-up. I'm very glad you rang." The voice became slightly reproachful. "We tried to contact you but you don't seem to be on the phone."

"No, I'm not. Is she—what did—how is my mother?"

"It's too early to say yet. They operated this afternoon at half past four."

"Operated? What *happened* to her?"

"A roof fell on her."

"?"

"The school gymnasium roof, I understand. She suffered from a head injury. . . . Where are you phoning from, Miss Meiklejohn?"

"I'm in Kent. I've only just got home and found your telegram."

"I think you should come here as soon as possible," Sister Crouch said.

Her voice was kind, human, sympathetic, but it frightened me to my roots. The relationship between Mother and myself was not a warm one, but we were each other's only relative; the prospect of a world without her seemed bleak indeed.

I dared not ask for any further details. My voice was only just under control—and I could feel the silent presence of Mrs. Charm, ghoulishly attentive, just behind my shoulder.

I said, "Wh-where is Stretford Hospital? How do I get to you?"

The sister seemed surprised at my ignorance but said, "You take a train from King's Cross. The fast trains take two hours."

"Thank you. I have to get up to London first, so I'm afraid I shan't be able to make it under four or five hours. Can you tell—is m-my mother conscious?"

"Not at present. If she does become conscious, I will tell her that you are on your way."

"Thank you, Sister," I said humbly, but she had rung off already.

"Eh, ye have tew go all the way up thrrough London, that's tairrible," said Mrs. Charm. "Why don't ye rring for a taxi to take ye tew the station while ye're heerr?"

That struck me as a good suggestion and an unusually kind thought. I did so.

But then Mrs. Charm rather spoiled the effect by saying, "Don't trrouble to pay me for the calls now, Miss Meeklejohn—I'll pewt them on yer rent bewk. Was it a car crash, then?" she asked hopefully.

"No—a roof fell on her," I said, and escaped, leaving her popeyed.

The taxi had said it would take twelve minutes to reach Parkside Villas, so I had time to finish my packing. Then, coming over faint and queer, I drank a cup of water and collapsed into one of my repulsive armchairs. They were from the art-deco period in the thirties—dirty-gray-upholstered semirockers of a curved shape, which tilted and slid back disconcertingly when one sat down in them; the sensation of the chair doing this under me added to my sick, terrified feeling that the whole *world* was about to cave in under me. I gazed around the ugly, dim room, with its orange dado, vomit-colored curtains, mustard wallpaper, and wondered if I would ever feel about it again as I had before the telegram came; my capacity to hope and plan for its regeneration seemed to have deserted me. The evening light had left the windows, and the room looked indescribably dismal.

I heard the crunch of a taxi's brakes in the road outside, jumped up, and hastily pushed a few last oddments into my bag, then left without a backward look. Mrs. Charm had a key to the place; let her come in after I had gone and find it untidy, as no doubt she would.

"Will you stop at the Theatre Royal first, please?" I asked the taxi driver.

Rickie would be there, for he lived an hour's motorbike ride outside Crowbridge and had said that he was going to stay in the theater and take a nap in the greenroom; I could give him a message for the rest of the cast.

I hated to wake him. He was fast asleep, curled up on a pile of leftover sacking, looking defenseless. When I shook him he sat up, tousled, rubbing his eyes; he could have been about fourteen years old. In fact he was twenty-two, six months younger than I, and highly experienced; he had been in various repertory companies since the age of sixteen.

"What's the row?" he said, yawning. "Anything wrong?"

"Rickie, I can't stay; I have to go. My mother's been badly hurt in an accident, and I have to get halfway across England. Will you please tell the others, and say how sorry I am?"

"Oh, my *god*." He gaped at me, slowly taking this in. "Oh, how terrible, Mike!" The same words that Mrs. Charm had used, but what a difference! "You

16

couldn't just wait till after the—No, of course you can't. You'd be worrying all the time. But how ever shall we manage without you?"

"You'll manage perfectly well." Rickie was my assistant. In most ways he was my equal, in some my superior. But I was touched by his look of devotion as he said, "Oh, but it won't be the *same* without you, Mike. It seems so unfair—Still, I can see that you've got to go." He gave me a hug and said, "Poor darling. How frightful for you! Where do you have to get to?"

"Stretford; I don't even know where it is."

"Oh, I know. My grandmother lived there. It's near Northampton. Are you on your way now?"

"Yes, I must go. I've got a taxi waiting."

"I can't *bear* that you have to miss this evening," he said miserably.

I couldn't bear it much myself, so I said again, "I must go."

"Wait—have you eaten anything?"

"No, but I'll get something at King's Cross. Tell the others how sorry I am. Say to Eve—"

"Here, take this—" He was thrusting a greasy package into my hands. "And a paperback—I bet you haven't got one, and the journey to Stretford takes forever—I should know—"

I tried to decline, but he overpowered my unspirited resistance and escorted me out to the taxi. "Are you all right for cash?" he said. "How about five pounds?"

Rickie was an unimpressive figure—short, frail, and consumptive-looking, his eyes myopic behind thick pebble glasses—I've never met anyone kinder or more reliable. I suddenly wished he could come all the way, longed to have his considerate company on the journey.

17

"I do *hope* you have good news when you get there," he said earnestly, shutting the taxi door on me.

I nodded, bit my lip, swallowed, and said, "I'll phone tomorrow."

"Yes, *do.*"

Then he went back inside—I hoped, to finish his interrupted nap.

The journey was quite as long and horrible as I'd expected. Trains from Crowbridge to Charing Cross are mostly slow, and this one was. London was crowded and disgusting, as usual. I battled across from one main-line station to the other as fast as I could, but it was now half past nine, and the tube trains were dismally infrequent. At King's Cross I found out that a train was due to start for Stretford in five minutes, which seemed at first like a piece of good fortune. I hurled myself into its corridor—of course it was full and there was no seat to be had—only to have it then spend half an hour sitting two hundred yards outside King's Cross before it hauled itself jerkily off northward. It proved to be another slow train, stopping at unheard-of, terrible little home-county stations with names like Scroop and Priddy's End and Moleham and Gazebo-on-the-Wold—places that nobody has ever heard of and where nobody could possibly want to live.

I was immeasurably grateful for Rickie's large, greasy slice of bacon between two chunks of stale brown bread, as the hours went by, and I stood lurching between two strangers in the narrow, dusty corridor flavored with cigarette butts and Coke trickles. The paperback Rickie had given me turned out to be *Candide*, which I knew too well and found too depressing, so I fell back on thoughts instead.

There were plenty of *them.*

18

I thought about how I'd feel if Mother died.

My relationship with her had been an arm's length one for years; it filled me at all times with guilt, often with sorrow. Now that I was grown up and earning my own living, we saw each other rarely; I had invited her several times to productions at the Theatre Royal, but her life as headmistress of the huge Market Broughton Comprehensive School was packed tight; any space left over from her school duties seemed to be spent at educational conferences, and she had never found time to come. And I on my part went to see her for two or three dutiful weekends each year; they were strained and uncomfortable, because our interests were so different that we had practically nothing to exchange. Even her house was not the one I had grown up in. When, after Father's death, she went back to teaching, her climb up the educational ladder, arduous, tough, but ultimately successful, had necessitated frequent moves from one school to another all over England. And I, in the meantime, had been sent off to boarding school (because she thought it would be bad for me to be in the same school where she taught). Then, later, of my own choice, I had gone to a drama school in France. Holidays, which might have been spent together, had more often than not been separate; Mother had found seminars and courses for me to attend, or she had been away on courses herself. And all these arrangements, I felt with unhappy certainty, had been made only to disguise an inner failure, the fact that Mother had no particular feeling for me, and, indeed, found me simply boring. The only real feeling she had, I was convinced, lay buried with my father and elder sister, who had died in the same year, though not together, when I was nine, long ago.

19

The fact that Mother had been obliged to go through the ordeal of their deaths on her own, for I was in Greece at the time, on a visit, had increased the distance between us. If only I had been with her at that time, I often thought, our relations would be different now.

Before Father's unexpected death I had been sent to stay with a Greek family on the island of Dendros. This had been Father's idea, in fact; he had spent time on Dendros during World War II, fell in love with the place, made friends, and wanted his children to share the experience. My sister, Drusilla, had gone some years earlier, but her visit had not been a success; she was delicate, hated heat, and wrote miserably, begging to come home. I, however, loved it there; I adored Father's friends, the Aghnides family; Calliope Aghnides, who was my age, became my special friend. When Father died, Mother found herself obliged to sell our house and move to a smaller one. (Father had been a singer, and taught singing and voice production, from which he had made a good though not lavish living.) Mother wrote to the Aghnides, explaining that the move would be even more distressing if I were there, getting in the way; Drusilla could give her all the help she needed; she asked if my visit could be extended a few months longer. Of course the Aghnides, in their kind and hospitable way, invited me to remain for as long as Mother wished.

And so the transfer from the house where I had been born and lived all my life took place when I was not there. I never entered it again. It was a big, pleasant farmhouse on the outskirts of Oxford. The loss of my father, who was kind, gay, gentle, fond of gardens, birds, and Victorian music-hall songs, together with

20

all the familiar surroundings of my childhood—even
my cat, Othello, had somehow got lost in the move—
was a strangely numbing shock. I used to dream wretch-
edly at night of my bedroom, with the irregular beams
in the ceiling and the view of the orchard; it seemed
impossible to believe that I would never go to sleep
in it again. (Years later, I went past the house and
wondered if I dared knock at the door and ask to see
inside, but courage failed me; it would have been too
painful.) Strangely enough, I never dreamed about
Father; it seemed as if he had sunk out of reach, down
to the very bottom of my mind.

The Aghnides were as kind as they could possibly
be during this time, and I was happy in Dendros; I
loved the Aghnides home, which was old and cool,
with orange trees growing round its pebbled courtyard;
I loved Calliope and enjoyed going to the Greek school
with her; in time the pain grew less painful. But then
came another pain; my sister, Drusilla, died in an accident at school on her seventeeth birthday. Mother wrote
this appalling news to the Aghnides and asked again if
my stay could be extended; to me she did not write at
that time. I was not told then, and had never, at any
later juncture, found myself able to ask Mother what
kind of accident had killed Dru.

This inability was, I suppose, a measure of the distance between Mother and myself. I knew she had preferred Dru to me. Dru was kind, reserved, serious,
hard-working, wanted to become a geologist; Dru took
after Mother, in fact; she had intended to go to Cambridge; whereas I, if I stayed in educational establish-
ments for twenty years, would never have turned into an
academic; I was not intelligent in that way. Also, I was
sure, Dru had been a planned child, whereas I was an

21

unexpected, inconvenient afterthought. At the age of ten I had grieved sadly for Dru, who had always been kind and loving to me, more like a third parent than a sister, because of the seven-year age gap between us; but I did not, as I had after the news of Father's death, wish that I could go home. The prospect, the thought, of all the changes that had taken place, the idea of being alone with Mother, was too frightening.

I acquiesced readily enough in the plan that I should stay on with the Aghnides at least until the following year. In the end, I remained in Dendros for nearly three years, and only returned to England because the Aghnides were planning a mass family visit to relatives in the U.S.A. They kindly suggested that I should go along with them, but Mother could not afford my fare, and although they offered to pay it, she could not allow herself to be beholden to them to such an extent. One of her primary qualities was a streak of granite independence. So at last, when I was twelve, I returned to England. By that time the Aghnides felt like my own family; I hated to part from them, hated to leave the hot, happy island.

It was a strange, sad return. Mother at that time was teaching history in a big school in Birmingham and had a flat near the school, so that was where I went. The flat had come furnished, so she had put all our furniture in storage and there was practically nothing in any of the three rooms to remind me of our home, save a box of my outgrown toys and books, which Mother had scrupulously saved for me. The worst part was that she and I seemed to be strangers to one another and remained so. She had arranged for me to begin the following week at a boarding school in the country, for, as she said, a flat in Birmingham was no place for a child; so, in a week, off I went, before we had had a chance to rediscover one another.

And, during the course of the following eleven years, the chance never did seem to come up. Mother did her duty by me, but her heart was now in her career, which she pursued with stoic tenacity and resolution. I looked up to her for this, I admired her, but I found it hard to love her, except in a remote and cautious and non-reciprocal way. She was so very unresponsive. I knew that she found it hard to get on close, relaxed, affectionate terms with anybody—she was a thorough Scot, and the double tragedy had the effect of accentuating her Scottishness and turning her inward even more. I felt it must devolve on me to bridge the gap between us, for I found contacts easier to make than she did, particularly after I was out in the world and mixing with congenial colleagues. But making contact with Mother still and always defeated me. I felt myself frozen by her reserve as soon as I ventured near. Consequently I kept deferring the effort until a time when I should have gained the required age and experience.

I hoped that I had not left it too late.

At last the train reached Stretford—a dark, flat, greasy industrial town that smelled, in the cool night, of breweries and tanneries and hot metal; the glow from its various factories splashed the sky with murky orange. It seemed a wealthy place—at least, there were taxis, quite a few of them, still waiting after midnight in the cobbled station yard; I asked one to take me to the hospital and was glad I had, for it proved to be a fifteen-minute ride to the outskirts of the town. Stretford, apparently, sat cheek-by-jowl on the Midland plain with Market Broughton, where Mother's school

23

was. I could have caught a train to Market Broughton just as easily, and it would have been faster.

Sister Crouch was still on duty in the casualty ward. She turned out to be a small, sharp-faced, sandy-haired, freckled woman, who took one look at me and said, "Eh, ye poor child, have ye been traveling ever since ye phoned me? Ye'd better come in my office and have a cup of tea and a warm-up. Yer mother's still unconscious, so there's no point in rushing in right away. I'm glad to have ye here, though. The time we'll want ye is when she comes round."

"What happened to her?" I asked again, sipping the scalding, tasteless hospital tea.

"It was a head injury. A beam fell on her. They had to mend a fracture in her skull and remove a clot."

"Was it—will she—" I gulped and began again. "What are her chances?"

Sister Crouch gave me a hard, measuring look. "Does your mother have no other relatives—no brothers, sisters, other children at all? No parents—grandparents? Just you?"

I nodded, terrified.

"You're very young," she said. "But you look sensible, I must say. Well, I'll tell you: the surgeon who operated thinks her chances are only about one in ten."

"Of surviving?"

"Of surviving—*or* of getting back to normal life. *But* —" she raised her hand, though I had not spoken; I was staring at her numbly—"*but*—I don't agree with him. Being a woman myself, I can understand better what kind of a person your mother is: I think she's tough, she has a very strong natural resistance. I think her chance is better than that. But it may be a long, slow job. And I may be wrong. Don't get your hopes

24

too high. Mr. Wintersmain has a lot of experience. It all depends how she comes through the next thirty-six hours."

"Yes, I see." I didn't see much, really.

Sister Crouch gave me a kind look and said, "You can come and see her now; then you might as well go home and get some rest."

Home? I thought bemusedly, following along the wide, glittering passage that smelled of warm drugs; where is home?

Thanks, no doubt, to her status as headmistress of M. B. Comprehensive, Mother had been placed in a private room, and there she lay, flat under a white cover, her head swathed in bandages, and various tubes connecting her to bottles clamped on tripod stands beside the bed. Her face, which, I was relieved to find, had not been injured (I had been nurturing some awful fears about that), was exactly as I had often seen it: pale, rather severe, the lips pressed tightly into a firm line; a slight frown creased her forehead as if, even in the depths of her unconsciousness, she had many anxious preoccupations. Her brow looked very high, under the bandage; then it came to me that, of course, they would have had to shave her head for the operation. Poor Mother—not that she attached any importance to physical appearances; but her hair had been pretty, a pale, Scottish straw-gold which, even in her early fifties, had not shown a single strand of gray. And she always had a look of great dignity; it was sad if that had been taken from her with her hair. Oh, well; there she lay—remote, forbidding, like a helmeted crusader on his tomb, her face the color of gray marble. I suddenly had a woeful childish longing to kneel down, bury my face in the side of her bed, and cry out, "Mother,

25

Mother, *say* something to me! Tell me you love me! Tell me you're going to be all right!"

Instead I leaned over and gently kissed her unconscious cheek.

Sister Crouch, looking as if she found such behavior irrational but humanly understandable, said, "Now ye'd best go home and get some sleep."

Where is home? I thought again, but she went on, "I'd call a hospital car to take ye, but it's only ten minutes from here to yer mother's house and a walk will help ye to sleep."

"I—I haven't a key to her house," I muttered confusedly, but Sister Crouch said, "We have her bag here; it was brought in with her; I daresay there's a key in it. When ye come in the morning, bring a little case, will ye, to take her clothes away; and I'll give ye a list of other things that she'll be needing. Of course we'll phone you directly there's any change if we think ye should come back. We have the number. It's very lucky ye're so near. And you call us any time, of course, if ye want to."

Very kind, Sister Crouch; she really wanted to do her best for me.

She gave me Mother's severe, executive-type, black handbag; and of course the keys were in it, along with a lot of other orderly belongings: diary, driver's license, and various professional cards.

Mother lived in the headmistress' house, on the edge of the huge school complex, which, as it happened, abutted on the hospital grounds. Not an ideal arrangement from the point of view of the patients, but nineteenth-century manufacturing towns had to grow where they could.

So I walked off through the solid Victorian suburbs

with their wide streets and manufacturers' villas, gothic-turreted and set about with cedars, araucarias, and rhododendrons, thinking how strange it was, that I should be entering Mother's house like a burglar at three in the morning; I had been there only once before, six months previously, driven over by some friends in the Birmingham Rep. Mother had not held the appointment long; less than a year.

The house, like the rest of the school buildings, was post-World War II, a small, square, plain block not much better than a glorified Council house. At least it was functional.

I let myself into the narrow hall and removed a large pile of business mail from the doormat to a side table. Sitting room on the right; behind it, dining room, which my mother used as an office; and kitchen straight ahead. The house smelled of nothing; it was strictly tidy and scrupulously clean. I went into the kitchen and poured myself a glass of milk; thought about making a cheese sandwich and abandoned the idea; turned the kitchen light off and went upstairs.

On the second floor the layout was identical: Mother's room, spare room over the office, bathroom over the kitchen. I left Mother's handbag in her bedroom, which, like the rest of the place, was ascetically bare and tidy, furnished with what I suppose must have been fashionable modernity in Mother's youth: blond, curved Swedish wood, rugs and curtains in pale buffs and grays. No ornaments, no treasures, souvenirs, or bits of nonsense. No photographs, either. Nothing to say the person who lives here once had a husband and children. Discouraged, I laid the bag on her tidily made bed, found the linen cupboard, took out sheets, and made up a bed in the spare room for myself. It would

27

have been more practical to sleep in Mother's room, where there was a phone extension, but I couldn't fancy the idea.

It was so quiet and lonely in that house that I found it almost impossible to get to sleep; I seemed to be the only person in the world. Night sounds from the town kept me awake, but they were disembodied, mechanical noises: trains shunting, factories grinding and wailing; they did nothing to allay my solitude.

Finally, at about ten to six, I fell into a heavy sleep, and was roused, almost at once, it seemed, by the phone ringing. Startled, confused, I stumbled into Mother's room and grabbed the receiver, expecting Sister Crouch to say, "Come at once," but the voice was unfamiliar.

"Gina Signorelli here," it announced without preliminaries. "I've just called the hospital and they say there's no change."

"What—who—?"

"That *is* Miss Meiklejohn, isn't it? They told me at the hospital that you were staying in your mother's house."

"Yes—yes, I am. I'm sorry, I've only just woken up." I looked at my watch. It was half past seven. "Who did you say you were?"

"Gina Signorelli. I'd like to call around in half an hour and collect Mrs. Meiklejohn's mail if you don't mind. There will be a lot of things that need answering. Is that all right?"

"Yes, of course," I said, vaguely remembering from the previous visit that Gina Signorelli was my mother's secretary and personal assistant.

"Can I bring you anything when I come?" she said, sounding less staccato, more human and friendly.

"Eggs? Bacon? It's a long way from you to the shops. Or are you a vegetarian, like your mother?"

"No, I'm not, but please don't bother, thanks; I'll go out and get something later."

"Sure? Good-by, then," she said and rang off briskly.

Still dazed from my short, broken sleep, I wandered shivering to the window and looked out. Here, more than half way up England, winter still had a firm grip on the landscape; icy, gray fog mostly concealed the town, but I could hear its industry revving up for the day: buses and trains rumbling along, factory hooters screeching, traffic snarling. I had a bath—cold, because I had failed to find the heating switch the night before, but at least it roused me; dressed, and was making a pot of coffee when Miss Signorelli arrived, announcing herself by a long peal at the front-door bell.

"I decided not to take you at your word," she said, dumping a carton of groceries on the kitchen table. "I daresay you're like your mother—hate to put people to trouble. But there's only food for rabbits in this house. And you need to eat to keep your strength up. Cheese and fruit may be all very well for *her*—goodness knows how she manages all she does on it—but I'm sure it won't do for you. It'll be a long day for you, I daresay.

She looked at me severely. She was a short, brisk person about my mother's age, high-colored, with snapping black eyes and dyed black curls. I remembered her now; she had taught shorthand and business methods at a school in Bath where Mother had been senior housemistress. Greatly impressed by Miss Signorelli's formidable efficiency, and liking her robust good temper, Mother, when she achieved her headship, had written and asked if Gina would be interested in the job of school secretary. Gina had accepted and moved

29

to Market Broughton with her invalid father. I vaguely supposed that in Mother's rather lonely and nomadic existence, Gina Signorelli was one of her few semi-friends, a small remaining link with an earlier epoch, about the closest thing to a confidante that she allowed herself. They even, I remembered, called each other by their Christian names.

Miss Signorelli seemed disposed to be friendly to me, and since she was evidently familiar with the house I was able to ask her where the various things were that I had been unable to find.

When I poured cups of coffee for us both, she went into the front office and collected a daunting stack of work for herself.

"There'll be three times as much to do, with your mother not here," she said. "I'll be over at the school all day, so give me a call if there's anything you want. And try not to worry too much about her," she added unconvincingly. "I'm sure she's putting up a terrific fight."

But I could see that she was sad and worried herself. "Can you tell me exactly what happened?" I asked. "The hospital didn't give me any details."

"It was the new gym roof." Miss Signorelli sat silent with her lips pressed together for a moment, then burst out, "Your mother told them and *told* them that the design was bad. But the board of governors insisted on accepting the lowest tender. Trust *them*. The cheapskates! Your mother was watching the end-of-term gym display yesterday afternoon, and suddenly there was an awful cracking from the roof and it started to sag in the middle. I wasn't there myself, but Emily Johns is a pal of mine—she's the gym mistress—and she told me what happened. There were about sixty people in the place—mostly children, a few parents—and four exits; Emily and your mother shouted to them to keep calm and make for the nearest door in an orderly way, but the roof collapsed before they were all out, and of course your mother stayed till the last—very properly, she'll get the Royal Humane Society medal or some such thing, damn those penny-pinching misers—one of the concrete girders broke in half and came down on her. I will say for the ambulance service here, they're efficient: they were round in ten minutes and she was in the hospital on the operating table in half an hour; all that *could* be done *was* done, but it shouldn't ever have happened in the first place. Hers was the only serious injury; otherwise it was nothing but cuts and bruises."

She paused with trembling lips and blinked at me furiously. "Well—I won't fuss you with all that. You've enough to bother you without going into whether it should have happened. Oh, when you go round to the hospital—I assume you'll be going fairly soon?—could you take your mother's Teachers' Provident Association card—they need the code numbers for their records, because she's in a private room; you'll find it in her desk, pigeonhole at the extreme right-hand end, the one marked PERSONAL. Right?"

"Yes, of course."

"Make yourself a decent breakfast first, though. And I hope they have better news for you by the time you get there," she said gruffly, and stumped away, clutching her bundle of papers.

I did not feel in the least hungry, but Miss Signorelli was right: it would be a long day; so I made myself

31

scrambled eggs and ate them fast. Hurriedly washing the dishes, I found in myself a neurotic urge to leave the kitchen as specklessly tidy as if Mother herself might walk in at any moment.

I left the kitchen immaculate and then did a quick check through the list that Sister Crouch had given me —nightwear, handkerchiefs, talcum, eau de cologne, slippers, dressing-gown, bed-jacket (not that she would be needing most of those for a while, I feared). Then I remembered the TPA card Miss Signorelli had mentioned. Carrying the little overnight case, I went into Mother's shadowy, unheated study and opened the desk, which was of the sloping-lid bureau type.

The contents were characteristically tidy and ordered—clean stationery neatly stacked underneath, tray full of pens, pigeonholes individually labeled, ACCOUNTS, TAX, BANK, HOUSE, UNPAID BILLS, TPA, SCHOOL, and the one on the far right indicated by Gina Signorelli, PERSONAL. I pulled out the bundle of papers it held, which were secured by an elastic band. There was a brown envelope marked Birth & Marriage Certificates, a passport (up to date and quite well used, due to Mother's frequent attendance at educational conferences), some National Insurance papers, and a plastic folder containing a few photographs.

So this was where she kept them. Filled with curiosity, I opened the folder and pulled out the half-dozen prints it contained. Here they were: two or three each of my father and sister, one of me, taken at the age of seven, holding Othello; my father had taken the picture, I remembered. Now I came to consider the matter, I was not even sure that Mother owned a camera; she certainly was not given to taking snapshots. That pic-

32

ture at age seven was the last I could remember having taken, apart from school and passport photographs.

I looked at the pictures of my father and sister. He was a thin-faced, smiling man with black hair, like mine, and a heavy mustache. The pictures of him were blurred and not very good—one had an impression of a young, gay, rather reckless character; that was about all. In one shot he was leaning back and laughing; in one he held a tennis racket, squinting at the sun; the third showed him in swimming trunks, a towel around his neck. He looked youthful, happy, carefree—not a strong personality, perhaps; yet not, surely, a man looking at whose picture you would say, "He will die at forty-one?"

And Drusilla? A serious girl—straight features, direct gaze; mouth set in a firm line, like Mother's, page-boy-style hair; rather a broad nose; wide-apart eyes, defenseless and concerned; I struggled to remember their color—gray, like Mother's? blue, like mine? This was a passport photo, taken, I thought, when she was sixteen, about the age when I remembered her last; all three prints were the same. My sister, Drusilla: why did she have to die before she had explored even the edge of her experience? What tide swept her away? Why were she and my father so lacking in stamina? Compared with them I felt vulgarly tenacious of life, full of obstinate health and vitality. I wondered if Mother shared this attribute? Or would she let go, as they had done? Shivering a little in the cold, gray room, I slipped the pictures back into their case and snapped the elastic band around the bundle again. A last envelope fell out from among the rest, one I had overlooked. I turned it over. On the front it bore a typed message:

33

TO BE GIVEN TO MY DAUGHTER PRISCILLA
MEIKLEJOHN IN THE EVENT OF MY DEATH.

I stared at this in a numb, stupid way for a long
time. To come across my formal name never fails—
as I have indicated—to throw me off balance. And to
have such an experience coupled with that freezing conclusion, that irrevocable period—"in the event of my
death"—that is enough to loosen the roots of one's
being at *any* time.

Suddenly I couldn't bear the sight of the envelope or
its inscription. I bundled it back under the elastic with
the other papers, removed the TPA card, which I put
in the case with Mother's toilet things, and rapped
the desk lid down. Then I hastily left the house, locking
up behind me, and hurried off to the hospital as if the
devil were on my heels.

Sister Crouch had gone off duty, of course. She had
been replaced by the day sister, a lugubrious, cowlike
woman called McCloy. Sister McCloy was kind in her
way, and doubtless an excellent nurse, but I missed
Sister Crouch's astringent common sense. Sister McCloy
seemed to be irresistibly attracted by doom, to assume
the worst as a foregone conclusion.

"Ach, not one in a hundred of those cases recover,"
she sighed, escorting me to Mother's bedside, where the
scene was unchanged. She fetched me an armchair and
left me alone in the melancholy little cube of a room,
whose features I came to know acutely well during the
next few days. Every hour or so, a nurse would come
in to check that the drip feed was working and that
Mother's temperature and pulse were unchanged. Otherwise Mother and I had the room to ourselves and I
sat looking at her marble profile, wondering what was

34

in that sealed envelope, what crucial piece of information, what terrifying fact, was so important to us both that it *must* be withheld from me throughout Mother's lifetime, and *must* be imparted to me after her death.

At half past eleven the surgeon who had operated on her, Mr. Wintersmain, came to look at her. He was a big, smooth man, like a gray seal, beautifully turned out, full of kindness and consideration, and I didn't like him. Everyone had assured me that he was a first-class surgeon, one of the best in the country, that Mother was uncommonly lucky he had been at hand after her accident—but I couldn't stand the way he called me "young lady" and assured me that everything possible was being done. It was all bedside manner, poured out as easily as cream from a silver jug; I couldn't believe a word he said. He, like Sister McCloy, had already prejudged my mother and dispatched her, in his mind, to the undertaker's parlor; to him, she was just an interesting case, and his only concern was to extract the maximum information from her state which he might use on some future occasion.

He discouraged me from remaining at Mother's bedside, making it plain he did not think she would come out of her coma. "It's not good for you to stay indoors all day," he said indulgently, as if I were about sixteen. "Why don't you go out and take a walk in the park, have lunch at a café, go to a movie? You could come back here at about teatime, but I really don't expect any change at present."

I said very well, without the least intention of following his advice, and stayed put. At noon I went down to the hospital canteen and ate a horrible sausage roll and a tasteless orange; then I returned to my vigil.

35

I imagined living in a bed-sitter in Crowbridge, pushing Mother along the promenade in her wheelchair once a day, paying Mrs. Charm to keep an eye on her. . . .

In the afternoon there came a message from the board of governors of Market Broughton School to say how terribly sorry for me they were and offering help of every kind; if there was anything at all that either Mother or I myself needed I was to let Miss Signorelli know . . . and of course all the medical bills would be taken care of by the school, I was not to have the least anxiety on that score.

"That's because they're scared your mother will sue —or you will," said Gina Signorelli, who had brought the message. She looked thin, feverish, and belligerent, in a bright-red plastic raincoat and hood trickling with drops, for a violent rainstorm had set in outside. "I'm quite surprised they offer to pay the bills; that's practically an admission of liability." She pinched her lips together. "How is she now?"

"No change."

She scowled at me and said, "You look terrible. How much did you sleep last night? I suggest that I drive you home this minute, otherwise you're going to get soaked. Come on. They'll call you fast enough if they want you."

"I don't like to trouble you."

"Bosh. I'll be glad to get away from my father for once. And I picked up your mother's car, which was having its M.O.T. test—you might as well have the use of it."

So she drove me home in Mother's little Renault and then came in and cooked spaghetti Bolognese for

36

us both, with the maximum speed, efficiency, mess, and clatter, banging saucepans about, frying onions till the kitchen reeked with blue smoke, leaving a trail of greasy dishes and tomatoey spoons behind her, smoking all the while, dropping cigarette ash on the floor, and onion peels and crumpled paper, meanwhile telling me tales of the parsimony and stupidity of the school governors; my mother, a very fastidious, tidy, silent worker, would have been thunderstruck at the chaos created all over her kitchen during the space of half an hour.

While we ate, still in the kitchen, which by now felt quite warm and friendly, as if it were in some other house, Gina Signorelli put questions to me about my job, displaying considerable knowledge of the theater. She had brought along a bottle of fierce red wine, which, together with the food and the cheerful conversation, helped me to forget, for half minutes at a time, the cause of my being there, the waiting that seemed to press on my shoulders and temples like a whole universe weighted with rocks of silence.

We drank all the wine between us and Gina became fierily lachrymose.

"I'm just so *angry* that such a thing should have happened to your mother, after all her battles and her struggles," she said several times over. "She is such a wonderful person. People often don't realize about her—they think she's tough."

"The thing is that Barbara's so bottled up inside herself," Gina continued, flushed and voluble, pulling grapes off a bunch she had brought and spitting out the pips. "Ever since your sister's suicide, she's been scared to invest affection in anything with more life in it than

37

a cactus—except in the most cautious, distant way—"

I could hear her sharp voice talking on, but what it said made no sense; the room had gone black and scarlet around me; I had to clutch the edge of the enamel table hard to prevent myself from toppling right off my chair. Gina, fortunately, noticed nothing; she was away into a dissertation about my mother's character: her sagacity, her pride, her judgment, her keen intelligence.

"Excuse me," I said, when I had somewhat recovered, seizing on a gap in this eulogy. "I'd forgotten you knew my sister."

Drusilla had been at the school in Bath.

"Well, I never actually taught her, dear, because she was in the science stream and I was tutoring in business methods at the Pulteney school, but of course I knew her to say hello to."

"I've never been told," I began, slowly, very cautiously, "what—what happened to her. What she actually—did. You remember, I was in Greece then. And Mother's never talked about it."

"I'm not at all surprised. It was dreadful for your poor mother. Dreadful! And so soon after she lost your father. . . . It was assumed that was why your sister did it. Poor girl. I suppose she just couldn't get over his death."

"What *did* she do?" I asked, swallowing. The taste of tomato and onion and wine burned in my throat.

"It was on her seventeenth birthday. That's a nervous age. And I suppose the anniversary upset her."

"She—?"

"She went to school as usual and locked herself in the chemistry lab and swallowed a bottle of sulphuric acid."

38

"Oh—"

The next thing I knew, I was lying on the floor among the onion skins and Gina Signorelli was worriedly wiping my face with a damp teacloth.

"Stupid ass I am," she said, wielding the cloth, angry and remorseful. "Shouldn't have told you that. Got carried away, thinking about it. Obviously Barbara felt it best to keep it from you, and quite right too. Here, drink this." She handed me a mug of hot, black coffee.

I said, "I'm glad you told me." I gulped the bitter, burning stuff, and added, "I'd have had to know some time. Mother couldn't have kept me insulated forever. I'm grown up now. Besides—" Besides, suppose Mother died, leaving me in ignorance? But perhaps she meant to? Or was that the message in the envelope? I stopped short, wondering this.

Gina said, "Yes, you're grown up—but you've enough to do with fighting your own battles, no need to be burdened by what's past and gone. That's why your mother's always kept you at a distance, you see; she wanted you to stay clear of it all." What all? I thought. "She was teaching at the Pulteney, remember, when Drusilla ki—died; they were together too much, Barbara thought, after it happened—they'd kept upsetting each other all over again, hadn't given the grief a chance to heal. And girls of seventeen are emotionally unbalanced, it's a tricky time—so Barbara was determined the same thing mustn't happen to you."

Well, she succeeded, I thought. Here I am, alive to tell the tale.

We washed up, sober and silent now, and Gina said she'd better be getting along. *"Don't* sit around brooding, now, dear; have a bath and get to bed."

39

Yes, I said, and thanked her; the same advice in one form or another had been given me a wearisome number of times in the past twenty-four hours. Why shouldn't I wear myself out if I wanted to?

But of course she was right.

It was still pouring, so when Gina had put herself back into her red plastic rainwear I drove her home— she lived with her aged father about a mile away in a different bit of suburb—and then came back via the hospital, stopping to inquire.

Still no change. Call again later if you like. Or to-morrow.

I re-entered Mother's house; the smell of onion and tomato and bayleaf had almost dispersed already, as if the secretive aura of the place were so dense that it expelled all common domestic vapors.

Then it occurred to me for the first time that day that, in my single-minded preoccupation over Mother's condition, I had completely forgotten my friends at the Crowbridge Theatre Royal. It would not be too late to phone them now.

I put a call through and asked to speak to Eve Kransky, who was our manager.

". . . Eve? This is Mike. I just rang to ask how it had all gone?"

"Mike! My *dear!* How are *you?* How's your mother?"

"No news yet; she's still in a coma. I'm just waiting about."

"Oh, how awful for you! We've all been thinking of you *so much*. We're so sorry for you."

"How did the play go?" I said quickly.

"My dear, a triumph! Really—all we'd hoped. Oh, well, Sam fluffed his lines, of course, and Mary came in too soon and was watery but—all in all—wonderful! And wonderful reviews—not only in the Crowbridge *Advertiser*—the Kent *Messenger* and the East Sussex *News* as well!"

"Really?" I was impressed. "That's marvelous."

"Special mention of your sets and costumes, too, dearie—we're really on the map. I'll send you stats of all the notices—or will you be coming back in the next couple of days, do you think—?"

She stopped awkwardly, and I said, "No, I don't see how I can get back at the moment; I'm terribly sorry to leave you all in the lurch like this—"

"Don't be absurd; we miss you, but we're managing. Hope the cuttings cheer you—they ought to. Keep your courage up, Mike, love; we're all thinking of you."

I thanked her, gulping, and rang off.

Then I started upstairs, walking very slowly.

I was thinking about my sister, Drusilla.

Drusilla was a *brave* girl, as I remembered her from thirteen years back. She had turned to face a charging bull, as I scrambled through a fence to safety. She had flown at a man who was hitting his small child in the Oxford High Street, and told him to stop or she would fetch the police. She had lanced her own boil when it was swelled up as big as a plum. What situation could have been so terrible that she was afraid to face it?

I am entitled to know about this, I thought, standing with my hand on the square-carved newel post at the head of the stairs.

Drusilla was my sister. I loved her too, even if she was seven years older. She used to bathe my knees when I fell down and grazed them, she dug splinters out of my fingers with a needle, she read to me when

41

I was in bed with measles, she made a set of Greek dresses for Katina, the doll she brought me.

Ever since I was nine, I had been cut off from my family. If it were not for the Aghnides—whom I had contrived to go on seeing occasionally after I left Dendros—my life would have been completely destitute of affection, dry as a bone. Nobody could help that; it was just misfortune; but the truth, at least, I am entitled to; and if the truth is in that envelope downstairs, I am going to have it now.

So I walked downstairs, entered Mother's study, took the packet from the PERSONAL pigeonhole, found the envelope, and opened it.

For a mean second, I was tempted to slide a pencil under the flap, or steam it open, so that, at a pinch, I could reseal the flap and pretend I had not tampered with it; then I thought: "Hell! If I can't be honest about a thing like this, there is no hope for me."

So I boldly tore the flap across and threw the crumpled envelope into the wastepaper basket.

Inside, there was a single sheet of typed paper. No date.

It said:

"My dear Priscilla,

I hope you will understand why I was never able to bring myself to talk to you about this.

The fact is that it was just too painful for me. And if you can't understand that—well, there is nothing to be done about it now.

You will be an adult by the time you read this letter, able, I hope, to stand distress and pain—because I have done my best to ensure that you had a peaceful, untroubled childhood in which to grow up without these troubles impinging on you.

You have a right to this information now, though.

Your father is not dead, as you have always understood. James Graffin is still alive, although he has changed his name. He is alive, but I must warn you: the *way* in which he is alive may be such a terrible shock to you that even the cushion of thirteen years'— or however much more it is—separation from him is not sufficient to prevent knowledge about him doing you profound psychological harm. Nor can I see that you could derive any benefit from knowing about him. So I do urge you, most earnestly—I *beg* you—to think very, very carefully before taking any step towards getting in touch with your ex-father.

If, however, you feel you must take this step—then you can write to Hazeler, Malling, and Tyrwhitt, Solicitors, at 87, Turl Street, Oxford, who are instructed to give you further information.

Believe that I did what I thought was best for you."

It was signed, *Mother*.

I was still reading the final paragraph when the telephone rang. The downstairs extension was on the wall by Mother's desk—about a foot from where I stood. Automatically I put a hand out to the receiver.

"Hullo?"

"Hullo, this is Sister Crouch. I think you should come down to the hospital, Miss Meiklejohn; your mother has begun moving a little, which might be the prelude to a return to consciousness."

"I'll be there in five minutes," I said.

43

It wasn't much more. Sister Crouch and a young doctor I didn't know were by her bedside when I slid into the room. Mother was stirring a little, restlessly; her fingers clenched and unclenched. Sister Crouch gave me a brief, approving nod, which both commended my speedy arrival and indicated that I had better sit down by the bed.

"It may be a while yet," she murmured. "And even if she does come around, she may not be very clear, of course; ye realise that? Ye've got to be prepared for *anything*. Ye've got to be tough."

I nodded, with a dry mouth, feeling about as tough as a mashed potato, and fixed my gaze on Mother's gray-marble profile, which was now, from time to time, disturbed by flickering frowns, brief contractions of the brow, as if she anticipated all the problems that awaited her just over the frontiers of consciousness.

In fact it was about fifteen minutes before she opened her eyes. When she did, she fixed them on me immediately, and a look of perplexity came over her face.

"Why, Prissy!" She hadn't called me that since I was about four. "What ever are *you* doing here?"

" 'Lo, Ma," I said. "I just thought I'd come and see how you were getting on."

I tucked my fingers around hers, which, for once, clasped mine quite firmly, but she said, "Oh, there was no need for that. That was very naughty of them—*very* naughty. Did they send for you? They shouldn't have made you come all this way—what about your first night?"

She was half whispering; her voice almost faded

44

away at this moment; she was plainly a good deal puzzled, trying to comprehend these unusual circumstances. Her eyes roamed about the room and she slightly moved a hand, as if to try to feel her head.

"It's all right, Mrs. Meiklejohn," Sister Crouch said firmly. "We want ye to lie *quite* still, if ye please. Ye're in hospital, and ye're going to be perfectly okay"—over Mother's recumbent form she gave me her short, brisk nod—"but in the meantime we want ye to co-operate, and not try to move about, just lie absolutely still. Will ye do that?"

"Yes, if I must," whispered Mother, with a touch of her usual dry manner. "But why did you fetch my daughter? There was no need for that."

"Naturally your daughter wished to see how ye were getting on," Sister Crouch said reprovingly. "Now we want ye to rest all ye can, Mrs. Meiklejohn."

"Oh, very well."

Mother's eyes moved back to mine. I did my best to give her a big, wide, cheerful smile, though I was feeling pretty beaten up, one way and another.

However, Mother seemed to accept my grin at face value and her own cheek muscles faintly crinkled in response. Her eyes were closing again, but she opened them momentarily to say, "What about your opening, though? Wasn't that tonight?"

"No, it was last night."

"Good gracious," she muttered in a perplexed tone. And then, "Did it go well?"

"Big success. I'll show you our press notices by and by."

"Good," she said, and then she floated off into what seemed to be an ordinary peaceful sleep.

"She'll be all right now," said Sister Crouch.

⨂ 2 ⨂

FUGUE

Julia Saint was moving slowly, idly, along Winston Churchill Street, enjoying the delicious warmth of the sun, and the smell, so strong that it was almost a taste, of orange blossoms mixed with souvlaki. The orange scent came from the municipal gardens, to her right, where, between the formally spaced and trained trees, bright scarlet hibiscus clashed madly with bougainvillea, which was the hideous color of black-currant purée mixed with milk. Chinaberry trees dangled clusters of lilac blossoms, which added their faint fragrance to that of the orange blossoms. Big, fat cacti writhed octopus tentacles, and the sandy grounds, already bare and dusty, seemed to exude a light, salt sweat.

The smell of souvlaki drifted from the harborside cafés ahead of Julia, where prelunch customers were already settled at the gaudily colored tables, sustaining themselves with coffee, ouzo, and Fix.

Julia surveyed the tables with leisurely satisfaction. Presently, when she had done all her shopping, she would return to the hotel and pick up Dikran, they would stroll back here and have a long, unhurried, enjoyable lunch at one of the harbor cafés —finding a sheltered spot, however, because, although the sun was powerful, the wind, as so often on Dendros in April, still blew keenly; waiters were darting among the little tables clamping down flapping tablecloths with metal clips. When, presently, Julia sat on one of the waterside benches to write some postcards, she found it necessary to tuck each card into her bag as soon as written, or they would have blown into the slapping, turquoise water, which bounced all the little red and blue and green boats up and down, and caused the masts of larger ships—cruise liners and yachts—moored farther out, to crisscross in a perpetually changing pattern of X's and Y's.

"Dendros is delicious," wrote Julia on a postcard to her brother. "We are having a charming time. Dikran is looking after me hand and foot. What a contrast! I feel I've never been pampered in my life before; am thoroughly appreciating it."

"Dendros is the most heavenly island in the world," she wrote to her daughter. "There are piles of oranges everywhere and a dusty camel sits perpetually outside the town gate for local color. I hope your finals aren't weighing on you too much. Give my love to Pa if you see him." Then she crossed out that line, x-ing it vigorously to ensure its illegibility. Though, no doubt, shrewd little Tansy would decipher it just the same.

48

To her son Julia wrote, "Darling Paul, Dendros is terrific. You would love the swimming. The interior is like trying to drive over Ryvitas turned edgeways on. I have collected some roots of plants for you. . . ."

Then she wrote to her best friend. "Dearest Dee, a second honeymoon is really a rejuvenating experience. I would never have believed that I could feel eighteen again. Dendros is the most wonderful island in the whole Mediterranean. Believe it or not!"

Having stuck stamps on all her cards, she carried them to the stately stone post office, which looked like the headquarters of the League of Nations, adorned with carved stone lions and blue-and-white flag fluttering overhead. There she posted them, bought more stamps, and walked on, at a slow, enjoyable pace, beside the harbor, under the crumbling, honey-colored stone arch, and so into Dendros Old Town, where the streets, become suddenly narrow and cobbled, ran steeply uphill or downhill, with distant views of the sea under Turkish arches, and were lined with dark, aromatic shops displaying, near the harbor front, everything the tourist heart could desire, and, farther away from the water, more commonplace household requisites for the natives themselves. There Julia bought muslin shirts for her daughter and nieces, silver jewelry for her friends, Turkish delight—only, of course, it was different here and called by a local, unpronounceable name—for her brother, who had a sweet tooth; records of Greek music for her son, and a scarf for herself. She wished to buy something for Dikran but could not fix on anything suitable; what can you give somebody who is rich enough to buy up the whole island if so minded? His wealth was delightful, but it did give rise to such problems from time to time. In the end she bought him a simple set of blue worry beads on a leather thong; very plain, but a beautiful blue.

By now she had reached the oldest part of the Old Town, where there were few shops but the houses had blossomed into the most exuberant colors possible; they were painted in sizzling lime greens, luminous powder blue with a touch of lilac, fondant pink, french-mustard ochre, lavender, and pea green. Roses, red lilies, sweet williams, and geraniums blazed and burgeoned in the tiny courtyards behind the secretive façades. Cascades of feathery green hung over the walls into the narrow alleys, and cats lay drowsing on stone doorsteps. Old ladies, dressed in black from head to toe, with faces brown, wrinkled, yet clear-cut as the lines of the ships in the harbor, plodded past in their canvas shoes and gave Julia brilliant smiles in return for her murmured greetings. I hope I look exactly like that when I am old, thought Julia, and also: What a pleasure not to be recognized anywhere, to be completely anonymous wherever I walk! What a comfort to slip through these narrow streets as unremarked as the old ladies in their black shawls! Probably not a soul in this island has heard of Lady Julia Gibbon, or of Arnold Gibbon, or of Lord Plumtree, or his wife, the sumptuous blonde Christian Plumtree. Well, no, that's not quite true, since English Sunday papers are on sale in the New Town bookshops, but, after all, who would be interested in their news stories here? The foreigners who come to Dendros do so for the sun, or for the music, or to buy furs, since Dendros has little to offer in its history or archaeology; and people who are interested in furs—or music—are generally interested in little else; which makes them dull but comfortable company for the heartsore and spiritually bruised.

We'll have lunch, thought Julia, hugging her armful of parcels in their frail, exotic foreign wrapping paper; a light lunch, just fish and salad; then we'll walk around the point to the western side of the island, where the waves are bigger, and swim—if Dirkan wants to; then a siesta; then a stroll, maybe round to the commercial harbor, where we saw the man with the radio-controlled boat the other day (damn, I forgot to mention that when I was writing Paul's postcard; must remember to tell him about it the next time I write, it's just the kind of thing he'd like); then dinner—perhaps at that place on the raft in the harbor that Dikran wants to try; and then we'll take a cab out to Helikon for the concert, the heavenly Haydn baryton trios, the best concert yet. . . .

It seemed hardly possible that a day *could* contain so much straight pleasure.

She left the Old Town regretfully and walked back along the harbor front. By now she was pleasantly tired, looking forward to a seat in the shade and her first sip of ouzo. She walked past a man and thought—with an old reflex acquired during the past nine months in England—Damn, he recognized me, before recalling with relief that the man had not recognized her because she was Lady Julia Gibbon but because she had been with Dikran yesterday when they saw him—no, the day before. It was the same man who had been operating the radio-controlled toy boat in the harbor, and that was the only reason why he had recognized her; he had smiled and waved his thanks when Dikran loosed the boat from a tangle of water-logged rope and set it free to return to its owner across the harbor.

51

She walked past the fishermen with their dark blue boat *Aphrodite* pulled up by the harbor wall, from which, with the aid of a pair of kitchen scales, they were selling their catch in paper cones as swiftly as customers could buy the small, wriggling fish and take them away. She passed the tourist shops with their beads, pottery, and postcards, and the car-rental offices, whose beach buggies sat inconveniently in the middle of the wide pavement.

Leaving the harbor, Julia walked purposefully out along Winston Churchill Street to where the Fleur de Lys Hotel stood by itself in somewhat somber isolation on a tree-grown spit of land extending into the Aegean. The Fleur de Lys had been built in the nineteenth century and patronized at that time by royalty; since those days, it had declined but still kept three stars and the blessing of Michelin because the staff and the cuisine were French, whereas the half dozen new, high-rise creations which had sprung up like groundsel at the south end of the island during the past few years had local staff, who came and went when the orange or olive crop demanded their attention, and menus that could be classified only as mongrel-tourist. Their gardens were cement slabs and potted geraniums, whereas the Fleur de Lys had handsome old ilex trees and rose-covered pergolas; shabby it might be, but it was also stately. It possessed its own beach, too, dotted with chunks of white concrete which would support thatched beach umbrellas when the wind dropped. Julia threaded her way among these, looking to see if her husband was still on the beach. Since the hour was now one-thirty, the sand was deserted; all the hotel's sedate residents were elsewhere, studying their lunch menus. Not a soul in sight. Julia walked through the garden and entered the dark, cool lobby. There she asked the desk clerk for the key of numéro quarante-cinq, but, as she had expected, he told her that Monsieur was *en haut,* doubtless waiting for her in their suite. Without troubling to wait for the slow, old elevator, Julia ran up the one flight of shallow, curving stairs and tapped on the door of 45.

She had to wait a moment or two; then the door was pulled open very suddenly. Dikran stood there. She felt immediately that there was something wrong about him, though she could not have defined precisely what was the matter. It frightened her, because it seemed a total wrongness. She noticed beads of sweat on his face, which looked drawn, aged by five years since she had left him after breakfast.

He said at once: "I'm all mixed up! What's happened this morning? I can't remember anything!"

He clutched both her hands violently, standing in the doorway as if he had been waiting for her there, on that spot, in a state of desperation, ever since she had left.

Julia was swamped at once by a flood of terror. So *this* is what has been in waiting! This, behind all the comfort and the luxury and pampering. I might have known it. I might have known that nothing lasts more than a few days, nothing is what it seems.

But, coinstantaneously, she was saying in a calm, confident voice, as she had so often to her children during many crises, "Come and sit down. Sit down and tell me what's the matter."

She pushed the door shut behind her and urged him through the entrance lobby into the sitting room beyond. Still clutching painfully at her hands he sat—awkwardly, sideways—on the tasseled velvet sofa and said again, "I'm all mixed up. I can't remember anything. What time is it?"

She told him and then said, "*What* can't you remember?"

She noticed that his hands were very cold, that he was shivering. On the low coffee table beside him was a mess of papers—tourist brochures, cruise advertisements, and the rental papers for the cars they had hired on the two previous days. Dikran turned these over in a perplexed, miserable, distracted way, peering at them as if they were written in Sanskrit.

"I've been trying to look through these, but I don't understand them! I can't remember anything. I'm all mixed up!" he said. "What time is it?"

"I've just told you."

"I've forgotten. What did you say?"

"A quarter to two."

"I'm all mixed up," he said again, hopelessly.

Deeply alarmed, but seizing on the nearest practical test, Julia tried to take him through their day. "Do you remember our having breakfast on the terrace? The coffee and croissants? Do you remember my saying that I'd prefer to go shopping on my own, because I thought you would be bored?"

"No, I don't. I don't remember *anything*. What time is it?"

"It's about ten minutes to two," she said once more. "I think you ought to see a doctor, darling."

"No. *No!* I don't want any doctor messing about with me!" he cried out in a wild panic. "Only, tell me what's happened. I'm all mixed up. I can't remember anything."

Julia looked at the gilt telephone, which stood on a marble table behind his shoulder. She was really terrified by now but did not know whether, if she tried to phone for a doctor, he might not physically stop her. So she suggested, diplomatically, "Don't you think you ought to put some warmer clothes on? You're shivering quite badly."

He was wearing a toweling beach shirt over cotton slacks. She noticed that his watch was not on his wrist. His feet, in *espadrilles,* were sockless. All this was most unusual for Dikran, whose sartorial habits were highly conventional; he would wear beach clothes only while actually on the beach, not a moment longer; not even in the privacy of their suite. He really disliked informal clothes.

"Did you go swimming, darling?" she asked him.

"I'm all mixed up. I can't remember," he said yet again, picking up the car-rental papers and despairingly shuffling them about.

"Come into the bathroom and get changed," Julia urged, endeavoring to hide her fear under the most soothing, matter-of-fact tone she could muster. She picked him a clean shirt from his closet and steered him in the direction of the bathroom. He came biddably enough and began to pull the toweling shirt over his head. As soon as she saw him thoroughly engaged in this operation, she flew back to the other room, partially pulling-to the door behind her, but not closing it completely in case he should feel himself shut in and become anxious.

Picking up the phone, she carried it to the length of its cord, out through the french doors, onto the balcony. Down below, the turquoise sea sparkled and bounced; along its edge the absurd row of short, phallic stone posts, painted powder pink, marched around the side of the paved promenade to the end of the point. Beyond the blue sea floated the coast of Turkey, mysterious and shadowy, with mountains wreathed in a few gauzy clouds. Everything was just as it had been half an hour before.

Feverishly joggling the receiver rest, Julia glanced back through the french windows; Dikran was still in the bathroom, thank heaven.

"Oui?" said a voice suddenly in her ear.

"Mon mari est malade," Julia murmured, fast and low-voiced. *"Je crois qu'il a un—un coup de soleil."* Was that the French for sunstroke? "Please, can you send me a doctor as fast as possible—a doctor who can speak some English, if there is one?"

"What are his symptoms? Does he have fever?" the clerk asked efficiently.

"No—no fever. But he is altogether confused. He does not know what has happened. I—I am very anxious about him."

"Remain tranquil, Madame. The doctor will attend you without delay."

"Thank you," she whispered, and put down the receiver, feeling just a little better. At least she had *done* something; taken some measures.

She went to the bathroom, where Dikran, having changed his clothes, was staring in a puzzled manner at the swimming trunks that he had just taken off.

Handling them, Julia observed that they were damp around the waist. Also, his *espadrilles,* bought two days before and so far unworn, had spots of tar and a little sand embedded in the rope soles.

"You were on the beach, then? You did go swimming? You said at breakfast you weren't sure you wanted to."

56

"I don't remember," he said doubtfully. "No, I didn't go swimming. I was on the balcony."

The balcony was now in shade, but it faced southeast and had had the full sun all through the morning. Perhaps he had gone swimming, come back, and then fallen asleep out there.

Julia said, "I think you have a touch of sunstroke."

"But the sun's not hot!" he said quickly and anxiously. "I wasn't out long. What time is it? I'm so confused." The alarm in his face was painful to see.

"Two o'clock," Julia said, looking at her watch, wondering if any quarter hour had ever gone so slowly before, and how soon the doctor could reasonably be expected.

She sat beside Dikran on the velvet sofa while he shivered, shifting restlessly, and looked with unhappy eyes around the cool, shady room with its dignified furniture. Every minute or so he asked, with the regularity of a metronome, "What time is it? I'm all mixed up."

"Do you know who I am?" Julia rather desperately inquired, hoping to shunt hs mental processes onto a new track.

But he said, "Of course I do," in an annoyed tone.

"Well, who am I, then? What's my name?"

This he would not answer; he began to fidget with the papers again, restlessly turning them over and over as if he hoped to find among them the clue to what had gone wrong with him. And she sat beside him, asking herself: Who is this man I lightheartedly married four weeks ago? Who is this stranger? What is going to happen next?

Within fifteen minutes there came a light tap on the door, and Julia, hugely relieved, hurried to open it.

The man who stood outside was dark, slight, and

dapper; he was, Julia noticed absently, dressed with great neatness and elegance; he carried a black doctor's bag. He gave her a look which contained solicitude and unfeigned admiration of her own appearance, nicely blended. "Mrs. Saint? I am Dr. Achmed Mustafa Adnan. The hotel inform me that you are anxious about your husband."

"Oh, I am! Do please come in!" She shut the door behind him and then, leading him into the main room, said to Dikran, "Darling, here's Dr. Adnan, who wants to talk to you."

Dikran instantly shrank back, alarmed and reluctant; his glance moved swiftly from one to the other of them.

"Mr. Saint?" The doctor gave him a shrewd, careful, assessing glance, and then laid down his bag on a gilt-and-marble table. "How do you do, Mr. Saint? How are you feeling now?"

"I'm all mixed up," Dikran said, for about the twentieth time. "I can't remember anything that's happened to me."

"So? We will soon fix that. Don't worry about it."

Dr. Adnan spoke English with great fluency and rapidity but with the slightest touch of an accent. He was evidently not Greek; Turkish, perhaps, Julia thought, or Lebanese. Quietly and efficiently he began to examine Dikran, testing his visual reflexes, face reflexes, and blood pressure.

"What's the *matter* with me?" Dikran kept asking miserably.

"We will soon find out. Tell me, what is your name?" Adnan inquired, banging on Dikran's patella, which responded sluggishly.

"Dikran."

"Dikran what?"

"Sareyan."

"He's changed it to Saint, actually," Julia murmured.

"You are nowadays called Mr. Saint?" Adnan suggested.

"Yes, Saint, Saint," Dikran agreed testily.

"Your age, Mr. Saint?"

Dikran gazed at him blankly, and after a pause Julia came to the rescue again.

"He's fifty-one, Doctor."

"Nationality?"

This time the answer came readily enough. "American."

"So? With a name like Sareyan, I had thought you to be Armenian. Of Armenian extraction, perhaps? And who is this lady?"

Who, indeed? thought Julia. But Dikran looked at her and replied, "She's Julia."

Adnan nodded. "So. She is Julia. And who do you think I am?"

"How should I know?" snapped Dikran fretfully. "What's the matter with me?"

"You have a slight touch of sunstroke, Mr. Saint, that is all, I am glad to inform you."

"*Sunstroke?* But the sun's not hot! I wasn't out very long!"

"None the less, sunstroke is what you have. The sun here is treacherous, when the wind blows especially, as today. Our air here on Dendros is so very clear that the ultraviolet rays come through like laser beams and can knock you cockeyed before you realize what is going on. Your case is by no means uncommon, if that is any comfort to you, Mr. Saint. Every summer, we have visitors suffering from this."

"Will he be all right?" Julia murmured anxiously.

But the doctor's air of imperturbable confidence was already doing her good.

"Sure, he will be all right! His blood pressure is up a little. I will give him now an injection to fix that, and to relieve his anxiety. It will make him sleep. He will sleep maybe five hours, then he will be right as rain, Mrs. Saint, don't you worry. He will just have to take things easy for a few days. Now just pull your pants down, if you please, Mr. Saint, and lie on your side on the bed."

Obediently Dikran moved to the bedroom and did so. Julia, following, watched the doctor administer what looked like a massive injection. "Largactil I give him, also Catapresan. Now also I leave you some pills, Mrs. Saint, which you make him take in two hours, in four hours, and last thing tonight before he goes to sleep. Furthermore, I think it advisable he stay in bed maybe thirty-six hours, and no alcohol at all, please, during that time. Is he a heavy drinker?"

"No, I would say moderate," Julia replied, thinking really how little she knew about Dikran's habits.

"Well, not even moderation for the time being, I beg!"

Julia accepted the pills and looked at Dikran, who was already lying back, his eyelids beginning to flicker drowsily and a more tranquil expression relaxing his aquiline features.

"You'll see; he will be asleep in two shakes," the doctor prophesied cheerfully, and led Julia back into the other room. "Now I am going to suggest," he went on in a lower tone, "that we transfer your husband to my clinic, and you too, if you wish, Mrs. Saint, for a few days. You stay in Dendros how long?"

"We have been here two weeks and are staying another fortnight."

"In the clinic he can be under my own observation and also have continual nursing care if necessary, until he is better, which is not so easy in a hotel. Better that way for you also—you are not tied to his bedside all the time. You agree?"

"Oh, I'm not sure—I don't mind looking after him —" Julia felt rather desperately that she was being hustled into an unknown situation.

"Naturally, naturally you want to look after him! You are on your honeymoon, yes? It is a most upsetting experience for you."

"Did you *guess?*" She blushed with annoyance, meeting his intelligent, plum-black eyes.

"No, Mrs. Saint. Or should I say, Lady Julia? I am not psychic! But I read the English papers. For quite a few years I was living in England, in Yorkshire to be precise; the *Sunday Times* and the *Observer* make me very nostalgic. And I recognize you at once as Lady Julia Gibbon. (May I now say that I greatly admire your work?)"

"Thank you," she murmured mechanically, trying to overcome a feeling of depression. Wherever one went, it caught up. No use trying to escape.

"Lady Julia Gibbon last month marries an American millionaire," said Dr. Adnan gaily, "and what more natural than to find the happy pair in our lovely island of Dendros, enjoying a peaceful honeymoon far from all the nuisance and turbulence of civilization? It is too bad that a small mischance like this should come to afflict you, but do not worry unduly; we shall soon have your husband again as fit as a flea."

He smiled at her with a flash of large, perfect teeth,

and her spirits lifted again, as irrationally as they had
sunk. In spite of his slightly odd and florid turn of
phrase, Dr. Adnan did inspire confidence in her. There
seemed genuine goodwill and friendliness under his
aplomb.

"So do not you think it best if you remove to my
clinic?" he repeated.

"Your clinic? Do you really think that necessary?"
she temporized. The thought of having to shift from
the comfortable Fleur de Lys to a strange clinic, with
all its rules and prohibitions, was very disagreeable.

"My dear Lady Julia." Now the plum-dark eyes were
suffused with sympathy and friendly understanding. "I
know how you must be feeling, believe me! You have
suffered already from most distressing publicity. A
horrible divorce ends what were, I am sure, many,
many years of happy married life. And then what? You
find and marry a kind, rich man, who will take care,
provide, cherish, look after all things. Your distress is
allayed. And what then? He is stricken down by sunstroke, becomes, all of a sudden, like a baby. Once
more you have all upon your shoulders. What a singularly demoralizing shock, just when all seemed set for
comfort and security! But do not be so troubled. I
assure you with all sincerity that your husband will
soon be quite okay again. Only—in the meantime—
how much better, do you not see, if he and you both
are in the care of my clinic? He must necessarily sleep
for many hours, during which you are alone and miserable in this Victorian dump of a hotel. Whereas in my
clinic you have company, you have the music, you have
me, to keep an eye on you—for I can see that you are
suffering from shock, almost as much as the unlucky

Mr. Saint. It is a very distressing experience that you have undergone."

"The music—?" She was bewildered. "What music? You mean—?"

"Ah—you did not know? I see you there several nights at the concerts, I thought you had known already. Yes, I run the medical side of Helikon, and my friend Joop Kolenbrander, he runs the musical side; and there, my dear Lady Julia, you shall be very welcome; we shall find a nice room for you and your husband, an orderly to sit by his bed and keep an eye on him, and this very evening you can be listening to the Haydn baryton trios, knowing that he is in good care instead of sitting here in this dismal room biting your nails with worry and loneliness. Does not this seem to you a sensible plan?"

It did, and tears pricked in Julia's eyes at his kindness. "You're perfectly right. I'll start packing right away."

"I'll phone at seven to see whether he has yet woken; and if he has, I will immediately send one of the clinic cars for you both. May I say"—Dr. Adnan contrived a neat, friendly bow while at the same time swiftly and tidily repacking his medical bag—"May I say how very honored we shall be by your residence at Helikon, Lady Julia? Perhaps while you are there our little repertory company might celebrate by performing an act from one of your beautiful plays? We should be very happy if you would consider permitting that?"

"Oh, I'm not certain—I'd really rather not have it known that I'm there—" she replied vaguely.

"Of course, of course not, just as you wish—"

Julia was wondering if the clinic was outrageously expensive—but of course such considerations were quite irrelevant, a thing of the past, out-of-date hang-ups from her previous life. The size of the clinic's fee was immaterial; Dikran could pay it with as little thought as he gave to the purchase of a concert ticket. An aged joke wandered back into her mind: "However much that doggie in the window costs, I can afford it."

"Till this evening, then," Adnan said, with another bow, another admiring glance; and he walked softly from the room.

He need not have taken such pains to be quiet, Julia reflected; Dikran was by now in a profound sleep. She covered him carefully with a cellular blanket from the closet and sat down in one of the armchairs, moving it so that she could see Dikran through the open bedroom door. She would have liked to be able to read and lose herself in a book for a couple of hours, but she had finished her own supply of paperbacks and Dikran had brought nothing but a history of gold in world financial markets, which proved totally unintelligible to her. She found a rumpled overseas *Telegraph* in the bottom of the closet and read that, but it lasted her only a short time, since she found herself unable to face the more depressing items, of which there were many, such as Yet Another Strike at Chrysler Plant, $4,000,000 Kidnapped Rittenhouse Baby Found Dead in Manhattan Basement, and Three-thousand-ton Tanker Aground on Ushant.

She decided to pack up their belongings, and was in the bathroom collecting Dikran's toilet things when he called out in a frightened voice, "Where are you?"

She went swiftly to his bedside, saying, "Here I am! It's all right!"

Taking his hand, she sat down on the bed. She was

64

not sure if he realized who she was, but her presence seemed to soothe him; he soon sank back into a peaceful slumber. She remained sitting by him on the bed for ten minutes or so, gently smoothing the strong, thick black hair with its faint sprinkling of silver, while her memory, rebelling against discipline, conjured up for her other rooms and other beds.

Two difficult tears found their way down her cheeks.

But Dikran slept again, and presently she called Room Service and asked for a sandwich and a glass of wine.

⸢3⸣

IMPROMPTU

I stood on the observation deck of the good ship *Monty Python*—which was carrying nine hundred assorted school kids along the Mediterranean to Ephesus, Heraklion, Rhodes, and other educational spots—gazing down thoughtfully into the bows and wondering what would be the best way of breaking to Mother the unpalatable news that she was not going to be allowed to take up her duties at Market Broughton School again for at least another two months.

The high sides of the Corinth Canal were sliding past us like giants' layer cake on either side. Down below, on the red-ochre foredeck, sailors darted about in a beautiful display of choreographic elegance and discipline, winding windlasses and arranging snowy-white ropes, getting the ship ready for Piraeus. The sight of their blue-clad forms against the red-brown background, among the dazzling white machinery and ropes, proved, as always, so distracting and enchanting that it prevented me from getting to grips with my problem.

Behind me Ted Toomey, the sports director, was giving a Yoga class to a batch of sixth formers.

"Breathe upward. Now downward. Now sideways. Now backward. Fill the bottom of your lungs with air," he said. "Now the middle. Now the top. Feel the air creep right up to your collarbones."

I followed his advice myself. The air crept up to my collarbones, but brought no intelligent ideas with it.

After a while Ted told his group to relax for five minutes, and came to lean on the rail by me.

"How's your mother today?" he inquired kindly.

"She's getting better all the time. It's quite fantastic how much progress she has been making! That's what's worrying me. Now she's beginning to feel all conscientious and responsible again, she hates being idle, and she's starting to make remarks about getting back to work."

It had been easy at first.

Grateful—as well as they might be—for Mother's not having died when the concrete beam fell on her head and for her not even having been blinded, paralyzed, crippled for life, or showing signs of intending to sue them for negligence and parsimony, the Stretfordshire County Council Education Department had offered—indeed practically forced on Mother—a free cabin on one of their educational cruise ships, plus free accommodation for companion-attendant (me) as soon as she was recovered enough to travel—which turned out to be about five weeks after her accident.

At the time this was fixed up, Mother was still in a docile, comatose state, under a bit of sedation; she

67

seemed quite pleased, for once in her hardworking life, to be looked after, cosseted, and planned for. "Everyone is so kind," she kept saying dreamily, as if she hadn't earned every scrap of their conscience-stricken attention and solicitude. One of the governors lent his Daimler to drive us from Stretford to Tilbury Dock, the others made sure that our cabin was supplied with books, magazines, flowers, fruit enough for a battalion of fruit-eating bats, mohair traveling rugs, portable radios, battery irons, and all the luxuries that mean and uninventive bureaucracy, racking its brains, could summon up. For the first couple of weeks on the *Monty Python*, while we whacked our way through the chilly Bay of Biscay and around the coasts of Spain and Portugal, this served well enough. Mother slept a great deal and was content to rest on her bed most of the time while I read aloud the works of Jane Austen to her.

"Are you sure this isn't a terrible bore for you, my dear child?" she would say from time to time. "I feel anxious about your being away from your job for so long."

But I had been able to show her letters from Eve Kransky about the success of our production, and the clippings from the Kent *Messenger* and other papers, even a letter from a London manager, which had made my heart beat high when I received it, for he asked if I'd be interested in doing some work with his company and invited me to go and have a talk with him some-time.

"Eve's keeping my job for me, that's all quite okay," I told Mother. "And I've got other irons in the fire too, so don't you fret; just concentrate on getting better. I'm planning to enjoy this time off. And I shan't get bored. I'll do some work with the kids to keep my hand in."

In fact, during some of the hours she spent napping, I had organized various theater workshops and a shipboard performance of *The Tempest*, which we scraped together in record time, cutting huge chunks and doubling parts. All things considered, it might have been worse. So Mother's anxieties in that respect were allayed. Provided she was satisfied that I was usefully occupied and acquiring professional experience in one form or another, she felt that all was well with me.

In fact, I was missing my Crowbridge friends a good deal and did, from time to time, feel lonely and cut off, but, what the hell! it was only for two months. And my improved relationship with Mother was a continual source of satisfaction and amazement. It could no longer be called a parent-child bond—that, I supposed, was gone for good—but it was growing into a cautiously affectionate (if simply based on day-to-day needs) link between two adults. Jane Austen and our joint purpose of getting Mother well again were all we had in common, and that was just enough.

But Mother's reviving urge to return to work created a complication.

The consultant at Stretford, and another who had been fetched in from London, had been highly categorical about the undesirability of her trying to do too much too soon. "A headmistress's position is one of constant pressure and strain—need for making decisions every minute of the day—long hours—dealing with hundreds of people—and so on and so on."

A letter giving the results of some final tests had been waiting for me at Venice. All was well, apparently, but it declared unequivocally that she must have at least three months away before she even began to consider going back to school.

Of course—it was true—they didn't know Mother, whose toughness had plainly been a surprise to Mr. Wintersmain; but still, one must defer to experts, you can't just toss their opinion out the window. And indeed it was plain to me that Mother, although rapidly repossessed of all her intelligence and clear-thinking capacities, had a long way still to go before she was really back to normal functioning. Much weaker than she liked to pretend, she still found it necessary to rest a great deal, and, in small matters, was much more gentle and biddable than I had ever known her. It seemed pretty plain to me that she did in fact need several more months of convalescence.

"What's your plan for her?" Ted asked. "You're not going home on the second leg of the cruise?"

Stretford County Education Authority organized their six-week cruises in two halves, so as to make maximum use of the ship while not taking the students out of school for too long. One lot of kids had the outward three weeks and were flown back from Dendros, where the airport was handily close to the harbor; another lot would have flown out and be waiting there, ready to embark. I felt fairly certain that Mother would have had enough and would not wish to revisit any of the places she had been; furthermore, if we went back on the *Monty Python,* that would get her back to England too soon to return to work. Added to this, I felt sure that, once she was in England again, it would be almost impossible to restrain her urge to get back into harness. So I had made other arrangements after I received the letter in Venice.

"I've fixed for her to go into Helikon," I told Ted.

"And I'm going along too, for a bit, just to get her settled in and keep an eye on her."

"Helikon? What's that? I've heard the name," he said vaguely. "But I thought it was a kind of music center like Tanglewood? Is it on Dendros?"

"Yes, it is. It's a music center and health clinic, both. They have music and drama festivals there, and students can work—they have regular seminars—but there's also a big residential clinic where people are treated for all kinds of ailments—lung and rheumatic troubles, or ulcers, or blood conditions, or overweight, or alcoholism, or heart disease—or, like Mother, people just go there to recuperate after illness and accidents. The music and stuff is going on all the time, and the public are allowed in to the concerts and dramatic performances, so it's becoming quite a tourist attraction to the island."

"It's an odd combination—music and medicine?" Ted's round, good-natured face looked a little puzzled.

"Not at all," I said firmly. "Lots of civilizations have mixed music with healing. Aesculapius said music was a cure for many ills. The Babylonians used to cure their mad people by music—primitive tribes do still. So I'm hoping that Mother will find the combination soothing and beneficial."

She had, I knew, a kind of brisk, no-nonsense fondness for the more cheerful, less introspective areas of classical music—Haydn symphonies and piano sonatas, Beethoven quartets (the early ones), the Brandenburg concertos, most of Mozart. I thought—hoped—that she would find enough at Helikon to keep her contented. At one time, long ago, she had played quite a competent voilin, and had enjoyed amateur chamber music, but she found less and less time for such activi-

71

ties during her climb up the educational ladder, and her violin had long since been put away; I could not remember even seeing it during the time I was staying in her house.

"Who founded this Helikon place?" Ted asked. "Has it been going long?"

"Eight or nine years, I think. It was founded by a famous pianist, Max Benovek—do you remember him?"

Ted said yes, but I was not sure if I believed him. However, he then added, "Benovek. Didn't he die, or something?" looking a bit more intelligent.

"He died, yes; he had leukemia, I believe. But before he died he had an unexpected long remission, and during that time he had the idea to start this place— probably doing so gave him an extra lease of life, gave him something to take his mind off his illness. So he lived in Dendros for a while and oversaw its beginnings. Some local Greek Croesus helped with a lot of cash— it's a fine thing for the island, of course. Gives quite a bit of employment and brings tourists. Benovek was a rich man himself and did a lot. He paid the medical director's salary and endowed funds for poor students, and so forth."

"Who's the medical director?"

"A very outgoing Turkish doctor called Adnan— Achmed Mustafa Adnan." I smiled a little at the thought of him. "It's due to him that the diet at Helikon is vegetarian."

"How come you know so much about this place?" Ted wanted to know.

"I've worked there, when they were holding seminars, in three different summers; washing up and doing odd jobs in exchange for drama classes. They get first-rate

72

people there, because it's such a lovely place. And of course, if you are working, you get to see and hear everything that's going on."

It had been Calliope's idea the first time; she had written to suggest it, so I would have an excuse to go back to Dendros. We had both worked up at Helikon, which was not far from the Aghnides' house. And that time had been so good that I had returned twice more, despite Mother's slight disapproval, and even after Calliope had married her cousin Dmitri and had gone off to live in Elizabeth, New Jersey. The first year on my own, I had stayed with Calliope's parents, but after her mother died, and her father became very old and frail, I moved into the center itself and became quite closely acquainted with several of the staff. Adnan was also a friend of the Aghnides family. So it had been easy enough to arrange for Mother's admission, in spite of the fact that the clinic was always booked up for months in advance.

"Well, that sounds a very good plan," said Ted, turning to give his group the office to collect up their muscles and put themselves vertical. "I'd have thought from the sound that it was the ideal place to convalesce— sun and air and music and fruit and so on. And a vegetarian diet ought to suit your Mother? What are you worried about?"

"It's just that Mother's so keen to get back to her school. I'm afraid she may jib when she hears about it. I haven't broken it to her yet. And so far we haven't fallen out over any major issue."

At the start of the trip, comatose and accepting, still under some sedation, she had not asked how long the cruise lasted or when we would get back. I had hoped that this state of mind would endure until we were safely installed at Helikon. Now I was not so sure that it would.

"Above all, don't let her get upset or overexcited," Consett-Smith, the London consultant, had warned me. "Humor her as much as you can in small ways."

I could see breakers ahead.

Another consequence of Consett-Smith's warning was that I had never yet found the courage, or thought the time right, to break to Mother the fact that I had read her not-to-be-opened-till-after-death message about Father. It just did not seem a suitable conversational topic for someone in a delicate state of health.

That lay on my conscience a good deal, but my conscience would have to take care of itself. Her steady recovery was obviously of more importance. Meanwhile, I had put the note into a plain envelope and replaced it among the other papers in the desk. Mother had not, in fact, even been back to the house, since it had been felt that the sight of her home might awaken undesirable cares and responsibilities; she had been driven straight from hospital to dockside and had made no inquiries about any business or personal affairs.

Naturally I had put in a good deal of time wondering about my father—in fact a large proportion of my scanty solitude was employed in this profitless occupation. Could he be in prison? I speculated. In a hospital for incurables? An institution for the mentally incapacitated? Living in disgraced seclusion because of some frightful social offense? What could he have done? Held up a bank? Raped a mother superior? Escaped to Russia with plans for a laser beam strong enough to disintegrate the Kremlin? What was the condition so outrageously shocking that Mother felt my whole mental balance might be endangered to tottering point if I knew about it?

Whatever it was, it could hardly outstrip my imaginings; and I did long to have some plain information on the matter. But obviously this topic came high in the category of things likely to upset or overexcite Mother, and so I had not spoken about it; I tried not even to think about it when I was with her. There it lay, notwithstanding, almost visibly between us, I sometimes thought, like a heavy lump of undigested trouble.

Had Drusilla's suicide, I wondered, been because she knew this terrible thing about Father?

But if Father was alive, why had he never made any attempt to get in touch with me? Had he perhaps given Mother a promise that he would not? If so, *why?* Because she thought it possible I too might kill myself if I knew about him? It seemed almost ludicrously improbable. I am naturally of a hopeful, energetic temperament—I couldn't even imagine wanting to kill myself. And yet Drusilla *had* killed herself—in the most dreadful way, too—or so Gina Signorelli had said and I had no reason to disbelieve her. Oh, Drusilla, my poor sister, how could you have been driven to such an awful step? I mourned inwardly, thinking of her many kindnesses to me, of the strong, determined, adult person she had seemed to me when I was seven or eight. Could she really have done it? Or was it an accident, unintentional? That was another thing I could not possibly ask Mother—at least until she was much more recovered—and yet I felt I had a right to know.

There was one person, though, who might be able to give me information on these matters, and that was Calliope's father, old Demosthenes Aghnides. When Mother had written to the Aghnides asking if I could go on living with them for another year and telling of Drusilla's death, she must have given some explanation for her request, some explanation which at the time had been withheld from me. Now I was resolved to ask for it. I loved Mr. Aghnides, he was one of the people I respected most in the world, and he had always been fond of me; he was a wonderful old man, wise as Socrates and honest as bread; I knew that he would tell me the truth if he thought it right to do so and had the information. Which was another good reason for going to Dendros. I was enormously looking forward to seeing him again.

Meanwhile I read aloud the works of Jane Austen and hoped that no serious showdown would come to disrupt our tranquillity.

It did not come just yet. We saw the factories at Piraeus and the gasworks at Heraklion. We listened to lectures on the city-states and the Persian wars and the Minoan civilization. Mother put on a few pounds in weight and I gave the kids some fencing lessons. And then, on the last evening before we docked at Dendros, the confrontation came, just when I was beginning to feel foolishly secure.

I had fallen into the habit of brewing Mother a mug of Ovaltine or Horlicks last thing at night. There was a small, unused stewards' pantry next door to our cabin, where I was able to cook up snacks; service on the boat was a bit sketchy, since it was primarily a utility cruise for the kids.

Mother began to sip her milk that evening and then said placidly, "I've been thinking, dear, that I'll fly back with the group who go home direct from Dendros. I don't want to waste another three weeks going back on the ship, I've had enough time off already—and you've wasted quite enough of *your* time looking after me—sweet of you though it has been, don't think me ungrateful—"

"Oh, but you can't—" I began, appalled.

"And why not, pray?"

Mother was still quite placid, a long distance from the kind of high-strung outrage she would once have generated if I had ventured on a flat negative like that. But she sounded uncommonly firm and definite.

"Well, for one thing, because Mr. Wintersmain absolutely forbade you to travel in a plane for nine months to a year after your operation. And you have to check with him first, then. Have you forgotten that?"

Plainly she *had* forgotten; or more probably, at the time when he laid it down, she had been in such a drowsy, sedated state that she hadn't really taken it in.

I saw a look of acute distress come over her face— quite obviously she was wondering what other important information had slipped past her during that time, before she was alert enough to take hold. I felt a pang of sympathy for her. Poor dear, she was used to being so independent and decisive—and she still looked so frail and vulnerable. Apart from anything else, her hair was taking a long time to grow back, in spite of the fact that I cautiously massaged her scalp every night with olive oil and various patent preparations. She now had a sort of golden-gray fuzz that made her look piteously like a day-old chick. Since she was outraged at the suggestion of wearing a wig, I had made her several head-hugging turbans out of black jersey, and she wore them all the time. They seemed oddly formal on the ship, and made her, with her large eyes and high cheekbones, look like some distinguished,

not to say formidable, character out of Russian literature. The close frame of black strongly accentuated
every shade of expression of her bony, lowland features.

She said, frowning a little and compressing her lips,
"Well, I certainly don't wish to stay on this ship for
another three weeks."

"No, I hadn't thought you'd wish to do that—"

"What, then, if I can't fly?" she said sharply. "Can we
get a train back from Athens?"

"We might do that presently, perhaps. We'll see!
But honestly, love, you aren't quite well enough for
long train journeys yet—think how tired you are by
the end of the day. So I've fixed for us to stay a few
weeks at Helikon," I said cheerfully.

But her face had turned the color of burned paper—
a kind of bluish white. I watched, hypnotized, as her
fingers loosened their grasp and the glass of malted
milk, slipping out of them, dolloped its gluey contents
over the brown carpet. I was just in time to catch her
before she slumped forward out of her chair in a dead
faint.

Somehow I managed to get her hoisted onto her
bunk, and then phoned through in a frenzy for the
ship's doctor, who came like lightning, bless his heart.
He was a young, cheerful character who rejoiced in the
improbable name of Dr. Albumblatt; he had been extremely kind and solicitous with his regular check-up
visits throughout the voyage, having been heavily
briefed, I suppose, by the board of governors and the
county education department.

Thank goodness he was fairly reassuring, after he
had made a careful examination of her. She was still
unconscious. "Nothing the matter that I can find. She's

still barely convalescent, don't forget. You say she was upset after hearing that she's not allowed to fly?"

"I suppose it might have been that."

"Might easily. She's a woman of strong character, your mother. Mortified at finding that she's not up to doing something she'd set her heart on. Don't you think that might be it?"

"I suppose it might," I said, wishing guiltily that the news had not come as such a last-minute surprise, that I had led up to it more carefully.

"To find there's something that's physically beyond her—after having led such an active, independent life —very upsetting."

"I shouldn't have let it come as such a shock," I lamented.

"You didn't know she'd forgotten she wasn't allowed to fly. Nor did you know what she was planning. Don't blame yourself. She'll get over it. Look, I'll give her a tranquilizing injection now. That will ensure her a quiet night. Then, when we reach Dendros, I'll phone the clinic to send an ambulance, and the whole move from ship to clinic can be carried out while she's still sedated, so as to upset her as little as possible. By the time she wakes up, she'll be there, snugly installed. Don't you think that's a good plan?"

It was certainly the easiest plan for me, though I felt very bad about poor Mother, once more practically kidnaped. She had accepted the cruise with great docility, but would she be so good-natured about Helikon? In spite of my longing to get her there and into Dr. Adnan's care, I felt it was unfair to her, though I knew Albumblatt meant it for the best.

"Well—I suppose you're right," I said slowly.

"Of course I am right," he said.

So he gave her the injection. I suppose things would have turned out very differently if I had not allowed him to do that.

⟨ 4 ⟩

BOURRÉE

The room allotted to Dikran and Julia at Helikon was, by Hotel Fleur de Lys standards, fairly austere. But it was comfortable enough. There were plain, low, flat twin beds, each of them simply a mattress set in a kind of wooden box. There were two plain Scandinavian armchairs, a writing desk, and a chest of drawers fitted against the wall. No balcony, but two windows, each with a window seat. An abstract picture on the wall and a plain, thin carpet. There was a tiny bathroom, functional but highly utilitarian.

Julia wondered how Dikran, accustomed all his life to luxury, would react to it when he woke. But Dikran was still asleep.

The outlook, though, was superior, she had to admit, kneeling on the window seat and leaning out to catch the early morning air, which was deliciously fresh.

81

Their two windows were at right angles, facing different ways. The one from which she was looking faced out over a stretch of intensively cultivated hillside, beyond which lay the sea. On her right grew a large and beautiful lemon orchard. Straight ahead the terraced vegetable beds dropped down the hillside, then came a narrow blacktop road, then a section of tomato plants protected from the wind by thick screens of reeds. Then a strip of beach, then the sea, today a pure, angelic blue. Across the sea the Turkish coast, far off today, a hazy, floating mirage. To the far right, beyond the lemon grove, a rocky hillside rose up to a saddlebacked headland. The hillside was all a mixture of dark and light foliage among rocks—dark little shapely cypresses like exclamation points rising from some low-growing gray shrub almost the color of lavender. Perhaps it *was* lavender, Julia thought happily. She resolved to go and investigate it at the first opportunity—after breakfast perhaps. If one was allowed breakfast at Helikon?

Dr. Adnan had told her the night before that it was a vegetarian establishment. "You prefer to share fully in our regime, I hope?" he said, strolling back with her after the concert. "Doing so will make you feel more one of our family while you remain here?"

"Certainly," Julia bravely replied, wondering what the regime involved.

"Good! Excellent! We meet at ten tomorrow and I show you round. In the meantime Zoé, our dear warden, will assign you your diet and treatment sheets."

"Do I really have to have *treatments?*" she said anxiously. "After all, I'm not ill!"

"You will be surprised!" He gave her his wide grin —it was beginning to remind her of Mr. Jackson in

The Tale of Mrs. Tittlemouse. "Aha—you think your-self in perfect health now. But—I can assure you—after three or four days here you will feel so different that you will be sorry for the poor self you brought here, with the big hollows under her eyes and the shaking hands"—he took one, held it a moment, then shook his head at her—"the pain in the back, the stiff neck, the bad dreams, the headaches, the sour taste in the mouth—"

"Stop, stop! All right, I'll take your treatments. I might as well, I suppose, while Dikran is recovering."

"Valiant lady! You will enjoy them, you will see. There is nothing at all to fear."

Just the same, she had gone to bed somewhat apprehensive, slept badly, worrying about Dikran, and waked early, wondering what the day's program held in store. She felt as nervous as on her first arrival at boarding school.

Ravished by the sudden sound of music, she looked around for its source and moved to the other window, which faced out, rather unexpectedly, into the quadrangle of Christchurch College, Oxford, England.

"Or, at any rate, as near as we could get it," Dr. Adnan had explained cheerfully. "We left out one side of the quadrangle, firstly to give a sight of the sea, secondly because we ran out of money. The quadrangle was the idea of Mr. Capranis, a local landowner who has endowed us very handsomely—indeed he gave all the land that the clinic stands on. The Christchurch layout was his idea; he is very attached to Oxford."

"He went to one of the colleges?"

"No, his first car was a Morris. It gave him a curiosity to go and see the place. And he liked it."

"The quadrangle seems very much at home here,"

83

Julia remarked thoughtfully. "I suppose, when one remembers the design of English colleges is based on early ecclesiastical architecture—"

"And that the early religious orders modeled their monasteries on forts and crusaders' castles—just so!"

"It's not surprising that it fits so well into this landscape. Though I *am* surprised that you have got grass to grow in your quadrangle."

"Well, we are lucky to have a spring behind the clinic that seldom dries up. Very good water! There is a most pretty path up the little valley—trees and waterfalls and nightingales. You must by no means neglect to take that walk. But in mid-summer, I must confess, our grass does not always survive. We do have, though, a fish in our fountain—very proper, just like the one in your Mercury pond at Oxford."

Looking out now, Julia could see an early-rising contingent of record players perched around the rim of the Mercury pond, playing some cheerful music by Handel, while a trio of dancers performed a series of intricate modern dance movements, standing on one spot close together and achieving their effects by skillful, controlled leanings and bendings. The statue of Mercury, waving his broken staff in the middle of the pond, seemed anxious to join them. "They look like willows," Julia thought. "Perhaps that is the intention." And then, "I'm going to like staying at Helikon, I think."

A light tap on the door deflected her attention from the dancers.

Dikran still slept. She went to open the door quietly and discovered that two cards had been tucked into the metal slot on the outside. They were marked with the day's date and, respectively, MR. D. SAINT and LADY

84

JULIA SAINT. Mr. D. Saint's said simply: "Bedrest. Massage. Consultant, Dr. A. Mustafa Adnan." Julia's had a whole lot of hieroglyphics which were meaningless to her, and presumably denoted various kinds of treatment. There was a square at the bottom marked *Diet*, which on both cards had the figure 1 added in ink.

Dikran stirred, mumbled something incomprehensible, and opened an eye. Julia went to him quickly. "Hullo, darling! How are you feeling today?"

He had waked briefly the previous night, had submitted in a somnambulistic way to being dressed and driven to Helikon, had swallowed a glass of fruit juice, and, as soon as he was back in bed, had fallen again into a profound and apparently restorative sleep. A student had been told off to sit by him, with orders to summon Adnan at once if he stirred or seemed distressed, while Julia, guilty but relieved, attended the Haydn concert. But the boy's report when she returned was that her husband had never moved, and he had passed the rest of the night in the same womb-like repose.

Now he was looking very much better, and more like the man with whom she had so lightheartedly started on her honeymoon. His dark eyes had regained their flash, and his mouth its firm line. But this appearance of being in control was considerably impaired when he looked around the Spartan little room in which he found himself. "Hey?" he demanded, staring about in astonished disbelief. "What's going on? What the devil's happened? Where are we?"

"Don't you remember?"

"Remember what?"

"You don't remember what happened yesterday?"

"We drove up to Skimi and then went on and had lunch at that fish place—Kalkos—Kalikos—"

"No, that was the day before, darling. Today is Thursday."

"What? . . . What do you mean?"

For a long time he refused to believe what she told him—that he had completely lost a day. He almost flew into a rage over it. But finally the plain fact that here they were, in completely new surroundings, vanquished him into a kind of grudging acceptance that *something* untoward must have happened.

His reaction then seemed strange to Julia. His main emotion, she thought, was terror—not so much of what had happened to him, but of what *might* have happened—what he might have done in his amnesiac state.

"It was perfectly all right, darling," Julia kept reassuring him—poor dear, perhaps he was afraid he might have committed some act of undignified folly—"I was with you almost the whole time, and you didn't do anything silly. You just seemed very miserable and confused."

Then she remembered that in fact she had *not* been with him yesterday morning, when, it seemed, from the evidence of his *espadrilles* and swiming trunks, he had gone out on the beach and perhaps swum—but she resolved to minimize this part of the episode, since the thought of it seemed to upset him so much.

"What caused it? What happened to me?" he kept saying.

"Well, Dr. Adnan thought you probably fell asleep on our balcony at the Fleur de Lys and were in the sun for too long. It's very sheltered there, it could have been really hot, out of the wind."

"But that's very frightening—very frightening" he muttered, staring past her, out the window. "Now there's part of my life that will always be hidden from me. I shall never know what happened."

Julia soothed him as best she could, and so did Adnan when he came in for a morning visit, but all their reassurances left Dikran only half satisfied. Julia was glad to escape from his anxieties for a little and slip away for her promised tour of inspection, leaving Dikran in the hands of a masseur.

Adnan had arranged to meet her in the quadrangle and, while waiting for him, she amused herself by studying a large number of statues that were placed around the rim of the lawn. Not much attempt had been made to choose pieces in keeping with the island's classic past; the statues were mostly ornate products of the nineteenth century, and she could only assume that they had been selected as examples for patients to aim at; the females tended to opulent bosoms and improbably sylphlike waists, the males bulged with muscle and virility. Here Hercules grappled with the Hydra, there Psyche simpered over a dove. Centaurs galloped, nymphs held modest, protecting hands over their exposed persons, gods and goddesses adopted strenuously athletic positions. Somehow she suspected that they had all been chosen by Dr. Adnan.

"Ah, here you are! I am sorry I keep you waiting," he said, bustling up to her. Today he was even more elegantly dressed, in a white denim suit with remarkable piping. There was something about it that reminded Julia of mashers in the eighteen nineties.

"Now—our concert hall you have already several times visited, so I will not take you there," he went on, waving a hand toward the impressive building at the upper end of the quadrangle. "I proceed. This wing to the right is all soundproof practice rooms for the musicians and dancers—" he flung open a door and displayed a monastic cell with nothing but a piano and a music stand. Another room beyond it, somewhat bigger, contained a *barre* and a floor-length mirror across one wall.

"Small recital hall here—lecture hall—two class-rooms, which can also be joined by removing a partition."

All these rooms were in vigorous use. A string quartet was practicing a modern piece in the recital hall, four singers were attempting Barber's *Hand of Bridge* in the lecture hall, accompanied by a single, harassed-looking pianist, a mime class was being conducted in one of the classrooms, and two jugglers were seriously working in the other.

"Now we go below," Adnan said. "What you have seen so far is only the tip of the iceberg."

He led her to the northeast corner of the quadrangle and down a flight of stone steps, following a sign that said TREATMENT AREAS and had a pointing arrow.

At the foot of the steps they entered a large, cool, circular stone hall brilliantly illuminated by concealed strip lighting. A carved marble font in the middle was wreathed in ferns and creepers. Twenty or so benches, wide and low and comfortably upholstered in white leather substitute, were disposed against the curving walls. In between these, passages led off in all directions, and a loudspeaker system was in operation.

"Mr. Klint to physiotherapy, please."

"Mrs. Helstron, Mrs. Psaros, Miss Jones, Mme. Jardine, to sauna."

"Herr Schneider for a mud bath, please."

88

"Mr. Kefauver for radiotherapy."

"Mrs. Mandelbaum for a wax bath."

"Miss McGregor for acupuncture."

"Mme. Beck for ultrasonic ray."

Around the walls, on the white seats, patients in terry-cloth robes sat waiting for their calls. The atmosphere was relaxed and cheerful. They chatted, read, the women knitted, children played on the floor. Some faces there were familiar, some were even famous. Julia recognized an English poet (as famous for his alcoholism as for his poetry), an Italian operatic tenor, and two members of the National Theatre Company. A pair of students, sitting cross-legged with their backs against the font, played softly on flute and guitar; the sound of their playing filtered gently away into the cavernous space.

Every minute, patients came and went to their various appointments.

"It seems extremely well organized," Julia said.

"We have now a computer," Adnan told her proudly. "Our local benefactor, Mr. Capranis, gave us that; it cuts down the waiting time. So patients seldom have more than ten minutes between one treatment and the next. If they *should* by chance have longer—then they can go upstairs and listen to somebody's recital, or watch a dance practice—or just sit in the sun."

"How civilized that is!" Julia thought of gloomy hours spent in the out-patient departments of English hospitals.

"Now, if you like, I show you some of the treatments," Adnan said, and led off along one of the passages, which were distinguished by numbers. The passage he selected was Number Three, which, according to a sign, led to Inhalation, Wax Baths, Sauna, and

Steam Baths. It took them, after a short walk, into a large, pillared region with a vaulted roof that was painted mustard yellow. The whole area was divided into cubicles of variable sizes by painted wooden screens. The atmosphere was warm and steamy, and smelled of soap and eucalyptus. Heavy rubber cables trailed and looped hither and thither. The colors of the screens, Julia noticed, were the same as those used on the Greek houses—brilliant, powdery blues, dazzling greens and lilacs and pinks. They, and the smell of eucalyptus, contributed a gay nursery-like air to the scene, which was competely different from the treatment areas of a hospital. Carefree, youthful-looking attendants in white smocks darted in and out among the screens. Uninhibited sounds came from all about the unseen regions—cheerful yells as patients encountered the heat of sauna or steam bath, the cold of shower or seaweed; splashes of water; the vigorous slip-slap, pummeling sound of massage; scraps of talk and expostulations:

"Take care, Mrs. Carmichael, that's my gouty toe!"

"Shall I turn over now, Mr. Elkin?"

"Is my five minutes up yet?"

"Hey, that's *cold*—much colder than you gave it to me last time!"

"Oh, how delicious!—can you pour it just a little higher up?"

Everybody seemed to be having a good time.

Julia was shown patients lying on their stomachs, wrapped in hot wax; patients immersed in mud; patients with their lesions being broken up by ultrasonic rays ("We have to be very careful with them," Adnan said. "More than fifty seconds and it melts your bones." Julia resolved on no account to have this treatment and to dissuade Dikran from having it either); patients apparently lying asleep with their exposed torsos stuck full of little bamboo darts.

Passing through the steam-bath area, Dr. Adnan paused by an elderly man who was completely encased in a large white enamel box about the size of a dishwasher. Only his head protruded, with a white towel swathed over it, turbanwise, and another wrapped around his neck and chin.

"Bonjour, M. Destrier, comment ça va?" Adnan inquired, and received a flood of French loquacity in return.

Julia moved on a few paces, out of politeness, but looked back with considerable interest.

"Is that *Annibal* Destrier," she inquired when Adnan caught up with her, "the composer?"

"He himself!" Adnan said with tremendous satisfaction. "Is he not a great old boy? He comes to us for a month every spring. This year will be his eighty-fifth birthday, so we plan to do him honor by a performance of one of his operas. A nice idea, no? I hope you remain for it?"

"Well—that depends on how soon you do it, I suppose, and how well my husband gets on. Which opera have you chosen? Will Enrico Gaspari be singing in it? Didn't I notice him back there in the waiting area?"

A slight cloud overshadowed Adnan's brow, she noticed, at this inquiry. He hesitated, then said, "It is not yet finally decided which opera is to be performed. We have difficulties at present. Now—here are Scottish douches. Here, doctors' consulting rooms. And here the stairs which lead to the Yoga and spinal exercise rooms. Such treatments are given above-ground."

They climbed up a different flight of steps into a kind of outside loggia, set about with more statuary and furnished with bamboo tables and chairs.

They were now, Julia realized, on the west side of the quadrangle—the treatment area occupied the whole of the space underneath it.

"We thought it cooler to have treatments underground, since in the summer it is so hot here," Adnan explained.

"Now I see what you mean about the tip of the iceberg."

He looked at his watch (which was amazingly ornate, studded with rubies; doubtless the gift of a grateful patient) and said, "At this hour the patients take their morning refreshment. You care to partake also?"

"Yes, thank you," said Julia, whose breakfast had consisted of a half glass of lemon juice.

"Our regime is small meals, but frequent, so that no one becomes dehydrated," he said seriously.

At one end of the loggia liquid refreshment was being dispensed by Zoé, the warden, whom Julia had already met. She was a pleasant, capable French girl with a round, dark face, upcurving mouth, and short, toffee-brown hair cut in a smooth cap. A marble table in front of her was set out with trays of little glasses and cups. There appeared to be a choice of lemon juice, grape juice, or a dollop of a brown, gluey substance onto which Zoé poured hot water from a huge brass can when requested to do so by a patient. Residents, wearing a motley mix of garments from formal wear to bikinis or bathrobes, assembled in an irregular queue to receive their drinks, and then stood or sat, sipping and chatting in the warm sun.

"What is that brown stuff?" Julia inquired.

"It is a vegetarian composition of my own invention called Rybomite—highly nutritious and beneficial. It contains no end of vitamin B, besides niacin, riboflavin, and thiamin."

"I'm sure it does," Julia said politely, and chose a glass of grape juice. She noticed that Adnan did likewise.

A stately old lady in a jade-green dressing gown was being pushed toward them in a wheelchair by another patient. She held a cane in her hand, which she waved commandingly at Dr. Adnan.

"Well, *Monsieur le Médecin,* are we going to have *Les Mystères d'Elsinore?* Has Enrico made up his mind yet?" she asked. She had a handsome, vigorous, hawklike face and bright, dark eyes; her white hair hung down her back in a thick plait.

"I have to discuss the matter with Joop, Mme. Athalie," Adnan replied. Julia thought his expression was somewhat evasive.

"What has Enrico decided?"

"Enrico does not wish to take part. He is on the point of leaving us, in fact. So all depends on whether Miss Farrell is able to come to us."

"You must persuade her, *mon cher Docteur!*"

"I will try my best," Adnan said.

A fat little woman was darting about, taking photographs. Julia was reminded by this of Dikran, who hated having his picture taken. "I must be keeping you from all sorts of important tasks," she said to Adnan.

He gave her his brilliant smile. "Please! My dear Lady Julia! What task could be more important than making sure that one of the most beautiful and distinguished visitors who has ever honored our clinic feels thoroughly at home? Besides," he added practically, "our staff are highly efficient; the place runs itself almost without my interference unless some slight crisis should arise."

"Then—if you still have time—I would like to ask you about my husband. Now that you have examined him more thoroughly, do you still think that it was a sunstroke?"

Around the perimeter of the quadrangle there was a wide path paved with flagstones; having finished their drinks, they turned and paced along it.

"May I, in return, ask you some questions about your husband, Lady Julia? Having examined him more closely, yes, I do still think it was a sunstroke, but it might have been augmented by some kind of shock. But, as to this, I am not able to be more explicit unless I know whether he is very susceptible to shocks. Can you give me a little background about him?"

She remained silent, looking at Adnan with troubled eyes.

To help her, he said gently, "For instance—please forgive my suggesting it if it is wide of the mark—but had you perhaps had some kind of quarrel or dispute before this happening?"

"No *indeed* we hadn't!" she answered in relief. "Unless you count my telling him that he would only be in the way while I was buying presents for my children. But he took that quite placidly."

"Then, we must look further for our explanation. Can you explain him to me a little?"

Somewhat embarrassed, she replied, "No, that's the trouble, you see. I can't. I really know very little about him. We have been married only four weeks. And before that, we had known each other only another month—which we did not spend together, though we were seeing each other very often."

"How did you come to meet?" he inquired, still in the same kind, quiet, solicitous manner. Since she remained silent, he added, "All that I know of you, Lady Julia, I read in the papers. I know that you were married for many happy years to the art critic Arnold Gibbon, that suddenly you are divorced because he wishes to marry the wife of a Labour peer—Lord Plumtree. So, without protest, you allow your husband his divorce, and he keeps the children too—which is uncommon, surely? Now that I see you, I understand this a little better, I think; I see that you are a gentle, chivalrous person who will not fight for your rights even in such a case of flagrant injustice. But still—*why* did you not fight for those rights?"

"Oh—" she said. "Various reasons. The children are nearly grown up in any case, they will soon be out in the world—I can see them when I like—I didn't want any more disgusting publicity and fuss, I wanted the whole thing over quickly—"

"Your ex-husband must be a remarkably undiscerning person," Dr. Adnan remarked with asperity. "I saw the pictures of his new wife when they were married—pffah!" He emitted an unreproducible noise of scorn. "A bourgeois British pig-blonde!—However, that is not to the purpose. You did not then agree to a divorce for your own ends?" And, as she looked puzzled, he added, "Because you had already encountered Mr. Saint?"

"My goodness, *no!*" She sounded completely taken aback by this idea, as if it had never entered her head that anyone might hold such a notion. "No, I didn't meet Dikran until after I was divorced."

"And—permit me to ask again—how *did* you meet?"

"Why," she replied slowly, blushing a little, "it was a pickup, really."

"Indeed? You surprise me!"

"We were both at a concert in the Elizabeth Hall. I'd moved out of Palace Gate—out of my husband's house—into a service flat. I was pretty lonely and miserable—I used to go to concerts almost every night, to cheer myself up. Didn't feel like seeing my friends. And, at this one, Dikran—Mr. Saint—happened to be sitting in front of me, and he dropped an envelope on the floor when he was getting program notes out of his pocket. He wasn't aware that he had dropped it, but I noticed it, so I picked it up and gave it to him— I was charmed by his name on the envelope, Dikran Salvador Saint—and made some remark about it— he was polite and grateful; it turned out that the envelope contained a very valuable stamp—he collects stamps among lots of other things—so he asked me to come and have a drink in the interval and—and we never went back for the second half of the concert."

"So you became acquainted. He will have recognized you and known who you were, I presume?"

"I—I'm not really sure," she said. "Well, of course, we soon exchanged names—so then he knew—and he asked me out to lunch next day, he knew by that time. I suppose he'd read about the case . . . I don't know," she ended, rather unhappily. "We didn't talk about that. We were both fond of music, we were both lonely— Dikran's first wife died years ago and he has no children, he couldn't have children—so we just gravitated together."

"Very natural," Adnan said. But then he added, "You did not feel he was drawn to you because you were a rich and well-known woman, several of whose plays have been performed in the West End? This was not your attraction for him?"

"Well—perhaps—a little," she said, deliberating in her mind with slow, careful honesty. "But not from the worldly or financial point of view! Dikran is a very rich man himself, absolutely rolling in money, in fact. He's certainly not a fortune hunter. Since we've been married he hasn't even allowed me to buy a packet of cigarettes. Up to yesterday."

"Indeed. Then you must forgive me for making such an ungallant inquiry. Irrelevant, too," he added. "No man who had seen your face would bother his head about your income." Julia blushed again. "Now," he pursued, "if it is not too prying—from what does your husband derive his wealth? Is it inherited? A business empire? Or what?"

"You'll find this almost incredible," she said. "I'm afraid you'll think me very dumb—but I simply don't know. I have a vague idea that he has a good many different business interests, mostly in America—so I suppose it is a kind of empire. I know it must seem uncommonly ignorant and unenterprising of me not to have found out—but Dikran is very uncommunicative about things like that. He came from an Armenian family, you see, and I suppose they have quite oriental ideas about the things that are and are not discussed with women. At any rate, he never *has* discussed his business affairs with me."

"So, for all you know, he is a leader of the Mafia," Adnan said cheerfully.

Julia laughed.

"Well—what kind of a man is he?" Adnan pursued. "If not about money—then, what *do* you talk about?"

The look he gave her was both quizzical and intent; for a moment, the space between them was heavily polarized by sexual currents. But then Julia said coolly, "Well—music a good deal; he's very knowledgeable about it. And my plays, which he has seen; he's interested in the theater. Books—poetry—Dikran writes poetry himself."

"Any good?" Adnan inquired briskly.

Really, he has a lot of *chutzpah,* this Dr. Adnan, Julia thought, why do I allow him to grill me like this about Dikran? But she had to admit that his intention seemed perfectly benevolent and disinterested; she answered in a moderate and considered tone, "Yes. Yes I think it is rather good."

"Not published, however?"

"He's never even bothered to try. He didn't need to. He just wrote for his own pleasure. But of course I know a good many English publishers. I'm going to show some of his work to— What is all this *about?*" she demanded, turning to face Adnan.

"Just trying to acquire a little background to the problem," he replied imperturbably, giving her a sphinx-like smile. "So what it amounts to, really, is that you know precious little about your Mr. Saint—except in honeymoon terms; you cannot therefore be expected to predict how he may behave in a situation of stress."

"No—not really," she agreed, strolling on. "I think I'd expect him to be quite tough—after all, he has either made or kept a very large fortune."

"True. You have not, however, seen him with business colleagues or employees? Does he have a house in England?"

"No, just a service flat in a big London block. He

told me he has a house in Iowa—or do I mean Illinois?—I always get those American states mixed. But he doesn't seem to spend much time there and I haven't been over yet. Well, there hasn't been time."

"Of course not! It is a whirlwind romance. So, while he is honeymooning, this empire looks after itself? He does not make long-distance phone calls? Display anxiety about it?"

"Not in the least. But he does display a great deal of anxiety about his present state: he gave me to understand that he feels he simply can't afford to get into amnesiac conditions."

"This I can readily understand. So do most of us feel, but especially so a man who runs many large and complicated affairs. Though probably he has the least need to worry, having, no doubt, many capable subordinates."

"I suppose so," she said doubtfully. "Do you think this state is likely to recur? That's what worries him, of course."

"No—I do not think it at all," Adnan said. "Knowing so little of him makes it less easy to predict, but his general health is evidently good; physically he is in excellent shape. In better shape, I should judge, than most men who have been through what he has."

"You mean the sunstroke?"

"No, I meant the concentration camp." She stared at him in such total surprise that he said, "You did not know this? Did you not observe the number on his arm?"

"Yes, but I didn't—I didn't—he said something about the Navy—"

"My dear Lady Julia! No navy in the world brands its ratings in such a way. For a lady of genius you seem singularly unobservant; but perhaps," he added thoughtfully, "that is what ladies of genius are like. I have not before encountered one. No, Lady Julia, that is a *Stalag* number."

"He never told me," she whispered.

"Then, I suppose I should not have done. No doubt he prefers to forget about it," Adnan said mildly. "But it seems certain you would have discovered sooner or later. There is nothing shameful about having been a prisoner of the Nazis. On the contrary! And—as to the amnesia—I do truly think that your husband has no cause to worry."

"I'm very glad," she said, relieved, though still startled at this new revelation of how very little she knew about Dikran.

Reaching the upper corner of the quadrangle, they entered a stone tunnel that led through past the concert hall. It was defended by a PRIVATE sign and brought them into a small walled garden which had been cut into the fairly steep hillside behind the hall.

"This is my private place," Adnan said. "I come here now and then for a little peace and quiet."

Julia looked around her in amused surprise. The garden was laid out in the English manner; there were no blazing cascades of color such as she had seen through doorways in Dendros Old Town; the atmosphere was quiet, and, in spite of the hot sunshine, a little melancholy. Wisteria grew on the walls and crept over a trellis; there were small rosebushes and stone-cobbled paths in a formal pattern; there was a sundial; lavender and other bushy, silvery, sweet-smelling flowerless shrubs grew profusely in the beds, but there were few flowers, except for small, inconspicuous things: rockroses and dwarf white cyclamens and daisies.

In the corner bed there was a small piece of sculpture on a marble plinth. It was very different from the opulent statuary in the quadrangle. It seemed, after a fashion, to represent a human figure, a person sitting with head on knees, hands around ankles, but the outline was rough and indistinct; the only feature directly recognizable as human was a pair of hands with fingers interlaced, which seemed to extend out of the stone base as if pleading for the rest of the figure inside to be released.

The statue vaguely reminded Julia of birth scenes in films—of a foal she had once helped deliver which had emerged feet first from its mother. There was something unhappy and claustrophobic for her about the carving—she did not like it at all. Underneath, on the plinth, she noticed that the name LUCY was carved, but, even if she had felt inclined to inquire about it—which she did not—a touch of melancholy and reserve in Adnan's expression as he stood regarding it would have prevented her from doing so.

"What a charming little place!" she said instead, looking around the garden. "You must often be thankful to have such a hidey-hole."

"Please, Lady Julia, feel free to visit it whenever you wish! I do not have time to come here much. But I shall be honored if you will make use of it." He picked a cluster of miniature pink roses and tucked them behind the statue's stone hands. Then he looked at Julia and smiled with great charm. "For you, I think, not the sweet roses but something more subtle. Such as this—" he picked a couple of sprigs from a feathery, sweet-scented gray shrub and added a couple

101

of white rockroses with yellow centers. "There! That seems more appropriate for the author of *Sharp, Flat, and Slightly Sweet.*"

"Thank you!" Julia said, laughing. Her slight feeling of depression was dissipated. She sniffed the posy and said, "It's delicious." Suddenly the warmth and quiet of the secluded little place and the spicy, aromatic scent of the tiny bouquet imbued her with a feeling of elation, and hope. Dikran would be all right—everything would turn out all right. "Do you know," she said, "it's odd, but yesterday I had a real premonition that I was going to be unhappy here. I could hardly bring myself to accept your invitation. Wasn't that silly? Now that I am here, I am sure that I was wrong."

"Ah, you English are always so full of superstitions," Adnan said indulgently. "That—it must be acknowledged—forms one part of your mysterious appeal. It is like the scent of these flowers—haunting, indefinable, and very, very far from logic!"

"What good English you speak," Julia remarked as they turned and strolled back through the stone passageway. Overhead, the bell in the clock tower could be heard striking ten.

"Ah, well, I have had many very good English friends—very dear friends," Adnan replied. Julia was aware in herself of a slight feeling of hostility toward these friends, whoever they were.

Re-entering the quadrangle, she saw that the bikini'd and terry-robed patients were now all making off purposefully in the direction of practice rooms and treatment areas. The trays of drinks had been removed from the loggia, and Helikon's routine was getting under way for the day. However, out on the grass, seven musicians were amusing themselves by racing through a Beethoven septet at breakneck speed, while two girls in leotards, equipped with staves, attempted to carry out a sequence of lunging exercises in time to the music. Julia lingered, amused, watching them, reluctant to leave the pleasant, sun-warmed scene.

But Adnan said briskly, "Now I am sure that you must wish to return to your husband; he will at present be resting after his massage. And I know that Zoé has a series of treatments worked out for you which I hope that you will enjoy and find of benefit. So I will say good-by for the moment—" He broke off and, looking across the grass, exclaimed, "My goodness gracious!"

Julia could see nothing remarkable in the girl walking rapidly toward them, who appeared to have been the cause of his ejaculation. She was on the small side, thin to scraggy, and wore the usual jeans and T shirt. Her short black hair was untidy, worn in no particular style, just pushed back off her forehead. She had a lot of freckles, and a pair of noticeable blue Irish eyes, her best feature; otherwise one could certainly not, Julia thought, call her pretty, though there was something cheerfully engaging about her expression.

Adnan, however, seemed quite enchanted at the sight of her.

"Mike! My dear little Mike! But how you have *grown*— how much you have improved! What a transformation!" He enveloped her in a tremendous hug, kissed each cheek, and, holding her off by the arms, surveyed her from top to toe and exclaimed, "But you are now so pretty! It is downright amazing!"

"That's not very polite of you, Uncle Achmed," the girl said gaily. "Wasn't I always pretty?"

"Are you kidding? At sixteen you were too fat—

hideous! And the glasses and the spots. At seventeen, too skinny, and wearing that atrocious brace on your teeth. At eighteen—still too skinny, the hair dyed and frizzed, the eyebrows plucked away to two bald patches—and as for the *clothes*—may Allah preserve me from English girls wearing dirty cotton nightdresses and wooden-soled shoes!"

"I dare say he will."

"But *now*—just right! It is wonderful what four years can do."

"Just you wait till you see me at twenty-four," she suggested.

His manner changed to kind solicitude. "And your mother? Has she made the transfer successfully? Is she settled in her room? I was sorry to hear that she had a fainting spell on the boat, but I feel sure it is no great matter. We will soon have her right as rain here, you will see. In one moment I will visit her. But first—let me introduce—" He stepped back so as to include Julia, who had politely removed herself a step or two, in the conversation. "Lady Julia, this is little Mike Meiklejohn, who has helped me on several summer seminars in the past and has now brought her mother here to be assisted back to health. And, Mike, my child, this is Lady Julia Gibb—Saint, whose plays, *The Blasted Heath, Midwinter,* and the rest, you without doubt know by heart and have seen many times over."

Julia saw the girl's eyes widen. "Oh, I have!" she said. "I—I'm happy to meet you, Lady Julia."

She looked as awe-stricken as if she had bumped into Shakespeare himself, which allayed Julia's slight feeling of anticlimax.

"Come, then, Mike my child," Adnan said, retaining the girl's hand. "We go to see your mother."

"Good-by for now, then, Dr. Adnan. And thank you very much for the interesting conducted tour," Julia said politely.

He bowed briskly, kissing the fingers of his left hand (the right still held that of Mike), and Julia walked away in the direction of Dikran's room, sniffing at her aromatic posy.

⨍ 5 ⨍

MINUET & TRIO

The ambulance which had been sent from Helikon for Mother was tiny but efficient, about the size of a horse box. There was just enough room inside for Mother, the attendant, and our luggage. So I sat in front, with the driver.

It was heaven to be back in Dendros again; despite my feelings of guilt and anxiety over Mother, I couldn't withstand a bursting sensation of happiness. Besides, I was sure that, once he got to work on her, Dr. Adnan would soon put her to rights. And Dendros was exactly its beautiful self, as I remembered it and had so often dreamed about it in the past four years: the honey-colored stone ramparts of the Old Town, the wide street near the harbor covered with bicycles and crazy little Fiats, the harbor water blue as the Greek flag, great big glossy orange and magnolia trees casting pools of shade, wafts of wonderful scent coming from the public gardens through the dry, hot, spicy air. All the old, black-dressed ladies were there along the quayside with their wise, wrinkled faces and their stalls covered with postcards and leather articles. I couldn't wait to get away and roam around, visit the Aghnides, eat an orange, swim in the no doubt icy Aegean.

"What's happening at Helikon?" I asked the driver, who was a cousin of Calliope's, a music student called George. I had been at school with him for a year. Now he was studying in Athens, but, of course, came back to Dendros for the holidays.

"Oh, things are much as usual. They still haven't fixed the leak in the swimming pool. A woman broke her collarbone diving in and threatened to sue the company, but Zoé talked her out of it. Adnan was very annoyed about it all. And he fell in love with an Italian film star last summer."

"Oh? Which one?" I asked suspiciously.

"Ghita Masolini—she was here losing weight after too much pasta."

"So, what happened?"

"She fell in love back, much more, and started sticking to him like glue. So then he got fed up and went off to Athens to buy ultrasonic-treatment equipment for six weeks. And she lost a lot more weight than she bargained for and went back to Rome."

"That's a good thing. Suppose he'd married her! She'd never have fitted in at Helikon. And he *couldn't* leave. I should think Helikon would just about collapse if Uncle Achmed weren't there to keep an eye. What else? Have they got any interesting visitors at the moment?"

107

My Greek was coming back in leaps and bounds, I was glad to find.

"Yes, we've got old Annibal Destrier, the composer who won the Hammarskøld Prize for Music. Uncle Achmed wants to put on one of his operas to celebrate his eighty-fifth birthday."

"What fun!" Instantly I wondered if there would be a chance for me to do the sets. Helikon had a small but well-equipped stage with several nice gadgets including a revolving bit in the middle. But of course the old boy's birthday might fall after Mother's and my departure. "Which opera are they going to do?"

"Well, old Annibal wants *Les Mystères d'Elsinore,* which is his favorite, apparently, but that's a bit awkward."

"Oh, why? Surely he ought to have the one he wants? After all, he may not be around for many more birthdays. What's the matter with it?"

Les Mystères was short, but very meaty, as I remembered it from reading the score and listening to radio productions. It was an operatic version of *Hamlet,* very emotional, Gallic, Gothic, and overwrought. Gertrude was a kind of belle Otero-cum-Phaedra, who yearns after her son and is filling in by having an affair with Polonius; Claudius a frozen French businessman-villain-cuckold, and Hamlet perfectly epicene and schizo. His part, I remembered, had been arranged for either male or female, tenor or contralto; in both the radio productions I'd heard, it had been sung by a woman.

"So, who'd sing Hamlet?" I asked, toying with the notion I'd been nursing for a long time of sets for *Hamlet* adapted from the paintings of Piero della Francesca. I can't remember what had originally given me the idea but, once conceived, it seemed ideally suitable—wide, watery landscapes filled with low hills and lakes in the distance, a few nobly plain buildings near at hand, such as the ones in his perspective drawing of an ideal town, and, for each scene, two or three Piero figures depicted as huge, impassive bystanders— the watchers from "The Flagellation," perhaps, and some of his angels, so severely beautiful, neither judging nor pitying but just calmly observant. I thought that to see Hamlet's difficulties taking place under the eyes of these Piero people would be interesting and show the story in a new perspective. Shakespeare, after all, would have been able to see Piero's paintings; wasn't he supposed to have taken a trip to northern Italy when he was young? But, to do designs for *Hamlet* was an ambition that I had resigned myself to not having fulfilled for years to come; this chance, if chance it was, seemed too good to miss.

"That's just it," George said. "Hamlet's part is where the difficulty comes in. Apparently there's a sort of hoodoo on *Les Mystères.*"

"What sort of hoodoo?"

"After each of the last two stage productions the singer who took Hamlet's part died, each time within a month. In one case it was a man—Orlando Lipschutz, the Austrian singer—and in one a woman, I can't remember who, but she was killed three weeks later in a plane crash. Lipschutz just died of heart failure. So now the opera has got a bad name—you know how superstitious singers are—and nobody's keen to take the part. Enrico Gaspari has been staying here, but he has made a lot of excuses and says he has to get back to London to rehearse for a BBC production. So then Joop wrote and asked Elisabet Maas if she'd do it, and at first she said yes but then she said her husband didn't want her to."

"Gosh! I wish I could sing. I'd do it like a shot."

"Well, you can't, we all know that, so there's no point in wishing," George said firmly.

It was true. I love music, but, like Mother—like Trilby—I've got plenty of voice but can't keep in tune for two consecutive notes.

George drove out along Winston Churchill Street, past the square, stuccoed, nineteenth-century villas painted in faded pinks and oranges and set about with palms and ilexes and chinaberry trees. It all looked good enough to eat.

"Isn't there *anybody* at Helikon—not a great singer, I mean just someone with a reasonable voice—who could take the part?" I was reluctant to lose my *Hamlet,* now I saw it in view.

"There were one or two possibles, but once they heard about Enrico Gaspari and Elisabet Maas, they changed their minds. Uncle Achmed was very annoyed about it."

"I can imagine," I said, grinning to myself. He hated being crossed. And he had no patience at all with supernatural beliefs or any such stuff.

"So now he's written to ask Kerry Farrell if she'd like to do it. She has visited Helikon once or twice in the past, so it seemed possible that she might, if she's not too busy and booked up."

"And what did she say?"

"Don't know. Maybe she hasn't answered."

"I think I heard her do it once on the radio," I said. "She'd be all right; she'd be fine, I think."

"Were you ever at Helikon when she came here?"

"No, I've never seen her or heard her live—only on

110

records or radio; but I feel she's got the right kind of voice: rather pure and colorless; better for sacred music than opera, really, but I should think for Hamlet she'd be just right."

I craned out the window for a view of the beautiful Dendros landscape, for we had now left the town and were shooting up over a shoulder of hillside before descending into the valley where Helikon lay. All the flat land was cultivated to within an inch of the beach—orange groves, vineyards, olive groves, set about with thin, spiky cypresses; then, above them, the bare, silvery hillsides with gray-green wild olives and figs. And then high, white mountains. And the blue, blue sea beyond and all around.

"Here we are," said George. "As I expect you remember."

It was hardly more than a ten-minute drive from the town, really. But the intervening hill gave the estate solitude and privacy. All this valley had belonged to a local millionaire called Capranis and he had given it, lock, stock, and barrel, or rather, rod, pole, and perch, to the Helikon Foundation. Of course Mother will love it here, I thought, loving every inch myself. Of course she will. Who could help doing so?

George drove through the arched entrance under the clock tower at one side of the main quadrangle and came to a halt by a service entrance. Mother was swiftly and expeditiously carried indoors on a stretcher. I would have followed her, but I caught sight of Adnan twenty yards away, and he gave me a wave and a welcoming shout, so I went to say hello.

He was talking to a strikingly beautiful woman whose face was vaguely familiar, so I thought, Aha! old Achmed's at it again. He always made a beeline for the handsome lady visitors and probably caused many a heartache by lavishing his fascinating Anatolian ways on them; though I am bound to admit that he was very agreeable to *all* his patients, and could make any female feel like a million dollars.

This one had a long, pointed face with hollows under the cheekbones, remarkable shallow eye sockets, a classically straight nose, and a most beautiful mouth —wide, tender, curving—her best feature, and all were good. Old Uncle Achmed does know how to pick them, I thought. Her hair, curly, dusty-fair, didn't interfere with or detract from the lovely mask of her face—just formed a cloudy, vague background to it. I noticed that she had very fine, long hands, too— tragic hands; I thought how I'd like to dress her in stiff Renaissance draperies and have her playing some doomed part, the Duchess of Malfi perhaps, against a lurid background of dark turrets and flames.

I was racking my brain to think why she looked so familiar, and when Achmed introduced her I thought, No *wonder* she looks so haunted. I'd read about her divorce in the papers and knew that after twenty-two years of happy marriage her highly intelligent, distinguished, and handsome husband had suddenly ditched her in favor of a fat blond political hostess without any apparent graces whatever. It must have been a terrible shock for Lady Julia. Maybe she constituted too much competition in the home, I thought. She certainly wrote first-rate plays, all of which I had both seen and read—and I felt impressed by my own luck in meeting her.

However, she didn't seem disposed to be in the least impressed by *me*, which was hardly surprising, and, after a brief acknowledgment of the introduction, said something about seeing how her husband was getting on and went off, walking with a long, graceful stride.

"Has she married again, then?" I said in surprise. "She didn't lose much time, surely?"

"No, I fear she remarried in a state of shock—on the rebound, as you would say—and may now repent at leisure."

"Why? What's the matter with her husband?"

"He is here suffering from a mild case of sunstroke."

"Poor chap." Sunstrokes on Dendros were very frequent. "But I meant, why will she repent at leisure? Is he nasty?"

"No," said Adnan thoughtfully. "No, in many ways I think he is an interesting character with many unusual qualities—judging from what I have seen of him, which is not a great deal. But their backgrounds are so dissimilar; what, I ask myself, is the magnetic force which has brought them together?"

"And the sixty-four-thousand-dollar answer to that is sex," I suggested. "Lady J. looks to me like one of those sirens who can call it out in any male unless he's actually blind or paralyzed. She's got a real aura, don't you think?"

"My dear Mike!" Adnan was scandalized. "You used to be a nice, proper young girl—demure, self-effacing, well-brought-up. What has happened to bring about this change in you?"

"I found that being demure, good, and whatever you said didn't get me anywhere. Besides, you forget that I've been out in the world earning my living for four years since I saw you last."

"Is it really four years? Well, do not let the Aghnides hear you talking about sex, or there will be the devil to pay."

"How is old Mr. Aghnides?" I asked eagerly. "I wrote to tell him that I was coming here, but he's never answered. Is he all right?"

"Not too good, I'm afraid. You will find that he is *very* old now. And he had a slight stroke last month. His sister from Athens is now living there, to look after him. But anyway, go to visit him. He misses Calliope—it will be a happy reminder for him to see you."

"I'll go right away—as soon as you've seen Mother and she's settled in."

But I was daunted to hear that Aunt Elektra had moved into the Aghnides house; she was the world's vinegar-puss.

I walked beside Adnan to Mother's room, thinking, Well, at least *he* hasn't changed, thank goodness! He was exactly the same as I'd remembered—square, dark, dandyishly dressed, teasingly cheerful, hiding, behind his big impassive dark eyes, a whole lot of secrets, but at least they were not *disagreeable* secrets. I had always felt safe with Uncle Achmed—as Calliope and I had fallen into the habit of calling him; he had a thoroughly kind heart, I knew, under his joky exterior, and, although he flirted with many, had never caused anybody permanent damage, so far as I knew. In fact, his had been the heart that got broken, long ago; apparently he had never recovered from that bygone affliction enough to become deeply involved with any other woman.

Calliope, when she was seventeen, had pined for him for a whole year, I knew, and had decided that, since he was plainly never going to take her seriously, her best recourse would be to clear out for pastures new, in Elizabeth, New Jersey. Besides, as I'd told her, he was far too old—at least thirty-four.

"Mr. Rochester was older than that," Calliope pointed out. "And I bet *you'd* take him like a shot—if you had the chance."

"Not likely! I wouldn't want to marry a blind, bad-tempered grouch with only one hand who lived in a damp thicket. Think of pushing him round in a wheelchair when he was seventy and you were fifty."

"Not Rochester; Achmed, you ass!"

"He'd never look at me. Besides, I've got to pursue my career and become one of the twentieth century's foremost stage designers."

So Calliope had gone to Elizabeth, New Jersey, and I had gone back to England. That had been four years ago.

Mother had never met Adnan, and I was marginally anxious about that, because she was such a serious person and I wasn't sure how his teasing ways would go down with her. But I needn't have worried. In no time he had her eating out of his hand.

She was just waking when we reached the double room on the ground floor that had been found for us; she seemed calm and drowsy and relaxed.

"Mother," I said, "this is Dr. Adnan that I've told you such a lot about."

"Oh, yes," she said, smiling faintly. "It was always Uncle Achmed this and Uncle Achmed that, and how kind you were—I hope you didn't let the child be a nuisance and tease you to death."

"Nuisance? She was often my right hand—even in the days when she dressed like a demented dervish! No, no, I am very devoted to this little Mike. She has been like a daughter to me. But now, my dear Mrs. Meiklejohn, let me have a look at you."

Feeling that it would be tactful to remove myself, I went out and sat on the grass in the quadrangle and listened to the sound, through a window, of somebody practicing a long, dismal setting by Respighi of a poem by Shelley about tragic love and a lady who pined for her dead sweetheart. It made me feel rather gloomy. Love, I thought, what an infernal nuisance it is, interfering with people's lives, making them rush half across the world to get away from it, or plant memorial gardens in witness to its never-fading pangs. I wandered into Achmed's little garden and then, when I judged a decent interval had elapsed, returned to Mother.

Adnan had gone and she was alone, lying on her bed by the window and gazing alternately at the beautiful lemon orchard outside and the pile of literature about Helikon that was left on the bedside table of every new inmate. There was a guest list, renewed every week, and menus of the different diets, all vegetarian and all scanty, that were supplied depending on the individuals's particular ailments and problems; descriptions of all the treatments and what they did; a list of concerts, recitals, and dramatic performances; descriptions of master-classes in piano, violin, solo singing, and so on, which varied from week to week as different artists came and went; lists of lectures, communal activities available, sight-seeing excursions, and entertainments in Dendros town; and finally a short list of prohibitions: smoking, eating own food, drinking anything but the fruit juice and mild Dendros wine supplied according to diet (Achmed was a realist and knew that if he omitted the wine some guests would

116

never return again), taking any medicines except those prescribed by the clinic, sex (not that Adnan disapproved of sex; it was simply that, he said, it played a disruptive part in the carefully controlled regime he had planned for his patients, so no sex while resident at Helikon, please), and nurturing unexpressed grudges or criticisms.

IF YOU HAVE COMPLAINTS, VOICE THEM! said a sign which was pinned prominently in the dining room, waiting area, library, and other public spots, and there was a regular period set aside after lunch every day for public discussion of any gripes that might arise, while Adnan himself was always available in his office from six to seven each evening to hear complaints that people might be too shy or nervous to voice publicly. By this means a remarkably serene atmosphere was successfully maintained, which was one of the great pleasures of Helikon. Each time I came back, I was amazed at the almost palpable warmth of friendliness and happiness that radiated from all the characters wandering about in their bathrobes and the performers wacking away at their cellos and pianos. And this despite the fact that they were all on a low diet of lemon juice, olives, grated carrot, and tomatoes! I didn't mind it for a while, but presently I did begin to long for a plate of scrambled egg or a chunk of feta cheese, or a crust of Greek bread. Adnan was firm, though: no animal foods or fats, no flour; he had a theory about expelling all the poison from the system before starting to build it up. Anyway, I knew Mother wouldn't mind the diet, as she always had been a vegetarian.

"He does seem a sweet person, I must say," she said when I asked how she had got on with Adnan. "I

can quite see why you've always been so fond of him."
This was uncommonly strong language, for Mother,
and encouraged me very much. The worst hurdle was
past.

"I really was sure that you'd like it here, once you
saw the place," I said.

"Yes, I'm sure I shall too—if I'm really not allowed
to go back yet—and you were a dear child to have
arranged it for me. I think it will do me a lot of good.
I only hope it dosen't cost a fortune."

"Oh, no. Adnan fixed a reduced rate because I'm
going to help again. But anyway Stretford County Ed.
said they'd take care of all this kind of thing."

"Well, you were a sly puss to arrange it all behind
my back, but it was very kind and thoughtful of you."

Better and better! With a huge load off my mind,
I asked if she'd like to come out and see the sights
of the place, or sit under the lemon trees, or listen to
some music, or watch some dancing. Anybody was free
to wander into any practice room at any time during
the day, though the formal recitals didn't begin until
the evening.

But Mother said she was still drowsy and would
prefer to rest on her bed for the moment and gaze
at the lemon trees from where she lay.

"In that case, perhaps I'll walk up the hill and pay
my respects to old Mr. Aghnides."

"Oh, do, dear; that's an excellent plan. Wait just
a minute and I'll write him a note explaining why I
can't come just yet."

So, presently, with a light heart, I was walking up
the path that threaded its way through the little valley
behind Helikon, with Mother's letter in my pocket.

The valley—deep and narrow, it was almost a

ravine, really—was all overgrown with shady trees—
oaks and sycamores and wild syringas smothered in
white blossoms that smelled hauntingly sweet. A few
cyclamens and early purple orchids were still flowering
there, in damp spots by the stream that tumbled in
cascades from one rocky pool to another. Nightingales in the syringa bushes were singing fortissimo, and
it was all so beautiful that if I hadn't had so many
other happinesses in store I would have liked to sit
down by the water's edge and just spend the day
there, looking at leaves and roots and ripples.

I'll come back and do that some other day, I thought,
when Mother is really settled in. One of those promises
that one makes to oneself and never keeps.

After fifteen minutes' climb—the path wound uphill
all the time—I came to where the stream gushed out
of a crack in the rock. I was hot by then, so I knelt
and had a good drink of the icy water. It tasted black
as ink, it was so cold.

Above this point the path climbed what was almost
a flight of rock steps, then emerged from the wood
and crossed a bare shoulder of hill covered with wiry,
low-growing aromatic scrub—various thymes, and sage,
and thistles. A couple of tethered goats were grazing.
Above me I could see the village where the Aghnides
had their house, perched on a ledge of hillside, set
about with dusty fig trees and dilapidated drystone
walls. The village was called Archangelos and consisted of about eight houses, each painted a different
beautiful color.

Presently I reached the road, which wound a slower,
zigzag way up the hillside, passed through the village,
and went on five miles farther to an archaeological site
up at the very top.

I panted around a last curve under the hot sun and then walked in among the houses, picking my way among hens and cats, saying a polite *kallimero* to each smiling old lady that I met. In this village they wore knee-high leather boots below their black skirts, and thick white head scarves, and carried themselves with stately pride, like Egyptians in wall paintings.

The Aghnides house was easily the biggest, set back from the street behind a white wall and a large, unkempt garden full of bougainvillaeas and cypresses. I rang the bell, and the door was answered by the old cook, Elena, who must have been about a hundred. She gave me a big hug and said that she would go and tell the *Kyrie* that I was there. But he was very, very old now, she added; I would see a sad change in him.

She left me in the central courtyard, which had a grapevine trained across above it for shade, and swags of roses, huge red and white lilies, geraniums and sweet williams, and something that smelt of cinnamon. A couple of supine tabby cats gazed at me somnolently through slit eyes.

Then, to my dismay, Aunt Elektra came stalking through an open door. Like all elderly Greek ladies, Aunt Elektra was dressed in black, but her dress had been bought in Athens, or even possibly in Paris, and was draped in elegant silken folds over her scraggy bones. She had a long, disapproving face, and her black eyes were by no means friendly.

"Ah," she said. "Priscilla. It would have been better to phone or to send a note before calling."

"I—I'm sorry," I said, much dashed. "I never thought. I was so anxious to see Kyrie Aghnides. Is he not well enough to see me?"

"He is very weak today. You may see him, as you

have come, but please stay only a moment, so as not to tire him unnecessarily."

"Yes, of course. I'm very sorry that he is so poorly."

Without replying, she led the way into the downstairs room where Calliope's father lay. The room was floored with tiny cobblestones set in a mosaic pattern, and there was a sleeping platform at one end covered with handsome ancient rugs and approached by a flight of four steps. Kyrie Aghnides was not on the platform, however, but on a high, old-fashioned brass bed, reclining against a pile of pillows.

My heart sank when I saw him. He looked terribly old, white, and frail, and was breathing in long, painful rasps; each breath seemed to cost him an almost unbearable effort.

"Hullo, Kyrie Aghnides," I said softly, approaching and planting a kiss on his cold old cheek above the patriarchal white mustache and beard. "Do you remember me? It's Mike—Calliope's friend. I am sorry that you are so tired."

His eyes opened slowly and he gave me a faint smile. But I saw that the fire and intelligence which had made him such an important person in my life were now died down to the lowest possible flicker. Today he was just a frail old man, not quite certain who I was, held together only by his habits of dignity and consideration.

"I'm Calliope's English friend," I said again. "Do you remember I used to stay with you, before Calliope went off to marry Dmitri?"

"Yes, yes—dear little Mike," he whispered. "Just as pretty as ever. I am glad to see you, my child— happy to see you—" His voice trailed into silence. His eyes closed.

"I've brought you a note from my mother," I said gently. "She and I are staying down at Helikon. Shall I read it to you?"

"Later, thank you, my child," he whispered after a moment. "Put it by for the moment. I am, just now, a little bit tired. Please thank your dear mother, however. Do not omit to do that. Is she as charming as ever?" he added vaguely.

Since I knew that he and Mother had never met, my heart sank still further. I could see now that there was not the slightest hope of my ever extracting any useful information from him about my father or Drusilla. Feeling bitterly grieved and disappointed—and also ashamed because now that I saw him my plan seemed so self-interested—I went back to the courtyard. I grieved for myself and I grieved for him, because this was just a travesty of the man I remembered.

Aunt Elektra was in the yard, grimly picking dead heads off the geraniums.

"Is he—is he always as tired and vague as this now?" I asked.

"Yes!" she snapped. "He is old, young lady. And he has had much to try him."

"I'm very sorry," I said truly. "What is his best time of day? I'd like to come again when he is not so tired, and then perhaps we could talk about Calliope."

"If Calliope had done her duty and stayed to look after her father, there would be no need to talk about her," said Elektra sourly. I could see this was a main part of her grievance, that she had had to leave Athens and return to this uncivilized spot because Calliope had gone to America. She added, "Visitors are not good for him, young lady. It is best that you do not come again."

"But I wanted to bring my mother—she so much wanted to meet him—to thank him—"

"No. There would be no purpose in his meeting a stranger."

Aunt Elektra ushered me, very definitively, out of the courtyard.

Just inside the front door I found Elena. "What's biting Kyria Elektra?" I whispered.

She gave a shrug, crossed herself, and made the sign to avert the evil eye. "Who can tell what gets into that one's head? All I know is that she does not approve of your family. But whatever faults your parents have are certainly no fault of *yours*, my little one. I find her exceedingly unreasonable. Alas, though, she has forbidden me to let you in again. I shall always be happy to talk to you in the street, though, or in the *taverna*; send a message by Apostoulos Adossides —or anybody you see about—and I'll come out and have a chat and tell you about the *Kyrie*. I fear he is not long for this world. Eh, me, those were happier days when the mistress was still alive, and you and Calliope were tumbling about the place like two young goats, upsetting my cooking pans and pulling the cats' tails.
. . ."

She probably would have gone on in this vein for a long time, but Aunt Elektra appeared in the hallway and gave me a hateful glare, so I hugged Elena once more, opened the big, chocolate-colored double doors, and slipped through, feeling both sore and puzzled.

I suppose I should have tackled Aunt Elektra then and there. It seemed quite out of the question, though, that she would be prepared to divulge any useful information. But what, in heaven's name, had made her so hostile? Why did she disapprove of my

123

family? What had we done to earn her condemnation? Mother worked hard at her profession and thought of little else; I worked hard at mine and lived a fairly thrifty and circumspect life; Drusilla was long dead; so who was there to disapprove of except . . . Father? If he was still alive?

I simply have to ask Mother about this soon, I resolved. Not while she's still prone to faint, obviously; I'll give her, say, a week at Helikon, and then tackle her about Father. This ought to be just the right environment in which to discuss the whole affair calmly and unemotionally; there will be Adnan to keep an eye on her, too, if she gets upset. I'll do that. Much better than trying to squeeze information out of old Aghnides.

In retrospect that plan now seemed an underhanded approach and I felt I had deserved Aunt Elektra's rebuff.

Having reached my decision, I felt better about the situation and walked lightheartedly back to Helikon, taking the longer way, down the road, which zigzagged down in acute, hairpin bends. It was a dangerous road to attempt in a car, because there was no room to pass and excursion buses were liable to come tearing down at mad speed, having visited the archaeological site up at the top of the hill, which was called Mount Atakos. The buses were supposed to make the ascent every other hour, but they were liable to become delayed when their passengers wandered off and got lost among the various Hellenic, pre-Hellenic, and early-Christian ruins up on the top, so it was never really safe to assume that a bus was not due. In fact, as I walked down, one of them roared past me, taking the outside of the bend with true Greek abandon, but as I was on foot I was able to dash up the bank and hold on to a wild fig while it whirled past leaving a wake of dust six feet high.

Strolling slowly after it, leaving the white cloud time to settle, I occupied myself by trying to put together all my childhood memories of Father. This was the first period of true solitude and peace I had had since Mother's accident, since I'd read her note, and it seemed an appropriate time for such an exercise.

Such odd, disconnected things one remembers about people—I sometimes wonder how biographies or memoirs are ever put together, how the writers possibly manage to assemble all those correct, suitable, and dignified recollections which appear to have gushed out on demand, like turning on a tap and releasing a flow of Earl Grey?

Scraping the bottom of my mind for memories, I came up with the fact that Father would not change his socks nearly often enough to please Mother; she was always scolding him about it. There was some family joke about how as soon as he took off the socks the cat would rush to them and start trampling on them. "Othello's sucking Father's socks again!" we used to shout. He got very impatient with me once when I would not drink my milk, and emptied the whole mug of it over my head. His anger was quickly aroused, quickly gone. Jokes. He made a lot of jokes—puns, ridiculous rhymes, spoonerisms, just bits of nonsense. "Da bakeda bean!" when it was beans on toast for our tea, he'd go into an Italian opera routine, hand on heart, eyes to heaven, twirling an imaginary mustache. But he worked very hard, used to come home late, hoarse and exhausted from his teaching; we didn't really see much of him. He had a wonderful gift of improvising on the piano; sometimes, at what seemed dead of night (really I daresay it was only half past eight or nine) on evenings when I'd have to go to bed before he got home from work, I would wake up hearing the piano, and lie comforted, knowing that he was in the house, listening to the tunes he was rattling off on our tinkling, sweet, old shallow-keyed piano. His tunes, I later realized, were considerably influenced by the school of Scott Joplin, but still they had a touch of true invention about them and a happy exuberance that carried me, entranced in my bed, to extremes of pleasure that I don't think I have ever sinced reached. I used to think that heaven could have nothing better to offer than lying in bed listening to Father play, on and on, forever. Socks, baked beans, tunes on the piano—he'd had a mustache but later shaved it off; he'd smoked a pipe, then cigarettes, then stopped smoking altogether; he'd drunk beer from a pewter tankard, then gave it up in favor of vermouth; he liked his eggs boiled for one minute only and was very fond of fish, "Fishes is delishes," he used to say and taught me how to expertly bone a mackerel or kipper. "James, just *do* it for her, we're in a hurry," Mother would say impatiently. "She's got to learn some time, Barbara," he would answer mildly, continuing to supervise my unskilled efforts. He called the cat Spinach—some private joke of his own.

Gentle—cheerful—fond of jokes and music—it was hard to imagine such a man in prison, in a madhouse, escaped behind the Iron Curtain with some disastrous secret? Yet my imagination would provide no other solution to the puzzle.

Arrived back in Helikon, I went to our room to

check on Mother but found a note there that said, "Having seaweed bath. See you at 1.00."

Delighted at this evidence of initiative, I went out to where I'd seen Zoé sitting at a table on the terrace, sorting herbs into bundles and labeling them. She said, *"Allo, allo, Mike, mon vieux—comment ça va?"*

I sat down to help her and we worked together while having a comfortable gossip. Zoé was very unlike everyone's stereotyped idea of a French girl: she was squarely built, with a round, dimpled, smiling face, and not particularly talkative; after we'd caught up on the basic information we fell into friendly silence. I had always felt great liking and respect for Zoé; she did a marvelous job as warden, looking after the whole establishment with amiable, serene, businesslike, unhurried efficiency.

From an open french window behind us we could hear the directions for a meditation class floating out. I glanced back inside the room and saw fifteen or so patients lying peacefully on straw mattresses.

"Think of a lake," the instructor said. "In the middle is an island. On the island grows a tree. Under the tree's roots lies a casket. In the still waters of the lake, mountains are reflected upside down. The tree, also, is reflected upside down. In the casket . . ."

In the casket, I thought. What is in the casket? Everybody has a casket inside them and its contents are unknown to anybody else.

I let my thoughts drift away in a different direction, to the *Mysteries of Elsinore*. Hamlet was really a homosexual, I (and evidently old Annibal, too) had decided; he discovers this unrealized identity in the course of the play: "Why did you laugh then, when I said 'man delights not me'?" "What should such fellows

127

as I do crawling between heaven and earth?" And to Ophelia—who, of course was played by a boy: "You jig, you amble, and you lisp, and nick-name God's creatures." And, later: "Give me that man . . . and I will wear him in my heart of heart, As I do thee." . . .

Poor Ophelia! No wonder she couldn't take it, had a breakdown, and threw herself in the river.

Old Annibal had obviously teetered between making Hamlet a man and a woman. Suppose he had been a girl? What would she have been like? As things were, no wonder he was queer, after an upbringing by Gertrude, not one of the world's shining examples of maternal intelligence and devotion.

"Now, imagine yourselves in a rose garden," said the instructor. "All the roses are yellow—that is the color of philosophy. Now the roses are red; that is the color of love. Now they are white—snow white; that is the color of peace."

He let the meditators rest on that for a while; then he played the Air for the G String, and the recumbent forms slowly came to life, picked themselves up, and ambled out into the sunshine. It was almost time for lunch; lemon juice for those on Diets 1, 2, and 3; shredded carrot and pulse for the lucky ones who had progressed to 4, 5, and 6.

Among the emerging meditators was old Annibal Destrier, clad in a striped bathrobe of great age and limping along slowly with a long staff. His beard and the robe made him look rather like Father Time.

Seeing Zoé, of whom he was very fond, he lowered himself with care onto the bench beside us.

"Les jolies demoiselles s'occupent en plein air . . ." he said gallantly and sniffed at a bundle of marjoram.

128

"Has it been decided which of your operas they are going to put on, M. Destrier?" I asked.

"Les Mystères, ma petite. Without doubt, *Les Mystères.* It is my wish. If they can only find a singer for Hamlet. Achmed has written off to Mlle. Kerry Farrell, but it seems she is traveling and cannot yet be located. If she can only come, there will be no difficulty, for she knows the part well and has sung it several times before on radio."

I thought of commenting, "She can't be superstitious, then?" decided not to, and asked instead, "Why did you design the part for a woman, monsieur?"

He launched into a disquisition about *castrati* and countertenors, and then into an analysis of the epicene qualities of Hamlet which so closely paralleled what I had just been thinking that I became very excited. We had a long argument about the play, agreeing with almost equal violence, while Zoé listened to us indulgently and got on with the herbs.

In the end, flown with the excitement of talking to him, and the warm sun, and the pleasure of being at Helikon, I hauled up my courage by its suspenders and asked if I might possibly be allowed to design the sets for the production. If they did *Les Mystères,* that was to say.

Old Annibal smiled at me benevolently. "I certainly have no objection, *mon enfant;* I shall be most curious to see what you do! But you must ask Joop Kolenbrander, of course."

"You'll tell him, though, that you don't mind? Oh, thank you, thank you, monsieur!" I could have hugged him, but refrained, out of consideration for his age and celebrity.

"Oh, to be twenty-two again!" he sighed.

"If I were as creative as you at eighty-four, I wouldn't worry about being twenty-two," I said. Then I saw Mother coming up the stairs from the treatment room, so I ran to meet her and grabbed her arm.

"M. Destrier says that I can do the sets for his birthday opera; isn't that *something?*"

"Oh, splendid, darling; I'm so pleased that you're finding plenty to occupy you," she said vaguely. The word *opera* always turns her off at once, as she can't stand it. But, still, she was very pleased for me. What she really wanted to do, however, was describe her seaweed bath and the wonderful massage that had preceded it. So I listened happily to her descriptions, while we drank our lemon-juice lunch, and managed to think my own thoughts as well.

❧ 6 ❧

NOCTURNE

"Won't you come out into the sunshine, darling?" Julia said to Dikran. "It seems a shame to spend such a lot of time in this room when it's so beautiful outside. Do come for a stroll!"

"No I won't!" he said snappishly. "It's too hot. Do you want me to get another sunstroke?"

Julia sighed. "It is seven o'clock in the evening," she pointed out. "Really, the sun can't be dangerously hot by now. I'm sure it would be safe enough. But if you like I'll call Adnan and ask him?"

This suggestion seemed to annoy Dikran still more. "What use would that be? If he said it was too hot it would just confirm what I've told you. And if he said it wasn't, I wouldn't believe him! When are we going to get out of this wretched hole?"

Helikon was not suiting Dikran. After three days

of its regime he was still protesting furiously. He did not care for the diet, he hated the lack of drink, he despised the accommodations, and in spite of undergoing every kind of treatment, he complained of headaches, constipation, claustrophobia, eyestrain, backache, and a dry mouth.

"But *every*body has a dry mouth for the first few days; they all say so," Julia told him. "I do too. It's the reduced diet. Then, after three or four days, your mouth clears and you feel like a million dollars. Everyone says that too. By tomorrow I'm sure you'll be another person." As the words left her mouth, she cursed herself, wishing she had chosen them more carefully. It was difficult to be tactful with Dikran at the moment; he was making her nervous and jumpy.

"By tomorrow I'll more likely be dead!" he growled. "I don't *want* to stay here a few more days. I want to leave now!"

Julia looked at him in worried silence. She was deeply troubled about him. He seemed so totally changed from the exuberant, gay, good-tempered man she had married that she frequently felt as if she were sharing the room with a complete stranger. In a way, she was.

Adnan had done his best to reassure her. "The aches and the eyestrain are some residual effects of the sunstroke; they will soon pass, have no fear! We must just keep him quiet and calm for a few days more."

It was all very well for Adnan to say that, Julia thought. He didn't have to spend his days and nights with her husband.

"Come into the orchard?" she said hopefully. "There's the most heavenly breeze blowing off the sea."

If he went out at all during the day, Dikran did

132

sometimes venture into the orchard, which was usually shady enough. But this evening he snarled, "Bloody Prokofiev! I'll stay where I am, thank you. It's bad enough here!"

Outside, under the lemon trees, Joop Kolenbrander was taking an enthusiastic group of students through *Peter and the Wolf,* while an old lady in a wheelchair, with a long plait of white hair trailing over her bathrobe, read out the narrative in ringing tones.

Julia would have liked to go out and listen to them at closer quarters. She started for the door, but Dikran said, "Come back and sit down! I hardly ever see you —you're always off having some goddamned treatment or talking to that bloody Turk."

Reluctantly, capitulating, Julia sat down on her bed. She told herself that she could hear *Peter and the Wolf* equally well from there.

" 'And what kind of a useless bird are you, if you can't swim?' said the duck."

A spirited duet broke out between the bird and the duck. Julia listened in delight. If only Dikran would get better, she thought, what a perfect spot this would be in which to spend a honeymoon.

After a moment or two he came and sat by her on the bed, and put his arms around her. "I'm sorry to be such a bear, my dear," he said miserably. "I don't mean to be—specially to you! It's just something that gets hold of me in this place."

He began kissing her, gently at first; soon, as she responded, with ravenous, demanding intensity. Then he pushed her back onto the bed, yanked off the loose cotton shirt she wore, and began fondling her breasts. There seemed something truly desperate about his pas-

133

sion, she thought, as if he were trying to submerge his identity in hers.

"Take your trousers off!" he ordered irritably, finding the fastener beyond his power to shift.

Obeying him, Julia listened dreamily to the velvet notes of the cat crawling through the long grass in Prokofiev's forest. Now Dikran was pressing her violently back against the hard Greek bolster, nuzzling her, biting her neck. Her body was automatically co-operating with his, she felt herself drifting nearer and nearer to the extremity of pleasure; without conscious intent she arched and clung, twined and untwined, clasped and unclasped. But all the time her mind remained disengaged.

She continued to listen to the narrator's voice outside.

"Soon after that, a great gray wolf *did* come out of the forest . . ."

Dikran tossed her farther down the bed, moving her body as easily as if it were a sack of straw.

Julia found herself imagining the joyful expressions on the faces of the three horn players as they waited for their cue to play the wolf theme.

"But the bird flew up into the tree . . ."

Dikran's face above her, furious, aquiline, and intent, looked like that of some avenging angel about to swoop down.

"Then, quick as a flash, he swallowed her up!" declaimed the old lady below, in ringing tones.

"Who, who can this man be?" wondered Julia, her body vibrating like an aspen leaf whirled down a weir. "What have I let myself in for?"

She cried out sharply in a voice not her own, as if possessed by devils; but her cry was lost in the clash of drums and kettledrums outside. Dikran lay spent and motionless on top of her while the hunters (shooting as they went) came marching through the forest, left, right, left, right.

Slowly Dikran's breathing leveled off, quieted down, became long and even; his heartbeats slowed, his head slumped down over Julia's shoulder into the pillow. His grasp relaxed. He slept.

Lying inertly under his weight, Julia heard Peter's tune break suddenly into lilting, perky waltz time: "Don't you worry! We've already caught the wolf!"

Flat, empty, almost anesthetized, she was surprised to find tears sliding backward out of her eyes and through her damp hair.

By degrees Peter's triumphal procession wound its way into the distance, through the forest.

"But what about the duck?" thought Julia in sudden agony. "He's forgotten about the duck!"

And then the parting line came back to her: "In his hurry the wolf swallowed the duck while she was still alive!"

It's a cruel, *horrible* tale, she thought—barbaric, just like the Russians themselves. They are a peasant race. They aren't civilized yet.

She waited until Dikran seemed totally oblivious, fathoms deep in sleep, then, carefully, inch by inch, slid herself out from under him. It took her a very long time. But he did not wake, and she knew that if she left him now, he would very likely remain asleep for eight or nine hours. Then he would probably get up and wander out by himself into the dark. That was the pattern of their life at present; exhausting bursts of passion, sleep, tension, quarrels, and more lovemaking. Often at night he went for long, roaming

135

walks, she did not know where; he refused to accompany her to the evening concerts, grumbling that he never listened to amateurs, or some other excuse obviously hatched up on the spur of the moment: he hated cellos, he couldn't stand French composers; he abused her because she would not join him on his night rambles, but she felt, just the same, that he was quite pleased to get away on his own. Likewise, although he complained about Helikon constantly and said he wished to leave, he took no real initiative about doing so; in a way, she suspected that he was finding the place as much of a refuge as she was herself.

For if they left Helikon, where could they go? To what kind of life could they return? To his flat in London? To hers? To New York, where he said he always spent part of his years, staying at the Plaza? To the house in Iowa (or was it Illinois)? They seemed to have no piece of the world that belonged to them both.

Standing under a cold shower, vigorously toweling herself, brushing her hair, putting on makeup, Julia admitted to herself, not for the first time, that she was both homesick and terrified. She longed for her lost husband, her lost children, her lost home.

Dikran seemed, sometimes, so totally irrational.

As when she had made the joke about the sunflower seeds.

She had discovered a small trail of them on the hotel bedroom carpet when she was packing up their clothes in the Fleur de Lys. Dikran had been sleeping off the effect of Dr. Adnan's tranquilizing shot.

A small trail of sunflower seeds across the carpet.

As if, she had said later, laughing, an absent-minded squirrel had passed that way. "I never knew that you had a secret passion for sunflower seeds!" she had teased Dikran. "Why didn't you let me know? I'd have kept a supply in my luggage."

But his face had turned so dark with rage that she was seriously afraid he might rupture a blood vessel.

"I hate sunflower seeds!" he roared at her. "I *hate* them. And don't you forget it!"

Next minute, he was cradling and fondling her, calling her his flower, and apologizing for scaring her. "Just don't ever mention those sunflower seeds again, that's all."

Trembling, Julia promised that she would not.

And, on another occasion, when she had offered to type out his poems—for she had brought a portable typewriter with her and a plot for a play, which was now sinking back into the sand—he had flown into another frightening paroxysm of rage. She had not even stretched out a hand toward his portfolio of papers—had not even glanced toward it—but he shouted at her, banging the table so savagely that a glass of lemon juice was jolted onto the floor.

"Don't you ever *touch* my papers, d'you hear? Don't you dare to go near that case!"

"I wouldn't dream of it!" she answered indignantly. "I wonder you dare talk to me in that tone!"

For, after all, she had her pride; who was she, Julia Gibbon, to be addressed in such a manner?

And again, at once, he was all contrition, caressed her and wrapped his arms around her, burying his face in her hair and calling her his English rose. "Forgive me, forgive me; I don't know what I am doing. It is this damned sunstroke, that is all."

But was it really the sunstroke? she wondered again, wrapping a shawl around her shoulders. Was it *only*

137

the sunstroke? Or would he have become like this in any circumstances?

Softly pulling the door to behind her, she ran down the stone stairs to the ground floor. It would be pleasant to encounter Adnan—who had, on several occasions, found time to play tennis with her or take her for walks when Dikran was sleeping or sulking—but the evening concert had already begun and he was probably in the hall.

At the foot of the stairs a paved passageway led right into the quadrangle, or left toward the orchard and vegetable gardens. She turned left, then right, and walked past the PRIVATE notice into Dr. Adnan's little formal garden. Preliminary chords from Schubert's *Magic Harp* overture were coming from the lighted windows of the concert hall above her; practically everybody would be there, attending the main music program of the evening. She could be alone here, to listen in peace and privacy.

Or, no: her heart leaped, then sank again. Somebody else was here in the small, dusk-filled place; somebody was at work. She heard the clink of a trowel and—peering through the twilight—could just distinguish a figure which seemed to be kneeling beyond the center bed, pulling plants from the ground and dropping them into a basket. The person, whoever it might be—child or girl—was too small to be Adnan.

"Oh, hullo," said Julia, rather put out but deciding that since she had come so far in she could hardly walk out again without making *some* remark. "Isn't it rather dark for weeding?"

"Yes, it is; you're right," said the girl, effortlessly straightening her back and standing up. It was the skinny child, what was her name, Mike something, who seemed to be a kind of protégée of Adnan's. "The dark creeps up on you when you're busy," she added. She looked down at the area she had cleared, stooped to remove a dying thistle, and explained, "I was just tidying up Lucy's flowerbed. Achmed has so little time."

"Lucy?"

"The statue."

"Oh. Oh yes. Who was she? Was Dr. Adnan married?"

"No, no. Or not that I ever heard," the girl said, sticking her weeding implement upright into the loose earth beside the statue's pedestal. "No, Lucy was a girl he fell in love with years ago in England."

"Oh, I see. What happened? Did she die?"

"Yes. It was very sad. She was a gifted pianist; Max Benovek was teaching her—or was going to teach her, I'm not quite sure of the details, but anyway he thought she was due to become a great player—and Uncle— Dr. Adnan fell in love with her and asked her to marry him. But she had a heart trouble, and before any of these things could happen, she died. She was quite young—younger than me, I believe."

"Poor Lucy." For the second time within an hour, Julia was surprised to find tears in her eyes. Why? What had produced in her this easy sensibility? Why should this simple and not uncommon tale affect her so?

"Did you know Lucy?"

"Oh, goodness, no! I expect I'd only have been about ten at the time. It was long before he came to Dendros. I didn't know Dr. Adnan then. Some Greek friends of his here told me about it once. He doesn't talk about her much—but he has mentioned her. After she died, he and Max Benovek wanted to make some kind of memorial to her, and that's how Helikon was started. Benovek donated quite a lot of money, and they fetched in a Greek millionaire called Capranis, who gave them this site. And Dr. Adnan sold a lot of very valuable pictures that he had. The girl's—Lucy's aunt was a painter, a primitive. Her name was Fennel Culpepper, maybe you've heard of her—"

"Oh, good heavens, yes. Some of her pictures are in the Tate, aren't they? They go for astronomic sums if they ever come on the market."

"Right. Adnan had acquired quite a lot of them, so he sold them all to the V & A and gave that money too. And that's how this place began."

"Quite a good memorial for little Lucy," Julia said rather drily, defying her own unreasonable emotion of two minutes before. "After all, she might never have become a great pianist."

"No. That's true," said Mike, in a mild and reflective tone.

"I wouldn't object to having such a memorial dedicated to me."

"No? But you," said Mike, "you don't need anyone's memorial, Lady Julia. Your plays will be enough to make people remember you."

Julia made no answer to this, only sighed, looking at the dim outline of the sculptured figure on its pedestal.

After a moment, Mike added diffidently, "I do hope you won't be offended—I suppose it must be very boring, people must be saying things like this all the time—but I would like to tell you how *very* much I admire your plays."

"Thank you," Julia answered mechanically.

Despite this lukewarm reception the girl went on. "They are so beautifully constructed. And—what I like best—they have such a marvelously condensed, suffocating feeling of *place*—that awful farm in *The Blasted Heath,* and the old man's flat in *Midwinter,* and the room over the station in *Sharp, Flat, and Slightly Sweet*—you can almost *smell* the trains—your plays don't really need sets at all, I can see, but just the same, I'd love to do the sets for one of them, some day."

"Is that your profession—stage design?" Julia inquired. In fact she had a vague memory of Adnan saying something about the child, but at the time, preoccupied and worried about Dikran, Julia had not paid much attention.

"Yes it is. I don't suppose I'll ever get to the top," the girl said resignedly. "There's a lot of competition. But I love it. Are you working on a play at the moment, Lady Julia?" She added, after a moment's hesitation, "If you are, it—it would be the most terrific privilege to hear you talk about it a little."

Julia's attention had been wandering again, but now it occurred to her that this child was actually the first person who had made any inquiry about her work since she had come to Dendros—since she had left England. Among all the actors, musicians, singers, and other artists assembled at Helikon, not one, except for this girl, had manifested the slightest interest in whether she was working on anything. Dikran certainly had not.

As a general rule Julia disliked talking too much about any project on which she was engaged—discussion of it often seemed to diminish the impetus—but now, touched and amused at finding professional interest in such a wholly unexpected quarter, she began to describe the play that was in her mind. And, as she did so, it moved sluggishly from its submerged domain, showing new features.

"It's called *The Buildings*. It's about a rich woman's bad relationship with the inhabitants of a tenement block near her house—in some northern industrial town—she's a kind of dried-out widow—"

"Hah!" Mike's attention was instantly engaged. "That sounds great! A big, tall, gaunt block, overlooking her house? Full of angry, suspicious, resentful people?"

They had turned and were walking out into the orchard, away from the ambagious strains of music bouncing out of the concert hall above them. Schubert had by now got well into his stride.

"That's it," Julia said. "I want there to be a member of different friction points—slum children climbing her fence, balls breaking her windows, arguments about loud music and dogs and motorbikes—added to which the widow has a rebellious son who wants to leave the university and join a circus and learn to be a tightrope walker—"

"A tightrope walker—oh, terrific!" breathed Mike. "I suppose you couldn't have him actually walk his tightrope on the stage?"

"I rather doubt it!" Julia said, laughing. "Though it would be a novelty! No, I had more in mind some kind of Ibsenesque downfall, offstage, where he gets killed, you know, in the last act—"

"Yes, I can see it would be too farcical to have him do it in full view," Mike said wistfully. "But what a scene! Maybe they can have it in the film version."

The orchard was all around them now. As they

strolled, they could feel the dry, soft grass crackle faintly under their feet. Huge stars flashed here and there among the dark leaves; the air was filled with a sharp scent of leaves and lemons.

"Do you like *Peter and the Wolf?*" Julia asked irrelevantly.

There was silence for a little while Mike reflected. "It's a job of work," she answered at length. "Lovely tunes. But I think Prokofiev never decided whose side he was on."

"Does that matter?"

"In a folk tale—or a children's story—yes, I think it's important, don't you?"

"Perhaps. I hadn't thought in those terms."

"But about your play—are you writing it now?"

"I'm thinking about it."

"When will you have finished it? When will it be put on?"

"I don't really know," Julia answered rather forlornly. "I've just got married again, you see; it's hard to plan ahead, with a new husband; one can't tell how much time there will be for work."

Beside her, in the dark, the girl gave a chuckle. "I suppose not! I hadn't thought of that as a reason against getting married, but now I see it must be quite a strong one."

"More so at my age, when time's beginning to get short. You're all right, you've still got plenty." She added, half idly, half enviously, "Perhaps you'll be designing sets for this play someday—heaven only knows how long it will take me to get it finished. By that time you may be halfway through your career."

"Oh, wouldn't that be marvelous!"

143

"Tell me what you've done—what experience you've had. Where are you working now?"

Talking, discussing, reminiscing, they walked to and fro under the lemon trees.

Presently the moon rose and threw long shadows over the limp, silvered grass.

"Do you know," said Julia, peering at her watch, "that we've been out here for two and a half hours?"

"Have we really? Gosh, I'd better go and see if Mother wants settling down for the night." She added diffidently, "I *have* enjoyed this talk."

"I have too.—Where are we?" Julia said. "I've clean lost my sense of direction under all these trees."

"Oh, I know where we are. We're right down at the bottom of the orchard—near the Dendros road—by the sun-bathing area. There's a path back to the main drive, if we go on in this direction."

"The sun-bathing area?"

"Nude—didn't you know? They've got two precincts —one for men, one for women. Uncle Achmed's a great stickler for propriety," Mike said, chuckling again. "You'd never think he was such a lady-killer in his private life. Here—this is the men's sun-bathing enclosure on our right, now, behind the bamboos."

They had reached a rock path. On their right, a barricade of bamboos and rushes, plaited and packed tightly between stakes, similar to the screens protecting the tomato beds, rose to a height of about nine feet.

"That's to keep out peeping Thomasinas," Mike explained. "Nobody from here would bother, of course. But I believe there are tales of people from Dendros— tourists probably—trying to poke spyglasses through the barricade. Silly, isn't it? I certainly can't imagine wanting to peep at male sun-bathers; most of the men who come here are no great shakes as far as looks go. Of course I'm not including your husband, Lady Julia. He's dreamy!"

Julia laughed. "The females aren't much better, if it comes to that. Who's the very fat woman with a blond bun who gets wheeled around in a wheelchair by a skinny dark boy?"

"That's Marion Hillel."

"The pianist? Whatever happened to her? It's years since she played."

"Some kind of spinal illness, I think. She couldn't even sit up, let alone walk. But Adnan's treatment is doing her so much good that she's begun practicing again—she plays Beethoven every morning," Mike said with pride.

"Hullo—what's that?"

Julia had stopped by the gate of the male sun-bathing enclosure. A large sign, white in the moonlight, said MEN ONLY. The gate stood open, and just inside it something light-colored had caught her eye.

"Nobody sun-bathing at this time of night," Mike said. "Unless they're moon-bathing."

She walked inside, glanced around, and stooped down.

"Somebody's clothes," she said, coming back. "But the somebody can't have been here for hours—the clothes are all damp and dewy. *Espadrilles*—jeans—T shirt—wonder how he got back to his room without them." She chuckled again. "Maybe he's a streaker! Anyway, I'll put these in Zoé's office—she can make an announcement about them at evening drinks or stick a note on the board."

"He'll probably remember and come back for them himself in the meantime," said Julia. "Most likely he had swimming trunks as well, and went down to the beach for a swim, and forgot these."

"Yes, probably that's it. Good night, then, Lady Julia," Mike said, and ran off in the direction of the office.

Nice child, Julia thought absently, looking after her. Tansy would like her. Seems to know what she's talking about.

And then Julia's attention was deflected from Mike by the sight of Dr. Adnan walking briskly toward her along the wide, flagged path among a group of emerging concert goers. He wore a velvet evening jacket and a flowered cravat. He was looking exceptionally pleased with himself. "Ah, there, Lady Julia! You do not attend our concert?"

"No," Julia replied coolly—but pleased that he had remarked her absence. "It was such a beautiful night that I've been walking with Mike in the orchard. You look very cheerful, Dr. Adnan?"

"Cheerful, yes indeed, I should say so. I have secured the services of Kerry Farrell for our small opera. Here at last is a singer of international caliber who is not subject to silly superstitions and shibboleths. She will sing the part extremely well—and the old Destrier will not be disappointed on his *jour de fête.*"

"Oh, that's very good news—I'm so pleased," said Julia, not with total truth, because she had never taken the least interest in opera. But she was pleased for Adnan's sake and added with sincerity, "Old Destrier's a splendid old boy, isn't he. Will you be able to get it rehearsed in time? When's his birthday?"

"In ten days from now. And, yes, I think so; we have rehearsed the minor parts already, in hopes. Joop knows the piece very well. I myself will take

146

the part of Horatio. But of course it has been an anxiety not knowing if we shall be able to proceed with it."

He suddenly burst into exuberant song.

"You can't do chromatics
With proper emphatics
When anguish your bosom is wringing!

When distracted with worries in plenty
And his pulse is a hundred and twenty
And his fluttering bosom the slave of mistrust is,
    A tenor can't do himself justice!

Julia laughed, thinking what an unexpected character he was; all serious professional consideration one minute, all lighthearted fooling and nonsense the next. What had that girl said—something about his being a lady-killer in private life?

He proved her point by dropping his musical-comedy manner and asking with the utmost kindness and gravity, "How is your husband this evening, Lady Julia? Do you think he is settling more to our ways?"

"Oh, I don't know, Dr. Adnan—sometimes I'm really puzzled and worried about him!" she burst out. "He seems—he seems in a rage against life itself sometimes—"

"That *would* seem ungrateful, just when life has presented him with such a beautiful partner," Adnan remarked, with a return to his former manner, but added more seriously, "Patience, my friend! He is a complicated character, that husband of yours. A few more days of our diet, though, a few more treatments, and we shall see a change, I am sure. You cannot ex-

147

pect recovery to be so simple in a man who has such a number on his arm."

"What kind of a number on whose arm?" Mike had come running lightly back along the flagged path from Zoé's office and now stood beside them. She spoke with casual friendliness, not from curiosity so much as to inform them of her arrival.

But Adnan, perhaps embarrassed at having been overheard speaking in a public place on a confidential matter, answered rather sharply, "My dear little Mike, small pitchers should not have enormous ears!" He pulled one of hers, not too gently. "Lady Julia and I were speaking privately."

Even in the moonlight, Julia could see Mike flush at the snub. "I'm sorry!" she said, trying to keep a quiver of hurt and anger out of her voice. "I didn't have the least intention of eavesdropping, I assure you! Zoé's wanted on the phone in her office—I only wanted to ask you if you knew where she was."

"Down in the steam room; somebody reported that the lid had jammed on one of the steam baths, and the plumber has come."

"Thank you," said Mike haughtily, and ran off toward the stair that led to the treatment area.

"Greek plumbers work long hours," Julia remarked.

"The plumber's cousin is a nurse here."

"I see.—What a nice child that little Mike is."

"Is she not?" Adnan agreed eagerly. He added with some remorse, "I'm sorry that I spoke to her unkindly —because I myself was caught in indiscretion! I will make it all right with her tomorrow."

"Oh, by tomorrow she'll have forgotten all about it. Is she your goddaughter."

148

"Goddaughter? No, indeed." He seemed taken aback at the suggestion.

Julia said good night and walked away in the direction of her bedroom.

I'm sure a touch of sunstroke wouldn't make *him* disagreeable, she thought, sighing. He never seems worried about anything. And yet plenty of responsibility must rest on his shoulders.

I hope we'll be able to fit in a game of tennis tomorrow. Or a walk. Or a drive.

She opened the door, fervently wishing that she might find Dikran asleep. Or, better still, gone out on one of his walks.

But he was wide awake, lying with open eyes fixed on the ceiling.

❧ 7 ❧

VARIATIONS

At least part of what I had hoped for now came to pass: Mother really did get into the spirit of Helikon, appreciated what it had to offer, and spent her days darting from one treatment to the next—seaweed baths, massage, manipulation, acupuncture, heat, cold, wax, mud—she was always in some mix or other. If I wanted to talk to her during the day, I had to thread my way through the treatment area, serenading like Blondel in search of Richard, and would find her behind some curtain, covered in hot wax and crinkly paper, or stuck full of bamboo darts and having a long conversation about education with kindly Mr. Twang, who did the acupunctures. She throve on the lemon juice and grated radish. She borrowed a violin, went to master classes, and practiced trios with two enthusiastic Latvian girls. Not a word of Latvian did she speak, they no English, but nonetheless they all managed to communicate as much as was necessary.

Apart from the Latvians, though, and me, and friendly consultations with Adnan, Mother did not involve herself in the social life of the place, which bubbled up among performers and patients in the form of lemon-juice parties on people's bedroom balconies and long, terry-robed gossip sessions on the lawns. Basically both shy and reserved, Mother was by no means a ready mixer; in fact she found it easy to talk to people only in her own professional slot. Nor did people find it easy to talk to her; they were frightened off, I thought, by her somewhat formidable appearance. She was also, I was saddened to discover, growing a little hard of hearing; alone with somebody in a room she could hear perfectly well, but put her among a chattering group and she was sunk. She would shrug, look defeated, and go back to her own room.

So, during the day, I did not see a lot of her, for I was quite busy myself, but I always gave her a scalp massage in the evenings. She would be tired by then; she never attended the main concerts, preferring to go to bed early and read. I hoped the scalp massages were doing her some good; her shaved hair was taking its time about growing back, and she still wore the black turbans, which did add a daunting air of formality among all the bikinis and bedroom slippers. By now she was fairly tanned (unlike me; all I do is freckle), but she looked frail and big-eyed and unlike herself, so that I still hesitated to burden her with questions relating to the tragic past (and the possible disagreeable and upsetting present). Besides—amid all the peaceful harmony and virtuous activities of Helikon—my wish to find out seemed like vulgar and selfish curiosity. So

I delayed and procrastinated and let it all lie fallow.

"I am a 'dull and muddy-mettled rascal, peak, like John-a-dreams, unpregnant of my cause,'" I thought sometimes, dropping in to watch the minor characters at their rehearsals of *Les Mystères d'Elsinore*. George, who had quite a pleasant light tenor, was standing in for the part of Hamlet, as their main singer hadn't arrived yet. She had some engagement in Berlin to fulfill first, but was due to appear any day. And there were still six days to go before old Annibal's birthday.

I was quite pleased with my sets.

I'd been given an empty barn as a workroom—a goat shed, I suppose it was really—and had bought a lot of wall paint in Archangelos village. The powdery blues and greens that the Greeks use for their houses were just the thing for my Piero distant backgrounds, and I had borrowed a book of reproductions from the main library in Dendros. I needed some dark reds and blacks, though, for the interiors and the castle walls; I was thinking, one morning as I surveyed my work, that I'd really have to co-opt somebody to go into Dendros with me and help carry stuff back. Zoé and a couple of Greek students were helping me with the costumes—and we were also lucky enough to have the advice of a professional dress designer, Graziella Vanzini, who, as it happened, was having her bursitis ameliorated at Helikon. But Zoé and the students were hard at work during the day, and Graziella was undergoing her treatment and not available to run errands. They worked hard in the evenings, though, and, despite the shortness of time, we were making good progress with the costumes, which, both from choice and necessity, were severely plain. We used the formal, fluted draperies and tunics that Piero characters mostly wear, with buttoned fronts and round collars and round, fifteenth-century hats like squashed cushions; they looked impressive and were very quick to make. Fortunately there was no shortage of material, for Zoé bought Greek cotton in twenty-bale lots for the Helikon sheets and cubicle curtains; all we had to do was dye it, and there was a small dye factory in a village called Skimi, five miles away, where they dipped all the material that was subsequently made up into shapeless garments of dazzling colors and sold to tourists in Dendros; so I borrowed Zoé's bike and cycled to Skimi and bought bags and bags of their dye powders. Then the two Greek students and I had a happy, splashy evening in one of Helikon's do-it-yourself laundry rooms, dyeing dozens of lengths of cloth and spinning them dry. By mixing and double dipping we achieved some rich and subtle shades that were highly satisfactory. I wanted, if possible, to match those shades in my backgrounds.

I was pondering over my sketches for the throne-room sets and deciding that the painted folds of curtain must be a dark plum red, when Adnan walked in.

He wandered about the shed, inspecting my flats, while I got silently on with my planning and made lists of things I wanted to buy.

"Hey-dey! We're not speaking today?" he observed, giving me a sharp look.

"I was thinking, that's all."

He gazed at the cliffs of Elsinore. "Very nice; v-e-r-y nice! Heads of cauliflower—am I right? Covered in your English white sauce, that ubiquitous, invaluable, all-purpose medium which can be used as a poultice, a paint-base, a makeup foundation, or as whitening for footmen's wigs."

"That's body color. And the sets are the cliffs of Elsinore," I said coldly.

"Of course, of course, fancy my making such a mistake. Tsk, tsk, so they are, so they are!" He inspected them a bit more and suddenly declaimed,

> It is the dreadful summit of the cliff
> That beetles o'er his base into the sea!

With Hadrian's villa on the top, no less! You don't think that is a *little* too classically Mediterranean for Denmark's seat of government?" He seemed extra nervous and fidgety, I thought; much more so than usual.

I said, "Certainly not. Shakespeare had *been* to Italy. He hadn't been to Denmark. I'm trying to follow *his* imagination."

"I see, I see." He began to sing,

> Tell me, where is fancy bread?
> Or in the heart, or in the head?
> Sesame, raisin, or honey-spread?
> But shut your eyes in holy dread
> For he on every kind hath fed
> And been by an-gels nourish-ed!

As I ignored this, he wandered about some more, balancing on toes and heels, muttering, "Not bad, not bad, they are really not at all bad. Has the old Destrier seen them?"

"Yes, he has," I said, and began gathering my brushes together.

"Hoity toity, we *are* on our high horse today, are we not? ((What a wonderful expression that is, hoity toity. What can it possibly *mean*? Now, if one were in

Brooklyn one would know: hoity, toity boids, oy, gevalt! But, then, we are not in Brooklyn. And as for the high horse—I like to think of you on *that,* my dear little Mike. It is almost, but not quite, as high as high dudgeon.)"

Turning a deaf ear to his teasing, I said, "Dr. Adnan, can I have about ten pounds' worth of drachmae from the petty cash to go into Dendros and buy some more paint, please?"

"Certainly you can; just tell Zoé I said so, but from where do you get all this Dr. Adnan stuff? How formal we are, all of a sudden! Old Uncle Achmed I used to be, once upon a time."

"That was when I was a child."

"And now we are very grown up, so elderly and dignified that we have to *stand* on our dignity, hmm?" I was hoping that he might offer to drive me into Dendros in his Volkswagen, which stood idle under the lemon trees most days, and he seemed on the point of doing so, for he said, "You will need quite a lot more paint, though, won't you? How do you propose to carry it all back? You can hardly pile that on the carrier of Zoé's bicycle. Is paint all you intend to buy?"

"No, I want some plaster of Paris and some tassels and stuff for the costumes as well."

"In that case," he said, "you had better borrow my car. And why do you not take Lady Julia with you? While her husband is having his treatments, I have observed that she is somewhat at a loose end; she does not take many treatments herself and I have seen her looking as if she does not know what to do with herself. I think she would be very pleased if you invited her."

"Oh—very well," I said, rather ungraciously, because that was not at all what I had had in mind.

He looked at me intently and said in a reproving manner, "Lady Julia is lonely and homesick and very sad and worried also. It would be kind in you to do this.—Besides, she likes you."

I had liked Lady Julia too, actually, and after our late-evening talk in the orchard, had rather hoped that I was going to have her for a friend. But during the past three or four days she and Adnan had seemed to be very much in each other's pockets. I sometimes wondered what her husband, the mysterious Mr. Saint, thought about this. Saint seemed of all names the most unsuitable for him, and plainly it was not his original designation—he looked more as if it should have been Saladin or Iskandar or Sheikh Somebody. He was a sultry-looking fellow, with a heavy blue jowl, Napoleonic, dark treacle-colored eyes, a thin, rather cruel (I thought) mouth, and a short, curved, beaky nose that seemed on the thin side for his fleshy face. I had remarked on this once to Matthieu, the masseur, where he was giving the shin I once broke in sixth-form hockey a bit of a rub, and Mat said at once, "Plastic surgery."

"Eh? How can you be sure?"

"O, *peuh,* I have seen dozens. In my father's health spa in Brussels we are all the time looking after ladies who have their noses improved or their double chins eliminated—there is a look—how can I say it?—some stiffness, skin not elastic—I can tell, always. Is like a drawing when lines have been rubbed out and redrawn."

Mat's father had sent him to Helikon for experience so that he could later on return and take over the parental business, but Mat himself intended to fill the

156

gap left by Breughel's passing. He was keen to help me with my sets, but although I was glad of his help I had to be constantly on the watch, to restrain him from suddenly putting in some feature that his inventive fancy had suggested: demons riding through the air, eggs exploding into monsters, touches of Bosch-like fantasy. "In Shakespeare's time, after all, folk believe in such things!" he would protest reproachfully.

"Mat, this is *Hamlet,* not *A Midsummer Night's Dream!"*

However, about plastic surgery and its effects I thought his knowledge was probably sound enough, and his observation had enhanced the sinister and mysterious aura that Mr. Saint seemed to carry around him. I'd cast him as Rochester, or Mr. Murdstone, I thought, or one of those fiends in Restoration drama. I could hardly imagine that he would take kindly to being neglected by his wife in favor of a smooth-spoken Turkish doctor. But perhaps he didn't realize what was happening; like Mother, he did not mix much; outside of his treatments, he seemed to spend a lot of time in his room. One saw him with Lady Julia in the big, light dining room, eating his little mounds of shredded nut and carrot with a look of disdainful, incredulous disgust; sometimes he could be seen briefly in the downstairs waiting area clad in a black robe of silk so stiff that it would have stood upright on its own—I longed to ask if I could borrow it for Hamlet. Otherwise Mr. Saint was not generally visible. Perhaps he was hardly aware that his wife played tennis and swam and so often went for strolls and evening drives with Adnan.

But, strangely enough, *I* found myself minding for him. Also, I had taken a liking to Lady Julia, and if

Adnan was regarding her as one of his regular flirts, I knew she would be in for a painful letdown. On the other hand, if it was more than a flirt, then everybody was in for trouble.

But why should one need to flirt on one's honeymoon?

None of this was my business, however, and I said to Adnan, who was now observing me very acutely, with a look that I did not greatly care for in his plumdark eyes—ironic, patronizing, quizzical—"I like Lady Julia too! And I admire her plays. If she wants to go into Dendros, that's okay by me. If she wouldn't prefer to swim or play tennis, I'll be glad to take her."

"Good," he said briskly. "Then, you can certainly borrow my car."

"Why don't you take her in yourself?" I couldn't resist saying.

He looked at me under his eyelashes—which were as thick and dark as a Jersey cow's—and said silkily, "Believe it or not, my dear little Mike, I have work to do, keeping an eye on Helikon. Besides, it is *your* trip to Dendros that is in question."

I wasn't going to pick that one up. Suddenly I felt tired of this conversation—tired altogether—in fact, really fatigued. I sat down on a packing case and said, "Very good. Tell Lady Julia—if you should see her—that I'd love her to come along if she wants to, and I plan to start about two o'clock. Dr. Adnan there's something I wanted to ask you about Mother."

Immediately he was kind, serious, attentive—a changed person. "What is it, Mike? Something is worrying you?"

Then of course I found it hard to go on. I looked

158

down at my paint-stained fingers and rubbed at a patch of explosive green on the back of my hand.

Seeing my difficulty, he, too, sat down on a box and said, quietly and sympathetically, "Do not look so distraught. Whatever it is, we try to fix it, hmn? It probably is not so bad as you imagine. Tell Papa Mustafa all your trouble."

I said, "You are a great friend of the Aghnides family. Did they ever tell you—anything of my family history?"

He looked at me very gravely and said, "No, Mike, they did not. Old Demosthenes Aghnides is the very soul of honor and discretion. Even supposing I were his blood brother, if he had been entrusted with any secret about your family, he would not tell it unless he had permission to do so. I do know that there was some tragedy connected with your family—that your father and sister both died, and that was the reason why you spent those years in Dendros when you were a child—but more than that, I do not know. It was long before I came to this island. But why do you ask?"

I could not tell him about Father being still alive—about my having read Mother's note. It wasn't my secret to give away; if old Mr. Aghnides could keep silent, so could I. But I did say, after a moment or two—during which he sat immovable, unspeaking, looking at me with the most penetrating attention—"I wasn't trying to *find out* from you—what happened to my father and Drusilla, I mean. It's just that there's this great, awful, undivulged secret which has always come between my mother and myself. It really has just about wrecked our relationship. Until now."

"You mean to say that *you* do not know what happened?" At this he did look really startled. His eyebrows—which were black, thick, and bushy—shot up like forklifts. He said, "She never *told* you what happened to your father and sister?"

"No."

"Ah, you English, you English!" Adnan exploded. "Never will I understand this race, never—not if I had lived in England for seventy years instead of just seven! Here you have a mother—an intelligent, educated lady who makes a fine career for herself, as what? as a *teacher,* directing young persons how they shall grow and learn and discover how to meet experience and make the best of their life. Here we have her child—a nice, funny, creative girl (never mind that she is also cursed with a black, censorious, puritanical, churlish temper)—" Dr. Adnan threw me a needle-sharp glance—even in his kindest moments one could never be quite safe from these darts—"and what does this lady do? Does she tell her troubles to her child, avail herself of this outlet, strengthen their relationship by mutual comfort, consolidation, solace, et cetera—"

"No," I said flatly. "She doesn't. She was trying to spare me from whatever it was, because it was all so dreadful."

He threw up his hands. "I say nothing! It is just a wonder that you have turned out—as you have turned out. Certainly I realize right away when I first see your mother that here is the very quintessence of English ladyhood: self-contained, reserved, independent, up-tight, and, above all, reluctant to make a fuss. Ah, this dread of fuss! It is the motivation behind all English history. Why did the Pilgrims go to America? To avoid fuss. Why did King Charles let his head be cut off? Too much of a gentleman to make a fuss. Why was Prince Albert—but I digress! So, all this time, your mother contains this terrible secret in her bosom. Whatever it was. No wonder she still looks so thin and frail, no wonder our Helikon regime is slow to take effect on her.'"

"It really has helped her, quite a lot," I assured him.

"Well, she must have a constitution like a musk ox—to retain all that anguish within her, the deaths of husband and daughter—*and* sustain a concrete beam dropping on her head as well. But, without doubt, this delays her recovery. Most definitely I think you should have a heart-to-heart conversation with her about it all. 'Mother, dear Mother,' you say to her, 'it may have escaped your attention that I am now a grown-up girl'—yes, my dear Mike, I have observed how she still behaves to you as if you were a little child, age twelve or less—'Mother,' you say, 'I am now an adult and it is my right that you reveal all.' Quite simply you say it—like that."

"Sure I do. Just like that."

"Well, my dear Mike, I know it takes a little courage, but courage you have in plenty. Faults you have in plenty too I do not deny—intolerance, suspicion, obstinacy, superiority—" He was well back in form now.

"Okay, okay," I said, standing up.

"But courage—this you do not lack. You are braver than I, indeed." He stood up too.

"I don't remember ever seeing *you* scared of *any*-thing."

"No? But some things do scare me, Mike, and several of them are right here in Helikon at this time."

I did not feel enough of the courage he attributed to me to ask what he meant by that, and when he said,

161

"Come, I will give you the car key," I followed him silently to his office. This was an austerely tidy place in the main building, with a secretary's room opening off it. Looking at his orderly files, dustless desk, pencils and pens tidily contained in a pottery mug, books neatly marshaled in bookshelves, I thought that, despite his explosion about the English, he and Mother did have quite a few traits in common.

Whereas I am really very untidy.

"Here." He opened a drawer and gave me the car key. "And here—" From a cashbox he gave me a fistful of Greek notes. "Buy your paint and trimmings. With what is left, treat yourself and Lady Julia to a glass of ouzo. Now run along. Have a—" he paused and then flashed his wide, beaming grin, "Have a nice time. That is the term, is it not?"

"Thank you," I said, and pocketed the money.

On his immaculate desk there stood one photograph. It was a head, not very big, simply framed in black. The print was fuzzy, as if it had been blown up from a much smaller snapshot: picture of a girl with a wide forehead, a thin, pointed face, and a spray of untidy, flax-pale hair. She was looking intently forward, eyes narrowed as if taking aim, and indeed, in the background, the stalls of a fair could vaguely be distinguished. It was, I knew, Adnan's lost love, Lucy; when I was much younger, he had occasionally let fall pieces of information about her. Rather a plain girl, Lucy was; but I thought I would have liked her. She looked an extremely determined character, who might ride roughshod over anyone who obstructed her; but she also looked as if she found plenty of things funny. She was not smiling in the picture, she was frowning slightly, and her lips were parted as she took aim, revealing the fact that her front teeth were rather endearingly crossed. I wondered what it was that she had been aiming at so carefully when the picture was taken, and whether she had hit it.

Adnan, following the direction of my gaze, said, "She has a little the look of Lady Julia, do you not think so?"

"No, I don't," I said shortly, and turned to leave the room.

Behind me, I heard him give a brief, sharp sigh. Then his phone rang, and instantly he was involved in a vigorous discussion about students' unions and the rates of holiday pay for part-time workers at Helikon. "Not a drach more do we give until we hear from the union about it! I am not in this business to support idle, good-for-nothing dropouts from the universities!" he snapped. Adnan could be quite tough when it suited him. He was by no means a simple character. But as I was going around the turn of the stairs, he put his head out of the study door and shouted, "Mike! Don't forget about the hand brake!"

I remembered then that the hand brake in his car, if applied too violently (and you had to apply it quite a bit, since the foot brake was not up to much) had a habit of opening the passenger door, which had caused unwary passengers to be catapulted out on bends. "All right, I'll remember!" I shouted back.

I went out into the sunshine with plenty to ponder about.

People were already assembling in the loggia for their lunchtime lemon juice. (Patients who were not yet into the solids were not subjected to the torture of going into the dining room and watching their better-fed companions chomping chick-peas). I picked up a

163

glass of juice and sat on the grass, waiting for Lady Julia to appear.

In the middle of the quadrangle Joop Kolenbrander was taking a batch of his compatriots through a Mozart wind octet. They were all different heights, and somehow, with their bulbous and tubular instruments, they looked irresistibly comic, like the Seven Dwarfs. Joop himself, pink-faced and egg-headed, was the shape of a stick of celery and had an outsize Adam's apple—an Adam's pineapple—which rushed up and down his throat all the time he conducted, as if it were some kind of glottal stop and wanted to be in on the act.

In between their bursts of carefree music I could hear conversation of the usual kind as patients wandered out of the dining room with plates of salad and sat on the grass crunching their carrots and sipping their juice.

". . . swelling's really going down at last."

". . . *always* comes in two bars early . . ."

". . . sore from all this harp practice—if I could possibly borrow your surgical spirit . . ."

". . . can't stand the woman who does the saunas—the big strapping one . . ."

". . . wind! I just fart *all* the time here . . ."

". . . Who doesn't? Adnan would say it's evil humors being released . . ."

". . . still haven't fixed the fourth steam bath. Greek plumbers . . ."

". . . first full rehearsal of *Elsinore,* now Miss Farrell's . . ."

". . . what wouldn't I give for a big steak and a plateful of . . ."

164

". . . joke if Kerry Farrell dropped dead in the part like the last two . . ."

". . . didn't actually die *during* the performance?"

". . . well, you know what I . . ."

". . . only ever sleep about four hours a night here—beds like planks—and as for dreams . . ."

It was true that one's sleep was thin and light on the low diet. But it did not seem to matter. Adnan's theory was that the life of stress and anxiety and regular overeating that most people subjected themselves to also caused them to sleep for unnecessarily long, even harmfully long periods of time, as a kind of escape. "Oversleeping is as bad as overeating," he often said severely. As a solace, or reward for the non-sleepers, he had a projection room at Helikon where early silent films were shown from midnight to 5 A.M. I seldom bothered to go in there; I quite enjoyed the sleepless hours and either went for night walks or lay on my bed peacefully planning the sets for all Shakespeare's plays.

Lady Julia came strolling out on to the grass wearing a plain, straw-colored silk dress and a big natural straw hat, and looking like a million dollars. It's no use, I thought; having a whole lot of money *does* make a difference, there's no getting away from the fact; expensive materials are just better than cheap ones.

But it was true that no amount of cash could have improved or made any difference to her long, beautiful face, framed by the cloudy, pre-Raphaelite hair.

For once, her husband was with her, and he stood regarding me impassively while I made my suggestion of the trip into town, feeling rather shy and foolish about it. Politeness impelled me to include him in the invitation: "And you too, of course, Mr. Saint, if you would like?"

"Thank you, but I'd better not," he said. "Walking around the streets of Dendros in hot sun is probably not what Dr. Adnan would recommend."

Did I imagine the sarcastic note in his voice?

Lady Julia, however, said that she would love to go, and vanished indoors to fetch her purse. I had thought her husband would go with her, but to my surprise he remained by my side and we kept up a slightly stilted conversation, waiting for her to return.

He asked how I came to be so well acquainted with Dendros, and I explained about my childhood visits. Then he said, "I hear that you are painting the sets for this *Hamlet* opera?"

Out of politeness, I think, he asked me about the job, so I described my Piero idea. Unexpectedly, he turned out to be very well informed about Piero; he did not, somehow, look the kind of man who would know about painters—I can't help it if that sounds snobbish—and our discussion had become quite animated by the time Lady Julia returned. It appeared that he had traveled all over Italy looking at Piero pictures in remote country churches, and had seen the great "Flagellation" at Urbino before it was stolen; he seemed as familiar with it as most people are with "When did you last see your father?"

"Do come and see my sets, any time," I said. "I'm sure you could give me lots of advice about them," and he said that he would very much like to.

Lady J. came back at last with her handbag and more lipstick on.

"Take care of yourself, my darling," she said, giving her husband a hasty peck, and then we went

166

off to the corner of the lemon grove, where Adnan's unassuming little auto lived. It was the same he'd had ever since I'd known him; many were the excursions I'd taken in it with him and Calliope. The smell of warm dust and gasoline and dirty upholstery gave me a queer, nostalgic feeling.

I remembered to warn Lady Julia about the hand-brake, and we swung off up the road into town, passing a bus in which an old lady was holding up her dead husband's picture to the window so that he could enjoy the ride too. I suddenly thought we should have brought Lucy along. Perhaps that's what Adnan would really have liked.

"I can see that my husband has taken a big fancy to you," Lady Julia said as we came within view of the flat, white roofs of Dendros town and the Aegean shining beyond them. She went on, "I do hope you'll talk to him some more. I don't think he knows any people your age and he's very shy with them. He's never had any children of his own, though I suspect he would have liked to very much."

Why didn't he, then? was the obvious question, but as there was presumably some sad reason for this I didn't ask it.

She added thoughtfully, more to herself than to me, "Perhaps, in a way, it's just as well. Millionaires' children must be in such a position of risk all the time."

"You mean kidnaping?" I said, working the car carefully along Winston Churchill Street, which had acquired several sets of traffic lights since last I'd been there. "Like the Getty boy, and that wretched little Rittenhouse baby that they found gnawed by rats."

She shivered and said, "I can't *bear* to think of that

167

case. I really just meant spoiling—the danger of having everything within reach, always—but there's kidnaping too, it's quite true."

I drove on past the post office and along the harborside. "Shall I park here, or would you like to go straight into the Old Town?"

"Whichever suits you better. I haven't anything special that I want to do," she said. "I just thought it would be nice to get away for a bit. I'll come and help you with your errands."

{8}

WATER MUSIC

As usual, when she got back, Julia found Dikran lying on his bed.

"I don't know why you didn't make an evening of it," he said in a surly tone. "Why didn't you go to a nightclub? Have dinner somewhere? Stay the night at the Fleur de Lys?"

"Mike wanted to get back and hear the *Hamlet* rehearsal," Julia replied coldly, affecting to be unaware of his sarcasm. "Kerry Farrell has arrived, and she's going to be singing tonight for the first time. I thought I'd go and listen, later on—do you want to come along?"

"You know I can't stand that man's music. Now," he said, "now, I suppose, what time you have left over from that little Turkish pimp is going to be spent puttering around with the girl—is that it?"

"Oh, Dikran—*don't!*"

"Don't what?"

"Don't *be* like this! She's a very nice girl—you liked her yourself, didn't you? You thought she was interesting—I could see. I just like her, that's all. What's wrong with going shopping with her?"

"Nothing—nothing—nothing!" he snarled, and, turning away from her, lay curled up with his face to the wall, sullen and silent. Julia gave a long, impatient, unhappy sigh. For the past two or three days Dikran's temper seemed to have been deteriorating hourly. He alternated between morose gloom and fairly active rage. Was it unreasonable that she wished to spend as little time as possible in his company?

Since she could think of nothing to say that was conciliating, she turned to leave the room.

"*Now* where are you off to?" he demanded.

"I'm due for a sauna in half an hour. I thought I'd go and listen to some music first. Why don't you come along?"

"Because I don't want to listen to any more goddamned amateurs!"

She shrugged and left him. No use to point out that many of the performers to be heard at Helikon were not amateurs at all but top-class professionals; in this mood Dikran was unsusceptible to reason.

Actually it was the amateur side of Helikon that Julia chiefly enjoyed. She loved to walk past a window, hear a burst of music, and, looking in, see three long-haired young persons in swimsuits playing a trio entirely for their own pleasure, lost to everything but the enjoyable noise they were making.

She loved being able to drop into any room, sit and listen to the music that was going on there, then, when she pleased, move on and dip elsewhere—or lie out under the lemon trees, with a distant, leaf-checkered view of the Aegean, and hear snatches of organ, flute, strings, or choir, from open windows or distant groups. The sense that all this joyful sound was free, given and taken purely for pleasure, added to her delight in it. Whereas for Dikran she feared that it worked in exactly the opposite way: his appreciation of anything went up in direct proportion to its cost; in a month's marriage she had already discovered that, and she occasionally asked herself, with unwonted bitterness, whether her own value to him had anything to do with personal attraction at all—or was it solely based on her status as playwright, celebrated ex-wife of a celebrated critic, well-known TV beauty of panel fame, much-photographed newspaper and magazine subject, conspicuous central figure in a notorious divorce case?

Perhaps, she thought gloomily, that was why Dendros had turned Dikran so sulky—because there were so few observers here to appreciate the prize he had acquired.

Running down the stairs, she turned right at random —she had really come out with no other intention than that of escaping from Dikran—and encountered Joop Kolenbrander carrying a suitcase and escorting an unfamiliar female with eager deference. His red face and unwontedly flustered demeanor aroused Julia's curiosity—could the newcomer be the much-discussed Kerry Farrell, the dauntless candidate for the part of Hamlet?

So it proved.

"Oh—Miss Farrell—have you met Lady Julia Gibbon—er—Lady Julia Saint?" Joop said. "Lady Julia, this is Miss Kerry Farrell, who has come so kindly at short notice to help us out of our difficulties."

"How do you do, Miss Farrell," Julia said, smiling. "I can't tell you how anxiously everyone has been waiting for your arrival!"

"And sorry I am I couldn't be here sooner," said the singer. " 'Twasn't the will that was lacking, I can tell you—if I had the choice I'd spend every minute of my time in this blessed spot. But I had a concert scheduled for last night in Berlin that I couldn't be cutting."

She spoke with a slight Irish lilt which Julia's sensitive ear diagnosed as being half artificial—a theatrical flourish. Though it was true that Kerry Farrell looked genuinely Irish. Despite the accent, she seemed pleasantly unaffected; she smiled frankly at Julia, putting out a large but shapely hand.

"And aren't you the clever one, Lady Julia, to be writing all those beautiful plays, each one of them better than the one before? Glory be to God, the time I've had, trying to get back to see them all, and I, as likely as not, stuck in some godforsaken corner of the globe singing my soul out to a lot of heathen who don't know Monteverdi from Monty Python."

Julia laughed. "Well, you won't find audiences like that here, I can tell you! Everyone's just panting to hear you."

"No, faith!" said Miss Farrell, rolling her eyes in mock despair, "it's terrified I am entirely at the thought of singing in front of such a set of experts."

"Oh, what nonsense you talk, Kerry," said Joop. "Come along with you now and meet M. Destrier."

The Irish accent seemed to be catching, Julia reflected as they went on their way.

172

The sound of piano and strings coming from a recital room caught Julia's attention as she wandered idly along the flagged path, and she turned through a door that stood open. Finding a canvas seat placed handily in a cool current of air near the entrance, she settled down to listen.

A woman sitting on another canvas chair gave her a welcoming smile; she was a fat little person with bright, rosy cheeks, and a row of black curls across her forehead, whom Julia had seen around for the past few days, taking a vociferous part in the talk of the livelier groups and using her immensely elaborate camera as a means of getting into conversation with others who might have wished to avoid her, which Julia had hitherto succeeded in doing. But she looked harmless enough. She wore a pink shirt and an ill-judged dirndl which did not suit her bun-shaped figure.

Julia smiled back with caution and turned her head in the direction of the players.

A quintet consisting of two violins, cello, viola, and piano were performing a work unfamiliar to Julia, but, to her chagrin, and as so often happens when one turns on radio music, she had no sooner settled herself than the piece came to its end.

The players all gathered around the piano to discuss the difficult passages.

"What *was* the quintet they were playing?" Julia murmured rashly to her neighbor.

"It's by Franz Schmidt—it's arranged for—" The little woman poured out a profuse flood of *sotto voce* information, not one word of which could Julia catch; her neighbor's voice, a kind of soft, chuckling coo, combined with a Missouri drawl, rendered what she said almost wholly incomprehensible.

Julia hopefully smiled and nodded and longed for the music to begin again.

The string players settled themselves to rest, and the pianist began on a solo. The music he played now was thoroughly familiar to Julia—the Bach-Busoni chaconne; nonetheless, there seemed something odd about it. For a few minutes, Julia found it hard to determine what was making her feel so uncomfortable; then she realized that the pianist was playing with his left hand only. He sometimes moved his right hand, as if unintentionally, toward the keyboard; then hastily checked himself and lowered it sharply to his side again. In spite of these hesitancies he played remarkably well; with considerable virtuosity indeed; if Julia had closed her eyes she would not have been been able to believe that such a flood of complicated contrapuntal music could be produced by five fingers only. But she could not close her eyes; she watched in rather tense fascination as the pianist pounded and slashed his way through the work; and she had a feeling of immense relief when he finally reached its end. After joining in the polite applause of his fellow players and the fat little woman, she was glad to make her escape—it was almost time for her sauna, in any case.

"Isn't he just wonderful?" To Julia's annoyance, the little woman had followed her out and now accompanied her toward the loggia. "Henk Willaerts, you know; he has such bad arthritis in his right hand that he had to give up playing with it; but Adnan thinks that with treatment here he can get back the use of it. That's why they were playing the Schmidt, before; that's arranged for left hand also."

Out in the open she spoke at normal pitch, and was intelligible; she continued to pour out a cascade of unwanted information about the players they had just left. Julia glanced at her watch, wondering how to get away.

"Oh, excuse me? I'm Miranda Schappin, I'm a professor of research into Social Divergences at Baton Rouge. Of course I know who *you* are: You're Julia Gibbon, aren't you? I'm just so *happy* to meet you; will you please allow me to say how much I admire your plays? They display a wonderful knowledge of human nature, if I may say so. I'd like to take your picture if you'll permit me?" Without waiting for verbal authority, Ms. Schappin extracted the elaborate camera from her large, loaded shoulder bag and took half a dozen snaps, darting about the terrace so as to get Julia from different angles. "You're a wonderful subject—but you must know that, of course! These will be developed in a couple of minutes if you've time to hang around," the little woman went on, twitching damp prints out of the camera. "Of course the full tone doesn't come up for half an hour, but you can see the outline. . . . I got a couple of your husband the other day, too; he's very photogenic, isn't he? Marvelous bones. Want to see?"

She rummaged again, among scarves, enormous pink sunglasses, quart-size containers of moisturizing cream, fly repellent, and the scores of late Beethoven quartets, and finally produced a large bundle of prints.

"There he is—see?—under the lemon trees. Isn't he just darling?"

Julia was amazed that the little woman knew they were husband and wife, still more that she had succeeded in taking pictures of Dikran, who was exceedingly camera-shy and greatly disliked being photographed even by his wife, let alone by a total stranger.

175

Possibly he had not noticed what was happening on this occasion, for it was a distant shot of him, taken probably from the driveway.

"I'll send you a print," promised Ms. Schappin, beaming. "*And* the ones of you, too, of course. This camera doesn't do color prints, but it does give a negative, so useful. . . . Now I must take all those gorgeous people—" for a stream of dancers were emerging from a nearby practice room.

Julia, with polite thanks and excuses, made her escape.

She ran down the stairs to the treatment area and heard her name called for a sauna just as she reached the circular waiting room.

The steam baths, seaweed baths, and sauna were all adjacent to one another in a big, vaulted region some distance from the central lobby. It was under the guest wing, and some basement windows looked out toward the lemon orchard but were kept curtained so as to preserve a dim, cosy gloom. The six steam baths stood in open-fronted cubicles screened by curtains along the wall. In front of the steam baths came a row of showers, accessible from either side. The three sauna cabins were in the middle, then another row of showers, and along the opposite wall, similarly cubicled, the row of marble tubs for seaweed baths. The whole area was illuminated by a dim infrared light in which patients and attendants flitted about softly like peaceful ghosts. The dim light made it possible for people to slip from tub to shower and back without anxieties as to nudity or propriety, since they were only visible at all from about five feet away and recognizable only at very close quarters.

Here vague figures wreathed in towels sat steaming

176

peacefully on benches or lay in cocoon-like hammocks; soft music came from the ceiling; the whole scene, Julia thought, resembled a sequence from Gluck's *Orpheo,* a greatly slowed-down Dance of the Blessed Spirits.

Passing in front of the steam baths (one of them still labeled OUT OF ORDER; evidently the plumber-cousin had not yet been able to fix whatever was wrong) Julia reached the saunas. These were sturdily constructed log cabins, their walls rising to the vaulted ceiling, with thick, insulated doors and an unrobing room at the side of each. The sauna bathers, in batches of four, first stripped and showered, then, wearing nothing but towels, entered the cabins, which contained wide, slatted wooden seats arranged in tiers like flights of stairs. The highest temperature was up at roof level, but the top step was seldom used; the bathers sat or lay on the other three benches, and the last one to enter, after having shut the door, poured a bucket of water onto a brazier full of electrically heated fire-bricks just inside the door, which instantly filled the cabin with steam. The bathers stayed in for about five minutes—or as long as they could stand the heat —then emerged for a cold shower, then returned to the sauna again, and so on, half a dozen times over. After that, wrapped to the chin in towels, they reclined in hammocks which were slung in a space beyond the cabins. They sipped lemon juice, dozed, or listened to the music from the ceiling, which was a taped record-ing of the previous night's concert. Julia found this ritual positively beatific; since her arrival at Helikon she had become greatly addicted to saunas and took one whenever there was an available slot. It was gen-erally possible to fit in one every day.

Two supervisors were in theoretical attendance, for fear any patient should turn faint, but since these attendants also had charge over the steam and seaweed baths, the sauna users were mostly left to their own devices, and it was possible to steam, shower in cold water, and steam again, lulled by the peaceful fragrance of hot, wet wood and clean, damp toweling, without any outside disturbance. Much, of course, depended on one's partners in the ritual; the enjoyment of a sauna could be greatly impaired by an uncongenial or intrusively chatty fellow bather, but Julia had hitherto been lucky, or else Helikon had put her into a friendly and accepting frame of mind. She had shared saunas with the old pianist, Marion Hillel, and Zoé, the warden, and little Mike, and a batch of girl dancers, and a harpist from Tel Aviv, and three teachers from a Paris music school; she had enjoyed sleepy, fragmentary conversations and undemanding silences, lying draped in towels or naked and relaxed on the baking, aromatic pine planks.

Today her fellow bathers were the two violin-playing Latvian girls, who were excellent company, in her opinion, since they seemed to speak no English at all. Blond and slender as Nordic goddesses, with their hair plaited in coronets, they restricted their communication to beaming smiles, friendly gestures, and a flow of soft, guttural conversation between themselves. The last member of the quartet was another Englishwoman, Mrs. Meiklejohn, the mother of little Mike. In the course of the past two days Julia had struck up a mild friendship with her, confined mainly to smiles and brief remarks about music. Certainly, her appearance when seen stripped was a little daunting, for she was haggardly slender and still wore on her head one of the black jersey turbans that she kept on all day long. This gave her a strangely incongruous appearance; all she needed, Julia felt, to complete the image of a Moulin Rouge dancer was black, elbow-length gloves and black stockings. But Mrs. Meiklejohn's expression did not recall the Moulin Rouge.

"Won't your turban get very wet?" Julia suggested, but Mrs. Meiklejohn answered with her usual reserve and brevity, "It doesn't matter. I have several."

She sat down primly on the bottom bench. Julia shrugged, and was about to climb to the middle bench when Mrs. Meiklejohn, evidently feeling that she had perhaps been too unforthcoming, added, "I have an ugly scar on my head, you see. I'm wearing a pad of medicated lint over it to keep it cool, and the turban helps. I had a head injury."

"In that case," said Julia, "you won't want the temperature too hot?"

"No—if you don't mind."

"Not a bit," said Julia, and altered the thermostat, having conveyed her intentions by signs to the two Latvian girls, who made agreeable, assenting gestures. She then poured water on the brazier and closed the door. Just like Renoir, she thought, surveying the shiny, pink, steam-wreathed forms dimly visible in the light from the thirty-watt red bulb.

"It really makes you feel good, doesn't it?" she murmured when she had settled herself on the middle bench.

"Very comfortable," Mrs. Meiklejohn agreed.

"No—I mean more than that—really *good,* as if all your imperfections are being sweated out of you."

"Er—what kind of imperfections did you have in mind?"

"Oh—all the useless, destructive ones: guilt, remorse, anxiety, hate—"

"Hate?" The other woman turned her black-swathed head on its thin neck and regarded Julia with thoughtful appraisal. "You don't—if I may say so—give the impression of a person who is capable of a great deal of hate?"

"Oh—I can hate, all right!" said Julia cheerfully.

"Whom?"

"Whom? Reviewers who say horrible things about my plays—people who prevent me from doing what I want—odious officials—people who take things away from me—my ex-husband's new wife—stupid people—rude, disagreeable people—"

She fell silent, thinking about Dikran. Sometimes, these days, she felt that she hated *him*—for letting her down by being other than she had expected, for imprisoning her in his cell of gloom.

She went on: "Come, now, Mrs. Meiklejohn, you must hate somebody in the world, surely? You are in the educational field; there must be all sorts of obstructive people, reactionary bureaucrats, dogmatic, hellfire, punitive people—?"

"Yes, but I don't hate them," replied Mrs. Meiklejohn in her precise, Scots voice. "I—just take what steps I can to make sure they do the minimum of harm."

"Ah, well—of course you are in a position of power, aren't you? If one has power, I suppose there is no need to hate. But in the past, before you had the power—?"

"In the past, yes, that's true," Mrs. Meiklejohn murmured thoughtfully.

"You're a Scot, I assume? I thought Scots made a specialty of long-standing feuds?"

"Feuds?" the Scotswoman took it up in her literal, repetitive way. "Eh—no, I don't believe I've ever had a feud with anybody. But I suppose I have hated; yes —there is one person whom I might say that I hate."

"That's the spirit!" Julia said encouragingly. "Why? What did he or she do to you? Is it a personal hate or a professional one?"

"Are you interested in *me,* Mrs. Saint, or are you collecting material for your plays?" Mrs. Meiklejohn inquired with her usual prudence.

"Oh, how can I divide that up?" Julia answered impatiently. "Of course I'm interested in you! And of course everything I see and hear all day long may— will—have its influence on my work, but never directly; rest assured that you won't ever find your character in any play of mine! What did this person do to you?"

"Stole something from me."

"You can't get it back?"

"Oh, good heavens, *no!* What was stolen was part of myself—and part of *them,* too; twenty years of my life."

"Ah—I see." Julia thought of Arnold Gibbon, of her own marriage. But she said, "Don't you think that's being a little unfair? An overemotional statement of the case? After all, you *had* those twenty years, while they were going on; and you still have the memory of them."

"You don't understand at all. The case is quite different from what you imagine." Mrs. Meiklejohn spoke with a cold, controlled intensity that did carry conviction.

181

Julia threw out her first hasty impression of a self-pitying injured wife determined to be a martyr; and indeed it had hardly accorded with Mrs. Meiklejohn's general demeanor. "What happened to this twenty years, then?" she inquired, more sympathetically.

"Oh, they were really lost—they were all turned inside out, in the most disgusting way imaginable."

"How?"

"You really are very inquisitive, Mrs. Saint," the other woman remarked, looking at Julia with a kind of unresentful surprise.

"I do like to know about people, it's true. Why not? It's my profession. Geologists study rocks, botanists look at plants. I'm interested in character. I don't think I use my knowledge harmfully. And I never indulge in gossip. Go on," Julia urged her, "spill the beans. It will do you good. Tell me what happened."

But Mrs. Meiklejohn still could not bring herself to do that. She thoughtfully crossed one thin, elegant leg over the other and said, "Imagine you thought you were living in a house—your own, private place—doing your normal job, pursuing your ordinary life, peaceful and unobserved—and suddenly you found that all the time you had really been a—a kind of exhibit at a zoo, with people studying everything you had done through a glass wall, laughing at you and everything connected with you, because it was so grotesque and peculiar?"

"I find it hard to imagine anybody laughing at *you*," Julia said, studying her with curiosity. "You have such a lot of natural dignity."

"Dignity! Hah! Nobody has dignity when they fall down in the street and the whole world can see they've forgotten to put any underclothes on! Nobody has

182

dignity when they're on the operating table with twenty medical students peering up their vagina."

Yes, she can hate, all right, Julia discovered with surprise. The jerky force with which the last words had come out told of a terrifyingly banked-up resentment burning underneath.

"You're very good at metaphors, Mrs. Meiklejohn. But couldn't you tell me what actually happened?— Was it a long time ago?"

The other woman remained silent.

"Where is this person now? Is he or she still alive?"

Mrs. Meiklejohn said bitterly, "Alive? Oh, yes, very much so. Flourishing like the green bay tree."

"Do you ever see them?"

"See them? I'd sooner *die*. It would be like—it would be like going back to some house where you had lived and been happy—and discovering that it was a brothel. *Had* been a brothel all along—"

Now, who'd have thought it? Julia reflected. Who would have expected that this quiet, controlled, elegant professional woman would have such a burning core in her?

Julia's professional curiosity was really roused by now; she longed to know Mrs. Meiklejohn's story. But the wretched woman was beginning to show distinct signs of strain, twisting her fingers and biting her lips. Filled with a certain compunction—for this was hardly the ideally relaxed atmosphere suitable to someone recovering from a head injury—Julia therefore slid the conversation sideways to quarrels based on misconceptions, hatred of tyranny, and the motives that make people cruel to one another.

She was resolved by one means or another to find out what lay behind these powerful feelings, but it

183

would be kinder—and more practical—to proceed slowly. Besides, there was always the possibility that she could get it all more easily from the daughter.

They took cold showers, came back for further steam sessions, and presently migrated to the hammock area, where an attendant helped them to wrap up in layers of toweling and then lie back, totally relaxed, with their beakers of lemon juice in easy reach. Muted strains of Mozart's Twenty-ninth Symphony came from overhead, and the dim red light lay over them like a soft extra covering. This is really back to the womb, Julia thought; I could spend half of every day like this with the greatest pleasure in the world. . . .

Mrs. Meiklejohn was being assisted by the nurse into the next hammock. Julia extended a lazy, friendly hand to help, and was surprised by the strength of the other woman's grip. The hand that caught hers was big-boned and firm; that impression of fragility that she gives is highly misleading, Julia mused! I bet Mrs. Meiklejohn is really quite a tough nut.

I wonder if Mike is fond of her mother? There's not much sign of affection between them. A bit of the mother in the daughter—feeling of resilience, a vigor—but Mike's got the creative streak; this woman has vitality, but she doesn't seem at all imaginative. I suppose the imagination came in with the father. Wonder who or what he was . . .

She closed her eyes, taking in through ears and pores the dreamlike, ethereal beauty of Mozart's adagio movement.

"Perhaps you're right," said Mrs. Meiklejohn's voice abruptly from the next hammock.

"Mmmh?"

"Perhaps it would do me good to get it off my chest. To tell you what happened."

"Of *course* it would." Julia was fully alert at once. "It *always* does good. Go ahead! There's no one in earshot. (Except the Latvians, and they don't understand English.) We're as private here as if we were in the vaults of the Bank of England. And you can trust me not to repeat a single word."

"Yes, I daresay." Having come to her decision, the other woman seemed hardly bothering to pay attention to Julia's words. She took a deep breath. "Well—you see, it was like this: I married at nineteen—"

But at this moment the screams began.

❦ 9 ❧

FANTASIA

A queer and haunting thing happened to me after I had returned from the excursion to Dendros with Lady Julia.

The first thing I did when I got back was to leave the things we had bought in my workroom. She had gone off to see how her mysterious husband was getting on. Then, feeling hot and dusty from town, I thought I would go and swim. So I collected a swimsuit and towel—Mother was having a treatment somewhere, presumably; at any rate, she was not around—and walked down to the shore, taking the sandy path between the rush-screened beds of tomato plants. This led out onto the flat, white beach, which, as ever, was completely empty; because there was a swimming pool alongside the practice rooms, the visitors to Helikon mostly appeared to think it not worth the trouble to walk five hundred yards for a dunk in the real McCoy. I had the Aegean to myself and it was wonderful; an afternoon breeze had sprung up, as it often did in Dendros, so that the waves rolling in from Turkey were quite large, and yet the water wasn't cold, just invigoratingly brisk.

I rolled and floated in the troughs of the waves, and let myself be slung and heaved over their tops, and gazed at the blue sky above me, and thought about how much I enjoyed the company of Julia Saint.

Away from the opposite sex, she became quite a different person, easier, more relaxed, and, it seemed to me, happier; she didn't bother to turn on her devastating sex appeal, or rather, I thought, reconsidering that, it switched itself off; it was just an automatic response to the presence of any male. When she was with one of her own ilk she was highly sympathetic, intelligent, and very entertaining, too. She could be funny in a farcical, primitive way that reminded me of my friends at school or the Crowbridge Rep. But also I became more and more convinced that, under her composed exterior, she was a sad and lonely woman.

I had enjoyed the trip to Dendros—and I thought she had too. We had strolled, and shopped, and gossiped; we had stood for a long time in front of a baker's oven in a back street, watching the people bring their food to be baked. It was a big, communal place, a huge hole in a wall, with three men operating long-handled, flat spades—"Like Hansel and Gretel," said Lady Julia—shoveling people's loaves and pies and legs of mutton in and out. Then, when we had bought all the things I needed, we had spent the rest of Adnan's money on ice cream, sitting at a table

187

under a huge laurel tree on the harbor front, stroking the skinny, agile harbor cats and talking about Jane Austen.

"She ought to have written plays," said Lady Julia. "Have you ever thought by what a narrow squeak she didn't? English literature only moved from plays to novels about fifty years before she began writing; it's probably thanks to Jane Austen that it has stuck at novels ever since. But she would have written plays equally well; think how naturally all her books fall into scenes between a few people. That's why they adapt so well for television. And all her main points are made verbally; her characters hardly ever indulge for long in deep introspection or private agony."

"Emma does," I said. "She cried all the way home in the carriage. And there is a point you've missed—how about Jane Austen's habit of condensing all her denouement and unraveling the whole plot in a huge letter from the offending villain—the one from Darcy, the one from Frank Churchill? That's not very dramatic." I thought about this a bit more, and added, "I bet she did that because of some awful happening in her own life that we don't know about. Probably the mysterious person she's suposed to have been engaged to, who jilted her, explained all *his* unfaithfulness in one long, dreadful letter, from which it took her nine years to recover. I think those letters in the novels are her greatest weakness—she makes use of them to shirk the real dramatic climax."

"Perhaps that's because she never had the real dramatic climax herself," said Lady Julia. "Or," she went on thoughtfully, "perhaps she couldn't bear to remember it.—But there isn't any letter in *Persuasion*."

"Yes there is! He proposes by letter. But also, perhaps by *Persuasion* she was beginning to get over whatever it was—the heartbreak. If she had lived long enough to finish *Sanditon,* perhaps she'd have done a real live denouement."

I finished my swim and wandered back up the dusty track, thinking about *Sanditon* and the enjoyable time Jane Austen had had settting up her scene in the seaside resort, setting her characters on the treeless, wind-blown hilltop with Waterloo Crescent in process of building, females sketching on campstools, and the sound of a harp to be heard here and there from an upper casement. Harps must have been a great deal easier to come by in 1817 than they are nowadays, for farther on in the story the Miss Beauforts, having overspent their allowance on clothes, are obliged to be content with a frugal holiday in Sanditon plus the hire of a harp and the purchase of some drawing paper.

It must, I was thinking, have been very pleasant to stroll through such a watering place as East Bourne or Brighthelmstone and hear the sound of all the young lady visitors practicing their harps behind the open casements. I wonder what kind of music they played?

Engaged in these speculations, I walked up the path between the practice rooms and the swimming pool. The faint sound of music coming from an upper window had probably, as Jane Austen would have said, given a turn to the course of my reflections. But as I came closer to the sound, and it grew more distinctly audible, it gave such a twitch to the course of my reflections that I forgot *Sanditon* entirely, and stood stockstill, suddenly overwhelmed by a huge wave of nostalgia. For the music that came from the upper casement (in actual fact a piano was being played, not a harp) took me back eighteen years to those nights of childhood when I had lain in my bed hugging Othello, looking at the shadowy slope of my bedroom ceiling, and listening to my father improvising his catchy, plaintive jazz tunes on the piano downstairs.

I stood still to listen. The tunes were, in fact, *extraordinarily* reminiscent of those Father used to play. How could anyone have picked up so exactly his very twirls and twiddles, his ornaments, flourishes, and hesitations? Perhaps this was a person who had also heard him? Perhaps . . .

And then came a tune that was unmistakably, irresistibly familiar, part of my whole childhood world; I felt as if it were unrolling inside me like an old phonograph cylinder; I could positively feel it emerging from the depths of my buried memory. I had always, to myself, for some probably Freudian reason called this tune "Tapioca"—something to do with the rhythm— not knowing Father's name for it, or even if it had a name . . .

Tum tiddle-tiddle-tiddle, tum tiddle-tiddle tum . . .
Surely *no one* but Father had ever played that tune?

Anybody watching me from the swimming pool would have been justified in thinking that I had suddenly gone crazy. Having stood riveted under the window, with my mouth open, I suddenly broke into a wild run. There wasn't an entrance to the practice block on this side. I had to go around two corners, along the path that circled the quadrangle, and in at the main entrance, which was halfway along the other side of the building. Then I had to go up two flights of stairs, for the music had been coming from the upper story.

Nobody was in sight. Upstairs, a gallery ran the length of the building, giving access to the doors of

190

the practice rooms. But which room had it been? I was not sure. The fourth or fifth from the end nearest the sea, perhaps. I began at the beach end and walked along, softly opening the soundproof doors and looking inside. Two rooms were empty. One had three absorbed men with a lot of electronic equipment. One had two flautists. One had old Marion Hillel playing Schumann—I was pretty sure that she was not my unknown pianist. Another room was empty, but the piano lid was open. Had somebody just left? I could have cried with disappointment and frustration. The next room had a pair of girls giggling their way through a Mozart duet—surely it had not been them? Now I was almost certain that I was too far along, but I went on. More empty rooms; a pair of guitarists . . . a couple who were making use of their proximity on two piano stools for a ten-minute kiss. And that was all. I had come to the end.

Feeling absolutely bereft, I ran down the stairs again at top speed. Perhaps somebody had just gone outside? In the lobby at the stair foot I found Adnan, looking, contrary to his usual habit, slightly irritated, as he stuck up on a board a notice relating to bulk purchase of honey from Hymettos.

"Has anybody just come down the stairs?" I asked him hastily.

"Who?"

"I don't know!"

He looked so very unreceptive and inaccessible to what I had been about to say that my impulse evaporated. "My dear Mike, have you gone off your chump?" he inquired tartly, "You look like Il Distratto."

I supposed I did, with my sandy hair, trailing a damp bathing towel.

"What is the matter?" he said.

"Nothing, nothing. It doesn't matter." For a moment, again, I considered telling him my wild idea, but it sounded too lunatic. Dejectedly I said, "It isn't important."

"Did you have a pleasant time in town?" he inquired courteously.

"Very; thank you," I rejoined with equal politeness. "Thank you for the loan of your car. I left the key in the ignition." (He often did, himself.) "And I bought all the stuff I need."

"Did Lady Julia also enjoy herself?"

"So far as I know. She seemed to," I said, and hurried out into the quadrangle to see if anybody still in the neighborhood looked as if they might have been the originator of my music. Two ladies were standing in the middle of the lawn having their pictures taken by the fat little sociology professor from Baton Rouge. A boy and girl were sitting on the grass arranging manuscript music. The nearest other person, strolling away at a measured pace, was Mr. Saint. Could some exchange with him have occasioned Adnan's annoyed expression? Could I ask Mr. Saint if he had been playing the piano? I walked rapidly after him, not certain of my resolution. Although in our brief exchanges he had been quite pleasant to me, there was something about him that made me very nervous. And when I saw his face, my courage failed me entirely; his thick brows were knitted, his thin lips were compressed in a tight line that boded no good to somebody. Not his wife, I hoped.

However, he greeted me civilly enough and, like

192

Adnan, asked if I had enjoyed myself in Dendros. Lady Julia's company was a guarantee of attention from everybody, it seemed.

I replied in kind. "Yes, thank you, we had a very pleasant time. I am sorry you couldn't come."

He looked so incredulous at this remark that I wondered if he suspected that his wife and I had slipped off to some den of assignation. In consequence, without having the least intention of doing so, I found myself launched into a description of our innocuous shopping and the baker's oven.

He listened, still with that same look of sour disbelief, as if he wondered whom I expected to take in with my far-fetched tale: baker's oven indeed! Who would want to stand for half an hour watching loaves of bread slid in and out on spades?

"You and my wife have made great friends?" he remarked with unmistakable distrust.

"Yes, isn't she nice?" I replied idiotically. "It's wonderful for me to have a chance to talk to her."

Quite evidently he was wondering what the devil *she* saw in *me*. This nettled me so much—though, of course, it was quite a reasonable point of view—that, without meaning to do so, I invited him to come and have a look at my sets. Now it was his turn to seem taken aback. But, to my great annoyance, he said, "Thank you. I should like that."

Gritting my teeth, I led him away to the workroom.

And then—as sometimes happens unexpectedly when two people are both ruffled and upset, but from causes not involving each other—we found that our relationship had, for reasons that were not in any way apparent, suddenly lifted from a very unpromising level to much more cordial terms.

He walked around examining my sets, praising, criticizing, and discussing them in a most knowledgeable manner. He asked what had given me the idea for using Piero in this way, and from that, by degrees, we found ourselves embarked on a general discussion about the effects of realizing that one's troubles and difficulties are being observed by strangers.

"Hamlet at least was in his own family," he said, which I found rather touching. "This aspect of Helikon I do not like at all. I am a private person, Miss Meiklejohn. I like to be alone with my wife, not to be all the time in a crowd of strangers. But she, I now begin to think, is a public person."

I felt for him very much in his difficulties, but I wasn't prepared to discuss Lady Julia with him, and when he said, "This Dr. Adnan, now. What kind of a person is he?" I limited myself to replying that Adnan was a man of high principles and a very good doctor and that he had always shown me, personally, very great kindness. Then, wishing to change the subject, I said that Lady Julia had told me Mr. Saint wrote poetry, and that I was very fond of poetry myself; what kind did he write?

To my great surprise, he said, "I write sonnets; nothing but sonnets. I have written a whole novel in sonnet form."

"Good heavens! That must have been very difficult, surely?" I thought also, privately, that it would be even more difficult to get such a work published.

He said, "Not difficult when you are, as I am, in the habit of the sonnet form," and quite matter-of-factly began to recite the last one he had written. It was very sad and complicated; it seemed to be about a dead child and a faithless lover; or perhaps the dead child was the sad, starved love that had perished prematurely and been devoured by the scavengers who lurk in darkness just out of sight, ready to prey on human weakness . . . his imagery was impressive and frightening and it shook me unexpectedly.

I made some appreciative, respectful comments, but I felt very strongly that I did not wish to hear any more of his verses just then, so I looked at my watch and said, "I'm just due for a spinal exercise class. Would you care to come along?"

I thought that might get rid of him; but also I vaguely felt that his mixing so little in all the activities of Helikon must account for some of his evident malaise and grouchiness; if he could only be beguiled into more participation, he might come to relax and enjoy himself a little.

To my astonishment—I had quite expected a fearful snub—he said, "All right, if it is not too athletic." He added, with a kind of nervous gloom, as if already wondering why he had made such a rash concession, "What do we have to do?"

"It isn't at all athletic," I reassured him. "Come along. It's in here."

I led him back to the quadrangle and into one of the downstairs practice rooms, where half a dozen people were lunging about in a lackadaisical way with staves in their hands. A fierce-looking old Scandinavian lady in a white chiton was calling out directions, but her class did not pay much heed to her; spinal exercises were a subject that few people took seriously, and the participants talked to each other freely as they lunged to left and right, or raised their staves with both hands above their heads. I collected a couple of staves and presented one end of each to Mr. Saint.

"Here. You take these. Now push and pull alternately with me, like pistons."

An unwilling smile replaced the scowl on his face, after a few minutes of this rather infantile exercise.

"What is it supposed to do?"

"Goodness knows. Loosen the shoulder blades, maybe."

Even if his shoulder blades weren't loosened, his expression certainly relaxed, as he watched an immensely fat man performing the piston exercise with a tiny, scrawny girl.

After ten minutes with the staves, we were instructed to take to the machines, nine or ten of which stood at the end of the room. They were hammock-shaped affairs made of jointed metal tubing, on which, after fitting hands and feet into holds at each end, one could, by dint of a certain amount of exertion, jackknife back and forth, bending one's spine forward and backward, which was supposed to benefit the hip and pelvic joints.

As there were not enough machines to go around, I sat out and watched Mr. Saint while he did a few, not very enthusiastic, jackknife exercises, and then he sat out and watched me.

"What do you and my wife talk about?" he inquired rather deliberately as I arched my back and then bent it. "What is the subject of your conversations when you are together?"

This was a bit of a facer. He really *is* suspicious of her, I thought. On their honeymoon! How very sad! And what a question to ask me! Is it because he is an Armenian—or whatever he is? Women's conversation not considered private? Or because he is a tycoon —anxious about vital secrets she might have given away? Or did he just envy our facility? Find conversation with her difficult? Maybe he wanted a bit of guidance? "Well—gosh—let me think—this afternoon we talked about plays quite a lot; and novels; and bread; and cats; and fishing; and life." (Life, I remembered, had also included Marriage, the desirability or undesireability of; but as that seemed a risky topic, I omitted it); "oh yes, and Jane Austen."

"Jane Austen?" For some inscrutable reason, this innocuous topic seemed to make him doubly suspicious. Perhaps he just plain didn't believe me. "What do you find to say about Jane Austen?"

"Oh," I said blithely, "let me think what we were saying. Lady Julia was talking about the dramatic structure of her books—how they might as well have been plays."

"Ah yes. So she would." His expression relaxed. "My wife sees a buried play in anything she looks at. That, already, in so few weeks of marriage, I have discovered."

"It must be quite strange, being married to someone like that," I remarked, bending my back forward, and then backward. "All the time, you must feel they have a whole inner life inside them to which you have no access; like a locked room and you haven't got the key." Though everybody is like it, really, I decided, thinking of Mother.

"That is so, indeed." Mr. Saint regarded me with surprise, and even a certain amount of respect, I thought.

I went on, "But we none of us know much about each other at all, do we? I'm here with my mother, you'd think I'd know her inside out, but I don't, not in the least; I doubt if I know much more about her than I do about you, Mr. Saint."

"And that is very little!" His glance at me was full of irony.

Old Miss Bjornsen banged two staves together to dismiss us, and we walked out into the evening air. I looked at my watch again. I was feeling full of useless regrets about my missed chance with the unseen pianist, and by this time quite badly wanted to escape from Mr. Saint; in spite of his new friendliness I found a long spell of his company somehow oppressive.

In ten minutes a full-scale rehearsal of *Les Mystères d'Elsinore* was due to commence with Kerry Farrell for the first time singing the main part. I intended to be there. But on the other hand I didn't want to offend Mr. Saint; my instinct told me that it was a good thing to keep conciliating him.

Our early-evening meal was being served from a buffet table in the loggia. As I had graduated to solids, I secured a couple of plates containing the customary nine or ten little heaps of grated this-and-that, and gave one to Mr. Saint, as he was standing near, with an irresolute expression on his hawklike countenance.

I began nibbling fast at my carrots and chestnuts. Little time was wasted on eating at Helikon. I am fond of leisurely eating as a rule—and protein—but at Helikon one did not feel the deprivation much, because so many alternatives were offered.

"Would you care to come to the *Elsinore* rehearsal?" I suggested to Mr. Saint, chomping away on my shredded raw beet and leeks and chick-peas and currants. I could see that he was looking around impatiently, for his wife no doubt, and she was not to be seen; Adnan was nowhere in view either, and I felt the suspicious husband was best kept distracted if possible.

198

"I am not sure," he said doubtfully. "I do not care for opera."

But I thought he might be willing to be persuaded, particularly if the alternative were solitary brooding about where his wife might have got to. (Of course I hoped that she was irreproachably taking a wax bath somewhere below ground.) To divert his thoughts from her, I began talking about *Hamlet*, reverting to our conversation in the workroom. "It would be interesting to see an uncut version of the play; of course in a way it's pretty irrelevant, all that stuff they usually cut out, with Voltimand and Cornelius and Fortinbras and Rosencrantz and Guildenstern and the letter to the King of England—the play stands just as well without it—"

I wasn't concentrating too hard on what I was saying, my mind had gone back to that tantalizing snatch of piano music. Who, *who* could have been playing just there, just then? "And then there's Hamlet's letter to Horatio—that's a fairly clumsy bit of business," I remarked, munching my last mouthful of chick-peas and glancing up at Mr. Saint, who was picking his way distastefully through his. "Oh, of course, that was another of the things that your wife and I were talking about—Jane Austen's letters."

"*What* do you say?"

I had tossed this out heedlessly enough, but he grasped my wrist so hard that if I had not swallowed my last chick-peas they would have been jerked all over the terrace.

"Jane Austen's letters?" I said, puzzled. "I mean the long, explanatory ones in her novels. You know, Frank Churchill writing to give an account of his secret engagement to Jane Fairfax—and so on." He looked at me as if what I was saying made no sense. Maybe he had never read any Jane Austen. Lots of people haven't. I went on nervously, "Nowadays I expect if a writer put such a device in a novel his editor would sling it back and tell him to turn it into direct action."

Then I blushed, thinking how conceited and opinionated I no doubt sounded, airing my superior views about Shakespeare and Jane Austen. If this made Mr. Saint wonder what his wife could possibly see in me, I didn't blame him. By now his expression really scared me; I had no clue at all to what he was thinking. Whatever it was, I was glad I was not sharing his thoughts. Though I couldn't for the life of me imagine why my frivolous reference to Jane Austen's letters should have engendered them.

He looked at me long and hard, and for several minutes said nothing at all. When he did speak, his words were not related to what had passed; he merely remarked, "After all, perhaps I will come to the rehearsal," and accompanied me across the grass to the big hall. At some point he had let go of my wrist, but it still ached so badly that I rubbed it surreptitiously as I went, while at the same time I tried to sort out my scared impressions. Such an atmosphere of cold seemed, sometimes, to emanate from him that I felt, when he was around, as if some large bird of prey had flown between me and the sun. But perhaps that was an evocation from his terrible past? For when he gripped my wrist I had seen a tattooed number on his, which must—mustn't it—be a constant reminder to him of hideous sufferings. Why, I wondered, did he not have it removed? If, as Mat the masseur believed, his face had been altered by plastic surgery, it would surely have been no problem to remove or replace that small patch of skin on his arm at the same time? But perhaps he *wanted* to be constantly reminded of the bad card that life had once dealt him? Perhaps—I thought—he might find it a justification for things he was doing now?

A chattering, anticipatory group had already assembled in the big hall. Here, in imitation of some English chapel, solid wooden seats like pews lined the walls, going up in tiers at right angles to the dais at the far end of the hall. Automatically I glanced around to see if Mother was there, but she was not, and I had not really expected her; opera and large gatherings ran each other close for first place among her dislikes. How did she stand school assemblies? Presumably because they were part of her profession, and, as such, to be endured. Lady Julia was not there either, so far as I could see. In itself that was no concern of mine, but the fact that Adnan was also absent did cause me some disquiet. Since he had been so proud of the fact that his personal intervention had been what persuaded Kerry Farrell to cancel an engagement in Basel and come here, I had expected that he would be in full plumage tonight, bustling about and organizing. Perhaps he intended to arrive escorting the diva? But no; that must be she on the dais already, talking to old Annibal and Joop Kolenbrander.

Curious to see her at closer range, I moved on toward the front of the hall, along the rows of sideways seats, and Mr. Saint followed me. Because of his company I did not go up on stage, as I otherwise might have done, but settled quietly down to watch on a bench near the front. Mr. Saint sat down silently by me. I could not see his face without screwing my neck sideways, but his silence was so fraught and ominous that I did not dare try to break it up with more chatter. I just observed the people on the stage and tried to pretend that I was not aware of the unspeaking thundercloud at my left elbow.

Joop was organizing the small orchestral ensemble, every now and then crossing the dais to ask Miss Farrell for her opinion and suggestions.

He was being his usual slow, lanky, efficient Dutch self, but his long, comic face had turned a dusky red and his Adam's apple was working overtime; it was plain that he was unusually keyed up. Old Annibal, established for the evening in his wheelchair and wrapped in a big blue Greek rug, looked very impressive and patriarchal, with his beard sweeping down over the blanket and his white, bushy hair standing on end; he seemed keyed up, too; his eyes sparkled and he was chatting away volubly to Kerry Farrell and the five or six other singers who stood nearby. None of them were in costume yet; we were to have a dress rehearsal the next day, and my conscience told me that I should be elsewhere, putting in some final touches, but the rest of me was determined to stay, at least for half an hour.

Kerry Farrell seemed very composed. I studied her with interest and perplexity, as one does when seeing a screen star for the first time in the flesh. I had heard her voice on the radio, and even had a Oiseau-Lyre record with some songs of hers on one side, but she was not in the least the way I had imagined, from her voice, that she would be. The voice was unusually powerful and clear—a kind of pure mezzo, without ornament or vibrato—and I had expected that, to match it, she would be a powerful-looking person. Not a bit of it. On the contrary, she looked rather slight and frail as she stood sniffing a syringa flower that she held between her fingers and laughing at something old Annibal had said. She was not very tall—even in high heels she hardly came up to Joop's shoulder. Her hair was black, and swept back in a high bouncy set that suited her narrow, pixyish, Irish face; I couldn't see the color of eyes from where I sat. Her face—not pretty, but sparkling—was one of the most lively and mobile I'd ever come across. She never kept one expression for more than an instant; at the same time, she twisted and pivoted, stepping from side to side, joking and chatting as if she were in her element in this central situation, enjoying every minute of it. The dress she wore was dark but flared, with a flash of lace jabot at the chin, and it emphasized her incessant movement, the skirt swishing around her, the frill catching the light as she leaned from side to side. I could see that her vivacity was infecting the people around her; there was an atmosphere of hectic gaiety, of heightened excitement and enthusiasm.

I wonder what Lady Julia will make of her? I suddenly thought. Can Helikon contain such a pair, both of prima-donna status?

While part of me—the conscious part—speculated about Kerry Farrell in this manner, another part, deeper down, was puzzled by some attribute of hers that seemed confusingly familiar. Could I, after all, have seen her somewhere long ago—on stage, on TV? —without remembering, without realizing it? Perhaps I had seen her before she was so well known—for I thought her name had only come into prominence within the past three or four years. I knew nothing about her past. She had appeared, she had become quite well known; that was all. Could she, perhaps, have taught, or given a lecture, at one of the sechools I had gone to? I thought I would have remembered if she had. Unless she had come in merely for a single occasion, or judged a singing contest? Could I have seen an article about her somewhere, with pictures? I could not recall doing so; and in any case that would not account for the peculiar familiarity I felt with the way she *moved*.

The more I teased my memory, however, the less co-operation I received from it; you know how it is sometimes when you try to remember a dream and your mind seems bent on throwing up obstacles, willfully scrambling the whole message.

Matthieu came stomping along the aisle and plumped himself down on my right.

"So she is here at last, our leading lady?" he muttered in my ear. "*Mon dieu,* what a complexion! She has the appearance to use boot polish instead of makeup foundation."

"It's her voice we're interested in, not her skin!"

"Me, I know nothing about voices," he said.

"Why are you here, then? Why aren't you massaging somebody?"

"There is trouble downstairs; they clear the steam area, massage rooms also. One of the steam baths misbehaves. So I come hoping to find a place by you," he said gallantly.

"Go on! *Quelle blague!*"

"Also, of course, hoping the witch's curse take effect and the prima donna she fall down dead," Mat said hopefully.

Mr. Saint, on my other side, had been watching the performers, as they moved and chatted on the dais, with, it seemed to me, a curiously rigid and fixed attention. I wondered if he, too, like me, was pursued

204

by some elusive, dodging memory. But at Mat's words he sat forward, looked past me, and said, "What's that about falling down dead?" very sharply indeed.

"Oh, ho," said Mat. "You do not know this tale?"

"What tale?"

"It is why they have such trouble casting this piece. The old Annibal Destrier is not always as you see him now, stuck on two crutches or in a wheelchair. No, when he is young he is very gay—I do not mean that he is a homo—"

"You mean gay in the sense of a gay Lothario," I suggested.

"*Quoi?* He is *homme du monde*. He has many *belles amies*. And one of them is a singer, a soprano called Minny Montherlant; when he is with her he compose this *Mystères d'Elsinore,* and she, she hope to sing the part of Ophélie at the first performance. Okay?"

"So what happened?" inquired Mr. Saint. He seemed greatly interested.

"*Enfin,* by the time it is put on, the old Annibal tire of this lady and leave her, as he had done all the rest. He live with her no longer, and, what is upsetting her much more, she do not get to sing the part of Ophélie, *moins plus.* She feel very bad and sad about it all, and she throw herself in the Seine, like all sad Parisian ladies."

"Not *quite* all, surely?" I said.

"But before she throw herself in, Minny Montherlant leave a note for Annibal. 'Me, I am gone,' it say. '*Et je m'en fiche,* I do not give a snap who play your silly Ophélie. But I wish, I wish from the bottom of my broken heart—'" Mat made a terrific gesture with his hands, as if he were tearing out his own heart and then breaking it like an egg—"'I 'ope from the bottom of my brroken 'earrt that bad luck come to your *opéra;* I 'ope you never 'ave a performance that go as it should.' "

"And he never has?" I said. "Really? Not ever?"

Mat shook his head. "First one thing, then another. And, *enfin,* after the two times when the 'Amlet 'e die soon after the performance, nobody care to put it on. That is why the old skunk ask to 'ave it perform here for his jour de fête, because 'e know otherwise 'e will likely not have the chance to 'ear it again in 'is lifetime."

"Surely," said Mr. Saint, "nobody seriously believes that any harm will come on account of that silly woman's letter?"

I said, "Kerry Farrell looks carefree enough, at all events."

Mat stuck out his lower lip, *"Les gens du théâtre sont toujours*—actors are always superstitious," he said, and gave a big, Belgian shrug. *Moi, non!* I don't believe. But if somebody is afraid they will die —then, maybe, they do die. Anyway—by and by we see, *n'est-ce pas?* If the performance go well—okay, the jinx is lifted. And if the 'Amlet die—okay by me also. It is no skin off my *poitrine.*"

He did not actually say *"poitrine."*

By now, action on the stage appeared imminent. Everyone except Kerry Farrell and the singer who was taking the Ghost's part had left and gone into the wings—or, rather, the choir stalls. The instrumentalists had finished their tuning, and the first violinist had given Kerry Farrell a note, which she sang, softly but clear as a bell.

She and the Ghost moved into their assigned positions, looking expectantly toward Joop, who raised his baton.

And then, when everybody, including myself, had reached a high point of nervous anticipation, I heard loud, clumping footsteps and the voice, from behind me, of Dr. Adnan, who called out, "I am very sorry to interrupt you, my friends, but I fear we must call a halt to this rehearsal, only temporarily I hope. There has been a very unfortunate accident in the treatment area. We have been obliged to fetch in the police, and they now wish to question everybody."

Commotion broke out at once. Everybody stood up, many people made for the exit, presumably with the idea of rushing down to the treatment area and discovering for themselves what had happened. But Adnan, climbing onto the stage, called for order through the rising buzz of nervous, hysterical chatter.

"Et alors?" said Mat. "Now what?"

"Please keep still!" Adnan demanded. "Do not all rush about like sheep! Captain Plastiras of the police requests that all the persons who are in this hall *remain* here unless specially requested to leave. The captain himself will be coming in here to interrogate you by and by. All the other Helikon guests are assembling in the dining hall, and the captain's assistant will be taking statements from them. What they will be wanting is any information you can give them about the steam area during the past few days. Can you therefore please try to have your memories sorted out, so as not to waste police time. This is a *deeply* regrettable occurrence, and I cannot tell you how much I wish that it had not happened. I can only ask you to be calm and patient, so that we can get through these formalities as fast as possible."

He added, "Mlle. Zoé is at the desk by the organ. Will you all file slowly past, and give her your names; then we shall have a knowledge of which guests are where."

The slow procession formed and began to move. Mr. Saint, behind me, looked very impatient. He said angrily, "It is ridiculous to keep us in here. I do not see my wife here—I shall wish to reassure her. She will find all this terribly upsetting."

"I expect she's with the other lot in the dining hall," I suggested soothingly. "She's probably just as worried about you."

He pressed his thin lips together irritably. "It is stupid. I myself have never taken a steam bath—why may not those like me give their names and leave at once?"

This seemed odd to me, as I myself had certainly seen him in the steam-bath area one day soon after I had arrived.

"I think it's not only people who have taken steam baths, but anyone who has been in the neighborhood."

However, Mr. Saint pushed off through the crowd, presumably to demand special treatment from Adnan, who was in the center of a group of vociferous inquirers.

Mat looked thoughtfully after Mr. Saint and remarked, "Always there is some guy who think he shall have all special, just for him alone!"

When, in my turn, I reached Zoé and gave her my name, she said,

"Ah, Mike. I have a message for you: you are to go to your mother in Achmed's office. Captain Plastiras has asked it. He will question you there."

"Why?" Unlike Mr. Saint, I was terrified by special

208

treatment, the more so as I had no notion why I should be singled out in this way.

Zoé shrugged. *"Sais pas, moi.* I just tell you what he asked."

As I slowly edged my way to the door, which was guarded by a cop, I heard a buzz of speculative conversation from the crowd waiting to give names.

"What happened?"

"One of the steam baths blew up."

". . . killed Marion Hillel."

". . . no, it was a man, *I* heard."

". . . bits of him blew about like confetti . . ."

". . . never did care for steam baths . . ."

". . . claustrophobia, okay, but not to be blown to . . ."

". . . who found him?"

". . . some woman . . ."

". . . no, it was the plumber, I heard . . ."

Everybody seemed better informed already than I was.

I left the hall after giving my name to the policeman and hurried in the direction of Adnan's office with deep anxiety in my heart, which was not allayed by the unwonted and frightening hush that reigned over the buildings and quadrangle. Normally the stone stairs and passages of Helikon resounded all day and half the night with cheerful chatter and bursts of music, but now, since all the residents were corralled in two spots, I felt a chill of isolation as I crossed the starlit, silent square of grass and then climbed the stairs toward Adnan's quarters. Loud, quick footsteps coming in my direction almost made me turn and retreat toward the safety of the crowded hall.

But it was only Adnan, looking angry and troubled.

His expression did not lift when he saw me, but he said, "Ah, Mike. That's good. Your mother is in my office."

"W-why?" I stammered nervously.

"She happened—quite by chance—to be the one of the first on the spot where the—the accident took place. She was upset."

Oh my god, I thought. Involvement in another accident—particularly one as gruesome as this sounds—is just the *last* thing she needed. This is hardly the cozy peace I promised her at Helikon.

"Is she—is she all right?"

"I think she will be so—yes," he said. "She has good stamina, your mother. But, what a thing to happen, my god! With all our safety precautions! And I am afraid Lady Julia was terribly shocked; she reacts violently to such things. It is to be expected."

"Lady Julia was there too? What—"

What *happened?* I wanted to know, regardless of etiquette, but Adnan, without paying any attention to my words, suddenly did a thing that disconcerted me very much: taking hold of my shoulders, he gripped them painfully hard, staring down at me—a long, long, piercing look—then he exclaimed harshly, "Oh, my dear Mike, why, *why* do you have to return to Helikon *now,* of all possible times? Why, if you were coming, could you not have done so three years ago, tell me that?" He almost shook me in his intensity, scowling at me as if I were too tiresome for words.

This behavior took me so much by surprise that I could only stammer, "It was because of my mother—"

"Oh, to hell with your mother!"

In the same harried and abrupt manner, he pulled me against him, wrapped his arms tightly around me, and buried his face in my hair; thus we stood for a brief, astonishing moment, with my nose jammed into his embroidered velvet waistcoat; I could hear his heart going pocketa-pocketa; I seemed myself to have lost the faculty of breathing, but that did not much matter, because I began to be convinced that I must be dreaming this whole unreal dialogue.

Then, with equal abruptness, Adnan let go of me, gave me another intent, scrutinizing look, and said, "Never mind! No matter! Forget it, please. Go to your mother."

Off he strode along the echoing passage, and I started in the other direction.

I was feeling shaken to my roots, it need hardly be said. But there was absolutely no time for self-analysis, as Mother and Lady Julia were sitting in Adnan's tidy office looking white and shocked, both of them, still wearing terry bathrobes and carrying bags of sauna equipment.

A young Greek police officer was solicitously plying them with coffee.

Mother, although she was pale and looked as if she might vomit, seemed reasonably collected and in control of herself. But Lady Julia looked deathly; her skin had a glazed, waxen shine, her eyes were dull and staring, she kept wiping beads of sweat off her forehead. The cloudy, curly hair, which usually made such a striking frame to her long, lovely face, was now a damp, matted tangle, and her mouth sagged. For once, she looked her age, which I happened to know. From time to time she jerked with nervous tension. When she did this, Mother patted her shoulder protectively, to my surprise, for Mother was not given to such gestures.

I went and sat beside them, and murmured, "What happened?" to Mother, but she gave me a bitten-off nod that signified, "Later, not now."

The young policeman poured me a cup of coffee, which, I must say, was as welcome as brandy from a St. Bernard, and just about as stimulating after days and days of lemon juice. Goodness knows where it had come from. Coffee was never served at Helikon, being considered a sinful, addictive, poisonous stimulant only about one degree up from heroin. Perhaps Zoé and the kitchen staff kept a secret supply for their own use.

While I sat sipping the thick, black, delicious brew (it was Greek coffee, solid with sugar), Captain Plastiras came into the room and smiled at me. He was a long-time friend of the Aghnides family—like most leading citizens of Dendros—and had played chess with old Kyrie Aghnides every Thursday for years, so he and I were well acquainted. He was a big, agreeable-looking man, the shine on his leather uniform belt equaled only by that on his bald head. He had opaque, thoughtful brown eyes under thick, bushy gray brows.

"And so here we have the little Mike," he said cordially. (He pronounced my name Meekay, it had been a family joke.) "We are so delighted to welcome you back to Dendros, though it is too bad that your visit should coincide with such a disagreeable occurrence."

"What actually happened?" I ventured, for what seemed like the fourth or fifth time.

Glancing at the faces of Mother and Lady Julia, he beckoned me into the secretary's room and closed the door.

"It seems," he said, "that some unfortunate visitor has been boiled in a steam bath."

"Oh my *god*. How on earth—"

In the light of this grisly news, all my other confused and untidy feelings about the earlier events of the evening—the nostalgic snatch of music, Mr. Saint's disconcerting behavior, Kerry Farrell's elusively haunting appearance, and—last but most emphatically not least—Adnan's wholly unexpected act—all these indigestible ingredients shook, and sank, for the moment, to the bottom of my mind.

"When did it happen?" I asked.

"It seems that about one hour ago one of the attendants downstairs, a half-trained girl called Ariadne Vasiliou, noticed that the sixth steam bath, the one at the end of the row, was switched on, though it had been reported as being out of order, and the safety lid was closed down and fastened. In fact the whole bath was covered by a tarpaulin, to remind everybody that it was not to be used—the thermostat had gone wrong, I understand. Anyway, Ariadne, who is a careful and conscientious girl, noticed that the switch was down, so she switched it up. After waiting ten minutes or so, she then apparently took off the tarpaulin and lifted the lid, presumably so as to allow the machine to cool down faster—and found this person inside. At which point she first screamed, and then fainted, falling and banging her head on a concrete plinth. That was when your mother and Lady Julia went to her assistance. She has now been taken off to hospital, as it is thought she may be suffering from concussion."

"Poor girl! What an awful thing to find. And who—who—"

"Who was the person in the steam bath? We think, a man. But that is a matter for the experts. The person —whoever it was—had been in the bath for quite a long time—possibly for days."

"Was the bath switched on all the time?" I asked, horrified.

Captain Plastiras gave me an approving look.

"No, it was not. The steam baths are all on one circuit. They can all be switched on at once by a master switch. But also it is possible to switch off each one individually, and to regulate it to the required temperature—as you doubtless know."

I nodded. I can't stand steam baths myself, and wouldn't ever climb into one. To climb into a big metal box and be shut in, helpless, with towels draped around you and a bowl of water on your knees, your hands inside too, so that you can't reach to open the lid—no, thank you, not for me! It is like the nastiest kind of nightmare. But I am familiar with the setup. The master switch was in a small office at the end of the treatment area, which was kept locked outside of treatment times, so that such potentially dangerous equipment as the steam baths and the ultrasonic ray could not be switched on accidentally.

Captain Plastiras pursued, "The steam bath, number six, had been switched off and covered up some days ago, as the thermostat had become defective and the temperature inside was uncontrollable, rising to dangerous heights. The plumber had inspected it, but a spare part was required which had to be obtained from Athens."

"And then somebody turned the switch on again, so that the bath kept automatically heating up again every time someone switched on the master switch?"

"Né," he said. "That is so. It may have been switched on for most of the day—perhaps for most of several days."

I wondered what would happen to a person who was

214

boiled in a steam bath for several days; my imagination gulped and retired from the resulting picture.

Another of his lieutenants came in, saluted, and handed Captain Plastiras a piece of paper.

He studied it thoughtfully for a while, then nodded. The man withdrew again. Captain Plastiras then looked at me in silence for a minute or two with a pondering, but not unfriendly, expression. I waited in nervous bewilderment, expecting him to go into a "When were you in the steam-bath area last?" routine, and I was wondering why he had chosen me to interrogate, for in fact I practically never went near the steam baths.

But Captain Plastiras did not ask me any questions about steam baths.

He said, "You left a small pile of clothes in Miss Pombal's room one evening."

"Oh, yes," I said, after a moment recollecting what he was talking about. "Yes, I did."

"Can you now recall which evening that was?"

I had to do a considerable amount of calculation. "Wait a minute—I'm getting there. It was the night they did Schubert's *Magic Harp* in the big hall—I know that because I was weeding in Dr. Adnan's little garden and listening to the music and then Lady Julia came in, that's right—and we went for a walk in the lemon orchard. And we found the clothes down at the bottom of the orchard by the men's sun-bathing enclosure. So it was about five days ago—last Monday or Tuesday. You can easily find out by checking the concert programs with Mr. Kolenbrander. Or Lady Julia might remember."

"Lady Julia is not in a very clear state at the moment," he said. "I will ask Mr. Kolenbrander."

He made a note on his tablets.

215

"But then—" the meaning of his question had taken some time to penetrate. "Do you mean—you think those were the clothes of the person in the steam bath? He has been there *all this time?*"

"We fear this may be so. You see—" Plastiras glanced at the piece of paper the man had brought him. It was a list of names. "We do now have a complete roster of all the guests and students at Helikon. Everyone is accounted for, nobody is missing. And, moreover, nobody ever claimed the pile of clothes that you left in Miss Pombal's room. They have remained there ever since."

"There was no identification on them—in them?"

"You yourself had already discovered that," he reminded me. "There was nothing at all in the trouser pockets—except a few sunflower seeds."

"That's not unusual at Helikon." Sunflower seeds were among the few permitted snacks. "But how on *earth* could an outsider, a stranger, make his way into the treatment area and accidentally get himself stuck in a steam bath?"

People did come into Helikon for single or day treatments, but it was not a practice encouraged by Adnan, who held that, in order to be any use at all, the Helikon regime, which was designed to benefit the whole system simultaneously, must be taken *in toto* for at least two weeks. And the treatment timetables drawn up by his cherished computer were so tightly scheduled that it seemed highly improbable an outsider could wander through and find his way to a vacant steam bath. Let alone get stuck in it. The security provisions around the treatment area were not obtrusive, but they were pretty thorough.

216

"Ah, well, this was no accident, I am afraid," Captain Plastiras said.

"No? You mean somebody *put him in there?*"

"It was a convenient circumstance that the defective steam bath was the only one situated beside a window—one of those basement windows looking out into the sunk area."

"Oh, I see," I said slowly. "And the area runs down alongside the lemon orchard—"

"Just so. In point of fact there are bushes and shrubs growing all over that sunk area; it would not be difficult for somebody—somebody of considerable strength —to climb down unobserved and lift another person through that window. The windows are not high. They are normally kept closed, but, on account of the overheating steam bath, that one had been left ajar during the past few days."

"Aren't there bars?"

"There are bars, yes, but two of them had been wrenched away at the bottom and were merely hanging loosely. Somebody had climbed in and put the person in the bath. And thanks to you, we shall now perhaps know when—one day early last week."

"But wouldn't he have been seen inside?"

"Not necessarily. While treatments were going on, and all the cubicle curtains were drawn, it would not have been too difficult to slip in and out again. The lights are very dim, as you know."

I gazed at Plastiras in silence, taking in the horrible implications of what he had said. He took a black-and-white photograph from a folder and showed it to me.

"Do you know this man?"

The picture was of a thin, dark, short man, wearing Levi's and a T shirt. He was walking along the harbor front in Dendros town; I recognized the Turkish arches of the harbor-master's office behind him. I also recognized the T shirt as the one I had picked up—or at least its twin; it had a design of rampant seahorses on a striped background.

"I don't know the man, but the shirt looks like the one we found."

"You have not seen this man around Helikon?"

"No, never."

"Well, if you *should* recall seeing him at any time —either here at Helikon or in the town—more particularly if you recall seeing him with anybody that you know—will you please not mention this to any person at all, but at once let me know?"

"Yes, of course."

"Very well; thank you, Mike, you have been very helpful," he said. The friendly, chestnut-brown eyes smiled at me again, and then he walked swiftly out of the passage door, neat and noiseless in spite of his large bulk. I went back into the other room.

Mother said, "Thank goodness he's done. I thought he was never going to finish talking to you. And I was afraid he might want to question Lady Julia again. I'm worried about her—we ought to put her to bed."

"Do you think we're allowed to leave here?" I said doubtfully. "Should we ask the cop?"

"If someone's ill they have to be looked after!" declared Mother, with a return to old habits of authority. Fortunately the matter was resolved by Adnan, who returned at that moment.

"Lady Julia needs to be put to bed!" Mother said to him truculently.

"Of course she does," he replied, taking the wind out of her sails with his usual imperturbability. "And I have sent for an attendant and a wheelchair to take her to her room, now that Captain Plastiras has said he will not want her again. You, yourself, Mrs. Meiklejohn, have also had a bad shock; I think your daughter should take you to your room. I will visit you there presently. It is probable that, like Lady Julia, you would benefit from a sedative."

The chair arrived now, and Lady Julia was wheeled off, drooping like a Madonna lily; Adnan bustled after with a bag of equipment. All the time he had been in the room, he had not once looked at me; apart from this, which was not customary with him, he had behaved as if that odd, brief moment at the head of the stairs had not taken place. He looked pale, grim, and set-faced; most unlike himself.

I took Mother to our room. In spite of her spurt of authority, she was fairly groggy, and glad enough to lean on my arm as we proceeded slowly down the stairs and across the quadrangle to the guest wing. People were now starting to trickle slowly out of the concert hall as interrogations finished, and knots gathered together outside doorways, engaged in nervous, excited discussion.

As we passed the main entrance to the concert hall, a small but distinguished procession debouched from it: old Annibal Destrier being pushed in his wheelchair by Joop Kolenbrander, accompanied by Kerry Farrell, walking alongside.

"Poor, poor devil," she was saying, in a clear voice that easily carried to where we were. "What a horribly bizarre way to die! Do you think, M. Destrier, that it *could* possibly have anything to do with the hoodoo on *Les Mystères d'Elsinore?*"

"Ah, mais, voyez-vous, Mme. Farrell, c'est de la folie, ça!"

At the sound of Kerry Farrell's voice, Mother had started violently, and gripped my arm so hard that I almost yelped; she had clutched exactly the same spot which had received such paralyzing treatment from Mr. Saint earlier on in the evening.

"Wait here a moment; don't move!" she said in a peremptory tone.

We stood still. We were about five yards away from them, half hidden in the shadows of a buttress.

"But you must admit, M. Destrier, that it is a bit of a coincidence! I am not superstitious myself . . ."

The little procession moved toward us, illuminated by the light streaming out the open door. Old Annibal's bush of white hair shone like a halo, and Joop's Adam's apple was clearly silhouetted, whereas we were in shadow. Nevertheless old Annibal recognized me, by the side of the path, and called a friendly good night.

"Et alors, demain—tomorrow we try your costumes, we forget all this sadness and see 'ow all will go together, *hein?"*

"You mean the performance is still going ahead?" I asked, very astonished. I had expected that all such festivities would be canceled.

"Pourquoi pas? No one may leave—Captain Plastiras require that every guest shall remain here until the inquiries are finished; but is that a reason for *tout le monde* to sit about as dumb as tortoises, as melancholy as giraffes?" Annibal demanded. *"Au contraire!* Everybody will need to be cheered up and have his mind distracted."

"Oh, well, I'm very glad to hear it. Good night, then, M. Destrier."

"Bon soir, mon enfant."

They moved on.

And we went in the other direction. When we reached our room, I was alarmed to see that Mother had turned as white as lint; she looked far worse now than she had when I first saw her in Adnan's office.

"Mother! You look terrible. You'd better get into bed at once. I'll make you some hot milk with whiskey in."

Milk was in disfavor at Helikon, but a few goats browsed in the ravine behind, and their scanty supply was available to those in the good graces of the kitchen staff. I ran off and begged a cupful from old Arachne, who was a sister-in-law of Elena, at the Aghnides. Mother and I kept a bottle of Glenlivet in our closet; Adnan would doubtless have disapproved, but Mother is too much of a Scot to travel anywhere without a dram for emergencies, and, knowing her views, I had stocked up before the cruise.

When I got back with my hot milk, she was looking a little better, and the posset helped. But still her manner seemed terribly strange. She would not get into bed, but sat in our armchair, staring away through the dark window with a set, fixed face and eyes that saw God knows what; things far off and long ago and even worse, it seemed, than the boiled victim in the steam bath.

"We'll have to leave," she said abruptly.

"We can't," I reminded her. "Didn't you hear what old Annibal said? We're fixed here till the police have finished investigating. Besides, honestly, Ma, you aren't fit to travel yet. I'm most *terribly* sorry about this horrible affair—it's not at *all* the kind of thing that usually

221

happens at Helikon—and it was just frightful that you happened to be first on the scene—"

Frightful, but not surprising. If screams were heard and someone was in trouble, naturally Mother would be first on the spot.

"Oh, it's not that," she said impatiently. She was not listening to me. She beat her clenched fist against the wooden arm of the chair. Then, "I'll have to stay in this room—just not leave it at all. Oh, why, why did I ever allow you to bring me here?"

With a remorseful pang, I remembered her sedated journey in the ambulance. She had really had no option in the matter. And I resolved that never again, even if it seemed to be for their own good, would I deprive anybody of the right of choice.

Which did not help in the present instance. But still I did not understand what was causing her deep distress. That, perplexingly enough, seemed not to be connected with the man in the steam bath.

"Mother, what is the trouble?" I said quietly. "I think you really must try to tell me."

I went and squatted in front of her chair and took hold of her thin hands.

"*Why* do you feel that you must stay in this room? What's worrying you so? Are you"—it seemed wildly improbable, but it was the only theory that presented itself to me—"are you afraid of somebody?"

"Afraid? No!" she said violently. "There's nothing to be *afraid* of! It's just disgusting!"

"What is?" I persisted. "Mother—I simply can't go on in the dark like this about what's making you feel so awful."

She took her haunted eyes away from the window and turned them on me. Still she said nothing.

"Who knows—perhaps I can help in some way," I said rather hopelessly.

She laid her hand briefly on my head. "You're a good child. But no," she said, as if to a stranger, "no, you can't help. You'll have to *know*, though, I suppose. I suppose I should have told you before—I just couldn't bear to."

"Told me *what?*" I asked with a fearful palpitation of the heart.

"As we were coming along," she said. "That person who was with the old man in the wheelchair—"

"Old Annibal Destrier?"

"No, not him—"

"Joop? The tall Dutchman who was pushing him, Joop Kolenbrander? Or the other person? Do you mean Kerry Farrell? She's the singer who's just come. She's taking the part of Hamlet."

Mother gave a violent shudder. A spasm twitched the corners of her mouth as if she had swallowed poison and felt it burning its fatal way into her system.

"You do mean Kerry Farrell?" I pressed, with a premonition of what was coming. "What about her?"

But inside me, as I asked, with the fearful velocity of a computer, everything began to add itself together. Digits flashed and slid, whole columns totaled up, shot themselves to the side, merged with other columns, exploded into fountains of zeros, and flung new rows of figures down to the bottom.

"*Her?*" Mother said. "Singer? That mincing, posturing, self-advertising little monster? That's not any *woman*—that's your *father!*"

I couldn't help it—the shock was too sudden and profound, the anticlimax too ludicrous—I burst into a fit of laughter, hysterical, I daresay. But I soon

223

stopped. Mother was sitting staring at me in rigid silence, her cheek muscles tight with strain, a tear in the corner of her large, round eye; she looked like some stricken, wild creature trapped in the dignity of death.

"I—I'm terribly sorry!" I gulped. "It was such a shock—not in the very least what I'd expected." I'd had some vague notion that perhaps Kerry Farrell was his mistress—that might account for her having picked up his mannerisms, his tunes on the piano . . . "Are you *sure?*" I wanted to say. But there was no uncertainty in that frozen face, those wide, inward-looking eyes. "You've just got to tell me all about it," I said resolutely. "That's really *Father?* What happened? His sex changed, somehow?" I'd heard of such things in a vague way. But it is not the sort of occurrence with which one expects ever to be intimately connected; one reads these cases in the newspaper; they happen to chemistry teachers in Leighton Buzzard or to film actors in Los Angeles; not to one's own father.

"His sex didn't 'somehow' change," Mother snapped. "He had it done. He had an operation."

"Oh, my god," I said slowly. "I see. He *wanted* to have it done. He wanted to become a woman."

"As if any man ever could!" said Mother with a vehement sniff.

Slowly, slowly, by painful degrees, I dragged the story out of her—or at least a thin, bloodstained thread of narrative; plainly there were many terrible passages, which, though preserved intact, I was sure, fossilized in Mother's wincing memory, would never be divulged by her, or at least not to me.

They had been married very young. He was twenty, she nineteen. Father had always toyed with this fantasy of becoming a woman—he had made no secret of

224

it, apparently—but Mother, with her blunt Scots common sense, had been sure that marriage and its responsibilities—and they did love each other, after all—fatherhood, a career, adult citizenship, she had thought, would soon knock all the nonsense out of his head.

But she had been wrong. The wish remained, the urge grew stronger and stronger; although they had an affectionate relationship, although he loved us when we began to grow, he could not rid himself of his longing.

"Didn't even *try*," Mother said, blinking furious tears away.

He was not a transvestite, not a homosexual; playacting—wearing women's clothes—was no good to him; he was not interested in the company of queers; what he wanted was the real thing. With every fiber of his being, he wanted to become a woman; he felt that, in all the most fundamental parts of him, he already *was* a woman.

"And, would you believe it," demanded Mother, staring at me with ferocious intensity, as if she were reliving endless, bitter old scenes of dispute, "not only did he want to have this disgusting operation done to him but he *then* expected to come home and live with us all just as before! As if nothing had happened! Can you imagine anything so horrible? He actually said he could live with me as if he were my sister, and go on having the same kind of relationship with you and Dru—" She stopped, gulping.

Oh, poor Dru, I thought. Poor, poor Dru, who loved Father so much. "It was just too much for Dru?" I asked, after a while. "She couldn't bear it? Was that why she killed herself?"

"How did you know *that*?" asked Mother on a

pounce. "You weren't supposed to. I always kept it from you."

I couldn't betray Gina Signorelli, so, rather evasively, I said, "Oh well, it got back to me in the end, the way things always do. I couldn't tell you that I knew."

What terrible things we expect each other to bear, I thought. Father honestly thought that there was nothing wrong with expecting them—us—to have him back at home. But was he so wrong? Perhaps we would have learned to adjust to the situation in time. People are probably more flexible than they imagine.

Sadly I wondered what Father had felt when he heard about Dru. How terrible it must have been for him!

Mother would not allow this, however. "Why should *he* feel anything?" she demanded. "He was too wrapped up in his own selfish concerns. Besides, if he did feel anything, it was only what he deserved, wasn't it?"

"But he was terribly fond of Dru. She was his favorite."

"Well? He should have thought of that sooner— before he robbed her of her father, turned the whole relationship into a horrible travesty."

In the end, I gathered, he had simply taken his own way. After settling all he could on Mother, he had gone off to a clinic in Sweden where they gave him preliminary treatment for some time—over a period of about eighteeen months, Mother thought—with hormones, before the climactic operation.

"And you've never seen him since?"

"What do you take me for? I told him I'd sooner die. I told him I'd get a divorce and change my name, that he must be prepared never to see his children again, that *he* must change *his* name, and completely disappear out of our lives. I wasn't going to have you and Dru—all of us—mixed up in revolting newspaper publicity, people coming and asking me how it felt to have a *woman* for a husband. Ugh!" She gave such a violent shudder of horror that I brought a blanket from the bed and draped it around her shoulders.

"You've never heard from him since? You didn't know the name he'd taken?"

"No, I didn't." *Could* I believe her? She went on, "He did write to me once or twice; he wrote care of the lawyers, and just signed with his initial, as he always had. Then he said that he missed us badly, and asked if he couldn't come back—just for a visit. But I—couldn't. I said no. After that I tore up his letters without reading them." Again that spasm of the mouth, as if she were suppressing nausea. "I'd thought he might have kept up connections with Dendros; that's why I never cared for your coming back here."

"Never cared" had been an understatement. There had been bitter rows over my first two visits to Helikon. But I, feeling there must be *some* advantage to be derived from my distant, cool relationship with Mother, had simply ignored her anger and gone; and presumably when she discovered that I had not run into Father here (by that time, no doubt, Kerry Farrell was becoming well known and had little chance to revisit old haunts) Mother's resistance died down; she became reconciled to my visits. When I gave up going, it was not through fear of her disapproval.

She went on, "Then—when I found you had brought me to Helikon—I was terrified that he might be here—but there was no sign of him, so I began to feel my fear had been a fuss about nothing."

And so it would have been, I thought, if only Elisabet

Maas or someone else had agreed to sing the part of Hamlet; if old Annibal hadn't been so set on having his *Mystères* performed; if Kerry Farrell hadn't managed to get out of her engagement in Basel—

His engagement.

What an extraordinary situation. That's no lady: that's my father.

Suddenly I felt a furious anger against both of them. How dared they rob me of my father in this arbitrary way? He had been one of the two first people in my childhood's world—someone with whom I shared happy games, songs, jokes, a whole loving relationship—and because *he* had this crazy longing, because *she* couldn't stand it—*wouldn't* stand it—because of their obstinacy, Dru must be driven to suicidal despair and I must be left to a lonely, virtually parentless childhood. Why didn't you think of *us* at all! I wanted to demand. But Mother would say that she *had* thought of us—the rigid silence, the impenetrable secrecy, the puritan reserve had been her way of protecting us. I felt that I would have been glad to exchange such protection for more love and the risk of publicity, of the world's curiosity—but how could I judge? Maybe she was right. And presumably she knew of her own endurance; she knew what she couldn't stand. The drawn expression of disgust about her mouth denoted plainly enough that her feelings were still as deep and bitter as they had ever been.

What a terrible, grotesque sort of rejection, I thought. To have a man say, "I don't want to go to bed with you any more, but I'd like to be a sister to you." All right for some women perhaps—but not for Mother, with her hot, fierce, sensitive Calvinist pride. With her deep, strong, inarticulate feelings. Think of having to share your memories of early sexual discoveries and happinesses with someone who had withdrawn from you in this way. No, I could see that it was not to be borne.

"I suppose Father didn't ever—well—marry again?" I asked with caution.

"God knows," said Mother with a curl of her nostril. "I suppose there might have been some man perverted enough to—I don't know. And I'd rather not know."

Enough of *that,* said the snap of her lips.

But it wasn't enough for me. And I felt that her acute disgust was a measure of how little she had allowed herself to discuss the subject—even *think* of it, probably—during the past twelve years. It had been unhealthily buried, deep down, festering. Who knows, if Father had had his way, if he had been allowed to live with us, she might in the end have become resigned—

But no, the idea was too squalid; there I did sympathize with Mother. I could not endure the thought, and pushed it away.

Poor Father, though. He had paid dearly for the realization of his dream. And how, I wondered, had he found it, being a woman? Had it come up to expectation? Satisfied his hopes? It seemed to me the most extraordinary wish imaginable—but how could I judge, being already endowed by nature with the estate he longed for? I tried to imagine longing to be a man—a yearning for the unattainable romance of being male—but my imagination could not bridge the gap; besides, I felt that I had already within reach all the desirable attributes of maleness—freedom, a career, the right to wear trousers, travel alone, sleep with whom I chose; the only exclusive male role remaining, it seemed to me, was the sexual decision, the right to attack, to make the first move, to take the plunge— and who in the world would want *that*, with its terrible anxieties and resonsibilities, terrible risks of failure, impotence, or plain rejection?

No, the more I thought about it, the more I felt a strong sympathy with Father's wish to opt out of the whole male rat race; I couldn't find it in my heart to blame him. But of course that was the last thing that Mother could be brought to understand, for hers was an intensely competitive nature. She thought that achievement was no more than one's duty, that one should be constantly overcoming challenges and grappling with circumstances. Maybe, if *she* could have chosen beforehand, she would have preferred to be a man?

Maybe that was what attracted Father to her?

But there was no profit in indulging in such speculations.

"Poor Ma! What a mess!" I sighed, leaning my head back against her knees. "It was lucky you were such a good teacher and had your career to occupy you. But didn't you ever think of marrying again?"

"Not likely!" she said with terrific intensity. "Do you think I'd run such a risk twice over?"

"A thing like that would hardly happen twice," I pointed out mildly.

"I'd had enough of men," she said with finality.

I didn't trouble to suggest that Father was hardly your typical man. I just felt sad for her. All her capacity for love wasted. And what about him? Did he never miss his male beginnings? Did they never miss each other? Didn't he ever long for the name "James" said as she used to say it?

230

But then, when I thought of Kerry Farrell, pacing so jauntily about the stage, swishing her flared skirt, teasing Joop Kolenbrander, and laughing at old Annibal's jokes, I could not feel that Father was much to be pitied; in fact some of Mother's disgust tinged the color of my thought. He had come a long way since he left our pleasant home near Oxford; he enjoyed his feminine role; he did not need us any more. I was glad at least that Mother had not watched that rehearsal; and I began to feel that she might be right to want to stay shut up in here.

Why should she be obliged to do that, though?

She had not committed any offense. Why must she remain cloistered up like a prisoner?

"You're quite sure you don't want to meet him— her?"

"I can't *stand* the idea!" Her expression, and the passionate intensity of her words, convinced me.

"Luckily I don't think there's much chance of his having recognized you. You look awfully different from your normal self in that black turban—and you're so thin just now."

"I recognized *him* at once," she said.

And at her tone of voice, I realized with a sad, transfixing stab of pain what had been staring me in the face all along. That she loved him still and completely, and always would. *That* was why she had never married again.

But nothing could be done about that.

"I know what," I said, jumping up. "I'll ask Adnan if we can't transfer to a hotel. I'll explain that there are acute personal reasons why it's necessary—I won't explain what—" as she looked daunted. "I'm sure it

231

will be all right; he can fix it with Captain Plastiras. As long as we stay on the island."

"Oh, no, I don't want a whole lot of fuss and special arrangements," Mother said exasperatingly.

"Of course the best thing would be if they just canceled the *Hamlet* opera—and really it does seem unsuitable to go on with it after that poor man's death. I could ask Adnan to suggest that to Annibal. If it were canceled I expect Kerry—Father—would just leave again."

How strange it was, I thought, that in all this personal denouement I had almost forgotten about the poor man and his grisly end. Yet that sinister problem still remained, waiting to be solved.

"No, I don't want you making any kind of suggestion to Adnan," said Mother, sounding even more obstinate. "I hate anything devious—underhand—"

I could have shaken her.

Luckily, just at that moment there came a tap on the door and Adnan walked in. I was unfeignedly glad to see him, though he was looking even grimmer, paler, and more fatigued than he had in his office. I felt it would be the last straw to burden him with our grotesque little problem.

"How are you now, Mrs. Meiklejohn?" he asked, walking over to Mother and laying a finger on her pulse.

I noticed his eye instantly take in the signs of our debauch: the two milk-rimmed cups, the bottle of Glenlivet on the table. The faintest possible grin momentarily lightened his expression. Then he became serious again.

"I am glad you are not too upset after such a shock, Mrs. Meiklejohn, but it is best you go to bed, I think."

"Thank you; I was about to go," said Mother with dignity. "And then I have a personal problem about which I should like to ask your advice, Dr. Adnan."

"I am delighted to be of any use," he said formally.

Well, that's certainly a massive step forward, I thought, helping Mother into bed. Though what poor Achmed will make of the business, heaven knows.

Adnan, meanwhile, had flung himself down in our armchair and was gazing moodily at the pile of paperback plays and poetry that I lug around with me, and the Piaget and Kornei Chukovsky and Winnicott with which Mother enlivens her leisure.

I was quite surprised that he acceded to Mother's request so readily, since there must be no end of horrible formalities requiring his attention.

Perhaps he was glad to escape them for a bit.

When Mother was all settled, "I have a message for you, Mike," he said. "I hesitated to give it, not knowing if your mother could spare you, but, if you do not object, Mrs. Meiklejohn, Lady Julia would be very glad to see your daughter for a few moments."

"Of course!" Mother said. "I'm quite all right now, and I'm sure Mike will be glad to go. Poor Lady Julia —is she still very upset?"

"Not good. For a person of her temperament— highly strung, imaginative—the shock was particularly severe."

I glanced at Mother to see how she received this implication that she, being of tougher, peasant stock, could be expected to weather the experience more easily, and our eyes met; she gave me a small smile, which suddenly cheered me up.

Also, I was now provided with an excuse for going off and leaving them together, which seemed a good thing; I felt sure that Mother would prefer to be alone with Adnan while she discussed the problem of her transmogrified husband with him. So I said, "Okay, I'll go right along now. Shan't be long, Mother. See you later. Good night, Ach—Dr. Adnan."

To tell the truth, I was glad to get away from that piece of revelation.

I went quietly out and closed the door on them.

╡ 10 ╞

ADAGIO

Julia lay weakly on her bed, gazing at the ceiling. Strident, random thoughts circled and collided inside her head like disordered hornets. Dikran was sitting in the far corner of the room with his back to her, as he had throughout Dr. Adnan's visit; he was being no help at all.

It was plain, thought Julia, from time to time, among the rest of her unprofitable reflections, that Dikran had never before found himself in the position of being required to look after anybody else; or not for a long time, she amended, remembering that number on his arm; for the latter part of his life his money had entitled him to all the service that was going; and he seemed as indignantly astonished and unhandy when asked to bring a box of tissues or to find her eau de cologne as if he had been expected to mop up vomit or empty a bedpan.

In consequence, Julia, on whom shock had had the effect of bringing to the surface all the buried griefs and distresses of the past two years, lay silently, painfully crying, and longing for her children, both so quiet, deft, and considerate when a parent was sick, or for her lost husband, who, with all his failings, had been a kindly, domesticated man, always amiably prepared to make a pot of tea or fill a hot-water bottle.

Adnan had provided her with a sedative, advice to stay in bed on the following day, and solicitous bedside manner but in the face of Dikran's silent, glowering hostility, he had kept his visit to the barest, polite minimum and had not stayed to supply any of the comforting, informative chat for which Julia had hoped.

"Is there anything more you need?" he had asked, casting a frowning, thoughtful glance at Dikran's unforthcoming back.

And Julia, terrified at the thought of being left to her husband's mercies for the next nine or ten hours, had said faintly, "I'd love to see Mike for a little. Do you think her mother could spare her to come and sit with me?"

"I will inquire. I do not see why she should not," Adnan said after a pause, and escaped. "Take the pill soon—try to sleep," he warned from the doorway. "I am afraid there will be police here all night long, trampling about, hunting for clues—though what clues they can expect to find in this nest of musicians, who are among the most untidy, haphazard creatures in creation—!" He flung up his hands and left the room.

"What did the police ask you?" Dikran inquired some time after Adnan had gone.

236

"Oh—if I had ever seen or heard anything odd in the steam room. Which I hadn't. And Captain Plastiras asked me if I knew about any feuds or antagonisms among people staying at Helikon."

"What did you say to that?" He had turned around. His face was very sallow. His dark eyes were fixed on her in a kind of angry irony.

"Antagonisms? How should I know? I said we hadn't been here long; I could not be expected to have picked up information about internal feuds."

Captain Plastiras had received that with skepticism. "Really?" he had remarked. "You have met nobody who so much as dislikes one single other person here?"

Guiltily Julia remembered that she had then—with some misgivings—mentioned Mrs. Meiklejohn's remark, brought out with such cold force: "Yes, there is one person whom I can say that I hate." But the moment after she mentioned it, she had felt angry with herself. For, after all, there was absolutely no indication that the person hated by Mrs. Meiklejohn was at Helikon; indeed, such an eventuality was highly improbable. Moreover Julia's recital of the incident had earned her a very strange look from Captain Plastiras—a look, it seemed to her, of disapproval, mixed with a sad, understanding pity. She preferred not to think about it. She had been glad to hurry out of the secretary's office, collapse into a chair, and forget about the interview.

"Was that all he asked you?"

"Yes, it was." Firmly, Julia suppressed the tale of the pile of clothes in the sun-bathing enclosure; she had never told Dikran about that, and had her own reasons for finding it too frightening to dwell on. She said, "What did Plastiras ask you?"

"Oh, nothing much. The same. About feuds and antagonisms. And had I used the steam room. I said no."

"Oh, but you have been there," Julia said incautiously. "Don't you remember the first time when you got up—when I showed you around?"

"So what of it?" he shouted with sudden fury. "Has not every person in this damned hole walked through there at one time or another?"

"I only meant—"

"Yes? What did you mean?"

Luckily, at this moment Mike tapped on the door and put her head around it, asking, "May I come in?"

"Oh, yes, do come in, Mike," Julia said with great relief. "This is very sweet of you—how is your mother? Are you sure it's all right to leave her?"

"Thank you, yes, she's better, and Dr. Adnan is sitting with her at the moment."

"Oh, so he does sit with other lady patients as well as with my wife?" Dikran observed sourly.

Mike threw him a rather startled glance and then, catching Julia's appealing expression, said, "Is there anything I can do for you, Lady Julia? We've been drinking hot milk and scotch—would you like some?"

"That's very kind of you, but I think I'd bring it up—the very thought of that awful sight nearly makes me vomit," Julia said with a gulp. "I'd love it if you'd just sit with me for a bit, though; and do you think you could possibly brush my hair? It feels such a horrible, dank mess."

"Of course I will."

Mike found a hairbrush, turned the bedside lamp so that its light did not shine in Julia's eyes, and gently set to work. Dikran watched all this with a cold, ironic eye. "It is exceedingly kind of Miss Meiklejohn to spare the time," he muttered.

"I'm glad to do it," said Mike, brushing away. "It must have been the most dreadful, dreadful shock for Lady Julia—finding that man—"

"I do not see why that stupid nurse-girl had to lift off the tarpaulin and open the machine," Dikran grumbled. "If she had waited for the engineer's arrival, like a person of sense—"

"Oh, well, it would have been bound to happen sooner or later. Let's hope the police quickly find out who did it. Poor Dr. Adnan! It's horrible publicity for his clinic."

"Such publicity often brings more customers, out of curiosity," Dikran said, and turned away again impatiently.

Wishing to change the subject, Julia asked Mike about the performance of *Les Mystères d'Elsinore*—was it still going forward?

"I think so," Mike said. "M. Destrier seemed to think there was no reason why it should not. So they will spend tomorrow rehearsing, and the performance will be on the day after, as scheduled. Perhaps the police will have finished their job by then."

"Oh, well, I'm glad you didn't have all your hard work in vain," Julia said. "I'm looking forward to seeing your sets. Dr. Adnan says they are highly original."

A closed, clouded expression came over Mike's face at that, but her only comment was, "He told *me* they looked like boiled cauliflower."

She glanced toward Dikran's back, as if she hoped for or expected some remark from him, but all he said, in an acid tone, was, "Dr. Adnan has a great sense of humor."

Julia wished that her husband would either take a

proper part in the conversation or leave the room; it created a very uncomfortable atmosphere to have him sitting there with his back half turned, doing nothing, but apparently monitoring all they said, and inserting his tart comments from time to time as a reminder that he was listening. Deliberately ignoring him, she asked Mike, "Have you been introduced to Kerry Farrell yet?"

The girl paused for a long moment before answering. The same guarded expression came down over her face; she said, "No. No, I haven't. I saw her in the hall just before the rehearsal was interrupted. I'm not really sure that I want to be introduced. It's awkward—I've found out something—" Then she stopped, bit her lip, and said, "Have you talked to her?"

"Yes, I did, before the rehearsal. You found out about her sex change, you mean?" Julia said. Without noticing Mike's shake of the head, she went on, "But that's all in the past, years ago now. I honestly don't think it would embarrass you in the least. It didn't me, a bit. I think that was such an incredibly brave thing to do, don't you? When I remember the disgusting publicity about my divorce, and how scarifying I found it all—and think what *she* must have gone through—I take off my hat to her, I really do. What a decision to make! And yet it's plain that it was the right decision, for her; she seems so *buoyantly* happy and at ease; one can see at once that she ended up where she belongs."

"You knew all about her, then?" Mike asked. "I'd never even heard—about it—I knew of her as a singer, of course. I—I suppose I was over here, at school in Greece, at the time when he—she—when it happened." She swallowed. After a moment she added, "Was there much publicity?"

"No; some. Photographs in cheaper papers—especially when she took up concert singing; and I remember an article in one of the color supplements about sex change in general, with some pictures of her. And a bit about the clinic in Sweden where it was done. Apparently they are doing more and more of these operations—as well as other kinds of plastic and cosmetic surgery. Anyway, it's done, it's over. She's a different person now."

"Did you *like* her?" Mike's tone was neutral, but she suspended the brushing for a moment while she waited for Julia's answer.

"Yes. Yes, I did!" Dikran raised his brows and, turning his head, directed an enigmatic look at his wife. But she had her back to him now and went on, "She was so lively and friendly. She seemed like a balanced, happy, *brave* person." Mike's suspended arm returned to its brushing. Julia went on, "I suppose she's the embodiment of the truth that most of us have a mix of both sexes in us and the really intelligent person must learn to assess their own balance and rectify it if it feels out of kilter."

"So I should be a woman, perhaps?" Dikran muttered, but not very loud.

"In fact I don't remember when I've felt so immediately *comfortable* with anybody," Julia continued. "You know what I mean? One didn't have, with her, the feeling that she—that she had any sexual ax to grind. It was easy and relaxed."

Dikran's grin became even more malicious. But Julia was lying on her stomach with her chin propped on her hands, enjoying the sensation of the brush gently teasing out her hair; she was remembering with an internal grin of her own that what she had actually

241

felt, after ten minutes' conversation with Miss Farrell, was that it would be very enjoyable to share a sauna with the singer. Here, in fact, was the perfect friend—somebody with whom one could gossip and chuckle on most complete terms, who would never attack, never be a rival, but who knew about *the other side;* who had a foot in both camps.

"I wonder where she lives?" Mike remarked quietly.

"In Ireland, I believe. Her accent's quite Irish. Of course she spends most of her time traveling from one engagement to another."

"Did the article—any of the articles you read—say anything about her private life?"

"You know something of it yourself, Miss Meiklejohn?" Dikran suddenly interjected.

Mike looked startled. "I? Why should you think so?"

"Just now you said you had found out something about her."

"Only a private piece of information that isn't my secret," Mike said quickly.

Julia yawned. "I don't remember that the article said anything about her private affairs. Dead silence as to whether she had a lover. Some vague indication that she'd had to leave a family when she took off for the opposite gender. Rather weird for them, poor things—but I suppose they're used to the situation by now. Better have Daddy turn into Aunty than find out he's really the Boston Strangler or one of the Moors Murderers."

"Cripes, so I should think!" Mike's tone was startled. "Why them? What far-out alternatives you pick!"

Dikran shot another narrow-eyed glance at his wife, but she, yawning again, rolled over onto her back and said, "Angel Mike—you really are a child of light!

242

You've actually made me feel sleepy with your conversation and your brushing—I never *ever* thought I'd be able to sleep again after that unutterably ghastly sight —Irish stew! Ugh! Now, could you be a love and fetch me a glass of water—give the glass a bit of a rinse first, I had cyclamens in it and they're almost certainly deadly poison—"

When Mike returned from the bathroom, Julia unclenched her hand, in which she had been holding Adnan's pill since he had given it to her.

"*Now* I shall sleep," she said, swallowing it with most of the water.

"Would you like me to stay till you drop off?" suggested Mike with a cautious glance at Dikran. Julia nodded, with a look of appeal, but Dikran again interposed.

"My dear Miss Meiklejohn, it is kind of you to make the offer, but that will be entirely unnecessary. Anything further that my wife requires, I can perform. She has taken an unfair amount of your time as it is— since your mother also is suffering—"

"Sure?" Mike was already poised to go. "Okay! I hope you'll have a good night and be much better in the morning. I'll come round at breakfast time to inquire—not too early."

"No, not too early," said Dikran, with his tightly controlled, muscular smile.

When he turned to speak to Julia, after closing the door, she lay silent, feigning sleep; and soon she was asleep in good earnest.

But Dikran sat up all night, motionless, in his chair, staring out the window, thinking. When light came, he got up and went out softly, leaving Julia still sleeping.

She woke with a start, some hours later, hearing a tap on the door, and called, "Come in!" anxiously, but it was only Mike again, carrying a glass of grape juice and some puréed fruit.

"Good morning. How did you sleep?"

"Like a log, thank you. I feel miles better," Julia said, stretching luxuriously. It was a great relief to find Dikran gone out, though she did not say so. Seizing the chance of his absence, she said, "Mike. Did you tell Captain Plastiras about finding that man's clothes?"

"Of course." Mike's tone was puzzled. "Didn't you?"

"Yes—I did. I wonder *why* they were left there?"

"I've been thinking about that. I suppose whoever killed that wretched man—he must have been murdered, mustn't he? No one would put someone else's body in a steam bath unless they had killed them first?"

"Might have been unconscious," Julia said grimly.

Mike shivered. "What a horrible idea! I hadn't thought of that. But the person who put him in must have done it hoping the body would be boiled till it was unidentifiable. I suppose he left the clothes in the men's sun-bathing place temporarily, thinking they wouldn't arouse any comment there and he could go back later and collect them and dispose of them permanently. But before he could get back, we came wandering along at dead of night and happened to see them. It was bad luck."

"Yes, it was bad luck," said Julia tonelessly. "The clothes didn't ring any bell with you—when the police questioned you—you didn't remember seeing anyone wearing them—either here or in Dendros?"

"No, Plastiras asked that," said Mike. "But I didn't —I'm sure I'd never seen them before. I would have remembered that shirt."

244

"Oh, well—" Julia's tone brushed the matter aside. "Maybe it was some wandering hippie who got bashed by one of his mates—some of the lot who sleep on the beach in Dendros—nothing to do with Helikon. Let's hope so. Thank you for the breakfast; it was sweet of you to bring it. Now I'm going to get up."

"You're sure you'll be all right?"

"Yes, fine, thanks—and your mother will be needing you, I expect."

"She's going to stay in bed today—take it easy," Mike said, accepting her dismissal and moving toward the door.

"I'll drop around and see her later."

Julia slowly dressed and went out into the quadrangle, thinking that it would be pleasant to encounter Kerry Farrell. More people than usual were standing and sitting in groups about the statue-studded grass. The heavenly, hot sun made yesterday's hidous discovery, and Dikran's strange behavior, seem like some half-forgotten nightmare, but there were still police around, and an uneasy atmosphere of gossip and speculation, to remind Julia that it had been no dream. Fellow guests eyed her with respectful commiseration, but few came to speak to her; evidently the news had gone around that it was she who had found the body, and people were shy of approaching her. Among the nervously whispering groups the shining, white, athletic statues leaned and watched and listened, as if waiting for a chance to take part in the discussion.

The sound of horns, violins, and a clear, carrying soprano voice floating from the main hall was a reminder that normal life was still proceeding, however. Julia moved irresolutely toward the concert-hall door, but before she reached it the rehearsal apparently broke up and the participants began to come out, laughing and chatting, evidently very pleased with themselves and each other. Old Annibal Destrier was among them hobbling on his two sticks today; he sank down on a bench in the sunshine and called to Joop Kolenbrander, "Be so good, *mon cher*, as to bring me some of that disgusting pseudo-beef drink from the loggia, will you? I wait for you here and rest my aged legs." Seeing Julia nearby, he gave her his gnome-like grin and said, "Aha, the beautiful Lady Julia! Expressly sent by *le bon Dieu* to cheer me after an exhausting *répétition*. Sit yourself here by me, and tell me about the rehearsings of your plays—you will 'ave seen many and they will all 'ave been 'orrible, is it not so?"

Julia, who had been feeling rather uncomfortably conspicuous and isolated, was glad to sit by him.

"Why," she said laughing, "was the rehearsal so very bad? I find that hard to believe. The musicians all seem first-rate—and I can't imagine that Kerry Farrell doesn't know her stuff?"

She glanced around for the singer as she spoke and saw her with Joop Kolenbrander, standing in the long, straggling queue that moved toward the hot-drinks table.

"*Pas mal*," Destrier confided. "No, I joke; the opera goes on in effect very well indeed. But—you know 'ow it is—players and singers are all obstinate as mules, self-willed as pigs—each wants his own way regardless of what is best for the ensemble."

"But I am sure they pay heed to you," Julia said soothingly.

"*Comme ci, comme ça!*"

"I'm afraid you will have a long wait for your *bouillon*," Julia remarked, observing the slow progress of the queue.

246

"No matter; what of it, when I am in such delightful company?"

Julia felt that the only appropriate reply to this would be, "La, sir, you are a sad flatterer, I vow!" She inclined her head, smiling.

Then in the distance she noticed Adnan, coming from the direction of his office. People streamed toward him, evidently asking him about the progress of the police investigations; he shook them off impatiently and came over to pay his respects to Annibal Destrier. He seemed to be doing it primarily out of a sense of duty; he asked civilly how the rehearsal had gone, but he looked pale and worried; his usual air of cheerful urbanity had quite left him. Julia felt fairly certain that, despite his informed and courteous inquiries, he was secretly wishing the aged composer and all his works at the devil. The presence of a whole batch of international celebrites at the time when such a horrible event had taken place at Helikon must add immensely to his problems and responsibilities.

Two pink-faced girl music students had summoned up the courage to approach Annibal Destrier and gigglingly ask for his autograph. Under cover of their chatter, Julia said to Adnan in a low tone, "I'd like to ask your advice sometime when you've a moment. I have a—a private problem that's worrying me."

His usual sympathy was noticeably lacking. He answered shortly, "Oh, very well—later, I will find time. After lunch."

"You seem very bothered."

He burst out, "It is all secrets, secrets! Everything at Helikon just now is somebody's secret. It is like 'The Fall of the House of Usher.' If only people would be

247

rather more communicative about their past lives, *my* life would be a great deal easier."

With which he turned on his heel and walked away, leaving Julia feeling hurt and snubbed. He had not even inquired how she felt.

But then, with a chill sensation at the pit of her stomach, she saw her husband, who had evidently arrived while she was talking to Adnan and taken his seat on a bench about fifteen yards away. He sat with his arms folded, watching her impassively.

The two autograph seekers had retreated, grateful, blushing, and stammering; Julia reflected rather disconsolately that it was a long time since she had been asked for her autograph; at Helikon, playwrights rated nowhere in comparison with musicians.

Annibal Destrier turned back to her and gave her another of his singular grins—shrewd, sharply observant, rather malicious; she fancied that, even while he was signing the girls' books, he had been aware of her overture to Adnan, Dikran's arrival, and Adnan's rebuff. He did not immediately allude to any of these events but embarked on some rambling remarks about Helikon, its beneficial treatments, and, in particular, its wonderfully serene ambiance.

"Indeed I have heard it said," he pursued, "that many, many people who come here regularly begin to find, after a while, that, in effect, Helikon is quite changing their natures."

"Really, M. Destrier? In what way?" Julia asked politely.

"They become, by degrees, more serene; less self-seeking. Now, you, madame," he said gallantly, watching her with his small, brilliant black eyes, "you are a very lovely woman, very intelligent, very creative, you are admired by *tout le monde*, accustomed at all times to 'ave your own way; but if you were many times in 'Elikon, I wonder if even you might not begin to ask yourself, 'Should not all this come perhaps to a stop? Maybe I am not to 'ave my own way so often? Maybe I should not expect to 'ave my cake and eat it quite so much?' You look upset—I think you do not agree with me?"

"I—I'm not really sure that I know what you mean." Julia was very much startled indeed, and her feelings were even more bruised than by Adnan's snub; she had expected more compliments from the old composer, not disconcerting home truths.

But he went on, gently and remorsefully, "I observe much, madame; I notice 'ow your very charming and 'armless flirtation with Achmed upset your 'usband— and this so soon after you are married, and when 'e is not well; this I find sad. Achmed *sans doute* can look after 'imself, but as to your 'usband, I am not so sure; if I were you I would treat that one with more care. Also, there are others concerned—I name no names!"

Julia opened her mouth to protest, but he checked her with an upraised hand. "Ah—ah! I am informed about your divorce, you see, also—for I am in England at that time, conducting the City of London Orchestra, and I rent a house in 'Olland Park from a lawyer who knows much about the case; I learn, what is not generally known, that it is not so much the 'usband who commit adultery, though *évidemment* 'e wish to marry 'is fat peeress, but, to my great astonishment, I find it is the beautiful, virtuous wife who 'ave commit so many indiscretions until at last 'er 'usband become fed up with 'er and throw 'er out."

249

Tears stood in Julia's eyes; an angry spot of color burned on each cheek.

"Now, you may say," continued old Annibal peacefully, "you may say, *et pour cause,* 'Why should this interfering old man, who 'ave 'ad many, many affairs *avec beaucoup de monde,* why should 'e presume to criticize a lovely, talented lady 'oo is young enough to be 'is daughter? Why is it okay for Annibal to commit *des folies* while I am denied this right?"

She could not speak, but swallowed and gave a slight nod, frowning to draw the tears back into her eyes. She felt wholly outraged, furious, *violated* by such an unprovoked attack; and done in public too, even in the presence of her husband!

"But, you see, it *is* different for me," Annibal ended with great complacence. "And the difference is that I do no 'arm to anybody, and I am 'appy myself."

No harm, thought Julia; what about the lady who threw herself into the Seine? For she too had encountered this legend as it floated around Helikon.

"I am 'appy myself," repeated Annibal. "But you, madame, you are not 'appy. Anyone can see that. And in your chagrin you pull and snatch at others, you inflict wounds—"

But Julia had had enough. She stood up, trembling.

"Monsieur Destrier," she said with what dignity she could muster, "I am sure you have meant this kindly. But you are quite right—it is no business of yours."

And she walked away from him, straight out across the lawn. The old man gazed after her with a sad and speculative air.

Dikran stood up leisurely and came to meet Julia. His appearance alarmed her inexpressibly: he was pale and sunken-eyed, as he had been on the day of his amnesia; he did not seem to have shaved. His expression as she came up to him was a frightening blend of fear and hostility; as if she were his life line but one he hated to make use of.

He said, "I cannot stand this silly place a day longer. We have to leave—"

"Dikran, we can't. Don't you remember—"

Immensely to Julia's relief, Kerry Farrell, who had been strolling in their direction carrying a mug of bouillon, at this moment greeted Julia with a friendly smile.

"Hallo! I hope you have recovered from your horrible experience?"

"Yes, thank you. I'm fine today. How did your rehearsal go?"

"Well—" The singer rolled her eyes in the direction of where old Annibal was drinking his bouillon and talking to Joop Kolenbrander; she then gave Julia a swift, conspiratorial grin. " 'Deed and he's an old Tartar, bless him! It would certainly go more easily without him there conducting an inquest into every note; he has me petrified entirely—but still! He's a great old boy and it is for his birthday—I daresay we'll survive."

"Poor you! He certainly is an old terror," Julia said in heartfelt agreement. Then, feeling Dikran's powerfully silent presence at her shoulder, "Oh, excuse me—this is my husband, Dikran; Miss Kerry Farrell."

"How do you do?" said Kerry Farrell with her frank smile. She held out a well-shaped, blue-veined hand, which was small for a man's but large for a woman's; after a moment's hesitation Dikran took it.

"Haven't we met before?" Kerry asked him. "Are you a musician? Your face is so familiar; I'm sure I know you from somewhere."

251

But he shook his head. "No, I am not a musician," he said stiffly. "I do not think we have met."

"Really? You weren't at Drottningholm last summer? I felt certain we'd met somewhere; I never forget a face."

"My husband isn't a muscian; he's a businessman," Julia said, and thought with annoyance how artificial her laugh sounded.

"Is that so? What kind of business?"

"Many kinds," Dikran answered briefly, returning Miss Farrell's look of lively interest with a lowering, frowning stare. "It would take too long to explain."

"And I've little head for business, faith!" the singer said laughing. "I'm always two years behind with my taxes, and keep my cash in an old teapot." She blew on her bouillon. "I wish this disgusting stuff would cool down; it's away too hot to drink yet, and me as parched as an old shoe after singing '*Être ou ne pas être*' thirty times over."

Mike walked swiftly across the grass carrying two cups of bouillon; she nodded, in response to Julia's wave, but did not stop, and disappeared into the guest wing.

"Who was that?" Kerry Farrell asked, looking after Mike.

"Oh, she's a dear child—haven't you met her yet? I'll introduce her when she comes back," said Julia. "She's got a lot of talent—and she's a darling, isn't she, Dikran?"

He grunted; but at this moment the two giggling autograph hunters came up, nudging each other like calves, even more pink and flustered than when they had approached Annibal Destrier.

"Oh, Miss Farrell—*could* we have your signature?"

Julia, who was feeling more and more apprehensive, looked at them with exasperation. But Kerry Farrell shrugged and laughed, accepting the autograph book that one of them handed her.

"Would you mind, just a moment?" she said gaily to Dikran, and passed him her steaming cup. "Which page—any?" she said, opening the book and delving in her shoulder bag for a ballpoint.

"Anywhere—yes, there—*thank* you, Miss Farrell!"

They stood in worshiping silence while she inscribed a baroque, flourishing signature in each book, then shouldered each other off again, triumphantly comparing signatures. As they did so, Julia noticed that a sudden hush had fallen over the lawn, like a silence in a hen run when a hawk sweeps overhead.

Glancing behind her, she saw that Captain Plastiras had appeared and was walking across the grass, glancing about him as if searching for some particular individual. When he saw Dikran and Julia, he quickened his pace and approached their group.

"Good morning!" Julia said nervously. "How are your inquiries proceeding?"

"Good morning, Mrs. Saint. I hope you are feeling better today?"

"Yes, thank you. Much better."

He greeted Kerry Farrell politely and, turning to Dikran, said, "Mr. Saint. I just wish to ask you one question. Yesterday I show you a photograph of a man, and you say you do not recall ever speaking to him?"

"Yes." Dikran was watchful, guarded; he eyed Plastiras with the wary look of a wrestler waiting to see which way his opponent will move. "That is so."

"Now, today, there has come into my possession

253

another picture, taken by a beach photographer, which I will be glad for you to do me the kindness of inspecting?"

He took a black-and-white print from an envelope. Dikran gazed at it impassively, but Julia saw that a muscle began to jump in his cheek. Filled with alarm, she moved around beside him and studied the picture. It showed Dikran on the beach in front of the Fleur de Lys Hotel; she recognized the thatched beach umbrellas and the garden behind. Dikran was wearing swimming trunks and carried a towel and a folded newspaper under his arm. He was talking to a man in a striped T shirt.

For a moment, Julia stared at the photograph as if she were paralyzed. Then she cried out, "But of *course* you didn't remember the man! Don't you see? There was only one day when you went on the beach in your swimming trunks, and that was the day you had your amnesia—when I was out shopping! Don't you remember? When I got back you had damp trunks on under your trousers! Of *course* he didn't remember the man," she repeated, turning to Captain Plastiras. "He was sick that day—he completely lost his memory. Dr. Adnan will be able to confirm that. And—" she added triumphantly, "you will be able to check the date from the headline on the newspaper that he is carrying. Won't you?"

"Yes, that is so," Captain Plastiras agreed. "In fact we have done that already." He said to Dikran, "Can you confirm that, Mr. Saint?"

Dikran looked at him haggardly. The muscle in his cheek was jumping even more. And his voice, when he answered, was full of exasperation. "How can I confirm anything?" he said. "I have no memory of that day."

Kerry Farrell, who had been an embarrassed spectator of this scene, now began to move away from it, looking suddenly troubled and uneasy.

"You don't want me, do you?" she said to Captain Plastiras. He shook his head. "Then, if you'll excuse me—I see M. Destrier going back into the hall. The rehearsal is going to start again."

She walked off to join Joop Kolenbrander.

╡ 11 ╞

MAESTOSO

I woke up next morning feeling horribly sad. I suppose the real essence of Mother's revelation about Father had taken time to sink right down into my subconscious; it had finally been assimilated while I slept.

Now I understood that, ever since reading Mother's open-after-my-death letter, I had, without realizing it, been filled with a crazy hope that—despite her warning—Father was not really lost to me but that I was going to be able to recover him in some form or other —blind, crippled, mad, exiled, disgraced, the circumstances had not seemed important. I thought that, so long as he was alive, we would ultimately be able to re-establish our old relationship.

But during my sleep—which was brief and troubled by dreams—my psyche had evidently absorbed the fact that Father was lost indeed; I surfaced from a nightmare of missing trains and hunting for mislaid luggage to a mood of almost unbearable depression and bereavement. My father, as he had been, was gone for good. I must learn to adjust to this fact.

Mother was still asleep when I woke. She had been sleeping when I returned from my rather uncomfortable session with Mr. Saint and Lady Julia the night before, so I still did not know whether she had confided in Adnan about our relationship with Kerry Farrell. Nor did I know whether I hoped she had. Talking about it to Adnan would certainly have helped her; for her sake, I supposed I hoped she had done so, for I had no doubt of his good sense and practicality; but on the other hand I was not at all sure that I wanted him to know this bizarre fact about my background; our relationship was already complicated enough, it seemed to me, without adding such a burden to its toppling structure. I felt it might be the last straw; he would wish to wash his hand of the Meiklejohns, parents and child, and I would not blame him.

Helikon, to which I had come with such high hopes and happy memories, now seemed like a cage, and I longed to leave it. Without a shadow of doubt, Mother did too. I wondered if, while she was talking to Adnan, she had broached the matter of our moving to a hotel.

Moodily I got up and dressed. Mother still slept, so I went down to the dining room and had a mug of grape juice, longing for coffee. I didn't speak to anyone, wasn't in the vein for sociability. Adnan did not appear in the dining room; nor did Kerry Farrell. I couldn't think of her as Father, didn't feel like trying. *She* was quite all right, I thought, infected by some of Mother's resentment; she had her fine new life, with all its successes and friends; she never gave a thought, probably, to the orphaned family she had left. To hell with her! I didn't want to see, hear, or converse with her; all I wanted to do was get right away, as far as possible, preferably back to my flat, my friends, and the Theatre Royal, Crowbridge. Which would never be the same again.

When I went back to our room after breakfast, Mother was still sleeping—it must have been a real knockout drop that Adnan gave her, which was probably a good thing—so I went and checked on Lady Julia, who seemed in a queer state, nervous and preoccupied. I had felt, the night before, that she was truly terrified of her husband—and in fact I was terrified of him myself. I wondered if she had made some awful discovery about him. Or was it just his evident bad temper that frightened her? Plainly she was not a woman who was used to being bossed around by her men. She preferred to take the initiative.—I thought of the odd story told me, in a moment of confidence, by my friend Rickie, who had been at school with Lady Julia's son, Paul. At sixteen or so the two boys had been friends, and Rickie was invited to stay at the Gibbon house. And one night his hostess had come, in the most matter-of-fact way, to his bed.

"What was really queer," he said, "was next morning at breakfast. There she was, behaving as if nothing had happened—teasing me and Paul, telling us to hurry and wash the dishes."

"Was that your first experience of sex?"

"Yes, it was," he said, "as a matter of fact."

"So what did you feel about it all?"

"I felt," he said, "that I couldn't have a relationship with Paul *and* his mother, both; and I didn't want to lose Paul; so I invented an interview for an imaginary

258

job and said I had to go that day. She laughed, she was quite good-natured about it, but I could see that she was annoyed. 'You'll never get on unless you learn to take the chances that you are given,' she told me when she was driving me to the station. But I felt I didn't want to get on if that was the only way it was to be done."

"I suppose she doesn't like people leaving before she's ready to let them go."

It seemed fairly plain now, from the mixture of dislike and irritation she displayed toward her husband, that she was ready to let *him* go; presumably she now realized what a hideous mistake she had made in getting married on the rebound from her divorce, and I imagined it wouldn't be long before she was in the market for another divorce.

Anyway, whatever she wanted this morning, it was not me, so, since she seemed to be reasonably recovered and able to fend for herself, I went back to Mother, who at last had waked up.

She, unlike Lady Julia, looked tired and pale and announced her intention of staying in bed all day. I provided her with breakfast and made her eat it, though she was reluctant.

Then, rather nervously, I asked her if she had confided in Adnan the night before and whether she'd asked him about our moving to a hotel. "I wouldn't suggest moving you today," I added, "but I do see that it's not on the cards for you to stay here at the same time as—as Father, and I'd think Adnan would see that too—"

"Yes, I did talk to him," Mother said.

I had stuck all our combined pillows behind her and she was reclining, propped against them, wearing the usual black turban and one of her plain white cotton nightdresses with long sleeves. It suddenly struck me that, though white with fatigue and hollow-eyed, she looked unusually serene, as if some knot had been untied inside her.

"He's a good man, your Achmed," she said reflectively. "I like him a lot. He's full of sound, solid sense, under that rather worldly exterior."

I refrained from pointing out how far from *mine* he was but concentrated on the rest of her remark. "Worldly? I wouldn't have called him that, exactly. How do you mean?"

"Oh—all those frilly shirts and velvet waistcoats," she said with indulgent scorn. She added, "However, I daresay he'll get over that stage," as if he were about seventeen. I could see that he was well into her good graces, and when she said, "In some ways I think the Turks are very like the Scots," I was quite thunderstruck and wondered by what arts he had contrived to wind her around his little finger.

"So, what did he have to say?"

"Well, we agreed that it would be quite unreasonable to ask James—to ask Kerry Farrell to cancel her performance now, after such a lot of effort has been put into it, besides being the old man's birthday treat—"

I was even more amazed that Adnan should seriously have considered such a step.

Mother went on, "When I suggested our going to a hotel, he seemed rather taken aback and said that was a lot of unnecessary trouble, as the performance will be over tomorrow and Ja—Kerry Farrell will be leaving again at once. He said if I didn't mind lying low for forty-eight hours—which I don't at all—he saw no

260

reason why there should be any awkwardness or embarrassment."

"But what did *you* feel?" I asked, amazed at all this sweet reason. She certainly had changed from the previous night.

"Oh—we had a long talk," said Mother vaguely. She was never much good at reporting the nuances of conversation. At the end of a committee meeting, clear as a clock striking she could announce, "So-and-so was proposed, such-and-such was discussed, this-and-that was decided," but the meanderings of emotional current were beyond her power to chart. She said, "I expect he'll tell you about it sometime." She added, after a pause, "But he did say that—for my own piece of mind—I ought to talk to James, at least once."

"Gosh!" I said, but internally, to myself. Aloud, after a moment, I merely asked, "*Could* you?"

"I don't know.—I'm thinking about it. It would be hard. I told Achmed so."

When did the pair of them get onto Christian-name terms? I wondered.

"But he pointed out," Mother went on calmly, "that I was doing both James and myself an injustice by not seeing him." A tinge of pink appeared in her cheeks. She went on, "He said—he said I might even *enjoy* seeing James."

This seemed to me a highly doubtful proposition. I said with caution, "Are you sure? Don't do anything in a hurry. Remember, you're still only convalescent. And you had that horrible shock yesterday. It might be drastically upsetting—for both of you. I don't think you should make any move to see him before the performance."

"Oh, dear me no. Of course not. I haven't come to

any conclusion yet about it. I'll go on thinking. But Achmed has made me feel better about the whole thing, I must say."

Oh, bless him, I thought, with loving exasperation. My thoughts warmed toward the maddening creature. How, I wondered, could he be so kind, so intelligent and understanding in one way, and so hopelessly, infernally dumb and infuriating in another?

"And he said," Mother continued, "that it was absolutely essential *you* should make yourself known to James. He said all your hang-ups—Father complex, Jocasta complex, feelings of insecurity and deprivation and so on—couldn't begin to be sorted out until you had faced the fact once and for all that your lost father had turned into someone completely different." She put on her reading glasses and peered curiously at me over them. "*Have* you got all those different complexes? I was quite surprised. You have always seemed unusually balanced and sensible to me, for a person of your age, I told Achmed."

She looked so thin and anxious in her black turban—so unlike my formidable Ma—that I felt a stab of compassion for her and only said gently, "I expect I put on a bit of a false front for you. What *is* a Jocasta complex, anyway?"

"Female form of an Oedipus complex."

"Oh, I see.—So old Achmed thinks I should rush to Kerry Farrell and throw my arms round her, crying, 'Daddy, Daddy, here's your little long-lost Priss!' does he?"

"Well, not before the performance, he thought."

"That's very considerate of Achmed!" I snapped, suddenly out of patience with him again. "Fine for Father, but what about me, having to go around for

262

two whole days, fixing the costumes and everything, with that load of dynamite inside me?"

"You can do it if you have to, dear," Mother said, suddenly giving me a firm, warm look of confidence and approval. "That was another thing Achmed said—that when it came to the point, you had a remarkably mature judgment and would be able to decide for yourself on the right moment to speak to your father. If you feel the situation is becoming too strained and artificial—then you'll have to speak out. Achmed said he felt sure you could be relied on to do it in a way that wouldn't be too upsetting for James."

"He did, did he? Well—I'll do some thinking, too." I looked at my watch. "Heavens! it's nearly twenty past eleven—I've already missed half the rehearsal. I'll get you a cup of broth and then I must dash."

"I don't want any of that disgusting bouillon. I've only just had breakfast."

"Rubbish! It's good for you."

"Oh, very well."

I ran down to the loggia and fetched it. When I returned—

"All this careful discussion and planning," Mother said, with her first full smile for two days, "but there's one possibility we haven't taken into account."

"What's that?" I asked, setting the steaming cup on her bedside table.

"Why, that James might simply recognize you. You're awfully alike."

So I ran back to the quadrangle with this new hazard to worry about.

By now the Helikon routine was getting back to normal. The police were less in evidence, people had stopped huddling and chattering and gone off to their dance or music practice or various treatments. In fact there was no one about in the quad, except, of course, God, and also Mr. Saint, who came out of the little telephone room by the loggia as I arrived, and stood brooding like a heron, with a suspended expression, as if he did not quite know what to do with himself.

As always with him, I had the instinctive feeling that he was better *occupied;* that if he were left to brood, Satan would find mischief still. So I said, "Why don't you come with me to the rehearsal and see if they get off to a better start than when we went last time?"

I didn't particularly want him with me—I had plenty to think about—but, as some Saki character observes, one must occasionally do things one dislikes. He gave me an odd look, glanced at his watch—then at the sky—and finally said, "Very well. But for ten minutes, no more."

So we went into the big hall together.

There were fewer spectators today. It was a time of day when most people were either in classes or having treatments; also, there had been an earlier session, which had probably satisfied such people as were simply out for sensation. There were only half a dozen watchers scattered among the pew-like seats. We stole softly down toward the front.

It was easy enough to do this without causing any disturbance: the King, the Queen, Polonius, and Ophelia were in the middle of their quartet and making quite a lot of noise. They were wearing my costumes, and the effect was just what I had intended, which cheered me somewhat.

As we settled ourselves, they sang down to a rousing conclusion and trooped off the dais. After a moment or two, Kerry Farrell came on. She was not in costume but wore black trousers and shirt, which seemed suitable enough for Hamlet. She looked extremely pale, but that might just be in contrast with all the black. I gazed at her, as old Annibal launched into a discussion with Joop about the previous scene, and thought, Yes, it's true, we are alike. The bones of that face are the same as the bones of mine, the eye sockets, jawbone, forehead are built in the same way as the structure of bone and muscle which contains my thoughts—how strange! How strange that is! That person up there has stolen the body of my father, whom I loved, and changed it into something different. The person there has gone to extreme trouble and expense—pain, shame, humiliation, the struggle of learning a whole new bodily language and set of skills—*simply to become what I already am.*

And what did I feel toward her? I really could not decide. Terror, partly—a wish to postpone our first meeting for as long as possible. But also longing— longing to cry, "Do you remember? Do you remember the games we used to play—the things we used to do? The pet names you had for me? Do you know who I *am?* I am Lady Goodheavens, Miss Fizz, the Timber-footed Wonder. I used to hold your hand all the way down the Banbury Road and along St. Giles's; you used to buy me sweets called Snowdrops and played me a special tune on the piano which you christened The Mad Marchioness's Funeral. And look at me now! I'm grown up! Listen while I tell you about all the things that have happened to me. . . ."

Watching her—although I still felt troubled, uncertain, bitterly sad, hostile, and confused—I began to have an inkling of the new kind of relationship which it might be possible to achieve with this person. All is

265

not lost, I thought. All is *never* lost. Matter can neither be created nor destroyed. It falls apart into fragments, and out of those fragments new shapes are formed, new organisms are born.

The orchestral group started to play their introduction. It trickled to a gentle close, and Kerry Farrell, standing in the middle of the stage, opened her mouth and lifted her voice into the first clear, thoughtful note of the aria. *"Être ou ne pas être . . ."* And pitched forward heavily on to her face, and lay still.

There was a horrified gasp from someone standing at the side of the stage, the singer who played Laertes. King Claudius and Queen Gertrude rushed out and knelt by the prone black figure.

I heard old Annibal, who was sitting just ahead of us, whisper, *"Ah, mon Dieu! Non—non—NON!"*

Joop dropped his baton. He jumped forward, his Adam's apple working convulsively. Everyone else in the scanty audience was up and moving toward the stage. Only my neighbor and I remained sitting still. A premonition, some kind of inner, instantaneous knowledge, had told me, in the moment of Kerry Farrell's collapse, that I need not have worried or tried to plan what I was going to say. I would never have the chance to express the things I had just been thinking.

Joop rose from his knees. His face was ashen.

"Fetch Dr. Adnan," he said hoarsely.

Somebody ran out at desperate speed. But I knew their bustle and activities were useless. Not Adnan nor anyone in the world had power to breathe life back into that motionless body. This time, Father was gone for good.

My silent neighbor stood up and took my arm in a firm clasp.

"Come," he said. "We can give no help here."

I did not resist when he led me out. I was in a state of shock, I suppose. Round and round my thoughts went, in a stupid circle. Why did it have to happen? I don't understand. Was the strain too great for her? But she was not afraid of the part. I *knew* this would happen. Right from the start, in my bones, I knew it. But why? I don't understand. Was the strain too great?

"Come," said Mr. Saint.

I didn't know where he was taking me but I followed mechanically, since I certainly had no other plan, either for my immediate future or for the rest of my life. I was in a state of suspended animation.

We walked under the clock arch to the shaggy bit of ground near the lemon orchard where Adnan's car stood. It was there, just as I had left it, with the keys in the ignition.

Mr. Saint opened the passenger door for me and himself got into the driver's seat. It's kind of him, I thought numbly; he's taking me for a drive in order to distract my mind. But how does he know that this affects me so particularly?

At the gate of the drive we passed a policeman, who looked as if he might stop us, but when we turned left he changed his mind. We went up the steep hill that would bring us presently to Archangelos and then on to the archaeological site at the top of Mount Atakos. Mr. Saint was driving quite fast—faster, indeed, than I would normally have considered safe, but he seemed to be a reasonably good driver and I was not in a critical mood. Stupidly I found myself crying; the beautiful figs and olives, the dark cypresses and pale, sage-green shrubs between them flowed past me in a tear-blurred haze.

Then we went through the village; rather too fast, I thought again; past the *taverna*, with its vine-draped pergola, where Calliope and I had once sneaked out to have our first ouzo with a couple of boys; unknown to her parents, we had thought, but of course the news had got back like lightning and there had been a terrific row; "I look on you as my child," Kyrie Aghnides had said, "so I chastise you as my child." Which I had accepted at the time as fair enough, but now, looking back, I felt that all my long sojourn in Greece had been *perfectly unnecessary;* all the time I had spent there mourning for Father, he had been still alive. What a stupid piece of deceit! If ever I have any children, I vowed, they shall learn to swallow the truth in great gulps, whether pleasant or unpleasant.

Mr. Saint drove on up toward the top of Mount Atakos.

I looked at my watch. "I'd pull off onto the next lay-by if I were you," I said.

"Why?" he asked in the disagreeable tone that drivers fall into when advised to stop by their passengers.

"Because it's a Sunday, even hours; you are likely to meet the excursion bus coming down, and they come at a terrific lick."

"Oh, very well." Still surly, he drove on a quarter mile and pulled off onto a rock platform that had been chewed out of the hillside by lowering the level of the road, so that the next bend was twice as steep. The little Volks was red hot and panting like a pug from the climb we had done already. Below us extended a terrific spread of coastline; there lay Helikon at the foot of its glen, square and gray, with the clock tower above and the orchard and gardens beyond; over to

268

the right, beyond a shoulder of mountain, a few of the roofs of Dendros town could just be seen, a bit of crusaders' castle and the green tip of a mosque; more rocky, cliffy coast to the left, and ahead the blue Aegean and the blue, mysterious coast of Turkey. For once the magnificent stretch of scenery failed to lift my heart; I wiped my eyes and observed it without enthusiasm.

"Why do you weep?" said my companion. "You cannot have been in any way devoted to that singer—you had not even met her."

"How do you know?" I asked childishly—as if it mattered.

"You said so yourself, last night."

"I might have met her this morning."

"But you had not. For we were talking at morning break time, my wife, and she, and I, and she asked who you were."

At this I wept afresh.

"Really, this is stupidity!" he said angrily. "I thought you were supposed to be unusually mature—unusually intelligent. My wife never ceases to sing your praises. So why carry on like a stage-struck child about someone of whom you know nothing?"

"I *do* know something about her—him." Stung by Mr. Saint's unjustified scorn, I turned to look at him resentfully. "He was my father!"

Just then, as I had foretold, the excursion bus came hell-for-leather down the hill, at a pace that scared the doves from the trees all along the road and left a cloud of scorching dust in the air behind it. I was glad I'd persuaded Mr. Saint to pull over.

The noise of its passing drowned his next remark,

269

which seemed to be an oath; he had turned very pale and stared at me incredulously.

"Your *father*? This I do not believe."

"It's true! His name used to be James Graffin. My name is really Graffin, but my mother and I went back to her maiden name when they were divorced."

"Your mother . . . Christ's bones!" he muttered. "What an entanglement!"

Mechanically he started the car again and drove on up the mountain road, negotiating bend after bend with the minimum of attention, so that I sat sweating slightly, with eyes glued to the windshield; if he had brought me on this ride with the object of distracting my thoughts, he was beginning to succeed, but I was not certain now that *had* been his aim; I was starting to wonder what he really did have in mind, and a nibble of fear began to make itself felt under my grief and shock.

"Well, look!" he said suddenly, making a wild swerve around another bend; I could feel the grit shoot from under our wheels as we skidded. "Look, I am sorry if he was your father, but, damn it, he was not *really* your father; you could not have seen him for many years, and what kind of a father is that? No good at all."

"It wasn't his fault! My mother wouldn't allow him to see us, because she thought it would be up—upsetting." I took a deep breath and blew my nose.

"Bones of god!" he muttered again. "What a crazy situation! If he had had any guts at all, he would have taken no notice of such a prohibition."

"I'd rather not discuss it, if you don't mind!"

To my utter astonishment, he then said, "Well, *I* will be a father to you." He snapped it out quite an-

270

grily, as if saddled with this tiresome obligation by circumstances that he saw no means of escaping.

I gaped at him as we missed death by a hair's breadth around another acute bend. Then I said, "Thank you for the offer, but I don't need a father any more."

"Of course you do! Every girl needs a father until she is married—to help her select a suitable partner."

I said resentfully, "I have no plans of that kind at present and I suggest you leave me to my own resources and look after your own children."

"I have no children," he said shortly. "They sterilized me in Dachau."

Shocked by this flat statement, I was silent for a moment, then muttered, "I'm sorry. I wouldn't have said that if I'd known."

"It does not matter. It is long ago. I have been rich for many years now—I could have adopted children if I had wished."

"That wouldn't be the same as your own."

"No." He glanced sideways at me, and again we narrowly missed death.

"*Please* keep your eyes on the road. We're about eight hundred feet up, here, and if we went off we'd roll right down to sea level."

He ignored that and went on moodily, "I suppose you think I could not be so good as your own father. But I assure you I would be a great deal better. I would look after you—pay for any education you wished— take you about the world—"

It seemed too rebuffing to tell him that I didn't particularly want any more education and certainly had not the least wish to travel about the world in his rather surly company. Besides, what would Lady Julia

271

have to say? But I was truly puzzled by this abrupt—
and, it seemed, reluctant—piece of generosity, and
couldn't resist asking, "Why? Why do you suddenly
make me this offer?"

"Oh, why! Why must you always ask *why?* Is it
not enough that I offer?" He added in a sharp, irritable
voice, "It is because I already have all I want, and it
is not enough. I have money for houses, travel, a beautiful, famous wife, cars, yachts, and so many treasures
that I could not begin to describe them to you. But
what is the use of it all if the health is not good and
the heart sad?"

He must have detected something that he interpreted
as skepticism in my expression, for he suddenly stopped
the car with a fearful screech of brakes, about ten
inches from a four-hundred-foot drop, and pulled a
little leather box from his pocket. It was about the
size of the kind that holds contact lenses. "Look!" he
said. Flipping up the lid, he exhibited its contents—a
drab-looking stamp. "Do you know what that is? It is
an 1848 Mauritius two-pence; one stamp was wrong
in every sheet printed. It should be a one-penny stamp.
At any dealer's, I could get twenty thousand pounds
for it. *Twenty thousand pounds!*"

"Oh? I'm not very interested in stamps, I'm afraid."

"No? But I have plenty of things that *would* interest
you," he said, putting the box away, furiously throwing
in the gear and driving on. "Art treasures—paintings—
curiosities of literature—for instance, I have a letter
from Jane Austen to her sister about the man she loved
who betrayed her—aha!" Triumphantly he caught my
eye. "*That* you would like to see!"

"I should think I would! But that must be *priceless*

—if it's genuine. Where in the world did you get hold of it?"

His face closed. He said, "I have my sources of supply. I do not reveal them."

"Are you going to publish the letter?"

"Never! I keep it to look at myself and enjoy the knowledge that I alone in the world can do so."

Privately I began now to wonder if he was a nut, which did not increase my confidence as we went on corkscrewing up those endless bends.

"Where do you keep your treasures?" I asked.

"In Switzerland. In a bank."

"Has Lady Julia seen them?"

"No. And she will not do so now," he said vindictively.

"Oh, why?"

"I leave her. She is a spoiled, selfish bitch. A man could not have a worse wife."

"Poor Lady Julia!" Though certainly I could not imagine a more ill-assorted couple; they were both well out of that marriage, I felt. "Does she know your intions?"

"I left her a note."

This struck me as odd; it seemed to indicate that he thought he had already left her—left Helikon. I said, with caution, "You didn't think this was the road into Dendros, did you?"

"*Hein?* No, we are going up the mountain."

"Oh, that's fine, then. So long as you knew that," I said rather absurdly. We described another fearsome U turn. I was glad that the bus had gone by. "Tell me about your other treasures," I suggested. They seemed a safer topic to occupy his mind than the failings of Lady Julia.

"Old masters I have many—Goya, Rembrandt, Titian, Tintoretto—"

"All in this bank?"

"All."

"You don't have any of them on display in your house?"

"Nup." He made a short, very emphatic negative noise. "Too dangerous."

"They might get stolen, you mean?"

To this he made no answer, and it struck me that possibly they already *were* stolen, which would account for his cagy behavior about them.

"Well," I said, "I hope they have good lighting in the bank."

I cheered up a little as I imagined it, the walls above the serious Swiss tellers covered with Rembrandts and Tintorettos.

"Do you have any Pieros?" I asked, remembering how well informed he had been about that painter.

"Yes, I have five."

"*Five?* But there are only *three* in the National Gallery!"

"Do you doubt me?" he asked coldly.

"Of course not, if you say so. What are their subjects?"

He did not answer, and I thought of the great paintings by Piero which had been stolen from the ducal palace in Urbino. Were only copies returned? Were the originals now reposing in a Swiss bank? I said, "I certainly would love to see those."

"If you do so, you will have to promise not ever in this world to reveal your knowledge about them."

I said—to cover the fearful chill on my heart caused by these words—"Oh, then, I think I'd rather

274

not, thank you. I don't like keeping other people's secrets. It's too much responsibility."

"But you keep the secret that Kerry Farrell was your father?"

My thoughts, which had temporarily been distracted by this crazy conversation, turned back to what had happened; the sense of loss engulfed me once more. I put my hands over my face, pressing fingers to the high, narrow forehead which was not mine only, and cried out, "Oh, why did he have to die just *now*, of all times?"

"I am afraid that was my doing," said Mr. Saint matter-of-factly, as if he were talking about a missed train. "I had to kill him."

It took a moment for the meaning of what he had said to sink in. Then I took my hands away from my face and stared at him.

We had reached the top of the mountain at last; there was a flat parking area, where the bus could turn around. He drove into it and stopped the car.

There was a pause.

"You *killed* him?" I said "You killed Kerry Farrell?"

"I regret so—yes."

"But why? *Why?*"

The hot sun beat ferociously down on the roof of the car. Mr. Saint got out, and I followed him automatically. "It was necessary," he said. "We were together once, in a room, in a clinic where at one time I had to have my appearance changed. It was a most unfortunate mischance. I had been under an anesthetic and was not conscious at first. When I discovered that we had been placed together, I was angry about it. But by that time he had left and I could not find what became of him. I thought perhaps we will not meet again so it does not matter—though I am not pleased to think there is a person in the world having this knowledge about me. But then we do meet again and he does recognize me. It is a pity."

"So—you—just—killed him?" I said slowly.

He made an impatient gesture. "What is one death to me? In Dachau every day one saw thousands go—do you think I should distress myself over one? But I am sorry he was your father. That is why I offer to make reparation."

"Thank you, but I don't want it."

I could not help looking at him curiously, though. Now I began to suspect that he was not exactly a nut but—which was more chilling—lived by standards completely alien to mine.

"What *are* you?" I asked. "A king of crime?"

"I have an organization," he said seriously. "And, at the moment, they are trying to seize my power. They believe that since my sunstroke I lost control. But they will find that they are wrong."

"I think I'm frightened of you."

"You are lucky," he said in an oddly paternal, indulgent manner. "Nothing frightens me since Dachau. There, every day, they would make us form into squares. Then some from each square would be taken off. One used to think about it at night."

"How old were you?"

"I was seventeen. Younger than you."

"So, after that, because nothing frightened you, you were able to devote yourself to getting rich."

"That is so."

"And now you have everything you want, and it isn't enough?"

He said irritably, "I shall find new things to do."

My attention wandered. That, I supposed, was why he had first been attracted to Lady Julia. She was a new thing for him—rich herself, beautiful, talented, notable; he could annex her, as he had the Rembrandts and the Jane Austen letter, but she would not have to be gloated over in secret like them; he could flaunt her all about the world. But then the plan had gone wrong; she turned out to be a person, after all, not a letter or a painting; she became bored, perhaps homesick, despised him and didn't bother to conceal it; in a mixed-up way I felt sorry for him.

And then, suddenly, cold with consternation, I saw, or thought I did, where this conversation was leading, where his plan for me fitted into all this. He was leaving Lady Julia, and he intended taking me along, not because he wanted me, but to spite her, because she had praised me and taken an interest in me and preferred my company to his. It was a final slap in the face for her.

I said, "Didn't Lady Julia know what you were— about your organization? How do you dare to leave her?"

"She knows nothing—nothing," he said. "She is interested in nothing but her own affairs."

"But when you had your amnesia? How can you be sure that you didn't let anything out to her during that time?"

A shadow of doubt crossed his face. I could see that he *was* worried on this head and possibly regretted that he had not killed her too. Maybe he had intended to but circumstances had prevented him.

He really was a bit unbalanced, I conjectured; doubtless the sunstroke had not helped his somewhat megalo-maniac personality.

"I shall go away," he said. "Take on a new name, a new life—then even if Julia knows anything about my organization—it does not matter."

"In that case, I don't see why you needed to kill my poor father."

Perhaps, I thought, he had done so out of a kind of meddling curiosity? To create a happening? I had a sudden, horrible suspicion that he might get some of his kicks out of murder as an art form.

Or had he just panicked?

"I suppose it was you who killed the man in the steam bath?"

"Ah, I had to kill that one," he explained. "It was a safety precaution."

"Oh, why?"

"He was my employee. He was supposed to come to Dendros to deliver this stamp." He tapped the pocket where the box reposed. "After that he should have left immediately. But he remained and was becoming a nuisance. He must have encountered me when I was having my amnesia—then he followed to Helikon—"

Mike, I said to myself, you are mad to stay here listening to this terrifying rubbish. Whether what he's telling you is the truth or not, he is the very last person with whom any sensible girl would wish to stand parleying on a deserted archaeological site.

I looked around us. It really was deserted. The ancient city of Archimandros sat on the flat top of nine-hundred-foot Mount Atakos. It had been a large town once, but sometime about 1300 B.C. the inhabitants decided that they would be more comfortable down below, and they moved down to Dendros, leaving behind them

278

a lot of tombs, a Phoenician temple, a temple to Athene, an early Christian basilica, a Turkish barracks (ruined), and an Orthodox monastery (remains of). Well, most of those buildings came later, but you get the gist.

In between the busloads of tourists there is not a soul about; the curator, who sits in his little box dealing out five-drachma tickets, comes up and down with the buses, no sense in wasting the time here in between, since precious few cars find their way up the terrifying climb, and if they do they are welcome to see the place for free.

There were no cars today apart from Achmed's Volks, and, looking over the edge, scanning such turns of the road below as were visible, I could see no vehicle making the ascent. I wondered whether our absence had been noted at Helikon. Possibly not, in the upset following Kerry Farrell's death.

"I'm getting quite hungry, Mr. Saint," I said, trying for what I hoped was the right blend of calm common sense and childish appeal. "Aren't you? It seems hours since breakfast, and all I had was grape juice anyway. Why don't we drive into Dendros for lunch? I'd love a change from vegetarian food."

"Into Dendros? Are you crazy?" he said. My heart sank. "You will get a meal by and by," he went on. "In Samsun. That is where my cousin lives."

"Samsun?"

It is mortifying how, in times of real crisis, one's mind blanks out; although there were plenty more important things to worry about, I could not stop myself feverishly ferreting around an imaginary atlas, scanning the shores of pale-blue seas and the sides of gray, furry mountain ranges. Samsun? Was it in Syria? the Lebanon? Thrace?

"Mr. Saint," I said rather hopelessly. "Don't think me ungrateful, but I'd really much rather just go back to Helikon. If I promise to forget all you've told me, couldn't we just go back—or I'll *walk* back if you want to stay here? I—I—I *enjoy* walking."

"No," he said. He had taken out a small gun, nicely chased with silver and a couple of rubies set in as well, but businesslike also, which was why I was feeling so hopeless. He made a gesture with it—a kind of shrug —and said, "Naturally I do not wish to use this so long as you do not make a fuss." (*Fuss,* I thought; don't I just wish Adnan were here!) "I think you are quite a nice girl," he went on. "I can see why my wife likes you." Bother Lady Julia! I thought ungratefully. Much good her favor has done me. "But if you make a fuss I shall be obliged to shoot you—in the knee, probably. It is very uncomfortable."

"Then, I won't make a fuss."

"Very well. So we wait."

"What for?"

"What for? Why, the helicopter, of course. I phoned for it just before the rehearsal. It should be here in" —he looked at his watch—"twenty minutes or so."

At that point I remembered with a hollow sensation that Samsun was in Turkey. I looked over the side of the mountain, thinking about Captain Plastiras. Calliope and I used to make fun of him, when he came to play those weekly chess games with old Demosthenes, and call him Plaster-Ass; now I felt quite apologetic about that, and only thought how very, very pleased I would be if I could catch a glimpse of his blue Mercedes chugging up one of the seventy bends of the mountain road.

And there it was. Chugging up one of the bends.

280

"Which direction will the helicopter be coming from?" I asked, feverishly hoping to distract Mr. Saint's attention from the mountainside.

I was still not sure, in point of fact, whether I believed in his helicopter. One two-penny Mauritius stamp (especially since I was so ignorant of philately that I could not tell the difference between the guinea stamp and a penny black) was not enough evidence to clinch my belief in his tales of Rembrandts, Jane Austen, and Swiss banks.

Maybe he just had a paranoid delusion about it all. If he'd had a rolled-up Piero with him it would have been different.

But then he said, "There is the helicopter coming now," and pointed northeast, toward the Turkish coast.

⟨ 12 ⟩

PRESTISSIMO

Julia went to Dr. Adnan's office. Nobody acknowledged her knock on the door, but she could hear voices inside, so she turned the handle and walked in. Adnan and Captain Plastiras were there with the little fat sociologist from Baton Rouge.

Julia would not have believed that Adnan could look so stricken. He was pale as death, his large, plum-dark eyes were dilated with anger and grief. The look he turned on Julia was far from friendly. "Lady Julia! We are having a private discussion in here. I wonder if you would be good enough to come back at some other time?"

But Julia, standing her ground, said, "Captain Plastiras. I am glad I found you. My husband has left me this note. I think you should see it." She passed over the sheet of paper.

While Plastiras read Dikran's note, she had time to study the papers on the desk between the two men, and saw that there were several photographs of her husband: the one with the man in the T shirt, one taken sitting in a deckchair in the garden of the Fleur de Lys Hotel, a couple walking with herself on Dendros harbor front, and others she did not know. "I suppose you're from Interpol?" Julia said to the little woman, visited by a sudden flash of illumination. Nobody answered, and she went on musingly, "I've been terribly stupid, haven't I? Anyone else would have realized that Dikran was a criminal long ago. I just shut my eyes to it.—What has he done?"

The three looked at one another. Then Plastiras said, "Many things. He has been responsible for giant art thefts—kidnapings—forgeries. Interpol have been on his track for some time. Then in this last week we have also received definite proofs of his connection with the Rittenhouse case."

"Oh, no!" Julia cried out in horror. "That awful case? The baby who died?"

"Yes, Mrs. Saint. Your husband made four million dollars out of that baby's death."

"I didn't know!" she whispered, and sat limply down in a chair, covering her face with her hands. "Thank god," she muttered, "at least I wasn't married to him then."

Captain Plastiras looked at her without much sympathy and picked up the desk telephone. While he was instructing someone to come immediately to the office, Adnan read Dikran's note and said softly to Julia, "What does Saint mean here? He says he is leaving and intends to take with him one of the only two things

283

you apparently found valuable in Helikon. What do you think he means by that crack?"

Julia said in a toneless voice, "I am afraid he might have meant *you*. That was why I came to your office—to see if you were all right. I was afraid—after I let myself understand that he must have killed the man in the steam bath—I was afraid he might have done something to you."

"As he did to Miss Farrell," Adnan said drily.

"He did *that?"* She was appalled. "It was not a heart attack?"

Adnan shook his head. "She was poisoned; almost certainly in the drink she had just before the rehearsal. Why, we do not yet know."

"Oh, my god," she muttered. "Why didn't I guess sooner about Dikran?"

A young policeman came in.

Miranda Schappin said cozily, taking the note from Adnan, "Never mind blaming yourself, honey; we can all be dumb at times. Just tell us what you think your husband means by this thing he intends to take with him? Is it some piece of your property—jewelry?"

Julia said dully, "No, I should think it's more likely he means the girl—Mike. He—he was jealous of our friendship, of the fact that I enjoyed her company more than I did his."

"What?" Adnan was on his feet staring at Julia, his face dark and congested with rage. "Saint has taken *Mike* with him?"

The young policeman, who was being questioned by Plastiras, said, "Yes, *Kyrie*. The suspected person went out at eleven forty-five with a young lady in blue jeans and a yellow shirt. They were driving Dr. Adnan's Volkswagen and proceeded in a westerly direction.

They were kept under observation and it was noted that they took the road up to the top of Mount Atakos."

"And you didn't send somebody to follow them?" said Plastiras, in a passion.

"What need, *Kyrie?* There is no other road down from that mountain. They are bound to come back the same way."

"Numbskull!" shouted Plastiras, and bounded from his chair.

He ran down the stairs, shouting orders behind him as he went. Adnan followed close behind. Julia hesitated.

"I'd stay here, honey, you can't do any good," counseled Miranda Schappin. "Keep from under their feet."

"But—Dikran is my husband, after all," said Julia, and ran after the two men. She found them getting into the police captain's blue Mercedes, which was parked under the clock arch.

"I want to come with you," she said breathlessly.

Adnan gave her an angry look. "That is not necessary, and your presence would be nothing but a hindrance," he snapped.

But Plastiras said, "Oh, let her come if she wants. If Saint has the girls holed up somewhere—this woman is his wife, it's true, she might be able to talk to him. Get in quickly, then," he ordered Julia, and she scrambled into the back of the car, feeling unwanted and humble.

The Mercedes took off with a spurt of gravel, shot down to the coast road, and turned left; another police car soon appeared and followed.

While driving up toward Archangelos at what seemed to Julia a terrifyingly reckless speed, Plastiras half turned his head and questioned her. "When did you

285

first suspect that your husband was other than he appeared to be?"

His question was inappropriately framed, Julia thought. Dikran had always appeared to be wild and strange; that was what had attracted her to him. But she said, "It was after his sunstroke, I suppose. That must have frightened him very much. He must suddenly have felt that he was losing his grip on—"

"On whatever he gripped," Plastiras said smoothly.

"Yes. I remember his saying something about the fact that a man in his position simply couldn't afford to have amnesia."

"Indeed not. For as soon as his subordinates realized this weakness, they would start to move in on him. And gossip travels fast here. The news that a wealthy visitor at the Fleur de Lys was afflicted by sunstroke would soon spread—through the waiters, the chambermaids, the bellboys."

The captain slowed, minimally, blasting on his horn, and then shot through Archangelos. Hens, donkeys, cats, dogs, and old ladies in black scattered to the sides of the road, which was, luckily, wide.

The blue Mercedes flashed between the little blue, pink, yellow, lavender, and lime-green houses; then they were on the shrubby hillside once more.

"Also, you recognized the man in the striped T shirt, did you not?" said Plastiras. "I could see, although you said no when I showed you the photographs, that his face meant something to you."

"Yes," Julia confessed without attempting to apologize. "Before Dikran's sunstroke we saw that man one day in the big, commercial harbor. He was on the outer bar with another man—they had a big, radio-controlled toy boat which they were demonstrating. I sup-

286

posed they were taking orders for some firm. They guided it round the harbor from where they stood, with a sort of control bar."

"Yes, I have seen them," Plastiras said. "They were cautioned about committing an offense because their gadget made such a loud noise, and they left next day; or one of them did."

Julia was vaguely surprised. The radio-control motor had indeed made a tremendous racket, like a power saw or a supercharged motorcycle—but she had yet to learn that the Greeks objected to loud noise.

"Miss Schappin was observing those men," the captain explained. "She had followed them here from Damascus."

"I see. Anyway, the boat came right across the harbor to us," Julia said, "and got caught in a tangle of driftwood on our side. Dikran set it free and turned it round, and the man waved to thank him. I remember—" she laughed a little hollowly, "I remember thinking at the time what a good method that would be for secret agents to pass on information."

"It was not information," said Plastiras quenchingly. "Merely a stolen two-penny stamp." He did not enlarge on this enigmatic statement and Julia did not ask what he meant. He was slowing down, and now pulling off the road onto one of the infrequent lay-bys.

"Why are you stopping?" asked Julia fretfully.

"To let *them* get by." Plastiras jerked his head toward the road behind. An armored car dashed past, and Plastiras swung the Mercedes out after it, remarking, "There are times when one needs the help of a specialist. Luckily we have a few of those in Dendros—just in case of an invasion by you-know-who." He dug Adnan amiably in the ribs with his elbow.

"What have they got that you haven't?" asked Julia, and he answered briefly, "An AA gun."

All this time, Adnan had sat containedly silent. But now he muttered, "Look . . ."

The dangling shape of a helicopter was proceeding slowly southward toward the line of surf along the coast; it seemed to hesitate in its deliberate, bumble-bee-like flight, then turned and moved purposefully inland toward the summit of Mount Atakos. The threatening stutter of its engines became louder and louder, almost drowning the screech of the armored car's gears on the bends above them.

"You don't mean," said Julia in horror, "you can't mean that's coming for *Dikran?* He can't do that, surely?"

Plastiras contrived to shrug, while throwing the Mercedes around, almost on its haunches, as they circled a particularly acute bend.

"You don't appear to have much awareness of your husband's potential, Mrs. Saint, if I may say so? He has many, many contacts in Asia Minor and the Arab countries."

"But he can't just take Mike and go off to one of those places? They could be extradited?"

"From Turkey? From Iran? From Kuwait?" Plastiras gave another tremendous shrug. "Perhaps! And perhaps not. How are we to know where he goes? He will not stay in that helicopter for long."

Adnan said, "You believe he will take Mike just to spite you, Lady Julia? He is not fond of her for herself?"

"I wouldn't have thought so," said Julia. "He has chatted with her once or twice, but never showed any particular interest in her; I've heard him being quite

288

disagreeable about her. And he didn't think she was at all pretty.—Well, she isn't!"

"He does not, in general, go after young girls?"

"How should I know?" Julia snapped angrily. "We were on our *honeymoon,* after all. I haven't noticed him doing so." Suddenly the voice of old Annibal came into her mind: "I see 'ow your flirtation with Achmed upset your 'usband—and this so soon after you are married; this I find sad." She fell silent. But, she thought, Dikran is a criminal. If I had known *that* about him, I'd never have married him. He was deceiving me all along. A cool, internal voice remarked, These arguments make no difference to the fact that your own behavior was unkind, inconsiderate, stupid, and bitchy. When are you going to stop landing yourself in this kind of mess?

From above them they heard two loud smacks of sound.

"That's the AA gun," remarked Plastiras. "Stephanos must have got up to the top already."

The helicopter had been out of sight, around the corner of the mountain; now it appeared, dodging back affrontedly, like a woman in a crinoline nipping away from the onset of a barking dog.

"Good for Stephanos," muttered Adnan.

"They won't shoot it down?" said Julia in horror.

"No, no. Merely fire warning shots. Unfortunately," said Captain Plastiras, "there is plenty of room on the mountaintop. The helicopter could go round to the south and land there."

"What's to stop Stephanos from going over there and chasing it off?"

"The fact that there is no road across the top. The road ends at the bus park. And beyond that are many trees—oaks and cypresses, old and large—besides a whole, complicated mass of crumbling ruins—no way through for vehicles."

He jammed his foot on the accelerator and almost pushed the Mercedes up the final slope to the flat, turnaround area.

In another moment he had brought the car to a stop, and they all tumbled out.

Adnan's Volkswagen was parked there, empty. Mr. Saint and the girl were not to be seen. The armored car was standing in the middle of the space, with two men at the AA gun; four more were along at the far end of the car park, scanning the thickly tree-grown area beyond. One of them ran to Plastiras. "They went that way, *Kyrie,* through the trees. Unfortunately, if we try to drive the car after them, we lose sight of the helicopter."

The helicopter was circling over the wood, quite a long way off. Evidently it had lost sight of its would-be passengers and was hunting for them.

"Vassili and Alexandros, go through the wood. Fire at the helicopter if you see it—not to hit, just to scare it off."

The men were carrying weapons that Julia supposed to be Tommy guns; she had never seen one close up before. "Don't fire at the man on the ground," Plastiras cautioned all the men. "He has a girl with him; you might hit her. Keep in radio communication."

They nodded and vanished into the trees.

All this show of mechanical efficiency ought to have reassured Julia, but in fact it terrified her. "Somebody's *sure* to get hurt," she found herself saying idiotically to Adnan.

He gave her a cold look. "If that girl is hurt because

290

of your husband, I can only hope he gets his head blown off!"

"Achmed!" she said miserably—the two of them were standing in the car park feeling painfully useless, while another carload of police and men in army uniforms arrived and dashed expertly about.

"Well, what?" he snapped.

"I wish you'd stop being so nasty to me! It isn't *my* fault that Dikran's gone off with that wretched girl."

"No?"

Another outburst of gunfire came from somewhere in the wood.

"Or if it is, it's yours just as much! You were quite prepared to—to flirt with me and play tennis—and so on."

"Yes," he said measuredly. "Which now I very much regret! It was irresponsible. But I was sorry for you— you seemed so lonely and unhappy. And at least *I* was not on my honeymoon. Nor was I then aware of your husband's particular disposition. If I had known of his pathological jealousy—if I had known that would ensue—wild horses would not have dragged me by my eyelids any nearer to you than the length of this car park!"

"Oh!"

"I am sorry," he went on more temperately. "But *you* know there was nothing ever—at any time—at all serious about our relationship! Your husband need not have troubled himself."

She sighed. "All right—I know."

"My affections are quite engaged—I think you know that too."

Startled, she turned to him, and for the first time took in the full significance of his haggard, sweating,

291

anxiety-racked face. "You are in love with that *girl*—with Mike?"

"Of course I am!" he said furiously. "I love her now for five years—may the devil fly away with her!"

As the words left his mouth, the distant figures of Saint and Mike broke out of the trees at the northern end of the car park. Saint was dragging the girl by the wrist. Her face was covered with blood. He turned and fired back into the trees, then forced Mike to race at top speed to the Volkswagen. He pushed her in, fired into the wood again, then flung himself in beside her; the engine started with a rattle of sound. The car spun around and shot toward the exit, passing close to where Adnan and Julia were standing.

Adnan shouted something at the top of his lungs, but the roar of the engine drowned it; Julia could not hear what he said. Mike, inside the car, was huddled out of sight; it was doubtful if she had heard him.

"What did you say?" asked Julia, but her question was lost in the rage of Plastiras, who was cursing his men for not immobilizing the Volkswagen.

"Come on!" he shouted to Adnan, and leaped back into the Mercedes. Adnan jumped in beside him, and they were off, without waiting for Julia, who found herself suddenly abandoned on the mountaintop with the crew of the AA gun. They were watching the helicopter, which was retreating rapidly from the mountain.

Julia ran to the edge of the car park and looked down the mountainside. On one bend of the hill she saw the blue Mercedes, and on another, much farther down, the red Volkswagen, skating recklessly around bends, zipping at a murderous speed along the straight sections of road.

The helicopter, hanging off the mountain, seemed to be observing its progress.

"Looking for another pickup spot," Julia thought in agony.

The men in the armored car, evidently realizing this or receiving new instructions by radio, started their engine and followed the Mercedes.

"They'll never catch Dikran," Julia thought. "There are plenty of flat places down below where he could drive out and the helicopter could pick him up."

But then, down toward the foot of the mountain, on a bend of the road just above Archangelos, she saw something that made the breath stick in her gullet as if it were a solid lump of impenetrable matter.

The excursion bus, driven at its usual, devil-may-care pace, was starting to climb the hill.

{ 13 }

CODA

I came to with very confused sensations.

I could remember seeing Achmed shouting.

"The hand brake!" were the words his mouth formed, though I couldn't hear them. I could remember our hurtling descent of the mountainside, with the helicopter watchfully accompanying our progress. And then I could remember the sudden vision of the yellow excursion bus, dead ahead on collision course, coming toward us. And I could remember dragging on the hand brake, which had the effect of opening the right-hand door. After that, memory came to a stop. I supposed I must have fallen out.

I tried to move, and found that it was impossible. Every bit of me seemed to be immobilized—strapped, tied, plastered, splinted. Which was probably just as well, for the least attempt to shift, as I soon discovered, brought such a cacophonous chorus of pains from all over me that I swiftly desisted. Parts of my body that I didn't even know about began to shriek and groan and gibber like the sheeted dead in the streets of Rome.

I lay quietly and sweated with agony.

Then it struck me that I had not yet tried to open my eyes.

Eyelids, it turned out, would move without pain, so, nervously, I raised them, expecting to see a thorny, rocky mountainside and bits of shattered Volkswagen.

Instead, to my surprise, I found myself staring straight into the faces of my mother and Adnan.

"Hello, Ma," I croaked. My voice worked, too, after a fashion, I was pleased to find.

"Priss!" There were tears in her eyes.

"Sorry about all the fuss," I muttered.

"*Fuss*—! Just be quiet, will you?" Adnan said, scowling down at me.

"You're going to be better soon, lovey," Mother said. "Don't worry. Just take it easy."

"First you, then me," I said, meaning beds in hospitals.

Adnan looked at Mother and said, "She is a tough nut, your daughter."

"What's the matter with me?" I asked.

"Broken collarbone, broken rib, broken arm, broken leg, concussion, and a scratched face," Adnan said. "You are going to have to refrain from meddling in other people's business for a long, long time."

"Oh!" I was outraged, but he was smiling at me in quite a friendly way.

He said, "See you later!" and walked out quietly.

Mother said, "Go to sleep, my dearest child. Everything is all right."

"Okay." Then I had a thought and said, "What's today? I mean, is it still Sunday?"

"No, it's Monday."

"Poor old Annibal's birthday. Will you wish him a happy *anniversaire* from me?"

"Yes, I will," said Mother. She cleared her throat and said, "*Now* go to sleep."

"Just one thing—what about the opera—what's happening?"

"Monsieur is going to take the part of Hamlet himself."

"Gosh!" I said. Then someone gave me an injection, and on the thought of a ninety-year-old Hamlet I drifted off into oblivion.

When I woke next time, things felt a little better. A Greek nurse appeared and supplied me with a big swig of lemon juice. I was, I learned, in the hospital in Hippokratous Street, as my breakages were a bit more than could be coped with at Helikon. I felt rather lonesome at that news, but quite soon Mother appeared again and explained that she had installed herself in a *pension* next door to the hospital so that she could spend most of the day with me.

"Me looking after you for a change," she said cheerfully. And she settled in without delay, giving me drinks at regular intervals, dealing expertly with bedpans, making me help her do the *Times* crossword, and reading aloud the works of Mrs. Gaskell.

I listened in a dreamy doze to long, hazy stretches of *Wives and Daughters,* every now and then breaking in to ask a question. "What's happened to Lady Julia?"

"She had to give a deposition to the police, but then

they allowed her to go back to England. She was missing her children. I like her very much," Mother said unexpectedly. "She's had a bad time, poor thing. But I'm sure that she's a devoted mother, and, fundamentally, a Thoroughly Nice Woman." Commendation from Mother could go no higher. "I shall keep in touch with her when I get back to England," Mother said, splicing two bits of wool together in her knitting.

I had a slightly bizarre vision of Mother, Gina Signorelli, and Lady Julia settling down *à trois* in some North Oxford house. After a pause, I said, "And Father?"

Mother said, "He was buried in the cemetery in Dendros. It's a very beautiful spot."

I nodded; or tried to. I knew it. There were tall, graceful eucalyptus trees, and chinaberry trees, and a lot of Turkish tombstones with turbans on them.

Mother said, "I'm sure he'd like that. The sea's only twenty yards off. He loved the sea."

I had shut my eyes, but a tear squeezed out. "If I could only have talked to him—just *once*—"

"Yes, I know. I konw," she said. "I feel exactly the same. But we didn't. We just have to accept it. And if we *had* talked just once," said Mother practically, "we'd now be wishing it was just twice. So there it is. —Achmed is going to have a tombstone put up with both his names and SINGER OF INTERNATIONAL RENOWN underneath."

"That's nice." Then I chuckled—which was a mistake, as my busted collarbone gave a shriek of rage. "Tell you what—"

"What?"

"They'll have a problem about his tombstone. It's turbans for males, plain for females. Which does he rate?"

"I'm sure he'd have wanted a plain one," said Mother austerely.

I couldn't ask her about Mr. Saint. For that, I waited until Adnan's next visit. He came in the evening, looking careworn and fatigued; he explained that there was an awful lot of bureaucratic paperwork to be got through in connection with the late dreadful goings on at Helikon.

So many things I wanted to ask him. A whole ocean of strange occurrences and unexplained happenings seemed to have rolled between us since the last time we had had a proper conversation. Actually, looking back, I could not remember *when* we had had a proper conversation. In the workroom when I was painting the cliffs of Elsinore? I hardly knew where to begin.

But he seemed to have no doubts on the matter. He took hold of my fingers, where they poked out from the cast, leaned over the bed, and very carefully and gently kissed me on the lips. "Oh, what a terrible time you give me, my treasure!" he said. "Once you are out of all that plaster and strapping, I do not know how I shall ever dare to let you out of my sight again!"

"Achmed! You mean—"

"I mean that for the last five years I have been loving you and waiting for you to grow from a naughty, impertinent, teasing child into an age of sense and come back to Helikon. Now you *do* come back, I begin to fear that you will *never* grow to an age of sense. So I asked your mother if I may pay my addresses to you, and she has said yes."

"She did, did she?" I remembered Mother's pronounced views on equality and Women's Lib.

Adnan grinned. "Even if she had said no, I would have paid them just the same. How do you pay an

298

address, though? I shall have to rely on you to instruct me." He sat down, still holding onto the finger.

I said, "But what about poor Lucy? You were going to love her forever?"

"She knows that I will always love her," he said comfortably. "There is room in my heart for both. Indeed, you are very alike, you wayward, teasing English creatures!"

"That's all right, then," I said. And I lay beautifully relaxed inside all my plasters and began to feel that soon I would be better. "Achmed—what happened to Mr. Saint?"

"Oh, well, I am afraid that when your car rolls over about forty times going down a mountain and you are inside it, there is not much left of you. He ended up in the little valley just above Helikon—smashed a lot of trees," Adnan said crossly. "Also, my car is a write-off."

"Poor Mr. Saint.—He wanted to adopt me, you know," I told Adnan. "And educate me and travel with me and show me a Jane Austen letter he had and a lot of Pieros in a numbered account."

"I would not have allowed it," Achmed said firmly. "He was really a very bad man, you know. He had done some dreadful things."

"I think I'd rather not hear about them just now. . . . Are you going to be one of those domineering husbands?" I asked suspiciously. ("We are going to be married, I assume?")

"Your assumption is correct. We are going to be married as soon as you can walk; unless you care to be married on a stretcher?"

"No, let's wait till I am vertical. Dr. Kalafilaikis says I'll be on crutches in ten days.—I wonder what will happen to all Mr. Saint's ill-gotten wealth? Does Lady Julia inherit that? Oh, my goodness," I said, remembering. "He had a two-penny Mauritius stamp on him that he said was worth twenty thousand pounds. I don't suppose anyone picked it up?"

"My treasure," said Achmed, "you might as well look for a pin in Pompeii after the volcano erupted on it. And the answer to your question before last is yes, and no; I shall domineer whenever I get the chance. Which will not be often."

"You know I intend to go on with my career?"

"Of course; that is understood."

"But how can we combine that with your being at Helikon?"

"To tell the truth," he said, "I was beginning to find Helikon a little quiet. (Until the last couple of weeks, that is to say.) I had been thinking of installing a suitable successor and returning to Western Europe in search of you, as you showed so little sign of coming here."

"I have my pride! You never showed that you wanted me to come.—Anyway, I did come in the end."

"Only because of your mother."

"Hah! It was the first excuse. Poor Mother!"

"It has done her a lot of good, being here," he said seriously. "Of course I will always love Helikon. But it must be admitted that the medical problems in Western Europe are more interesting."

"But I've been dreaming of coming back here for five years! We'll have to come here for all our holidays."

"It is the place, not me, you love, in other words?"

I bit his finger, which happened to be handily acces-

300

sible. "*Oh,* how angry I was with you. Flirting so with Lady Julia!"

"And what about you—so cool, so distant—thorny and prickly as an acacia—calling me Dr. Adnan and behaving as if we had never met before?"

"You were worse. You were much, much worse! You must promise never to tease me again."

"You know that I have a roving eye."

"Well, kindly don't let it rove!"

"The eye may rove," he said, "the heart remains in one spot." He gave me a long, long, serious look. It made me so happy that I had to lie breathing deeply and quietly; otherwise, I felt, I might have exploded right out of my plaster casts.

Then a thought struck me. "Achmed! When we are married—will you expect me to turn vegetarian?"

Our eyes met, measuringly, and then at the same moment we both burst out laughing.

Which did no good at all to my busted rib and collarbone.

THE BEST OF THE BESTSELLERS
FROM WARNER BOOKS!

BIG STICK-UP AT BRINK'S by Noel Behn   (81-500, $2.50)
Hailed as "the best book about criminals ever written,"
BRINK'S recreates a real-life caper more exciting, more en-
grossing than any crime novel. It's the most fun you can have
from a bank robbery without taking the money!

PASSION AND PROUD HEARTS   (82-548, $2.25)
by Lydia Lancaster
The sweeping saga of three generatons of a family born of a
great love and torn by the hatred between North and South.
The Beddoes family—three generations of Americans joined
and divided by love and hate, principle and promise.

SUMMERBLOOD by Ann Rudeen   (82-535, $2.25)
The four exquisite women of Land's End . . . sweet with
promise . . . wild with passion . . . and bound forever to one
lonely man tortured by his terrible past. A big, lush contempo-
rary novel hot with searing sexuality.

THE FAN by Bob Randall   (82-471, $2.25)
A masterpiece of humor, suspense and terror as an aging
Broadway actress is pursued by an adoring fan whose obsession with love and death leads him deeper and deeper into
madness. A **New York Times** bestseller, Literary Guild Alter-
nate, Reader's Digest Condensed Book, and serialized in
Photoplay.

━━━

Please send me the books I have checked.

Enclose check or money order only, no cash please. Plus 50¢
per copy to cover postage and handling. N.Y. State residents
add applicable sales tax.

Please allow 2 weeks for delivery.

WARNER BOOKS
P.O. Box 690
New York, N.Y. 10019

Name ....

Address ....

City .... State .... Zip ....

_____ Please send me your free mail order catalog

THE BEST OF THE BEST SELLERS
FROM WARNER BOOKS!

THE KINGDOM by Ron Joseph   **(81-467, $2.50)**
The saga of a passionate and powerful family who carves out of the wilderness the largest cattle ranch in the world. Filled with both adventure and romance, hard-bitten empire building and tender moments of intimate love, **The Kingdom** is a book for all readers.

BLUE SKIES, NO CANDY by Gael Greene   **(81-368, $2.50)**
"How in the world were they able to print **Blue Skies, No Candy** without some special paper that resists Fahrenheit 451? (That's the burning point of paper!) This sizzling sexual odyssey elevates Ms. Greene from her place at the head of the food-writing list into the Erica Jong pantheon of sexually liberated fictionalists."—Liz Smith, New York Daily News

THESE GOLDEN PLEASURES   **(82-416, $2.25)**
by Valerie Sherwood
From the stately mansions of the east to the freezing hell of the Klondike, beautiful Roxanne Rossiter went after what she wanted—and got it all! By the author of the phenomenally successful **This Loving Torment**.

THE OTHER SIDE OF THE MOUNTAIN 2   **(82-463, $2.25)**
by E. G. Valens
Part 2 of the inspirational story of a young Olympic contender's courageous climb from paralysis and total helplessness to a useful life and meaningful marriage. An NBC-TV movie and serialized in **Family Circle** magazine.

- -

Please send me the books I have checked.

Enclose check or money order only, no cash please. Plus 50¢ per copy to cover postage and handling. N.Y. State residents add applicable sales tax.

Please allow 2 weeks for delivery.

WARNER BOOKS
P.O. Box 690
New York, N.Y. 10019

Name ....

Address ....

City .... State .... Zip ....

_____ Please send me your free mail order catalog

IN 1918 AMERICA FACED AN ENERGY CRISIS

UNCLE SAM NEEDS THAT EXTRA SHOVELFUL

Help Uncle Sam to Win the War

An icy winter gripped the nation. Frozen harbors blocked the movement of coal. Businesses and factories closed. Homes went without heat. Prices skyrocketed. It was America's first energy crisis now long since forgotten, like the winter of '76 '77 and the oil embargo of '73 '74. Unfortunately, forgetting a crisis doesn't solve the problems that cause it. Today, the country is relying too heavily on foreign oil. That reliance is costing us over $40 billion dollars a year. Unless we conserve, the world will soon run out of oil, if we don't run out of money first. So the crises of the past may be forgotten, but the energy problems of today and tomorrow remain to be solved. The best solution is the simplest conservation. It's something every American can do.

ENERGY CONSERVATION -
IT'S YOUR CHANCE TO SAVE, AMERICA

Department of Energy, Washington, D.C.

A PUBLIC SERVICE MESSAGE FROM WARNER BOOKS, INC.